SO-AZJ-546

THE ORDEAL OF
RICHARD FEVEREL

THE ORDEAL
OF
RICHARD
FEVEREL

BY

GEORGE MEREDITH

THE
MODERN LIBRARY
NEW YORK

Random House IS THE PUBLISHER OF

THE MODERN LIBRARY

BENNETT A. CERF · DONALD S. KLOPFER · ROBERT K. HAAS

Manufactured in the United States of America

Printed by Parkway Printing Company   Paper by Richard Bauer & Co.

Bound by H. Wolff

CONTENTS

CHAPTER   PAGE

I. THE PILGRIM'S SCRIP 1

II. A GLIMPSE BEHIND THE MASK . . . 13

III. MRS. MALEDICTION 21

IV. THE INMATES OF RAYNHAM ABBEY . . 26

V. SHOWING HOW THE FATES SELECTED THE FOURTEENTH BIRTHDAY TO TRY THE STRENGTH OF THE SYSTEM 41

VI. THE MAGIAN CONFLICT 53

VII. ARSON 58

VIII. ADRIAN PLIES HIS HOOK 70

IX. JUVENILE STRATAGEMS 75

X. DAPHNE'S BOWER 83

XI. THE BITTER CUP 89

XII. A FINE DISTINCTION 98

XIII. RICHARD PASSES THROUGH HIS PRELIMINARY ORDEAL, AND IS THE OCCASION OF AN APHORISM 104

XIV. IN WHICH THE LAST ACT OF THE BAKEWELL COMEDY IS CLOSED IN A LETTER . 112

XV. THE BLOSSOMING SEASON 119

XVI. THE MAGNETIC AGE 132

XVII. AN ATTRACTION 142

XVIII. FERDINAND AND MIRANDA 149

XIX. UNMASKING OF MASTER RIPTON THOMPSON 160

CONTENTS

CHAPTER   PAGE

XX. GOOD WINE AND GOOD BLOOD 170

XXI. THE SYSTEM ENCOUNTERS THE WILD OATS SPECIAL PLEA 177

XXII. A SHADOWY VIEW OF CŒLEBS PATER GOING ABOUT WITH A GLASS-SLIPPER . . . 181

XXIII. A DIVERSION PLAYED ON A PENNY-WHISTLE 192

XXIV. CELEBRATES THE TIME-HONOURED TREATMENT OF A DRAGON BY THE HERO . . 196

XXV. RICHARD IS SUMMONED TO TOWN TO HEAR A SERMON 218

XXVI. INDICATES THE APPROACHES OF FEVER . 229

XXVII. CRISIS IN THE APPLE-DISEASE 245

XXVIII. OF THE SPRING PRIMROSE AND THE AUTUMNAL 262

XXIX. IN WHICH THE HERO TAKES A STEP . . 268

XXX. RECORDS THE RAPID DEVELOPMENT OF THE HERO 290

XXXI. CONTAINS AN INTERCESSION FOR THE HEROINE 306

XXXII. RELATES HOW PREPARATIONS FOR ACTION WERE CONDUCTED UNDER THE APRIL OF LOVERS 310

XXXIII. IN WHICH THE LAST ACT OF A COMEDY TAKES THE PLACE OF THE FIRST . . 330

XXXIV. CELEBRATES THE BREAKFAST 344

XXXV. THE PHILOSOPHER APPEARS IN PERSON . 357

XXXVI. PROCESSION OF THE CAKE 367

XXXVII. NURSING THE DEVIL 387

XXXVIII. CONQUEST OF AN EPICURE 399

CONTENTS

CHAPTER   PAGE

XXXIX. CLARE'S MARRIAGE 422

XL. A DINNER PARTY AT RICHMOND . . . 439

XLI. MRS. BERRY ON MATRIMONY 457

XLII. AN ENCHANTRESS 471

XLIII. THE LITTLE BIRD AND THE FALCON: A
BERRY TO THE RESCUE! 497

XLIV. CLARE'S DIARY 517

XLV. AUSTIN RETURNS 535

XLVI. NATURE SPEAKS 548

XLVII. AGAIN THE MAGIAN CONFLICT 558

XLVIII. THE LAST SCENE 568

XLIX. LADY BLANDISH TO AUSTIN WENTWORTH . 587

THE ORDEAL
OF
RICHARD FEVEREL

CHAPTER I

THE PILGRIM'S SCRIP

SOME years ago was printed, and published anonymously, dedicated to the author's enemies, a small book of original Aphorisms, under the heading, THE PILGRIM'S SCRIP. The book was noticeable for its quaint earnestness, and a perversity of view regarding Women, whom the writer seldom extolled, and appeared with all conscience to rank as creatures still doing service to the Serpent: bound to their instincts, and happily subordinate in public affairs, though but too powerful in their own walk. Modern Aphorists are accustomed to make their phrases a play of wit, flashing antithetical brilliancies, rather than condensing profound truths. This one, if he did not always say things new, evidently spoke from reflection, feeling, and experience: the Triad which gives a healthy utterance to Wisdom: and omitting one of which, or with the three not in proper equipoise and junction, admirable sentences may survive as curiosities, and aptly quoted may clinch a debate, but are as Dead Sea Apples to a thirsting mind, and to men at large incomprehensible juggleries usurping dominion of their understandings without seal of authority. His thoughts were sad enough; occasionally dark; here and there comical in their oddness: nevertheless there ran through the volume a fire of Hope; and they did him injustice who said he lacked Charity.

1

Thus he wrote:

'I am happy when I know my neighbour's vice.'

And it was set down as the word of a cynic; when rightly weighed, it was a plea for tolerance.

He said again:

'Life is a tedious process of learning we are Fools.'

And this also is open to mild interpretation, if we do not take special umbrage at the epithet. For, as he observes, by way of comment: 'When we know ourselves Fools, we are already something better.'

He made no pretension to Novelty. 'Our new thoughts have thrilled dead bosoms,' he wrote; by which avowal may be seen that Youth had manifestly gone from him, since he had ceased to be jealous of the ancients, his forefathers. There was a half sigh floating through his pages for those days of intellectual coxcombry, when Ideas come to us affecting the embraces of Virgins, and swear to us, they are ours alone, and no one else have they ever visited: and we believe them.

On the subject of Women, certainly, the Aphorist seemed to lose his main virtue. He was not splenetic: nay, he proved in the offending volume he could be civil, courteous, chivalrous, towards them: yet, by reason of a twist in his mental perceptions, it was clear he looked on them as domesticated Wild Cats, ready, like the lady in the fable, to resume their natural habits when there was a little mouse to tear, and, after they had done so, not to be allowed to reappear as the seraphs we thought them when they had a silly male mortal to lure: in fact, to be stamped Wild Cats, to the dissipation of Illusion.

He gravely declared, as one whose postulate was accepted universally:

'I expect that Woman will be the last thing civilized by Man.'

And from this tremendous impertinence, he stalked on like a Colossus to treat of other matters, worldly and spiritual, with the calm of a superior being who has avowed a most hopeful opinion: as indeed it was. He conceived that the Wild Cats would some day be actually tamed. At present it was best to know what they were.

Singular to say, the one dangerous and objectionable feature in this little volume, preserved it from limbo. Men read, and tossed it aside, amused, or weary. They set the author down as a Sentimentalist jilted; commonly known to be a savagely vindictive wretch, who deserves to be listened to solely when he dresses a gay shaft, and that for the fun. They were angry at his ponderous intentness. They, let us suppose, were Sentimentalists not yet jilted.

By the ladies, however, who took the Dedication to themselves, he was welcomed otherwise. These extraordinary creatures, whose moves it is impossible to predict, and who will, now and then, love, or affect to love, their enemies better than their friends, cherished his book, and asked for him. He had fortunately not put his name to the title-page. In the place of a signature of authorship, stood a Griffin between Two Wheatsheaves. It became a question, then, whether this might be symbolic, or a family crest. Several ladies detected symbolism in the aspect of the Griffin, which had a snarling hostile air to them, and seemed to mean that the author was a double-animal, and could do without them, being well fortified by Life's Wherewithal to right and left. Other ladies, arguing from the latent vanity in man, would insist upon the Crest. Bodies of ladies made application to the publisher, who maintained the good repute of his craft in keeping his secret, and was not to be seduced, and increased the mystery.

'Thou that thinkest thyself adored,' says THE PILGRIM'S SCRIP, 'O Fool! it is not Thou she loveth, but the Difficulty.'

To manifest the truth in which, one adventurous fair one betook herself to the Herald's College, and there, after immense labour, ascertained that a Griffin between Two Wheatsheaves formed the crest of Sir Austin Absworthy Bearne

Feverel, Baronet, of Raynham Abbey, in a certain Western County folding Thames: a man of wealth, and honour, and a somewhat lamentable history.

The discovery of a Secret implies no obligation to retain it; and the lady in question treated her capture as a prisoner of war, whom, like Tamerlane, she exhibited in a cage to her friends: that is,. it was shared with them, and was presumed to belong to her: but they, considering a Secret to be of so rich an essence that it can only be enjoyed diluted, had also their confidences, and the Secret soon broke through its solemn bars and evaporated in soft whispers, by which in the end Sir Austin Feverel, much to his amazement, became famous as The Griffin, and learnt what it was to give Woman a clue.

The Baronet became famous, and tasted the fruits of celebrity. His breakfast-table grew odoriferous with dainty notes from fair correspondents, deploring their non-intimacy, and begging the favour of a Copy of his Beautiful Book, while remonstrating humbly against the severity of his judgment pronounced on a sex, which, whatever its short-comings, could, and did, reverence a Sage. Showers of the enthusiastic rose-pink descended on Raynham. One lady addressed the Aphorist as England's Christian La Roche-foucauld. One went so far as to propose herself to him as An Uncorrupted Eve: and there is no knowing what a disinher-ison of Posterity may have sprung from his persistent eva-sion of their pointed flatteries. For he was a soured Adam whom not even an uncorrupted Eve might tempt.

"We live and learn," said the Baronet to young Adrian Harley, his nephew and intimate; "but it is odd that, when we whip her, Madam should love us the more."

"You have propounded it frequently, Sir," replied that clever youth, "in the GREAT SHADDOCK DOGMA." (For so, on account of its constant and ungenerous citation of the primal slip in Paradise, Adrian chose to entitle THE PIL-GRIM'S SCRIP). "You say:

" 'Woman when she wrestles for supremacy with every one she encounters, is but seeking her Master.'

"She's a Tyrant till she's reduced to bondage, and a rebel till she's well beaten. She worships strength, whether of the physic or of the intellect, and likes to feel it. Poet, Philosopher, or Athlete, come not amiss to her; and could she get the three in one—"

"Ay, then," Sir Austin took him up, "farewell Duty! Women are born Pagans, ever on the look-out for material Gods!"

"Whom, if they can't discover, they create!" added Adrian. "Witness many a gentle joy of an Ass. To be distinguished by Woman is to wear Bully Bottom's Garland."

"Preserve me from that!" exclaimed the Baronet, shuddering devoutly.

His own written enunciations were adverse to his chances of escape, and Adrian capitulated them:

" 'Man is the speculative animal: Woman the practical.'

"Wherefore:

" 'Tempt her not to swear to her soul she will have thee —thou art lost!' "

But he had written a book; he had made himself an object: Miss Blewins was in the field; the lean, the long-nosed, the accomplished, the literary: Miss Joy Blewins, sister to the aforesaid, was in the field; the half-man, who cut her hair short, and parted it on the left side: Lady Blandish was in the field; the fairest sweetest sensible widow ever seen, a dead shot with her eyes, when she used them: The Hon. Mrs. Breakyeline was in the field; who had in her time plunged through countless ethical hedges and ditches, without apparent discomfiture to her muslin. A dozen emulous young persons in, or just out of, pinafores, swift-runners, had taken the field. Half the number of habituated old ones were there, formidable with experience and wigs. Poetesses, authoresses, heiresses, were there. In the field, too, was Mrs. M'Murphy, an Irish Giantess, who made a point of asking

directly of men whatever she wanted; terrible to deal with!
Mrs. Cashentire, a banker's wife, who behaved as if she
had been his relict: Lady Attenbury, who followed the
fashion. Lastly, Camilla Duvergey, the fastest young
woman of the day. All these female harriers were in the
field prepared to give chase to the Griffin.

Miss Blewins said, he must be converted to a nobler conception of the Dignity of Woman, and her Mission.

Mrs. M'Murphy averred, "she should be dis'pinted if
she didn't marr' him," and, hearing that he was already
married, shrieked "Ow;" for which the Hon. Mrs. Breakyeline sneered at her, and scandalously declared he was still
to be had: but Lady Blandish, and Lady Attenbury, were
neighbours of his, and knew that the game was scarce tract-
able.

In pursuance of their resolve, the hardiest of these terrible persecutors announced their intention of coming down
to Raynham to sit at Gamaliel's feet and drink of wisdom
from its source.

"What am I to do?" cried the unhappy Griffin, when
the news reached him.

"Hire a Boy and a Mantle, Sir. I see nothing else for
it," said Adrian.

The Baronet stroked his brow, as if he already felt Bully
Bottom's Garland.

"But when they have read my opinion of them," he exclaimed fretfully, "what do they want with me?"

"That's it," Adrian remarked. "They want to change
it. Sheba once made a far journey!"

Solomon shook his head.

The ladies were true to their threat. Miss Blewins, the
long-nosed, the literary, was the first to arrive. Her followed
the short-haired Joy, the half-man. Then came Mrs. Cashentire, succeeded by the bony big Celt, and the swift Camilla,
and nameless worshipers, who all introduced themselves, and

claimed admittance on the strength of their admiration of THE PILGRIM'S SCRIP.

Sir Austin did his best to receive them graciously, and his sister, Mrs. Doria Forey, the female Head of his house, kept her eyes in wakeful watch on them. They came, and did not go. They formed a Court about him; listening to him eagerly, and sighing at his inveterate conclusions: hoping higher things of Woman, and meekly combating till they fell. A Tournament was held nightly.

Miss Blewins, the long-nosed, the literary, elected herself spokeswoman, and held the post in spite of vehement obstructions from Mrs. M'Murphy.

"Oh, Sir Austin," she ejaculated, "it is surely our Education which causes us to shine at such a disadvantage! You make dolls of us! puppets! Are we not something—something more?"

"Aren't we yer mothers?" shouts the M'Murphy.

"Are we not delegated to a higher office in conjunction with Man?" continued the Maiden, heedless of the vulgar interruption. "Is it only for our beauty you take us?" And she lifted her length of nose pathetically.

"You compel us," stammered Miss Joy, who knew the sequence.

"You compel us," Miss Blewins caught her by the skirt, "you compel us to lean on our acquirements utterly, and you wonder that Woman deprived of inner life, is found wanting in moral self-support!"

This was not going to the root of the matter. The Baronet would smile in pity, and put a case to her.

"A woman, Madam, the sole representative of her sex! Suppose her upon an Island peopled by nothing but men.—"

"Horrut!" the M'Murphy howls, and the exclamation was repeated in English by the whole Court.

"I ask you," he calmly resumed, "to accord me your candid opinion how that woman would be treated, even though the men were hinds—all but savages?"

The Court mutely consulted, and Miss Blewins was approved in observing, that she really did honestly think that the single representative of her sex would—shocking as her situation must be deemed—be treated with due respect, and esteem, if not with reverence, nay, worship!

Then the ladies, warming to the notion, cried out with one voice, that it would be delightful! that she would be a Queen, a Priestess among them. Numbers pined for such a fate. The swift Camilla vowed she never should be happy till she reigned in that blissful Island.

"Good!" said Sir Austin. "And now reverse the case. Conceive an Island peopled by Women, and but one Man in their Society: tossed there, say, by shipwreck.—Hem!" and the Aphorist looked arch. "What course of treatment might that one Man anticipate at their hands?"

Silence, and abashed blushes, and smothered silver laughter, received this second Supposition. How indeed would he be treated? To which of the ladies would he belong? A shipwrecked mariner is not easily made a Priest of; and if they crowned him King, the prime consideration still remained at issue—to whom would he belong? He must belong to some one of them! The Court was split. A few ladies faintly maintained that he would be prudently impounded till such time as they could make suitable use of him, and despatch him in safety, sound of limb, from the Isle. Lady Blandish, too, suggested the present instance of an Aphorist, and a hostile one, alone in their company, and undamaged, she hoped: and Miss Blewins desperately attempted to claim the triumph of the illusion for Woman; inasmuch as it was admitted, that Woman would leaven the male mass by her presence, whereas a feminine community, hitherto smiling and uncorrupt, was, by the inauspicious sea-gift of one of the opposite sex, depraved. It was barely necessary that Sir Austin should expose her as a sophist, to stride victorious through the field. A Majority of the ladies, headed by Mrs. M'Murphy, who was very outspoken about the claims she should put forth to the Man, let it be seen that in their gentle bosoms they believed that unfortunate male would fare sadly, if he did not ultimately suffer the fate of a celebrated mythic Singer. Torn in pieces! was the all but unanimous Verdict on the Wretch. There was no Chivalry in Woman. So these ladies confessed. Her spirit of appropriation was too strong!

That some great things are done without design, and that certain wonderful victories may be found more costly than a defeat, it were loss of time to insist upon. The ladies who formed the Court at Raynham had doubtless no conspiracy to succumb to the insult of the SHADDOCK DOGMA, thereby to ensnare and make foolish its pronouncer; and the Baronet assuredly entertained no idea that an uninterrupted career of logical conquest endangered his stability. He thought, naturally, that the more he overthrew her in argument, the safer his position. Nevertheless, he was melting to Woman. Woman appreciated his Aphorisms, and Man did not. That was possibly a reason. When the inferior creature appreciates us, we cease to despise her. When the inferior creature acknowledges her fault, she is already rising in the scale. She exhibits Intelligence; she gives proof of Humility; two excellent bases for the building of a better hope for her. The change was insensible in Sir Austin; a work of months and years. He was surrounded by an admiring circle of sweet women, and against the charm of their society what Shaddock Dogmatist, however soured and reluctant, can hold out lastingly? It is an opposite extreme of the peril of entire abstraction from them, which has ruined renowned Saints, who had trusted that way to solve man's problem. Sir Austin's state was nearly as precarious as Saint Anthony's. The vision of a single young woman is said to have overcome the inflammable Monk: twenty of these were now besetting our fire-proof Baronet. The fact of a Shaddock Dogmatist resisting them to any extent, may account for his being so pertinaciously pursued. Be it

said, for the honour of the sex, Women esteem not easy
game. Adonis is wished for his beauty, and Lovelace for
his naughty character: but Beauty and Wickedness, though
desirable, are small deer. It is the rank misogynist, who
flees them, whom they hunt down as far as he will go. Him
they regard as the noble stag of the forest, and to catch him
they disencumber themselves of many garments retained in
a common chase.

From THE PILGRIM'S SCRIP, it was clear that Sir Austin
knew them mighty hunters: as thus:

'The Amazon cut off a breast to battle: How will not
Woman disfigure and unsex herself to gain her end?'

And further, mournfully:

'To withstand them, must we first annihilate our Mothers
within us: die half!'

The poor gentleman, seriously believing Woman to be a
Mistake, had long been trying to do so. Had he succeeded,
he would have died his best half, for his mother was strong
in him. The very acridity of the Aphorisms, the GREAT
SHADDOCK DOGMA itself, sprang from wounded softness,
not from hardness. It may be that the unerring scent of the
hounds in pursuit told them this. One who really despised
them had left them in peace.

Beyond dispute, Sir Austin must have fallen a prey to
them, and they were to have added a Griffin to their Zoolog-
ical Garden of tributaries: the greater his æsthetic, the
more positive their earthy, triumphs: and he might say, 'If
I fall, I fall perforce of spiritual superiority, for they can but
tempt my baser nature, and were they to rise to me, there
would be no jeopardy.' He must have been ultimately betrayed by his softness, but, as often happens, he was fully
armed at his weakest point; namely, the heart. He had a
son, and his heart was filled by him. He had a son, and
he was incubating a System.

To the Son, and to the System, the stranger ladies of the
Court were introduced. In the former, they beheld a hand-

some, graceful, boy, not unlike other boys, but looking the pick of them. The latter was a puzzle.

Sir Austin explained it in his Aphoristic fashion.

"Sin is an alien element in our blood. 'Tis the Apple-Disease with which Nature has striven since Adam. To treat Youth as naturally sinful, is, therefore, false, and bad; as it is bad, and false, to esteem it radically pure. We must consider that we have forfeited Paradise, but were yet grown there.

"Belonging, then, by birth to Paradise, our tendency should even be towards it: allowing no lower standard than its Perfection.

"The Triumph of man's intellect, the proof of his power, is to make the Serpent who inhabits us fight against himself, till he is destroyed.

"My son possesses Pride, say. Human Pride is a well-adjusted mixture of Good and Evil. Well; it tempts him to conceive that he is more than his fellows. Let it, as it can, lift him to *be* more than his fellows, and at once he will cease to conceive it: the fight will have been fought: the Devil will be dead.

"For this is our divine consolation: that Evil may be separated from Good: but Good cannot be separated from Evil: the Devil may, the Angel will not, be driven out from us. A truly good man is possible upon Earth: a thoroughly bad man is not possible. This you admit?"

The poor ladies murmured, that they admitted it. Man! Man! Man! they began to feel in their souls a dreadful antagonism to Man.

"Well!" and the Baronet sententiously pursued.

He did right to preach to women: men would not have listened to him. As it was, Miss Joy Blewins, and Mrs. M'Murphy, were restive.

The gist of the System set forth: That a Golden Age, or something near it, might yet be established on our sphere, when fathers accepted their solemn responsibility, and studied human nature with a Scientific eye, knowing what a high Science it is, to live: and that, by hedging round the Youth from corruptness, and at the same time promoting his animal health, by helping him to grow, as he would, like a Tree of Eden; by advancing him to a certain moral fortitude ere the Apple-Disease was spontaneously developed, there would be seen something approaching to a perfect Man, as the Baronet trusted to make this one Son of his, after a receipt of his own.

What he exactly meant by the Apple-Disease, he did not explain: nor did the ladies ask for an explanation. Intuitively they felt hot when it was mentioned.

Miss Blewins said the idea was very original.

"A gigantic task!" said Mrs. Cashentire.

"It's more than ye'll do though. Take my word for it," said the M'Murphy, and the Hon. Mrs. Breakyeline vowed, "She liked a man to be a man." She was evidently not the Uncorrupted Eve.

But whatever folly there was in the System, it saved its author for awhile, at least, and cleansed his Court of such ladies as had come there for a lower motive than the Adoration of Wisdom. The swift Camilla wished she could have waited for the youth. She could not, she declared, and retired, followed in her secession by the M'Murphy, who plainly told Sir Austin, that, now young men had got the taste for Apples, they would bite at them. Ohers departed to combat the GREAT SHADDOCK DOGMA in books, and justify it by their acts. The System was left with a few occasionally-visiting old Maids, and eccentric wives, and the neighbouring fair Widow Blandish, to work itself out, and then was peace again at Raynham Abbey.

CHAPTER II

A GLIMPSE BEHIND THE MASK

FAME, the chief retainer of distinguished families, has first sounded the origin of the Feverels where their line of Ancestry blossoms with a Baronet; and Rumour, the profane vagabond, who will not take service in any respectable household, whispers that he was a Villain. At all events, for this proud race, behind his dazzling appearance sits Darkness and democratic Adam, and they cling to him as an ark of pure aristocracy. Sir Pylcher Feverel, they will tell you, assuming a Norman air to deliver it, spelt his name (or meant to spell it) Fiervarelle; a name hearing which you seem to hear a trumpet blown remote, from the Conqueror's ranks, in the morning, in the mists, over Pevensey: youthful Feverels of the latest generation have been known to challenge the Saxon towards the same hour, by announcing themselves as formidably. This luminous Knight (still to follow the traditions of the family, for the sake of avoiding a challenge), having quarters on the Welsh frontier, mixed his blood with the royal blood ap Gruffudh: from whose fair Princess the Welsh estates were inherited, and who must at the same time have endowed them with that Cymric tinge to their habits and mental cast observable in the fortunes of the race. At what period they quitted Cheshire and settled upon Thames is a matter of family controversy, and History, unable to decide, has declined to speak on the point. They were great on their pedigree, and held that an old Baronetcy is worth any new Dukedom, and that good blood is Heaven's first-gift. Occasionally in its downward course the blood branched into many channels: and again it shrunk into one. Sir Caradoc Feverel, the predecessor of Sir Austin, was an only son; twice, it was said, on the verge of death before he had a successor, and then they came in

numbers. There was a Mrs. Malediction in the House
(bequeathed by the great Sir Pylcher). Often had she all
but cut them off from their old friend, Time, and they revived again. Whether it was the Apple-Disease, or any
other, strong constitutions seemed struggling in them with
some peculiar malady. Of course, members of the family
were foremost in spilling loyal blood on Marston Moor,
that great field of phlebotomy to so many Cavaliers. With
the increase of their wealth, owing to the discovery of
mineral treasures on their ap Gruffudh grounds, they sank
into quiescent Tories, and spent the better portion of their
time in essays at Agriculture and Park-planting at home,
while abroad they did battle on behalf of Protection.

The house they lived in, called an Abbey from some tradition of its site, was a heterogeneous architectural jumble,
which nevertheless presented a generous front to a broad
westward valley of green pastures, fruitful tillage, and a
pure-flowing wave; and seen from the river, on its platform
of greensward, backed by lofty pines and flanked with beech-
woods midway down a hillocky roll of grass, that ended in
flat rich meadows extending to the river-side, deserved some
better title than that of Raynham Ramshackle, as the Papworths, old political antagonists of the Feverels, delighted
to term it. A child, with two perpendicular lines and one
horizontal, could have designed the mansion of Sir Miles
Papworth, shining down the valley, towards Lobourne; and
a child, too, might have designed Sir Miles, and accurately
sketched him when it drew a round impending upon a round
of exaggerated girth, from which two stumpy down-strokes
stuck forth to prop the fabric. Sir Miles was a Saxon born
and bred, and (though not consequently) a Whig. He was
a mature specimen of modern England's vaunted race: or
let us say, the vaunted race of modern England's novelists.
He was the heroic grain they cut types from. In his youth
he had amassed good muscle, and sank down on it, in his
decline, to drink Port. Prosperous, pig-headed, and just in

proportion: bald and rubicund: corpulent, hearty, and bandy: a domestic despot, a staunch subject, a fair-dealing father, a foe to innovation and ideas, a devoted worshiper of himself against the world, this old hero was the contrast of the Head of the Fiervarelles, and fought the Battle of Hastings with him more than once, and beat him on one field. Sir Austin was unhappy in his Marriage, and Sir Miles, entrenched in a well-drilled, many-childed, timid little shadow of a wife, vastly enjoyed his social advantage over the lord of Raynham. Not to have mastered a woman, he thought the meanest confession a man could make, and, apart from political feud, he had no pity for his wretched rival Baronet, though, between his port, he vented much damnable condolence. THE PILGRIM'S SCRIP he held in contempt, being an admirer of Woman, whom he said, he never had any difficulty in understanding. His way of reading them was decidedly straightforward. On the field of politics, he had to lay down his arms to Sir Austin. Feverel was the richer man, and the County was agricultural and Tory. Hence their dissension. The battle was well-fought, and, though beaten, the Saxon did not give in: but he was no match for the Conqueror's Cook. The strategy of Raynham's Dining-hall overpowered him. Of that hall, at least, the Papworths could say nothing derogatory without betraying miserable envy. Jolly farmers had sighed in it; influential tradesmen with a taste for land, had there been kindled into high enthusiasm for the Old Blood. The legs of devoted plumpers had grown weak under Raynham's famous mahogany, and their heads strong. Sir Austin's Cook thrice returned him to Parliament.

The Dining-hall had been closed seven years when THE PILGRIM'S SCRIP appeared: closed seldom to hear revel again. There at one end drooped two mouldy standards, wrung from the foeman by a Feverel on the battle-field: between them a Golden Torque set in a frame, said to have belonged once to a warrior of the ap Gruffudh. A sense of

cobwebs and the reign of the spider hung about its heavy
oak-carvings. The music of glasses, the laughter of free-
men, was dumb there. The place seemed to have forgotten
how once within the jovial four walls Britons had been
touched to the quick by the great wines, shrewd dishes! how
whiskers had been widened by the grin!

In those days Sir Austin Feverel was thought a royal man,
and was in a fair way to be beloved. He was frank and
warm with his friends; generous to the poor, and above all,
delicate with them, who have the keenest instinct for a
gentleman, and venerated him accordingly. When his
disaster befell him, and his home was suddenly desolate, it
was as though his tree of life had shrunk under a blight.
He shut himself up as he did his Dining-hall; relinquished
Parliament, and bade a mute adieu to Ambition. People
were astonished at the utter change wrought in so apparently
proud and self-reliant a man: but old folks, that knew the
family, said, they expected it some day or other. It was in
the blood, they said: Sir Caradoc, his father, was a strange
hand, and so was his father, Sir Algernon, before him: they
were all sure to turn out a little wrong some day or other.
And the old folks tapped their foreheads meaningly.

Sir Austin also came to their conclusion, that it was in
his blood; a superstition he had aforetime smiled at. He had
regarded his father, Sir Caradoc, as scarce better than a
madman when he spoke of a special Ordeal for their race;
and when, in his last hour (the sails of the knightly bark
then loosening to the night wind on the fast-ebbing tide),
the old Baronet caught his elder son's hand, and desired him
to be forewarned, Austin had. while bowing respectfully,
wondered that Reason was not vouchsafed to his parent at
that supreme instant. From the morning hills of existence
he beheld a clear horizon. He was no sooner struck hard
than Sir Caradoc's words smote him like a revelation. He
believed that a curse was in his blood; a poison of Retribution, which no life of purity could expel; and grew, perhaps,

more morbidly credulous on the point than his predecessor: speaking of the Ordeal of the Feverels, with sonorous solemnity, as a thing incontrovertibly foredecreed to them. Vainly his friends argued, that men commonly calculated on wounds and bruises, and were not disappointed. Sir Austin, strong in the peculiar sharpness of the sting darted into him, held that there was an entire distinction in their lot: that other men were tried by puny ailments; were not searched and shaken by one tremendous shock, as of a stroke of Heaven's lightning. He indicated that the Fates and Furies were quite as partial as Fortune. Stricken Pride, and a feverish blood, made him seek consolation in this way.

The outline of the Baronet's story was by no means new. He had a wife, and he had a friend. His marriage was for love; his wife was a beauty; his friend was a poet. Sir Austin Feverel did nothing by halves. His wife had his whole heart, and his friend all his confidence. When he selected Denzil Somers from among his College chums, it was not on account of any similarity of disposition between them, but from his intense worship of Genius, which made him overlook the absence of principle in his associate, for the sake of such brilliant promise. Denzil had a small patrimony to lead off with, but that he dissipated before he left College, and thenceforth he was dependent upon his admirer, with whom he lived, filling a nominal post of bailiff to the estates, and launching forth Verse of some satiric and sentimental quality; for being inclined to vice, and occasionally, in a quiet way, practising it, he was, of course, a sentimentalist and a satirist, entitled to lash the Age, and complain of human nature. His earlier Poems, published under the pseudonym of Diaper Sandoe, were so pure and bloodless in their love-passages, and at the same time so biting in their moral tone, that his reputation was great among the virtuous, who form the larger portion of the English book-buying public. Election-seasons called him to ballad-poetry on behalf of the Tory party, and lines of his on "Sir Miles Paunch," adapted to the dialect of the County (wherein two Countrymen meet to discuss the nation's affairs, and contend, in iambics, one, that all goes wrong for want of a Head in Parliament—a clear allusion to the Feverel faction—the other, that the country labours lacking Paunch there—grotesquely describing the Papworth minority—and the arguments of the two end in a fight, when the Head-man finishes by doubling-up the Paunch-man), appealed triumphantly to popular British humour, and shared in routing the Saxon at the hustings. Diaper possessed undoubted fluency, but did little, though Sir Austin was ever expecting much of him.

A pale, languishing, inexperienced, woman, whose husband, in mental, and in moral, stature is more than the ordinary height above her, and who, now that her first romantic admiration of his lofty bearing has worn off, and her little fretful refinements of taste and sentiment are not instinctively responded to, is thrown into no wholesome household collision with a fluent man, fluent in prose and rhyme. Lady Feverel, when she first entered on her duties at Raynham, was jealous of her husband's friend, and moved the very foundation-stones of the house to get his dismissal; ineffectually: Sir Austin reasoned with her,—an insult in such cases, as a woman knows, and that she does not pardon. Diaper remained, and led his old chrysalis life from which he was some day to emerge a resplendent butterfly. Good cellars, choice company, a house in town, pocket-money at command, one may believe (Sir Austin did) that it was not he who sought the ruin, and courted temptation. By degrees the lady tolerated him. In time he touched his guitar in her chamber, and they played Rizzio and Mary together.

> "For I am not the first who found
> The name of Mary fatal!"

says a subsequent sentimental alliterative love-poem of Diaper's.

Such was the outline of the story. But the Baronet could fill it up. He had opened his soul to these two. He had been noble Love to the one, and to the other perfect Friendship. He had bid them be brother and sister, whom he loved, and live a Golden Age with him at Raynham. In fact, he had been prodigal of the excellencies of his nature, which it is not good to be, and, like Timon, he became bankrupt, and fell upon bitterness.

"Didn't he expect his luck?" cried Sir Miles.

The old Saxon understood women, he did. And he affirmed that the best way to continue their warm admirer was to keep the bit well in their mouths, and lay on the whip now and then. They laugh who win. His wife was a faithful woman.

The faithless lady was of no particular family—an orphan daughter of an Admiral who educated her on his half-pay, and her conduct struck but at the man whose name she bore.

After five years of Marriage, and twelve of Friendship, Sir Austin was left to his loneliness with nothing to ease his heart of love upon save a little baby-boy in a cradle. He forgave the man: he put him aside as poor for his wrath. The woman he could not forgive. She had sinned everyway. Simple ingratitude to a benefactor was a pardonable transgression, for he was not one to recount, and crush the culprit under the heap of his good deeds. But her he had raised to be his equal, and he judged her as his equal. She had blackened the world's fair aspect for him.

In the presence of that world, so different to him now, he preserved his wonted demeanour, and made his features a flexible mask. Mrs. Doria Forey, his widowed sister, said: "Austin might have retired from his Parliamentary career for a time, and given up gaieties, and that kind of thing: her opinion, founded on observation of him in public and private, was, that the light thing that had taken flight was but a feather on her brother's Feverel-heart,—and his ordinary course would be resumed." There are times when common men cannot bear the weight of just so much. Hippias Feverel thought him immensely improved by his misfortune, if the loss of such a person could be so designated; and seeing that Hippias received in consequence free quarters at Raynham, and possession of the wing of the Abbey she had inhabited, it is profitable to know his thoughts. If the Baronet had given two or three blazing dinners in the great Hall, he would have deceived people generally, as he did his relations and intimates. He was too sick for that: fit only for passive acting.

A stern cold man, it was said: touched in his Pride—nowhere but there.

The nursemaid waking in the night, beheld a solitary figure darkening a lamp above her little sleeping charge, and became so used to the sight as never to wake with a start. One night she was strangely aroused by a sound of sobbing. The Baronet stood beside the cot in his long black cloak and travelling-cap. His fingers shaded a lamp, and reddened against the fitful darkness that ever and anon went leaping up the wall. She could hardly believe her senses to see the austere gentleman, dead silent, dropping tear upon tear before her eyes. She lay stone-still in a trance of terror and mournfulness, mechanically counting the tears as they fell, one by one. The hidden face, the fall and flash of those heavy drops in the light of the lamp he held, the upright, awful figure, agitated at regular intervals, like a piece of clockwork, by the low murderous catch of his breath: it was so painfully piteous to her poor human nature that her heart began wildly palpitating. Involuntarily the poor girl cried out to him, "Oh, Sir!" and fell a-weeping. Sir Austin turned the lamp on her pillow, and harshly bade her go to sleep, striding from the room forthwith.

To express sympathy for a Feverel during his Ordeal, was a grave misdemeanour: to surprise the Head of the family unmanned was a mortal offence. Dian was not more chastely jealous of her bath, than Sir Austin of the moment when his knightly chainmail was removed, and his heart stood bare.

Poor Polly-Actæon was summoned to the Baronet's study next morning, and was shortly afterwards deported from the Abbey by his man, like a guilty thing whose touch to the rest of the inmates was contagion: her cheeks in a deluge, and a seal on her mouth.

CHAPTER III

MRS. MALEDICTION

ON one occasion in the year, the old Hall tried to know itself again. The logs blazed, and the table was laid to celebrate young Richard's birthday. October summoned every connection of the Feverels to this festivity. The boy's uncles, Algernon, the guardsman, Cuthbert, the sailor, Vivian, the diplomatist and beau, made a point of coming, for not to be present on that great day of the golden month, was to encounter a cold eye and a colder forefinger when they at other times required the Baronet's consideration and an order on his Bankers. Hippias was always on the spot, prepared to drink anybody's health. The ladies of the family were likewise assembled. Notwithstanding their goodwill in seconding the gentlemen, it was a frigid feast. Sir Austin sat in the presence of a phantom. He brightened after dinner, as the young heir was trotted in to hear himself toasted. Possibly that was his one happy moment of the year. Mr. Justice Harley, the husband of a Feverel, proposed the toast; supported by Colonel Wentworth, another husband of a Feverel. The ladies smiled, nodded, and kissed the boy. The Baronet drank him solemnly exuberant.

Then a glass of wine is poured out for Master Richard, and his father's one happy moment is over.

"You have given him port, Algernon," he says. "I think it not good for him."

"Better accustom him to the best at once," pleads Algernon.

"A little mulled claret, very weak," the Baronet suggests.

"Deprave his young taste?" cries Vivian.

"Let it be half water," the Baronet falters.

"Worst thing for his health!" growls Hippias, deep in his second bottle.

Sir Austin still hesitating, Mr. Justice Harley cites a Greek proverb pointing out the deadliness of water to the soul: Colonel Wentworth comes down on him with a camp-couplet sparkling with the virtues of the pure vintage: minor cousins and remote Feverels raise a hum of supplication for the little gaping fellow. Simultaneously Vivian and Cuthbert announce, that they expect to be thanked in form, and that it's only once a year.

"Only once a year!" echo the ladies. "Only one glass!" And those born Pagans carry the day. The wine is applied to little Ricky's mouth, who sucks and sucks, winking fearful satisfaction under his father's alarmed eyes, and coughing violently halfway down the glass, which fortunate interposition rescues him from the remaining portion; every Feverel declaring that he does it like a man: whereupon the young heir is kissed half out of his scarlet frock by the women, and, after giving an honest fist to the men all round, and an embrace to his father, marches off to bed, and stomach-ache.

It may be conceived, that while Sir Austin could hesitate and permit himself to be overborne in his judgment of what was good for his son, his System was not yet ripe. In fact, it grew as the boy grew. On Richard's seventh birthday, it was excited to some definite shape, and was not so pliable. The members of the family were at breakfast with little

Richard, and Sir Austin had joked his brother-in-law Wentworth on his habit of excessive early rising, as his man had
seen the Colonel coming across the Park, apparently from
the village, at six in the morning: to which the Colonel
carelessly replied, that he could not sleep, and the matter
was passing off, when Ricky cries out: "Oh, Papa! and I
couldn't sleep, too! Oh, you know, I was dreaming all
night long! And first I dreamed I was a ship sailing on
the sea, like Nurse sings. And then I dreamed I was a
bird, and flew, and felt so funny—just here," traversing his
birthday diaphragm with a finger. "And then I dreamed—
what was it? Oh! up I started in bed, and there was a
beautiful lady! beautifuller than my Nurse, or you, or you,
or you," pointing to his Aunts, "and she kissed me."

Sir Austin had listened with a pleased attention to his
boy's prattle. The mention of the Lady changed his face.

"Kissed you, my child?" he asked anxiously.

"Yes, Papa. On the forehead—here."

The Baronet turned sharply to his sister. "Have they
been talking to him of ghosts?"

"Certainly not," replied Mrs. Doria, "They dared not.
I think you had better let it drop, before the children."

Sir Austin held back his son, as the other young ones
flew forth to their games, and took him to a window.

"Kissed you, my son? where?"

"Here, Papa." The boy touched the centre of his forehead.

"And what then? what did she do then?"

"I don't remember any more, Papa. I was so sleepy."

"You are sure she did not speak to you, my son?"

"Oh, yes, Papa! quite sure of that."

Little Richard had spoken what he knew, but observing
an inquiring hesitation linger in his father's eyes, and loath
to let it go unsatisfied, he drew upon his imagination instantly, and began to pour forth what he now remembered
the Lady next did, and next did, with astounding readiness.

"And then she stood me up in bed, and said, 'I could kiss you all to rags, you darling pet—how you're growing!' And she said, 'If I had you with me, wouldn't you have nice things.' And told me she would give me a pony, a better one than you're going to give me, Papa—all white, with a spot between his eyes, and a silver bit, and a gold bridle. And he's called Prince Jack!"

Sir Austin listened credulously to it all, and was only persuaded to let the child follow his playmates, by Mrs. Doria's impetuous assurance that he was ruining his son.

"Can you not perceive, Austin," she said, "you are teaching him to invent?"

"Helen!" returned the Baronet. "What he has seen, has been seen in this house before, and is not a good omen. I do not perhaps altogether believe in supernatural visitations. Call it an optical delusion. It is in the habit of coming to us when something is about to happen."

Master Richard threw gallons of cold water on the pleasures of the day by his morning's eloquence, and had his enjoyments thwarted at every turn. His uncle Cuthbert had proposed to take him for a sail on the river. A peremptory message arrived just as they were getting ready, that the boy was on no account to go on the water. His tears were dried by the promise of a ride on horseback with his uncle Vivian, and the horse was brought round, Vivian in the saddle, and the boy just being lifted up to him, when Sir Austin appeared, and forbade it, to the grief and rage of the poor little fellow. Then he was to have fired off his own handsome beautiful pieces of small brass cannon, his uncle Algernon's birthday present, and again his father was on the spot, and would only allow him to take hold of Algernon's coat-skirt while the match was applied. On the cricketing field, whither he went later in the day, to witness the match played by the lads of Lobourne, with his uncle Algernon, against the lads of Bursley, and a terrible-swift bowler, his temper was so put to it that he exhibited the gravest sign of precocious intelligence: he swore. He had requested the favour of an ice: but was begged by his father to consider that it would not agree with him. He petitioned for a cake, and Reason again stept forward, like a detestable friend, to ask him to withstand his inclinations till dinner-time. Ricky bore it. He was in that calm mood when the cup is full. Now fell a Lobourne-wicket to Bursley's terrible-swift bowler, and, amid cheers from the spectators, Captain Algernon Feverel shouldered his bat, and leisurely strode to his innings, the Hope of Lobourne. He was settling his preliminaries (the most important of which seemed to be to attain an extreme salient posture of his manly person in the eyes of the ladies), when a messenger reached Sir Austin, and spoke a few words to him, who now, jogging his son's hand, said in a cheerful voice; "Come along, my son! the Doctor is waiting for us."

"The Doctor!" exclaimed sweet Lady Blandish, standing by with her old lord not yet gone. "Whatever can the dear boy want with a Doctor?"

"He is seven years old to-day, Madam," replied Sir Austin. "I wish him to be examined medically from head to foot, that I may be sure he is physically sound for his second seven-years' march, as he is morally promising."

The Baronet smiled down on his son, and beheld a cloud not at all morally promising on the brows of him.

"Come!" he said.

"No!" cried Richard, releasing his hand.

"Come!" his father repeated, while his brows went up.

Richard fell back sullenly.

"I desire you to come, my boy," said his father, with the gentle severity of a last command.

And the young seven-year-old, wrought to the furthest pitch of endurance, stamped his loot, and flushed, as he cried, looking his father full in the face, "I won't! Damned if I do!"

Of course, he had to go; but when he came back, approved

robust, he was covered with the caresses of the field, and enjoyed an enraptured hug from Lady Blandish: the lady provoking thereby those reflections in THE PILGRIM'S SCRIP, 'On the Popularity of the Forbidden Fruit, and the preference we have for it, provided an Innocent offer it us.'

Little Ricky returned from his Examination in time to witness the Catastrophe of the day. His Uncle Algernon was still in, batting gloriously: his elegant figure and fine legs deservedly admired by the ladies. A shot from Bursley's terrible-swift bowler took him on the forward thigh, and he was seen limping towards the tents with considerable lack of grace, and a ruefully animated expression. Dr. Clifford of Lobourne was present, and perused the bruise. He had him conveyed immediately to the house, where, towards night, it was debated whether there was to be a leg less in the family, as was soon the case.

"Said I not, Something would happen?" remarked Sir Austin, not altogether dissatisfied.

"Oh, confound Mrs. Malediction!" Algernon groaned to Colonel Wentworth.

"You're as staunch a believer in her now as Austin," said the Colonel. "It's true that the boy did see a woman."

"What woman?" asked Algernon.

"His mother!" replied the Colonel.

"Confound the women, then!" cried the poor one-legged Guardsman.

Colonel Wentworth did not make this revelation to Sir Austin, and the latter from that day incorporated a little of his superstition with his System.

CHAPTER IV

THE INMATES OF RAYNHAM ABBEY

RICHARD's Uncles pass out of his history after this sacrifice of a leg for him. Cuthbert, the sailor, perished in a spirited boat-expedition against a slaving Negro-chief up the Niger. Some of the gallant lieutenant's trophies of war decorated the little boy's play-shed at Raynham, and he bequeathed his sword to Richard, whose hero he was. The diplomatist and beau, Vivian, ended his flutterings from flower to flower by making an improper marriage, as is the fate of many a beau, and was struck out of the list of visitors. Algernon generally occupied the Baronet's disused Town house, a wretched being, dividing his time between horse, and card, exercise: possessed, it was said, of the absurd notion, that a man who has lost his balance by losing his leg, may regain it by sticking to the Bottle. At least, whenever he and Hippias got together, they never failed to try whether one leg, or two, stood the Bottle best, and it was known that the ardour of the contest now and then put them both in a position not to require balance. They were stout drinkers, and the primogenital cellars were not niggard of their stores. Much of a Puritan as Sir Austin was in his habits, he was too good a host, and too thorough a gentle· man, to impose them upon his guests. The brothers, and other relatives, might do as they would while they did not disgrace the name, and then it was final: they must depart to behold his countenance no more.

Algernon Feverel was a simple sort of man, who felt, subsequent to his misfortune, as he had perhaps dimly fancied it before, that his career lay in his legs, and was now irrevocably cut short. He taught the boy boxing, and shooting, and the arts of fence, and superintended the direction of his animal vigour with a melancholy vivacity. The remaining energies of Algernon's mind were devoted to animadversions on Swift-bowling. He preached it over the County, struggling through laborious literary compositions, addressed to sporting newspapers, on the Decline of Cricket. In Adrian Harley's words, he bored everybody so that he took off the bales of Forbearance and knocked down the stumps of Patience. It was Algernon who witnessed and chronicled Richard's first fight, a very plucky combat with young Tom Blaize of Belthorpe Farm, three years the boy's senior, whom, with the aid of Science, he defeated.

Hippias Feverel was once thought to be the genius of the family. It was his ill luck to have strong appetites and a weak stomach; and, as one is not altogether fit for the Battle of Life who is engaged in a perpetual contention with his dinner, Hippias forsook his prospects at the Bar, and, in the embraces of dyspepsia, compiled his ponderous work on the Fairy Mythology of Europe. He had little to do with the Hope of Raynham, beyond what he endured from his juvenile tricks.

A venerable lady, known as Great-Aunt Grantley, who had money to bequeath to the Heir, and whom Adrian called The Eighteenth Century, occupied with Hippias the back ground of the house, and shared her caudles with him. These two were seldom seen till the dinner-hour, for which they were all day preparing, and probably all night remembering: for The Eighteenth Century was an admirable trencherman, and cast age aside while there was a dish on the table.

Very much against her will, Mrs. Doria Forey, though the female head of the house, was not allowed to come to the fore, while the System was at work, as she would have done in any other establishment but that of the author of THE PILGRIM'S SCRIP. She was the elder of the three sisters of the Baronet, a florid affable woman, with fine teeth, exceedingly fine light wavy hair, a Norman nose, and a reputation for understanding men, which, with these practical creatures, always means, the art of managing them. She had married an expectant younger son of a good family, who deceased before fulfilment; and, casting about in her mind the future chances of her little daughter, the sole child, Clare, she marked down a probability; and the far sight, the deep determination, the resolute perseverance, of her sex, where a daughter is to be provided for, and a man to be overthrown, instigated her to invite herself to Raynham, and, with that daughter, she fixed herself there, to watch the System, and sap it. Not that she did not love her brother, Austin; she thought him an incomparable man, and tenderly pitied him: but that she deemed the System Nonsense: its interdict against the espousals of cousins, Nonsense: all experiments in education, Nonsense.

'Women,' says THE PILGRIM'S SCRIP, 'are, by nature, our staunchest Conservatives. We must look on them as the Bulwarks of Society.'

Which may, or may not, be true, but is surely in a manner complimentary, and was true in Mrs. Doria's case. She had never forgiven Cromwell the execution of the Martyr Charles; and to extenuate the conduct of the great Roundhead Captain, was to make Mrs. Doria despise and detest you, if you did not lie direct in her line of tactics for the time being: in which instance she would sigh, and deplore your mistake, and draw melting pictures of the sufferings of her Martyr, and ask you whether you had a heart. Adrian Harley, who sided with the Commonwealth, not from any sympathy, for he abjured politics, as a Wise Youth should, but for the pleasure of taking an adverse view, and to tease her,—him she was, during the first period of her residence at Raynham, inclined for that sole reason to hate, till she perceived his influence with the Baronet, and then she said, lamenting for him, he had no heart: but Austin Wentworth, the Colonel's son, a Republican on principle, as true a Christian and kindly a spirit as ever walked the earth, who had small influence with the Baronet, she for her sole reason quite hated, and conscientiously damaged him wherever she could; not shrinking from frequent hints and amplifications of an unhappy story of the poor youth's, in support of the Cause of her Martyr; and it is certain that Mrs. Doria's constant insinuations made the Baronet look dubiously on one who was ever his son's best friend.

Austin's story was of that wretched character which to

be comprehended, that justice should be dealt him, must be told out, and openly; which no one dares now do.

For a fault in early youth, redeemed by him nobly, according to his light, he was condemned to undergo the world's harsh judgment: not for the fault—for its atonement.

"—Married his mother's housemaid," whispered Mrs. Doria, with a ghastly look, and a shudder at Republicans.

And women gave the young man a cold shoulder. Marble-cold they can make that lovely feature of their persons, when they please; in a way unknown to men. What right had he, for a whim, for a folly, to destroy for ever his prospects? —and theirs? It was true, he was not rich. Still he had an independence. And he was extremely presentable: fair-haired, with a smile sweet as a woman's: gentle as a child: a face set with the seal of a courageous calm: so pure a face that looking on it you seemed to see into his soul. You could not misdoubt him. And he had gone and ruined himself: married that creature! The world of women turned from him as from a blighted rose.

'The compensation for Injustice,' says THE PILGRIM'S SCRIP, 'is, that in that dark Ordeal we gather the worthiest around us.'

And Lady Blandish, and some few true men and women held Austin Wentworth high.

"He was, I think—I do not know—mistaken," the fair widow pleaded for him to the Baronet, "but I cannot blame him. It is so rare to meet that nobleness in men."

Her widow's privilege permitted her to distantly allude to the circumstances of the case.

Sir Austin was a man to estimate and welcome nobleness. He ranked it more, and it was more akin to him, than Intellect. Very different for young Richard would it have been had Austin taken his right place in the Baronet's favour: but Austin had offended against the Baronet's main crotchet: who said, in answer to Lady Blandish, that, to ally oneself randomly was to be guilty of a crime before Heaven greater

than the offence it sought to extinguish; and he had heard
that his nephew was the one seduced. Wherefore he was
doubly foolish; a thing in Sir Austin's opinion, he said,
almost equal to depravity.

"Think, Madam," he argued, "think of the children."

"There may be none," she said.

"They live apart: the woman is vicious, true," the Baronet
resumed. "Think then, Madam—I may speak to you,—
think that he, a young man of excellent qualities, has madly
disinherited his future, and is barren to posterity, while
knaves are propagating. I do not forgive him. The nobler
he, the worse his folly. I do not forgive him."

This it was to look on Life as a Science.

Adrian Harley, who had no views of his own on the subject, except that it was absurd when you were in the mud
to plunge in deeper instead of jumping out, cleverly interpreted his Chief's, and delighted him with swelling periods.

"Marriage," flourished Adrian, "is more than a creation
of the Laws. As the solemn deed of Life, the culminating
act of our existence, an anticipation of its ordinances is not
to be cancelled by seeking their countenance; which endeavour may expose penitence in the offender, but generates
for him Retribution rather than Absolution, in lives unborn,
misbegotten, in a callous companion, in an outraged future
bearing with it a life-long ill-assortedness." And so forth.

Adrian, the Wise Youth Adrian, would never have made
such a mistake. Some people are born green: others yellow.
Adrian was born yellow. He was always on the ripe sensible side of a question.

'In action,' THE PILGRIM'S SCRIP observes, 'Wisdom goes
by majorities.'

Adrian had an instinct for the majorities, and as the world
invariably found him enlisted in its ranks, his appellation of
Wise Youth was generally acquiesced in.

The Wise Youth, then, had the world with him, but no
friends. Nor did he wish for those troublesome appendages

of success. He caused himself to be required by people who could serve him; feared by such as could injure. Not that he went out of the way to secure his end, or risked the expense of a plot. He did the work as easily as he ate his daily bread. Adrian was an Epicurean: one whom Epicurus would have scourged out of his Garden, certainly: an Epicurean of our modern notions. To satisfy his appetites without rashly staking his character, was the Wise Youth's problem for life. He had no intimates save Gibbon and Horace, and the society of these fine aristocrats of literature helped him to accept humanity as it had been, and was; a Supreme Ironic Procession, with Laughter of Gods in the background. Why not Laughter of Mortals also? Adrian had his laugh in his comfortable corner. He possessed peculiar attributes of a Heathen God. He was a disposer of men: he was polished, luxurious, and happy—at their cost. He lived in eminent self-content, as one lying on soft cloud, lapt in sunshine. Nor Jove, nor Apollo, cast eye upon the maids of earth with cooler fire of selection, or pursued them in the covert with more sacred impunity. And he enjoyed his reputation for virtue, as something additional. Stolen fruits are said to be sweet. Undeserved rewards are very exquisite.

The best of it was, that Adrian made no pretences. He did not solicit the favourable judgment of the world. Nature and he attempted no other concealment than the ordinary mask men wear. And yet the world would proclaim him moral, as well as wise, and the pleasing converse everyway of his disgraced cousin, Austin. Adrian had a logical contempt for creatures who do things for mere show, as losing, he said, the core of enjoyment for the rind of respectability. The world might find itself in the wrong: it would find him the same. His ambition, within the reserved limits, was to please himself, as being the best judge and the absolute gainer. Placed on Crusoe's Island, his first cry would have been for clean linen: his next for the bill-of-fare: and then, for that Grand Panorama of the Mistress of the World falling to wreck under the barbarians, which had been the spur and the seal to his mind: twittering Horace in Roman feast-attendant's tunic, twanging his lyre, might charm him to sleep, careless of the morrow, since the day was good.

In a word Adrian Harley had mastered his philosophy at the early age of one-and-twenty. Many would be glad to say the same at that age twice-told: they carry in their breasts a burden with which Adrian's was not loaded. Mrs. Doria was nearly right about his heart. A singular mishap (at his birth, possibly, or before it)· had unseated that organ, and shaken it down to his stomach, where it was a much lighter, nay, an inspiring, weight, and encouraged him merrily onward. Throned in that region, it looked on little that did not arrive to gratify it. Already that region was a trifle prominent in the person of the Wise Youth, and carried, as it were, the flag of his philosophical tenets in front of him. A fat Wise Youth, digesting well: charming after dinner, with men, or with women: soft, dimpled, succulent-looking as a sucking-pig: delightfully sarcastic: perhaps a little too unscrupulous in his moral tone, but that his moral reputation belied him, and it must be set down to generosity of disposition.

Such was Adrian Harley, another of Sir Austin's intellectual favourites, chosen from mankind to superintend the education of his son at Raynham. Adrian had been destined for the Church. He did not enter into Orders. He and the Baronet had a conference together one day, and from that time Adrian became a fixture in the Abbey. His father, Mr. Justice Harley, died in his promising son's College term, bequeathing him nothing but his legal complexion, and Adrian became stipendiary officer in his Uncle's household.

The Wise Youth spread out his mind to the System like a piece of blank paper.

Another chief personage of the establishment was Benson,

the butler: Heavy Benson, Adrian called him, from the mace-like fashion with which he wielded his respectability, and the fact of a connubial misfortune. The latter had recommended him to his patron. Benson was the GREAT SHADDOCK DOGMA condensed in a look: potential with silence:— a taciturn hater of Woman; burly, flabby, and implacable. In him Sir Austin had his only faithful believer, and Adrian his solitary rival. When, after THE PILGRIM'S SCRIP was published, the fair ladies, its admirers, swarmed down to form a Court at Raynham, they were soon taught to stand in fear of Heavy Benson, who read their object, and, if one by chance got closeted with the Baronet, as they were all seeking to do, a knock was sure to come, and Heavy Benson obtruded his glum person into the room on pressing business, and would not go till he had rescued the prey. As Dragons of old guarded the dwellings of beautiful princesses, Heavy Benson stood sentinel over the Baronet. He held the door to them, as they severally departed, and took their discomfiture to his own praise.

With these intimates young Richard Feverel lived in the great House, unconscious of the tight jacket he was gathering flesh to feel. The System hung loosely on his limbs at first. The Curate of Lobourne attended to his rudimentary lessons: a Papworth being sometimes invited to Raynham to play with him, who said, he was a lucky fellow not to be sent to school, and tried to make the boy think so, for which purpose he had, perhaps, been brought over. Now and then a well-meaning friend of Sir Austin's ventured to remonstrate on the dangerous trial he was making in modelling any new plan of Education for a youth, but the Baronet was firm. He pointed to his son, and said, "Match him."

Towards his fourteenth year, however, the young Experiment began to grow exceedingly restless. The Curate of Lobourne sent in a report that Master Richard's lessons were contumaciously disregarded: that in his Latin and

Greek he was retrograding: in propriety of behaviour like-wise; for witness, exhibiting a broken slate and a broken window of the room set apart for his studies. Heavy Benson also laid a portentous book on the Baronet's table, found by him in Master Richard's bedroom, proving to be a Lemprière, and a rather grave sign in Sir Austin's estimation.

"What can this be?" the Baronet meditated, and referred to his Note-Book (a famous and much-feared Instrument at Raynham, which held the bare bones of THE PILGRIM'S SCRIP), wherein the youth's progressionary phases were mapped out in sections, from Simple Boyhood to the Blossoming Season, The Magnetic Age, The Period of Probation, from which, successfully passed through, he was to emerge into a Manhood worthy of Paradise. It was now Simple Boyhood; The Ante-Pomona Stage, as Adrian named it. A slate sent through a window was mere insubordination: a Lemprière in the bedroom looked like precocity,—looked like Pomona in person. Supposing the boy to be precocious, the whole System was disorganized; based as it was upon concordant Nature, after that saying of THE PILGRIM'S SCRIP:

'Health is the Body's Virtue: Truth, the Soul's; Valour springs but from the unison of these twain.'

Sir Austin consulted with his young Achates, and old Dr. Clifford, who were not so perplexed in arriving at a simple conclusion as the philosopher, and said, that the boy only wanted companions of his own age.

"Some one to rub his excessive vitality against, you mean?" asked the Baronet.

"Ay, Sir," Adrian replied. "He is now laden with that superabundant energy which makes a fool of a man, and a scapegrace of a boy, and he wants to work it off."

"Too much Health," added the Doctor, "is inductive Disease."

"Scarcely sound. Scarcely sound," remarked the Baronet, "on that ground you tolerate much. You give human nature

but a short tether. Our Virtues, then, are pigmies, Doctor,
that daren't grow for fear of the sty?"

"Circe looks out for strapping fellows, I fancy," said
Adrian, and closed the session with laughter.

Sir Austin continued to meditate some days, and then
requested the Wise Youth's advice on a proposition conceived by him, to have a boy of Richard's age to stay with
him in the house and be his comrade.

"I think your idea excellent," said Adrian, giving him all
the credit of it. "And I know the very boy that will suit.
Thompson, your solicitor, has a son. Poor fellow! only one,
I believe, and about a dozen girls with parchment exteriors
and snub noses. The whole family's a genesis of sheepskin.
But they're well brought up. You might try the lad, Sir.
The Thompsons stuck by my father in his Brief days."

Sir Austin determined to try the lad whose sisters were
so innocuous. A message was forwarded to Mr. Thompson,
for the loan of his son for a term; and, his son's holidays
being in that season, his son was, in compliance, joyfully
packed down to Raynham Abbey, big with anticipations of
aristocratic intimacies. In this way Richard was gifted with
a comrade, and Master Ripton Thompson became an in-
mate of Raynham.

Master Ripton Thompson was quite a common boy; shy,
and awkward, and prepared to be totally subservient to the
young Prince whose Court he had come to. His hair and
his eyes were of no colour, and everybody said, there was
nothing in him; to which Mrs. Doria excepted 'sound principle,' finding that he had the proper Old Lawyer's view of
Life and History, and sincerely thought her Charles a
Martyr. Sound principle was all Sir Austin required of
him in his probational contact with the Hope of Raynham.
The two boys soon assumed their relative positions. Richard
led, and Ripton followed. Ripton thought one or two things
in his leader rather odd: for instance, his proficiency in
manly sports and exercises, joined to his habit of calling his

father, Papa, and not Governor, and his entire ignorance about the ways of the girls, and indifference to them; but he concealed his surprise, having been primed by his parents to behave acquiescently, whatever he saw to astonish him.

On the morning of the fourteenth birthday, Ripton had to stow away loud bursts of laughter in the capacious sleeve his provident parents had furnished him with. The day was to be a great day. The boys were to join the Lobourne Eleven against swift-bowling Bursley: dinner on the field; fireworks at night; supper in the Hall: the Cornucopia of Raynham Abbey playing on them exhaustlessly from morning to night. If this were the System, Ripton thought it a fine thing. He was standing waiting for the favoured boy on the gravel-walk fronting the breakfast-room from which he had escaped five minutes before, when forth started Richard, and, catching him by the arm, bore him hurriedly towards the darkest corner of the clustered beeches, and then told him, he would see nobody—he would leave Raynham—he would quit the country, if he could—be a sailor—a cabin-boy—a common soldier—anything, that he might never be seen there again. All this he uttered between a gnawing of the lips, and a blinking of the eyes, a flushing of the cheeks, and a clenching of the fists, showing a frenzy of shamefacedness. He seemed in the gripe of his birthday devil, as they called it at Raynham, where, till that day, he was generally a brisk happy boy.

Ripton kindly endeavoured to console him, but was silenced by a fiercer repetition of the threats.

"Well, then—what is it?" Ripton jerked out at last. "What ever's the matter?"

"I have been insulted," cried Richard; "insulted by my own father. Lucky it wasn't anyone else! Come along!" and he dragged Ripton further into the covert.

"But what is it?" asked Ripton once more, when he could grasp at a halt. "You may as well tell a friend."

"I tell you I've been insulted! Isn't that enough?"

Richard replied. "Come along!" and Ripton had to resume his trot.

By-and-by, after deep dark hints, under the deepest darkest shelter of the foliage, the intimacy of boys brought it all out.

Sir Austin had asked his son to submit to medical examination, and strip!

"Don't laugh!" shouted Richard menacingly, as he saw the great mute O of Ripton's mouth stretch its length towards explosion.

With an effort that cost him tears, Ripton swallowed his guffaw.

"And don't speak of it, or allude to it, if you don't wish mortally to offend me," said the outraged youth. "Come along!" and poor Ripton was soon far from the preparations for the festivities dear to his ears.

The author of the System sat in his study with old Dr. Clifford, much aggrieved.

"A boy who has no voice but mine, Doctor," he said; "whose spirit is clear to me as day—he enters another Circle of nature, and I require to be assured of his bodily well-being, and this boy, educated in the seclusion of a girl, refuses—nay, swears he will not."

"From which, my dear Sir Austin, you have to learn, that your son is no longer a child," was the Doctor's comment.

"A beautiful shamelessness is not necessarily dependent upon a state of childhood," returned the Baronet. "In a boy properly looked to, as this boy has been, there should not be the most distant sense of indelicacy in such a request. He registers revolt, too, with an oath:—The old way! The moment he breaks from me, in a moment he is like the world, and claims Cousinship with an oath for his password."

Sir Austin put a finger to his temple and stared at the fire.

"What do you attribute it to, Doctor?" he asked presently.

"The System, Sir," quietly replied the Doctor.

"Excellent!" Sir Austin exclaimed. "It is I who teach him bad language?"

"At a school," said the Doctor, "there are the two extremes: good boys, and the reverse. Your son does not see that distinction here. He is a heathen as to right and wrong. Good from instinct—not from principle: a creature of impulse. A noble lad, I admit, but—you know, I am of the old school, Sir Austin. I like boys to be boys, and mix together. Christians are not born in hermitages."

"Very well said, Doctor!" remarked the Baronet, always alive to a phrase, even in his tribulation. "A spice of the Devil, then, is necessary for a Christian?"

Dr. Clifford stroked his chin. "I don't say that," he replied. "But I don't mind saying that a fair stand-up fight with him is."

"For a boy, Doctor?"

"For a boy, Sir Austin. He can't have it out too soon."

"Listen, Doctor," said the Baronet, after turning in his chair uneasily two or three times.

"I think you none of you understand my System. My good Doctor! I am not preparing my son to avoid the fight. I know it is inevitable. I brace him for the struggle."

"By keeping him out of his element?" quoth the Doctor.

"By giving him all the advantages of Science," Sir Austin emphasized. "By training him. Our theory is the same, with this difference: that you set the struggle down at an earlier date than do I. It may be true I sacrifice two or three little advantages in isolating him at present: he will be the better fortified for his trial to come. You know my opinion, Doctor: we are pretty secure from the Serpent till Eve sides with him. I speak, of course, of a youth of good pure blood."

"I don't think the schools would harm such a youth," said the Doctor.

"The schools are corrupt!" said the Baronet.

Dr. Clifford could not help thinking there were other temptations than that one of Eve. For youths and for men, Sir Austin told him. She was the main bait: the sole to be dreaded for a youth of good pure blood: the main to resist.

Dr. Clifford inquired whether it was good for such a youth to be half a girl? Whereat Sir Austin smiled a laugh.

"You see him one instant a shamefaced girl, and the next, a headlong boy," the Doctor explained. "Is that good?"

"Yes, yes; I caught your meaning," said Sir Austin. "You suppose shame to be the property of innocence, and therefore of womankind. A wonderful double deduction!" He went into scientific particulars which would reduce the reader to greater confusion than it did the Doctor. They then fell upon the question of Richard's marrying.

"He shall not marry till he is thirty!" was the Baronet's Spartan Law.

"He need not marry at all," said Dr. Clifford. "Birth and death are natural accidents: Marriage we *can* avoid!" The Doctor had been jilted by a naughty damsel.

"On my System he must marry," said the Baronet, and again dissected the frame of man, and entered into scientific particulars: ending their colloquy: "However! I thank you, Doctor, for speaking as you think, and the proof that I know how to profit by it, is seen in my admission of the boy, Thompson, to my household. Perhaps our only difference, after all, is not a pathologic one. I acknowledge your diagnosis, but mollify the prescription. I give the poison to my son in small doses; whereas you prescribe large ones. You naturally contend with a homœopathist—Eh? You are inimical to that heresy?"

"With your permission, Sir Austin, I hate that humbug." The Doctor nodded grimly, and the Baronet laughed, in his stiff way, to have turned the tables on his staunch old adversary, calling him forth into the air to look after the boy, and inspect the preparations for his day's pleasure.

CHAPTER V

SHOWING HOW THE FATES SELECTED THE FOURTEENTH BIRTHDAY TO TRY THE STRENGTH OF THE SYSTEM

OCTOBER shone royally on this day of the completion of the Second Seven years' march of the Hope of Raynham. The brown beechwoods and golden birches glowed to a brilliant sun. Banks of moveless cloud hung about the horizon, mounded to the West, where slept the wind. Promise of a great day for Raynham, as it proved to be, though not in the manner Raynham had marked out.

Already archery booths and cricketing tents were rising on the lower grounds towards the river, whither the lads of Bursley and Lobourne, in boats and in carts, shouting for a day of ale and honour, jogged merrily to match themselves anew, and pluck at the living laurel from each other's brows, like manly Britons. The whole park was beginning to be astir and resound with holiday cries. Sir Austin Feverel, a thorough good Tory, was no game-preserver, and could be popular whenever he chose, which Sir Miles Papworth, a fast-handed Whig and terror to poachers, never could be. Half the village of Lobourne was seen trooping through the avenues of the park. Fiddlers and gypsies clamoured at the gates for admission: white smocks, and slate, surmounted by hats of serious brim, and now and then a scarlet cloak, smacking of the old country, dotted the grassy sweeps to the levels.

And all the time the star of these festivities was receding further and further, and eclipsing himself with his reluctant serf, Ripton, who kept asking, what they were to do, and where they were going, and how late it was in the day, and suggesting that the lads of Lobourne would be calling out for them, and Sir Austin requiring their presence, without getting any attention paid to his misery or remonstrances. For in Richard's bosom a fate was working, and the shame of the insult, as he thought it, rankled.

Now it happened that, as the two boys wandered kicking the clods disconsolately, they started a pheasant. The bird, with its fellow in the brake, drummed, and whirred, and to the misfortune of its species made its plumage seem a prize to them.

"I know what we'll do," cries Richard, his features suddenly lighting up, "we'll have a day's shooting! We'll shoot all day, and we won't go home till night."

He turned to his friend to see how his proposal was received. Master Ripton, whose mind was set on Raynham and the fun there, listened but half cheerfully, and hinted that any other day would do for shooting.

"No!" said Richard, "look what a day it is. We shall kill lots of birds, and give everybody the slip. You'll have a gun and I'll have a gun, and we'll have better fun than any of them at Raynham. Come along!" And he made Ripton moodily retrace his steps. It seemed mad and stupid to Ripton's sense of reason, but he was a bondsman and bound to acquiesce. He mumbled something about not having a license, and was putting that in for a plea against the expedition, till Richard assured him positively that every gentleman had a license, and Ripton, who deeply delighted in the notion of belonging to that privileged class, and walked with tight boots, and underwent daily tortures, to induce the world to accept him as one, admitted it was the case that every gentleman had a license, and therefore he must have one.

So back they ran to the Abbey, dodged the Baronet, armed themselves, got the old pointer Mark'em (named after his profession and the keeper at a blow) close to their heels, and, by skirting outhouses and slinking under walls, escaped in the security that favours the commencement of adventures of this sort, and made for the coverts of the park.

Rearward of the Abbey lay a lake that took the morning sun, and the shadow of a solitary cypress, planted by some sad-minded Ancestress. The boys had to round the lake before they could plunge into perfect concealment, and as they did so, Richard cried out, "Look! do you see how that shadow follows me?—just look."

Ripton cast a dissatisfied eye on the phenomenon, not a whit inclined to express any wonder, if he felt it.

"Do you see it, Rip?" Richard moved forward and back on the brink of the lake, pretending that the reflection of the cypress pointed after him.

"What do you think!" he continued. "They say in our family that when we any of us come across it in this way— like this, look!—there's going to be mischief. My father doesn't believe in that kind of thing: nor more do I. But it's strange, isn't it? Look!" The boy held to the spot like one fascinated. "It's true my great-grandfather, Sir Algernon Feverel, noticed it pointing at him as he passed the morning he fought the duel, and was killed. And he went half round the lake. Of course I don't believe there's anything in it. Do you?"

Ripton said, he did not, because all shadows seemed to do the same, in a modified way: but there, Richard assured him, he was wrong, as this cypress was the only tree ever known to do it.

"Though I don't believe it means anything," he added. "Mind you hold your gun properly and don't shoot me, and I'll take care I don't shoot you. If we get lots of birds we'll take some over to Lady Blandish to-morrow, and she'll ask us to dine there, and she has capital wine, and no Benson, and all sorts of fun, and you may do as you like there."

"Any girls?" asked Ripton.

"I don't know." The young gentleman was violently contemptuous in his reply.

They entered the wood, and from its eastern border could see the people of Lobourne trooping along the main road to Raynham: horsemen and horsewomen; carriages, carts, cricketers, from whose entertainment the heart was running away. He had a little touch of compunction as he beheld them; but immediately putting the blame on his father, branched off in a contrary direction, and so eulogized the house of Lady Blandish to Ripton, and the reception she would give them and their birds to-morrow, that the unlucky youth began to get consoled. Richard shouldered his own gun, a light single-barrel, suitable for his years. Ripton had made free with Captain Feverel's. He was rather short-sighted and inexperienced in guns, though it was out of the question he should admit the fact, every gentleman being familiar with guns from his birth. It was not in bravado that he carried a rifle instead of a fowling-piece. Both boys were warming at the prospect of sport. Old Mark'em joined in the conspiracy nose and tail; a dog's equivalent for heart and soul; generally one as good.

"Are you a prime shot?" said Richard.

Ripton nodded knowingly, and answered, "Pretty good."

"Then we'll have a dozen brace apiece to-day," said Richard.

On nosed old Mark'em, bent upon work. Out of the wood into a field of stubble, and onward they went at a trot, and down plumped old Mark'em, true as the needle to the pole. Then the cat-like steps of the juvenile sportsmen were fine to see. Ripton surpassed his comrade in velvety paw and professional attitude, crouching his body in the most hopeful manner. But when this moment of exquisite expectancy was cut short by the birds rising, the hapless youth suddenly remembered he had forgotten to load. Earth reeled round his figure of confusion as Richard fired. He fired, but old Mark'em made no blithe bounds in advance. The sagacious old dog looked sulky and disgusted. A dead miss! Richard reproached his friend bitterly.

"Why did you bawl out just as I was aiming? Who can aim with a fellow bawling in his ear? I've lost the birds through it. At least I should have had one of the two."

Ripton explained humbly that he had forgotten to load.

"Always load at home," said Richard. "Then you're ready for anything. And don't make that noise another time."

His eye fell on the instrument Ripton carried to make war on the feathery creation, and he recognized his Uncle's rifle.

"Do you know what you've got in your hands?" he said.

"I think it's not the right gun," stammered Ripton.

"You *think* it's not! Well! You must be accustomed to sport."

He looked scornfully, and the next minute called his friend, Ripton, a fool.

Now Ripton was not in the best of tempers. He was a disappointed boy that morning, and a Briton in bondage— a very dangerous animal at all times. Richard had added the emphasis of conviction to the insulting epithet. A boy does not like to be called a fool, and is usually ready to try the question with his fists when a doubt is once cast on him; as of old Valour asserted the spotlessness of fair dames; and if he conquers it is clear that he cannot be a fool. These primitive courts of appeal despise casuistries.

Feeling that circumstances were making him look wonderfully like one, Ripton lifted his head and retorted defiantly, "I'm not!"

This angry contradiction, so very uncalled-for, offended Richard, who was still smarting at the loss of his birds, and was really the injured party. He therefore bestowed the abusive epithet on Ripton anew, and with increase of emphasis.

"You shan't call me so, then, whether I am or not," says Ripton, and sucks his lips, looking wicked.

This was becoming personal. Richard sent up his brows,

and stared at his defier an instant. He then informed him that he certainly should call him so, and would not object to call him so twenty times.

"Do it, and see!" returns Ripton, rocking on his pins, and breathing quick.

With a gravity of which only boys and other barbarians are capable, Richard went through the entire number stressing the epithet to increase the defiance and avoid monotony, as he progressed, while Ripton bobbed his head every time in assent, as it were, to his comrade's accuracy, and as a record for his profound humiliation. Old Mark'em gazed at the extraordinary performance with interrogating wags of the tail.

Twenty times, duly and deliberately, Richard repeated the obnoxious word.

At the twentieth solemn iteration of Ripton's capital short-coming, old Mark'em started up to action. Ripton had delivered a smart backhander on Richard's mouth, and squared precipitately; perhaps sorry when the deed was done, for he was a kind-hearted lad, and as Richard simply bowed in acknowledgment of the blow, he thought he had gone too far. He did not know the young gentleman he was dealing with. Richard was extremely cool.

"Shall we fight here?" he said.

"Anywhere you like," replied Ripton.

"A little more into the wood, I think. We may be interrupted." And Richard led the way with a courteous reserve that somewhat chilled Ripton's ardour for the contest. On the skirts of the wood, Richard threw off his jacket and waistcoat, and, quite collected, waited for Ripton to do the same. The latter boy was flushed and restless; older and broader, but not so tight-limbed and well-set. The gods, sole witnesses of their battle, betted dead against him. Richard had mounted the white cockade of the Feverels, and there was a look in him that asked for tough work to extinguish. His brows, slightly lined upward at the temples, converging to a knot about the well-set straight nose; his full grey eyes, open nostrils, and planted feet, and a gentlemanly air of calm and alertness, formed a spirited picture of a young combatant. As for Ripton, he was all abroad, and fought in schoolboy style: that is, he rushed at the foe head foremost, and struck like a windmill. He was a lumpy boy. When he did hit, he made himself felt; but he was at the mercy of Science. To see him come dashing in, blinking, and puffing, and whirling his arms abroad while the felling blow went straight between them, you perceived that he was fighting a fight of desperation, and knew it. For the dreaded alternative glared him in the face that, if he yielded, he must look like what he had been Twenty Times calumniously called; and he would die rather than yield, and swing his windmill till he dropped. Poor boy! he dropped pretty frequently. The gallant fellow fought for appearances, and down he went. The gods favour one of two parties. Prince Turnus was a noble youth; but he had not Pallas at his elbow. Ripton was a capital boy, but he had no Science. Minerva turned her back on him. He could not, could not prove he was not a fool! When one comes to think of it, Ripton did choose the only possible way, and we should all of us have considerable difficulty in proving the negative by any other. Ripton came on the unerring fist again and again, and if it was true, as he said in short colloquial gasps, that he required as much beating as an egg to be beaten thoroughly, a fortunate interruption alone saved our friend from resembling that substance. The boys heard summoning voices, and beheld Mr. Morton of Poer Hall and Austin Wentworth stepping towards them.

A truce was sounded, jackets were caught-up, guns shouldered, and off they trotted in concert through the depths of the wood, not stopping till that and half-a-dozen fields and a larch plantation were well behind them.

When they halted to take breath, there was a mutual study of faces. Ripton's was much discoloured and looked fiercer with its natural war-paint than the boy felt. Nevertheless he squared up dauntlessly on the new ground, and Richard, whose wrath was appeased, could not refrain from asking him whether he had not really had enough.

"Never!" shouts the noble enemy.

"Well, look here," said Richard, appealing to common sense, "I'm tired of knocking you down. I'll say you're not a fool, if you'll give me your hand."

Ripton demurred an instant to consult with Honour, who bade him catch at his chance.

He held out his hand. "There!" and the boys grasped hands and were fast friends. Ripton had gained his point, and Richard decidedly had the best of it. So they were on equal ground. Both could claim a victory, which was all the better for their friendship.

Ripton washed his face and comforted his nose at a brook, and was now ready to follow his friend wherever he chose to lead. They continued to beat about for birds. The birds on the Raynham estates were found singularly cunning, and repeatedly eluded the aim of these prime shots, so they pushed their expedition into the lands of their neighbours, in search of a stupider race, happily oblivious of the laws and conditions of trespass; unconscious too that they were poaching on the demesne of the notorious farmer Blaize, the free-trade farmer under the shield of the Papworths, parent of Richard's first defeated foe, and no worshiper of the Griffin between Two Wheatsheaves: destined to be much allied with Richard's fortunes from beginning to end. Farmer Blaize hated poachers, and especially young chaps poaching, who did it mostly from impudence. Farmer Blaize heard the audacious shots popping right and left, and going forth to have a glimpse at the intruders, and observing their size, swore he would teach my gentlemen a thing, lords or no lords.

Richard had brought down a beautiful cock-pheasant, and was exulting over it, when the farmer's portentous figure burst upon them, cracking an avenging horsewhip. His salute was ironical.

"Havin' good sport, gentlemen, are ye?"

"Just bagged a splendid bird!" radiant Richard informed him.

"Oh! y'ave!" Farmer Blaize gave an admonitory flick of the whip. "Jest let me clap eye on 't, then."

"Say, please," interposed Ripton, who, not being the possessor of the bird, was not blind to doubtful aspects.

Farmer Blaize threw up his chin, and grinned grim.

"Please to yew, Sir? Why, my chap, yew looks as if ye din't much mind what come t' yer nose, I reckon. Yew looks an old poacher, yew do. Tall ye what 'tis!" He changed his banter to business, "Bird's mine! Now yew jest hand 'un over, and sheer off, ye dam young scoundrels! I knows ye!" And he became exceedingly opprobrious and uttered contempt at the name of Feverel.

Richard opened his eyes.

"If ye wants to be horse'upp'd, ye'll stay where y'are!" continued the farmer irate. "Giles Blaize never stands no nonsense!"

"Then we'll stay," quoth Richard.

"Good! so be't! If ye wull have't, have't, my men! Have't, ye young suckin' poachers!"

As a preparatory measure, Farmer Blaize seized a wing of the bird, on which both boys flung themselves desperately, and secured it minus the pinion.

"That's your game," cried the farmer. "Here's a taste of horse'up for ye. I never stands no nonsense," and sweetch went the mighty whip, well swayed. The boys tried to close with him. He kept his distance, and lashed without mercy. Black blood made Farmer Blaize that day! The boys wriggled, in spite of themselves. It was like a relentless serpent coiling, and biting, and stinging their young veins to madness. Probably the boys felt the disgrace of the contortions they were made to go through, more than the pain, but the pain was fierce, for the farmer laid about from a practised arm, and did not consider that he had done enough till he was well breathed and his ruddy jowl inflamed. He paused, to receive the remainder of the cock-pheasant in his face.

"Take your beastly bird," cried Richard.

"Money, my lads, and interest," roared the farmer, lashing out again.

Shameful as it was to retreat, there was but that course open to them. They decided to surrender the field.

"Look! you big brute," Richard shook his gun, hoarse with passion, "I'd have shot you, if I'd been loaded. Mind! if I come across you when I'm loaded, you coward! I'll fire."

The un-English nature of this threat exasperated Farmer Blaize, and he pressed the pursuit in time to bestow a few farewell stripes as they were escaping, tight-breeched, into neutral territory. At the hedge they parleyed a minute, the farmer to inquire if they had had a mortal good tanning and were satisfied, for when they wanted a further instalment of the same, they were to come for it to Belthorpe Farm, and there it was in pickle: the boys meantime exploding in menaces and threats of vengeance, on which the farmer contemptuously turned his back. Ripton had already stocked an armfull of flints for the enjoyment of a little skirmishing. Richard, however, knocked them all out, saying, "No! a gentleman don't fling stones: leave that to the blackguards."

"Just one shy at him?" pleaded Ripton, with his eye on Farmer Blaize's broad mark, and his whole mind drunken with a sudden revelation of the advantages of light troops in opposition to heavies.

"No," said Richard, imperatively, "no stones," and marched briskly away. Ripton followed with a sigh. His leader's magnanimity was wholly beyond him. A good spanking mark at the farmer would have relieved Master Ripton: it would have done nothing to console Richard

Feverel for the ignominy he had been compelled to submit
to. Ripton was familiar with the rod, a monster much
despoiled of his terrors by intimacy. Birch-fever was past
with this boy. The horrible sense of shame, self-loathing,
universal hatred, impotent vengeance, as if the spirit were
steeped in abysmal blackness, which comes upon a courageous
and sensitive youth condemned for the first time to taste this
piece of fleshly bitterness and suffer what he feels is a de-
filement, Ripton had weathered, and forgotten. He was
seasoned wood, and took the world pretty wisely; not reckless of castigation, as some boys become, nor over-sensitive as
to dishonour, as his friend and comrade beside him was.

Richard's blood was poisoned. He had the fever on him
severely. He would not allow stone-flinging, because it was
a habit of his to discountenance it. Mere gentlemanly considerations had scarce shielded Farmer Blaize, and certain
very ungentlemanly schemes were coming to ghastly heads
in the tumult of his brain; rejected solely from their glaring
impracticability even to his young intelligence. A sweeping
and consummate vengeance for the indignity alone should
satisfy him. Something tremendous must be done, and done
without delay. At one moment he thought of killing all the
farmer's cattle: next of killing him; challenging him to
single combat with the arms, and according to the fashion,
of gentlemen. But the farmer was a coward; he would
refuse. Then he, Richard Feverel, would stand by the
farmer's bedside, and rouse him; rouse him to fight with
powder and ball in his own chamber, in the cowardly midnight, where he might tremble, but dare not refuse.

"Lord!" cried simple Ripton, while these hopeful plots
were raging in his comrade's brain, now sparkling for immediate execution, and anon lapsing disdainfully dark in
their chances of fulfilment, "how I wish you'd have let me
notch him, Ricky!—I'm a safe shot. I never miss. I
should feel quite jolly, if I'd spanked him once. We should
have had the best of him at that game.—I say!" and a sharp

thought drew Ripton's ideas nearer home: "I wonder whether my nose is as bad as he says? Where can I see myself? Gracious! what shall I do when we get to Raynham, if it is? What'll the ladies think of me? O lord, Ricky! suppose it turns blue?"

Ripton moved a meditative forefinger down the bridge of his nose, as this horrible suspicion clouded him. Farmer Blaize passed from his mind. The wretched boy called aloud in agony that his nose was turning blue. "Oh, if I had a bit of raw meat to lay across it!" he cried. "What a fool I was to fight!—Won't I learn boxing!—What shall I look like?" To these doleful exclamations Richard was deaf, and trudged steadily forward, facing but one object.

After tearing through innumerable hedges, leaping fences, jumping dykes, penetrating brambly copses, and getting dirty, ragged, and tired, Ripton awoke from his dream of Farmer Blaize and a blue nose, to the vivid consciousness of hunger; and this consciousness grew with the rapidity of light upon him, till in the course of another minute he was enduring the extremes of famine, and ventured to question his leader whither he was being conducted. Raynham was out of sight. They were a long way down the valley, miles from Lobourne, in a country of sour pools, yellow brooks, rank pasturage, desolate heath. Solitary cows were seen; the smoke of a mud-cottage; a cart piled with peat; a donkey grazing at leisure, oblivious of an unkind world; geese by a horsepond, gabbling as in the first loneliness of Creation: uncooked things that a famishing boy cannot possibly care for, and must despise. Ripton was in despair.

"Where *are* you going to?" he inquired with a voice of the last time of asking, and halted resolutely.

Richard now broke his silence to reply, "Anywhere."

"Anywhere!" Ripton took up the moody word. "But ain't you awfully hungry?" he gasped vehemently in a way that showed the total emptiness of his stomach.

"No," was Richard's brief response.

"Not hungry!" Ripton's amazement lent him increased vehemence. "Why, you haven't had anything to eat since breakfast! Not hungry? Well! that beats me! Why, I declare I'm starving. I feel such a gnawing I could eat dry bread and cheese!"

Richard sneered: not for reasons that would have actuated a similar demonstration of the philosopher.

"Come," cried Ripton, "at all events, tell us where you're going to stop?"

Richard faced about to make a querulous retort. The injured and hapless visage that met his eye disarmed him. The lad's unhappy nose, though not exactly of the dreaded hue, was really becoming discoloured. To upbraid him would be cruel. Richard lifted his head, surveyed the position, and exclaiming, "Here!" dropped down on a withered bank, leaving Ripton to contemplate him as a puzzle whose every new move was a worse perplexity.

CHAPTER VI

THE MAGIAN CONFLICT

AMONG boys there are laws of honour and chivalrous codes, not written, or formally taught, but intuitively understood by all, and invariably acted upon by the loyal and the true. The race is only half civilized, we must remember. Thus, not to follow your leader whithersoever he may think proper to lead; to back out of an expedition because the end of it frowns dubious, and the present fruit of it is discomfort; to quit a comrade on the road, and return home without him: these are tricks which no boy of spirit would be guilty of, let him come to any description of mortal grief in consequence. Better so, than have his own conscience denouncing him sneak. Some boys who behave boldly enough, are not troubled by this conscience, and the eyes and the lips of their fellows have to supply the deficiency. They do it with just as haunting, and even more horrible, pertinacity than the inner voice, and the result, if the probation be not very severe and searching, is the same. The leader can rely on the faithfulness of his host: the comrade is sworn to serve. Master Ripton Thompson was naturally loyal. The idea of turning off and forsaking his friend, never once crossed his mind, though his condition was desperate, and his friend's behaviour that of a Bedlamite. He announced several times impatiently that they would be too late for dinner. His friend did not budge. Dinner seemed nothing to him. There he lay plucking grass, and patting old Mark'em's nose, as if incapable of conceiving what a thing hunger was. Ripton took half-a-dozen turns up and down, and at last flung himself down beside the taciturn boy, accepting his fate.

Now the chance that works for certain purposes sent a smart shower from the sinking sun, and the wet sent two strangers for shelter in the lane behind the hedge where the boys reclined. One was a travelling Tinker, who lit a ·pipe and spread a tawny umbrella. The other was a burly young countryman, pipeless, and tentless. They saluted with a nod, and began recounting for each other's benefit the day-long doings of the weather, as it had affected their individual experience, and followed their prophecies. Both had anticipated and foretold a bit of rain before night, and therefore both welcomed the wet with satisfaction. A monotonous betweenwhiles kind of talk they kept droning in harmony with the still hum of the air. From the weather theme they fell upon the blessings of Tobacco; how it was the poor man's friend: his company, his consolation, his comfort, his refuge at night, his first thought in the morning.

"Better than wife!" chuckled the Tinker. "No curtain-lectu'rin' with pipe. Pipe an·t shrew. Pipe's sweet creetur."

"That be ut!" the other chimed in. "Doan't tax ye wi'

pot'us. Doan't mak' ye out wi' all the cash Saturday evenin', pipe doan't."

"Take one," said the Tinker, in the enthusiasm of the moment handing a grimy short clay. Speed-the-Plough filled from the Tinker's pouch, and continued his praises.

"Pipe's a rare 'un! Penny a day, and there y'are! primed! Better than wife? ha, ha! Shud think 'twaws! Pipe an't no vexation."

"And you can get rid of it, if ye wants for to, and when ye wants," added Tinker.

"So ye can!" Speed-the-Plough took him up, "So ye can! And ye doan't want for to. Leastways, t'other case. I means pipe."

"And," continued Tinker, comprehending him perfectly, "it don't bring repentance after it."

"Not nohow, master, it doan't! And,"—Speed-the-Plough cocked his eye,—"it doan't eat up half the victuals, pipe doan't."

Here the honest yeoman gesticulated his keen sense of a clincher, which the Tinker acknowledged; and having, so to speak, sealed up the subject by saying the best thing that could be said, the two smoked for some time in silence to the drip and patter of the shower.

Ripton solaced his wretchedness by watching them through the briar hedge. He saw the Tinker stroking a white cat, and appealing to her, every now and then, as his Missus, for an opinion, or a confirmation: and he thought that a curious sight. Speed-the-Plough was stretched at full length, with his boots in the rain, and his head amidst the Tinker's pots, smoking profoundly contemplative. The minutes seemed to be taken up alternately by the grey puffs from their mouths.

It was Tinker who renewed the colloquy. Said he: "Times is bad!"

His companion assented: "Sure-ly!"

"But it somehow comes round right," resumed the Tinker.

"Why, look here. Where's the good o' moping? I sees it all come round right and tight. Now I travels about. I've got my beat. 'Casion calls me t'other day to Newcastle!— Eh?"

"Coals!" ejaculated Speed-the-Plough, sonorously.

"Coals!" echoed the Tinker. "Y' ask what I goes there for, mayhap? Never you mind. One sees a mort o' life in my trade. Not for coals it isn't. And I don't carry 'em there, neither. Anyhow, I comes back. Lunnon's my mark. Says I, I'll see a bit o' the sea, and steps aboard a collier. We were as nigh wracked as the prophet Paul."

"A—who's him?" the other wished to know.

"Read your Bible," said the Tinker. "We pitched and tossed—'tain't that game at sea 'tis on land, I can tell ye. I thinks, down we're a-going—Say your prayers, Bob Tiles! That was a night, to be sure! But God's above the Devil, and here I am, ye see."

Speed-the-Plough lurched round on his elbow and regarded him indifferently. "Moighty foin, that be! D'ye call that Doctrin'? He bean't al'ays, or I shoon't be scrapin' my heels wi' nothin' to do, and what's warse, nothin' to eat. Why, look heer. Luck's luck, and bad luck's the con-trary. Varmer Bollop, t'other day, has 's rick burnt down. Next night his gran'ry's burnt. What do he tak' and go and do? He takes, and goes, and hangs unsel', and turns us out o' 'ploy. God warn't above the Devil then, I thinks, or I can't make out the reckonin'."

The Tinker cleared his throat, and said, it was a bad case.

"And a darn'd bad case. I'll tak' my oath on 't?" cried Speed-the-Plough. "Wall! look heer. Heer's another darn'd bad case. I threshed for Varmer Blaize—Blaize o' Beltharpe—afore I goes to Varmer Bollop. Varmer Blaize misses pilkins. He swears soam o' our chaps steals pilkins. 'Twarn't me steals 'em. What do *he* tak' and go and do? He takes and tarns us off, me and another, neck and crop, to scuff about and starve, for all *he* keers. God warn't above the Devil then, I thinks? Not nohow, as I can see!"

The Tinker shook his head, and said, that was a bad case also.

"And ye can't mend us," added Speed-the-Plough. "Ut's bad, and there ut be. But I'll tall ye what, master. Bad wants payin' for." He nodded and winked mysteriously. "Bad has ut's wages as well's honest work, I'm thinkin'. Varmer Bollop I don't owe no grudge to: Varmer Blaize I do. And I shud like to stick a Lucifer in his rick soam dry windy night." Speed-the-Plough screwed up an eye villainously. "He wants hittin' in the wind,—jest where the pocket is, master, do Varmer Blaize, and he'll cry out 'Oh, Lor!' Varmer Blaize wull. Ye won't get the better o' Varmer Blaize by no means, as I makes out, if you doan't hit into 'un jest there."

The Tinker sent a rapid succession of white clouds from his mouth and said, that would be taking the Devil's side of a bad case. Speed-the-Plough observed energetically that, if Farmer Blaize was on the other, he should be on that side.

There was a young gentleman close by, who thought with him. The Hope of Raynham had lent a careless, half-compelled, attention to the foregoing dialogue, wherein a common labourer and a travelling Tinker had propounded and discussed one of the most ancient theories of trans-mundane dominion and influence on mundane affairs. He now started to his feet, and came tearing through the briar hedge, calling out for one of them to direct him the nearest road to Bursley. The Tinker was kindling preparations for his tea, under the tawny umbrella. A loaf was set forth, on which Ripton's eyes, stuck in the hedge, fastened ravenously. Speed-the-Plough volunteered information that Bursley was a good three mile from where they stood, and a good eight mile from Lobourne.

"I'll give you half-a-crown for that loaf, my good fellow," said Richard to the Tinker.

"It's a bargain," quoth the Tinker, "eh, Missus?"

Missus replied by humping her back at old Mark'em.

The half-crown was tossed down, and Ripton, who had just succeeded in freeing his limbs from the briar, prickly as a hedgehog, collared the loaf.

"Those young squires be sharp-set and no mistake," said the Tinker to his companion. "Come! we'll to Bursley after 'em, and talk it out over a pot o' beer." Speed-the-Plough was nothing loath, and in a short time they were following the two lads on the road to Bursley, while a horizontal blaze shot across the Autumn land from the western edge of the rain-cloud.

CHAPTER VII

ARSON

SEARCH for the missing boys had been made everywhere over Raynham, and Sir Austin was in grievous discontent. None had seen them save Austin Wentworth and Mr. Morton. The Baronet sat construing their account of the flight of the lads when they were hailed, and resolved it into an act of rebellion on the part of his son. At dinner he drank the young heir's health in ominous silence. The Wig of Mr. Justice Harley was low, and Adrian stood up in his place to propose the health. His speech was a fine piece of rhetoric. He warmed in it till, after the Ciceronic model, inanimate objects were personified, and Richard's table-napkin and vacant chair were invoked to follow the steps of a peerless father, and uphold with his dignity the honour of the Feverels. Austin Wentworth, whom also a soldier's death compelled to take his father's place in support of the toast, was tame after such magniloquence. But the reply, the thanks which young Richard should have delivered in person were not forthcoming. Adrian's oratory had given but a momentary life to napkin and chair. The company

of honoured friends, and Aunts, and Uncles, and remotest
Cousins, were glad to disperse and seek amusement in music
and tea. Sir Austin did his utmost to be hospitably cheerful,
and requested them to dance. If he had desired them to
laugh, he would have been obeyed, and in as hearty a manner.

"How triste!" said Mrs. Doria Forey to Lobourne's
Curate, as that most enamoured automaton went through his
paces beside her with professional stiffness.

"One who does not suffer can hardly assent," the Curate
answered, basking in her beams.

"Ah, you are good!" exclaimed the lady. "Look at my
Clare. She will not dance on her cousin's birthday with
any one but him. What are we to do to enliven these
people?"

"Alas, Madam! you cannot do for all what you do for
one," the Curate sighed, and wherever she wandered in
discourse, drew her back with silken strings to gaze on his
enamoured soul.

He was the only gratified stranger present. The others
had designs on the young heir. Lady Attenbury of Long-
ford House, had brought her highly polished specimen of
market-ware, the lady Juliana Jaye, for a first introduction
to him, thinking he had arrived at an age to estimate and
pine for her black eyes and pretty pert mouth. The lady
Juliana had to pair off with a dapper Papworth, and her
Mama was subjected to the gallantries of Sir Miles, who
talked land and Steam-Engines to her till she was sick, and
had to be impertinent in self-defence. Lady Blandish sat
apart with Adrian, and enjoyed his sarcasms on the company. By ten at night, the poor show ended, and the rooms
were dark, dark as the prognostics multitudinously hinted
by the disappointed and chilled guests, concerning the probable future of the Hope of Raynham. Little Clare kissed
her Mama, curtsied to the lingering Curate, and went to
bed like a very good girl. Immediately the maid had de-

parted, little Clare deliberately exchanged night attire for that of day. She was noted as an obedient child. Her light was always allowed to burn in her room for half an hour, to counteract her fears of the dark. She took the light, and stole on tiptoe to Richard's room. No Richard was there. She peeped in further and further. A trifling agitation of the curtains shot her back through the door and along the passage to her own bed-chamber with extreme expedition. She was not much alarmed, but feeling guilty she was on her guard. In a short time, she was prowling about the passages again. Richard had slighted and offended the little lady, and was to be asked whether he did not repent such conduct towards his cousin; not to be asked whether he had forgotten to receive his birthday kiss from her; for if he did not choose to remember that, Miss Clare would never remind him of it, and to-night should be his last chance of a reconciliation. Thus she meditated, sitting on a stair, and presently heard Richard's voice below in the hall, shouting for supper.

"Master Richard has returned," old Benson tolled out intelligence to Sir Austin.

"Well?" said the Baronet.

"He complains of being hungry," the butler hesitated, with a look of solemn disgust.

"Let him eat."·

Heavy Benson hesitated still more as he announced that the boy had called for wine. It was an unprecedented thing. Sir Austin's brows were portending an arch, but Adrian suggested that he wanted possibly to drink his birthday, and Claret was conceded.

The boys were in the vortex of a partridge-pie when Adrian strolled in to them. They had now changed characters. Richard was uproarious. He drank a health with every glass. His cheeks were flushed, and his eye brilliant. Ripton looked very much like a rogue on the tremble of detection, but his honest hunger and the partridge-pie shielded him awhile from Adrian's scrutinizing glance. Adrian saw there was matter for study, if it were only on Master Ripton's betraying nose, and sat down to hear and mark.

"Good sport, gentlemen, I trust to hear?" he began his quiet banter, and provoked a loud peal of laughter from Richard.

"Ha, ha! I say, Rip! 'Havin' good sport, gentlemen, are you?' You remember the farmer? Your health, Parson! We haven't had our sport yet. We're going to have some first-rate sport. Oh, well! we haven't much show of birds. We shot for pleasure, and returned them to the proprietors. You're fond of game, Parson! I wish I'd thought of it. Rip took uncle's rifle out on purpose to knock down his birds clean for you. And he didn't miss, either. He's a dead shot in what cousin Austin calls the Kingdom of 'Would-have-done,' and 'Might-have-been.' Up went the birds, and, cries Rip, 'I've forgotten to load!' O ho!—Rip! some more claret.—Do just leave that nose of yours alone.—Your health, Ripton Thompson! The birds hadn't the decency to wait for him, and so, Parson, it's their fault, and not Rip's, you haven't a dozen brace at your feet. What have you been doing at home, Cousin Rady?"

"Playing Hamlet, in the absence of the Prince of Denmark. The day without you, my dear boy, must be dull, you know."

> "'He speaks: can I trust what he says is sincere?
> There's an edge to his smile which cuts much
> like a sneer.'

Sandoe's poems! You know the couplet, Mr. Rady. Why shouldn't I quote Sandoe? You know you like him, Rady. But if you've missed me, I'm sorry. Rip and I have had a beautiful day. We've made new acquaintances. We've seen the world. I'm the monkey that has seen the world, and I'm going to tell you all about it. First, there's a gentleman who takes a rifle for a fowling-piece. Next, there's a farmer who warns everybody, gentleman and beggar, off his premises. Next, there's a tinker and a ploughman, who think that God is always fighting with the Devil which shall command the kingdoms of the earth. The tinker's for God, and the ploughman—"

"I'll drink your health, Ricky," said Adrian, interrupting.

"Oh, I forgot, Mr. Parson!—I mean no harm, Adrian. I'm only telling what I've heard."

"No harm, my dear boy," returned Adrian. "I'm perfectly aware that Zoroaster is not dead. You have been listening to a common creed. Drink the Fire-worshipers, if you will."

"Here's to Zoroaster, then!" cried Richard. "I say, Rippy! we'll drink the Fire-worshipers to-night, won't we?"

A fearful conspiratorial frown, that would not have disgraced Guido Fawkes, was darted back from the plastic features of Master Ripton.

Richard gave his lungs loud play.

"Why, what did you say about Blazes, Rippy? Didn't you say it was fun?"

Another hideous silencing frown was Ripton's answer. Adrian watched the innocent youths, and knew that there was talking under the table. 'See,' he thought: 'This boy has tasted his first scraggy morsel of life to-day, and already he talks like an old-stager, and has, if I mistake not, been acting too. My respected Chief,' he apostrophized Sir Austin, 'combustibles are only the more dangerous for compression. This boy will be ravenous for Earth when he is let loose, and very soon make his share of it look as foolish as yonder game-pie!'—a prophecy Adrian kept to himself.

Uncle Algernon shambled in to see his nephew before the supper was finished, and his more genial presence brought out a little of the plot.

"Look here, Uncle!" said Richard. "Would you let a

churlish old brute of a farmer strike you without making
him suffer for it?"

"I fancy I should return the compliment, my lad," replied his Uncle.

"Of course you would! So would I. And he shall suffer
for it." The boy looked savage, and his Uncle patted him
down.

"I've boxed his son; I'll box him," said Richard, shouting
for more wine.

"What, boy! Is it old Blaize has been putting you up?"

"Never mind, Uncle!" the boy nodded mysteriously.

"Look there!" Adrian read on Ripton's face, "he says
'never mind,' and lets it out!"

"Did we beat to-day, Uncle?"

"Yes, boy; and we'd beat them any day they bowl fair.
I'd beat them on one leg. There's only Natkins and Feather-
dene among them worth a farthing."

"We beat!" cries Richard. "Then we'll have some more
wine, and drink their healths."

The bell was rung; wine ordered. Presently comes in
Heavy Benson to say, supplies are cut off. One bottle, and
no more. The Captain whistles: Adrian shrugs.

"Don't you know it's my birthday, Benson?"

Benson knew it, but had positive orders.

He withdraws, and to the delight of all present, Adrian,
ever provident, puts his hand behind him and leads forth
a flask, saying that he had anticipated this possibility.

One subject was at Richard's heart, about which he was
reserved in the midst of his riot. Too proud to inquire
how his father had taken his absence, he burned to hear
whether he was in disgrace. He led to it repeatedly, and
it was constantly evaded by Algernon and Adrian. At last,
when the boy declared a desire to wish his father good
night, Adrian had to tell him that he was to go straight to
bed from the supper-table. Young Richard's face fell at that,

und his gaiety forsook him. He marched to his room without another word.

Adrian gave Sir Austin an able version of his son's behaviour and adventures; dwelling upon this sudden taciturnity when he heard of his father's resolution not to see him. The Wise Youth saw that his Chief was mollified behind his moveless mask, and went to bed and Horace, leaving Sir Austin in his study. Long hours the Baronet sat alone. The house had not its usual influx of Feverels that day. Austin Wentworth was staying at Poer Hall, and had only come over for the day. At midnight the house breathed sleep. Sir Austin put on his cloak and cap, and took the lamp to make his rounds. He apprehended nothing special, but with a mind never at rest, he constituted himself the sentinel of Raynham. He passed the chamber where the Great-Aunt Grantley lay, who was to swell Richard's fortune, and so perform her chief business on earth. By her door he murmured, "Good creature! you sleep with a sense of duty done," and paced on, reflecting, "She has not made Money a demon of discord," and blessed her. He had his thoughts at Hippias's somnolent door, and to them the world might have subscribed. Algernon challenged him, and was quieted by two knocks which he knew. Algernon's voice was thick. Sir Austin excused the cause. "He saved my son that day!" the Baronet murmured, and devoutly believed it.

"A monomaniac at large, watching over sane people in slumber!" thinks Adrian Harley, as he hears Sir Austin's footfall, and truly that was a strange object to see, but one not so strange in his service. Where is the fortress that has not one weak gate? where the man who is sound at each particular angle? "Ay," meditates the recumbent cynic, "more or less mad is not every mother's son? Favourable circumstances; good air, good company, two or three good rules rigidly adhered to; keep the world out of Bedlam. But let the world fly into a passion, and is not Bedlam its

safest abode? What seemed inviolable barriers are burst
asunder in a trice: men, God's likeness, are at one another's
throats, and the Angels may well be weeping. In youth,
'tis love, or lust, makes the world mad: in age, 'tis prejudice. Superstition holds a province; Pride an empire.
Tinker's right! There's a battle raging above us. One
can't wonder at Ploughman's contrary opinion, as to which
is getting the upper hand. If we were not mad, we should
fight it for ourselves, and end it. We are; and we make
Life the disease, and Death the cure. Good night, my
worthy Uncle! Can I deem the man mad who holdeth
me much?" And Adrian buried a sleepy smile in his pillow,
and slept, knowing himself wise in a mad world.

Sir Austin ascended the stairs, and bent his steps leisurely
towards the chamber where his son was lying in the left
wing of the Abbey. At the end of the gallery which led
to it, he discovered a dim light. Doubting it an illusion, Sir
Austin accelerated his pace. This wing had aforetime a bad
character. Notwithstanding what years had done to polish
it into fair repute, the Raynham kitchen stuck to tradition
still, and preserved certain stories of ghosts seen there, and
thought to have been seen, that effectually blackened it in the
susceptible minds of new housemaids and under-cooks, whose
fears would not allow the sinner to wash his sins. Sir Austin
had heard of the tales circulated by his domestics underground. He cherished his own belief, but discouraged theirs,
and it was treason at Raynham to be caught traducing the
left wing. As the Baronet advanced, the fact of a light
burning was clear to him. A slight descent brought him
into the passage, and he beheld a poor human candle standing outside his son's chamber. At the same moment a door
closed hastily. He entered Richard's room. The boy was
absent. The bed was unpressed: no clothes about: nothing
to show that he had been there that night. Sir Austin felt
vaguely apprehensive. "Has he gone to my room to await
me?" thought the father's heart. Something like a tear

quivered in his arid eyes as he meditated and hoped this
might be so. His own sleeping-room faced that of his son.
He strode to it with a quick heart. It was empty. "My
son! my son! what is this?" he murmured. Alarm dis-
lodged anger from his jealous heart, and dread of evil put
a thousand questions to him that were answered in air.
After pacing up and down his room, he determined to go
and ask the boy Thompson, as he called Ripton, what was
known to him.

The chamber assigned to Master Ripton Thompson was
at the northern extremity of the passage, and overlooked
Lobourne and the valley to the west. The bed stood between the window and the door. Sir Austin found the door
ajar, and the interior dark. To his surprise, the boy Thompson's couch, as revealed by the rays of his lamp, was likewise
vacant. He was turning back, when he fancied he heard
the sibilation of a whispering in the room. Sir Austin
cloaked the lamp and trod silently towards the window.
The heads of his son Richard and the boy Thompson were
seen crouched against the glass, holding excited converse
together. Sir Austin listened, but he listened to a language
of which he possessed not the key. Their talk was of Fire,
and of delay: of expected agrarian astonishment: of a
farmer's huge wrath: of violence exercised towards gentlemen, and of vengeance: talk that the boys jerked out by fits,
and that came as broken links of a chain impossible to
connect. But they awoke curiosity. The Baronet condescended to play the spy upon his son.

Over Lobourne and the valley lay black night and innumerable stars.

"How jolly I feel!" exclaimed Ripton, inspired by Claret;
and then, after a luxurious pause, "I think that fellow has
pocketed his guinea, and cut his lucky."

Richard allowed a long minute to pass, during which the
Baronet waited anxiously for his voice: hardly recognizing
it, when he heard its altered tones.

"If he has, I'll go, and I'll do it myself."

"You would?" returned Master Ripton. "Well, I'm hanged!—I say, if you went to school, wouldn't you get into rows! Perhaps he hasn't found the place where the box was stuck in. I think he funks it. I almost wish you hadn't done it, upon my honour—eh? Look there! what was that? That looked like something.—I say! do you think we shall ever be found out?"

Master Ripton intoned this abrupt interrogation very seriously.

"I don't think about it," said Richard, all his faculties bent on signs from Lobourne.

"Well, but," Ripton persisted, "suppose we are found out?"

"If we are, I must pay for it.'

Sir Austin breathed the better for this reply. He was beginning to gather a clue to the dialogue. His son was engaged in a plot, and was moreover the leader of the plot. He listened for further enlightenment.

"What was the fellow's name?" inquired Ripton.

His companion answered, "Tom Bakewell."

"I'll tell you what," continued Ripton. "You let it all clean out to your cousin and Uncle at supper.—How capital Claret is with Partridge Pie! What a lot I ate!—Didn't you see me frown?"

The young sensualist was in an ecstasy of gratitude to his late refection, and the slightest word recalled him to it. Richard answered him:

"Yes. And felt your kick. It doesn't matter. Rady's safe, and Uncle never blabs."

"Well, my plan is to keep it close. You're never safe if you don't.—I never drank much Claret before," Ripton was off again. "Won't I now, though! Claret's my wine. You know, it may come out any day, and then we're done for," he rather incongruously appended.

Richard only took up the business-threads of his friend's rambling chatter, and answered:

"You've got nothing to do with it, if we are."

"Haven't I, though! I didn't stick in the box, but I'm an accomplice, that's clear. Besides," added Ripton, "do you think I should leave you to bear it all on your shoulders? I ain't that sort of chap, Ricky, I can tell you."

Sir Austin thought more highly of the boy Thompson. Still it looked a detestable conspiracy, and the altered manner of his son impressed him strangely. He was not the boy of yesterday. To Sir Austin is seemed as if a gulf had suddenly opened between them. The boy had embarked, and was on the waters of life in his own vessel. It was as vain to call him back as to attempt to erase what Time has written with the Judgment Blood! This child for whom he had prayed nightly in such a fervour and humbleness to God, the dangers were about him, the temptations thick on him, and the Devil on board piloting. If a day had done so much, what would years do? Were prayers and all the watchfulness he had expended, of no avail?

A sensation of infinite melancholy overcame the poor gentleman: a thought that he was fighting with a fate in this beloved boy.

He was half disposed to arrest the two conspirators on the spot, and make them confess, and absolve themselves: but it seemed to him better to keep an unseen eye over his son: Sir Austin's old system prevailed.

Adrian characterized this system well, in saying that Sir Austin wished to be Providence to his son.

If immeasurable Love were perfect Wisdom, one human being might almost impersonate Providence to another. Alas! Love, divine as it is, can do no more than lighten the house it inhabits: must take its shape, sometimes intensify its narrowness: can spiritualize, but not expel, the old life-long lodgers above-stairs and below.

Sir Austin decided to continue quiescent.

The valley still lay black beneath the large Autumnal stars, and the exclamations of the boys were becoming fevered and impatient. By-and-by one insisted that he had seen a twinkle. The direction he gave was out of their anticipations. Again the twinkle was announced. Both boys started to their feet. It was a twinkle in the right direction now.

"He's done it!" cried Richard in great heat. "Now you may say old Blaize'll soon be old Blazes, Rip. I hope he's asleep."

"I'm sure he's snoring!—Look there! He's alight fast enough. He's dry. He'll burn.—I say," Ripton reassumed the serious intonation, "do you think they'll ever suspect us?"

"What if they do? We must brunt it."

"Of course we will. But I say! I wish you hadn't given them the scent, though. I like to look innocent. I can't, when I know people suspect me. Lord! look there! Isn't it just beginning to flare up!"

The farmer's grounds were indeed gradually standing out in sombre shadows.

"I'll fetch my telescope," said Richard. Ripton, somehow not liking to be left alone, caught hold of him. "No, don't go and lose the best of it. Here, I'll throw open the window, and we can see."

The window was flung open, and the boys instantly stretched half their bodies out of it: Ripton appearing to devour the rising flames with his mouth: Richard with his eyes.

Opaque and statuesque stood the figure of the Baronet behind them. The wind was low. Dense masses of smoke hung amid the darting snakes of fire, and a red malign light was on the neighbouring leafage. No figures could be seen. Apparently the flames had nothing to contend against, for they were making terrible strides into the darkness.

"Oh!" shouted Richard, overcome by excitement, "if I

had my telescope! We must have it! Let me go and fetch it! I will!"

The boys struggled together, and Sir Austin stepped back. As he did so, a cry was heard in the passage. He hurried out, closed the chamber, and came upon little Clare lying senseless along the floor.

CHAPTER VIII

ADRIAN PLIES HIS HOOK

In the morning that followed this night, great gossip was interchanged between Raynham and Lobourne. The village told how farmer Blaize, of Belthorpe farm, had had his rick feloniously set fire to; his stables had caught fire, himself been all but roasted alive in the attempt to rescue his cattle, of which numbers had perished in the flames. Raynham counterbalanced Arson with an authentic Ghost seen by Miss Clare in the left wing of the Abbey; the Ghost of a Lady, dressed in deep mourning, a scar on her forehead, and a bloody handkerchief at her breast, frightful to behold! and no wonder the child was frightened out of her wits and lay in a desperate state awaiting the arrival of the London Doctors. It was added that the servants had all threatened to leave in a body, and that Sir Austin to appease them had promised to pull down the entire left wing, like a gentleman; for no decent creature, said Lobourne, could consent to live in a haunted house.

Rumour for the nonce had a stronger spice of truth than usual. Poor little Clare lay ill, and the calamity that had befallen farmer Blaize, as regards his rick and his cattle, was not much exaggerated. Sir Austin caused an account of it to be given him at breakfast, and appeared so scrupulously anxious to hear the exact extent of injury sustained by the farmer, that Heavy Benson went down to inspect the scene.

Mr. Benson returned, and, acting under Adrian's malicious advice, framed a formal Report of the Catastrophe, in which the farmer's breeches figured, and certain cooling applications to a part of the farmer's person. Sir Austin perused it without a smile. He took occasion to have it read out before the two boys, who listened very demurely, as to an ordinary newspaper incident: only when the Report particularized the peculiar garments damaged, and the unwonted distressing position farmer Blaize was reduced to in his bed, an indecorous fit of sneezing laid hold of Master Ripton Thompson, and Richard bit his lip and burst into loud laughter, Ripton joining him, lost to consequences.

"I trust you feel for this poor man," said Sir Austin to his son, somewhat sternly.

"I'm sorry about the poor horses, Sir," Richard replied, looking anything but sorry about the poor man.

It was a difficult task for Sir Austin to keep his old countenance towards the Hope of Raynham, knowing him the accomplice-incendiary, and believing the deed to have been unprovoked and wanton. But he must do so, he knew, to let the boy have a fair trial against himself. Be it said, moreover, that the Baronet's possession of his son's secret flattered him. It allowed him to act, and in a measure to feel, like Providence; enabled him to observe and provide for the movements of creatures in the dark. He therefore treated the boy as he commonly did, and young Richard saw no change in his father to make him think he was suspected.

The game was not so easy against Adrian. Adrian did not shoot or fish. Voluntarily he did nothing to work off the destructive nervous fluid, or whatever it may be, which is in man's nature; so that two culprit boys once in his power were not likely to taste the gentle hand of Mercy, and Richard and Ripton paid for many a trout and partridge spared. At every minute of the day Ripton was thrown into sweats of suspicion that discovery was imminent, by some stray remark or message of Adrian. He was as a fish with the hook in his gills, mysteriously caught without having nibbled; and dive into what depths he would, he was sensible of a summoning force that compelled him perpetually towards the gasping surface, which he seemed inevitably approaching when the dinner-bell sounded. There the talk was all of farmer Blaize. If it drooped, Adrian revived it, and his caressing way with Ripton was just such as a keen sportsman feels towards the creature that has owned his skill and is making its appearance for the world to acknowledge the same. Sir Austin saw the manœuvres, and admired Adrian's shrewdness. But he had to check the young natural lawyer, for the effect of so much masked examination upon Richard was growing baneful. This fish also felt the hook in its gills, but this fish was more of a pike, and lay in different waters, where there were old stumps and black roots to wind itself about, and defy alike strong pulling and delicate handling. In other words, Richard showed symptoms of a disposition to take refuge in lies.

"You know the grounds, my dear boy," Adrian observed to him. "Tell me. Do you think it easy to get to the rick unperceived? I hear they suspect one of the farmer's turned-off hands."

"I tell you I don't know the grounds," Richard sullenly replied.

"Not?" Adrian counterfeited courteous astonishment. "I thought Mr. Thompson said you were over there yesterday?"

Ripton, glad to speak a truth, hurriedly assured Adrian that it was not he had said so.

"Not? You had good sport, gentlemen, hadn't you?"

"Oh, yes!" mumbled the wretched victims, reddening as they remembered, in Adrian's slightly drawled rusticity of tone, farmer Blaize's first address to them.

"I suppose you were among the Fire-worshipers last night, too?" persisted Adrian. "In some countries, I hear, they manage their best sport at night-time, and beat up for game with torches. It must be a fine sight. After all, the Country would be dull if we hadn't a rip here and there to treat us to a little conflagration."

"A rip!" laughed Richard, to his friend's disgust and alarm at his daring: "You don't mean this Rip, do you?"

"Mr. Thompson fire a rick? I should as soon suspect you, my dear boy.—You are aware, young gentlemen, that it is rather a serious thing—Eh? In this country, you know, the landlord has always been the pet of the Laws. By the way," Adrian continued, as if diverging to another topic, "You met two gentlemen of the road in your explorations yesterday, Magians. Now, if I were a magistrate of the County, like Sir Miles Papworth, my suspicions would light upon those gentlemen. A tinker and a ploughman, I think you said, Mr. Thompson. Not? Well, say two ploughmen."

"More likely two tinkers," said Richard.

"Oh! if you wish to exclude the ploughman—was he out of employ?"

Ripton, with Adrian's eyes inveterately fixed on him, stammered an affirmative.

"The tinker, or the ploughman?"

"The ploughm—." Ingenuous Ripton looking about, as if to aid himself whenever he was able to speak the truth, beheld Richard's face blackening at him, and swallowed back half the word.

"The ploughman!" Adrian took him up cheerily. "Then we have here a ploughman out of employ. Given a ploughman out of employ, and a rick burnt. The burning of a rick is an act of vengeance, and a ploughman out of employ is a vengeful animal. The rick and the ploughman are advancing to a juxtaposition. Motive being established, we have only to prove their proximity at a certain hour, and our ploughman voyages beyond seas."

"Dear me! is it transportation for rick-burning?" inquired Ripton aghast.

Adrian spoke solemnly: "They shave your head. You are manacled. Your diet is sour bread and cheese-parings. You work in strings of twenties and thirties. ARSON is branded on your backs in an enormous A. Theological works are the sole literary recreation of the well-conducted and deserving. Consider the fate of this poor fellow, and what an act of vengeance brings him to! Do you know his name?"

"How should I know his name?" said Richard, with a stubborn assumption of innocence sad to see.

Sir Austin remarked that no doubt it would soon be known, and Adrian perceived that he was to quiet his line, marvelling a little at the Baronet's blindness to what was so clear. He would not tell, for that would ruin his future influence with Richard; still he wanted some present credit for his discernment and devotion. The boys got away from dinner, and, after deep consultation, agreed upon a course of conduct, which was, to commiserate farmer Blaize loudly, and make themselves look as much like the public as it was possible for two desperate young malefactors to look, one of whom already felt Adrian's enormous A devouring his back with the fierceness of the Promethean Eagle, and isolating him for ever from mankind. Adrian relished their novel tactics sharply, and led them to lengths of lamentation for farmer Blaize. Do what they might, the hook was in their gills. The farmer's whip had reduced them to bodily contortions; these were decorous compared with the spiritual writhings they had to perform under Adrian's skilful manipulation. Ripton was fast becoming a coward, and Richard a liar, when next morning Austin Wentworth came over from Poer Hall bringing news that one Mr. Thomas Bakewell, yeoman, had been arrested on suspicion of the crime of Arson and lodged in jail, awaiting the magisterial pleasure of Sir Miles Papworth. Austin's eye rested on Richard, as he spoke these terrible tidings. The Hope of Raynham returned his look, perfectly calm, and had, moreover, the presence of mind not to look at Ripton.

CHAPTER IX

JUVENILE STRATAGEMS

As soon as they could escape, the boys got away together into an obscure corner of the park, and there took counsel of their extremity.

"Whatever shall we do now?" asked Ripton of his leader.

Scorpion girt with fire was never in a more terrible prison-house than poor Ripton, around whom the raging element he had assisted to create seemed to be drawing momently narrower circles.

"There's only one chance," said Richard, coming to a dead halt, and folding his arms resolutely.

His comrade inquired with the utmost eagerness, what that chance might be?

Richard fixed his eyes on a flint, and replied: "We must rescue that fellow from jail."

"Rescue him from jail!" Ripton gazed at his leader, and fell back with astonishment. "My dear Ricky! but how are we to do it?"

Richard still perusing his flint, replied: "We must manage to get a file in to him, and a rope. It can be done, I tell you. I don't care what I pay. I don't care what I do. He must be got out."

"Bother that old Blaize!" exclaimed Ripton, taking off his cap to wipe his frenzied forehead, and brought down his friend's severe reproof.

"Never mind old Blaize now. Talk about letting it out. Look at you. I'm ashamed of you. You talk about Robin Hood and King Richard! Why, you haven't an atom of courage. Why, you let it out every second of the day. Whenever Rady begins speaking, you start, I can see the perspiration rolling down you. Are you afraid?——And then you contradict yourself. You never keep to one story.

Now, follow me. We must risk everything to get him out. Mind that! And keep out of Adrian's way as much as you can. And keep to one story."

With these sage directions, the young leader marched his companion-culprit down to inspect the jail where Tom Bakewell lay groaning over the results of the super-mundane conflict, and the victim of it that he was.

In Lobourne Austin Wentworth had the reputation of the poor man's friend; a title he earned more largely ere he went to the reward God alone can give to that supreme virtue. Dame Bakewell, the mother of Tom, on hearing of her son's arrest, had run to comfort him and render him what help she could; but this was only sighs and tears, and, Oh deary me! which only perplexed poor Tom, who bade her leave an unlucky chap to his fate and not make him feel himself a thundering villain. Whereat the dame begged him to take heart, and he should have a true comforter. "And though it's a gentleman that's coming to you, Tom— for he never refuses a poor body," said Mrs. Bakewell, "it's a true Christian, Tom! and the Lord knows if the sight of him mayn't be the saving of you, for he's light to look on, and a sermon to listen to, he is!"

Tom was not prepossessed by the prospect of a sermon, and looked a sullen dog enough when Austin entered his cell. He was surprised at the end of half an hour to find himself engaged in man-to-man conversation with a gentleman and a Christian. When Austin rose to go, Tom begged permission to shake his hand.

"Yew've doan me good, Sir," said Tom, "and made me feel—there! I knows I'm a sinner, though yew an't said ut —that's where't is!—like a man! And a man I intends to be let coam what coam may! Now, Sir, Muster Went'orth! you knows what a bad chap I be. But I an't a blackguard. Now, Sir, 'skews me for sayin' I moight 'a doan your fam'ly a bad turn. But I an't a-goin' to. Leastways, if I was ever a-minded to, which I warn't. Leastways, not now, I an't.

Yew tak' and tall young Measter up at t 'Abbey, that I an't the chap to peach. He'll know. He's a young gentleman as'll mak' any man do as he wants 'em! He's a mortal wild young gentleman! And I'm a Ass! That's where 'tis. But I an't a blackguard. Tall'n that, Sir! That'll mak' un easy, or he'll mayhap be funkin'-loike. They knows at Beltharpe ut's all on moy shoolders. I did ut. Thay're bad 'nough. Tall'n that, Sir. Sure-ly they be!" And Tom shook his much-burdened shoulders with a grin.

This was how it came that Austin eyed young Richard seriously while he told the news at Raynham. The boy was shy of Austin more than of Adrian. Why, he did not know; but he made it a hard task for Austin to catch him alone, and turned sulky that instant. Austin was not clever like Adrian: he seldom divined other people's ideas, and always went the direct road to his object; so instead of beating about and setting the boy on the alert at all points, crammed to the muzzle with lies, he just said, "Tom Bakewell told me to let you know he does not intend to peach on you," and left him.

Richard repeated the intelligence to Ripton, who cried aloud that Tom was a brick.

"He shan't suffer for it," said Richard, and pondered on a thicker rope and sharper file.

"But will your cousin tell?" was Ripton's reflection.

"He!" Richard's lip expressed contempt. "A ploughman refuses to peach, and you ask if a Feverel will?"

Ripton stood for the twentieth time reproved on this point.

The boys had examined the outer walls of the jail, and arrived at the conclusion that Tom's escape might be managed, if Tom had spirit, and the rope and file could be any-way reached to him. But to do this, somebody must gain admittance to his cell, and who was to be taken into their confidence?

"Try your cousin," Ripton suggested, after much debate.

Richard, smiling, wished to know if he meant Adrian?
"No, no!" Ripton hurriedly reassured him. "Austin."

The same idea was knocking at Richard's head.

"Let's get the rope and file first," said he, and to Bursley
they went for those implements to defeat the law, Ripton
procuring the file at one shop, and Richard the rope at
another; with such masterly cunning did they lay their
measures for the avoidance of every possible chance of detection. And better to assure this, in a wood outside
Bursley Richard stripped to his shirt and wound the rope
round his body, tasting the tortures of anchorites and penitential friars, that nothing should be risked to make Tom's
escape a certainty. Sir Austin saw the marks at night, as his
son lay asleep, through the half-opened folds of his bed-
gown, and wondered afresh, but decided still to watch.

It was a severe stroke when, after all their stratagems and
trouble, Austin Wentworth refused the office the boys had
zealously designed for him. Time pressed. In a few days
poor Tom would have to face the redoubtable Sir Miles,
and get committed, for rumours of overwhelming evidence
to convict him were rife about Lobourne, and farmer Blaize's
wrath was unappeasable. Again and again young Richard
begged his cousin not to see him disgraced, and to help him
in this extremity. Austin was firm in his refusal.

"My dear Ricky," said he, "there are two ways of getting
out of a scrape: a long way, and a short way. When you've
tried the roundabout method, and failed, come to me, and
I'll show you the straight route."

Richard was too entirely bent upon the roundabout method
to consider this advice more than empty words, and only
ground his teeth at Austin's unkind refusal.

He imparted to Ripton, at the eleventh hour, that they
must do it themselves, to which Ripton heavily assented.

On the day preceding poor Tom's doomed appearance
before the magistrate, Dame Bakewell had an interview with
Austin, who went to Raynham immediately, and sought

Adrian's counsel what was to be done. Homeric laughter and nothing else could be got out of Adrian when he heard of the doings of these desperate boys: How they had entered Dame Bakewell's smallest of retail shops, and purchased tea, sugar, candles, and comfits of every description, till the shop was clear of customers: how they had then hurried her into her little back-parlour, where Richard had torn open his shirt and revealed the coils of rope, and Ripton displayed the point of a file from a serpentine recess in his jacket: how they had then told the astonished woman that the rope she saw and the file she saw were instruments for the liberation of her son; that there existed no other means on earth to save him, they, the boys, having unsuccessfully attempted all: how upon that Richard had tried with the utmost earnestness to persuade her to disrobe and wind the rope round her own person; and Ripton had aired his eloquence to induce her to secrete the file: how, when she resolutely objected to the rope, both boys began backing the file, and in an evil hour, she feared, said Dame Bakewell, she had rewarded the gracious permission given her by Sir Miles Papworth to visit her son, by tempting Tom to file the Law. Though, thanks be to the Lord! Dame Bakewell added, Tom had turned up his nose at the file, and so she had told young Master Richard, who swore very bad for a young gentleman.

"Boys are like monkeys," remarked Adrian, at the close of his explosions, "the gravest actors of farcical nonsense that the world possesses. May I never be where there are no boys! A couple of boys left to themselves will furnish richer fun than any troop of trained comedians. No: nc Art arrives at the artlessness of Nature in matters of Comedy. You can't simulate the Ape. Your antics are dull. They haven't the charming inconsequence of the natural animal. Look at these two! Think of the shifts they are put to all day long! They know I know all about it, and yet their serenity of innocence is all but unruffled in my presence.—You're sorry to think about the end of the business, Austin? So am I! I dread the idea of the curtain going down. Besides, it will do Ricky a world of good. A practical lesson is the best lesson."

"Sinks deepest," said Austin, "but whether he learns good or evil from it is the question at stake."

Adrian stretched his length at ease.

"This will be his first nibble at Experience, old Time's fruit, hateful to the palate of youth! for which season only hath it any nourishment! Experience! You know Coleridge's capital simile?—Mournful you call it? Well! all Wisdom is mournful. 'Tis therefore, coz, that the Wise do love the Comic Muse. Their own high food would kill them. You shall find great poets, rare philosophers, night after night on the broad grin before a row of yellow lights and mouthing masks. Why? because all's dark at home. The Stage is the pastime of great minds. That's how it comes that the Stage is now down. An Age of rampant little minds—pshaw! my dear Austin! how I hate that cant of yours about an Age of Work—you, and your Mortons, and your parsons Brawnley, rank Radicals all of you, base Materialists! What does Diaper Sandoe sing of your Age of Work? Listen!

> "'An Age of petty tit for tat,
>   An Age of busy gabble:
> An Age that's like a brewer's vat
>   Fermenting for the rabble!

> "'An Age that's chaste in Love, but lax
>   To virtuous abuses:
> Whose gentlemen and ladies wax
>   Too dainty for their uses.

> "'An age which drives an Iron Horse
>   Of Time and Space defiant:
> Exulting in a Giant's Force,
>   And trembling at the Giant.

> "'An Age of Quaker hue and cut,
>   By Mammon misbegotten;
> See the mad Hamlet mouth and strut!
>   And mark the Kings of Cotton!
>
> "'From this unrest, lo, early wreck'd,
>   A Future staggers crazy,
> Ophelia of the Ages, deck'd
>   With woful weed and daisy!'"

Murmuring, "Get your parson Brawnley to answer that!"
Adrian changed the resting-place of a leg, and smiled. The
AGE was an old battlefield between him and Austin.

"My parson Brawnley, as you call him, has answered it,"
said Austin, "not by hoping his best, which would probably
leave the Age to go mad to your satisfaction, but by doing
it. And he has and will answer your Diaper Sandoe in
better verse, as he confutes him in a better life."

"You don't see Sandoe's depth," Adrian replied. "Consider that phrase, 'Ophelia of the Ages!' Is not Brawnley,
like a dozen other leading spirits—I think that's your term—
just the metaphysical Hamlet to drive her mad? She, poor
maid! asks for Marriage and smiling babes, while my lord
lover stands questioning the Infinite, and rants to the
Impalpable."

Austin laughed. "Marriage, and smiling babes she would
have in abundance, if Brawnley legislated. Wait till you
know him. He will be over at Poer Hall shortly, and you
will see what a Man of the Age means. But now pray
consult with me about these boys."

"Oh, these boys!" Adrian tossed a hand. "Are there
boys of the Age as well as men? Not? Then boys are
better than men: boys are for all Ages. What do you think,
Austin? They've been studying Latude's Escape. I found
the book open in Ricky's room, on the top of Jonathan Wild.
Jonathan preserved the secrets of his profession, and taught

them nothing. So they're going to make a Latude of Mr.
Tom Bakewell. He's to be Bastille Bakewell, whether he
will or no. Let them. Let the wild colt run free! We
can't help them. We can only look on. We should spoil
the play. Keep out of it, if you're wise, Austin, or possibly
they'll be turning from Tom to you and insist on your
swallowing the famous file to save Tom from transportation."

Adrian always made a point of feeding the fretful beast,
Impatience, with pleasantries; a not congenial diet; and
Austin, the most patient of human beings, began to lose
his self-control.

"You talk as if Time belonged to you, Adrian. We have
but a few hours left us. Work first, and joke afterwards.
The boy's fate is being decided now."

"So is everybody's, my dear Austin!" yawned the Epicurean.

"Yes, but this boy is at present under our guardianship:
under yours especially."

"Not yet! not yet!" Adrian interjected languidly. "No
getting into scrapes when I have him. The leash, young
hound! The collar, young colt! I'm perfectly irresponsible
at present."

"You may have something different to deal with, when you
are responsible, if you think that."

"I take my young Prince as I find him, coz: a Julian, or
a Caracalla: a Constantine, or a Nero. Then if he will
play the fiddle to a conflagration, he shall play it well: if he
must be a disputatious apostate, at any rate, he shall understand logic and men, and have the habit of saying his
prayers."

"Then you leave me to act alone?" said Austin, rising.

"Without a single curb!" Adrian gesticulated an
acquiesced withdrawal. "I'm sure you would not, still
more certain you cannot, do harm. And be mindful of my
prophetic words: Whatever's done, Old Blaize will have to

be bought off. There's the affair settled at once. I suppose I must go to the Chief to-night, and settle it myself. We can't see this poor devil condemned, though it's nonsense to talk of a boy being the prime instigator."

Austin cast an eye at the complacent languor of the Wise Youth, his cousin, and the little that he knew of his fellows told him he might talk for ever here, and not be comprehended. The Wise Youth's two ears were stuffed with his own wisdom. One evil only Adrian dreaded, it was clear: the action of the Law. Austin saw it sadly, and foreboded of Richard's future.

As he was moving away, Adrian called out to him, "Stop, Austin! There! don't be anxious! You invariably take the glum side. I've done something. Never mind what. If you go down to Belthorpe, be civil, but not obsequious. You remember the tactics of Scipio Africanus against the Punic elephants? Well, don't say a word:—in thine ear, coz: I've turned Master Blaize's elephants. If they charge, 'twill be a feint, and back to the destruction of his serried ranks! You understand. Not? Well, 'tis as well. Only let none say that I sleep. If I must see him to-night, I go down knowing he has not got us in his power." The Wise Youth yawned, and stretched out a hand for any book that might be within his reach. Austin left him, to look about the grounds for Richard.

CHAPTER X

DAPHNE'S BOWER

A LITTLE laurel-shaded Temple of white marble looked out on the river from a knoll bordering the Raynham beech-woods, and was dubbed by Adrian Daphne's Bower. To this spot Richard had retired, and there Austin found him with his head buried in his hands, a picture of Desperation whose last shift has been defeated. He allowed Austin to greet him, and sit by him, without lifting his head. Perhaps his eyes were not presentable.

"Where's your friend?" Austin began.

"Gone!" was the answer, sounding cavernous from behind hair and fingers. An explanation presently followed, as Ripton's due, that a summons had come for him in the morning from Mr. Thompson; and that Ripton had departed against his will.

In fact Ripton had protested that he would defy his parent and remain by his friend in the hour of adversity and at the post of danger. Sir Austin signified his opinion that a boy should obey his parent, by giving orders to Heavy Benson for Ripton's box to be packed and ready before noon; and Ripton's alacrity in taking the Baronet's view of filial duty, was as little feigned as his offer to Richard to throw filial duty to the winds. He rejoiced that the Fates had agreed to remove him from the very hot neighbourhood Lobourne, while he grieved, like an honest lad, to see his comrade left to face calamity alone. The boys parted amicably as they could hardly fail to do, when Ripton had sworn fealty to the Feverels with a fervour that made him declare himself bond and due to appear at any stated hour and at any stated place to fight all the farmers in England, on a mandate from the heir of the house.

"So you're left alone," said Austin, contemplating the boy's shapely head. "'I'm glad of it. We never know what's in us till we stand by ourselves."

There appeared to be no answer forthcoming. Vanity, however, replied at last: "He wasn't much support."

"Remember his good points, now he's gone, Ricky."

"Oh! he was staunch," the boy grumbled.

"And a staunch friend is not always to be found. Now, have you tried your own way of rectifying this business, Ricky?"

"I've done everything."

"And failed!"

There was a pause, and then the deep-toned evasion, "Tom Bakewell's a coward!"

"I suppose, poor fellow," said Austin, in his kind way, "he doesn't want to get into a deeper mess. I don't think he's a coward."

"He is a coward," cried Richard fiercely. "Do you think, if I had a file, I would stay in prison? I'd be out the first night! The miserable churl! And he might have had the rope, too—a rope thick enough for a couple of men his size and weight. Ripton and I and Ned Markham swung on it for an hour, and it didn't give. He's a coward, and deserves his fate. I've no compassion for a coward."

"Nor I much," said Austin.

Richard had raised his head in the heat of his denunciation of poor Tom. He would have hidden it, had he known the thought in Austin's clear eyes while he faced them.

"I never met a coward myself," Austin continued. "I have heard of one or two. One let an innocent man die for him."

"How base!" exclaimed the boy.

"Yes, it was bad," Austin acquiesced.

"Bad!" Richard scorned the poor contempt. "How I would have spurned him! He was a coward!"

"I believe he pleaded the feelings of his family in his excuse, and tried every means to get him off. I have read also in the Confessions of a celebrated philosopher, that in his youth he committed some act of pilfering, and accused a young servant-girl of his own theft, who was condemned and dismissed for it, pardoning her guilty accuser."

"What a coward!" shouted Richard. "And he confessed it publicly?"

"You may read it yourself."

"He actually wrote it down, and printed it?"

"You have the book in your Father's library. Would you have done so much?"

Richard faltered. No! he admitted that he never could have told people.

"Then who is to call that man a coward?" said Austin. "He expiated his cowardice, as all who give way in moments of weakness, and are not cowards, must do. The coward chooses to think 'God does not see. I shall escape.' He who is not a coward, and has succumbed, knows that God has seen all, and it is not so hard a task for him to make his heart bare to the world. Worse, I should fancy it, to know myself an impostor when men praised me."

Young Richard's eyes were wandering on Austin's gravely cheerful face. A keen intentness suddenly fixed them, and he dropped his head.

"So I think you're wrong, Ricky, in calling this poor Tom a coward, because he refuses to try your means of escape," Austin resumed. "A coward hardly objects to drag in his accomplice. And where the person involved belongs to a great family, it seems to me that for a poor ploughlad to volunteer not to do so, speaks him anything but a coward."

Richard was silent. Altogether to surrender his Rope and File was a fearful sacrifice, after all the time, trepidation, and study, he had spent on those two saving instruments. If he avowed Tom's manly behaviour, Richard Feverel was in a totally new position. Whereas, by keeping Tom a coward, Richard Feverel was the injured one, and to seem injured is always a luxury; sometimes a necessity, whether among boys or men.

In Austin the Magian conflict would not have lasted long. He had but a blind notion of the fierceness with which it raged in young Richard. Happily for the boy, Austin was not a preacher. A single insistance, a cant phrase, a fatherly manner, might have wrecked him, by arousing ancient, or latent, opposition. The born preacher we feel instinctively to be our foe. He may do some good to the wretches that have been struck down, and lie gasping on the battle-field; he rouses deadly antagonism in the strong. Richard's nature, left to itself, wanted little more than an indication of the proper track, and when he said, "Tell me what I can do, Austin?" he had fought the best half of the battle. His voice was subdued. Austin put his hand on the boy's shoulder.

"You must go down to farmer Blaize."

"Well!" said Richard, sullenly divining the deed of penance.

"You'll know what to say to him when you're there."

The boy bit his lip, and frowned. "Ask a favour of that big brute, Austin? I can't!"

"'Just tell him the whole case, and that you don't intend to stand by and let the poor fellow suffer without a friend to help him out of his scrape."

"But, Austin!" the boy pleaded, "I shall have to ask him to help off Tom Bakewell! How can I ask him, when I hate him?"

Without seeking to confute this logical proposition, Austin bade him go, and think nothing of the consequences till he got there.

Richard groaned in soul.

"You've no pride, Austin."

"Perhaps not," Austin calmly avowed.

"You don't know what it is to ask a favour of a brute you hate."

Richard stuck to that view of the case, and stuck to it the faster the more imperatively the urgency of a movement dawned upon him.

"Why," continued the boy, "I shall hardly be able to keep my fists off him!"

"Surely you've punished him enough, boy?" said Austin.

"He struck me!" Richard's lip quivered. "He dared not come at me with his hands. He struck me with a whip. He'll be telling everybody that he horsewhipped me, and that I went down and begged his pardon. Begged his pardon! A Feverel beg his pardon! Oh, if I had my will!"

"The man earns his bread, Ricky. You poached on his grounds. He turned you off, and you fired his rick."

"And I'll pay him for his loss. And I won't do any more."

"Because you won't ask a favour of him?"

"No! I will not ask a favour of him."

Austin looked at the boy steadily. "You prefer to receive a favour from poor Tom Bakewell?"

At Austin's slow enunciation of this obverse view of the matter, Richard raised his brow. Dimly a new light broke in upon him. "Favour from Tom Bakewell, the ploughman? How do you mean, Austin?"

"To save yourself an unpleasantness, you permit a country lad to sacrifice himself for you? I confess I should not have so much pride."

"Pride!" shouted Richard, stung by the taunt, and set his sight hard at the blue ridges of the hills.

Not knowing for the moment what else to do, Austin drew a picture of Tom in prison, and repeated Tom's volunteer statement. The picture, though his intentions were far from designing it so, had to Richard, whose perception of humour was infinitely keener, a horrible chaw-bacon smack about it. Visions of a grinning lout, open from ear to ear, unkempt, coarse, splay-footed, rose before him and afflicted him with the strangest sensations of disgust and comicality, mixed up with pity and remorse: a sort of twisted pathos. There lay poor Tom; hob-nail Tom! a bacon-munching, reckless, beer-swilling animal! and yet a man; a dear brave human heart notwithstanding; capable of devotion and un-selfishness. The boy's better spirit was touched, and kindled his imagination to realize the abject figure of poor clodpole Tom, and surrounded it with a halo of mournful light. His soul was alive. Feelings he had never known streamed in upon him, as from an ethereal casement: an unwonted tenderness: an embracing humour: a consciousness of some ineffable glory: an irradiation of the features of humanity. All this was in the bosom of the boy, and through it all, the

vision of an actual hob-nail Tom, coarse, unkempt, open.
from ear to ear; whose presence was a finger of shame to
him, and an oppression of clodpole; yet towards whom he
felt just then a loving-kindness beyond what he felt for any
living creature. He laughed at him, and wept over him.
He prized him, while he shrank from him. It was a genial
strife of the Angel in him with constituents less divine; but
the Angel was uppermost and led the van: extinguished loath-
ing: humanized laughter: transfigured Pride—Pride that
would persistently contemplate the corduroys of gaping Tom,
and cry to Richard, in the very tone of Adrian's ironic voice:
'Behold your benefactor!'

Austin sat by the boy, unaware of the sublimer tumult he
had stirred. Little of it was perceptible in Richard's countenance. The lines of his mouth were slightly drawn; his
eyes still hard set into the distance. He remained thus many
minutes. Finally he jumped to his legs, saying, "I'll go at
once to old Blaize, and tell him."

Austin grasped his hand, and together they issued out of
Daphne's Bower, in the direction of Lobourne.

CHAPTER XI

THE BITTER CUP

FARMER Blaize was not so astonished at the visit of
Richard Feverel, as that young gentleman expected him to be.
The farmer, seated in his easy chair in the little low-roofed
parlour of an old-fashioned farmhouse, with a long clay-pipe
on the table at his elbow, and a veteran pointer at his feet,
had already given audience to three distinguished members
of the Feverel blood, who had come separately, according
to their accustomed secretiveness, and with one object. In
the morning it was Sir Austin himself. Shortly after his
departure, arrived Austin Wentworth; close on his heels,

Algernon, known about Lobourne as, the Captain, popular wherever he was known. Farmer Blaize reclined in considerable elation. He had brought these great people to a pretty low pitch. He had welcomed them hospitably, as a British yeoman should; but not budged a foot in his demands: not to the Baronet: not to the Captain: not to the good young Mr. Wentworth. For farmer Blaize was a solid Englishman, and on hearing from the Baronet a frank confession of the hold he had on the family, he determined to tighten his hold, and only relax it in exchange for tangible advantages: compensation to his pocket, his wounded person, and his still more wounded feelings: the total indemnity being, in round figures, three hundred pounds, and a spoken apology from the prime offender, young Mister Richard. Even then, there was a reservation. Provided, the farmer said, nobody had been tampering with any of his witnesses. In that case, farmer Blaize declared, the money might go, and he would transport Tom Bakewell, as he had sworn he would. And it goes hard, too, with an accomplice, by Law, added the farmer, knocking the ashes leisurely out of his pipe. He had no wish to bring any disgrace anywhere, had farmer Blaize. He respected the inmates of Raynham Abbey, as in duty bound. He should be sorry to see them in trouble. Only no tampering with his witnesses. He was a man for Law. Rank was much: money was much: but Law was more. In this country, Law was above the sovereign. To tamper with the Law was treason to the realm.

"I come to you direct," the Baronet explained: "I tell you candidly in what way I discovered my son to be mixed up in this miserable affair. I promise you indemnity for your loss, and an apology that shall, I trust, satisfy your feelings, assuring you that to tamper with witnesses is not the province of a Feverel. All I ask of you in return is, not to press the prosecution. At present it rests with you. I am bound to do all that lies in my power for this imprisoned man. How and wherefore my son was prompted to suggest, or assist in, such an act, I cannot explain, for I do not know."

"Hum!" said the farmer. "I think I do."

"You know the cause?" Sir Austin stared. "I beg you to confide it to me."

"—Least, I can pretty nigh neighbour it with a guess," said the farmer. "We an't good friends, Sir Aust'n, me and your son, jest now: not to say cordial. I, ye see, Sir Aust'n, I'm a man as don't like young gentlemen a-poachin' on his grounds without his permission,—in 'special when birds is plentiful on their own. It appear he do like it. Consequently I has to flick this whip—as them fallers at the racers: All in this 'ere Ring's mine! as much as to say; and who's been hit, he's had fair warnin'. I'm sorry for 't, but that's jest the case."

Sir Austin retired to communicate with his son, when he should find him.

Algernon's interview passed off in Ale and promises. He also assured farmer Blaize that no Feverel could be affected by his proviso.

No less did Austin Wentworth. The farmer was satisfied. "Money's safe, I know," said he; "now for the 'pology!" and Farmer Blaize thrust his legs further out, and his head further back.

The farmer naturally reflected that the three separate visits had been conspired together. Still the Baronet's frankness, and the Baronet's not having reserved himself for the third and final charge, puzzled him. He was considering whether they were a deep, or a shallow, lot, when young Richard was announced.

A pretty little girl with the roses of thirteen springs in her cheeks, and abundant beautiful bright tresses, tripped before the boy, and loitered shyly by the farmer's arm-chair to steal a look at the handsome new-comer. She was introduced to Richard as the farmer's niece, Lucy Desborough, the daughter of a lieutenant in the Royal Navy, and, what was better, though the farmer did not pronounce it so loudly, a real good girl.

Neither the excellence of her character, nor her rank in life, tempted Richard to inspect the little lady. He made an awkward bow, and sat down.

The farmer's eyes twinkled. "Her father," he continued, "fought and fell for his coontry. A man as fights for's coontry, 's a right to hould up his head—ay! with any in the land. Desb'rough's o' Dorset! d' ye know that family, Master Feverel?"

Richard did not know them, and, by his air, did not desire to become acquainted with any offshoot of that family.

"She can make puddens and pies," the farmer went on, regardless of his auditor's gloom. "She's a lady, as good as the best of 'em. I don't care about their being Catholics—the Desb'roughs o' Dorset are gentlemen. And she's good for the pianer, too! She strums to me of evenin's. I'm for the old tunes: she's for the new. Gal-like! While she's with me, she shall be taught things use'l. She can parleyvoo a good 'un and foot it, as it goes: been in France a couple o' year. I prefer the singin' of 't, to the talkin' of 't. Come, Luce! toon up—eh?—Ye wun't? That song about the Viffendeer—a female"—farmer Blaize volunteered the translation of the title—"who wears the—you guess what! and marches along with the French sojers: A pretty brazen bit o' goods! I sh'd fancy."

Mademoiselle Lucy corrected her uncle's French, but objected to do more. The handsome cross boy had almost taken away her voice for speech, as it was, and sing in his company she could not; so she stood, a hand on her uncle's chair to stay herself from falling, while she wriggled a dozen various shapes of refusal, and shook her head at the farmer with fixed eyes.

"Aha!" laughed the farmer, dismissing her, "they soon learn the difference 'twixt the young 'un and the old 'un. Go along, Luce! and learn yer lessons for tomorrow."

Reluctantly the daughter of the Royal Navy glided away. Her uncle's head followed her to the door, where she dallied to catch a last impression of the young stranger's lowering face, and darted through.

Farmer Blaize laughed and chuckled. "She an't so fond of her uncle as that, every day! Not that she an't a good nurse—the kindest little soul you'd meet of a winter's walk! She'll read t' ye, and make drinks, and sing, too, if ye likes it, and she won't be tired. A obstinate good 'un, she be! Bless her!"

The farmer may have designed, by these eulogies of his niece, to give his visitor time to recover his composure, and establish a common topic. His diversion only irritated and confused our shame-eaten youth. Richard's intention had been to come to the farmer's threshold: to summon the farmer thither, and in a loud and haughty tone then and there to take upon himself the whole burden of the charge against Tom Bakewell. He had strayed, during his passage to Belthorpe, somewhat back to his old nature; and his being compelled to enter the house of his enemy, sit in his chair, and endure an introduction to his family, was more than he bargained for. He commenced blinking hard in preparation for the horrible dose to which delay and the farmer's cordiality added inconceivable bitters. Farmer Blaize was quite at his ease: nowise in a hurry. He spoke of the weather and the harvest: of recent doings up at the Abbey: glanced over that year's cricketing: hoped that no future Feverel would lose a leg to the game. Richard saw and heard Arson in it all. He blinked harder, as he neared the cup. In a moment of silence, he seized it with a gasp.

"Mr. Blaize! I have come to tell you that I am the person who set fire to your rick the other night."

An odd contraction formed about the farmer's mouth. He changed his posture, and said, "Ay? that's what ye're come to tall me, Sir?"

"Yes!" said Richard firmly.

"And that be all?"

"Yes!" Richard reiterated.

The farmer again changed his posture. "Then, my lad, ye've come to tall me a lie!"

Farmer Blaize looked straight at the boy, undismayed by the dark flush of ire he had kindled.

"You dare to call me a liar!" cried Richard, starting up.

"I say," the farmer renewed his first emphasis, and smacked his thigh thereto, "that's a lie!"

Richard was mounting the white cockade of the Feverels. He held out his clenched fist. "You have twice insulted me. You have struck me: you have dared to call me a liar. I would have apologized—I would have asked your pardon, to have got off that fellow in prison. Yes! I would have degraded myself that another man should suffer for my deed—"

"Quite proper!" interposed the farmer.

"And you take this opportunity of insulting me afresh. You're a coward, Sir! nobody but a coward would have insulted me in his own house."

"Sit ye down, sit ye down, young Master," said the farmer, indicating the chair and cooling the outburst with his hand. "Sit ye down. Don't ye be hasty. If ye hadn't been hasty t'other day, we sh'd a been friends yet. Sit ye down, Sir. I sh'd be sorry to reckon you out a liar, Mr. Feverel, or anybody o' your name. I respects yer father, though we're opp'site pol'tics. I'm willin' to think well o' you. What I say is, that as you say an't the trewth. Mind! I don't like you none the worse for 't. But it an't what is. That's all! You knows it as well's I!"

Richard, disdaining to show signs of being pacified, angrily reseated himself. The farmer spoke sense, and the boy, after his late interview with Austin, had become capable of perceiving vaguely that a towering passion is hardly the justification for a wrong course of conduct.

"Come," continued the farmer, not unkindly, "what else have you to say?"

Here was the same bitter cup he had already once drained, brimming at Richard's lips again! Alas, poor human nature! that empties to the dregs a dozen of these evil drinks, to evade the single one Destiny, less cruel, had insisted upon.

The boy blinked, and tossed it off.

"I came to say, that I regretted the revenge I had taken on you for your striking me."

Farmer Blaize nodded.

"And now ye've done, young gentleman?"

Still another cupful!

"I should be very much obliged," Richard formally began: but his stomach was turned; he could but sip and sip, and gather a distaste which threatened to make the penitential act impossible. "Very much obliged," he repeated: "much obliged, if you would be so kind," and it struck him that had he spoken this at first, he would have given it a wording more persuasive with the farmer and more worthy of his own pride: more honest, in fact: for a sense of the dishonesty of what he was saying, caused him to cringe and simulate humility to deceive the farmer, and the more he said, the less he felt his words, and feeling them less, he inflated them more. "So kind," he stammered, "so kind" (fancy a Feverel asking this brute to be so kind!) "as to do me the favour" (*me* the favour!) "to exert yourself" (it's all to please Austin) "to endeavour to—hem! to" (there's no saying it!)

The cup was full as ever. Richard dashed at it again.

"What I came to ask is, whether you would have the kindness to try what you could do" (what an infamous shame to have to beg like this!) "do to save—do to ensure—whether you would have the kindness—" It seemed out of all human power to gulp it down. The draught grew more and more abhorrent. To proclaim one's iniquity: to apologize for one's wrong-doing: thus much could be done: but to beg a favour of the offended party—that was beyond the self-abasement any Feverel could consent to. Pride, however, whose inevitable battle is against itself, drew aside the curtains of poor Tom's prison, crying a second time, 'Behold your Benefactor!' and with the words burning in his ears Richard swallowed the dose:

"Well, then! I want you, Mr. Blaize,—if you don't mind —will you help me to get this man Bakewell off his punishment?"

To do farmer Blaize justice, he waited very patiently for the boy, though he could not quite see why he did not take the gate at the first offer.

"Oh!" said he, when he heard and had pondered on the request: "Hum! hah! we'll see about it t'morrow. But if he's inn'cent, ye know, we shan't make'n guilty."

"It was I did it!" Richard declared.

The farmer's half-amused expression sharpened a bit.

"So, young gentleman! and yer sorry for the night's work?"

"I shall see that you are paid the full extent of your losses."

"Thank'ee," said the farmer drily.

"And if this poor man is released tomorrow, I don't care what the amount is."

Farmer Blaize deflected his head twice in silence. 'Bribery,' one motion expressed: 'Corruption,' the other.

"Now," said he, leaning forward, and fixing his elbows on his knees, while he counted the case at his fingers' ends, "ascuse the liberty, but wishin' to know where this 'ere money's to come from, sh'd like jest t' ask if so be Sir Aust'n know o' this?"

"My father knows nothing of it," replied Richard.

The farmer flung back his chair. 'Lie number Two,' said his shoulders, soured by the British aversion to being plotted at, and not dealt with openly.

"And ye've the money ready, young gentleman?"

"I shall ask my father for it."

"And he'll hand 't out?"

"Certainly he will!"

Richard had not the slightest intention of ever letting his father into his counsels.

"A good three hundred pounds, ye know?" the farmer suggested.

No consideration of the extent of damages, and the size of the sum, affected young Richard, who said boldly, "He will not object to pay it, when I tell him."

It was natural Farmer Blaize should be a trifle suspicious that a youth's guarantee would hardly be given for his father's readiness to disburse such a thumping bill, unless he had previously received his father's sanction and authority.

"Hum!" said he, "why not 'a told him before?"

The farmer threw an objectionable shrewdness into his query, that caused Richard to compress his mouth and glance high.

Farmer Blaize was positive 't was a lie.

"Hum!" "Ye still hold to 't you fired the rick?" he asked.

"The blame is mine!" quoth Richard, with the loftiness of a patriot of old Rome.

"Na, na!" the straightforward Briton put him aside. "Ye did 't, or ye didn't do 't. Did ye do 't, or no?"

Thrust in a corner, Richard said, "I did it."

Farmer Blaize reached his hand to the bell. It was answered in an instant by little Lucy, who received orders to fetch in a dependant at Belthorpe going by the name of the Bantam, and made her exit as she had entered, with her eyes on the young stranger.

"Now," said the farmer, "these be my principles. I'm a plain man, Mr. Feverel. Above board with me, and ye'll find me handsome. Try to circumvent me, and I'm a ugly customer. I'll show you I 'ven't any-mosity. Your father pays—you 'pologize. That's enough for me! I'm a plain man. Let Tom Bakewell fight 't out with the Law, and I'll look on. The Law wasn't on the spot, I suppose? so

the Law ain't much witness. But I am. Leastwise the
Bantam is. I tell you, young gentleman, the Bantam saw 't!
It's no mortal use whatever your denyin' that ev'dence. And
where's the good, Sir, I ask? What comes of 't? Whether
it be you, or whether it be Tom Bakewell—ain't all one?
If I holds back, ain't it sim'lar? It's the Trewth I want!
And here 't comes," added the farmer as Miss Lucy ushered
in the Bantam, who presented a curious figure for that rare
divinity to enliven.

CHAPTER XII

A FINE DISTINCTION

In build of body, gait, and stature, Giles Jinkson, the
Bantam, was a tolerably fair representative of the Punic
Elephant, whose part, with diverse anticipations, the generals
of the Blaize, and Feverel, forces, from opposing ranks, expected him to play. Giles, surnamed the Bantam, on account
of some forgotten sally of his youth or infancy, moved and
looked elephantine. It sufficed that Giles was well fed, to
assure that Giles was faithful—if uncorrupted. The farm
which supplied to him ungrudging provender, had all his vast
capacity for work in willing exercise: the farmer who held
the farm his instinct reverenced as the fountain-source of
Beef and Bacon, to say nothing of Beer, which was plentiful at Belthorpe, and good. This, farmer Blaize well knew,
and reckoned consequently that here was an animal always
to be relied on—a sort of human composition out of dog,
horse, and bull, a cut above each of these quadrupeds in
usefulness, and costing proportionately more, but on the
whole worth the money, and therefore invaluable, as everything worth its money must be to a wise man. When the
stealing of grain had been made known at Belthorpe, the
Bantam, a fellow-thresher with Tom Bakewell, had shared

with him the shadow of the guilt. Farmer Blaize, if he hesitated which to suspect, did not debate a second as to which he would discard; and when the Bantam said he had seen Tom secreting pilkins in a sack, farmer Blaize chose to believe him, and off went poor Tom, told to rejoice in the clemency that spared his appearance at Sessions.

The Bantam's small sleepy orbits saw many things, and just at the right moment, it seemed. He was certainly the first to give the clue at Belthorpe on the night of the conflagration, and he may, therefore, have seen poor Tom retreating stealthily from the scene, as he averred he did. Lobourne had its say on the subject. Rustic Lobourne hinted broadly at a young woman in the case, and, moreover, told a tale of how these fellow-threshers had, in noble rivalry, one day turned upon each other to see which of the two threshed the best; whereof the Bantam still bore marks, and malice, it was said. However, there he stood, and tugged his forelocks to the company, and if Truth really had concealed herself in him, she must have been hard set to find her unlikeliest hiding-place.

"Now," said the farmer, marshalling forth his elephant with the confidence of one who delivers his ace of trumps, "tall this young gentleman what ye saw on the night of the Fire, Bantam!"

The Bantam jerked a bit of a bow to his patron, and then swung round, fully obscuring him from Richard.

Richard fixed his eyes on the floor, while the Bantam in rudest Doric commenced his narrative. Knowing what was to come, and thoroughly nerved to confute the main incident, Richard barely listened to his barbarous locution: but when the recital arrived at the point where the Bantam affirmed he had seen "T'm Baak'll wi 's owen hoies," Richard faced him, and was amazed to find himself being mutely addressed by a series of intensely significant grimaces, signs, and winks.

"What do you mean? Why are you making those faces at me?" cried the boy, indignantly.

Farmer Blaize leaned round the Bantam to have a look at him, and beheld the stolidest mask ever given to man.

"Bain't makin' no faces at nobody," growled the sulky elephant.

The farmer commanded him to face about and finish.

"A see T'm Baak'll," the Bantam recommenced, and again the contortions of a horrible wink were directed at Richard. The boy might well believe this churl was lying, and he did, and was emboldened to exclaim,

"You never saw Tom Bakewell set fire to that rick!"

The Bantam swore to it, grimacing an accompaniment.

"I tell you," said Richard, "I put the lucifers there myself!"

The suborned elephant was staggered. He meant to telegraph to the young gentleman that he was loyal and true to certain gold-pieces that had been given him, and that in the right place and at the right time, he should prove so. Why was he thus suspected? Why was he not understood?

"A thowt I see 'un, then," muttered the Bantam, trying a middle course.

This brought down on him the farmer, who roared, "Thought! Ye thought! What d'ye mean? Speak out, and don't be thinkin'. Thought? What the devil's that?"

"How could he see who it was on a pitch dark night?" Richard put in.

"Thought!" the farmer bellowed louder. "Thought— Devil take ye, when ye took yer oath on 't. Hulloa! what are ye screwin' yer eye at Mr. Feverel for?—I say, young gentleman, have you spoke to this chap before now?"

"I?" replied Richard, "I have not seen him before."

Farmer Blaize grasped the two arms of the chair he sat on, and glared his doubts.

"Come," said he to the Bantam, "speak out, and ha' done wi' t. Say what ye saw, and none o' yer thoughts. Dam yer thoughts! Ye saw Tom Bakewell fire that there rick!" The farmer pointed at some musk-pots in the window.

"What business ha' you to be a-thinkin'? You're a witness! Thinkin' an't ev'dence. What 'll ye say tomorrow before magistrate? Mind! what you says today, you'll stick by tomorrow."

Thus adjured, the Bantam hitched his breech. What on earth the young gentleman meant, he was at a loss to speculate. He could not believe that the young gentleman wanted to be transported, but if he had been paid to help that, why, he would. And considering that this day's evidence rather bound him down to the morrow's, he determined, after much ploughing and harrowing through obstinate shocks of hair, to be not altogether positive as to the person. It is possible that he became thereby more a mansion of Truth than he previously had been; for the night, as he said, was so dark that you could not see your hand before your face; and though, as he expressed it, you might be mortal sure of a man, you could not identify him upon Oath, and the party he had taken for Tom Bakewell, and could have sworn to, might have been the young gentleman present, especially as he was ready to swear to it upon Oath.

So ended the Bantam.

No sooner had he ceased, than Farmer Blaize jumped up from his chair, and made a fine effort to lift him out of the room from the point of his toe. He failed, and sank back groaning with the pain of the exertion, and disappointment.

"They're liars, every one!" he cried. "Liars, Perj'rers, Bribers, and C'rrupters!—Stop!" to the Bantam, who was slinking away. "You've done for yerself already! You swore to it!"

"A din't!" said the Bantam, doggedly.

"You swore to 't," the farmer vociferated afresh.

The Bantam played a tune upon the handle of the door, and still affirmed that he did not; a double contradiction at which the farmer absolutely raged in his chair, and was hoarse, as he called out a third time that the Bantam had sworn to it.

"Noa!" said the Bantam, ducking his poll. "Noa!" he repeated in a lower note; and then, while a sombre grin betokening idiotic enjoyment of his profound casuistical quibble worked at his jaw:—

"Not up'n O-ath!" he added, with a twitch of the shoulder and an angular jerk of the elbow.

Farmer Blaize looked vacantly at Richard, as if to ask him what he thought of England's peasantry after the sample they had there. Richard would have preferred not to laugh, but his dignity gave way to his sense of the ludicrous, he let fly an irrepressible peal. The farmer was in no laughing mood. He turned a wide eye back to the door, "Lucky for 'm!" he exclaimed, seeing the Bantam had vanished, for his fingers itched to break that stubborn head. He grew very puffy, and addressed Richard solemnly:

"Now, look ye here, Mr. Feverel! You've been a-tampering with my witness. It's no use denyin'! I say y' 'ave, Sir! You, or some of ye. I don't care about no Feverel! My witness there has been bribed. The Bantam's been bribed," and he shivered his pipe with an energetic thump on the table—"Bribed! I knows it! I could swear to 't—"

"Upon oath?" Richard inquired, with a grave face.

"Ay, upon oath!" said the farmer, not observing the impertinence.

"I'd take my Bible oath on 't! He's been corrupted, my principal witness! Oh! it's dam cunnin', but it won't do the trick. I'll transport Tom Bakewell, sure as a gun. He shall travel, that man shall. Sorry for you, Mr. Feverel—sorry ye haven't seen how to treat me proper—you, or yours. Money won't do everything—no! it won't. It'll c'rrupt a witness, but it won't clear a felon. I'd ha' 'scused you, Sir! You're a boy and 'll learn better. I asked no more than payment and a 'pology; and that I'd ha' taken content—always provided my witnesses weren't tampered with. Now you must stand yer luck, all o' ye."

Richard stood up, and replied, "Very well, Mr. Blaize."

"And if," continued the farmer, "Tom Bakewell don't drag you into 't after 'm, why, you're safe, as I hope ye'll be, sincere!"

"It was not in consideration of my own safety that I sought this interview with you," said Richard, head erect.

"Grant ye that," the farmer responded. "Grant ye that! Yer bold enough, young gentleman—comes of the blood that should be! If y' had only ha' spoke Trewth!—I believe yer father—believe every word he said. I do wish I could ha' said as much of Sir Aust'n's son and heir."

"What!" cried Richard with an astonishment hardly to be feigned, "you have seen my father?"

But Farmer Blaize had now such a scent tor lies, that he could detect them where they did not exist, and mumbled gruffly.

"Ay, we knows all about that!"

The boy's perplexity saved him from being irritated. Who could have told his father? The old fear came upon him, and a touch of the old inclination to revolt.

"My father knows of this?" said he, very loudly, and staring, as he spoke, right through the farmer. "Who has played me false? Who would betray me to him? It was Austin! No one knew it but Austin. Yes, and it was Austin who persuaded me to come here, and submit to these indignities. Why couldn't he be open with me? I shall never trust him again!—"

"And why not you with me, young gentleman?" said the farmer. "I sh'd trust you if ye had."

Richard did not see the analogy. He bowed stiffly and bade him good afternoon.

Farmer Blaize pulled the bell. " 'Company the young gentleman out, Lucy," he waved to the little damsel in the doorway. "Do the honours. And Mr. Richard, ye might ha' made a friend o' me, Sir, and it's not too late so to do. I'm not crool, but I hate lies. I whipped my boy Tom, big-

ger than you, for not bein' above-board, only yesterday,—ay!
made 'un stand within swing o' this chair, and take 's measure. Now, if ye'll come down to me, and speak Trewth
before the Trial—if it's only five minutes before 't; or if Sir
Aust'n, who's a gentleman, 'll say there's been no tamperin'
with any o' my witnesses, his word for 't—well and good!
I'll do my best to help off Tom Bakewell. And I'm glad,
young gentleman, you've got a conscience about a poor man,
though he's a villain. Good afternoon, Sir."

Richard marched hastily out of the room, and through
the garden, never so much as deigning a glance at his wistful little guide, who hung at the garden gate to watch him
up the lane, wondering a world of fancies about the handsome proud boy.

CHAPTER XIII

RICHARD PASSES THROUGH HIS PRELIMINARY ORDEAL, AND IS THE OCCASION OF AN APHORISM

To have determined upon an act something akin to heroism in its way, and to have fulfilled it by lying heartily, and
so subverting the whole structure built by good resolution,
seems a sad downfall if we forget what human nature, in its
green weedy Spring, is composed of. Young Richard had
quitted his cousin Austin fully resolved to do his penance
and drink the bitter cup; and he had drunk it; drained
many cups to the dregs; and it was to no purpose. Still they
floated before him, brimmed, trebly bitter. Away from
Austin's influence, he was almost the same boy who had
slipped the guinea into Tom Bakewell's hand, and the
Lucifers into Farmer Blaize's rick. For good seed is long
ripening; a good boy is not made in a minute. Enough
that the seed was in him. He chafed on his road to Raynham, at the scene he had just endured, and the figure of

Belthorpe's fat tenant burnt like hot copper on the tablet
of his brain, insufferably condescending, and, what was
worse, in the right. Richard, obscured as his mind's eye
was by wounded pride, saw that clearly, and hated his
enemy for it the more.

Heavy Benson's tongue was knelling Dinner, as Richard
arrived at the Abbey. He hurried up to his room to dress.
Accident, or design, had laid the book of Sir Austin's
Aphorisms open on the dressing-table. Hastily combing his
hair, Richard glanced down, and read:

'The Dog returneth to his Vomit: the Liar must eat his
Lie.'

Underneath was interjected in pencil: 'The Devil's
mouthful!'

Young Richard ran downstairs feeling that his father had
struck him in the face.

Sir Austin marked the scarlet stain on his son's cheek-
bones. He sought the youth's eye, but Richard would not
look, and sat conning his plate, an abject copy of Adrian's
succulent air at that employment. How could he pretend
to the relish of an Epicure, when he was painfully endeavour-
ing to masticate The Devil's Mouthful?

Heavy Benson sat upon the wretched dinner. Hippias,
usually the silent member, as if awakened by the unnatural
stillness, became sprightly, like the goatsucker owl at midnight, and spoke much of his book, his digestion, and his
dreams; and was spared both by Algernon and Adrian.
One inconsequent dream he related, about fancying himself
quite young and rich, and finding himself suddenly in a
field cropping razors around him, when, just as he had, by
steps dainty as those of a French dancing-master, reached
the middle, he to his dismay beheld a path clear of the
bloodthirsty steel-crop, which he might have taken at first
had he looked narrowly; and there he was.

Hippias's brethren regarded him with eyes that plainly said they wished he had remained there. Sir Austin, however, drew forth his note-book, and jotted down a reflection. A composer of Aphorisms can pluck blossoms even from a razor-crop. Was not Hippias's dream the very counterpart of Richard's position? He, had he looked narrowly, might have taken the clear path: he, too, had been making dainty steps till he was surrounded by the grinning blades. And from that text Sir Austin preached to his son when they were alone. Little Clare was still too unwell to be permitted to attend the dessert, and father and son were soon closeted together.

It was a strange meeting. They seemed to have been separated so long. The father took his son's hand. They sat without a word passing between them. Silence said most. The boy did not understand his father: his father frequently thwarted him: at times he thought his father foolish: but that paternal pressure of his hand was eloquent to him how warmly he was beloved. He tried once or twice to steal his hand away, conscious it was melting him. The spirit of his pride, and old Rebellion, whispered him to be hard, unbending, resolute. Hard he had entered his father's study: hard he had met his father's eyes. He could not meet them now. His father sat beside him gently; with a manner that was almost meekness, so he loved this boy. The poor gentleman's lips moved. He was praying internally to God for him.

By degrees an emotion awoke in the boy's bosom. Love is that blessed wand which wins the waters from the hardness of the heart. Richard fought against it, for the dignity of old Rebellion. The tears would come; hot and struggling over the dams of Pride. Shamefully fast they began to fall. He could no longer conceal them, or check his sobs. Sir Austin drew him nearer and nearer, till the beloved head was on his breast.

An hour afterwards, Adrian Harley, Austin Wentworth, and Algernon Feverel, were summoned to the Baronet's study.

Adrian came last. There was a style of affable omnipotence about the Wise Youth as he slung himself into a chair, and made an arch of the points of his fingers, through which to gaze on his blundering kinsmen. Careless as one may be whose sagacity has foreseen, and whose benevolent efforts have forestalled, the point of danger at the threshold of his apprehensive fellows, Adrian crossed his legs, and only intruded on their introductory remarks so far as to hum half audibly at intervals,

'Ripton and Richard were two pretty men,'

in parody of the old Ballad. Young Richard's red eyes, and the Baronet's ruffled demeanour, told him that an explanation had taken place, and a reconciliation. That was well. The Baronet would now pay cheerfully. Adrian summed and considered these matters, and barely listened when the Baronet called attention to what he had to say: which was, elaborately to inform all present what all present very well knew: that a rick had been fired: that his son was implicated as an accessory to the fact: that the perpetrator was now imprisoned: and that Richard's family were, as it seemed to him, bound in honour to do their utmost to effect the man's release.

Then the Baronet stated that he had himself been down to Belthorpe, his son likewise: and that he had found every disposition in Blaize to meet his wishes.

The lamp which ultimately was sure to be lifted up to illumine the acts of this secretive race, began slowly to dispread its rays; and as statement followed statement, they saw that all had known of the business: that all had been down to Belthorpe: all save the Wise Youth Adrian, who, with due deference and a sarcastic shrug, objected to the proceeding, as putting them in the hands of the man Blaize. His wisdom shone forth in an oration so persuasive and aphoristic, that, had it not been based on a plea against Honour, it would have made Sir Austin waver. But its basis was Expediency, and the Baronet had a better Aphorism of his own to confute him with.

" 'Expediency is man's wisdom, Adrian Harley. Doing Right is God's.' "

Adrian curbed his desire to ask Sir Austin whether an attempt to counteract the just working of the Law, was Doing Right. The direct application of an Aphorism was unpopular at Raynham.

"I am to understand, then," said he, "that Blaize consents not to press the prosecution."

"Of course he won't," Algernon remarked. "Confound him! he'll have his money, and what does he want besides?"

"These agricultural gentlemen are delicate customers to deal with. However, if he really consents—"

"I have his promise," said the Baronet, fondling his son.

Young Richard looked up to his father, as if he wished to speak. He said nothing, and Sir Austin took it as a mute reply to his caresses, and caressed him the more. Adrian perceived a reserve in the boy's manner, and as he was not quite satisfied that his Chief should suppose him to have been the only idle, and not the most acute and vigilant, member of the family, he commenced a cross-examination of him by asking, who had last spoken with the tenant of Belthorpe?

"I think I saw him last," murmured Richard, and relinquished his father's hand.

Adrian fastened on his prey. "And left him with a distinct and satisfactory assurance of his amicable intentions?"

"No," said Richard.

"Not?" the Feverels joined in astounded chorus.

Richard sidled away from his father, and repeated a shamefaced "No."

"Was he hostile?" inquired Adrian, smoothing his palms, and smiling.

"Yes," the boy confessed.

Here was quite another view of their position. Adrian, generally patient of results, triumphed strongly at having evoked it, and turned upon Austin Wentworth, reproving him for inducing the boy to go down to Belthorpe. Austin looked grieved. He feared that Richard had failed in his good resolve.

"I thought it his duty to go," he observed.

"It was!" said the Baronet emphatically.

"And you see what comes of it, Sir," Adrian put in "These agricultural gentlemen, I repeat, are delicate customers to deal with. For my part I would prefer being in the hands of a policeman. We are decidedly collared by Blaize. What were his words, Ricky? Give it in his own Doric."

"He said he would transport Tom Bakewell."

Adrian smoothed his palms, and smiled again. Then they could afford to defy Mr. Blaize, he informed them significantly, and made once more a mysterious allusion to the Punic Elephant, bidding his relatives to be at peace. They were attaching, in his opinion, too much importance to Richard's complicity. The man was a fool, and a very extraordinary Arsonite to have an accomplice at all. It was a thing unknown in the annals of rick-burning. But one would be severer than Law itself to say that a boy of fourteen had instigated to crime a full-grown man. At that rate the boy was 'father of the man' with a vengeance, and one might hear next that 'the baby was father of the boy.' They would find Common Sense a more benevolent ruler than Poetical Metaphysics.

When he had done, Austin, with his customary directness, asked him what he meant.

"I confess, Adrian," said the Baronet, hearing him expostulate with Austin's stupidity, "I for one am at a loss.

I have heard that this man, Bakewell, chooses voluntarily not to inculpate my son. Seldom have I heard anything that so gratified me. It is a view of innate nobleness in the rustic's character which many gentlemen might take example from. We are bound to do our utmost for the man." And saying that he should pay a second visit to Belthorpe, to inquire into the reasons for the farmer's sudden exposition of vindictiveness, Sir Austin rose.

Before he left the room, Algernon asked Richard if the farmer had vouchsafed any reasons, and the boy then spoke of the tampering with the witnesses, and the Bantam's "Not upon oath!" which caused Adrian to choke with laughter. Even the Baronet smiled at so cunning a distinction as that involved in swearing a thing, and not swearing it upon oath.

"How little," he exclaimed, "does one yeoman know another! To elevate a distinction into a difference, is the natural action of their minds. I will point that out to Blaize. He shall see that that idea is native born."

Remorsefully Richard saw his father go forth. Adrian, too, was ill at ease.

"This trotting down to Belthorpe spoils all," said he. "The affair would pass over tomorrow—Blaize has no witnesses. The old rascal is only standing out for more money."

"No, he isn't," Richard corrected him. "It's not that. I'm sure he believes his witnesses have been tampered with, as he calls it."

"What if they have, boy?" Adrian put it boldly. "The ground is cut from under his feet."

"Blaize told me that, if my father would give his word there had been nothing of the sort, he would take it. My father will give his word."

"Then," said Adrian, "you had better stop him from going down."

Austin looked at Adrian keenly, and questioned him, whether he thought the farmer was justified in his suspicions. The Wise Youth was not to be entrapped. He had only been given to understand that the witnesses were tolerably unstable, and like the Bantam, ready to swear lustily, but not upon the Book. How given to understand, he chose not to explain, but he reiterated that the Chief should not be allowed to go down to Belthorpe.

Sir Austin was in the lane leading to the farm, when he heard steps of some one running behind him. It was dark, and he shook off the hand that laid hold of his cloak, roughly, not recognizing his son.

"It's I, Sir," said Richard, panting. "Pardon me. You mustn't go in there."

"Why not?" said the Baronet, putting his arm about him.

"Not now," continued the boy. "I will tell you all to-night. I must see the farmer myself. It was my fault, Sir. I—I lied to him—the Liar must eat his Lie. Oh, forgive me for disgracing you, Sir. I did it—I hope I did it to save Tom Bakewell. Let me go in alone, and speak the truth."

"Go, and I will wait for you here," said his father.

The wind that bowed the old elms, and shivered the dead leaves in the air, had a voice and a meaning for the Baronet, during that half-hour's lonely pacing up and down under the darkness, awaiting his boy's return. The solemn gladness of his heart gave Nature a tongue. Through the desolation flying overhead—the wailing of the Mother of Plenty across the bare-swept land—he caught intelligible signs of the beneficent order of the universe, from a heart newly confirmed in its grasp of the principle of human goodness, as manifested in the dear child who had just left him: confirmed in its belief in the ultimate Victory of Good within us, without which Nature has neither music, nor meaning, and is rock, stone, tree, and nothing more.

In the dark, the dead leaves beating on his face, he drew forth the Note-book, and with groping fingers traced out:

'There is for the mind but one grasp of Happiness: from that uppermost pinnacle of Wisdom, whence we see that this world is well-designed.'

CHAPTER XIV

IN WHICH THE LAST ACT OF THE BAKEWELL COMEDY IS CLOSED IN A LETTER

OF all the chief actors in THE BAKEWELL COMEDY, Master Ripton Thompson awaited the fearful morning which was to decide Tom's fate, in dolefulest mood, and suffered the gravest mental terrors. Adrian on parting with him, had taken casual occasion to speak of the position of the Criminal in modern Europe, assuring him that International Treaty now did what Universal Empire had aforetime done, and that among Atlantic Barbarians now, as among the Scythians of old, an offender would find precarious refuge, and an emissary haunting him. In the paternal home, under the roofs of Law, and removed from the influence of his conscienceless young Chief, the staggering nature of the act he had put his hand to, its awful felonious aspect, overwhelmed poor Ripton. He saw it now for the first time. "Why it's next to murder!" he cried out to his amazed soul, and wandered about the house with a prickly skin. Thoughts of America, and commencing life afresh as an innocent gentleman, had crossed the agitated brain of Ripton. He wrote to his friend Richard, proposing to collect disposable funds, and embark, in case of Tom's breaking his word, or of accidental discovery. He dared not confide the secret to his family, as his leader had sternly enjoined him to avoid any weakness of that kind; and being by nature honest and communicative, the restriction was painful, and melancholy fell upon the boy. Mama Thompson attributed it to love. The daughters of parchment rallied him concerning Miss Clare Forey. His hourly letters to Raynham, his silence as to everything and everybody there, his loss of appetite, nervousness, and unwonted propensity to sudden inflammation of the cheeks, were set down for sure signs of the passion. Miss Letitia Thompson, the pretty and least parchmenty one, destined by her Mama for the heir of Raynham, and perfectly aware of her brilliant future, up to which she had, since Ripton's departure, dressed, and grimaced, and studied cadences (the latter with such success, though not yet fifteen, that she languished to her maid, and melted the very marrow of the small factotum footman),—Miss Letty, whose insatiable thirst for intimations about the young heir, Ripton could not satisfy, tormented him daily in revenge, and once, quite unconsciously, gave the lad a fearful turn: for after dinner, when Mr. Thompson read the paper by the fire preparatory to sleeping at his accustomed post, and Mama Thompson and her submissive female brood sat tasking the swift intricacies of the needle, and emulating them with the tongue, Miss Letty stole behind Ripton's chair, and introduced between him and his book the Latin initial letter, large and illuminated, of the theme she supposed to be absorbing him, as it did herself. The unexpected vision of this accusing Captain of the Alphabet, this resplendent and haunting A, fronting him bodily, threw Ripton straight back in his chair, while Guilt, with her ancient indecision what colours to assume on detection, flew from red to white, from white to red, across his fallen chaps. Letty laughed triumphantly.

"Ah—a!" she sang, "you are found out, Mr. Mum!" and innocently followed up the attack, by asking him how he would wear his badge, before, or behind? which precipitated Ripton from the room, in sick certainty that he was discovered, and thrilled the motherly heart of Mama Thompson with the blissful prospect of marrying two of her brood to the House of Feverel.

"Why, what does A stand for? Silly!" said Letitia, after

rallying her brother next morning at breakfast, "For **Angel**, doesn't it?"

"Yes: and for America," Ripton answered gloomily.

"Yes, and you know what else!" rejoined his persecutor, while another sister, previously instructed, presumed it might possibly stand for Amor.

"And for Arson," added the deep paternal voice, unwittingly springing a mine under poor Ripton.

Letty's study of the aspects of love, and of the way young people should look, and of the things they should do, under the dominion of the passion, was not much assisted by its outward development in the supposed love-stricken youth. "I'm sure," she thought, "I shall never be like that. He bounds in his seat. He never looks comfortable. He seems to hate us all, and does nothing but mumble his food, and growl, and frown. If that's love, I can't do it!" she sorrowfully concluded her reflections.

The delivery of a letter into Master Ripton's hands, however, furnished her with other and likelier appearances to study. For scarce had Ripton plunged his head into the missive, than he gave way to violent transports, such as the healthy-minded little damsel, for all her languishing cadences, deemed she really could express, were a downright declaration to be made to her. The boy did not stop at table. Quickly recollecting the presence of his family, he rushed to his own room. And now Miss Letty's ingenuity was tasked to gain possession of that letter. In love, it is said, all stratagems are fair, and many little ladies transverse the axiom by applying it to discover the secrets of their friends. Letty ransacked the drawers in Ripton's rooms, she dived her hands into the pockets of his garments lying about, she turned down the pillow, she spied under the mattress of his bed, with an easy conscience; and if she found nothing, of course, as she was doing a wrong, she did not despair of gaining her object, and soon knew that Ripton carried it about in his left jacket-pocket, persecuting

Ripton with her caresses, till she felt the tantalizing treasure
crack beneath her fingers. Some sisters would have coaxed
him for a sight of it. Letty was not so foolish: she did not
allude to it, and was still hovering round the pocket, at a
loss to devise any new scheme, when accident bestowed on
her what artifice denied. They were standing on a hill
together, and saw some people of their acquaintance coming
up in a pony-chaise. Letty told Ripton to wave his handkerchief, which he snatched from the very pocket, and
waved vigorously, and continued waving, heedless that his
sister had on a sudden lost her interest in the pony-chaise.
Indeed she presently commanded him to turn a contrary
way, and was voluble with reasons for getting home immediately, though they had set out for a long walk into the
country. Once home, Letitia darted up stairs to be alone
with her naughty self. She had the letter. Ripton had
dropped it as he drew forth his handkerchief. With the
eyes of amazement, she read this foreign matter:—

"Dear Ripton,
     "If Tom had been committed I would have shot old
Blaize. Do you know my father was behind us that night
when Clare saw the Ghost and heard all we said before the
fire burst out. It is no use trying to conceal anything from
him. Well as you are in an awful state I will tell you all
about it. After you left Ripton I had a conversation with
Austin and he persuaded me to go down to old Blaize and
ask him to help off Tom. I went for I would have done
anything for Tom after what he said to Austin and I defied
the old churl to do his worst. Then he said if my father
paid the money and nobody had tampered with his witnesses
he would not mind if Tom did get off and he had his chief
witness in called the Bantam very like his master I think
and the Bantam began winking at me tremendjously as you
say and said he had sworn he saw Tom Bakewell but not
upon Oath. He meant not on the Bible. He could swear

to it but not on the Bible. I burst out laughing and you should have seen the rage old Blaize was in. It was splendid fun. Then we had a consultation at home Austin Rady my father Uncle Algernon who has come down to us again and your friend in prosperity and adversity R. D. F. My father said he would go down to old Blaize and give him the word of a gentleman we had not tampered with his witnesses and when he was gone we were all talking and Rady says he must not see the farmer. I am as certain as I live that it was Rady bribed the Bantam. Well I ran and caught up my father and told him not to go in to old Blaize but I would and eat my words and tell him the truth. He waited for me in the lane. Never mind what passed between me and old Blaize. He made me beg and pray of him not to press it against Tom and then to complete it he brought in a little girl niece of his and says to me she's your best friend after all and told me to thank her. A little girl twelve years of age. What business had she to mix herself up in my matters. Depend upon it Ripton wherever there is mischief there are girls I think. She had the insolence to notice my face and ask me not to be unhappy. I was polite of course but I would not look at her. Well the morning came and Tom was had up before Sir Miles Papworth. It was Sir Miles gout gave us the time or Tom would have been had up before we could do anything. Adrian did not want me to go but my father said I should accompany him and held my hand all the time. I shall be careful about getting into these scrapes again. When you have done anything honourable you do not mind but getting among policemen and magistrates makes you ashamed of yourself. Sir Miles was very attentive to my father and me and dead against Tom. We sat beside him and Tom was brought in. Sir Miles told my father that if there was one thing that showed a low villain it was rick-burning. What do you think of that. I looked him straight in the face and he said to me he was doing me a service in getting Tom committed and clearing the country of such fellows and Rady began laughing. I hate Rady. My father said his son was not in haste to inherit and have estates of his own to watch and Sir Miles laughed too. I thought we were discovered at first. Then they began the examination of Tom. The Tinker was the first witness and he proved that Tom had spoken against old Blaize and said something about burning his rick. I wished I had stood in the lane to Bursley with him alone. Our country lawyer we engaged for Tom cross-questioned him and then he said he was not ready to swear to the exact words that had passed between him and Tom. I should think not. Then came another who swore he had seen Tom lurking about the farmer's grounds that night. Then came the Bantam and I saw him look at Rady. I was tremendjously excited and my father kept pressing my hand. Just fancy my being brought to feel that a word from that fellow would make me miserable for life and he must perjure himself to help me. That comes of giving way to passion. My father says when we do that we are calling in the devil as doctor. Well the Bantam was told to state what he had seen and the moment he began Rady who was close by me began to shake and he was laughing I knew though his face was as grave as Sir Miles. You never heard such a rigmarole but I could not laugh. He said he thought he was certain he had seen somebody by the rick and it was Tom Bakewell who was the only man he knew who had a grudge against farmer Blaize and if the object had been a little bigger he would not mind swearing to Tom and would swear to him for he was dead certain it was Tom only what he saw looked smaller and it was pitch dark at the time. He was asked what time it was he saw the person steal away from the rick and then he began to scratch his head and said supper-time. Then they asked what time he had supper and he said nine o'clock by the clock and we proved that at nine o'clock Tom was drinking in the ale-house with the Tinker at Bursley and Sir Miles swore and said he was

afraid he could not commit Tom and when he heard that
Tom looked up at me and I say he is a noble fellow and no
one shall sneer at Tom while I live. Mind that. Well
Sir Miles asked us to dine with him and Tom was safe and
I am to have him and educate him if I like for my servant
and I will. And I will give money to his mother and make
her rich and he shall never repent he knew me. I say Rip.
The Bantam must have seen *me*. It was when I went to
stick in the Lucifers. As we were all going home from Sir
Miles's at night he has lots of red-faced daughters but I
did not dance with them though they had music and were
full of fun and I did not care to I was so delighted and
almost let it out. When we left and rode home Rady said
to my father the Bantam was not such a fool as he was
thought and my father said one must be in a state of great
personal exaltation to apply that epithet to any man and
Rady shut his mouth and I gave my pony a clap of the heel
for joy. I think my father suspects what Rady did and
does not approve of it. And he need not have done it after
all and might have spoilt it. I have been obliged to order
him not to call me Ricky for he stops short at Rick so that
everybody knows what he means. My dear Austin is going
to South America. My pony is in capital condition. My
father is the cleverest and best man in the world. Clare is a
little better. I am quite happy. I hope we shall meet soon
my dear old Rip and we will not get into any more tremend-
jous scrapes will we.

> "I remain
> "Your sworn friend
> "RICHARD DORIA FEVEREL.

"P.S. I am to have a nice River Yacht. Good bye Rip.
Mind you learn to box. Mind you are not to show this to
any of your friends on pain of my displeasure.

"N.B. Lady B. was so angry when I told her that I had

not come to her before. She would do anything in the world for me. I like her next best to my father and Austin. Good bye old Rip."

Poor little Letitia, after three perusals of this ingenuous epistle, where the laws of punctuation were so loftily disregarded, resigned it to one of the pockets of her brother Ripton's best jacket, deeply smitten with the careless composer. And so ended the last act of the Bakewell Comedy, on which the curtain closes with Sir Austin's pointing out to his friends the beneficial action of the System in it from beginning to end.

CHAPTER XV

THE BLOSSOMING SEASON

LAYING of Ghosts is a public duty, and as the mystery of the Apparition that had frightened little Clare was never solved on the stage of events at Raynham, where dread walked the Abbey, let us go behind the scenes a moment. Morally superstitious as the Baronet was, the character of his mind was opposed to anything like spiritual agency in the affairs of men, and when the matter was made clear to him, it shook off a weight of weakness, and restored his mental balance; so that from this time he went about more like the man he had once been, grasping more thoroughly the great truth that, This World is well designed. Nay, he could laugh on hearing Adrian, in reminiscence of the ill luck of one of the family members at its first manifestation, call the uneasy spirit, Algernon's Leg. Mrs. Doria was outraged. She maintained that her child had seen—. Not to believe in it was almost to rob her of her personal property. After satisfactorily studying his old state of mind in her, Sir Austin, moved by pity, took her aside one day, and showed her that her Ghost could write words in the flesh. It was a letter from the unhappy lady who had given Richard birth, —brief cold lines, simply telling him his house would be disturbed by her no more. Cold lines, but penned by what heart-broken abnegation, and underlying them what anguish of soul! Like most who dealt with him, Lady Feverel thought her husband a man fatally stern and implacable, and she acted as silly creatures will act when they fancy they see a fate against them: she neither petitioned for her right, nor claimed it: she tried to ease her heart's yearning by stealth, and now she renounced all. Mrs. Doria, not wanting in the family tenderness and softness, shuddered at him for accepting the sacrifice so composedly: but he bade her to think how distracting to this boy would be the sight of such relations between mother and father. A few years, and as man he should know, and judge, and love, her. "Let this be her penance, not inflicted by me!" Mrs. Doria bowed to the System for another, not opining when it would be her turn to bow for herself.

Further behind the scenes we observe Rizzio and Mary grown older, much disenchanted: she discrowned, dishevelled, —he with gouty fingers on a greasy guitar. The Diaper Sandoe of promise lends his pen for small hires. His fame has sunk; his bodily girth has sensibly increased. What he can do, and will do, is still his theme; meantime the juice of the juniper is in requisition, and it seems those small hires cannot be performed without it. Returning from her wretched journey to her wretcheder home, the lady had to listen to a mild reproof from easy-going Diaper,—a reproof so mild that he couched it in blank verse: for seldom writing metrically now, he took to talking it. With a fluent sympathetic tear, he explained to her that she was damaging her interests by these proceedings; nor did he shrink from undertaking to elucidate wherefore. Pluming a smile upon his succulent mouth, he told her that the poverty she lived in was utterly unbefitting her gentle nurture, and that he had reason to believe—could assure her—that an annuity was on the point of being granted her by her husband. And Diaper broke his bud of a smile into full flower, as he delivered the radiant information. She learnt that he had applied to her husband for money. It is hard to have one's last prop of self-respect cut away just when we are suffering a martyr's agony at the stake. There was a five-minutes' tragic colloquy in the recesses behind the scenes,— totally tragic to Diaper, who had fondly hoped to bask in the warm sun of that annuity, and re-emerge from his state of grub. The lady then wrote the letter Sir Austin held open to his sister. I think the atmosphere behind the scenes is not wholesome, so, having laid the Ghost, we will return and face the curtain.

That infinitesimal dose of THE WORLD which Master Ripton Thompson had furnished to the System with such instantaneous and surprising effect, was considered by Sir Austin to have worked well, and to be for the time quite sufficient, so that Ripton did not receive a second invitation to Raynham, and Richard had no special intimate of his own age to rub his excessive vitality against, and wanted none. His hands were full enough with Tom Bakewell. More-over, his father and he were heart in heart. The boy's mind was opening, and turned to his father affectionately reverent. At this period, when the young savage grows into higher in-fluences, the faculty of worship is foremost in him. At this period Jesuits stamp the future of their chargeling flocks; and all who bring up youth by a System, and watch it, know that it is the malleable moment. Boys possessing any mental or moral force to give them a tendency, then predestinate their careers; or, if under supervision, take the impress that is given them: not often to cast it off, and seldom to cast it off altogether.

In Sir Austin's Note-book was written: 'Between Simple Boyhood, and Adolescence—The Blossoming Season—on the threshold of Puberty, there is one Unselfish Hour: say, Spiritual Seed-time.'

He took care that good seed should be planted in Richard, and that the most fruitful seed for a youth, namely, Example, should be of a kind to germinate in him the love of every form of nobleness.

"I am only striving to make my son a Christian," he said, answering them who persisted in expostulating with the System. And to these instructions he gave an aim: "First be virtuous," he told his son, "and then serve your country with heart and soul." The youth was instructed to cherish an ambition for Statesmanship, and he and his father read History and the Speeches of British Orators to some purpose; for one day Sir Austin found him leaning cross-legged and with his hand to his chin, against a pedestal supporting the Bust of Chatham, contemplating the Hero of our Parliament, his eyes streaming with tears.

People said, the Baronet carried the principle of Example so far, that he only retained his boozing dyspeptic brother Hippias at Raynham, in order to exhibit to his son the woful retribution Nature wreaked upon a life of indulgence: poor Hippias having now become a walking Complaint. This was unjust, but there is no doubt he made use of every illustration to disgust, or encourage, his son, that his neighbourhood afforded him, and did not spare his brother, for whom Richard entertained a contempt in proportion to his admiration of his father, and was for flying into penitential extremes, which Sir Austin had to soften.

The boy prayed with his father morning and night.

"How is it, Sir," he said, one night, "I can't get Tom Bakewell to pray?"

"Does he refuse?" Sir Austin asked.

"He seems to be ashamed to," Richard replied. "He wants to know, What is the good? and I don't know what to tell him."

"I'm afraid it has gone too far with him," said Sir Austin, "and until he has had some deep sorrows he will not find the divine want of Prayer. Strive, my son, when you represent the People, to provide for their education. He feels everything now through a dull impenetrable rind. Culture is halfway to Heaven. Tell him, my son, should he ever be brought to ask how he may know the efficacy of Prayer, and that his prayer will be answered, tell him (he quoted The Pilgrim's Scrip):

" 'Who rises from Prayer a better man, his prayer *is* answered.' "

"I will, Sir," said Richard, and went to sleep happy.

Happy in his father and in himself the youth now lived. Conscience was beginning to inhabit him, and he carried some of the freightage known to men; though in so crude a form that it overweighed him, now on this side, now on that.

The Wise Youth Adrian observed these further progressionary developments in his pupil, soberly cynical. He was under Sir Austin's interdict not to banter him, and eased his acrid humours inspired by the sight of a felonious young rick-burner turning Saint, by grave affectations of sympathy and extreme accuracy in marking the not widely-distant dates of his various changes. The Bread-and-water phase lasted a fortnight: the Vegetarian (an imitation of his cousin Austin), little better than a month: the religious, somewhat longer: the religious-propagandist (when he was for converting the Heathen of Lobourne and Bursley, and the domestics of the Abbey, including Tom Bakewell), longer still, and hard to bear: he tried to convert Adrian! All the while Tom was being exercised like a raw recruit. Richard had a drill-serjeant from the nearest barracks down for him, to give him a proper pride in himself, and marched him to and fro with immense satisfaction, and nearly broke his heart trying to get the round-shouldered rustic to take in the rudiments of letters: for the boy had unbounded hopes for Tom, as a hero in grain.

Richard's pride also was cast aside. He affected to be, and really thought he was, humble. Whereupon Adrian, as by accident, imparted to him the fact that men were animals, and he an animal with them.

"*I* an animal!" cries Richard in scorn, and for weeks he was as troubled by this rudiment of self-knowledge as Tom by his letters. Sir Austin had him instructed in the Wonders of Anatomy, to restore his self-respect.

SEED-TIME passed thus smoothly, and Adolescence came on, and his cousin Clare felt what it was to be of an opposite sex to him. She too was growing, but nobody cared how she grew. Outwardly even her mother seemed absorbed in the sprouting of the green off-shoot of the Feverel Tree, and Clare was his handmaiden, little marked by him.

The ladies of the Court who had not published, or put their names to what they published denouncing Sir Austin and his System, wrote for tidings, and were overjoyed to hear of its success. Lady Blandish was the only lady by to witness it. She honestly loved the boy. She would tell him: "If I had been a girl, I would have had you for my husband." And he with the frankness of his years would reply: "And how do you know I would have had you?" causing her to laugh and call him a silly boy, for had he not heard her say, She would have had him? Terrible words, he knew not then the meaning of!

"You don't read your father's Book," she said. Her own Copy was bound in purple velvet, gilt-edged, as decorative ladies like to have holier books, and she carried it about with her, and quoted it, and (Adrian remarked to Mrs. Doria) hunted a noble quarry, and deliberately aimed at him, therewith, which Mrs. Doria chose to believe, and regretted her brother would not be on his guard.

"See here," said Lady Blandish, pressing an almondy finger-nail to one of the Aphorisms, which instanced how

Age and Adversity must clay-enclose us ere we can effectually resist the Magnetism of any human creature in our path. "Can you understand it, child?"

Richard informed her that when she read he could.

"Well, then, my Squire," she touched his cheek and ran her fingers through his hair, "learn as quick as you can not to be all hither and yon with a hundred different attractions, as I was before I met a wise man to guide me."

"Is my father very wise?" Richard asked.

"I think so," the lady emphasized her individual judgment.

"Do you——" Richard broke forth, and was stopped by a beating of his heart.

"Do I—what?" she calmly queried.

"I was going to say, do you——I mean, I love him so much."

Lady Blandish smiled and slightly coloured.

They frequently approached this theme, and always retreated from it; always with the same beating of heart to Richard, accompanied by the sense of a growing Mystery, which however did not as yet generally disturb him.

Life was made very pleasant to him at Raynham, as it was part of Sir Austin's principle of education, that his boy should be thoroughly joyous and happy; and whenever Adrian sent in a satisfactory report of his pupil's advancement, which he did pretty liberally, diversions were planned, just as prizes are given to diligent schoolboys, and Richard was supposed to have all his desires gratified, while he attended to his studies. The System flourished. Dr. Clifford had nothing but his old stock phrases to reply with: the boy was a living argument against him. Tall, strong, bloomingly healthy, he took the lead of his companions on land and water, and had more than one bondsman in his service besides Ripton Thompson—the boy without a Destiny! Perhaps the boy with a Destiny, was growing up a trifle too conscious of it. His generosity to his occasional companions was princely, but was exercised something too much in the manner of a Prince; and notwithstanding his contempt for baseness, he would overlook that more easily than an offence to his pride, which demanded an utter servility when it had once been rendered susceptible. If Richard had his followers, he had also his feuds. The Papworths were as subservient as Ripton, but young Ralph Morton, the nephew of Mr. Morton, and a match for Richard in numerous promising qualities, comprising the noble science of fisticuffs, this youth spoke his mind too openly, and moreover would not be snubbed. There was no middle course for Richard's comrades between high friendship, or absolutely slavery. He was deficient in those cosmopolite habits and feelings which enable boys and men to hold together without caring much for each other; and, like every insulated mortal, he attributed the deficiency, of which he was quite aware, to the fact of his possessing a superior nature. Young Ralph was a lively talker: therefore, argued Richard's vanity, he had no intellect. He was affable; therefore he was frivolous. The women liked him: therefore he was a butterfly. In fine, young Ralph was popular, and our superb Prince, denied the privilege of despising, ended by detesting, him.

Early in the days of their contention for leadership, Richard saw the absurdity of affecting to scorn his rival. Ralph was an Eton boy, and hence, being robust and shrewd, a swimmer and a cricketer. A swimmer and a cricketer is nowhere to be scorned in youth's Republic. Finding that manœuvre would not do, Richard was prompted once or twice to entrench himself behind his greater wealth, and his position; but he soon abandoned that also, partly because his chilliness to ridicule told him he was exposing himself, and chiefly that his heart was too chivalrous. And so he was dragged into the lists by Ralph, and experienced the luck of champions. For cricket, and for diving, Ralph bore away the belt: Richard's middle-stump tottered before his ball, and he could seldom pick up more than three eggs under-

water to Ralph's half-dozen. He was beaten, too, in jumping and running. Why will silly mortals strive to the
painful pinnacles of championship? Or why, once having
reached them, not have the magnanimity and circumspection
to retire into private life immediately? Stung by his de-
feats, Richard sent one of his dependent Papworths to Poer
Hall, with a challenge to Ralph Barthrop Morton; match-
ing himself to swim across the Thames and back, once, twice,
or thrice, within a less time than he, Ralph Barthrop Morton, would require for the undertaking. It was accepted,
and a reply returned, equally formal in the trumpeting of
Christian names, wherein Ralph Barthrop Morton acknowledged the challenge of Richard Doria Feverel, and was his
man. The match came off on a Midsummer morning, under
the direction of Captain Algernon. Sir Austin was a spec-
tator from the cover of a plantation by the riverside, unknown to his son, and, to the scandal of her sex, Lady
Blandish accompanied the Baronet. He had invited her attendance to try her, and she, obeying her frank nature, and
knowing what THE PILGRIM'S SCRIP said about Prudes, at
once agreed to view the match, pleasing him mightily. For
was not here a woman worthy the golden Ages of the
world? one who could look upon man as a creature divinely
made, and look with a mind neither tempted, nor taunted,
by the Serpent! Such a woman was rare. Sir Austin did
not discompose her by uttering his praises. She was conscious of his approval only in an increased gentleness of
manner, and something in his voice and communications, as
if he were speaking to a familiar, a very high compliment
from him. While the lads were standing ready for the
signal to plunge from the steep decline of greensward into
the shining waters, Sir Austin called upon her to admire
their beauty, and she did, and even advanced her head above
his shoulder delicately. In so doing, and just as the start
was given, a bonnet became visible to Richard. They saw
him suddenly catch his hand to his side, and hesitate. Young

Ralph was heels in air before he moved, and then he dropped like lead. He was beaten by several lengths.

The result of the match was unaccountable to all present, and Richard's friends unanimously pressed him to plead a false start. But though the youth, with full confidence in his better style and equal strength, had backed himself heavily against his rival, and had lost his little river-yacht to Ralph, he would do nothing of the sort. It was the Bonnet had beaten him, not Ralph. The Bonnet, typical of the Mystery that caused his heart those violent palpitations, the Bonnet was his dear, detestable enemy. He took a savage pleasure in attributing his evil luck to the Bonnet. It distilled an exquisite bitter-sweet, the notion that he was the victim of the Bonnet!

And now as he progressed from mood to mood, his ambition turned towards a field where Ralph could not rival him, and where the Bonnet was etherealized, and reigned glorious mistress. A check to the pride of a boy will frequently divert him to the path where lie his subtlest powers. Richard gave up his companions, servile, or antagonist: he relinquished the material world to young Ralph, and retired into himself, where he was growing to be lord of kingdoms: where Beauty was his Handmaid, and History his Minister, and Time his ancient Harper, and sweet Romance his Bride: where he walked in a realm vaster and more gorgeous than the great Orient, peopled with the heroes that have been. For there is no princely wealth, and no loftiest heritage to equal this early one that is made bountifully common to so many, when the ripening blood has put a spark to the imagination, and the earth is seen through rosy mists of a thousand fresh-awakened nameless and aimless desires, panting for bliss, and taking it as it comes; making of any sight or sound, perforce of the enchantment they carry with them, a key to infinite, because innocent, pleasure. The passions then are gambolling cubs; not the ravaging gluttons they grow to. They have their teeth and their talons, but they

neither tear nor bite. They are in counsel and fellowship
with the quickened heart and brain. The whole sweet
system moves to music.

Something akin to the indications of a change in the spirit
of his son, which were now seen, Sir Austin had marked
down to be expected, as due to his plan. The blushes of the
youth, his long vigils, his clinging to solitude, his abstraction,
and downcast, but not melancholy, air, were matters for rejoicing to the prescient gentleman. "For it comes," said he
to Dr. Clifford, after consulting him medically on the youth's
behalf and being assured of his soundness, "it comes of a
thoroughly sane condition. The blood is healthy, the mind
virtuous: neither instigates the other to evil, and both are
perfecting toward the flower of manhood. If he reach that
pure—in the untainted fulness and perfection of his natural
powers, I am indeed a happy father! But one thing he will
owe to me: that at one period of his life he knew Paradise,
and could read God's handwriting on the earth! Now those
abominations whom you call precocious boys—your little
pet monsters, Doctor!—and who can wonder that the world
is what it is, when it is full of them!—as they will have
no divine time to look back upon in their own lives, how
can they believe in innocence and goodness, or be other than
sons of selfishness and the Devil? But my boy," and the
Baronet dropped his voice to a key that was touching to
hear, "my boy, if he fall, will fall from an actual region
of purity. He dare not be a sceptic as to that. Whatever
his darkness, he will have the guiding light of a memory
behind him. So much is secure."

To talk nonsense, or poetry, or the dash between the two,
in a tone of profound sincerity, and to enunciate solemn dis-
cordances with received opinion so seriously as to convey the
impression of a spiritual insight, is the peculiar gift by which
monomaniacs, having first persuaded themselves, contrive to
influence their neighbours, and through them to make conquest of a good half of the world, for good or for ill. Sir

Austin had this gift. He spoke as if he saw the Truth, and persisting in it so long, he was accredited by those who did not understand him, and silenced them that did. "We shall see," was now all the argument left to Dr. Clifford, and other unbelievers.

So far certainly the experiment had succeeded. A comelier, braver, better boy, was nowhere to be met. His promise was undeniable. The vessel, too, though it lay now in harbour, and had not yet been proved by the buffets of the elements on the great Ocean, had made a good trial trip, and got well through stormy weather, as the records of the Bakewell Comedy witnessed to at Raynham. No augury could be hopefuler. The Fates must indeed be hard, the Ordeal severe, the Destiny dark, that could destroy so bright a Spring! But bright as it was, the Baronet relaxed nothing of his vigilant supervision. He said to his intimates: "Every act, every fostered inclination, almost every thought, in this Blossoming Season, bears its seed for the Future. The living Tree now requires incessant watchfulness." And acting up to his light, Sir Austin did watch. The youth submitted to an hour's examination every night before he sought his bed; professedly to give an account of his studies; but really to recapitulate his moral experiences of the day. He could do so, for he was pure. Any wildness in him that his father noted, any remoteness, or richness, of fancy in his expressions, was set down as incidental to the Blossoming Season. The Blossoming Season explained and answered for all. There is nothing like a Theory for blinding the wise. Sir Austin, despite his rigid watch and ward, knew less of his son than the servant of his household. And he was deaf, as well as blind. Adrian thought it his duty to tell him that the youth was consuming paper. Lady Blandish likewise hinted at his mooning propensities. Sir Austin from his lofty watch-tower of the System, had foreseen it, he said. But when he came to hear that the youth was writing Poetry, his wounded heart had its reasons for being disturbed.

"Surely," said Lady Blandish, "you knew he scribbled?"

"A very different thing from writing Poetry, Madam," said the Baronet. "No Feverel has ever written Poetry."

"I don't think it's a sign of degeneracy," the lady remarked. "He rhymes very prettily to me."

A London Phrenologist, and a friendly Oxford Professor of Poetry quieted Sir Austin's fears.

The Phrenologist said, he was totally deficient in the imitative faculty; and the Professor, that he was equally so in the rhythmic, and instanced several consoling false quantities in the few effusions submitted to him. Added to this, Sir Austin told Lady Blandish, that Richard had, at his hest, done what no poet had ever been known to be capable of doing: he had, with his own hands, and in cold blood, committed his virgin Manuscript to the flames: which made Lady Blandish sigh forth, "Poor boy!"

Killing one's darling child is a painful imposition. For a youth in his Blossoming Season, who fancies himself a poet, to be requested to destroy his first-born, without a reason (though to pretend a reason cogent enough to justify the request were a mockery), is a piece of abhorrent despotism, and Richard's blossoms withered under it. A strange man had been introduced to him, who traversed and bisected his skull with sagacious stiff fingers, and crushed his soul while, in an infallible voice, declaring him the animal he was: making him feel such an animal! Not only his blossoms withered, his being seemed to draw in its shoots and twigs. And when, coupled thereunto (the strange man having departed, his work done), his father, in his tenderest manner, stated that it would give him pleasure to see those same precocious, utterly valueless, scribblings among the cinders, the last remaining mental blossoms spontaneously fell away. Richard's spirit stood bare. He protested not. Enough that it could be wished! He would not delay a minute in doing it. Desiring his father to follow him, he went to a drawer in his room, and from a clean-linen recess, never suspected by Sir Austin, the secretive youth drew out bundle after bundle: each neatly tied, named, and numbered: and despicably pitched them into the flames. And so Farewell my young Ambition! and with it Farewell all true confidence between Father and Son.

CHAPTER XVI

THE MAGNETIC AGE

IT was now, as Sir Austin had written it down, The Magnetic Age: the Age of violent attractions; when to hear mention of Love is dangerous, and to see it, a communication of the disease. People at Raynham were put on their guard by the Baronet, and his reputation for wisdom was severely criticized in consequence of the injunctions he thought fit to issue through butler and housekeeper down to the lower household, for the preservation of his son from any visible symptom of the passion. A footman and two housemaids are believed to have been dismissed on the report of Heavy Benson that they were in, or inclining to, the state; upon which an under-cook and a dairymaid voluntarily threw up their places, averring that "they did not want no young men, but to have their sex spied after by an old wretch like that," indicating the ponderous butler, "was a little too much for a Christian woman," and then they were ungenerous enough to glance at Benson's well-known marital calamity, hinting that some men met their deserts. So intolerable did Heavy Benson's espionage become, that Raynham would have grown depopulated of its womankind, had not Adrian interfered, who pointed out to the Baronet what a fearful arm his butler was wielding. Sir Austin acknowledged it despondently. "It only shows," said he, with a fine spirit of justice, "how all but impossible it is to legislate where there are women!"

"I do not object," he added, "I hope I am too just to object to the exercise of their natural inclinations. All I ask from them is discreetness."

"Ay," said Adrian, whose discreetness was a marvel.

"No gadding about in couples," continued the Baronet, "no kissing in public. Such occurrences no boy should witness. Whenever people of both sexes are thrown together, they will be silly, and where they are high-fed, uneducated, and barely occupied, it must be looked for as a matter of course. Let it be known that I only require discreetness."

Discreetness, therefore, was instructed to reign at the Abbey. Under Adrian's able tuition, the fairest of its domestics acquired that virtue.

Discreetness, too, was enjoined to the upper household. Sir Austin, who had not previously appeared to notice the case of Lobourne's hopeless curate, now desired Mrs. Doria to interdict, or at least discourage, his visits, for the appearance of the man was that of an embodied sigh and groan.

"Really, Austin!" said Mrs. Doria, astonished to find her brother more awake than she had supposed, "I have never allowed him to hope."

"Let him see it then," replied the Baronet, "let him see it."

"The man amuses me," said Mrs. Doria. "You know, we have few amusements here, we inferior creatures. I confess I should like a barrel-organ better: that reminds one of town and the Opera; and besides, it plays more than one tune. However, since you think my society bad for him, let him stop away."

The sight of the Note-Book backing a sardonic smile, caused Mrs. Doria her unusual flash of irony; and truly it was hard upon a lady to mark this cold Rhadamanthus deliberately and openly jotting her down to fire judgment and condemnation at her sex in some future edition of the Verdicts. With the self-devotion of a woman, she abjured it, and grew patient and sweet the moment her daughter Clare was spoken of, and the business of her life in view. Mrs. Doria's maternal heart had betrothed the two cousins, Richard and Clare; had already beheld them espoused, and fruitful. For this she yielded the pleasures of town: for this she immured herself at Raynham: for this she bore with a thousand follies, exactions, inconveniences, things abhorrent to her, and Heaven knows what forms of torture and self-denial, which are smilingly endured by that greatest of voluntary martyrs, a mother with a daughter to marry. Mrs. Doria, an amiable widow, had surely married but for her daughter Clare. The lady's hair no woman could possess without feeling it her pride. It was the daily theme of her lady's-maid,—a natural aureole to her head. She was gay, witty, still physically youthful enough to claim a destiny: and she sacrificed it to accomplish her daughter's! sacrificed, as with heroic scissors, hair, wit, gaiety—let us not attempt to enumerate how much! more than may be said. And she was only one of thousands: thousands who have no portion of the hero's reward: for he may reckon on applause, and condolence, and sympathy, and honour; they, poor slaves! must look for nothing but the opposition of their own sex, and the sneers of ours. Oh, Sir Austin! had you not been so blinded, what an Aphorism might have sprung from this point of observation! Mrs. Doria was coolly told, between sister and brother, that, during the Magnetic Age, her daughter's presence at Raynham was undesirable. Instead of nursing offence, her sole thought was, the mountain of prejudice she had to contend against. She bowed, and said, Clare wanted sea-air—she had never quite recovered the shock of that dreadful night. How long, Mrs. Doria wished to know, might the Peculiar Period be expected to last?

"That," said Sir Austin, "depends. A year perhaps. He is entering on it. I shall be most grieved to lose you, Helen. Clare is now—how old?"

"Seventeen."

"She is marriageable."

"Marriageable, Austin! at seventeen! don't name such a thing. My child shall not be robbed of her youth."

"Our women marry early, Helen."

"My child shall not!"

The Baronet reflected a moment. He did not wish to lose his sister.

"As you are of that opinion, Helen," said he, "perhaps we may still make arrangements to retain you with us. Would you think it advisable to send Clare—she should know discipline—to some Establishment for a few months? . . ."

"To an Asylum, Austin?" cried Mrs. Doria, controlling her indignation as well as she could.

"To some select superior Seminary, Helen. There are such to be found."

"Austin!" Mrs. Doria exclaimed, and had to fight with a moisture in her eyes. "Unjust! absurd!" she murmured. The Baronet thought it a natural proposition that Claire should be a bride, or a schoolgirl.

"I cannot leave my child." Mrs. Doria trembled. "Where she goes, I go. I am aware that she is only one of our sex, and therefore of no value to the world, but she is my child. I will see, poor dear, that you have no cause to complain of her."

"I thought," Sir Austin remarked, "that you acquiesced in my views with regard to my son."

"Yes—generally," said Mrs. Doria, and felt culpable that she had not before, and could not then, tell her brother that he had set up an Idol in his house—an Idol of flesh! more retributive and abominable than Wood, or Brass, or Gold. But she had bowed to the Idol too long,—she had too entirely bound herself to gain her project by subserviency, to enjoy that gratification now. She had, and she dimly perceived it, committed a greater fault in tactics, in teaching her daughter to bow to the Idol also. Love of that kind, Richard took for tribute. He was indifferent to Clare's soft eyes. The parting kiss he gave her was ready and cold as his father could

desire, and Sir Austin had hardly slept overnight for thinking of the effect it might have on the Magnetic youth. He
caressed his son as if Richard had done something virtuous.
Compensation his boy should have for any trifling crosses to
his feelings. He should have yachts, horses, whatever he
fancied. Sir Austin now grew eloquent to him in laudation
of manly pursuits: but Richard thought his eloquence barren,
his attempts at companiohsnip awkward, and all manly pursuits and aims, life itself, vain and worthless. To what
end? sighed the blossomless youth, and cried aloud, as soon
as he was relieved of his father's society, what was the good
of anything? Whatever he did—whichever path he selected,
led back to Raynham. And whatever he did, and however
wretched and wayward he showed himself, only confirmed
Sir Austin more and more in the truth of his previsions.
Tom Bakewell, now the youth's groom, had to give the
Baronet a report of his young master's proceedings, in common with Adrian, and while there was no harm to tell, Tom
spoke out. "He do ride like fire every day to Pig's Snout,"
naming the highest hill in the neighbourhood, "and stand
there, and stare, never movin', like a mad'un. And then
hoam again all slack as if he'd been beaten in a race by
summody."

To the interrogation—Did he look East, or West? Tom,
dreading a snare, replied, that he had not marked: "He
seemed for to look where he could look fur away."

"There is no woman in that!" mused the Baronet. "He
would have ridden back as hard as he went," reflected this
profound Scientific Humanist, "had there been a woman in
it. He would shun vast expanses, and seek shade, concealment, solitude. The desire for distances betokens emptiness
and undirected hunger: when the heart is possessed by an
image we fly to wood and forest, like the guilty."

Adrian's report accused his pupil of an extraordinary access of cynicism.

"Exactly," said the Baronet. "Just so. As I foresaw.

At this period an insatiate appetite is accompanied by a fastidious palate. Nothing but the quintessences of existence, and those in exhaustless supplies, will satisfy this craving, which is not to be satisfied! Hence his bitterness. Life can furnish no food fitting for him. The strength and purity of his energies have reached to an almost divine height, and roam through the Inane. Poetry, Love, and such-like, are the drugs Earth has to offer to high natures, as she offers to low ones Debauchery. 'Tis a sign, this sourness, that he is subject to none of the empiricisms that are afloat. Now to keep him clear of them!"

The Titans had an easier task in storming Olympus. As yet, however, it could not be said that Sir Austin's System had failed. On the contrary, it had reared a youth, handsome, intelligent, well-bred, and, observed the ladies, with acute emphasis, innocent. Where, they asked, was such another young man to be found?

"Oh!" said Lady Blandish to Sir Austin, "if men could give their hands to women unsoiled—how different would many a marriage be! She will be a happy girl who calls Richard, husband."

"Happy indeed!" was the Baronet's caustic ejaculation. "But where shall I meet one equal to him, and his match?"

"I was innocent when I was a girl," said the lady.

Sir Austin bowed a reserved opinion.

"Do you think no girls innocent?"

Sir Austin gallantly thought them all so.

"No, that you know they are not," said the lady, stamping. "But they are more innocent than boys, I am sure."

"Because of their Education, Madam. You see now what a youth can be. Perhaps, when my System is published, or rather—to speak more humbly—when it is practised, the balance may be restored, and we shall have virtuous young men."

"It's too late for poor me to hope for a husband from one of them," said the lady, pouting and laughing.

"It is never too late for Beauty to awaken Love," returned the Baronet, and they trifled a little. They were approaching Daphne's Bower, which they entered, and sat there to taste the coolness of a descending Midsummer day.

The Baronet seemed in a humour for dignified fooling; the lady for serious converse.

"I shall believe again in Arthur's knights," she said. "When I was a girl I dreamed of one."

"And he was in quest of the San Greal?"

"If you like."

"And showed his good taste by turning aside for the more tangible San Blandish?"

"Of course you consider it would have been so," sighed the lady, ruffling.

"I can only judge by our generation," said Sir Austin, with a bend of homage.

The lady gathered her mouth. "Either we are very mighty, or you are very weak."

"Both, Madam."

"But whatever we are, and if we are bad, bad! we love virtue, and truth, and lofty souls, in men: and when we meet those qualities in them, we are constant, and would die for them—die for them. Ah! you know men, but not women."

"The knights possessing such distinctions must be young, I presume?" said Sir Austin.

"Old, or young!"

"But if old, they are scarce capable of enterprise?"

"They are loved for themselves, not for their deeds."

"Ah!"

"Yes—Ah!" said the lady, mocking him. "Intellect may subdue women—make slaves of them; and they worship Beauty perhaps as much as you do. But they only love for ever and are mated when they meet a noble nature."

Sir Austin looked at her wistfully.

"And did you encounter the knight of your dream?"

"Not then." She lowered her eyelids. It was prettily done.

"And how did you bear the disappointment?"

"My dream was in the Nursery. The day my frock was lengthened to a gown I stood at the altar. I am not the only girl that has been made a woman in a day, and given to an ogre instead of a true knight."

"Good God!" exclaimed Sir Austin, "women have much to bear."

Here the couple changed characters. The lady became gay as the Baronet grew earnest.

"You know it is our lot," she said. "And we are allowed many amusements. If we fulfil our duty in producing children, that, like our virtue, is its own reward. Then, as a widow, I have wonderful privileges."

"To preserve which, you remain a widow?"

"Certainly," she responded. "I have no trouble now in patching and piecing that rag the world calls—a character. I can sit at your feet every day unquestioned. To be sure, Miss Blewins and Mrs. Cashentire do the same, but they are female eccentrics, and have cast off the rag altogether: mine mends itself."

Sir Austin drew nearer to her. "You would have made an admirable mother, Madam."

The lady smiled. This from Sir Austin was very like positive wooing.

"It is," he continued, "ten thousand pities that you are not one."

"Do you think so?" She spoke with an extreme humility.

"I would," he went on, "that Heaven had given you a daughter."

"Would you have thought her worthy of Richard?"

"Our blood, Madam, should have been one!"

The lady tapped her toe with her parasol, blushing. "But I am a mother," she said.

Sir Austin's brows started up.

"Richard is my son."

Sir Austin looked relieved. That he could look relieved by so presumptuous a speech, was a sign how far the lady had gone with him.

"Yes! Richard is my boy," she reiterated.

Sir Austin most graciously appended: "Call him ours, Madam," and held his head as if to catch the word from her lips, which, however, she chose to refuse, or defer. They made the coloured West a common point for their eyes several minutes, and then Sir Austin said: "Listen, Madam."

Lady Blandish turned to him very sweetly.

"As you will not say 'ours,' Madam, let me. And as you have therefore an equal claim in the boy, I will confide to you a project I have lately conceived."

The announcement of a project hardly savoured of a coming proposal, but for Sir Austin to confide one to a woman was almost tantamount to a declaration. So Lady Blandish thought, and so said her soft, deep-eyed, smile, as she perused the ground while listening to the project. It concerned Richard's nuptials. He was now nearly eighteen. He was to marry when he was five-and-twenty. Meantime a young lady, some years his junior, was to be sought for in the homes of England, who would be every way fitted by education, instincts, and blood—on each of which qualifications Sir Austin unreservedly enlarged—to espouse so perfect a youth and accept the honourable duty of assisting in the perpetuation of the Feverels. The Baronet went on to say that he proposed to set forth immediately, and devote a couple of months, to the first essay in his Cœlebite search.

"I fear," said Lady Blandish, when the project had been fully unfolded, "you have laid down for yourself a difficult task. You must not be too exacting."

"I know it." The Baronet's shake of the head was piteous. "Even in England she will be rare. But I confine myself to no class. If I ask for blood, it is for untainted, not what you call high blood. I believe many of the middle classes are frequently more careful—more pure-blooded—than our aristocracy. Show me among them a God-fearing family who educate their children—I should prefer a girl without brothers and sisters—as a Christian damsel should be educated—say, on the model·of .my son, and she may be penniless, I will pledge her to Richard Feverel."

Lady Blandish bit her lip. "And what do you do with Richard while you are absent on this expedition?"

"Oh!" said the Baronet, "he accompanies his father."

"Then give it up. His future bride is now pinafored, and bread-and-buttery. She romps, she cries,·she dreams of play and pudding. How can he care for her? He thinks more at his age of old women like me. He will be certain to kick against her, and destroy your plan, believe me, Sir Austin."

"Ay? ay? do you think that?" said the Baronet.

Lady Blandish gave him a multitude of reasons.

"Ay! true," he muttered. "Adrian said the same. He must not see her. How could I think of it. The child is naked woman. He would despise her. Naturally!"

"Naturally!" echoed the lady.

"Then, Madam," and the Baronet rose, "there is one thing for me to determine upon. I must, for the first time in his life leave him."

"Will you, indeed?" said the lady.

"It is my duty, Madam, having thus brought him up, to see that he is properly mated,—not wrecked upon the quicksands of Marriage, as a youth so delicately trained might be; more easily than another! Betrothed, he will be safe from a thousand snares. I may, I think, leave him for a term. My precautions have saved him from the temptations of his season."

"And under whose charge will you leave him?" Lady Blandish inquired.

She had emerged from the Temple, and stood beside Sir Austin on the upper steps, under a clear Summer twilight.

"Madam!" he took her hand, and his voice was gallant and tender, "under whose but yours?"

As the Baronet said this, he bent above her hand, and raised it to his lips.

Lady Blandish felt that she had been wooed and asked in wedlock. She did not withdraw her hand. The Baronet's salute was flatteringly reverent. He deliberated over it, as one going through a grave ceremony. And he, the scorner of women, had chosen her for his homage! Lady Blandish forgot that she had taken some trouble to arrive at it. She received the exquisite compliment in all its unique honey-sweet: for in love we must deserve nothing, or the fine bloom of fruition is gone.

The lady's hand was still in durance, and the Baronet had not recovered from his profound inclination, when a noise from the neighbouring beechwood startled the two actors in this courtly pantomime. They turned their heads, and beheld the Hope of Raynham on horseback, surveying the scene aghast. The next moment he had galloped away.

CHAPTER XVII

AN ATTRACTION

ALL night Richard tossed on his bed with his heart in a rapid canter, and his brain bestriding it, traversing the rich untasted world, and the great Realm of Mystery, from which he was now restrained no longer. Months he had wandered about the gates of the Bonnet, wondering, sighing, knocking at them, and getting neither admittance nor answer. He had the key now. His own father had given it him. His heart was a lightning steed, and bore him on and on over limitless regions bathed in superhuman beauty and strangeness, where cavaliers and ladies leaned whispering upon close green swards, and knights and ladies cast a splendour upon savage forests, and tilts and tourneys were held in golden Courts lit to a glorious day by ladies' eyes, one pair of which, dimly visioned, constantly distinguishable, followed him through the boskage and dwelt upon him in the press, beaming while he bent above a hand glittering white and fragrant as the frosted blossom of a May-night. Awhile the heart would pause and flutter to a shock: he was in the act of consummating all earthly bliss by pressing his lips to the small white hand. Only to do that, and die! cried the Magnetic Youth: to fling the Jewel of Life into that one cup, and drink it off! He was intoxicated by anticipation. For that he was born. There was, then, some end in existence, something to live for! to kiss a woman's hand, and die! He would leap from the couch, and rush to pen and paper to relieve his swarming sensations. Scarce was he seated, when the pen was dashed aside, the paper sent flying, with the exclamation, "Have I not sworn I would never write again?" Sir Austin had shut that safety-valve. The nonsense that was in the youth might have poured harmlessly out, and its urgency for ebullition was so great that he was repeatedly oblivious of his oath, and found himself seated under the lamp in the act of composition, before Pride could speak a word. Possibly the pride even of Richard Feverel had been swamped if the act of composition were easy at such a time, and a single idea could stand clearly foremost; but myriads were demanding the first place; chaotic hosts, like ranks of stormy billows, pressed impetuously for expression, and despair of reducing them to form, quite as much as pride, to which it pleased him to refer his incapacity, threw down the powerless pen, and sent him panting to his outstretched length and another head-long career through the rosy-girdled land.

Towards morning the madness of the fever abated somewhat, and he went forth into the air. A lamp was still burning in his father's room, and Richard thought, as he looked up, that he saw the ever-vigilant head on the watch.

Instantly the lamp was extinguished, the window stood cold against the hues of dawn. Had he cast a second glance at his own chamber, he might then have seen the ever-vigilant head on the watch. Sir Austin had slept no more than his son. Beholding him so early abroad, his worst fears were awakened. He hurried to gaze at the forsaken couch, a picture of tempest: the papers, with half-written words ending in reckless tails and wild dashes, strewn everywhere about, blankly eloquent: chairs upset, drawers left open, companion slippers astray about the room. The abashed Baronet dared not whisper to his soul what had thus distracted the youth. As little could he make self-confession that it was impossible for him to face his son for some time to come. No doubt his conscious eye looked inward, and knew; but he chose to juggle with it, and say to himself, that not an hour must be lost in betrothing Richard, and holding him bond to virtue, and therefore he would immediately depart on his expedition. The pain of not folding the beloved son to his breast before he went, was moreover a fortunate beguilement of the latent dread that his going just now was a false step. It would be their first separation. Sir Austin ascended to the roof of the Abbey, and descried him hastening to the boat-house by the river-side. Ere he was out of sight, the Baronet's sense of sacrifice had blinded his conscious eye, and enabled him to feel altogether a martyr to Duty.

Strong pulling is an excellent medical remedy for certain classes of fever. Richard took to it instinctively. The clear fresh water, burnished with sunrise, sparkled against his arrowy prow: the soft deep shadows curled smiling away from his gliding keel. Overhead solitary morning unfolded itself, from blossom to bud, from bud to flower; still delicious changes of light and colour, to whose influences he was heedless as he shot under willows and aspens, and across sheets of river-reaches, pure mirrors to the upper glory, himself the sole tenant of the stream. Somewhere at the founts of the world lay the land he was rowing towards: something of its shadowed lights might be discerned here and there. It was not a dream, now he knew. There was a secret abroad. The woods were full of it; the waters rolled with it, and the winds. Oh, why could not one in these days do some high knightly deed which should draw down ladies' eyes from their heaven, as in the days of Arthur! To such a meaning breathed the unconscious sighs of the youth, when he had pulled through his first feverish energy.

He was off Bursley, and had lapsed into that musing quietude which follows strenuous exercise, when he heard a hail and his own name called. It was no lady, no fairy, but young Ralph Morton, an irruption of miserable masculine prose. Heartily wishing him abed with the rest of mankind, Richard rowed in and jumped ashore. Ralph immediately seized his arm, saying that he desired earnestly to have a talk with him, and dragged the Magnetic Youth from his water-dreams, up and down the wet mown grass. That he had to say seemed to be difficult of utterance, and Richard, though he barely listened, soon had enough of his old rival's gladness at seeing him, and exhibited signs of impatience; whereat Ralph, as one who branches into matter somewhat foreign in his mind, but of great human interest and importance, put the question to him:

"I say, what woman's name do you like best?"

"I don't know any," quoth Richard indifferently. "Why are you out so early?"

In answer to this, Ralph suggested that the name of Mary might be considered a pretty name.

Richard agreed that it might be: the housekeeper at Raynham, half the women cooks and all the housemaids enjoyed that name: the name of Mary was equivalent for woman at home.

"Yes, I know," said Ralph. "We have lots of Marys. It's so common. Oh! I don't like Mary best. What do you think of Lucy?"

Richard thought it just like another.

"Do you know," Ralph continued, throwing off the mask and plunging into the subject, "I'd do anything on earth for some names—one or two. It's not Mary, or Lucy. Clarinda's pretty, but it's like a novel. Claribel I like. Names beginning with 'Cl' I prefer. The 'Cl's' are always gentle and lovely girls you would die for! Don't you think so?"

Richard had never been acquainted with any for them to inspire that emotion. Indeed these urgent appeals to his fancy in feminine names at five o'clock in the morning, slightly surprised him, though he was but half awake to the outer world. By degrees he perceived that Ralph was quite changed. Instead of the lusty boisterous boy, his rival in manly sciences, who spoke straightforwardly and acted up to his speech, here was an abashed and blush-persecuted youth, who sued piteously for a friendly ear wherein to pour the one idea possessing him. Gradually, too, Richard apprehended that Ralph likewise was on the frontiers of the Realm of Mystery, perhaps further towards it than he himself was; and then, as by a sympathetic stroke, was revealed to him the wonderful beauty and depth of meaning in feminine names. The theme appeared novel and delicious, fitted to the season and the hour. But the hardship was that Richard could choose none from the number; all were the same to him; he loved them all.

"Don't you really prefer the 'Cl's'?" said Ralph, most persuasively.

"Not better than the names ending in 'a' and 'y,'" Richard replied, wishing he could, for Ralph was evidently ahead of him.

"Come under these trees," said Ralph. And under the trees Ralph unbosomed. His name was down for the army: Eton was quitted for ever. In a few days he would have to join his regiment, and before he left he must say good-bye to his friends . . . would Richard tell him Mrs. Forey's address? he had heard she was somewhere by the sea. Richard did not remember the address, but said he would willingly take charge of any letter and forward it.

"Will you?" cried Ralph, diving his hand into his pocket, "here it is. But don't let anybody see it."

"My aunt's name is not Clare," said Richard, perusing what was composed of the exterior formula.

"Ah! why, you've addressed it to Clare herself."

"Have I?" murmured Ralph, hiding his hot face in a stumble, and then peeping at the address to verify. "So I have. The address, you know. . . . It's because I like to write the name of Clare," he added hurriedly, by way of excellent justification.

"Is that the name you like best?"

Ralph counterqueried, "Don't you think it very nice—beautiful, I mean?"

"Not so good as Clara," said Richard.

"Oh! a hundred times better," shouted young Ralph in a fervour.

Richard meditated unwittingly: "I suppose we like the names of the people we like best."

No answer from Ralph.

"Emmeline Clementina Matilda Laura, Countess Blandish," Richard continued in a low tone, transferring the names, and playing on them like musical strings.

"Eh?" quoth Ralph.

"I'm certain," said Ralph, as he finished his performance, "I am certain we like the names of the people we like best." And having made this great discovery for himself, he fixed his eyes on blushing Ralph. If he discovered anything further, he said nothing, but bade him good bye, jumped back into his boat, and pulled down the tide. The moment Ralph was hidden by an abutment of the banks, Richard perused the address. For the first time it struck him that his cousin Clare was a very charming creature: he remembered the look of her eyes, and especially the last reproachful glance she gave him at parting. What business, pray, had Ralph to write to her? Did she not belong to him, Richard Feverel? He read the words again and again: Clare Doria Forey. Why, Clare was the name he liked best: nay, he loved it. Doria, too: she shared his own name with him. Away went his heart, not at a canter now, at a gallop, as one who sights the quarry. He felt too weak to pull. Clare Doria Forey—oh, perfect melody! Sliding with the tide, he heard it flung in the bosom of the hills.

When Nature has made us ripe for Love it seldom occurs that the Fates are behindhand in furnishing a Temple for the flame.

Above green-flashing plunges of a weir, and shaken by the thunder below, lilies, golden and white, were swaying at anchor among the reeds. Meadow-sweet hung from the banks thick with weed and training bramble, and there also hung a daughter of Earth. Her face was shaded by a broad straw-hat with a flexile brim that left her lips and chin in the sun, and sometimes nodding, sent forth a light of promising eyes. Across her shoulders, and behind flowed large loose curls, brown in shadow, almost golden where the ray touched them. She was simply dressed, befitting decency and the season. On a closer inspection you might see that her lips were stained. This blooming young person was regaling on dewberries. They grew between the bank and the water. Apparently she found the fruit abundant, for her hand was making pretty progress to her mouth. Fastidious youth, which shudders and revolts at woman plumping her exquisite proportions on bread-and-butter, and would (we must suppose) joyfully have her quite scraggy to have her quite poetical, can hardly object to dewberries. Indeed the act of eating them is dainty and induces musing. The dewberry is a sister to the lotos, and an innocent sister. You eat; mouth, eye, and hand, are occupied, and the undrugged mind free to roam. And so it was with the damsel who knelt there. The little skylark went up

above her, all song, to the smooth southern cloud lying
along the blue: from a dewy copse standing dark over her
nodding hat, the blackbird fluted, calling to her with thrice
mellow note: the kingfisher flashed emerald out of green
osiers: a bow-winged heron travelled aloft, searching solitude: a boat slipped towards her, containing a dreamy
youth, and still she plucked the fruit, and ate, and mused,
as if no fairy prince were invading her territories, and as
if she wished not for one, or knew not her wishes. Surrounded by the green shaven meadows, the pastoral summer buzz, the weir-fall's thundering white, amid the
breath and beauty of wildflowers, she was a bit of lovely
human life in a fair setting: a terrible attraction. The Magnetic Youth leaned round to note his proximity to the weir-
piles, and beheld the sweet vision. Stiller and stiller grew
Nature, as at the meeting of two electric clouds. Her posture was so graceful that, though he was making straight
for the weir, he dared not dip a scull. Just then one most
enticing dewberry caught her eye. He was floating by un-
heeded, and saw that her hand stretched low, and could not
gather what it sought. A stroke from his right brought
him beside her. The damsel glanced up dismayed, and her
whole shape trembled over the brink. Richard sprang from
his boat into the water. Pressing a hand beneath her foot,
which she had thrust against the crumbling wet sides of
the bank to save herself, he enabled her to recover her
balance, and gain safe earth, whither, emboldened by the
incident, touching her finger's tip, he followed her.

CHAPTER XVIII

FERDINAND AND MIRANDA

HE had landed on an Island of the still-vexed Bermoothes.
The world lay wrecked behind him: Raynham hung in

ιnists, remote, a phantom to the vivid reality of this white
hand which had drawn him thither away thousands of
leagues in an eye-twinkle. Hark, how Ariel sung overhead! What splendour in the Heavens! What marvels of
beauty about his enchanted head! And, O you Wonder!
Fair Flame! by whose light the glories of being are now
first seen. . . . . Radiant Miranda! Prince Ferdinand is
at your feet.

Or is it Adam, his rib taken from his side in sleep, and
thus transformed, to make him behold his Paradise, and
lose it? . . .

The youth looked on her with as glowing an eye. It
was the First Woman to him.

And she—mankind was all Caliban to her, saving this
one princely youth.

So to each other said their changing eyes in the moment
they stood together; he pale, and she blushing.

She was indeed sweetly fair, and would have been held
fair among rival damsels. On a magic shore, and to a youth
educated by a System, strung like an arrow drawn to the
head, he, it might be guessed, could fly fast and far with
her. The soft rose in her cheeks, the clearness of her eyes,
bore witness to the body's virtue; and health, and happy
blood was in her bearing. Had she stood before Sir Austin
among rival damsels, that Scientific Humanist, for the consummation of his System, would have thrown her the handkerchief for his son. The wide summer-hat nodding over
her forehead to her brows, seemed to flow with the flowing
heavy curls, and those fire-threaded mellow curls, only half-
curls, waves of hair, call them, rippling at the ends, went
like a sunny red-veined torrent down her back almost to
her waist: a glorious vision to the youth, who embraced it
as a flower of beauty, and read not a feature. There were
curious features of colour in her face for him to have read.
Her brows, thick and brownish against a soft skin showing
the action of the blood, met in the bend of a bow, extend-

ing to the temples long and level: you saw that she was
fashioned to peruse the sights of earth, and by the pliability
of her brows, that the wonderful creature used her faculty,
and was not going to be a statue to the gazer. Under the
dark thick brows an arch of lashes shot out, giving a
wealth of darkness to the full frank blue eyes a mystery
of meaning—more than brain was ever meant to fathom:
richer henceforth than all mortal wisdom to Prince Ferdinand. For when Nature turns artist, and produces contrasts of colour on a fair face, where is the Sage, or what
the Oracle, shall match the depth of its lightest look?

Prince Ferdinand was also fair. In his slim boating-attire
his figure looked heroic. His hair, rising from the parting
to the right of his forehead, in what his admiring Lady Blandish called his plume, fell away slanting silkily to the
temples across the nearly imperceptible upward curve of
his brows there—felt more than seen, so slight it was—and
gave to his profile a bold beauty, to which his bashful breathless air was a flattering charm. An arrow drawn to the
head, capable of flying fast and far with her! He leaned
a little forward to her, drinking her in with all his eyes,
and young Love has a thousand. Then truly the System
triumphed, just ere it was to fall; and could Sir Austin
have been content to draw the arrow to the head, and let
it fly, when it would fly, he might have pointed to his
son again, and said to the world, "Match him!" Such
keen bliss as the youth had in the sight of her, an innocent
youth alone has powers of soul in him to experience.

'O Women!' says The Pilgrim's Scrip, in one of its
solitary outbursts, 'Women, who like, and will have for
hero, a rake! how soon are you not to learn that you have
taken bankrupts to your bosoms, and that the putrescent
gold that attracted you, is the slime of the Lake of Sin.'

If these two were Ferdinand and Miranda, Sir Austin

was not Prospero, and was not present, or their fates might have been different.

So they stood a moment, changing eyes, and then Miranda spoke, and they came down to earth, feeling no less in heaven.

She spoke to thank him for his aid. She used quite common simple words; and used them, no doubt, to express a common simple meaning; but to him she was uttering magic, casting spells, and the effect they had on him was manifested in the incoherence of his replies, which were too foolish to be chronicled.

The couple were again mute. Suddenly Miranda, with an exclamation of anguish, and innumerable lights and shadows playing over her lovely face, clapped her hands, crying aloud, "My book! my book!" and ran to the bank.

Prince Ferdinand was at her side. "What have you lost?" he said.

"My book! my book!" she answered, her long delicious curls swinging across her shoulders to the stream. Then turning to him, divining his rash intention, "Oh, no, no! let me entreat you not to," she said. "I do not so very much mind losing it." And in her eagerness to restrain him, she unconsciously laid her gentle hand upon his arm, and took the force of motion out of him.

"Indeed I do not really care for the silly book," she continued, withdrawing her hand quickly, and reddening. "Pray do not!"

The young gentleman had kicked off his shoes. No sooner was the spell of contact broken, than he jumped in. The water was still troubled and discoloured by his introductory adventure, and, though he ducked his head with the spirit of a dabchick, the book was missing. A scrap of paper floating from the bramble just above the water, and looking as if fire had caught its edges and it had flown from one adverse element to the other, was all he could lay hold of, and he returned to land disconsolately, to hear

Miranda's murmured mixing of thanks and pretty expostulations.

"Let me try again," he said.

"No, indeed!" she replied, and used the awful threat: "I will run away if you do," which effectually restrained him.

Her eye fell on the fire-stained scrap of paper, and brightened, as she cried, "There—there! you have what I want. It is that. I do not care for the book.—No, please! You are not to look at it. Give it me."

Before her playfully-imperative injunction was fairly spoken, Richard had glanced at the document, and discovered a Griffin between Two Wheatsheaves: his Crest, in silver: and below, O wonderment immense! his own handwriting! remnant of his burnt Offering! a page of the sacrificed Poems! one Blossom preserved from the deadly universal blight.

He handed it to her in silence. She took it, and put it in her bosom.

Who would have said, have thought, that, where all else perished, Odes, fluttering bits of broad-winged Epic, Idyls, Lines, Stanzas, this one Sonnet to the Stars should be miraculously reserved for such a starry fate! passing beatitude!

As they walked silently across the meadow Richard strove to remember the hour, and the mood of mind, in which he had composed the notable production. The stars were invoked, as seeing, and foreseeing, all, to tell him where then his love reclined, and so forth; Hesper was complacent enough to do so, and described her in a couplet:

> '*Through sunset's amber see me shining fair,*
> *As her blue eyes shine through her golden hair.*'

And surely no words could be more prophetic. Here were two blue eyes, and golden hair; and by some strange chance, that appeared like the working of a divine finger, she had become the possessor of the prophecy, she that was to fulfil it! The youth was too charged with emotion to speak. Doubtless the damsel had less to think of, or had some trifling burden on her conscience, for she seemed to grow embarrassed. At last she threw up her chin to look at her companion under the nodding brim of her hat (and the action gave her a charmingly freakish air), crying, "But where are you going to? You are wet through. Let me thank you again, and pray leave me, and go home, and change instantly."

"Wet?" replied the Magnetic muser, with a voice of tender interest, "not more than one foot, I hope? I will leave you while you dry your stocking in the sun."

At this she could not withhold a shy and lovely laugh.

"Not I, but you. You know you saved me, and would try to get that silly book for me, and you are dripping wet. Are you not very uncomfortable?"

In all sincerity he assured her that he was not.

"And you really do not feel that you are wet?"

He really did not: and it was a fact that he spoke truth. She pursed her sweet dewberry mouth in the most comical way, and her blue eyes lightened laughter out of the half-closed lids.

"I cannot help it," she said, her mouth opening, and sounding harmonious bells of laughter in his ears. "Pardon me, won't you?"

His face took the same soft smiling curves in admiration of her.

"Not to feel that you have been in the water, the very moment after!" she musically interjected, seeing she was excused.

"It's true," he said; and his own gravity then touched him to join a duet with her, which made them no longer feel strangers, and did the work of a month of intimacy. Better than sentiment Laughter opens the breast of Love;

opens the whole breast to his full quiver, instead of a corner here and there for a solitary arrow. Hail the occasion Propitious, O ye British young! and laugh, and treat Love as an honest God, and dabble not with the spiritual rouge. These two laughed, and the souls of each cried out to other, 'It is I,' 'It is I.'

They laughed and forgot the cause of their laughter, and the sun dried his light river-clothing, and they strolled towards the blackbird's copse, and stood near a stile, in sight of the foam of the weir, and the many-coloured rings of eddies streaming forth from it.

Richard's boat, meanwhile, had contrived to shoot the weir, and was swinging, bottom upwards, broadside with the current down the rapid backwater.

"Will you let it go?" said the damsel, eyeing it curiously.

"Yes," he replied, and low, as if he spoke in the core of his thought: "What do I care for it now?"

His old life was whirled away with it, dead, drowned. His new life was with her, alive, divine.

She flapped low the brim of her hat. "You must really not come any further," she softly said.

"And will you go, and not tell me who you are?" he asked, growing bold as the fears of losing her came across him: "And will you not tell me before you go," his face burned, "how you came by that—that paper?"

She chose to select the easier question to reply to: "You ought to know me; we have been introduced." Sweet was her winning off-hand affability.

"Then who, in Heaven's name, are you? Tell me! I never could have forgotten you."

"You have, I think," she said demurely.

"Impossible that we could ever have met, and I forget you!"

She looked up to him quickly.

"Do you remember Belthorpe?"

"Belthorpe! Belthorpe!" quoth Richard, as if he had to

touch his brain to recollect there was such a place. "Do you mean old Blaize's farm?"

"Then I am old Blaize's niece." She tripped him a soft curtsey.

The Magnetized youth gazed at her. By what magic was it that this divine sweet creature could be allied with that old churl!

"Then what—what is your name?" said his mouth, while his eyes added, "O wonderful creature! How came you to enrich the earth?"

"Have you forgot the Desboroughs of Dorset, too?" she peered at him archly from a side bend of the flapping brim.

"The Desboroughs of Dorset?" a light broke in on him. "And have you grown to this? That little girl I saw there!"

He drew close to her to read the nearest features of the vision. She could no more laugh off the piercing fervour of his eyes. Her volubility fluttered under his deeply wistful look, and now neither voice was high, and they were mutually constrained.

"You see," she murmured, "we are old acquaintances."

Richard, with his eyes still intently fixed on her, returned: "You are very beautiful!"

The words slipped out. Perfect simplicity is unconsciously audacious. Her overpowering beauty struck his heart, and like an instrument that is touched and answers to the touch, he spoke.

Miss Desborough made an effort to trifle with this terrible directness: but his eyes would not be gainsaid, and checked her lips. She turned away from them, her bosom a little rebellious. Praise so passionately spoken, and by one who has been a damsel's first d_eam, dreamed of nightly many long nights, and clothed in the virgin silver of her thoughts in bud, praise from him is coin the heart cannot reject, if it would. She quickened her steps to the stile.

"I have offended you!" said a mortally wounded voice across her shoulder.

That he should think so were too dreadful.

"Oh, no, no! you would never offend me." She gave him her whole sweet face.

"Then why—why do you leave me?"

"Because," she hesitated, "I must go."

"No. You must not go. Why must you go? Do not go."

"Indeed, I must," she said, pulling at the obnoxious broad brim of her hat; and, interpreting a pause he made for his assent to her sensible resolve, shyly looking at him, she held her hand out, and said, "Good-bye," as if it were a natural thing to say.

The hand was pure white: white and fragrant as the frosted blossom of a May-night. It was the hand whose shadow, cast before, he had last night bent his head reverentially above, and kissed—resigning himself thereupon over to execution for payment of the penalty of such daring: by such bliss well rewarded.

He took the hand, and held it; gazing between her eyes.

"Good-bye," she said again, as frankly as she could, and at the same time slightly compressing her fingers on his in token of adieu. It was a signal for his to close firmly upon hers.

"You will not go?"

"Pray let me," she pleaded, her sweet brows suing in wrinkles.

"You will not go?" Mechanically he drew the white hand nearer his thumping heart.

"I must," she faltered piteously.

"You will not go?"

"Oh yes! yes!"

"Tell me. Do you wish to go?"

The question was subtle. A moment or two she did not answer, and then forswore herself, and said, Yes.

"Do you—do you wish to go?" He looked with quivering eyelids under hers.

A fainter, Yes, responded to his passionate repetition.

"You wish—wish to leave me?" His breath went with the words.

"Indeed I must."

Her hand became a closer prisoner.

All at once an alarming delicious shudder went through her frame. From him to her it coursed, and back from her to him. Forward and back Love's electric messenger rushed from heart to heart, knocking at each, till it surged tumultuously against the bars of its prison, crying out for its mate. They stood trembling in unison, a lovely couple under these fair Heavens of the morning.

When he could get his voice, it was, "Will you go?"

But she had none to reply with, and could only mutely bend upward her gentle wrist.

"Then, farewell," he said, and dropping his lips to the soft fair hand, kissed it, and hung his head, swinging away from her, ready for death.

Strange, that now she was released she should linger by him. Strange, that his audacity, instead of the executioner, brought blushes and timid tenderness to his side, and the sweet words, "You are not angry with me?"

"With you, O Beloved!" cried his soul. "And you forgive me, Fair Charity!"

She repeated her words in deeper sweetness to his bewildered look; and he, inexperienced, possessed by her, almost lifeless with the divine new emotions she had realized in him, could only sigh, and gaze at her wonderingly.

"I think it was rude of me to go without thanking you again," she said, and again proffered her hand.

The sweet Heaven-bird shivered out his song above him. The gracious glory of Heaven fell upon his soul. He touched her hand, not moving his eyes from her, nor speaking, and she, with a soft word of farewell, passed across the stile, and up the pathway through the dewy shades of the copse, and out of the arch of the light, away from his eyes.

And away with her went the wild enchantment: he looked on barren air. But it was no more the world of yesterday. The marvellous splendours had sown seeds in him, ready to spring up and bloom at her gaze; and in his bosom now the vivid conjuration of her tones, her face, her shape, makes them leap and illumine him like fitful summer lightnings— ghosts of the vanished Sun.

There was nothing to tell him that he had been making love and declaring it with extraordinary rapidity: nor did he know it. Soft-flushed cheeks! sweet mouth! strange sweet brows! eyes of softest fire! how could his ripe eyes see you, and not plead to keep you? Nay, how could he let you go? And he seriously asks himself that question.

Tomorrow this spot will have a memory—the river, and the meadow, and the white, falling weir: his heart will build a temple here; and the skylark will be its high-priest, and the old blackbird its glossy-gowned chorister, and there will be a sacred repast of dewberries. Today the grass is grass: his heart is chased by phantoms, and finds rest nowhere. Only when the most tender freshness of his flower comes across him, does he taste a moment's calm; and no sooner does it come than it gives place to keen pangs of fear that she may not be his for ever.

Ere long he learns that her name is Lucy. Ere long he meets Ralph, and discovers that in a day he has distanced him by a sphere. Ere long, he, and Ralph, and the Curate of Lobourne, join in their walks, and raise classical discussions on ladies' hair, fingering a thousand delicious locks, from those of Cleopatra to the Borgia's. "Fair! fair! all of them fair!" sighs the melancholy Curate, "as are those women formed for our perdition! I think we have in this country what will match the Italian, or the Greek." His mind flutters to Mrs. Doria: Richard blushes before the vision of

Lucy: and Ralph, whose heroine's hair is a dark luxuriance, dissents, and claims a noble share in the slaughter of men for dark-haired Wonders. They have no mutual confidences, but they are singularly kind to each other, these three children of instinct.

CHAPTER XIX

UNMASKING OF MASTER RIPTON THOMPSON

LADY BLANDISH, and others who professed an interest in the fortunes and future of the systematized youth, had occasionally mentioned names of families whose alliance, according to apparent calculations, would not degrade his blood; and over these names, secretly preserved on an open leaf of the Note-Book, Sir Austin, as he neared the Metropolis, distantly dropped his eye. There were names historic, and names mushroomic; names that the Conqueror might have called in his muster-roll; names that had been, clearly, tossed into the upper stratum of civilized life by a mill-wheel, or a merchant-stool. Against them the Baronet had written M., or Po., or Pr.: signifying, Money, Position, Principles: favouring the latter with special brackets. The wisdom of a worldly man, which he could now and then adopt, determined him, before he commenced his round of visits, to consult and sound his Solicitor and his Physician thereanent: Lawyers and Doctors being the rats who know best the merits of a House, and on what sort of foundation it is standing.

Sir Austin entered the great City with a sad mind. The memory of his misfortune came upon him vividly, as if no years had intervened, and it were but yesterday that he found the letter telling him that he had no wife, and his son no mother. He wandered on foot through the streets the first night of his arrival, looking strangely at the shops, and shows, and bustle of the World from which he had divorced himself; feeling as destitute as the poorest vagrant. He had almost forgotten how to find his way about, and came across his old mansion in his efforts to regain his hotel. The windows were alight; signs of merry life within. He stared at it from the shadow of the opposite side. It seemed to him he was a ghost gazing upon his living past. And then the Phantom which had stood there mocking while he felt as other men—the Phantom now flesh and blood Reality seized and convulsed his heart, and filled its unforgiving crevices with bitter ironic venom. He remembered by the time reflection returned to him that it was Algernon, who had the house at his disposal, probably giving a card-party, or something of the sort. In the morning, too, he remembered that he had divorced the World to wed a System, and must be faithful to that exacting Spouse, who, now alone of things on earth, could fortify and recompense him.

Mr. Thompson received his client with the dignity and emotion due to such a rent-roll and the unexpectedness of the honour. He was a thin stately man of Law, garbed as one who gave audience to acred Bishops, and carrying on his countenance the stamp of paternity to the parchment-skins, and of a Virtuous attachment to port-wine sufficient to increase his respectability in the eyes of moral Britain. After congratulating Sir Austin on the fortunate issue of two or three suits, and being assured that the Baronet's business in town had no concern therewith, Mr. Thompson ventured to hope that the young heir was all his father could desire him to be, and heard with satisfaction that he was a pattern to the youth of the Age.

"A difficult time of life, Sir Austin!" said the old lawyer, shaking his head. "We must keep our eyes on them—keep awake! The mischief is done in a minute!"

"We must take care to have seen where we planted, and that the root was sound, or the mischief will do itself in spite of, or under the very spectacles of, Supervision," said the Baronet.

His legal adviser murmured "Exactly," as if that were his own idea; adding, "It is my plan with Ripton, who has had the honour of an introduction to you, and a very pleasant time he spent with my young friend, whom he does not forget. Ripton follows the Law. He is articled to me, and will, I trust, succeed me worthily in your confidence. I bring him into town in the morning: I take him back at night. I think I may say that I am quite content with him."

"Do you think," said Sir Austin, fixing his brows, "that you can trace every act of his to its motive?"

The old lawyer bent forward and humbly requested that this might be repeated.

"Do you," Sir Austin held the same searching expression, "do you establish yourself in a radiating centre of intuition— do you base your watchfulness on so thorough an acquaintance with his character—so perfect a knowledge of the instrument, that all its movements—even the eccentric ones—are anticipated by you, and provided for?"

The explanation was a little too long for the old lawyer to entreat another repetition. Winking with the painful deprecation of a deaf man, Mr. Thompson smiled urbanely, coughed conciliatingly, and said he was afraid he could not affirm that much, though he was happily enabled to say that Ripton had borne an extremely good character at school.

"I find," Sir Austin remarked, as sardonically he relaxed his inspecting pose and mien, "there are fathers who are content to be simply obeyed. Now I require not only that my son should obey, I would have him guiltless of the impulse to gainsay my wishes: feeling me in him stronger than his undeveloped nature, up to a certain period, where my responsibility ends and his commences. Man is a self-acting machine. He cannot cease to be a machine; but, though self-acting, he may lose the powers of self-guidance, and in a wrong course his very vitalities hurry him to perdition.

Young, he is an organism ripening to the set mechanic diurnal round, and while so he needs all the Angels to hold watch over him that he grow straight, and healthy, and fit for what machinal duties he may have to perform. . . ."

Mr. Thompson agitated his eyebrows dreadfully. He was utterly lost. He respected Sir Austin's estates too much to believe for a moment he was listening to downright folly. Yet how otherwise explain the fact of his excellent client being incomprehensible to him? For a middle-aged gentleman, and one who has been in the habit of advising and managing, will rarely have a notion of accusing his understanding, and Mr. Thompson had not the slightest notion of accusing his. But the Baronet's condescension in coming thus to him, and speaking on the subject nearest his heart, might well affect him, and he quickly settled the case in favour of both parties, pronouncing mentally that his honoured Client had a meaning, and so deep it was, so subtle, that no wonder he experienced a difficulty in giving it fitly significant words.

Sir Austin elaborated his theory of the Organism and the Mechanism, for his lawyer's edification. At a recurrence of the word, healthy, Mr. Thompson caught him up:

"I apprehend you! Oh, I agree with you, Sir Austin! Entirely! Allow me to ring for my son Ripton. I think, if you condescend to examine him, you will say that regular habits, and a diet of nothing but law-reading—for other forms of literature I strictly interdict—have made him all that you instance."

Mr. Thompson's hand was on the bell. Sir Austin arrested him.

"Permit me to see the lad at his occupation," said he.

Our old friend Ripton sat in a room apart with the confidential clerk, Mr. Beazley, a veteran of Law, now little better than a Document, looking already signed and sealed, and shortly to be delivered, who enjoined nothing from his pupil and companion save absolute silence, and sounded his

praises to his father at the close of days when it had been
rigidly observed—not caring, or considering, the finished dry
old Document that he was, under what kind of spell a turbu-
lent commonplace youth could be charmed into stillness six
hours a day. Ripton was supposed to be devoted to the
study of Blackstone. A tome of the classical legal Com-
mentator lay extended outside his desk; under the partially
lifted lid of which nestled the assiduous student's head—
Law being thus brought into direct contact with his brain-
pan. The office-door opened, and he heard not: his name
was called, and he remained equally moveless. His method
of taking in Blackstone seemed absorbing as it was novel.

"Comparing notes, I dare say," whispered Mr. Thompson
to Sir Austin. "I call that study!"

The Confidential Clerk rose, and bowed obsequious senility.

"Is it like this every day, Beazley?" Mr. Thompson asked
with parental pride.

"Ahem!" the old Clerk replied, "He is like this every
day, Sir. I could not ask more of a mouse."

Sir Austin stepped forward to the desk. His proximity
roused one of Ripton's senses, which blew a call to the
others. Down went the lid of the desk. Dismay, and the
ardours of Study, flashed together in Ripton's face. He
slouched from his perch with the air of one who means rather
to defend his position than welcome a superior, the right hand
in his waistcoat pocket fumbling a key, the left catching at
his vacant stool.

Sir Austin put two fingers on the youth's shoulder, and
said, leaning his head a little on one side, in a way habitual
to him, "I am glad to find my son's old comrade thus profit-
ably occupied. I know what Study is myself. But beware
of prosecuting it too excitedly! Come! you must not be
offended at our interruption—you will soon take up the
thread again. Besides, you know, you must get accustomed
to the visits of your Client."

So condescending and kindly did this speech sound to Mr. Thompson, that seeing Ripton still preserve his appearance of disorder and sneaking defiance, he thought fit to nod and frown at the youth, and desired him to inform the Baronet what particular part of Blackstone he was absorbed in mastering at that moment.

Ripton hesitated an instant, and blundered out, with dubious articulation, "The Law of Gravelkind."

"What Law?" said Sir Austin, perplexed.

"Gravelkind," again rumbled Ripton's voice.

Sir Austin turned to Mr. Thompson for an explanation. The old lawyer was shaking his law-box.

"Singular," he exclaimed. "He will make that mistake!— What Law, Sir?"

Ripton read his error in the sternly painful expression of his father's face, and corrected himself: "Gavelkind, Sir."

"Ah!" said Mr. Thompson, with a sigh of relief. "Gravel-kind, indeed! Gavelkind!—An old Kentish——" he was going to expound, but Sir Austin assured him he knew it, and a very absurd Law it was: adding, "I should like to look at your son's notes, or remarks on the judiciousness of that family arrangement, if he has any."

"You were making notes, or referring to them, as we entered," said Mr. Thompson to the suckling lawyer; "a very good plan, which I have always enjoined to you. Were you not?"

Ripton stammered that he was afraid he had not any Notes to show—worth seeing.

"What were you doing, then, Sir?"

"Making notes," muttered Ripton, looking incarnate subterfuge.

"Exhibit!"

Ripton glanced at his desk, and then at his father: at Sir Austin, and at the confidential clerk. He took out his key. It would not fit the hole.

"Exhibit!" was peremptorily called again.

In his praiseworthy efforts to accommodate the keyhole, Ripton discovered that the desk was already unlocked. Mr. Thompson marched to it, and held the lid aloft. A book was lying open within, which Ripton immediately hustled among a mass of papers and tossed into a dark corner: not before the glimpse of a coloured frontispiece was caught by Sir Austin's eye.

The Baronet smiled, and said, "You study Heraldry, too? Are you fond of the Science?"

Ripton replied that he was very fond of it—extremely attached; and threw a further pile of papers into the dark corner.

The Notes had been less conspicuously placed, and the search for them was tedious and vain. Papers, not legal, or the fruits of study, were found that made Mr. Thompson more intimate with the conditions of his son's exchequer: nothing in the shape of a Remark on the Law of Gavelkind.

Mr. Thompson suggested to his son that they might be among those scraps he had thrown carelessly into the dark corner. Ripton, though he consented to inspect them, was positive they were not there.

"What have we here?" said Mr. Thompson, seizing a neatly folded paper addressed to the Editor of a Law publication, as Ripton brought them forth, one by one. Forthwith Mr. Thompson fixed his spectacles and read aloud:

'*To the Editor of the Jurist.*

    'Sir,

'In your recent of observations on the great case of Crim—'

Mr. Thompson hem'd! and stopped short like a man who comes unexpectedly upon a snake in his path. Mr. Beazley's feet shuffled. Sir Austin changed the position of an arm.

"It's on the other side, I think," gasped Ripton.

Mr. Thompson confidently turned over, and intoned with emphasis.

'To Absalom, the son of David, the little Jew usurer of
Bond Court, Whitecross Gutters, for his introduction to
Venus, I.O.U. Five Pounds, when I can pay.

'Signed: RIPTON THOMPSON.'

Underneath this fictitious legal instrument was discreetly
appended:

'(Mem. Document not binding.)'

There was a pause: an awful under-breath of sanctified
wonderment and reproach passed round the office.   Sir
Austin assumed an attitude.   Mr. Thompson shed a glance
of severity on his confidential clerk, who parried by throwing up his hands.

Ripton, now fairly bewildered, stuffed another paper under
his father's nose, hoping the outside perhaps would satisfy
him: it was marked 'Legal Considerations.'   Mr. Thompson
had no idea of sparing or shielding his son.   In fact, like
many men whose self-love is wounded by their offspring, he
felt vindictive, and was ready to sacrifice him up to a certain
point, for the good of both.   He therefore opened the paper,
expecting something worse than what he had hitherto seen,
despite its formal heading, and he was not disappointed.

The 'Legal Considerations' related to the Case regarding
which Ripton had conceived it imperative upon him to address a letter to the Editor of the 'Jurist,' and was indeed a
great case, and an ancient; revived apparently for the special
purpose of displaying the forensic abilities of the Junior
Counsel for the Plaintiff, Mr. Ripton Thompson, whose
assistance the Attorney-General, in his opening statement,
congratulated himself on securing; a rather unusual thing,
due probably to the eminence and renown of that youthful
gentleman at the Bar of his country.   So much was seen
from the Copy of a Report purporting to be extracted from
a Newspaper, and prefixed to the Junior Counsel's Re-

marks, or Legal Considerations, on the Conduct of the Case, the admissibility and non-admissibility of certain Evidence, and the ultimate Decision of the Judges.

Mr. Thompson, Senior, lifted the paper high, with the spirit of one prepared to do execution on the criminal, and in the voice of a town-crier, varied by a bitter accentuation and satiric sing-song tone, deliberately read:

'VULCAN v. MARS.

'The Attorney-General, assisted by Mr. Ripton Thompson, appeared on behalf of the Plaintiff. Mr. Serjeant Cupid, Q.C., and Mr. Capital Opportunity, for the Defendant.'

"Oh!" snapped Mr. Thompson, Senior, peering venom at the unfortunate Ripton over his spectacles, "your Notes are on that issue, Sir! Thus you employ your time, Sir!"

With another side-shot at the Confidential Clerk, who retired immediately behind a strong entrenchment of shrugs, Mr. Thompson continued to read:

'This Case is too well known to require more than a partial summary of particulars . . .'

"Ahem! we will skip the particulars, however partial," said Mr. Thompson. "Ah?—what do you mean here, Sir, by the 'chief of the Olympic games,' which you eulogize?"

"Not I," answered Ripton, from under his head. "It's Mr. Cap— Mr. Opp— It's the Defendant's Counsel. I'm against."

Outraged by hearing the culprit speak at all, his father broke in, "How dare you talk so unblushingly, Sir!"

Ripton dropped his head a degree lower.

"Enough!" cried Mr. Thompson, appealing mutely to all present, and elongating his syllables with a vehement sneer; "I think we may be excused your Legal Considerations on

such a Case. This is how you employ your Law-studies,
Sir! You put them to this purpose! Mr. Beazley! you
will henceforward sit alone. I must have this young man
under my own eye. Sir Austin! permit me to apologize to
you for subjecting you to a scene so disagreeable. It was a
father's duty not to spare him!"

Mr. Thompson wiped his forehead, as Brutus might have
done after passing judgment on the scion of his house.

"These papers," he went on, fluttering Ripton's precious
lucubrations in a wavering judicial hand, "I shall retain.
The day will come when he will remark them with shame.
And it shall be his penance, his punishment, to do so! Stop!"
he cried, as Ripton was noiselessly shutting his desk, "have
you more of them, Sir! of a similar description? Rout them
out. Let us know you at your worst. What have you there
—in that corner?"

Ripton was understood to say, he devoted that corner to
old briefs on important cases.

Mr. Thompson thrust his trembling fingers among the
old briefs, and turned over the volume Sir Austin had observed, but without much remarking it, for his suspicions
had not risen to print.

"A Manual of Heraldry?" the Baronet politely inquired,
before it could well escape.

"I like it very much," says Ripton, clutching the book in
dreadful torment.

"Allow me to see that you have our Arms and Crest correct." The Baronet proffered a hand for the book.

"A Griffin between two Wheatsheaves," cries Ripton, still
clutching it nervously.

Mr. Thompson, without any notion of what he was doing,
drew the book from Ripton's hold; whereupon the two
Seniors laid their grey heads together over the title-page. It
set forth in attractive characters beside a coloured frontispiece, which embodied the promise displayed there, the en-
trancing Adventures of Miss Random, a strange young lady.

Had there been a Black Hole within the area of those Law regions to consign Ripton to there and then, or an Iron Rod handy to mortify his sinful flesh, Mr. Thompson would have used them. As it was, he contented himself by looking Black Holes and Iron Rods at the detected youth, who sat on his perch insensible to what might happen next, collapsed.

Mr. Thompson cast the wicked creature down with a "Pah!" He, however, took her up again, and strode away with her. Sir Austin gave Ripton a forefinger, and kindly touched his head, saying, "Good-bye, boy! at some future date Richard will be happy to see you at Raynham."

Undoubtedly this was a great triumph to the System!

CHAPTER XX

GOOD WINE AND GOOD BLOOD

THE conversation between Solicitor and Client was resumed.

"Is it possible," quoth Mr. Thompson, the moment he had ushered his client into his private room, "that you will consent, Sir Austin, to see him, and receive him, again?"

"Certainly!" the Baronet replied. "Why not? This by no means astonishes me. When there is no longer danger of contamination to my son, he will be welcome as he was before. He is a schoolboy. I knew it—I expected it. The results of your principle, Thompson!"

"One of the very worst books of that abominable class!" exclaimed the old lawyer, opening at the coloured frontispiece, from which brazen Miss Random smiled bewitchingly out, as if she had no doubt of captivating Time and all his veterans on a fair field. "Pah!" he shut her to with the energy he would have given to the office of publicly slapping her face; "from this day I diet him on bread and water—rescind his pocket-money!—How he could have got hold of

such a book! How he—! And what ideas! Concealing
them from me as he has done so cunningly. He trifles with
Vice! His mind is in a putrid state! I might have believed
—I did believe—I might have gone on believing my son
Ripton to be a moral young man!" The old lawyer interjected on the delusions of fathers, and sat down in a lamentable abstraction.

"The lad has come out!" said Sir Austin. "His adoption
of the legal form is amusing. He trifles with Vice, true:
people newly initiated are as hardy as its intimates, and a
young sinner's amusements will resemble those of a confirmed debauchee. The satiated, and the insatiate, appetite
alike appeal to extremes. You are astonished at this revelation of your son's condition. I expected it—though assuredly—believe me—not this sudden and indisputable proof
of it. But I knew that the seed was in him, and therefore
I have not latterly invited him to Raynham. School, and
the corruption there, will bear its fruits, sooner or later. I
could advise you, Thompson, what to do with him: it would
be my plan—"

Mr. Thompson murmured, like a true courtier, that he
should esteem it an honour to be favoured with Sir Austin
Feverel's advice: secretly resolute, like a true Briton, to
follow his own.

"Let him, then," continued the Baronet, "see Vice in its
nakedness. While he has yet some innocence, nauseate him!
Vice, taken little by little, usurps gradually the whole
creature. He has sisters?—"

"Four," said the old lawyer, with melancholy voice. "But
would you, Sir Austin, really advise?—"

"My counsel to you, Thompson, would be, to drag him
through the sinks of Town! Then, when he is sickened,
let his sisters do the rest—the recovering work."

"Good girls! good girls!" muttered the old lawyer. "Boys
will be boys, I suppose!"

"A palliation, remember, which is frequently an incentive."

Mr. Thompson began to wink again.

"Oh, I shall punish him, Sir Austin! Do not fear me, Sir. I have no tenderness for Vice."

"That is not what is wanted, Thompson. You mistake me. He should be dealt with gently. Heavens! do you hope to make him hate Vice, by making him a martyr for its sake? Totally wrong, Thompson! You must descend from the pedestal of Age to become his Mentor: cause him to see how certainly and pitilessly Vice itself punishes: accompany him into its haunts——"

"Over Town?" broke forth Mr. Thompson.

"Over Town," said the Baronet.

"But, my dear Sir Austin," the old lawyer interposed, "what would Mrs. Thompson say? at me?——"

"Mrs. Thompson!" the Baronet ejaculated very scornfully. "I really doubt!" Mr. Thompson saw that he had slipped in citing the possible disapproval of his spouse, and diverted drearily to the figure he would cut in the haunts of Vice.

Sir Austin said he should not hesitate.

Mr. Thompson declared that whoso could do it, he honoured. In his heart, he thought it the most ridiculous idea in the world.

"And depend upon it," added the Baronet, "that until fathers act thoroughly up to their duty, we shall see the sights we see in great cities, and hear the tales we hear in little villages, with death and calamity in our homes, and a legacy of sorrow and shame to the generations to come. I do aver," he exclaimed, becoming excited, "that, if it were not for the duty to my son, and the hope I cherish in him, I, seeing the accumulation of misery we are handing down to an innocent posterity—to whom, through our sin, the fresh breath of life will be foul—I—yes! I would hide my name! For whither are we tending? What home is pure absolutely? What cannot our Doctors and Lawyers tell us?"

Mr. Thompson acquiesced significantly.

"And what is to come of this?" Sir Austin continued "When the sins of the fathers are multiplied by the sons, is not Perdition the final sum of things? And is not Life, the boon of Heaven, growing to be the Devil's game utterly? But for my son, I would hide my name. I would not bequeath it to be cursed by them that walk above my grave!"

This was indeed a terrible view of existence. Mr. Thompson felt uneasy. There was a dignity in his Client, an impressiveness in his speech, that silenced remonstrating Reason and the cry of long years of comfortable respectability, Mr. Thompson went to Church regularly; paid his rates and dues without overmuch, or at least more than common, grumbling. On the surface he was a good citizen, fond of his children, faithful to his wife, devoutly marching to a fair seat in Heaven on a path paved by something better than a thousand a year. But here was a man sighting him from below the surface, and though it was an unfair, unaccustomed, not to say un-English, method of regarding one's fellow-man, Mr. Thompson was troubled by it. What though his Client exaggerated? Facts were at the bottom of what he said. And he was acute—he had unmasked Ripton! Since Ripton's exposure he winced at a personal application in the text his Client preached from. Possibly this was the secret source of part of his anger against that peccant youth.

Mr. Thompson shook his head, and with dolefully puckered visage, and a pitiable contraction of his shoulders, rose slowly up from his chair. Apparently he was about to speak, but he straightway turned and went meditatively to a side-recess in the room, whereof he opened a door, drew forth a tray, and a decanter labelled PORT, filled a glass for his Client, deferentially invited him to partake of it; filled another glass for himself, and drank.

That was his reply.

Sir Austin never took wine before dinner. Thompson had looked as if he meant to speak: he waited for Thompson's words.

Mr. Thompson saw that, as his Client did not join him in his glass, the eloquence of that Porty reply was lost on his Client.

Having slowly ingurgitated, and meditated upon, this precious draught and turned its flavour over and over with an aspect of potent Judicial Wisdom (one might have thought that he was weighing mankind in the balance), the old lawyer heaved, and said, sharpening his lips over the admirable vintage, "The world is in a very sad state, I fear, Sir Austin!"

His Client gazed at him queerly.

"But that," Mr. Thompson added immediately, ill-concealing by his gaze the glowing intestinal congratulations going on within him, "that is, I think you would say, Sir Austin—if I could but prevail upon you—a tolerably good character wine!"

"There's Virtue somewhere, I see, Thompson!" Sir Austin murmured, without disturbing his legal adviser's dimples.

The old lawyer sat down to finish his glass, saying, that such a wine was not to be had everywhere.

They were then outwardly silent for a space. Inwardly one of them was full of riot and jubilant uproar: as if the solemn fields of Law were suddenly to be invaded and possessed by troops of Bacchanals: and to preserve a decently wretched physiognomy over it, and keep on terms with his companion, he had to grimace like a melancholy clown in a pantomime.

Mr. Thompson brushed back his hair. The Baronet was still expectant. Mr. Thompson sighed deeply, and emptied his glass. He combated the change that had come over him. He tried not to see Ruby. He tried to feel miserable, and

it was not in him. He spoke, drawing what appropriate
inspirations he could from his Client's countenance, to show
that they had views in common: "Degenerating sadly, I
fear!"

The Baronet nodded.

"According to what my wine-merchants say," continued
Mr. Thompson, "there can be no doubt about it."

The Baronet stared.

"It's the grape, or the ground, or something," Mr. Thompson went on. "All I can say is, our youngsters will have a
bad look-out! In my opinion Government should be compelled to send out a Commission to inquire into the cause.
To Englishmen it would be a Public Calamity. It surprises
me—I hear men sit and talk despondently of this extraordinary disease of the Vine, and not one of them seems to think
it incumbent on him to act, and do his best to stop it." He
fronted his Client like a man who accuses an enormous
public delinquency. "Nobody makes a stir! The apathy of
Englishmen will become proverbial. Pray try it, Sir Austin!
Pray allow me. Such a wine cannot disagree at any hour.
Do! I am allowanced two glasses three hours before dinner.
Stomachic. I find it agree with me surprisingly. Quite a
new man. I suppose it will last our time. It must! What
should we do? There's no Law possible without it. Not
a Lawyer of us could live. Ours is an occupation which
dries the blood. We require—Ahem! have I taken my
second glass?"

Mr. Thompson meditated; conceived that he had, and
again that he had not. The same luxury of indecision occurred daily, and daily another glass solved the difficulty.

"Too much is decidedly bad," he continued, looking firmly
convinced. "But just the quantum makes men of us."

Launched on the theme, he determined to overbear his
Client vinously.

"Now that very wine, Sir Austin—I think I do not err
in saying, that very wine your respected father, Sir Pylcher

Feverel, used to taste whenever he came to consult my
father, when I was a boy. And I remember one day being
called in, and Sir Pylcher himself poured me out a glass.
I wish I could call in Ripton now, and do the same. No!
Leniency in such a case as that!—The wine would not hurt
him—I doubt if there be much left for him to welcome his
guests with. Ha! ha! Now if I could persuade you, Sir
Austin, as you do not take wine before dinner, some day to
favour me with your company at my little country cottage—
I have a wine there—the fellow to that—I think you would,
I do think you would"—Mr. Thompson meant to say, he
thought his Client would arrive at something of a similar
jocund contemplation of his fellows in their degeneracy that
inspirited lawyers after potation, but condensed the sensual
promise into, "highly approve."

Sir Austin speculated on his legal adviser with a sour
mouth comically compressed.

It stood clear to him that Thompson before his Port,
and Thompson after, were two different men. To indoc-
trinate him now was too late: it was perhaps the time to
make the positive use of him he wanted.

Drawing forth the Note-Book, and pencilling roughly:
'Two prongs of a fork: the World stuck between them: Port,
and the Palate: 'Tis one which fails first—Down goes
World:' and again the hieroglyph—'Port-spectacles:' he said:
"I shall gladly accompany you this evening, Thompson,"—
words that transfigured the delighted lawyer—and restored
the skeleton of a great Aphorism to his pocket, there to
gather flesh and form, with numberless others in a like
condition.

"I came to visit my lawyer," he said to himself. "I think
I have been dealing with The World in epitome!"

CHAPTER XXI

THE SYSTEM ENCOUNTERS THE WILD OATS SPECIAL PLEA

THE Rumour circulated that Sir Austin Feverel, the Recluse of Raynham, the rank misogynist, the rich Baronet, was in Town, looking out a Bride for his only son and uncorrupted heir. Doctor Benjamin Bairam was the excellent authority. Doctor Benjamin Bairam had safely delivered Mrs. Deborah Gossip of this interesting bantling, which was forthwith dandled in dozens of feminine laps. Doctor Benjamin Bairam could boast the first interview with the famous Recluse: he had it from his own lips that the object of the Baronet was, to look out a Bride for his only son and uncorrupted heir: "and," added the Doctor, "she'll be lucky who gets him." Which was interpreted to mean, that he would be a catch; the Doctor probably intending to allude to certain extraordinary difficulties in the way of a choice.

A demand was made on the publisher of THE PILGRIM'S SCRIP, for all his outstanding copies. Conventionalities were defied. A summer-shower of cards fell on the Baronet's table. The old feminine enthusiasm for his productions revived. He was threatened with the formation of a new Court at his hotel. Miss Joy Blewins, now an Authoress of greater celebrity than her sister, and even more the man than formerly, came to him repentant of her attacks on his private history (which she called her exhibition of their common difference of view regarding Woman, whose champion she was acknowledged to be), trusting to convert him to support her. The swift Camilla, transformed by tricksy Time into the fat wife of a wheezy Squire, paid him a flying visit during the wretched two weeks she was annually allowed in Town, to call his attention to a tiny paragon daughter she possessed, with none of its father's complaints and all her youthful energies. Mrs. M'Murphy also, after writing innumerable novels of which he was the villain and

she the heroine, tried to get admittance to him, but the
Baronet shudderingly gave orders to be denied to her, and
the rest of them. As in other interesting cases, no Irish were
tolerated.

He had few male friends. He shunned the Clubs as nests
of scandal. The cards he contemplated were mostly of that
sex, with the husband, if there was a husband, evidently
dragged in for Propriety's sake. He read their cards, and
smiled. He knew their purpose. What terrible light
Thompson and Bairam had thrown on some of them!
Heavens! in what a state was the blood of this Empire.

Before commencing his campaign, he called on two ancient
intimates, Lord Heddon, and his distant cousin Darley Absworthy, both Members of Parliament, useful men, though
gouty, who had sown in their time a fine crop of Wild Oats,
and advocated the advantage of doing so, seeing that they
did not fancy themselves the worse for it. He found one
with an imbecile son, and the other with consumptive
daughters. "So much," he wrote in the Note-book, "for the
Wild Oats theory!"

Darley was proud of his daughters' white and pink skins.
"Beautiful complexions," he called them. The eldest was
in the market, immensely admired. Sir Austin was introduced to her. She talked fluently and sweetly. A youth not
on his guard, a simple schoolboy youth, or even a man, might
have fallen in love with her, she was so affable and fair.
There was something poetic about her. And she was quite
well, she said, the Baronet frequently questioning her on that
point. She intimated that she was robust; but towards the
close of their conversation, her hand would now and then
travel to her side, and she breathed painfully an instant,
saying, "Isn't it odd? Dora, Adela, and myself, we all feel
the same queer sensation—about the heart I think it is—
after talking much."

Sir Austin nodded, and blinked sadly; exclaiming to his
Soul, "Wild Oats! Wild Oats!"

He did not ask permission to see Dora and Adela.

Lord Heddon vehemently preached Wild Oats.

"It's all nonsense, Feverel," he said, "about bringing up a lad out of the common way. He's all the better for a little racketing when he's green—feels his bone and muscle—learns to know the world. He'll never be a man if he hasn't played at the old game one time in his life, and the earlier the better. I've always found the best fellows were wildish once. I don't care what he does when he's a green-horn:—besides he's got an excuse for it then. You can't expect to have a man, if he doesn't take a man's food. You'll have a milksop. And depend upon it, when he does break out, he'll go to the Devil, and nobody pities him. Look what those fellows, the grocers, do when they get hold of a young—what d'ye call 'em?—apprentice. They know the scoundrel was born with a sweet tooth. Well! they give him the run of the shop, and in a very short time he soberly deals out the goods, a devilish deal too wise to abstract a morsel even for the pleasure of stealing. I know you have contrary theories. You hold that the young grocer should have a soul above sugar. It won't do! Take my word for it, Feverel, it's a dangerous experiment, that of bringing up flesh and blood in harness. No colt will bear it, or he's a tame beast. And look you: take it on medical grounds. Early excesses the frame will recover from: late ones break the constitution. There's the case in a nutshell. How's your son?"

"Sound and well!" replied Sir Austin. "And yours?"

"Oh, Lipscombe's always the same!" Lord Heddon sighed peevishly. "He's quiet—that's one good thing; but there's no getting the Country to take him, so I must give up hopes of that."

Lord Lipscombe entering the room just then, Sir Austin surveyed him, and was not astonished at the refusal of the Country to take him.

"Wild Oats! Wild Oats!" again thinks the Baronet, as

he contemplates the headless, degenerate, weedy, issue and result.

Both Darley Absworthy and Lord Heddon spoke of the marriage of their offspring as a matter of course. "And if I were not a coward," Sir Austin confessed to himself, "I should stand forth and forbid the banns! This universal ignorance of the inevitable consequence of Sin is frightful! The Wild Oats plea is a torpedo that seems to have struck the world, and rendered it morally insensible." However, they silenced him. He was obliged to spare their feelings on a subject to him so deeply sacred. The healthful image of his noble boy rose before him, a triumphant living rejoinder to any hostile argument.

He was content to remark to his Doctor, that he thought the third generation of Wild Oats would be a pretty thin crop!

Families against whom neither Thompson, lawyer, nor Bairam, physician, could recollect a progenitorial blot, either on the male, or female, side, were not numerous. "Only," said the Doctor, "you really must not be too exacting in these days, my dear Sir Austin. It is impossible to contest your principle, and you are doing mankind incalculable service in calling its attention to this the gravest of its duties: but as the stream of civilization progresses, we must be a little taken in the lump, as it were. The world is, I can assure you—and I do not look only above the surface, you can believe—the world is awakening to the vital importance of the question."

"Doctor," replied Sir Austin, "if you had a pure-blood Arab barb, would you cross him with a hack?"

"Decidedly not," said the Doctor.

"Then permit me to say, I shall employ every care to match my son according to his merits," Sir Austin returned. "I trust the world is awakening, as you observe. I have been to my publisher, since my arrival in Town, with a Manuscript 'Proposal for a New System of Education of

our British Youth,' which may come in opportunely. I
think I am entitled to speak on that subject—eh?"

"Certainly," said the Doctor. "You will admit, Sir
Austin, that, compared with continental nations—our neighbours for instance—we shine to advantage, in morals, as
in everything else. I hope you admit that?"

"I find no consolation in shining by comparison with a
lower standard," said the Baronet. "If I compare the enlightenment of your views—for you admit my principle—
with the obstinate incredulity of a country Doctor's, who
sees nothing of the world, you are hardly flattered, I presume?"

Doctor Bairam would hardly be flattered at such a comparison, assuredly, he interjected.

"Besides," added the Baronet, "the French make no pretences, and thereby escape one of the main penalties of
hypocrisy. Whereas we!—but I am not their advocate,
credit me. It is better, perhaps, to pay our homage to
Virtue. At least it delays the spread of entire corruptness."

Doctor Bairam wished the Baronet success, and diligently
endeavoured to assist his search for a mate worthy of the
pure-blood barb, by putting several Mamas, whom he visited,
on the alert.

CHAPTER XXII

A SHADOWY VIEW OF CŒLEBS PATER GOING ABOUT
WITH A GLASS-SLIPPER

ONE of these Mamas favoured by Doctor Benjamin
Bairam, was Mrs. Caroline Grandison, said to be a legitimate descendant of the great Sir Charles: a lady who, in
propriety of demeanour and pious manners, was the petti-
coated image of her admirable ancestor. The clean-linen of
her morality was spotless as his. As nearly she neighboured

Perfection, and knew it as well. Let us hope that her History will some day be written, and the balance restored in Literature which it was her pride to have established for her sex in Life.

Mrs. Caroline was a colourless lady of an unequivocal character, living upon drugs, and governing her husband and the world from her sofa. Woolly Negroes blest her name, and whiskered John-Thomases deplored her weight. The world was given to understand that Sorrows and Disappointments had reduced her to the contemplative posture which helped her to consider the urgent claims of her black fellow-creatures, and require the stalwart services of her white. In her presence the elect had to feel how very much virtue is its own reward; for if they did not rightly esteem the honour she did them, they had little further encouragement from Mrs. Caroline Grandison. On the other hand her rigour towards vice was unsparing; especially in the person of one of her own sex, whom she treated as Heaven treats fallen Angels. A sinful man—why Mrs. Caroline expected nothing better: but a sinful woman—Oh! that was a scandal, a shame! And you met no sinful woman at Mrs. Caroline Grandison's parties. As a consequence, possibly, though one hardly dares suppose it, her parties were the dullest in London, and gradually fell into the hands of popular preachers, Specific Doctors, raw Missionaries with their passage paid for, and a chance Dean or so; a non-dancing, stout-dining congregation, in the midst of which a gay young guardsman was dismally out of his element, and certainly would not have obtruded his unsodden spirit, had there been no fair daughters.

The completeness of the lady's reputation was rounded by the whispers of envious tongues; which, admitting the inviolability of her character, remarked that indeed she was a little too careful to appear different from others, and took an ascetic delight in the contrast. There is no doubt that she took a great deal of medicine. Dr. Bairam may have contributed towards her asceticism somewhat. The worthy Doctor may even, perhaps, have contributed a trifle towards her perfection.

In her sweet youth this lady fell violently in love with the great Sir Charles, and married him in fancy. The time coming when maiden fancy must give way to woman fact, she compromised her reverent passion for the hero by declaring that she could never change the name he had honoured her with, and must, if she espoused any mortal, give her widowed hand to a Grandison. Accordingly two cousins were proposed to her; but the moral reputation of these Grandisons was so dreadful, and such a disgrace to the noble name they bore, that she rejected them with horror. Woman's Mission, however, being her perpetual precept, she felt, at the age of twenty-three, bound to put it in practice, and as she was handsome, and most handsomely-endowed, a quite unobjectionable gentleman was discovered who, for the honour of assisting her in her Mission, agreed to disembody himself in her great name, and be lost in the blaze of Sir Charles. With his concurrence, she rapidly produced eight daughters. A son was denied to them. This was the second generation of Grandisons denied a son. Her husband, the quite unobjectionable gentleman, lost heart after the arrival of the eighth, and surrendered his mind to more frivolous pursuits. She also appeared to lose heart. It was her saintly dream to have a Charles. So assured she was that he was coming at last, that she prepared male baby-linen with her own hands for the disappointing eighth. When, in that moment of creative suspense, Dr. Bairam's soft voice, with sacred melancholy, pronounced, "A Daughter, Madam!" Mrs. Caroline Grandison covered her face, and wept. She afterwards did penance for her want of resignation, and relapsed upon Religion and little dogs.

Mrs. Caroline Grandison appeared to lose heart. But people said, she was not really solaced by Religion and little dogs. People said, that her repeated consultations with Dr.

Bairam had one end in view, and that all those quantities
of medicine were consumed for a devout purpose. Eight is
not a number to stop at. Nine if you like, but not eight.
No one thinks of stopping at eight. People said, that the
pertinacity of her spirit weakened her mind, and that she
consulted cards and fortune-tellers, and cast horoscopes, to
discover if there would be a ninth, and that ninth a Charles.
They might truly have said, that the potency of Dr. Bairam's
prescriptions weakened the constitution. Mrs. Caroline
Grandison grew fretful, and reclined on an invalid couch,
while her name hunted foxes. Time flew: the faint-hearted
Unobjectionable refused to participate in Dr. Bairam's prescriptions: there was a close to all concert between them:
instead of a Charles, barebacked poodles and pendent fox-
tails reigned in the House of Grandison.

The disappointing Eighth was on the verge of her teens
when Sir Austin visited Town. None of Mrs. Caroline
Grandison's daughters had married: owing, it was rumoured,
to the degeneracy of the males of our day. The elder ones
had, in their ignorance, wished to marry young gentlemen of
their choosing. Mrs. Caroline Grandison bade them wait till
she could find for them something like Sir Charles; she was
aware that such a man would hardly be found alive again.
If they rebelled, as model young ladies occasionally will, Mrs.
Caroline Grandison declared that they were ill, and called
in Dr. Bairam to prescribe, who soon reduced them. Physic
is an immense ally in bringing about filial obedience.

No lady living was better fitted to appreciate Sir Austin,
and understand his System, than Mrs. Caroline Grandison.
When she heard of it from Dr. Bairam, she rose from her
couch, and called for her carriage, determined to follow him
up and come to terms with him. All that was told her of
the Baronet conspired to make her believe that he was Sir
Charles in person fallen upon evil times: the spirit of Sir
Charles revived to mix his blood with hers and produce a
race of moral Paladins after Sir Charles's pattern. She

reviewed her daughters. Any one of the three younger ones would be a suitable match, and if he wanted perfectly-educated young women, where else could he look for them? But he was difficult to hunt down. He went abroad shyly. He was never to be met in general Society. The rumour of him was everywhere, and an extremely unfavourable rumour it was, from mothers who had daughters, and hopes for their daughters, which a few questions of his had kindled, and a discovery of his severe requisitions extinguished. It appeared that he had seen numerous young ladies. He had politely asked them to sit down and take off their shoes; but such monstrous feet they had mostly, that he declined the attempt to try on the Glass Slipper, and politely departed; or tried it on, and with a resigned sad look declared that it would not, would not fit!

"And I assure you, my dear," said Mrs. Rectangle, one of these outraged mothers, to Mrs. Caroline Grandison, "he does not scruple to ask the most abominable things of you, where this son of his is concerned. He made me quite blush, and but for his manner, which, I admit, is dignified, I should have been indignant. He asked absolutely—" and she sank her voice. "I really now believe everything Miss Joy and Mrs. M'Murphy say of him. What does the man want?"

"What none of you can give him," was Mrs. Caroline Grandison's mental ejaculation.

Some of the young ladies had been to schools. Their feet were all enormously too big, and there was no need for them to take off their shoes. Some had been properly educated at home; and to such, if Bairam, physician, and Thompson, lawyer, did not protest, the Slipper was applied; but by occult arts of its own it seemed to find out that their habits were somehow bad, and incapacitated them from espousing the Fairy Prince. The Slipper would not fit at all.

Unsuspecting damsels were asked, at what time they rose in the morning; and would reply, at any hour. Some said, they finished in the morning the Romance they had relin-

quished to sleep overnight; little considering how such a
practice made the feet swell. Selina Rectangle thought it
a fine thing to tell him, she took Metastasio to bed with her
and pencilled translations of him when she awoke.

There was a damsel closer home, who did not take Metastasio to bed with her, and who ate dewberries early in the
morning, whose foot, had Sir Austin but known it, would
have fitted into the intractable Slipper as easily and neatly
as if it had been a soft kid glove made to her measure.
Alas! the envious Sisters were keeping poor Cinderella out
of sight. Dewberries still abounded by the banks of the
river; and thither she strolled, and there daily she was met
by one who had the test of her merits in his bosom; and
there, on the night the Scientific humanist conceived he had
alighted on the identical house which held the foot to fit
the Slipper, there, under consulting stars, holy for ever more
henceforth, the Fairy Prince, trembling and with tears, has
taken from her lips the first ripe fruit of Love, and pledged
himself hers.

A night of happy augury to Father and Son. They were
looking out for the same thing; only one employed Science,
the other Instinct; and which hit upon the right it was for
Time to decide. Sir Austin dined with Mrs. Caroline
Grandison. They had been introduced by Sir Miles Papworth.

"What!" said Sir Miles, when Mrs. Caroline expressed
her wish for an introduction, "you want to know Feverel?
Aha! Why, you are the very woman for him, Ma'am. It's
one of the strong-minded he's after. So you shall. So you
shall. I'll give a dinner tomorrow. And let me tell you
in confidence, that the value of his mines is increasing,
Ma'am. You needn't be afraid about his crotchets. Feverel
has his eye on the main chance as well as the rest of us."

"You do not believe, Sir Miles, that one may esteem him

for his principles, and sympathize with his object?" said Mrs. Caroline.

"Well, Ma'am," Sir Miles returned, "I'm a plain man. I said to my wife the other day—she was talking something in that way—and I said to her, If Feverel had five hundred, instead of fifty thousand, a-year—he's got that clear, Ma'am, and it'll double—how about his principles then? Aha! A rich man can play the fool if he likes, and you women clap your hands, and cheer him. Now if I were to have a System for all my rascals, you'd call me something like what I should be—eh? You would, though! And I wish I had sometimes, for they're every one of 'em in scrapes, and I've got to pay the piper. But that's part of their education, to my mind, so down goes the money."

"Have you seen much of his son?" Mrs. Caroline inquired, restraining an appearance of particular interest.

"Not much, Ma'am; not much. Aha! I expect it's the mothers'll be asking about *his* son, and the daughters about mine—eh?" Sir Miles indulged in a stout laugh.

"He's a fine lad. I'll say that for him, Ma'am. He'll go a long way when he's once loose, that lad will. I came to hear the other day that I was pretty near transporting him once, the young villain!"

Sir Miles told Mrs. Caroline certain facts that had gradually become public intelligence about his neighbourhood concerning the Bakewell Comedy.

Mrs. Caroline threw her hands aloft.

"Have I frightened you a bit, Ma'am?" said twinkling Sir Miles; but the perverse woman, with the downfall of her hands, checked his exultation by exclaiming: "Is it not a proof of his father's wisdom to watch him so rigorously!"

Next day, at Sir Miles Papworth's hastily-ordered dinner, Mrs. Caroline Grandison, who had summoned her great dormant energies successfully to stand upon her feet, was handed down by Sir Austin. They sat together, and talked together. Those who were near and could catch scraps of their conversation, said, that they were engaged in mutually dissecting the frame of man: which perhaps was the origin of Mrs. Caroline's fame as a proficient in Anatomy, and of the honourable mention made of her in Miss Joy Blewins' pamphlet 'On the Educational Claims of Woman,' wherein Mrs. Caroline Grandison was cited as a woman, pure, delicate, beautiful, a pattern Wife and Mother, who had superintended many cuttings-up, and knew Man from top to toe, as was the undoubted right, Miss Joy vehemently urged, of every Woman upon earth.

At all events, Sir Austin and Mrs. Caroline discovered that they had in common from an early period looked on life as a Science: and having arrived at this joint understanding, they, with the indifference of practised dissectors, laid out the world and applied the knife to the people they knew. In other words, they talked most frightful scandal. It is proverbial what a cold Torturer Science can be. Malice is nothing to it. They reviewed their friends. Pure blood was nowhere. Sir Austin hinted his observations since his arrival in town, and used a remark or two from Bairam and Thompson. Mrs. Caroline cleverly guessed the families, and still further opened his eyes. Together they quashed the Wild-Oats special plea. Mrs. Caroline gave him a clearer idea of his system than he had ever had before. She ran ahead of his thoughts like nimble fire. She appeared to have forethought them all, and taken a leap beyond. When he plodded and hesitated on his conception, she, at a word, struck boldly into black and white, making him fidget for his Note-Book to reverse a sentence or two on Woman. And she quoted THE PILGRIM'S SCRIP.

"How true are some of the things you say, Sir Austin! And how false, permit me to add, are others!" she deprecatingly remarked. "That for instance on Domestic Differences. How could you be so cynical as to say, that '*In a dissension between man and wife, that one is in the right who has most friends.*' It really angered me. Cannot one be absolutely superior—notoriously the injured one?" (Mrs. Caroline was citing her own case against the faint-hearted fox-hunting Unobjectionable.) "But you amply revenge it. You say: *'Great Hopes have lean offspring.'* How true that is! How I know it myself! How true every disappointed woman must know it to be! And what you say of the Instincts and the Mind—something—that our Instincts seek Stability here below, and are always casting anchor—something—without the Captain's consent—and that it is at once the fruitful source of unhappiness and the proof of immortality—I'm making nonsense of it, but I appreciated the Wisdom fully."

In this way she played with him. The Theorist was dazzled, delighted. Lady Blandish was too like a submissive slave to the System. Mrs. Caroline wedded it on the equal standing of an English wife, who gives her half, and more, to the union.

Her name appeared on his card-table the day after the dinner. Six of her eight daughters and a sprinkling of her little dogs, were ready for his visit by the afternoon, or fashionable morning. Charlotte and Harriet were absent. Clementina was the elder in attendance, and the rest presented fairly decreasing heights down to the disappointing last, Carola, called as near Charles as was permissible, a rigid ruddy young woman out of the Nursery.

"We receive you into the family," the fond mother leaned on her elbows maternally smiling, to welcome her visitor. "I wished my daughters to share with me the pleasure of your acquaintance."

"And knew well, Madam, how to gratify me most." Sir Austin bowed to the ceremony of introduction, and took a hand of each, retaining Carola's.

"This is your youngest, Madam?"

"Yes!" Mrs. Caroline suppressed a sigh.

"And how old are you, my dear?"

Carola twisted, and tried to read the frill of her trousers. She was dressed very young.

"My child!" her mother admonished her; whereat Carola screwed out a growl: "Thirteen."

"Thirteen this day," said her mother.

"Allow me to congratulate you, my dear." Sir Austin bent forward, and put his lips to her forehead.

Carola received the salute with the stolidity of a naughty doll.

"She is not well today," said Mrs. Caroline. "She is usually full of life and gaiety; almost too much of an animal, I sometimes think."

"At her age she can scarcely be that," observed Sir Austin.

"She's the maddest creature I ever knew," Mrs. Caroline immediately went upon his tack with unction. "Today she is shy. She is not herself. Possibly something has disagreed with her."

"That nasty medicine, it is, Mama," mumbled wilful Carola, swinging her frock.

Sir Austin turned to Mrs. Caroline, and inquired anxiously if the child took much medicine.

"The smallest occasional doses," Mrs. Caroline remarked, to an accompaniment of interjectory eyebrows and chins from all her younger daughters, and a reserved demure aspect of the elder ones.

"I do not like much medicine for children," said the Baronet, a little snappishly.

"Only the smallest occasional doses?" Mrs. Caroline repeated, making her voice small, and the doses sound sweet.

"My son has had little, or nothing," said the Baronet.

The young ladies looked on the father of that son with interest.

"Will you come and see our gymnasium?" Mrs. Caroline asked quickly.

"It is," she added, rising with heroic effort, "not to be compared to our country one. But it is of excellent use, and all my girls exercise in it, when in Town, once a day, without intermission. My principle is, that girls require a development of their frames as well as boys; and the more muscle they have, the better women they make. I used it constantly till disappointment and sorrow broke the habit."

"On my honour, Madam," said the enraptured Baronet, "you are the only sensible woman I have met," and he offered his arm to conduct the strenuous invalid.

Daughters and little dogs trooped to the Gymnasium, which was fitted up in the court below, and contained swing-poles, and stride-poles, and newly invented instruments for bringing out special virtues: an instrument for the lungs: an instrument for the liver: one for the arms and thighs: one for the wrists: the whole for the promotion of the Christian accomplishments.

Owing, probably, to the exhaustion consequent on their previous exercises of the morning, the young ladies, excepting Carola, looked fatigued, and pale, and anything but well-braced; and for the same reason, doubtless, when the younger ones were requested by their mother to exhibit the use of the several instruments, each of them wearily took hold of the depending strap of leather, and wearily pulled it, like mariners oaring in the deep sea; oaring to a haven they have no faith in.

"I sometimes hear them," said their Mama, "while I am reclining above, singing in chorus. 'Row, brothers, row,' is one of their songs. It sounds pretty and cheerful."

The Baronet was too much wrapped up in the enlightenment of her principle, to notice the despondency of their countenances.

"We have a Professor of Gymnastics, who comes twice a week to superintend," said Mrs. Caroline, breathing fresh fumes to the pleased reverie of her guest.

"How old did you say your daughter is, Madam?" the Baronet abruptly interrogated her.

"Which?—Oh!" she followed his eye and saw it resting

on ruddy Carola, "thirteen. She this day completes her thirteenth year. That will do, dears; much of it is not good after your dinners."

The Baronet placidly nodded approval of all her directions, and bestowed a second paternal kiss upon Carola.

"They talk of the Future Man, Madam," he said. "I seem to be in the house of the Future Woman."

"Happy you that have a son!" exclaimed Mrs. Caroline, and, returning to the Drawing-room, they exchanged Systems anew, as a preparatory Betrothal of the Objects of the Systems.

CHAPTER XXIII

A DIVERSION PLAYED ON A PENNY-WHISTLE

AWAY with Systems! Away with a corrupt World! Let us breathe the air of the Enchanted Island!

Golden lie the meadows: golden run the streams: red gold is on the pine-stems. The Sun is coming down to Earth, and walks the fields and the waters.

The Sun is coming down to Earth, and the fields and the waters shout to him golden shouts. He comes, and his heralds run before him, and touch the leaves of oaks, and planes, and beeches, lucid green, and the pine-stems redder gold; leaving brightest foot-prints upon thickly weeded banks, where the foxglove's last upper-bells incline, and bramble-shoots wander amid moist rich herbage. The plumes of the woodland are alight; and beyond them, over the open, 'tis a race with the long-thrown shadows; a race across the heaths and up the hills, till, at the farthest bourne of mounted eastern cloud, the heralds of the sun lay rosy fingers, and rest.

Sweet are the shy recesses of the woodland. The ray treads softly there. A film athwart the pathway quivers many-hued against purple shade fragrant with warm pines, deep moss-beds, feathery ferns. The little brown squirrel drops tail, and leaps: the inmost bird is startled to a chance tuneless note. From silence into silence things move.

Peeps of the revelling splendour above, and around, enliven the conscious full heart within. The flaming West, the crimson heights, shower their glories through voluminous leafage. But these are bowers where deep bliss dwells, imperial joy, that owes no fealty to yonder glories in which the young lamb gambols, and the spirits of men are glad. Descend, Great Radiance! embrace Creation with beneficent fire, and pass from us! You, and the vice-regal Light that succeeds to you, and all heavenly pageants, are the ministers and the slaves of the throbbing Content within.

For this is the home of the Enchantment. Here, secluded from vexed shores, the Prince and Princess of the Island meet; here like darkling nightingales they sit, and into eyes, and ears, and hands, pour endless ever-fresh treasures of their souls.

Roll on, grinding wheels of the world: cries of ships going down in a calm; groans of a System which will not know its rightful hour of exultation; complain to the Universe. You are not heard here.

He calls her by her name, Lucy: and she, blushing at her great boldness, has called him by his, Richard. Those two names are the key-notes of the wonderful harmonies the Angels sing aloft.

"Lucy! my beloved!"

"O Richard!"

Key-notes of the harmonies Earth even now revolves to, shadowing slowly to its bright-eyed kindred.

Out in the world there, on the skirts of the woodland, a sheep-boy pipes to meditative Eve on a penny-whistle.

Love's musical Instrument is as old, and as poor; it has but two stops; and yet, you see, the Cunning Musician does thus much with it!

Other speech they have little; light foam playing upon waves of feeling, and of feeling compact, that bursts only when the sweeping volume is too wild, and is no more than their sigh of tenderness spoken.

Perhaps Love played his tune so well, because their natures had unblunted edges, and were keen for bliss, confiding in it as natural food. To gentlemen and ladies he fine-draws upon the viol, ravishingly; or blows into the mellow bassoon; or rouses the heroic ardours of the trumpet; or, it may be, commands the whole Orchestra for them. And they are pleased. He is still the Cunning Musician. They languish, and taste ecstasy: but it is, however sonorous, an earthly concert. For them the spheres move not to Two Notes. They have lost, or forfeited and never known, the first supersensual spring of the ripe senses into passion; when they carry the soul with them, and have the privileges of spirits to walk disembodied, boundlessly to feel. Or one has it, and the other is a dead body! Ambrosia let them eat, and drink the Nectar: here sit a couple to whom Love's simple Bread and Water is a finer feast.

Pipe, happy sheep-boy, Love! Irradiated Angels, unfold your wings and lift your voices!

They have outflown Philosophy. Their Instinct has shot beyond the ken of Science. Imperiously they know we were made for this Eden: and would you gainsay them who are outside the Gates, and argue from the Fall?

"And this divine Gift was in store for me!"

So runs the internal outcry of each, clasping each: their recurring refrain to the harmonies. How it illumined the years gone by, and suffused the living Future!

"You for me: I for you!"

"We are born for each other!"

They believe that the Angels have been busy about them from their cradles. The celestial hosts have worthily striven to bring them together. And, O Victory! O Wonder! after toil, and pain, and difficulties exceeding, the celestial hosts have succeeded!

"Here we two sit who are written above as one!"

Pipe, happy Love! pipe on to these dear Innocents!

The tide of colour has ebbed from the upper-sky. In the West the sea of sunken fire draws back; and the stars leap forth, and tremble, and retire before the advancing moon, who slips the silver train of cloud from her shoulders, and, with her foot upon the pine-tops, surveys Heaven.

"Lucy, did you never dream of meeting me?"

"O Richard! yes; for I remembered you."

"Lucy! and did you pray that we might meet?"

"I did!"

Young as when she looked upon the Lovers in Paradise, the Fair Immortal journeys onward. Fronting her, it is not Night but veiled Day. Full half the sky is flushed. Not Darkness; not Day; the Nuptials of the twain.

"My own! my own for ever! You are pledged to me? Whisper!"

He hears the delicious music.

"And you are mine?"

A soft beam travels to the fern-covert under the pine-wood where they sit, and for answer he has her eyes: turned to him an instant, timidly fluttering over the depths of his, and then downcast; for through her eyes her soul is naked to him.

"Lucy! my bride! my life!"

The night-jar spins his dark monotony on the branch of the pine. The soft beam travels round them, and listens to their hearts. Their lips are locked.

Pipe no more, Love, for a time! Pipe as you will you cannot express their first kiss; nothing of its sweetness, and of its sacredness nothing. St. Cecilia up aloft, before the silver organ-pipes of Paradise, pressing fingers upon all the notes of which Love is but one, from her you may hear it.

So Love is silent. Out in the world there, on the skirts

of the woodland, the self-satisfied sheep-boy delivers a last complacent squint down the length of his penny-whistle, and, with a flourish correspondingly wry-faced, he also marches into silence, hailed by supper. The woods are still. There is heard but the night-jar spinning on the pine-branch, circled by moonlight.

CHAPTER XXIV

CELEBRATES THE TIME-HONOURED TREATMENT OF A DRAGON BY THE HERO

ENCHANTED Islands have not yet rooted out their old brood of Dragons. Wherever there is Romance, these Monsters come by inimical attraction. Because the Heavens are certainly propitious to true lovers, the Beasts of the Abysses are banded to destroy them; stimulated by innumerable sad victories; and every love-tale is an Epic War of the Upper, and Lower, Powers. I wish Good Fairies were a little more active. They seem to be cajoled into security by the happiness of their favourites; whereas the Wicked are always alert, and circumspect. They let the little ones shut their eyes to fancy they are not seen, and then commence.

These appointments and meetings, involving a start from the dinner-table at the hour of contemplative digestion and prime Claret; the hour when the Wise Youth Adrian delighted to talk at his ease—to recline in dreamy consciousness that a work of good was going on inside him; these abstractions from his studies, excesses of gaiety, and glumness, heavings of the chest, and other odd signs, but mainly the disgusting behaviour of his pupil at the dinner-table, taught Adrian to understand, though the young gentleman was clever in excuses, that he had somehow learnt there was another half to the divided Apple of Creation, and had embarked upon the great voyage of discovery of the difference between the two halves. With his usual coolness Adrian debated whether he might be in the philosophic, or the practical, stage of the voyage. For himself, as a man and a philosopher, Adrian had no objection to it being either; and he had only to consider which was temporarily most threatening to the ridiculous System he had to support. Richard's absence annoyed him. The youth was vivacious, and his enthusiasm good fun; and besides, when he left table, Adrian had to sit alone with Hippias and the Eighteenth Century, from both of whom he had extracted all the amusement that could be got, and he saw his digestion menaced by the contagious society of two ruined stomachs, who bored him just when he loved himself most. Poor Hippias was now so reduced that he had profoundly to calculate whether a particular dish, or an extra-glass of wine would have a bitter effect on him and be felt through the remainder of his years. He was in the habit of uttering his calculations half aloud, wherein the prophetic doubts of experience, and the succulent insinuations of appetite, contended hotly. It was horrible to hear him, so let us pardon Adrian for tempting him to a decision in favour of the moment.

"Happy to take wine with you," Adrian would say, and Hippias would regard the decanter with a pained forehead, and put up the Doctor.

"Drink, nephew Hippy, and think of the Doctor tomorrow!" the Eighteenth Century cheerily ruffles her cap at him, and recommends her own practice.

"It's this literary work!" interjects Hippias, handling his glass of Remorse. "I don't know what else it can be. You have no idea how anxious I feel. I have frightful dreams. I'm perpetually anxious."

"No wonder," says Adrian, who enjoys the childish simplicity to which an absorbed study of his sensational existence has brought poor Hippias. "No wonder. Ten years of Fairy Mythology! Could any one hope to sleep in peace after that? As to your digestion, no one has a digestion who is in the Doctor's hands. They prescribe from dogmas, and don't count on the system. They have cut you down from two bottles to two glasses. It's absurd. You can't sleep, because your system is crying out for what it's accustomed to."

Hippias sips his Madeira with a niggardly confidence, but assures Adrian, that he really should not like to venture on a bottle now: it would be rank madness to venture on a bottle now, he thinks. Last night only, after partaking, under protest, of that rich French dish, or was it the duck?— Adrian advised him to throw the blame on that vulgar bird.—Say the duck, then. Last night, he was no sooner stretched in bed, than he seemed to be of an enormous size: all his limbs—his nose, his mouth, his toes—were elephantine! An elephant was a pigmy to him. And his hugeousness seemed to increase the instant he shut his eyes. He turned on this side; he turned on that. He lay on his back; he tried putting his face to the pillow; and he continued to swell. He wondered the room could hold him— he thought he must burst it—and absolutely lit a candle, and went to the looking-glass to see whether he was bearable.

By this time Adrian and Richard were laughing uncontrollably. He had, however, a genial auditor in the Eighteenth Century, who declared it to be a new disease, not known in her day, and deserving investigation. She was happy to compare sensations with him, but hers were not of the complex order, and a potion soon righted her. In fact, her system appeared to be a debatable ground for aliment and medicine, on which the battle was fought, and, when over, she was none the worse, as she joyfully told Hippias. Never looked ploughman on prince, or village belle on Court Beauty, with half the envy poor Nineteenth-Century Hippias expended in his gaze on the Eighteenth. He was too serious to note much the laughter of the young men.

"I fancy, Uncle, you have swallowed a Fairy," says Richard. "You know what malicious things they are. Is

there a case in the Mythology of anybody swallowing a
Fairy?"

Hippias grimly considered, and thought, there was not.

"Upon my honour," Adrian composes his features to remark, "I think Ricky has hit the right nail. You have not
only swallowed one, you have swallowed the whole Mythology! I'm not astonished you suffer so. I never could, I
confess, so they don't trouble me; but, if I had, I should
pour a bottle of the best on him every night. I should
indeed."

"Can my Uncle," Richard meditates, his eyes on Hippias's
weazened face, "ever have been, as my father says, happy,
and like other men? Was he ever in love?"

Alas, and alack a day! Yes! Love had once piped even
to Hippias in dewy shade. He was once an ardent youth,
the genius of the family, master of his functions. 'Which,
when one ceases to be,' says The Pilgrim's Scrip, 'one is no
longer man:' and appends that 'it is the tendency of very
fast people to grow organically *downward.*' Pity the sorrows of a poor dyspepsy! Like an Actinia, poor Hippias
had grown to be all stomach—though not so pretty to look at.

"You will drink a bottle and drown the Fairy on the
day Ricky's married," says Adrian, eyeing the traitor blush
he calls up on the ingenuous cheeks.

Hippias realizes distant consequences immediately, and
contracts his jaw to stipulate for it at night, then: not in
the morning at the breakfast. He is capable of nothing but
very weak tea and dry toast, or gruel, in the morning. He
adds that, how people can drink wine at that early hour,
amazes him. "I should," he exclaims energetically, "I
should be afraid to go to bed that night, if I did such a
thing!"

Adrian leans to Richard, and bids the blush-mantled youth
mind he does not swallow his Fairy, or he may have a similar unbewitching fear upon him on the awful occasion.

Richard cocks his ear. His hour has struck. His Heaven awaits him in the wood, and he is off.

This 'Tragedy of a Cooking-Apparatus,' as Adrian designated the malady of Hippias, was repeated regularly every evening. It was natural for any youth to escape as quick as he could from such a Table of Stomachs.

Adrian bore with his conduct considerately, until a letter from the Baronet, describing the house and maternal System of Mrs. Caroline Grandison, and the rough grain of hopefulness in her youngest daughter, spurred him to think of his duties, and see what was going on. He gave Richard half-an-hour's start, and then put on his hat to follow his own keen scent, leaving Hippias and the Eighteenth Century to piquet.

In the lane near Belthorpe he met a maid of the farm not unknown to him, one Molly Davenport by name, a buxom lass, who, on seeing him, invoked her Good Gracious, the generic Maid's Familiar, and was instructed by reminiscences vivid, if ancient, to giggle.

"Are you looking for your young gentleman?" Molly presently asked.

Adrian glanced about the lane like a cool brigand, to see if the coast was clear, and replied to her; "I am, Miss. I want you to tell me about him."

"Dear!" said the buxom lass, "was you coming for me tonight?"

Adrian rebuked her: for her bad grammar, apparently.

" 'Cause I can't stop out long tonight," Molly explained, taking the rebuke to refer altogether to her bad grammar.

"You may go in when you please, Miss. Is that any one coming? Come here in the shade."

"Now, get along!" said Miss Molly.

It was hard upon the Wise Youth, and he felt it so, that she would not accept his impeccability. He said austerely: "I desire you to know, Miss, that, notwithstanding your unprotected situation and the favouring darkness, a British female, in all places, and at all seasons, may confidently repose the precious Jewel—"

The buxom lass interrupted the harangue by an explosion of giggles. "I declare," she cried, "I used for to believe you at fust; and when you begin you looks like it now. You're al'ays as good as a play. I say—don't you remember—"

Adrian spoke with resolution. "Will you listen to me, Miss Davenport!" He put a coin in her hand which had a medical effect in calming her to attention. "I want to know whether you have seen him at all?"

"Who? Your young gentleman? I sh'd think I did. I seen him tonight only. Ain't he growed handsome. He's al'ays about Beltharp now. It ain't to fire no more ricks, I gesses. He's afire 'unself. Ain't you seen 'em together? He's after the missis, and you're after the—"

Adrian checked the audacious accusation. He requested Miss Davenport to be respectful, and confine herself to particulars. The buxom lass then told him that her young Missis was farmer Blaize's niece, and that she and Adrian's young gentleman were a pretty couple, and met one another every night. The girl swore for their innocence.

"As for Miss Lucy, she haven't a bit of art in her, nor have he."

"They're all nature, I suppose," said Adrian. "How is it I don't see her at Church?"

"She's a Catholic, or somethink," said Molly. "Her feyther was, and a leftenant. She've a Cross in her bedroom. She don't go to Church. I see you there last Sunday a-lookin' so solemn," and Molly stroked her hand down her chin to give it length.

Adrian insisted on her keeping to facts. It was dark, and in the dark he was indifferent to the striking contrasts suggested by the buxom lass, but he wanted to hear facts, and he again bribed her to distil nothing but facts. Upon which she told him further, that her young lady was an innocent artless creature who had been to school upwards of three years with the nuns, and had a little money of her own, and was beautiful enough to be a lord's lady, and had been in love with Master Richard ever since she was a little girl. Molly had got from a friend of hers up at the Abbey, Mary Garner, the housemaid who cleaned Master Richard's room, a bit of paper once with the young gentleman's handwriting, and had given it to her Miss Lucy, and Miss Lucy had given her a gold sovereign for it—just for his handwriting! Miss Lucy did not seem happy at the farm, because of that young Tom who was always leering at her, and to be sure she was quite a lady, and could play, and sing, and dress with the best.

"She looks like a Angel in her nightgown!" Molly wound up.

"Can one be favoured with the opportunity . . .?" said Adrian.

"That you shan't," Molly cried.

"I only want to see, and worship," said Adrian.

"Worship—you!" Molly stepped jeeringly back from him.

The next moment she ran up close, and, speaking for the first time as if there were a distinction of position between them, as well as gender, petitioned: "Mr. Harley! yon won't go for a-doin' any harm to 'em 'cause of what I said, will you now? Do say, you won't now, Mr. Harley? She is good, though she's a Catholic. She was kind to me when I was ill, and I wouldn't have her crossed —I'd rather be showed up myself, I would!"

The Wise Youth gave no positive promise to the buxom lass, and she had to read his consent in a relaxation of his austerity. The noise of a lumbering foot plodding down the lane caused her to be abruptly dismissed. Molly took to flight, the lumbering foot accelerated its pace, and the pastoral appeal to her flying skirts was heard: "Moll, yau, theyre! It be I—Bantam!" But the sprightly Silvia would not stop to his wooing, and Adrian turned away laughing at these Arcadians.

Adrian was a lazy Dragon. All he did for the present was to hint, and tease. "It's the Inevitable!" he said, and asked himself why he should seek to arrest it. He had no faith in the System. Heavy Benson had. Benson of the slow thick-lidded Antediluvian eye and loose-crumpled skin: Benson, the Saurian, the Woman-hater: Benson was wide awake. A sort of rivalry existed between the Wise Youth and Heavy Benson. The fidelity of the latter dependant had moved the Baronet to commit to him a portion of the management of the Raynham estate, and this Adrian did not like. No one who aspires to the honourable office of leading another by the nose, can tolerate a party to his ambition. Benson's surly instinct told him he was in the Wise Youth's way, and he resolved to give his Master a striking proof of his superior faithfulness. For some weeks the Saurian eye had been on the two secret creatures. Heavy Benson saw letters come and go in the day, and now the young gentleman was off and out every night, and seemed to be on wings. Heavy Benson knew whither he went and the object he went for. It was a woman, that was enough. The Saurian eye had actually seen the sinful thing lure the Hope of Raynham into the shades. He composed several epistles of warning to the Baronet of the work that was going on; but before sending one, he wished to record a little of their guilty conversation; and for this purpose the faithful fellow nightly trotted over the dews to eavesdrop, and thereby aroused the Good Fairy, in the person of Tom Bakewell, the sole confidant of Richard's state.

Tom said to his young Master: "Do you know what, Sir? You be watched!"

Richard, in a fury, bade him name the wretch, and Tom hung his arms, and aped the respectable protrusion of the butler's head.

"It's he, is it?" cried Richard. "He shall rue it. Tom! if

I find him near me when we're together, he shall never forget it."

"Don't hit too hard, Sir," Tom suggested. "You hit mortal hard when you're in earnest, you know."

Richard averred he would forgive anything but that, and told Tom to be within hail tomorrow night—he knew where. By the hour of the appointment it was out of the lover's mind.

Heavy Benson's Epistle of Warning, addressed to Sir Austin Absworthy Bearne Feverel, Bart., and containing an extraordinary travesty of the mutual converse of two love-sick beings, specially calculated to alarm a moral parent, was posted and travelling to Town. His work was done. Unluckily for his bones, he had, in the process, acquired a prurient taste for the service of spy upon Cupid; and, after doing duty at table, he was again out over the dews, hoping to behold the extreme wickedness of the celestial culprit.

Lady Blandish dined that evening at Raynham, by Adrian's pointed invitation. According to custom, Richard started up and off, with few excuses. The lady exhibited no surprise. She and Adrian likewise strolled forth to enjoy the air of the Summer night. They had no intention of spying. Still they may have thought that, by meeting Richard and his inamorata, there was a chance of laying a foundation of ridicule to sap the passion. They may have thought so—they were on no spoken understanding.

"I have seen the little girl," said Lady Blandish. "She is pretty—she would be telling if she were well set up. She speaks well. How absurd it is of that class to educate their women above their station! The child is really too good for a farmer. I noticed her before I knew of this. She has enviable hair. I suppose she doesn't paint her eyelids. Just the sort of person to take a young man. I thought there was something wrong. I received, the day before yesterday, an impassioned poem evidently not intended for me. My hair was gold: my meeting him was foretold. My eyes were homes of light fringed with night. I sent it back, correcting the colours."

"Which was death to the rhymes," said Adrian. "I saw her this morning. The boy hasn't bad taste. As you say, she is too good for a farmer. Such a spark would explode any System. She slightly affected mine. The Huron is stark mad about her."

"But we must positively write, and tell his father," said Lady Blandish.

The Wise Youth did not see why they should exaggerate a trifle. The lady said she would have an interview with Richard, and then write, as it was her duty to do. Adrian shrugged, and was for going into the scientific explanation of Richard's conduct, in which the lady had to discourage him.

"Poor boy!" she sighed. "I am really sorry for him. I hope he will not feel it too strongly. They feel strongly, father and son."

"And select wisely?" Adrian slyly appended.

"That's another thing," said Lady Blandish. "You have heard about the Grandisons, I presume?"

"Yes. A perfect woman, mirrored in her progeny."

"I detest a perfect woman," said Lady Blandish.

"I should like her better than her progeny."

"I pity her husband," said Lady Blandish.

"As THE PILGRIM'S SCRIP would remark—There's his recompense."

"I'm afraid some one is easily hoodwinked," said Lady Blandish.

The Wise Youth smiled.

Their talk was then of the dulness of neighbouring county people, about whom, it seemed, there was little or no scandal afloat: of the lady's loss of the Season in Town, which she professed not to regret, though she complained of her general weariness: of whether Mr. Morton of Poer Hall would propose to Mrs. Doria, and of the probable despair of the hapless

Curate of Lobourne; and other gossip, partly in French.

They rounded the lake, and got upon the road through the park to Lobourne. The moon had risen. The atmosphere was warm and pleasant.

"Quite a lover's night," said Lady Blandish.

"And I, who have none to love—pity me!" The Wise Youth attempted a sigh.

"And never will have," said Lady Blandish curtly. "You *buy* your loves."

"Good Heavens, Madam!" Adrian protested. This was Science with a vengeance. However, he did not plead verbally against the impeachment, though the lady's decisive insight astonished him. He began to respect her—scarce relishing her exquisite contempt—and reflected that Widows were terrible creatures.

He had hoped to be a little sentimental with Lady Blandish, knowing her romantic. This mixture of the harshest Common Sense and an air of, "*I* know you men," with Romance and refined temperament, subdued the Wise Youth more than a positive accusation supported by witnesses would have done. He looked at the lady. Her face was raised to the moon. She knew nothing—she had simply spoken from the fulness of her human knowledge, and had forgotten her words. Perhaps, after all, her admiration, or whatever feeling it was, for the Baronet was sincere, and really the longing for a virtuous man. Perhaps she had tried the opposite set pretty much. Adrian shrugged. Whenever the Wise Youth encountered a mental difficulty he instinctively lifted his shoulders to equal altitudes, to show that he had no doubt there was a balance in the case,—plenty to be said on both sides, which was the same to him as a definite solution.

At their tryst in the wood abutting on Raynham Park, wrapped in themselves, piped to by tireless Love, Richard and Lucy sat, toying with the eternal moments. How they seem as if they would never end! What mere sparks they are when they have died out! And how in the distance of time

they revive, and extend, and glow, and make us think them
full the half, and the best of the fire, of our lives!

With the onward flow of intimacy, the two happy lovers
ceased to be so shy of common themes, and their speech did
not reject all as gross that was not pure gold of emotion.
Lucy was very inquisitive about everything and everybody
at Raynham. Whoever had been about Richard since his
birth, she must know the history of, and he for a kiss will
do her bidding.

Thus goes the tender duet.

"You should know my cousin Austin, Lucy.—Darling!
Beloved!"

"My own! Richard!"

"You should know my cousin Austin. You shall know
him. He would take to you best of them all, and you to
him. He is in the Tropics now, looking out a place—it's a
secret—for poor English working-men to emigrate to and
found a colony in that part of the world—my white Angel!"

"Dear love!"

"He is such a noble fellow! Nobody here understands
him but me. Isn't it strange? Since I met you I love him
better! That's because I love all that's good and noble better
now—Beautiful! I love—I love you!"

"My Richard!"

"What do you think I've determined, Lucy? If my father
—but no! my father does love me—No! he will not; and we
will be happy together here. And I will win my way with
you. And whatever I win will be yours; for it will be
owing to you. I feel as if I had no strength but yours—
none! and you make me—Oh, Lucy!"

His voice ebbs. Presently Lucy murmurs:

"Your father, Richard."

"Yes? my father?"

"Dearest Richard! I feel so afraid of him."

"He loves me, and will love you, Lucy."

"But I am so poor and humble, Richard."

"No one I have ever seen is like you, Lucy."

"You think so, because you—"

"What?"

"Love me," comes the blushing whisper, and the duet gives place to dumb variations, performed equally in concert.

It is resumed.

"You are fond of the knights, Lucy. Austin is as brave as any of them.—My own bride! O how I adore you! When you are gone, I could fall upon the grass you tread upon, and kiss it. My breast feels empty of my heart.— Lucy! if we lived in those days, I should have been a Knight, and have won honour and glory for you. Oh! one can do nothing now. My lady-love! My lady-love!—A tear!— Lucy?"

"Dearest! Ah, Richard! I am not a lady."

"Who dares say that? Not a lady—the Angel I love!"

"Think, Richard, who I am."

"My beautiful! I think that God made you, and has given you to me."

Her eyes fill with tears, and, as she lifts them heaven-ward to thank her God, the light of Heaven strikes on them, and she is so radiant in her pure beauty that the limbs of the young man tremble.

"Lucy! O heavenly spirit! Lucy!"

Tenderly her lips part: "I do not weep for sorrow."

The big bright drops lighten, and roll down, imaged in his soul.

They lean together: shadows of ineffable tenderness play-ing on their thrilled cheeks and brows.

He dare not touch her lips. He lifts her hand, and presses his mouth to it. She has seen little of mankind, but her soul tells her this one is different from others, and at the thought, in her great joy, tears must come fast, or her heart will break: tears of boundless thanksgiving. And he, gazing on those soft, ray-illumined, dark-edged, eyes, and the grace of her loose falling tresses, feels a scarce-sufferable holy fire streaming through his members.

It is long ere they speak in open tones.

"Oh happy day when we met!"

What says the voice of one, the soul of the other echoes.

"Oh glorious Heaven looking down on us!"

Their souls are joined, are made one for evermore beneath that bending benediction.

"Oh Eternity of bliss!"

Then the diviner mood passes, and they drop to earth.

"Lucy! come with me tonight, and look at the place where you are some day to live. Come, and I will row you on the lake. You remember what you said in your letter that you dreamt?—that we were floating over the shadow of the Abbey to the nuns at work by torchlight felling the Cypress, and they handed us each a sprig. Why, darling, it was the best omen in the world, their felling the old trees. And you write such lovely letters. So pure and sweet they are. I love the nuns for having taught you."

"Ah, Richard! See! we forget! Ah!" she lifts up her face pleadingly, as to plead against herself, "even if your father forgives my birth, he will not my Religion. And, dearest, though I would die for you, I cannot change it. It would seem that I was denying God; and, oh! it would make me ashamed of my love."

"Fear nothing!" He winds her about with his arm. "Come! He will love us both, and love you the more for being faithful to your father's creed. You don't know him, Lucy. He seems harsh and stern—he is full of kindness and love. He isn't at all a bigot. And besides, when he hears what the nuns have done for you, won't he thank them as I do? And, Oh! I must speak to him soon, and you must be prepared to see him soon, for I cannot bear your remaining at Belthorpe, like a jewel in a sty. Mind! I'm not saying a word against your Uncle. I declare I love everybody and everything that sees you and touches you.

Stay! it *is* a wonder how you could have grown there. But you were not born there, and your father had good blood. Desborough!—there was a Colonel Desborough—never mind! Come!"

She dreads to. She begs not to. She is drawn away.

The woods are silent, and then:

"What think you of that for a pretty pastoral?" says a very different voice.

Adrian reclined against a pine overlooking the fern-covert. Lady Blandish was recumbent upon the brown pine-droppings, gazing through a vista of the lower greenwood which opened out upon the moon-lighted valley, her hands clasped round one knee, her features almost stern in their set hard expression.

She did not answer. A movement among the ferns attracted Adrian, and he stepped down the decline across the pine-roots to behold Heavy Benson below shaking fern-seed and spidery substances off his crumpled skin.

"Is that you, Mr. Hadrian," called Benson, starting, as he puffed, and exercised his handkerchief.

"Is it *you*, Benson, who have had the audacity to spy upon the Mysteries, and are not struck blind?" Adrian called back, and coming close to him, added: "You look as if you had just been well thrashed."

"Isn't it dreadful, Sir?" snuffled Benson. "And his father in ignorance, Mr. Hadrian!"

"He shall know, Benson! He shall know how you have endangered your valuable skin in his service. If Mr. Richard had found you there just now, I wouldn't answer for the consequences."

"Ha!" Benson spitefully retorted. "This won't go on, Mr. Hadrian. It shan't, Sir. It will be put a stop to tomorrow, Sir. I call it corruption of a young gentleman like him, and harlotry, Sir, I call it. I'd have every jade flogged that made a young innocent gentleman go on like that, Sir."

"Then why didn't you stop it yourself, Benson? Ah, I

see! you waited for the worst—eh? Hm!—or what? Benson? This is not the first time you have been attendant on Mr. Apollo and Miss Dryope? You have written to headquarters, have you? Nothing like zeal, Benson!"

"I did my dooty, Mr. Hadrian."

"Don't let it rob you of your breath, Benson."

The Wise Youth returned to Lady Blandish, and informed her of Benson's zeal. The lady's eyes flashed. "I hope Richard will treat him as he deserves," she said.

"Shall we home?" Adrian inquired.

"Do me a favour," the lady replied. "Get my carriage sent round to meet me at the park-gates."

"Won't you—?"

"I want to be alone."

Adrian bowed, and left her. She was still sitting with her hands clasped round one knee, gazing towards the dim ray-strewn valley.

"An odd creature!" muttered the Wise Youth. "She's as odd as any of them. She ought to be a Feverel. I suppose she's graduating for it.—Hang that confounded old ass of a Benson! He has had the impudence to steal a march on me! Not a bad suggestion of the Blandish. We'll see about it."

The shadow of the Cypress was lessening on the lake. The moon was climbing high. As Richard rowed the boat, Lucy sung to him softly. She sang first a fresh little French song; reminding him of a day when she had been asked to sing to him before, and he did not care to hear. "Did I live?" he thinks. Then she sang to him a bit of one of those majestic old Gregorian chants, that, wherever you may hear them, seem to build up cathedral walls about you. The young man dropped the sculls. The strange solemn notes gave a religious tone to his love, and wafted him into the Knightly Ages and the reverential Heart of Chivalry.

Hanging between two Heavens on the lake: floating to her voice; the moon stepping over and through white shoals of soft high clouds above, and below: floating to her voice—no other breath abroad! His soul went out of his body as he listened.

They must part. He rows her gently shoreward.

"I never was so happy as tonight," she murmurs.

"Look, my Lucy. The lights of the old place are on the Lake. Look, where you are to live."

"Which is your room, Richard?"

He points it out to her.

"Oh, Richard! that I were one of the women who wait on you! I should ask nothing more. How happy she must be!"

"My darling Angel-love! You shall be happy, but all shall wait on you, and I foremost, Lucy."

"Dearest! may I hope for a letter?"

"By eleven tomorrow. And I?"

"Oh! you will have mine, Richard."

"Tom shall wait for it. A long one, mind! Did you like my last song?"

She puts her hand quietly against her bosom, and he knows where it rests. Oh, Love! Oh, Heaven!

They are aroused by the harsh grating of the bow of the boat against the shingle. He jumps out, and lifts her ashore.

"See," she says, as the blush of his embrace subsides: "See!" and prettily she mimics awe and feels it a little, "the Cypress does point towards us. Oh, Richard! it does!"

And he, looking at her rather than at the Cypress, delighting in her arch grave ways:

"Why, there's hardly any shadow at all, Lucy. She mustn't dream, my darling! or dream only of me."

"Dearest! but I do."

"Tomorrow, Lucy! The letter in the morning, and you at night. Oh, happy tomorrow!"

"You will be sure to be there, Richard?"

"If I am not dead, Lucy."

"Oh, Richard; pray, pray do not speak of that. I shall not survive you."

"Let us pray, Lucy, to die together, when we are to die. Death, or Life, with you!—Who is it, yonder? I see some one—is it Tom?—It's Adrian!"

"Is it Mr. Harley?" The fair girl shivered.

"How dare he come here!" cried Richard.

The figure of Adrian, instead of advancing, discreetly circled the lake. They were stealing away, when he called. His call was repeated. Lucy entreated Richard to go to him, but the young man preferred to summon his attendant Tom from within hail, and send him to know what was wanted.

"Will he have seen me? Will he have known me?" whispered Lucy tremulously.

"And if he does, love?" said Richard.

"Oh! if he does, dearest—I don't know, but I feel such a presentiment. You have not spoken of him tonight, Richard. Is he good?"

"Good?" Richard clutched her hand for the innocent maiden phrase. "He's very fond of eating; that's all I know of Adrian."

Her hand was at his lips when Tom returned.

"Well, Tom?"

"Mr. Adrian wishes particular to speak to you, Sir," said Tom, emphasizing his achievement of a four-syllable word.

"Do go to him, dearest. Do go!" Lucy begs him.

"Oh, how I hate Adrian!" The young man grinds his teeth.

"Do go!" Lucy re-urges him. "Tom—good Tom—will see me home. Tomorrow, dear love! Tomorrow!"

"You wish to part from me?"

"Oh, unkind! but you must not come with me now. It may be news of importance, dearest. Think, Richard!"

"Tom! go back!"

At the imperious command the well-drilled Tom strides

off a dozen paces, and sees nothing. Then the precious charge is confided to him. A heart is cut in twain.

Richard made his way to Adrian. "What is it you want with me, Adrian?"

"Are we seconds, or principals, O fiery one?" was Adrian's answer. "I want nothing with you, except to know whether you have seen Benson."

"Where should I see Benson? What do I know of Benson's doings?"

"Of course not—such a secret old fist as he is! I want some one to tell him to order Lady Blandish's carriage to be sent round to the park-gates. I thought he might be round your way over there—I came upon him accidentally just now in Abbey-wood—Hey! what's the matter, boy?"

"You saw him *there?*"

"Hunting Diana, I suppose. He thinks she's not so chaste as they say," continued Adrian. "Are you going to knock down that tree?"

Richard had turned to the cypress, and was tugging at the tough wood. He left it, and went to an ash.

"You'll spoil that weeper," Adrian cried. "Down she comes!—all but! Good night, Ricky! If you see Benson, mind you tell him."

Doomed Benson following his burly shadow hove in sight on the white road while Adrian spoke. The Wise Youth chuckled and strolled round the lake, glancing over his shoulder every now and then.

It was not long before he heard a bellow for help—the roar of a Dragon in his throes. Adrian placidly sat down on the grass, and fixed his eyes on the water. There, as the roar was being repeated, amid horrid resounding echoes, the Wise Youth mused in this wise:

" 'The Fates are Jews with us when they delay a punishment,' says THE PILGRIM'S SCRIP, or words to that effect. Not a bad idea, that of the Fates being Jews—Jewesses more classically speaking. The Heavens evidently love Ben-

son, seeing that he gets his punishment on the spot. He don't
like it. What a lovely night! Those two young ones do it
well. Master Ricky is a peppery young man. Love and
War come as natural to him as bread and butter. He gets
it from the ap Gruffudh. I rather believe in race. What
a noise that old ruffian makes! He'll require poulticing
with THE PILGRIM'S SCRIP. We shall have a message tomorrow, and a hubbub, and perhaps all go to Town, which
won't be bad for one who's been a prey to all the desires
born of dulness for a decade. Benson howls: there's life in
the old dog yet! He bays the moon. Look at her. She
doesn't care. It's the same to her whether we coo like turtle-
doves, or roar like twenty lions. Most beauteous Moon!
How complacent she looks! How admirably equable! And
yet she has just as much sympathy for Benson as for Cupid.
She would smile on if both were being birched. She is Perfect Justice. Was that a raven or Benson? He howls no
more. It sounds guttural: frog-like—something between old
brek-kek-kek and the hoarse raven's croak. That fellow'll
be killing him. It's time to be to the rescue. A deliverer
gets more honour by coming in at the last gasp, than if he
forestalled catastrophe.—Ho, there! What's the matter?"

So saying, the Wise Youth rose, and leisurely trotted to the
scene of battle, where stood St. George puffing over the
prostrate Dragon.

"Holloa, Ricky! is it you?" said Adrian. "What's this?
Whom have we here?—Benson, as I live!"

"Make this beast get up," Richard returned, breathing
hard, and shaking his great ash-branch. "Make him get up."

"He seems incapable, my dear boy. What have you been
up to?—Benson! Benson!—I say, Ricky, this looks bad."

"He's shamming!" Richard clamoured like a savage.
"Spy upon me, will he? I tell you, he's shamming. He
hasn't had half enough. Nothing's too bad for a spy. Let
him get up! Let him get up!"

"Insatiate youth! do throw away that enormous weapon."

"He has written to my father," Richard shouted. "The miserable spy! Let him get up! Let him get up!"

"Ooogh! I won't," huskily groaned Benson. "Mr. Hadrian, you're a witness he's murdered—my back!"—Cavernous noises took up the tale of his maltreatment.

"I dare say you love your back better than any part of your body now!" Adrian muttered. "Come, Benson! be a man. Mr. Richard has thrown away the stick. Come, and get off home, and let's see the extent of the damage."

"Ooogh! he's a devil! Mr. Hadrian, Sir, he's a devil!" groaned Benson, turning half over in the road to ease his aches.

Adrian caught hold of Benson's collar and lifted him to a sitting posture. He then had a glimpse of what his hopeful pupil's hand could do in wrath. The wretched butler's coat was slit and welted; his hat knocked in; the stain of a tremendous blow across his nose, which made one of his eyes seem gone; his flabby spirit so broken that he started and trembled if his pitiless executioner stirred a foot. Richard stood over him with folded arms, grasping his great stick: no dawn of mercy for Benson in any corner of his features.

Benson screwed his neck round to look up at him, and immediately gasped, "I won't get up! I won't get up! He's ready to murder me again!—Mr. Hadrian! if you stand by and see it you're liable to the law, Sir—I won't get up while he's near." No persuasion could induce Benson to try his legs while his executioner stood by.

Adrian took Richard aside: "You've almost killed the poor devil, Ricky. You must be satisfied with that. Look at his face."

"The coward bobbed while I struck," said Richard. "I marked his back. He ducked. I told him he was getting it worse."

At this civilized piece of savagery, Adrian opened his mouth to shake out a coil of laughter.

"Did you really? I admire that. You told him he was getting it worse? I thought you were in a passion. Beautifully cool! Bravo!—You are politely informed that if you take that posture, in the nature of things, and by reasonable calculation, you will get it worse."

Adrian opened his mouth again to shake another coil of laughter out.

"Come," he said, "Excalibur has done his work. Pitch him into the lake. And see—here comes the Blandish. You can't be at it again before a woman. Go and meet her, and tell her the noise was an ox being slaughtered. Or say, Argus."

With a whirr that made all Benson's bruises moan and quiver, the great ash-branch shot aloft, and Richard swung off to intercept Lady Blandish.

Adrian got Benson on his feet. The heavy butler was disposed to summon all the commiseration he could feel for his bruised flesh. Every half step he attempted was like a dislocation. His groans and grunts were frightful.

"How much did that hat cost, Benson?" said Adrian, as he put it on his head.

"A five-and-twenty shilling beaver, Mr. Hadrian!" Benson caressed its injuries.

"The cheapest policy of Insurance I remember to have heard of!" said Adrian. "Never part with that hat, Benson! Love it as you love yourself."

Benson staggered, moaning at intervals to his cruel comforter:

"He's a devil! Mr. Hadrian. He's a devil, Sir, I do believe, Sir. Ooogh! he's a devil!—I can't move, Mr. Hadrian. I must be fetched. And Dr. Clifford must be sent for, Sir. I shall never be fit for work again. I haven't a sound bone in my body, Mr. Hadrian."

"You see, Benson, this comes of your declaring war upon Venus. 'Twas Venus, Venus struck the deadly blow! I hope the maids will nurse you properly. Let me see—you are friends with the housekeeper, aren't you? All depends upon that."

"I'm only a faithful servant, Mr. Hadrian," the miserable butler snarled.

"So you've got no friend but your bed. Get to it as quick as possible, Benson."

"I can't move." Benson made a resolute halt. "I must be fetched," he whinnied. "It's a shame to ask me to move, Mr. Hadrian."

"You will admit that you are heavy, Benson," said Adrian, "so I can't carry you. However, I see Mr. Richard is very kindly returning to help me."

At these words Heavy Benson instantly found his legs, and shambled on.

Lady Blandish met Richard in dismay.

"I have been horribly frightened," she said. "Tell me, what was the meaning of those cries I heard?"

"Only some one doing justice on a spy," said Richard, and the lady smiled, and looked on him fondly, and put her hand through his hair.

"Was that all? I should have done it myself if I had been a man. Kiss me."

CHAPTER XXV

RICHARD IS SUMMONED TO TOWN TO HEAR A SERMON

By twelve o'clock at noon next day, the inhabitants of Raynham Abbey knew that Berry, the Baronet's man, had arrived post haste from Town, with orders to conduct Mr. Richard thither, and that Mr. Richard had refused to go: had sworn he would not, defied his father, and despatched Berry to the shades. Berry, the Baronet's man, was all that Benson, the butler, was not. Whereas Benson hated Woman, Berry admired her warmly. Second to his own stately person, Woman occupied his reflections, and commanded his homage. Berry was of majestic port, and used dictionary words. Among the maids of Raynham his conscious conquering calves produced all the discord and the frenzy those adornments seem destined to create in tender bosoms. He had, moreover, the reputation of having suffered terribly for the sex; which assisted his object in inducing the sex to suffer terribly for him. What with his calves, and his dictionary words, and the attractive halo of the mysterious vindictiveness of Venus surrounding him, this Adonis of the lower household was a mighty man below, and he moved as one.

On hearing the tumult that followed Berry's arrival, Adrian sent for him, and was informed of the nature of his mission, and its result.

"You should come to me first," said Adrian. "I should have imagined you were shrewd enough for that, Berry?"

"Pardon me, Mr. Adrian," Berry doubled his elbow to explain. "Pardon me, Sir. Acting recipient of special injunctions, I was not a free agent."

Adrian tacitly acknowledged the choiceness of the phraseology, and asked, if he had seen Benson.

"I have enjoyed an interview with Mr. Benson, Sir."

"I dare say you did enjoy it, Berry!"

Berry protested: "On my honour, Sir! From the plenitude of health and spirits, I regarded Mr. Benson with profound—a—profound—" a word fine enough for his emotion seemed wanting.

"Mr. Richard have shattered his ganglions, Sir."

"His what?" Adrian asked.

Berry corrected the casual error: "I should say, his idioshincrazy, Sir."

"Accentuate the fourth, not the fifth, syllable, Berry."

"Exactly, Sir. His idihoshincrazy. I may have my own retrospections against Mr. Benson; but, hem! as homo,"—

and Berry ventured a familiar smile as he joined Adrian on classical ground; "as homo, Sir, I am concerned."

"But if you discovered that Benson dogged you in the woods with Betsy Sommersault—eh, Berry? How then?"

"O fie, Mr. Adrian! a Spy, Sir?" Berry expanded his magnificent chest, and stated his opinion that, "That quite altered the catastrophe."

"Benson wishes it did, no doubt," said Adrian. "So Mr. Richard refuses to go?"

"Voiciferously, Sir."

"What did he say?"

"His accentuation was of the wildest. Sir. Erratic."

"Trochaic, you mean, Berry! On the first syllable altogether, I suppose? Trochaic running into the anapæstic," Adrian suggested, drumming the measure.

That was what Berry meant. On the first syllable altogether! Trochaic.

Adrian soon got tired of Berry, who was poor fun to him, and occupied the rank in his order of household amusement that a pun does to wit.

"Go to him again, Berry. There will be a little confusion if he holds back. Just go to him, and perhaps you had better throw out a hint or so of apoplexy. A slight hint will do. And here—Berry! when you return to Town, you had better not mention anything—to quote Johnson—of Benson's spiflication."

"Certainly not, Sir."

Berry retired, saying to himself: "What I like, is to confabulate with educated people. You always learn something new from them." And he drew forth his pocket-Johnson that he might commit the new words he had learnt to memory.

The Wise Youth's hint had the desired effect on Richard. He dashed off a hasty letter by Tom to Belthorpe, and mounting his horse, galloped to the Bellingham station.

Sir Austin was sitting down to a quiet early dinner at his

hotel, when the Hope of Raynham burst into his room.

The Baronet was not angry with his son. On the contrary, for he was singularly just and self-accusing while Pride was not up in arms, he had been thinking all day after the receipt of Benson's letter, that he was deficient in cordiality, and did not, by reason of his excessive anxiety, make himself sufficiently his son's companion: was not enough, as he strove to be, Mother and Father to him; Preceptor and Friend; Previsor and Associate. He had not to ask his conscience where he had lately been to blame towards the System. He had slunk away from Raynham in the very crisis of the Magnetic Age, and this young woman of the parish (as Benson had termed sweet Lucy in his letter) was the consequence.

Yes! Pride and Sensitiveness were his chief foes, and he would trample on them. To begin, he embraced his son: hard upon an Englishman at any time—doubly so to one so shamefaced at emotion in cold blood, as it were. It gave him a strange pleasure, nevertheless. And the youth seemed to answer to it: he was excited. Was his love, then, commencing to correspond with his father's, as in those intimate days before the Blossoming season?

But when Richard, inarticulate at first, in his haste, cried out: "My dear, dear father! You are safe! I feared—You are better, Sir? Thank God!" Sir Austin stood away from him.

"Safe?" he said, "What has alarmed you?"

Instead of replying, Richard dropped into a chair, and seized his hand, and kissed it, murmuring again, that he thanked God.

Sir Austin took a seat, and waited for his son to explain.

"Those Doctors are such fools!" Richard broke out. "I was sure they were wrong. They don't know headache from apoplexy. It's worth the ride, Sir, to see you. You left Raynham so suddenly—But you are well! It was not an attack of real apoplexy?"

His father's brows contorted, and he said, "No, it was not." Richard pursued.

"If you were ill, I couldn't come too soon, though, if Coroners' inquests sat on Horses, those Doctors would be found guilty of mareslaughter. Cassandra 'll be knocked up. I was too early for the train at Bellingham, and I wouldn't wait. She did the distance in four hours and three quarters. Pretty good, Sir, wasn't it?"

"It has given you an appetite for dinner, I hope," said the Baronet, not so well pleased to find that it was not simple obedience that had brought the youth to him in such haste.

"I'm ready," replied Richard. "I shall be in time to return by the last train to-night. I will leave Cassandra in your charge for a rest."

His father quietly helped him to soup, which he commenced gobbling with an eagerness that might pass for appetite.

"All well at Raynham?" said the Baronet.

"Quite, Sir."

"Nothing new?"

"Nothing, Sir."

"The same as when I left?"

"No change whatever!"

"I shall be glad to get back to the old place," said the Baronet. "My stay in Town has certainly been profitable. I have made some pleasant acquaintances who may probably favour us with a visit there in the late Autumn—people you may be pleased to know. Hem! They are very anxious to see Raynham."

"I love the old place," cried Richard. "I never wish to leave it."

"Why, boy, before I left, you were constantly begging to see Town."

"Was I, Sir? How odd! Well! I don't want to remain here. I've seen enough of it."

"How did you find your way to me?"

Richard laughed, and related his bewilderment at the miles of brick, and the noise, and the troops of people: concluding: "There's no place like home!"

The Baronet watched his symptomatic brilliant eyes, and favoured him with a double-dealing sentence:

"To anchor the heart by any object, ere we have half traversed the world, is Youth's Foolishness, my son. Reverence Time! A better maxim, that, than your Horatian."

"He knows all!" thought Richard, and instantly drew away leagues from his father, and threw up fortifications round his love and himself.

Dinner over, Richard looked hurriedly at his watch, and said, with much briskness, "I shall just be in time, Sir, if we walk. Will you come with me to the station?"

The Baronet did not answer.

Richard was going to repeat the question, but found his father's eyes fixed on him so meaningly, that he wavered, and played with his empty glass.

"I think we will have a little more claret," said the Baronet.

Claret was brought, and they were left alone.

The Baronet then drew within arm's-reach of his son, and began:

"I am not aware what you may have thought of me, Richard, during the years we have lived together: and indeed, I have never been in a hurry to be known to you: and, if I had died before my work was done, I should not have complained at losing half my reward, in hearing you thank me. Perhaps, as it is, I never may. Everything, save selfishness, has its recompense. I shall be content, if you prosper."

He fetched a breath, and continued: "You had, in your infancy, a great loss." Father and son coloured simultaneously. "To make that good to you, I chose to isolate myself from the world, and devote myself entirely to your welfare; and I think it is not vanity that tells me now, that the son I have reared is one of the most hopeful of God's creatures. But for that very reason, you are open to be tempted the most, and to sink the deepest. It was the First of the Angels who made the road to Hell."

He paused again. Richard fingered at his watch.

"In our House, my son, there is peculiar blood. We go to wreck very easily. It sounds like superstition,—I cannot but think we are tried as most men are not. I see it in us all. And you, my son, are compounded of two races. Your passions are violent. You have had a taste of Revenge: You have seen, in a small way, that the pound of Flesh draws rivers of Blood. But there is now in you another power. You are mounting to the Table-land of Life, where mimic battles are changed to real ones. And you come upon it laden equally with force to create and to destroy." He deliberated to announce the intelligence, with deep meaning: "There are women in the world, my son!"

The young man's heart galloped back to Raynham.

The Baronet gravely repeated his last sentence.

"It is when you encounter them that you are thoroughly on trial. It is when you know them that Life is either a mockery to you, or, as some find it, a gift of blessedness. They are our Ordeal. Love of any human object is the soul's Ordeal; and they are ours, loving them, or not."

The young man heard the whistle of the train. He saw the moon-lighted wood, and the vision of his beloved. He could barely hold himself down, and listen.

"I believe," the Baronet spoke with little of the cheerfulness of belief, "good women exist."

Oh, if he knew Lucy!

"But," and the Baronet gazed on Richard intently, "it is given to very few to meet them on the threshold. I may say, to none. We find them after hard buffeting, and usually we find the one fitted for us, when our madness has misshaped our destiny, our lot is cast! For women are not the end, but the means, of life. In youth we think them the former, and thousands, who have not even the excuse of youth, select a mate—or worse—with that sole view. I believe women punish us for so perverting their uses. They punish Society."

The Baronet put his hand to his brow as his mind travelled into Consequences.

'Our most diligent pupil learns not so much as an earnest teacher,' says The Pilgrim's Scrip; and Sir Austin, in schooling himself to speak with moderation of women, was beginning to get a glimpse of their side of the case.

Cold Blood now touched on Love to hot Blood.

Cold Blood said, "It is a passion coming in the order of Nature, the ripe fruit of our animal being."

Hot Blood felt: "It is a Divinity! All that is worth living for in the world."

Cold Blood said: "It is a fever which tests our strength, and too often leads to perdition."

Hot Blood felt: "Lead whither it will, I follow it!"

Cold Blood said: "It is a name men and women are much in the habit of employing to sanctify their appetites."

Hot Blood felt: "It is Worship; Religion; Life!"

And so the two parallel lines ran on.

The Baronet became more personal:

"You know my love for you, my son. The extent of it you cannot know; but you must know that it is something very deep and—I do not wish to speak of it—but a father must sometimes petition for gratitude, since the only true expression of it is his son's moral good. If you care for my love, or love me in return, aid me with all your energies to keep you what I have made you, and guard you from the snares besetting you. It was in my hands once. It is ceasing to be so. Remember, my son, what my love is. It is different, I fear, with most fathers: but I am bound up in your welfare: what you do affects me vitally. You will take no step that is not intimate with my happiness, or my misery. And I have had great disappointments, my son."

So far it was well. Richard loved his father, and even in his frenzied state he could not without emotion hear him thus speak.

Unhappily, the Baronet, who by some fatality never could see when he was winning the battle, thought proper in his wisdom to water the dryness of his sermon with a little jocoseness, on the subject of young men fancying themselves in love, and when they were raw and green, absolutely wanting to be—that most awful thing, which the wisest and strongest of men undertake in hesitation and after self-mortification and penance—married! He sketched the Foolish Young Fellow—the object of general ridicule and covert contempt. He sketched the Woman—the strange thing made in our image, and with all our faculties—passing to the rule of one who in taking her proved that he could not rule himself, and had no knowledge of her save as a choice morsel which he would burn the whole world, and himself in the bargain, to possess. He harped upon the Foolish Young Fellow, till the Foolish Young Fellow felt his skin tingle and was half suffocated with shame and rage.

After this, the Baronet might be as wise as he pleased: he had quite undone his work. He might analyze Love, and anatomize Woman. He might accord to her her due position, and paint her fair: he might be shrewd, jocose, gentle, pathetic, wonderfully wise: he spoke to deaf ears.

Closing his sermon with the question, softly uttered: "Have you anything to tell me, Richard?" and hoping for a confession, and a thorough re-establishment of confidence, the callous answer struck him cold: "I have not."

The Baronet relapsed in his chair, and made diagrams of his fingers.

Richard turned his back on further dialogue by going to the window. In the section of sky over the street twinkled two or three stars; shining faintly, feeling the moon. The moon was rising: the woods were lifting up to her: his star of the woods would be there. A bed of moss set about flowers in a basket under him breathed to his nostril of the woodland keenly, and filled him with delirious longing.

A succession of great sighs brought his father's hand on his shoulder.

"You have nothing you could say to me, my son?—Tell me, Richard! Remember, there is no home for the soul where dwells a shadow of untruth!"

"Nothing at all, Sir," the young man replied, meeting him with the full orbs of his eyes.

The Baronet withdrew his hand, and paced the room.

At last it grew impossible for Richard to control his impatience, and he said: "Do you intend me to stay here, Sir? Am I not to return to Raynham at all tonight?"

The Baronet was again falsely jocular:

"What? and catch the train after giving it ten minutes start?"

"Cassandra will take me," said the young man earnestly. "I needn't ride her hard, Sir. Or perhaps you would lend me your Winkelried? I should be down with him in little better than three hours."

"Even then, you know, the park-gates would be locked."

"Well, I could stable him in the village. Dowling knows the horse, and would treat him properly.—May I have him, Sir?"

The cloud cleared off Richard's face as he asked. At least, if he missed his love that night, he would be near her, breathing the same air, marking what star was above her bed-chamber, hearing the hushed night-talk of the trees about her dwelling: looking on the distances that were like Hope half-fulfilled and a bodily presence bright as Hesper, since he knew her. There were two swallows under the eaves shadowing Lucy's chamber-windows: two swallows, mates in one nest, blissful birds who twittered and cheep-cheeped to the sole-lying beauty in her bed. Around these birds the lover's heart revolved, he knew not why. He associated them with all his close-veiled dreams of happiness. Seldom a morning passed when he did not watch them leave the nest on their breakfast-flight, busy in the happy stillness of dawn. It seemed to him now that if he could be at Raynham to see them in tomorrow's dawn, he would be compensated for his incalculable loss of tonight: he would forgive and love his father, London, life, the world. Just to see those purple backs and white breasts flash out into the quiet morning air! He wanted no more.

The Baronet's trifling had placed this enormous boon within the young man's visionary grasp.

He still went on trying the temper of poor Tantalus:

"You know there would be nobody ready for you at Raynham. It is unfair to disturb the maids."

Richard overrode every objection.

"Well, then, my son," said the Baronet, preserving his half-jocular air, "I must tell you that it is my wish to have you in town."

"Then you have not been ill at all, Sir!" cried Richard, as in his despair he seized the whole plot.

"I have been as well as you could have desired me to be," said his father.

"Why did they lie to me?" the young man wrathfully exclaimed.

"I think, Richard, you can best answer that," rejoined Sir Austin, kindly severe.

Dread of being signalized as the Foolish Young Fellow prevented Richard from expostulating further. Sir Austin saw him grinding his passion into powder for future explosion, and thought it best to leave him for awhile.

CHAPTER XXVI

INDICATES THE APPROACHES OF FEVER

FOR three weeks Richard had to remain in town and endure the teachings of the System in a new atmosphere. He had to sit and listen to men of science who came to renew their intimacy with his father, and whom of all men his father wished him to respect and study: practically scientific men being, in the Baronet's estimation, the only minds thoroughly mated, and enviable. He had to endure an introduction to the Grandisons, and meet the eyes of his kind, haunted as he was by the Foolish Young Fellow. The idea that he might by any chance be identified with him held the poor youth in silent subjection. And it was horrible. For it was a continued outrage on the fair image he had in his heart. The notion of the world laughing at him because he loved sweet Lucy stung him to momentary frenzies, and developed premature misanthropy in his spirit. Also the System desired to show him whither young women of the Parish lead us, and he was dragged about at nighttime to see the sons and daughters of darkness, after the fashion prescribed to Mr. Thompson: how they danced and ogled down the high-road of Perdition. But from this sight possibly the teacher learnt more than his pupil, since we find him seriously asking his meditative hours, in the Note-Book: 'Wherefore Wild Oats are only of one gender?' a question certainly not suggested to him at Raynham; and again: 'Whether men might not be attaching too rigid an importance? . . .' to a subject with a dotted tail apparently, for he gives it no other in the Note-Book. But, as I apprehend, he had come to plead in behalf of women here, and had deduced something from positive observation. To Richard the scenes he witnessed were strange wild pictures, likely if anything to have increased his misanthropy, but for his love.

Mrs. Grandison appeared to be in raptures with the son of a System. What her daughters thought of a young gentleman who did nothing but frown and bite his lips in their company, may be imagined. With Carola, however, he got on better.

Riding in the park one morning, Carola beheld her intended galloping furiously down the Row, and left her sister Clementina's side to waylay him. He pulled up smartly, and this young person's frank accost was:

"I say! are you afraid of girls?"

He stared at her, and did his salute laughing: upon which she said:

"No, I see you're not. My sisters all say you are. I should think you were not afraid of anything. A man afraid of girls! I never heard the like!"

"Well!" said Richard, "at all events I'm not afraid of you. Are you a girl?"

Carola immediately became pensive.

"Yes," she sighed, striping her pony's ears with her whip, "I'm afraid I am! I used to keep hoping once that I wasn't. I'm afraid it's no use." She seriously shook her curls, and looked up at him. Richard shouted with laughter.

"But what do you want to be?" he asked, scrutinizing the comical young person.

"A boy, to be sure!" said Carola, and pouted proudly, as if the wish had raised her out of her sex. At this Richard laughed again, and took to the young woman. They trotted on in company. Within five minutes he had all the secrets of the family.

"When I like anybody," said Carola, "I always speak out everything I know."

"And you like me?"

"Yes, I do.—What do you think they call your father?— the Griffin! That's what they call him. I don't know why. I like him. Do you know who gave me this pony? He did, to be sure! He bought it the day after my birthday.

He's fonder of me than you are.—I like fathers better than mothers. My Pa and Ma don't agree. I say! what may I call you?"

Richard gave her permission to call him what she pleased.

"Well, then, Richard—if you don't really mind.—What a nice fellow you are, and we all thought you so nasty!— I was going to say, I wish they'd let us ride our ponies strideways?"

Richard, with all the muscles of his face in play, lamented the severe restriction.

"It's so much handier," Carola continued. "Look at this! all on one side!—I used to when I was little, though. Not here, you know,—in the country. And Ma knew of it. She didn't interfere. She wanted me to be a boy, Ma did.—What do you think?—Ma smokes! Not before people! She says, it's for her complaint. I wish she had a little of our medicine instead. She gives us all such quantities of medicine—the big ones as well as me. I shall smoke for my complaint when I grow up—see if I don't! If I call you Richard, you'll call me Carl, won't you? That's the German for Charles. In the country the boys call me, Charley.—Can't I ride slapping?"

"Capital!" said Richard. "Let's have a gallop."

After a short heat, Carola slackened her pace to re-commence:

"Do you know why none of my sisters 'll have you? Because they've all got lovers themselves—all but me. And they have letters from them, too, and write back. I shouldn't know what to say. Ma would let us have you, but she wouldn't let us have anybody else."

"Really?" said Richard.

"Yes," Carola nodded. "Ma says, you're going to be a hero. One of us is to be married to you.—Do you call me good-looking?"

Richard complimented her by saying, he thought she would grow to be a very handsome chap.

Carola assured him, she could not think it. "My nose turns up, and my cheeks are so red. Pa calls them cabbage-roses.—I don't mind the 'roses,' but I can't bear the 'cabbage!'—Why is it you laugh so?"

"Because you're such a funny fellow, Carl."

"Am I? Do you like funny fellows?"

"Of course I do. The funny fellows are always my best friends."

"Why, now, that's just like me," exclaimed Carola. "We're just alike. I hate people who mope. I thought you moped at first. I suppose you were only a little put out—weren't you?"

"Only a little!" sighed poor Richard.

"I declare if you don't talk exactly like my sister Clem!—She's moping in love, you know.—Richard!"

"Well, old friend?"

"You don't hear me. Why are you so sad in a minute? Why do you call me 'old friend'?"

"Because"—he bent down and put his hand on her neck—"because, because—well! why?—I suppose it's because I like you better than any of my new friends."

"Do you?" cried the joyful Carola, clapping her hands. "That's right! I'm so glad. Mind you always do, Richard! —won't you? And I will you.—Are you fond of theatres?"

Richard informed her, he had never been to one in his life, which caused lively astonishment to Miss Carl.

"Then you don't know what a beautiful lady is, if you've never been to a theatre," she said authoritatively.

"I'm afraid I do!" replied the lover.

"There you are again—just like Clem!—Are you in love, too? Oh, I hope it isn't with Clem! She'll never have you. I heard her say, she'd die first. I did indeed!—It's a secret—his name's Walter. I've seen her letters: Lieutenant Papworth, in the Hussars. She begins them—'Dearest Dearest Walter!'—and they take her hours to write.—I shouldn't write like that. I should say, 'Dear Richard! I

love you. I hope we shall be married soon. Your faithful
Carl!' That would do—wouldn't it?"

Richard looked down on her with something like veritable
affection. Almost every turn in the artless little maid's
prattle touched a new mood in him, and beguiled away his
melancholy.

"That would just do," he said. "All we want is to be
married soon!"

Carola flushed up, and was quiet. Clementina cantered to
join them, bowing distantly to Richard, as if anything like
familiarity involved the fate of her adoring hussar.

After this conversation with the daughter of a System,
Richard informed his father that he thought girls were very
like boys.

"I think they are," said his father. "I am beginning to
think that the subsequent immense distinction is less one of
sex than of education. They are drilled into hypocrites."

"When they much prefer riding strideways," said Richard, and repeated some of his young friend's remarks, which
his father evidently thought charming, and chuckled over
frequently. A girl so like a boy was quite his ideal of a
girl.

Certain sweet little notes from Lucy sustained the lover
during the first two weeks of exile. Suddenly they ceased;
and now Richard fell into such despondency that his father
in alarm had to take measures to hasten their return to
Raynham. At the close of the third week Berry laid a
pair of letters, bearing the Raynham postmark, on the
breakfast-table, and after reading one attentively the Baronet
asked his son if he was inclined to quit the metropolis.

"For Raynham, Sir?" cried Richard, and relapsed, saying, "As you will!" aware that he had given a glimpse of
the Foolish Young Fellow.

Berry accordingly received orders to make arrangements
for their instant return to Raynham.

The letter Sir Austin lifted his head from to bespeak

his son's wishes, was a composition of the Wise Youth Adrian's. and ran thus:

"Benson is doggedly recovering. He requires great indemnities. Happy when a faithful fool is the main sufferer in a household! I quite agree with you that a faithful fool is the best servant of great schemes. Benson is now a piece of history. I tell him that this is indemnity enough, and that the sweet Muse usually insists upon gentlemen being half flayed before she will condescend to notice them; but Benson, I regret to say, ignobly rejects the comfort so fine a reflection should offer, and had rather keep his skin and live opaque. Heroism seems partly a matter of training. Faithful folly is Benson's nature: the rest has been thrust upon him.

"The young person has resigned the neighbourhood. I had an interview with the Fair Papist myself, and also with the man, Blaize. They were both very sensible, though one swore, and the other sighed. She is pretty. I hope she does not paint. As to her appearance she would affect Adam more than me; but as I did not see her as Eve was seen, I cannot tell how the likeness may be. I can affirm that her legs are strong, for she walks to Bellingham twice a week to take her Scarlet bath, when, having confessed and being made clean by the Romish unction, she walks back the brisker, of which my Protestant muscular system is yet aware. It was on the road to Bellingham I engaged her. She is well in the matter of hair. Madam Godiva might challenge her: it would be a fair match. Has it never struck you that Woman is nearer the *vegetable* than Man?— Mr. Blaize intends her for his son—a junction that every lover of Fairy Mythology must desire to see consummated. Young Tom is heir to all the *agrémens* of the Beast. The maids of Lobourne say (I hear) that he is a very Proculus among them. Possibly the envious men say it for the maids. Beauty does not speak bad grammar—and altogether she is

better out of the way. Allow me to congratulate you on
having found Richard's Unripe Half in good condition, and
rosy. I shall be glad to see the Original Man again, to
whom his Tutor's salute and benediction."

The other letter was from Lady Blandish, a lady's letter,
and said:

"I have fulfilled your commission to the best of my ability,
and heartily sad it has made me. She is indeed very much
above her station—pity that it is so! She is almost beautiful—*quite* beautiful at times, and not in *any way* what you
have been led to fancy. The poor child had no story to
tell. I have again seen her, and talked with her for an
hour as kindly as I could. I could gather nothing more than
we know. It is just a woman's history as it invariably commences (not with *all*—Is it fortunate for us, or the reverse?). Richard is the God of her idolatry. She will re-
nounce him, and sacrifice herself for his sake. Are we so
bad? She asked me what she was to do. She would do
whatever was imposed upon her—all but pretend to love
another, and that she never would, and I believe *never will*.
You know I am sentimental, and I confess we dropped a
few *tears* together. Her Uncle has sent her for the Winter to
the Institution where it appears she was educated, and where
they are very fond of her and want to keep her, which it
would be a good thing if they were to do. The man is a
good sort of man. She was entrusted to him by her father,
and he never interferes with her Religion and is very scrupulous about all that pertains to it, though, as he says, he
is a Christian himself. In the Spring (but the poor child
does not know this) she is to come back, and be married to
his lout of a son. I am *determined* to prevent that. May
I not reckon on your promise to aid me? When you see
her, I am sure you will. It would be sacrilege to look on
and permit such a thing. You know, they are *cousins*. She

asked me, where in the world was there one like Richard?
What could I answer? They were your own words, and
spoken with a depth of conviction! I hope he is really
calm. I shudder to think of him when he comes, and discovers what I have been doing. I hope I have been really
doing right! A good deed, you say, never dies; but we cannot always know—I must rely on you. Yes, it is, I should
think, easy to suffer martyrdom when one is sure of one's
cause! but then one *must* be sure of it. I have done nothing
lately but to repeat to myself that saying of yours, No. 54.,
C. 7., P. S.: and it has consoled me, I cannot say why, except
that all wisdom consoles, whether it applies directly or
not:

" 'For this reason so many fall from God, who have attained to him; that they cling to him with their Weakness,
not with their Strength.'

"I like to know of what you were thinking when you
composed this or that saying—what *suggested* it. May not
one be admitted to inspect the machinery of Wisdom? I
feel curious to know how thoughts—*real* thoughts are born.
Not that I hope to win the secret. Here is the beginning of
one (but we poor women can never put together even two
of the three ideas which you say go to form a thought):
'When a wise man makes a false step, will he not go further
than a fool?' It has just flitted through me.

"I cannot get on with Gibbon, so wait your return to
re-commence the readings. I dislike the *sneering essence* of
his writings. I keep referring to his face, until the dislike
seems to become personal. How different is it with Wordsworth! And yet I cannot escape from the thought that
he is always solemnly thinking of himself (but I *do* reverence him). But this is curious: Byron was a greater egotist,
and yet I do not feel the same with him. He reminds me
of a beast of the desert, savage and beautiful: and the former

is what one would imagine a superior donkey reclaimed from the heathen, to be—a *very* superior donkey, I mean, with great power of speech and great natural complacency, and whose stubbornness you must admire as part of his mission. The worst is that no one will imagine anything sublime in a superior donkey, so my simile is unfair and false. Is it not strange? I love Wordsworth best, and yet Byron has the greater power over me. How is that?"

('Because,' Sir Austin wrote beside the query in pencil, 'Women are cowards, and succumb to Irony and Passion, rather than yield their hearts to Excellence and Nature's Inspiration.')

The letter pursued:
"I have finished Boiardo and have taken up Berni. The latter offends me. I suppose we women do not really care for humour. You are right in saying we have none ourselves, and 'cackle' instead of laugh. It is true (of me, at least) that 'Falstaff is only to us an incorrigible fat man.' I want to know what he *illustrates*. And Don Quixote— what end can be served in making a noble mind ridiculous? —I hear you say—practical! So it is. We are very narrow, I know. But we like wit—practical again? Or in your words (when I really *think* they generally come to my aid— perhaps it is that it is often all *your thought*): we 'prefer the rapier thrust, to the broad embrace, of Intelligence.' By the way, is there a characteristic in Mrs. Grandison? Or is she only *good?* If so, how tired you must be! I hope Richard really *is* beginning to take an interest in the child. I sincerely trust that this young creature is *not so good as her mother*. I wish indeed the Experiment were well 'launched through the surf,' as you do us the honour to term it.

"Heigho! I have given up a Season to you. What is to be my reward?—"

Something, no doubt, the Baronet had in store for her, and possibly the lady's instinct made her meditate the day when Richard should be 'launched through the surf' in earnest.

He trifled with the letter for some time, re-reading chosen passages as he walked about the room, and considering he scarce knew what. There are ideas language is too gross for, and shape too arbitrary, which come to us and have a definite influence upon us, and yet we cannot fasten on the filmy things and make them visible and distinct to ourselves, much more to others. Why did he twice throw a look into the glass in the act of passing it? Why did he for a moment stand with erect head facing it? His eyes for the nonce seemed little to peruse his outer features: the grey-gathered brows and the wrinkles, much action of them had traced over the circles half up his high straight forehead: the iron-grey hair that rose over his forehead and fell away in the fashion of Richard's plume. His general appearance showed the tints of years, but none of their weight, and nothing of the dignity of his youth was gone. It was so far satisfactory, but his eyes were wide, as one who looks at his essential self through the mask we wear. Perhaps he was speculating as he looked, on the sort of aspect he presented to the lady's discriminative regard. Of her feelings he had not a suspicion. But he knew with what extraordinary lucidity women can, when it pleases them, and when their feelings are not quite boiling under the noonday sun, seize all the sides of a character, and put their fingers on its weak point. He was cognizant of the total absence of the humorous in himself (the want that most shut him out from his fellows), and perhaps the clear-thoughted intensely self-examining gentleman filmily conceived: 'Me also, in common with the poet, she gazes on as one of the superior—greybeasts!'

He may have so conceived the case: he was capable of that great-mindedness, and could at times snatch very luminous glances at the broad Reflector which the world of

Fact lying outside our narrow compass holds up for us to
see ourselves in when we will. Unhappily, the faculty of
laughter, which is due to this gift, was denied him; and having once seen, he, like the companion of friend Balaam, could
go no further. For a good wind of laughter had relieved
him of much of the blight of self-deception, and oddness,
and extravagance; had given a healthier view of our atmosphere of life: but he had it not.

Journeying back to Bellingham in the train, with the
heated brain and brilliant eye of his son beside him, Sir
Austin tried hard to feel infallible, as a man with a System
should feel; and because he could not do so, after much
mental conflict, he descended to entertain a personal antagonism to the young woman who had stepped in between
his Experiment, and success. He did not think kindly of
her. Lady Blandish's encomiums of her behaviour and her
beauty annoyed him. Forgetful that he had in a measure
forfeited his rights to it, he took the common ground of
fathers, and demanded, Why he was not justified in doing
all that lay in his power to prevent his son from casting
himself away upon the first creature with a pretty face he
encountered. Deliberating thus, he lost the tenderness he
should have had for his Experiment—the living, burning,
youth at his elbow, and his excessive love for him took a
rigorous tone. It appeared to him politic, reasonable, and
just, that the Uncle of this young woman who had so long
nursed the prudent scheme of marrying her to his son, should
not only not be thwarted in his object, but encouraged, and
even assisted. At least, not thwarted. Sir Austin had no
glass before him while these ideas hardened in his mind,
and he had rather forgotten the letter of Lady Blandish.

Father and son were alone in the railway carriage. Both
were too pre-occupied to speak. As they neared Bellingham,
the dark was filling the hollows of the country. Over the
pine-hills beyond the station a last rosy streak lingered across
a green sky. Richard eyed it while they flew along. It

caught him forward: it seemed full of the spirit of his love, and brought tears of mournful longing to his eyelids. The sad beauty of that one spot in the heavens seemed to call out to his soul to swear to his Lucy's truth to him: was like the sorrowful visage of his fleur-de-luce, as he called her, appealing to him for faith. That tremulous tender way she had of half-closing and catching light on the nether-lids, when sometimes she looked up in her lover's face—a look so mystic-sweet it had grown to be the fountain of his dreams: he saw it yonder, and his blood thrilled.

Know you those wand-like touches of I know not what, before which our grosser being melts, and we, much as we hope to be in the Awaking, stand etherealized, trembling with new joy? They come but rarely; rarely even in Love, when we fondly think them Revelations. Mere Sensations they are, doubtless: and we rank for them no higher in the spiritual scale than so many translucent glorious *polypi* that quiver on the Celestial Shores, the hues of Heaven running through them. Yet in the harvest of our days it is something for the animal to have had such mere fleshly polypian experiences to look back upon, and they give him an horizon,—pale seas of luring splendour. One who has had them (when they do not bound him), may find the Isles of Bliss sooner than another. Sensual faith in the upper glories is something. 'Let us remember,' says THE PILGRIM'S SCRIP, 'that Nature, though heathenish, reaches at her best to the footstool of the Highest. She is not all dust, but a living portion of the spheres. In aspiration it is our error to despise her, forgetting that through Nature only can we *ascend*. Cherished, trained, and purified, she is then partly worthy the Divine mate who is to make her wholly so. St. Simeon saw the Hog in Nature, and took Nature for the Hog.'

It was one of these strange bodily exaltations which thrilled the young man, he knew not how it was, for his sadness and his forebodings vanished. The soft wand touched him. At that moment had Sir Austin spoken openly, Richard might have fallen upon his heart. He could not. He chose to feel injured on the common ground of fathers, and to pursue his System by plotting. Lady Blandish had revived his jealousy of the creature who menaced it, and jealousy of a System is unreflecting and vindictive as jealousy of woman.

Heath-roots and pines breathed sharp in the cool Autumn Evening about the Bellingham Station. Richard stood a moment as he stepped from the train, and drew the country air into his lungs with large heaves of the chest. Leaving his father to the felicitations of the Station-Master, he went into the Lobourne road to look for his faithful Tom, who had received private orders through Berry to be in attendance with his young master's mare, Cassandra, and was lurking in a plantation of firs unenclosed on the borders of the road, where Richard, knowing his retainer's zest for conspiracy too well to seek him anywhere but in the part most favoured with shelter and concealment, found him furtively whiffing tobacco.

"What news, Tom?—Is she well? Is she ill? Is she safe?"

Tom smuggled his pipe into his pocket. He sent his undress cap on one side to scratch at Dilemma, an old agricultural habit to which he was still a slave in moments of abstract thought, or sudden difficulty.

"No, I don't want the rake, Mr. Richard," he whinnied with a deprecating false grin, as he beheld his master's eye vacantly following the action. "You're looking uncommon well, Sir."

"D'you hear, Tom?" cried Richard, imperatively. "I haven't had a letter for a week! How is she? Where is she?"

Tom stepped back to Cassandra's hind-quarters, and round to her fore-feet, pretending to be spying after furze-thorns.

Between anger and alarm at Tom's hesitation to answer honestly, a quality that served for patience restrained his master; but Tom saw that this trifling would not do, and he got up from the mare's loins, and said, holding forth both hands open, "There, Sir! I don't mind saying it. I know I ought for to have powsted a letter, tall'n you all of it as much as I'd come to hear—but there, Mr. Richard, I do writ so shocken bad, and that's the truth, I wasn't the man for't. Well, Sir," Tom warmed to speak out now he had begun, "I shewd 'a stopped her. I know that, Sir. I know'd how it'd knock you down. But I ain't a scholar! I ain't what you thinks, or hopes for—bain't a bit of a hero! I never can do anything 'less it's in company. I can't do't by myself. *I'm* no hero. I know very well Lord Nelson 'd a' done it," continued Tom, remembering, doubtless, many a lecture on the darling hero of Britain. *"He'd* 'a done it. So'd the Duke o' Wellington, or any o' them Peninsoolar War chaps. But I hadn't the speert to step in and say—You shan't take her away! I thought about 't, but there—I couldn't! There's no more mistakes between us now, Mr. Richard. You see, I ain't a bit better than any other chap."

Thus Richard learnt the news. He took it with surprising outward calm, only getting a little closer to Cassandra's neck, and looking very hard at Tom without seeing a speck of him, which had the effect on Tom of making him sincerely wish his master would punch his head at once rather than fix him in that owl-like way.

"Go, on, Tom!" said Richard huskily. "Yes? She's gone! Well?"

Tom was brought to understand he must make the most of trifles, and recited how he had heard from a female domestic at Belthorpe of the name of Davenport, formerly known to him, that the young lady never slept a wink from the hour she knew she was going, but sat up in her bed till morring crying most pitifully, though she never com-

plained. Hereat the tears unconsciously streamed down
Richard's cheeks. Tom said he had tried to see her, but
Mr. Adrian kept him at work ciphering at a terrible sum—
that and nothing else all day! saying it was to please his
young master on his return. "Likewise something in Lat'n,"
added Tom. "Nom'tive Mouser!—'nough to make ye mad,
Sir!" he exclaimed with pathos. The wretch had been put
to acquire a Latin declension.

Tom saw her on the morning she went away, he said:
she was very sorrowful-looking, and nodded kindly to him
as she passed in the fly along with young Tom Blaize. "She
have got uncommon kind eyes, Sir," said Tom, "and cryin'
don't spoil them." For which his hand was violently
wrenched.

Tom had no more to tell, save that, in rounding the road,
the young lady had hung out her hand, and seemed to move
it forward and back, as much as to say, Good-bye, Tom!
"And though she couldn't see me," said Tom, "I took off
my hat. I did take it so kind of her to think of a chap
like me." Tom was at high-pressure sentiment, what with
his education for a hero, and his master's love-stricken state.

"You saw no more of her, Tom?"

"No, sir. That was the last!" said Tom, imitating the
forlornness of his master's voice.

"That was the last you saw of her, Tom?"

"Well, Sir! I saw nothin' more."

"You didn't go to the corner of the road to see—?"

"Dash'd if I thought o' doin' that, Sir!"

"And so she went out of sight, Tom?"

"Clean gone, that she were, Sir!"

"Why did they take her away? what have they done
with her? where have they taken her to?"

These red-hot questionings were addressed to the universal heaven rather than to Tom.

"Why didn't she write?" they were resumed. "Why did
she leave? She's mine! She belongs to me! Who dared

take her away? Why did she leave without writing?——
Tom!"

"Yes, Sir," said the well-drilled recruit, dressing himself up to the word of command. He expected a variation
of the theme from the change of tone with which his name
had been pronounced, but it was again, "Where have they
taken her to?" and this was even more perplexing to Tom
than his hard sum in arithmetic had been. He could only
draw down the corners of his mouth hard, and glance up
queerly.

"She *had* been crying—you saw that, Tom?"

"No mistake about that, Mr. Richard. Cryin' all night
and all day, I sh'd say."

"And she was crying when you saw her?"

"She looked as if she'd just done for a moment, Sir," Tom
insinuated.

"But her face was white?"

"White as a sheet."

Richard paused to discover whether his instinct had caught
a new view from these facts. He was in a cage, always
knocking against the same bars, fly as he might. Her tears
were the stars in his black night. He clung to them as golden
orbs. Inexplicable as they were, they were at least pledges
of love. She could not have been too miserable to please
him.

"Tom!" he said, "I'll follow her at once."

"Better wait," Tom advised, "till I search out where the
young lady is—hadn't you, Sir?"

The hues of sunset had left the West. No light was
there but the steadfast pale eye of twilight. Thither he was
drawn: thither he must go. He had not listened to Tom's
sound sense, but it appeared to guide him, for he mounted
Cassandra, saying: "Tell them something, Tom. I shan't
be home to dinner," and rode off towards the forsaken home
of light over Belthorpe, wherein he saw the wan hand of his

Lucy, waving farewell, receding as he advanced. His Jewel
was stolen,—he must gaze upon the empty box.

CHAPTER XXVII

CRISIS IN THE APPLE-DISEASE

NIGHT had come on as Richard entered the old elm-shaded,
grass-bordered, lane leading down from Raynham to Belthorpe. The pale eye of twilight was shut. The wind had
tossed up the bank of western cloud, which was now flying
broad and unlighted across the sky, broad and balmy,—the
charioted South-west at full charge behind his panting
coursers. As he neared the farm his heart fluttered and
leapt up. He was sure she must be there. She must have
returned. Why should she have left for good without writing? He caught suspicion by the throat, making it voiceless, if it lived: he silenced Reason. Her not writing was
now a proof she had returned. He listened to nothing but
his imperious passion, and murmured sweet words for her,
as if she were by: tender cherishing epithets of love in the
nest. She was there,—she moved somewhere about like a
silver flame in the dear old house doing her sweet household
duties. His blood began to sing: O happy those within, to
see her and be about her! By some extraordinary process
he contrived to cast a sort of glory round the burly person
of farmer Blaize himself. And Oh! to have a companionship with a seraph one must know a seraph's bliss, and was
not young Tom to be envied? The smell of late clematis
brought on the wind enwrapped him, and went to his brain,
and threw a light over the old red-brick house, for he remembered where it grew, and the winter rose-tree, and the
jessamine, and the passion-flower: the garden in front with
the standard-roses tended by her hands; the long wall to the
left striped by the branches of the cherry; the peep of ↄ

further garden through the wall, and then the orchard, and
the fields beyond—the happy circle of her dwelling! it flashed
before his eyes while he looked on the darkness. And yet it
was the reverse of hope which kindled this light and inspired
the momentary calm he experienced: it was despair exag-
gerating delusion, wilfully building up on a groundless basis.
'For. the tenacity of true passion is terrible,' says THE PIL-
GRIM'S SCRIP, 'it will stand against the hosts of Heaven,
God's great array of Facts, rather than surrender its aim, and
must be crushed before it will succumb—sent to the lowest
pit!'—He knew she was not there: she was gone. But the
power of a will strained to madness fought at it, kept it
down, conjured forth her ghost, and would have it as he
dictated. Poor youth! the great array of Facts was in due
order of march.

He had breathed her name many times, and once overloud;
almost a cry for her escaped him. He had not noticed the
opening of a door, and the noise of a foot along the gravel-
walk. He was leaning over Cassandra's uneasy neck watching the one window intently, when a voice addressed him
out of the darkness.

"Be that you, young gentleman?—Mr. Fev'rel?"

Richard's trance was broken. "Mr. Blaize!" he said,
recognizing the farmer's voice.

"Good even'n' t' you, Sir," returned the farmer. "I knew
the mare, though I didn't know you. Rather bluff t' night
it be. Wull ye step in, Mr. Fev'rel? it's beginnin' to spit—
goin' to be a wildish night, I reckon."

Richard dismounted. The farmer called one of his men
to hold the mare, and ushered the young man in. Once
there Richard's conjurations ceased. There was a deadness
about the rooms and passages that told of her absence. The
walls he touched—these were the vacant shell of his divinity.
He had never been in the house since he knew her, and now,
what strange sweetness, and what pangs!

Young Tom Blaize was in the parlour squared over the

table in open-mouthed examination of an ancient book of the
Fashions for a Summer month which had elapsed during his
mother's minority. Young Tom was respectfully studying
the aspects of the radiant beauties of the polite work. He
also was a thrall of woman, newly enrolled, and full of
wonder.

"What, Tom!" the farmer sung out as soon as he had
opened the door; "there ye be! at yer Folly agin, are ye?
What good'll them Fashens do to *yew,* I'd like t' know?
Come, shut up, and go and see Mr. Fev'rel's mare taken
into stables.—He's al'ays at that ther' Folly now," the
farmer addressed Richard, as he of the seraph's bliss sullenly
cast the Fashions among the musk-pots, and stumped off
mumbling unintelligible grumblings. "I say there never
were a better name for a book than that ther' Folly! Talk
about attitoods! Why, they're all attitood! they're nothin'
else!" The farmer laughed broadly. "If we went about
in that style I don't think we sh'd do much work, and get
much t' eat—in style o' that ther' Folly!—ha, ha! 'counts
for ther' bein' se thin, mayhap—ha, ha, ha! Thin ain't lis-
some, though, in style o' that ther' Folly."

The farmer laughed his fat sides into a chair and motioned
his visitor to do likewise.

"It's a comfort they're most on'em females," he pursued,
sounding a thwack on his knee as he settled himself agreeably
in his seat. "It don't matter much what they does—'cept
pinchin' in—waspin' it—at the waist. Give me Natur', I
say—woman as she's made! eh, young gentleman?"

A blush went over Richard: he was thinking—'Is this the
chair she sat in?'—She seemed to put her arms about him,
and say, 'Suppose I have gone? Shall I not soon be back
to you? Why are you so downcast?'

"I asks 'un," the farmer was unable to quit the subject
his humour had fixed on, "I asks 'un, what he expects out
of a Folly but fools? And take care he don't get among
'em!—Seems Folly's a new name for them Fashens. So

they tells me. Not a bad 'un, I think!—Hope yer father's
well, Mr. Fev'rel? Ah, if he'd been the man he bid fair
to be—though we was opp'site pol'tics—well! it's a loss anyhow!—Not the first time you've bin in this apartment, young
gentleman?"

"No, Mr. Blaize! it is not," Richard now spoke. "I
think I ought to have—you see, that was my book of Folly,
and I shall be glad to think it's closed."

To this proper speech, the farmer replied drily: "Wall!
so long as that sort of Folly don't grow to be the Fashen!
'somever that's over and past—no more said about 't!"

A rather embarrassing silence ensued, broken by a movement of legs changing places, like evolutions of infantry
before the dread Artillery opens.

"You seem very lonely here," said Richard, glancing
round, and at the ceiling.

"Lonely?" quoth the farmer. "Well, for the matter o'
that, we be!—jest now, so 't happens; I've got my pipe,
and Tom's got his Folly. He's on one side the taable,
and I'm on t'other. He gaapes, and I gazes. We are a bit
lonesome. But there—it's *for* the best!"

Richard resumed: "I hardly expected to see you tonight,
Mr. Blaize."

"Y' acted like a man in coming, young gentleman, and I
does ye honour for it!" said farmer Blaize with sudden
energy and directness.

The thing implied by the farmer's words caused Richard
to take a quick breath. They looked at each other, and then
looked away, the farmer thrumming on the arm of his
chair.

Above the mantel-piece, surrounded by tarnished indifferent miniatures of high-collared well-to-do yeomen of the
anterior generation, trying their best not to grin, and high-
waisted old ladies smiling an encouraging smile through
plentiful cap-puckers, there hung a passably executed half-
figure of a Naval Officer in uniform, grasping a telescope

under his left arm, who stood forth clearly as not of their kith and kin. His eyes were blue, his hair light, his bearing that of a man who knows how to carry his head and shoulders. The artist, while giving him an epaulette to indicate his rank, had also recorded the juvenility which a Lieutenant in the Naval service can retain after arriving at that position, by painting him with smooth cheeks and fresh ruddy lips. To this portrait Richard's eyes were directed. Farmer Blaize observed it, and said:

"Her father, Sir!"

Richard moderated his voice to praise the likeness.

"Yes," said the farmer, "pretty well. Next best to havin' *her,* though it's a long way off that!"

"An old family, Mr. Blaize—is it not?" Richard asked in as careless a tone as he could assume.

"Gentlefolks—what's left of 'em," replied the farmer, with an equally affected indifference.

"And that's her father?" said Richard, growing bolder to speak of her.

"That's her father, young gentleman!"

"Mr. Blaize," Richard turned to face him, and burst out, "where is she?"

"Gone, Sir! packed off!—Can't have her here now." The farmer thrummed a step brisker, and eyed the young man's wild face resolutely.

"Mr. Blaize," Richard leaned forward to get closer to him. He was stunned, and hardly aware of what he was saying or doing: "Where has she gone? Why did she leave?"

"Ye needn't to ask, Sir—ye know," said the farmer with a side shot of his head.

"But *she* did not—it was not her wish to go?"

"No! I think she likes the place. Mayhap she likes 't too well?"

"Why did you send her away to make her unhappy, Mr. Blaize?"

The farmer bluntly denied it was he was the party who

made her unhappy. "Nobody can't accuse *me*. Tall ye what, Sir. I wunt have the busybodies set to work about her, and there's all the matter. So let you and I come to an understandin'."

A blind inclination to take offence made Richard sit upright. He forgot it the next minute, and said humbly: "Am I the cause of her going?"

"Wall!" returned the farmer, "to speak straight—ye be!"

"What can I do, Mr. Blaize, that she may come back again?" the young hypocrite asked.

"Now," said the farmer, "ye're coming to business. Glad to hear ye talk in that sensible way, Mr. Fev'rel. You may guess I wants her bad enough. The house ain't itself now she's away, and I ain't myself. Wall, Sir! This ye can do. If yew gives me yew're promus not to meddle with her at all—I can't mak' out how ye come to be acquainted—not to try to get her to be meetin' you—and if you'd 'a seen her when she left, ye would—when did ye meet?—last grass wasn't it?—your word as a gentleman not to be writing letters, and spyin' after her—I'll have her back at once. Back she shall come!"

"Give her up?" cried Richard.

"Ay, that's it!" said the farmer. "Give her up."

The young man checked the annihilation of Time that was on his mouth.

"You sent her away to protect her from me, then?" he said savagely.

"That's not quite it, but that'll do," rejoined the farmer.

"Do you think I shall harm her, Sir?"

"People sim to think she'll harm you, young gentleman," the farmer said with some irony.

"Harm *me*—she? What people?"

"People pretty intimet with you, Sir."

"What people? Who spoke of us?" Richard began to scent the plot, and would not be baulked.

"Wall, Sir, look heer," said the farmer. "It an't no

secret, and if it be, I don't see why I'm to keep it. It
appear your eddication's peculiar." The farmer drawled out
the word as if he were describing the figure of a snake. "You
an't to be as other young gentlemen. All the better! You're
a fine bold young gentleman, and your father's a right to be
proud of ye. Wall, Sir—I'm sure I thank him for 't—he
comes to hear of you and Luce, and of course he don't want
nothin' o' that—more do I. I meets him there! What's
more I won't have nothin' of it. She be my gal. She were
left to my pertection. And she's a lady, Sir. Let me tall
ye, ye won't find many on 'em so well looked to as she be—
my Luce! Well, Mr. Fev'rel, it's you, or it's her—one of
ye must be out o' the way. So we're towld. And Luce—I
do believe she's just as anxious about yer eddication as yer
father—she says she'll go, and wouldn't write, and 'd break
it off for the sake o' your eddication. And she've kep her
word, haven't she?—Ah! she's a true 'n. What she says
she'll do!—True blue she be, my Luce! So now, Sir, you
do the same, and I'll thank ye."

Any one who has tossed a sheet of paper into the fire,
and seen it gradually brown with heat, and strike to flame,
may conceive the mind of the lover as he listened to this
speech.

His anger did not evaporate in words, but condensed and
sank deep. "Mr. Blaize," he said between his set teeth,
"this is very kind of the people you allude to, but I am of
an age now to think and act for myself.—I love her, Sir!"
His whole countenance changed, and the muscles of his face
quivered.

"Wall!" said the farmer appeasingly, "we all do at your
age—somebody or other. It's nat'ral!"

"I love her!" the young man thundered afresh, too much
possessed by his passion to have a sense of shame in the confession.—"Farmer!" his voice fell to supplication, "will you
bring her back?"

Farmer Blaize made a queer face. He asked—what for?

and where was the promise required! But was not the lover's argument conclusive? He said he loved her! and he could not see why her uncle should not in consequence immediately send for her, that they might be together.—All very well, quoth the farmer, but what's to come of it?— What was to come of it? Why, love, and more love!—And a bit too much! the farmer added grimly.

"Then you refuse me, farmer," said Richard. "I must look to you for keeping her away from me, not to—to—these people. You will not have her back, though I tell you I love her better than my life?"

Farmer Blaize now had to answer him plainly, he had a reason and an objection of his own. And it was, that her character was at stake, and God knew whether she herself might not be in danger. He spoke with a kindly candour, not without dignity. He complimented Richard personally, but young people were young people: Baronets' sons were not in the habit of marrying farmers' nieces.

At first the son of a System did not comprehend him. When he did, he said: "Farmer! if I give you my word of honour, as I hope for Heaven, to marry her when I come of age, will you have her back?"

He was so fervid that, to quiet him, the farmer only shook his head doubtfully at the bars of the grate, and let his chest fall slowly. Richard caught what seemed to him a glimpse of encouragement in these signs, and observed: "It's not because you object to me, Mr. Blaize?"

The farmer signified it was not that.

"It's because my father is against me," Richard went on, and undertook to show that love was so sacred a matter that no father could entirely and for ever resist his son's inclinations. Argument being a cool field where the farmer could meet and match him, the young man got on the tramroad of passion, and went ahead. He drew pictures of Lucy, of her truth, and his own. He took leaps from Life to Death, from Death to Life, mixing imprecations and prayers in a torrent. Perhaps he did move the stolid old Englishman a little, he was so vehement, and made so visible a sacrifice of his pride.

Farmer Blaize tried to pacify him, but it was useless. His Jewel he must have.

The farmer stretched out his hand for the pipe that allayeth botheration.—"May smoke heer now," he said. "Not when—somebody's present. Smoke in the kitchen then. Don't mind smell?"

Richard nodded, and watched the operations while the farmer filled, and lighted, and began to puff, as if his fate hung on them.

"Who'd 'a thought, when you sat over there once, of it's comin' to this!" ejaculated the farmer, drawing ease and reflection from tobacco. "You didn't think much of her that day, young gentleman? I introdooced ye. Wall! things comes about. Can't ye wait till she returns in doo coorse, now?"

This suggestion, the work of the pipe, did but bring on him another torrent.

"It's queer," said the farmer, putting the mouth of the pipe to his wrinkled up temples.

Richard waited for him, and then he laid down the pipe altogether as no aid in perplexity, and said, after leaning his arm on the table and staring at Richard an instant:

"Look, young gentleman! My word's gone. I've spoken it. I've given 'em the 'surance she shan't be back till the spring, and then I'll have her, and then—wall! I do hope, for more reasons than one, ye'll both on ye be wiser—I've got my own notions about her. But I ain't the man to force a gal to marry 'gainst her inclines. 'Pend upon it I'm not yer enemy, Mr. Fev'rel. Yer jest the one to mak' a young gal proud. So jest wait,—and see. That's my 'dvice. Jest tak' and wait. I've no more to say."

Richard's impetuosity had made him really afraid of speak-

ing his notions concerning the projected felicity of young
Tom, if indeed they were serious.

The farmer repeated that he had no more to say, and
Richard with, "Wait till the spring! Wait till the spring!"
dinning despair in his ears, stood up to depart. Farmer
Blaize shook his slack hand in a friendly way, and called out
at the door for young Tom, who, dreading allusions to his
Folly, did not appear. A maid rushed by Richard in the
passage, and slipped something into his grasp, which fixed
on it without further consciousness than that of touch. The
mare was led forth by the Bantam. A light rain was falling
down strong warm gusts, and the trees were noisy in the
night. Farmer Blaize requested Richard at the gate to give
him his hand, and say all was well. He liked the young
man for his earnestness and honest outspeaking. Richard
could not say all was well, but he gave his hand, and knit
it to the farmer's in a sharp squeeze, when he got upon
Cassandra, and rode into the tumult.

A calm clear dawn succeeded the roaring west, and threw
its glowing grey image on the waters of the Abbey-lake. Before sunrise Tom Bakewell was abroad, and met the missing youth, his master, jogging Cassandra leisurely along the
Lobourne park-road, a sorry couple to look at. Cassandra's
flanks were caked with mud, her head drooped: all that was
in her had been taken out by that wild night. On what
heaths and heavy fallows had she not spent her noble
strength, recklessly fretting through the darkness!

"Take the mare," said Richard, dismounting and patting
her between the eyes. "She's done up, poor old gal! Look
to her, Tom, and then come to me in my room."

Tom asked no questions. He saw that he was in for the
first Act of the new Comedy.

Three days would bring the anniversary of Richard's
birth, and though Tom was close, the condition of the mare,
and the young gentleman's strange freak in riding her out
all night becoming known, prepared everybody at Raynham

for the usual bad-luck birthday, the prophets of which were full of sad gratification. Sir Austin had an unpleasant office to require of his son: no other than that of humbly begging Benson's pardon, and washing out the undue blood he had spilt in taking his Pound of Flesh. Heavy Benson was told to anticipate the demand for pardon, and practised in his mind the most melancholy Christian deportment he could assume on the occasion. But while his son was in this state, Sir Austin considered that he would hardly be brought to see the virtues of the act, and did not make the requisition of him, and Heavy Benson remained drawn up solemnly expectant at doorways, and at the foot of the staircase, a Saurian Caryatid, wherever he could get a step in advance of the young man, while Richard heedlessly passed him, as he passed everybody else, his head bent to the ground, and his legs bearing him like random instruments of whose service he was unconscious. It was a shock to Benson's implicit belief in his patron; and he was not consoled by the philosophic explanation, 'That Good in a strong many-compounded nature is of slower growth than any other mortal thing, and must not be forced.' Damnatory doctrines best pleased Benson. Benson was ready to pardon, as a Christian should, but he did want his enemy before him on his knees. And now, though the Saurian Eye saw more than all the other eyes in the house, and saw that there was matter in hand between Tom and his master to breed exceeding discomposure to the System, Benson, as he had not received his indemnity, and did not wish to encounter fresh perils for nothing, held his peace.

Sir Austin partly divined what was going on in the breast of his son, without conceiving the depths of distrust his son cherished towards him, and all, or quite measuring the intensity of the passion that consumed him. He was very kind, and tender with him. Like a cunning physician who has, nevertheless, overlooked the change in the disease superinduced by one false dose, he meditated his prescriptions carefully and confidently, sure that he knew the case, and was a match for it. He decreed that Richard's erratic behaviour should pass unnoticed. Two days before the birthday, he asked him whether he would object to the Grandisons coming, and having company? To which Richard said: "Have whom you will, Sir." The preparation for festivity commenced accordingly.

On the birthday eve he dined with the rest. Lady Blandish was there, and sat penitently at his right. Hippias prognosticated certain indigestion for himself on the morrow. The Eighteenth Century wondered whether she should live to see another birthday. Adrian drank the two-years' distant term of his tutorship, and Algernon went over the list of the Lobourne men who would cope with Bursley on the morrow. Sir Austin gave ear and a word to all, keeping his mental eye for his son. To please Lady Blandish also, Adrian ventured to make trifling jokes about Mrs. Grandison; jokes delicately not decent, but so delicately so that it was not decent to perceive it. He desired to know whether Berry was in sufficient muscular condition to transport the lady up stairs and down; and being told that no doubt Berry would be, were the service required of him, Adrian appeared to reflect profoundly, and thought that on no account must the precious freight be consigned to the inflammable Berry; in support of which Adrian mildly cited certain grievous instances in the Pagan mythology of breach of trust, even when the offenders were Gods, which Berry had no pretence to be, utter animal that he was.

"Then you must do it," said Richard, just waking up, and for want of something to say.

"Even I dare not! Such an Ordeal as that!"—Adrian gravely replied, shaking a meek sinner's head, and it was impossible to help laughing at his solemn manner. Algernon, knowing him better than the others, laughed aloud.

"I suppose I must be the man!" he said.

"Remember," said Adrian, "that you have already had your Ordeal."

"Well, then, Hip!" Algernon turned to his melancholy brother, "Hip will do for it exactly."

"Happy one!" Adrian apostrophized Hippias reverently, "behold in his arms the fruit of a thousand indigestions!"

And at this picture of the virtuous lady borne as a prize by the Dyspepsy, there was laughter all round the board, Sir Austin himself reticently joining in.

After dinner Richard left them. Nothing more than commonly peculiar was observed about him, beyond the excessive glitter of his eyes, but the Baronet said, "Yes, yes! that would pass." He, and Adrian, and Lady Blandish, took tea in the library, and sat till a late hour discussing casuistries relating mostly to the Apple-Disease. Converse very amusing to the Wise Youth, who could suggest to the two chaste minds situations of the shadiest character, with the air of a seeker after truth, and lead them, unsuspecting, where they dare not look about them. The Aphorist had elated the heart of his constant fair worshiper with a newly-rounded, if not newly-conceived, sentence, when they became aware that they were four. Heavy Benson stood among them. He said he had knocked, but received no answer. There was, however, a vestige of surprise and dissatisfaction on his face beholding Adrian of the company, which had not quite worn away, and gave place, when it did vanish, to an aspect of flabby severity.

"Well, Benson? well?" said the Baronet, not understanding the interruptions, and impatient at Benson's presence.

Benson persisted in the flabby-severe without speaking, and the appearance of this strange owl presiding stupidly over them, was so astonishing as to keep them all looking at him. They had disconcerted Benson, who was of slow wit, by being three, instead of two, and he was troubled what to say for himself. At last he said the thing he would have said had they been but two, and one of the two a born Pagan.

"If you please, Sir Austin! it's very late."

Benson regarded the impression he had made. It was not a very distinct one. Lady Blandish laughed and said: "I see. Benson wishes to have us up early in the morning! Hasn't my maid gone to bed?"

"She has gone, my Lady."

"Are you sure?" said Adrian.

"To the best of my knowledge, Mr. Hadrian, she has gone to her bed." Benson's tone defied misconstruction or imputation.

"Then I will follow soon to mine, Benson," said Lady Blandish.

This should have satisfied Benson, but still he did not go.

"Well, Benson? well?" said the Baronet.

The unmoving man replied: "If you please Sir Austin— Mr. Richard!"

"Well?"

"He's out!"

"Well?"

"With Bakewell!"

"Well?"

"And a carpet-bag!"

Benson had judged his climax properly. And a carpet-bag! The Baronet looked blank. Adrian raised his brows. Lady Blandish glanced at one, and at the other.

Out he was, and with a carpet-bag, which Tom Bakewell carried. He was on the road to Bellingham, under heavy rain, hasting like an escaped captive, wild with joy, while Tom shook his skin, and grunted at his discomforts. The mail-train was to be caught at Bellingham. He knew where to find her now, through the intervention of Miss Davenport, and thither he was flying, an Arrow loosened from the bow: thither, in spite of fathers, and friends, and plotters, to claim her, and take her, and stand with her against the world.

They were both thoroughly wet when they entered Bellingham, and Tom's visions were of hot drinks. He hinted the necessity for inward consolation to his master, who could answer nothing but, "Tom! Tom! I shall see her tomorrow!" It was bad—travelling in the wet, Tom hinted again, to provoke the same insane outcry, and have his arm seized and furiously shaken into the bargain. Passing the principal Inn of the place, Tom spoke plainly for brandy.

"No!" cried Richard, "there's not a moment to be lost!" and as he said it, he reeled, and fell against Tom, muttering indistinctly of faintness, and that there was no time to lose. Tom lifted him in his arms, and got admission to the Inn. Brandy, the country's specific, was advised by host and hostess, and forced into his mouth, reviving him sufficiently to cry out, "Tom! the bell's ringing: we shall be late," after which he fell back insensible on the sofa where they had stretched him. Excitement of blood and brain had done its work upon him. The poor youth suffered them to undress him and put him to bed, and there he lay, forgetful even of Love; a drowned weed borne onward by the tide of the hours. There his father found him.

Was the Scientific Humanist remorseful? Not he. He had looked forward to such a crisis as that point in the disease his son was the victim of, when the body would fail and give the spirit calm to conquer the malady, knowing very well that the seeds of the evil were not of the spirit. Moreover to see him, and have him, was a repose after the alarm Benson had sounded. Anxious he was, and prayerful; but with faith in the physical energy he attributed to his System. This providential stroke had saved the youth from Heaven knew what! "Mark!" said the Baronet to Lady Blandish, "when he recovers, he will not care for her."

The lady had accompanied him to the Bellingham Inn on first hearing of Richard's seizure.

"Oh! what an iron man you can be," she exclaimed, smothering her intuitions. She was for giving the boy his bauble; promising it him, at least, if he would only get well and be the bright flower of promise he once was.

"Can you look on him," she pleaded, "can you look on him, and persevere?"

It was a hard sight for this man who loved his son so deeply. The youth lay in his strange bed, straight and motionless, with fever on his cheeks, and altered eyes.

"See what you do to us!" said the Baronet, sorrowfully eyeing the bed.

"But if you lose him?" Lady Blandish whispered.

Sir Austin walked away from her, and probed the depths of his love. "The stroke will not be dealt by me," he said.

His patient serenity was a wonder to all who knew him. Indeed to have doubted and faltered now was to have subverted the glorious fabric just on the verge of completion. He believed that his son's pure strength was fitted to cope with any natural evil: that such was God's Law. To him Richard's passion was an ill incident to the ripeness of his years, and his perfect innocence; and this crisis the struggle of the poison passing out of him—not to be deplored. He was so confident that he did not even send for Dr. Bairam. Old Dr. Clifford of Lobourne was the medical attendant, who, with head-shaking, and gathering of lips, and reminiscences of ancient arguments, guaranteed to do all that leech could do in the matter. The old Doctor did admit that Richard's constitution was admirable, and answered to his prescriptions like a piano to the musician. "But," he said, at a family consultation, for Sir Austin had told him how it stood with the young man, "drugs are not much in cases of this sort. Change! That's what's wanted, and as soon as may be. Distraction! He ought to see the world, and know what he's made of. It's no use my talking, I know," added the Doctor.

"On the contrary," said Sir Austin. "I am quite of your persuasion. And the world he shall see—now."

"We have dipped him in Styx, you know, Doctor," Adrian remarked.

"But, Doctor," said Lady Blandish, "have you known a case of this sort before?"

"Never, my lady," said the Doctor, "they're not common in these parts. Country people are tolerably healthy-minded."

"But people—and country people—have died for love, Doctor?"

The Doctor had not met any of them.

"Men, or women?" inquired the Baronet.

Lady Blandish believed, mostly women.

"Ask the Doctor whether they were healthy-minded women," said the Baronet. "No! you are both looking at the wrong end. Between a highly-cultured being, and an emotionless animal, there is all the difference in the world. But of the two, the Doctor is nearer the truth. The healthy nature is pretty safe. If he allowed for organization he would be right altogether. To feel, but not to feel to excess, that is the problem."

> "If I can't have the one I chose,
> To some fresh maid I will propose,"

Adrian hummed a country ballad.

"That couplet," said Sir Austin, "exactly typifies the Doctor's hero. I think he must admire Agamemnon—eh, Doctor? Chryseïs taken from us, let us seize Bryseïs!—Children cry, but don't die, for their lumps of sugar. When they grow older, they—"

"Simply have a stronger appreciation of the sugar, and make a greater noise to obtain it," Adrian took him up, and elicited the smile which usually terminated any dispute he joined.

CHAPTER XXVIII

OF THE SPRING PRIMROSE AND THE AUTUMNAL

WHEN the young Experiment again knew the hours that rolled him onward, he was in his own room at Raynham. Nothing had changed: only a strong fist had knocked him down and stunned him, and he opened his eyes to a grey world. He had forgotten what he lived for. He was weak, and thin, and with a pale memory of things. His functions were the same, everything surrounding him was the same: he looked upon the old blue hills, the far-lying fallows, the river, and the woods: he knew them, but they seemed to have lost recollection of him. Nor could he find in familiar human faces the secret intimacy of heretofore. They were the same faces: they nodded and smiled to him. What was lost he could not tell. Something had been knocked out of him! He was sensible of his father's sweetness of manner, and he was grieved that he could not reply to it, for every sense of shame and reproach had strangely gone. He felt very useless. In place of the fiery love for one, he now bore about a cold charity to all.

Thus in the heart of the young man died the Spring Primrose, and while it died another heart was pushing forth the Primrose of Autumn.

The wonderful change in Richard, and the wisdom of her admirer, now positively proved, were exciting matters to Lady Blandish. She was rebuked for certain little rebellious fancies concerning him that had come across her enslaved mind from time to time. For was he not almost a prophet? It distressed the sentimental lady that a love like Richard's could pass off in mere smoke, and words such as she had heard him speak in Abbey-wood resolve to emptiness. Nay, it humiliated her personally, and the Baronet's shrewd prognostication humiliated her. For how should he know, and

dare to say, that Love was a thing of the dust that could
be trodden out under the heel of Science? But he had said
so, and he had proved himself right. She heard with wonderment that Richard of his own accord had spoken to his
father of the folly he had been guilty of, and had begged
his pardon. The Baronet told her this, adding that the
youth had done it in a cold unwavering way, without a
movement of his features: had evidently done it to throw
off the burden of the duty he had conceived, and thereafter
passed by. He had thought himself bound to acknowledge
that he had been the Foolish Young Fellow, wishing, possibly, to abjure the fact by an act of penance. He had also
given satisfaction to Benson, and was become a renovated
peaceful spirit, whose main object appeared to be to get up
his physical strength by exercise and no expenditure of
speech. In her company he was composed and courteous:
even when they were alone together, he did not exhibit a
trace of melancholy. Sober he seemed, as one who has recovered from a drunkenness and has determined to drink no
more. The idea struck her that he might be playing a part,
but Tom Bakewell, in a private conversation they had, informed her, that he had received an order from his young
master, one day while boxing with him, not to mention the
young lady's name to him so long as he lived: and Tom
could only suppose that she had offended him. Theoretically
wise Lady Blandish had always thought the Baronet: she
was unprepared to find him thus practically sagacious. She
fell many degrees: she wanted something to cling to: so
she clung to the man who struck her low. Love, then, was
earthly: its depth could be probed by Science! A man lived
who could measure it from end to end; foretell its term;
handle the young cherub as were he a shot owl! We who
have flown into cousinship with the empyrean, and disported
among immortal hosts, our base birth as a child of Time is
made bare to us!—our wings are cut! Oh, then, if Science
is this victorious enemy of Love, let us love Science! was the

logic of the lady's heart: and secretly cherishing the assurance that she should confute him yet, and prove him utterly wrong, she gave him the fruits of present success, as it is a habit of women to do: involuntarily partly. The fires took hold of her. She felt soft emotions such as a girl feels, and they flattered her. It was like youth coming back. Pure women have a second youth. The Autumn primrose flourished.

We are advised by THE PILGRIM'S SCRIP that:

'The ways of women, which are Involution, and their practices, which are Opposition, are generally best hit upon by guess-work, and a bold word:'—it being impossible to track them and hunt them down in the ordinary style.

So that we may not ourselves become involved and opposed, let us each of us venture a guess and say a bold word as to how it came that the lady, who trusted Love to be eternal, grovelled to him that shattered her tender faith, and loved him.

Hitherto it had been simply a sentimental dalliance, and gossips had maligned the lady. Just when the gossips grew tired of their slander, and inclined to look upon her charitably, she set about to deserve every word they had said of her: which may instruct us, if you please, that gossips have only to persist in lying to be crowned with verity, or that one has only to endure evil mouths for a period to gain impunity. She was always at the Abbey now. She was much closeted with the Baronet. It seemed to be understood that she had taken Mrs. Doria's place. Benson in his misogynic soul perceived that she was taking Lady Feverel's; but any report circulated by Benson was sure to meet discredit, and drew the gossips upon himself; which made his meditations tragic. No sooner was one woman defeated than another took the field! The object of the System was no sooner safe than its great author was in danger! Benson alone was sincere, and wretched! Consequently he turned prophet. He foretold the Downfall of the System, and carried it in his face. There was no escaping from his horrible heaviness. The Baronet complained of it. At a time of exuberant self-congratulation, a dear lady worshiping, a beloved boy obedient, a System triumphant, and scoffers confounded, Benson's dead weight was offensive.

"I can't think what has come to Benson," he said to Adrian.

"He seems to have received a fresh legacy of several pounds of lead," returned the Wise Youth, and imitating Dr. Clifford's manner, "Change is what he wants! distraction! send him to Wales, Sir, for a month, and let Richard go with him. The two victims of Woman may do each other good."

"Unfortunately I can't do without him," said the Baronet.

"Then we must continue to have him on our shoulders all day, and on our chests all night!" Adrian ejaculated.

"I think while he preserves this aspect, we won't have him at the dinner-table," said the Baronet.

Adrian thought that would be a relief to their digestions; and added: "You know, Sir, what he says?"

Receiving a negative, Adrian delicately explained to him that Benson's excessive ponderosity of demeanour was caused by anxiety for the safety of his master.

"You must pardon a faithful fool, Sir," he continued, for the Baronet became red, and exclaimed:

"His stupidity is past belief! I have absolutely to bolt my study-door against him."

"Have you indeed, Sir!" said Adrian, and at once beheld a charming scene in the interior of the study, not unlike one that Benson had visually witnessed. For, like a wary prophet, Benson, that he might have warrant for what he foretold of the future, had a care to spy upon the present: warned haply by THE PILGRIM'S SCRIP, of which he was a diligent reader, and which says, rather enigmatically: 'Could we see Time's full face we were wise of him.' Now to see Time's full face, it is sometimes necessary to look through keyholes, the veteran having a trick of smiling peace to you on one cheek, and grimacing confusion on the other, behind the curtain. Decency and a sense of honour restrain most of us from being thus wise, and miserable, for ever. Benson's excuse was that he believed in his master, who was menaced. And moreover, notwithstanding his previous tribulation, to spy upon Cupid was sweet to him. So he peeped, and he saw a sight. He saw Time's full face; or, in other words, he saw the wiles of woman and the weakness of man: which is our history, as Benson would have written it, and a great many poets and philosophers have written it.

Yet it was but the plucking of the Autumn primrose that Benson had seen: a somewhat different operation from the plucking of the Spring one: very innocent! Our staid elderly sister has paler blood, and has, or thinks she has, a reason or two about the roots. She is not all instinct. 'For this high cause, and for that I know men, and know him to be the flower of men, I give myself to him!' She makes that lofty inward exclamation while the hand is detaching her from the roots. Even so strong a self-justification she requires. She has not that blind glory in excess which her younger sister can gild the longest leap with. And if, moth-like, she desires for the star, she is nervously cautious of candles. Hence her circles about the dangerous human flame are wide and shy. She must be drawn nearer and nearer by a fresh *reason*. She loves to sentimentalize. Lady Blandish had been sentimentalizing for ten years. She would have preferred to pursue the game. The dark-eyed dame was pleased with her smooth life and the soft excitement that did not ruffle it. Not willingly did she let herself be won.

'Sentimentalists,' says THE PILGRIM'S SCRIP, 'are they who seek to enjoy Reality, without incurring the Immense Debtorship for a thing done.'

'It is,' the writer says of Sentimentalism elsewhere, 'a happy pastime, and an important science, to the timid, the idle, and the heartless: but a damning one to them who have anything to forfeit.'

However, one who could set down, Dying for Love, as a Sentimentalism, can hardly be accepted as a clear authority. Assuredly he was not one to avoid the incurring of the immense Debtorship in any way: but he was still a bondsman to the woman who had forsaken him, and a spoken word had made it seem duty to face that public scandal which was the last evil to him. What had so horrified the virtuous Benson, Richard had already beheld in Daphne's Bower; a simple kissing of the fair white hand! Doubtless the keyhole somehow added to Benson's horror. The two similar performances, so very innocent, had wondrous opposite consequences. The first kindled Richard to adore Woman: the second destroyed Benson's faith in Man. But Lady Blandish knew the difference between the two. She understood why the Baronet did not speak: excused, and respected him for it. She was content, since she must love, to love humbly, and she had, besides, her pity for his sorrows to comfort her. A hundred fresh reasons for loving him arose and multiplied every day. He read to her the secret book in his own handwriting, composed for Richard's Marriage Guide: containing Advice and Directions to a Young Husband, full of the most tender wisdom, and delicacy: so she thought: nay, not wanting in poetry, though neither rhymed nor measured. He expounded to her the distinctive character of the divers ages of Love, giving the palm to the flower she put forth, over that of Spring, or the Summer Rose. And while they sat and talked, "My wound has healed," he said. "How?" she asked. "At the fountain of your eyes," he replied and drew the joy of new life from her blushes, without incurring further debtorship for a thing done.

CHAPTER XXIX

IN WHICH THE HERO TAKES A STEP

LET it be some apology for the damage caused by the careering hero, and a consolation to the quiet wretches dragged along with him at his chariot-wheels, that he is generally the last to know when he has made an actual start: such a mere creature is he, like the rest of us, albeit the head of our fates. By this you perceive the true hero, whether he be a prince or a pot-boy, that he does not plot: Fortune does all for him. He may be compared to one to whom, in an electric circle, it is given to carry the *battery*. We caper and grimace at his will: yet not his the will, not his the power. 'Tis all Fortune's, whose puppet he is. She deals her dispensations through him. Yea, though our capers be never so comical, he laughs not. Intent upon his own business, the true hero asks little services of us here and there; thinks it quite natural that they should be acceded to, and sees nothing ridiculous in the lamentable contortions we must go through to fulfil them. Probably he is the elect of Fortune, because of that notable faculty of being intent upon his own business: 'Which,' says THE PILGRIM'S SCRIP, 'with men to be valued equal to that force which in water *makes a stream.*' This prelude was necessary to the present chapter of Richard's history.

It happened that in the turn of the year, and while old Earth was busy with her flowers, the fresh wind blew, the little bird sang, and Hippias Feverel, the Dyspepsy, amazed, felt the Spring move within him. He communicated his delightful new sensations to the Baronet, his brother, whose constant exclamation with regard to him, was: "Poor Hippias! All his machinery is bare!" and had no hope that he would ever be in a condition to defend it from view.

Nevertheless Hippias had that hope, and so he told his brother, making great exposure of his machinery to effect the explanation. He spoke of all his physical experiences exultingly, and with wonder. The achievement of common efforts, not usually blazoned, he celebrated as mighty triumphs, and, of course, had Adrian on his back very quickly. But he could bear him, or anything, now. It was such ineffable relief to find himself looking out upon the world of mortals instead of into the black phantasmal abysses of his own complicated frightful structure. "My mind doesn't so much seem to haunt itself, now," said Hippias, nodding shortly and peering out of intense puckers to convey a glimpse of what hellish sufferings his had been: "I feel as if I had come aboveground."

A poor Dyspepsy may talk as he will, but he is the one who never gets sympathy, or experiences compassion: and it is he whose groaning petitions for charity do at last rout that Christian virtue. Lady Blandish, a charitable soul, could not listen to Hippias, though she had a heart for little mice and flies, and Sir Austin had also small patience with his brother's gleam of health, which was just enough to make his disease visible. He remembered his early follies and excesses, and bent his ear to him as one man does to another who complains of having to pay a debt legally incurred.

"I think," said Adrian, seeing how the communications of Hippias were received, "that when our Nemesis takes lodgings in the stomach, it's best to act the Spartan: smile hard, and be silent."

"Exactly," replied the Baronet. "Mankind has some instinctive disgust for the victims of their appetites. We pity any other functional derangement than that."

Richard alone was decently kind to Hippias; whether from opposition, or real affection, could not be said, as the young man was mysterious. He advised his uncle to take exercise, walked with him, cultivated cheerful impressions in him, and pointed out innocent pursuits. He made Hippias visit with him some of the poor old folks of the village, who bewailed the loss of his cousin, Austin Wentworth, and did his best to waken him up, and give the outer world a stronger hold on him. He succeeded in nothing but in winning his Uncle's gratitude. The Season bloomed scarce longer than a week for Hippias, and then began to languish. The poor Dyspepsy's eager grasp at beatification relaxed: he went underground again. He announced that he felt "spongy things"—one of the more constant miseries of his malady. His bitter face recurred. He chewed the cud of horrid hallucinations. He told Richard he must give up going about with him: people telling of their ailments made him so uncomfortable—the birds were so noisy, pairing—the rude bare soil sickened him.

"Besides," said Hippias, "it's singular, but at this time of the year, Richard, I always have the same idea. I can't go out and see a garden without thinking I ought to be upside down, and have the bulbous part underneath me, like those— what do you call those flowers?—yes, like those crocuses. And you can't imagine how distressing it really is when you think those things in earnest."

Richard treated him with a gravity equal to his father's. He asked what the Doctors said.

"Oh! the Doctors!" cried Hippias with vehement scepticism. "No man of sense believes in medicine for chronic disorder. Do you happen to have heard of any new remedy, then, Richard? No? They advertise a great many cures for Indigestion, I assure you, my dear boy. I wonder whether one can rely upon the authenticity of those signatures? I see no reason why there should be *no* cure for such a disease?—Eh? And it's just one of the things a quack, as they call them, would hit upon sooner than one who is in the beaten track. Do you know, Richard, my dear boy, I've often thought that if we could by any means appropriate to our use some of the extraordinary digestive power that a Boa Constrictor has in his gastric juices, there is really no

manner of reason why we should not comfortably dispose
of as much of an ox as our stomachs will hold, and one
might eat French dishes without the wretchedness of thinking what's to follow. And this makes me think that those
fellows *may,* after all, have got some truth in them; some
prodigious secret that, of course, they require to be paid for.
We distrust each other in this world too much, Richard.
I've felt inclined once or twice—but it's absurd!—If it only
alleviated a few of my sufferings *I* should be satisfied. I've
no hesitation in saying that I should be quite satisfied if it
only did away with one or two, or left me free to eat and
drink as other people do. Not that I mean to try them.
It's only a fancy—Eh? What a thing health is, my dear
boy! Ah, if I were like you! I was in love once!"

"Were you!" said Richard coolly regarding him.

"I've forgotten what I felt!" Hippias sighed. "You've
very much improved, my dear boy."

"So people say," quoth Richard.

Hippias looked at him anxiously: "If I go to town and
get the Doctor's opinion about trying a new course—Eh,
Richard? will you come with me? I should like your company. We could see London together, you know. Enjoy
ourselves," and Hippias rubbed his hands.

Richard smiled at the feeble glimmer of enjoyment promised by his Uncle's eyes, and said he thought it better they
should stay where they were,—an answer that might mean
anything. Hippias immediately became possessed by the be-
guiling project. He went to the Baronet, and put the
matter before him, instancing Doctors as the object of his
journey, not quacks, of course; and requesting leave to take
Richard. Sir Austin was getting uneasy about his son's
manner. It was not natural. His heart seemed to be
frozen: he had no confidences: he appeared to have no
ambition—to have lost the virtues of youth with the poison
that had passed out of him. He was disposed to try what
effect a little travelling might have on him, and had himself

once or twice hinted to Richard that it would be good for him to move about; the young man quietly replying that he did not wish to quit Raynham at all; which was too strict a fulfilment of his father's original views in educating him there entirely. On the day that Hippias made his proposal, Adrian, seconded by Lady Blandish, also made one. The sweet Spring season stirred in Adrian as well as in others: not to pastoral measures: to the joys of the Operatic world and bravura glories. He also suggested that it would be advisable to carry Richard to town for a term, and let him know his position, and some freedom. Sir Austin weighed the two proposals. He was pretty certain that Richard's passion was consumed, and that he was now only under the burden of its ashes. He had found against his heart, at the Bellingham Inn, a great lock of golden hair. He had taken it, and the lover, after feeling about for it with faint hands, never asked for it. The precious lock (Miss Davenport had thrust it into his hand at Belthorpe as Lucy's last gift), what sighs and tears it had weathered! The Baronet laid it in Richard's sight one day, and beheld him take it up, turn it over, and drop it down again, calmly as if he were handling any common curiosity. It pacified him on that score. The young man's love was dead. Dr. Clifford said right: he wanted distractions. The Baronet determined that Richard should go. Hippias and Adrian then pressed their several suits as to which should have him. Hippias, when he could forget himself, did not lack sense. He observed that Adrian was not at present a proper companion for Richard, and would teach him to look on life from the false point.

"You don't understand a young philosopher," said the Baronet.

"A young philosopher's an old fool!" returned Hippias, not thinking that his growl had begotten a phrase.

His brother smiled with gratification, and applauded him loudly: "Excellent! worthy of your best days! That is as good a thing as I have heard, Hippias. You're wrong, though, in applying it to Adrian. He has never been precocious. All he has done has been to bring sound common sense to bear upon what he hears and sees. I think, however," the Baronet added, "he may want faith in the better qualities of men." And this reflection inclined him not to let his son be alone with Adrian. He gave Richard his choice, who saw which way his faher's wishes tended, and decided so to please him. Naturally it annoyed Adrian extremely. He said to his chief:

"I suppose you know what you are doing, Sir. I don't see that we derive any advantage from the family name being made notorious for twenty years of obscene suffering, and becoming a by-word of our constitutional tendency to stomachic distension before we fortunately encountered O'Quackem's Pill. My Uncle's tortures have been huge, but I would rather society were not intimate with them under their several headings." Adrian enumerated some of the most abhorrent. "You know him, Sir. If he conceives a duty, he will do it in the face of every decency,—all the more obstinate because the conception is rare. If he feels a little brisk the morning after the Pill, he sends the letter that makes us famous! We go down to posterity with heightened characteristics, to say nothing of a contemporary celebrity nothing less than our being turned inside-out to the rabble. I confess I don't desire to have my machinery made bare to them."

Sir Austin assured the Wise Youth that Hippias had arranged to go to Dr. Bairam. He softened Adrian's chagrin by telling him, that in about two weeks they would follow to London; hinting also at a prospective Summer campaign. The day was fixed for Richard to depart, and the day came. Madam The Eighteenth Century called him to her chamber and put into his hand a fifty-pound note, as her contribution towards his pocket expenses. He did not want it, he said, but she told him he was a young man, and would soon make that fly when he stood on his own feet. The old lady did not approve of the System in her heart, and she gave her grand-nephew to understand that, should he require more, he knew where to apply, and secrets would be kept. His father presented him with a hundred pounds, which also Richard said he did not want—he did not care for money. "Spend it or not," said the Baronet, perfectly secure in him. All he desired of him was, to go and see the Grandisons, and give his love to little Carola.

"I wonder how my cabbage-rose is looking," Richard remarked. "She was disappointed at not seeing me when she came, wasn't she, Sir?"

"Well, she cried about you," said the Baronet, content to hear his son add: "Poor little thing!" however coldly.

Hippias had a few injunctions to observe, beyond that of going to the Grandisons. They were to take up quarters at the hotel, Algernon's general run of company at the house not being altogether wholesome. The Baronet particularly forewarned Hippias of the imprudence of attempting to restrict the young man's movements, and letting him imagine he was under surveillance. Richard having been, as it were, pollarded by Despotism, was now to grow up straight, and bloom again, in complete independence, as far as he could feel. So did this Sage decree: and we may pause a moment to reflect how wise were his previsions and how successful they must have been, had not Fortune, the great foe to human cleverness, turned against him.

The departure took place on a fine March morning. The bird of Winter sang from the budding tree; in the blue sky sang the bird of Summer. Adrian rode between Richard and Hippias to the Bellingham station, and vented his disgust on them after his own humorous fashion, because it did not rain and damp their ardour. In the rear came Lady Blandish, and the Baronet, conversing on the calm summit of Success.

"You have shaped him exactly to resemble yourself," she

said, pointing with her riding-whip to the grave stately figure of the young man.

"Outwardly, perhaps!" he answered, and led to a discussion on Purity, and Strength, the lady saying that she preferred Purity.

"But you do not," said the Baronet. "And there I admire the always true instinct of woman, that they *all* worship Strength in whatever form, and seem to know it to be the child of Heaven; whereas Purity is but a characteristic, a garment, and can be spotted—how soon! For there are questions in this life with which we must grapple, or be lost; and when, hunted by that cold eye of intense inner-consciousness, the clearest soul becomes a cunning fox, if it have not courage to stand and do battle. Strength indicates a boundless nature—like the Maker. Strength is a God to you: Purity a toy. A pretty one, and you seem to be fond of playing with it," he added with unaccustomed slyness.

The lady listened pleased at the sportive malice which showed that the constraint on his mind had left him. It was for women to fight their fight now: she only took part in it for amusement. This is how the ranks of our enemies are thinned: no sooner do poor women put up a champion in their midst than she betrays them.

"I see," she said archly, "we are the lovelier vessels: you claim the more direct descent. Men are seedlings: Women —slips!—Nay, you have said so," she cried out at his gestured protestation, laughing.

"But I never printed it."

"Oh! what you speak answers for print with me."

Exquisite Blandish! He could not choose but love her.

"Tell me, what are your plans?" she asked. "May a woman know?"

He replied: "I have none, or you would share them." No longer the old watchful nervous air about him, as of one who dared not sleep upon advantage. "I shall study him in the world. This indifference must wear off. I shall mark his inclinations now, and he shall be what he inclines to. Occupation will be his prime safety. That, and the feeling of guardianship to this child. His cousin Austin's plan of life appears most to his taste, and he can serve the people that way as well as in Parliament, should he have no stronger ambition. The clear duty of a man of any wealth is to serve the people as he best can. He shall go among Austin's set, if he wishes it, though personally I find no pleasure in rash imaginations, and undigested schemes built upon the mere instinct of principles."

"Look at him now," said the lady. "He seems to care for nothing; not even for the beauty of the day."

"Or Adrian's jokes," added the Baronet.

Adrian could be seen to be trying zealously to torment a laugh, or a confession of irritation, out of his hearers, stretching out his chin to one, and to the other, with audible Asides. Richard he treated as a new instrument of destruction about to let loose on the slumbering Metropolis; Hippias as one in an interesting condition: and he got so much fun out of the notion of these two journeying together, and the mishaps that might occur to them, that he esteemed it almost a personal insult for his hearers not to laugh. The Wise Youth's dull life at Raynham had afflicted him with many peculiarities of the professional joker.

"Oh! the Spring! the Spring!" he cried, as in scorn of his sallies they exchanged their unmeaning remarks on the sweet weather across him. "You seem both to be uncommonly excited by the operations of turtles, rooks, and daws. Why can't you let them alone?

> *"Wind bloweth,*
> *Cock croweth,*
> > *Doodle-doo:*
> *Hippy verteth,*
> *Ricky sterteth,*
> > *Sing Cuckoo!*

"There's an old native pastoral!—Why don't you write a
Spring sonnet, Ricky? The asparagus-beds are full of
promise, I hear, and eke the strawberry. No lack of inspiration for you. Berries I fancy your Pegasus has a taste
for. What kind of berry was that I saw some verses of
yours about once?—amatory verses to some kind of berry—
yewberry, blueberry, glueberry! I can't remember rightly.
Pretty verses, though decidedly warm. Lips, eyes, bosom,
legs—legs? I don't think you gave her any legs. No legs
and no nose. That appears to be the poetic taste of the day.
It shall be admitted that you create the very beauties for a
chaste people.

> "'O might I lie where leans her lute!'

and offend no moral community. I say, that's not a bad
image of yours, my dear boy:

> "'Her shape is like an antelope
> Upon the Eastern hills.'

"But as a candid critic, I would ask you if the likeness
can be considered correct when she has no legs? But you will
see at the Ballet, that you are quite in error about women
at present, Richard. That admirable institution which our
venerable elders have imported from Gallia for the in-
struction of our gaping youth, will edify, and astonish you.
I assure you I used, from reading THE PILGRIM'S SCRIP,
to imagine all sorts of things about them, till I was taken
there, and learnt that they are very like us after all, and
then they ceased to trouble me. Mystery is the great danger
to youth, my son! Mystery is woman's redoubtable weapon,
O Richard of the Ordeal! I'm aware that you've had your
lessons in Anatomy, but nothing will persuade you that an
anatomical figure means flesh and blood. You can't realize
the fact. Do you intend to publish when you're in town?

It'll be better not to put your name. Having one's name to a Volume of Poems is as bad as to an advertising Pill. My uncle, I dread, is madly bent upon returning thanks publicly for the Pill, so you must be content to let Ignotus wear your laurels, or the critics will confound you together. 'Notwithstanding the deplorable state of this gentleman's stomach,' they will say, 'the Muse and Cupid have taken so strong a hold on him, that he is evidently one of those who, to avoid more punishable transgressions, must commit verse, and we prefer to attribute any shortcomings which it may be our duty to indicate, rather to the utter distraction of his internal economy than to a want of natural propensity.'"

"I will send you an early copy, Adrian, when I publish," quoth Richard. "Hark at that old blackbird, Uncle."

"Yes!" Hippias quavered, looking up from the usual subject of his contemplation, and trying to take an interest in him, "fine old fellow!"

"What a chuckle he gives out before he flies! Not unlike July nightingales. You know that bird I told you of— the blackbird that had its mate shot, and used to come to sing to old dame Bakewell's bird from the tree opposite. A rascal knocked it over the day before yesterday, and the dame says her bird hasn't sung a note since."

"Extraordinary!" Hippias muttered abstractedly. "I remember the verses."

"But where's your moral?" interposed the wrathful Adrian. "Where's Constancy Rewarded?

> *"The ouzel-cock so black of hue,*
> . *With orange-tawny bill;*
> *The rascal with his aim so true;*
> *The Poet's little quill!*

"Where's the moral of that? except that all's game to the poet! Certainly we have a noble example of the devotedness of the female, who for three entire days refuses to make herself heard, on account of a defunct male. I suppose that's what Ricky dwells on."

"As you please, my dear Adrian," says Richard, and points out larch-buds to his Uncle, as they ride by the young green wood.

The Wise Youth was driven to extremity. Such a lapse from his pupil's heroics to this last verge of Arcadian coolness, Adrian could not believe in. "Hark at this old blackbird!" he cried, in his turn, and pretending to interpret his fits of song:

"O what a pretty comedy!—Don't we wear the mask well, my Fiesco?—Genoa will be our own tomorrow!— Only wait until the train has started—jolly! jolly! jolly! We'll be winners yet!

"Not a bad verse—eh, Ricky? my Lucius Junius!"

"You do the blackbird well," said Richard, and looked at him in a manner mildly affable.

Adrian shrugged. "You're a young man of wonderful powers," he emphatically observed; meaning to say that Richard quite beat him: for which opinion Richard gravely thanked him, and with this they rode into Bellingham.

There was young Tom Blaize at the station, in his Sunday beaver and gala waistcoat and neckcloth, coming the lord over Tom Bakewell, who had preceded his master in charge of the baggage. He likewise was bound for London. Richard, as he was dismounting, heard Adrian say to the Baronet: "The Beast, Sir, appears to be going to fetch Beauty;" but he paid no heed to the words. Whether young Tom heard them or not, Adrian's look took the lord out of him, and he shrunk away into obscurity, where the nearest approach to the Fashions which the tailors of Bellingham could supply to him, sat upon him more easily, and was not unaccountably stiffened by the eyes of the superiors whom he sought to rival. The Baronet, Lady Blandish, and Adrian, remained on horseback, and received Richard's adieux across the palings. He shook hands with each of them in the same kindly cold way, eliciting from Adrian a marked encomium on his style of doing it. The train came up, and Richard stepped after his uncle into one of the carriages.

Now surely there will come an Age when the presentation of Science at war with Fortune and the Fates, will be deemed the true Epic of modern life; and the aspect of a Scientific Humanist who, by dint of incessant watchfulness, has maintained a System against those active forces, cannot be reckoned less than sublime, even though at the moment he but sit upon his horse, on a fine March morning such as this, and smile wistfully to behold the son of his heart, his System incarnate, wave a serene adieu to tutelage, neither too eager nor morbidly unwilling to try his luck alone for a term of two weeks. At present, I am aware, an audience impatient for Blood and Glory scorns the stress I am putting on incidents so minute, a picture so little imposing. One will come to whom it will be given to see the elementary machinery at work: who, as it were, from some slight hint of the straws, will feel the winds of March when they do not blow. To them will nothing be trivial, seeing that they will have in their eyes the invisible conflict going on around us, whose features a nod, a smile, a laugh, of ours perpetually changes. And they will perceive, moreover, that in real life all hangs together: the train is laid in the lifting of an eyebrow, that bursts upon the field of thousands. They will see the links of things as they pass, and wonder not, as foolish people now do, that this great matter came out of that small one.

Such an audience, then, will participate in the Baronet's gratification at his son's demeanour, wherein he noted the calm bearing of Experience not gained in the usual wanton way: and will not be without some excited apprehension at his twinge of astonishment, when, just as the train went sliding into swiftness, he beheld the grave, cold, self-

possessed, young man throw himself back in the carriage
violently laughing. Science was at a loss to account for it.
Sir Austin checked his mind from inquiring, that he might
keep suspicion at a distance, but he thought it odd, and the
jarring sensation that ran along his nerves at the sight, remained with him as he rode home.

Lady Blandish's tender womanly intuition bade her say:
"You see, it was the very thing he wanted. He has got
his natural spirits already."

"It was," Adrian put in his word, "the exact thing he
wanted. His spirits have returned miraculously."

"Something amused him," said the Baronet, with an eye
on the puffing train.

"Probably something his Uncle said or did," Lady
Blandish suggested, and led off at a gallop.

Her conjecture chanced to be quite correct. The cause
for Richard's laughter was simple enough. Hippias, on
finding the carriage-door closed on him, became all at once
aware of the bright-haired Hope who dwells in Change, for
one who does not woo her too frequently; and to express his
sudden relief from mental despondency at the amorous prospect, the Dyspepsy bent and gave his hands a sharp rub
between his legs: which unlucky action brought Adrian's
pastoral,

> *'Hippy verteth,*
> *   Sing cuckoo!'*

in such comic colours before Richard, that a demon of
laughter seized him.

> *'Hippy verteth!'*

Every time he glanced at his Uncle the song sprang up, and
he laughed so immoderately that it looked like madness
come upon him.

"Why, why, why, what are you laughing at, my dear boy," said Hippias, and was provoked by the contagious exercise to a modest "Ha! ha!"

"Why, what are *you* laughing at, Uncle?" cried Richard.

"I really don't know," Hippias chuckled.

"Nor I, Uncle! Sing, Cuckoo!"

They laughed themselves into the pleasantest mood imaginable. Hippias not only came aboveground, he flew about in the very skies, *verting* like any blithe creature of the season. He remembered old legal jokes and anecdotes of Circuit; and Richard laughed at them all, but more at him—he was so genial, and childishly fresh, and innocently joyful at his own transformation, while a lurking doubt in the bottom of his eye now and then, that it might not last, and that he must go underground again, lent him a look of pathos and humour which tickled his youthful companion irresistibly, and made his heart warm to him.

"I tell you what, Uncle," said Richard. "I think travelling's a capital thing."

"The best thing in the world, my dear boy," Hippias returned. "It makes me wish I had given up that Work of mine, and tried it before, instead of chaining myself to a task. We're quite different beings in a minute. I am. Hem! What shall we have for dinner?"

"Leave that to me, Uncle. I shall order for you. You know, I intend to make you well.—How gloriously we go along! I should like to ride in a Railway every day."

Hippias assumed a mysterious sadness, and remarked:—

"They say, I've heard, Richard, that it rather injures the digestion."

"Nonsense! see how you'll digest tonight, and write tomorrow."

"Perhaps I shall do something yet!" sighed Hippias, alluding to the vast literary fame he had aforetime dreamed: "I hope I shall have a good night tonight."

"Of course you will! What! after laughing like that?"

"Ugh!" Hippias grunted, "I dare say, Richard, you sleep the moment you get into bed!"

"The instant my head's on my pillow, and up the moment I wake. Health's everything!"

"Health's everything!" echoed Hippias, from an immense distance.

"And if you'll put yourself in my hands," Richard continued, "you shall do just as I do. You shall be well and strong, and sing 'Jolly!' like Adrian's blackbird. You shall, upon my honour, Uncle!"

He specified the hours of devotion to his Uncle's recovery —no less than twelve a day—that he intended to expend, and his cheery robustness almost won his Uncle to leap up recklessly and clutch Health as his own.

"Mind," quoth Hippias, with a half-seduced smile, "mind your dishes are not too savoury!"

"Light food, and claret! Regular meals, and amusement! Lend your heart to all, but give it to none!" exclaims Young Wisdom, and Hippias mutters, "Yes! yes!" and intimates that the origin of his malady lay in his not following that maxim earlier.

"Love ruins us, my dear boy," he said, thinking to preach Richard a lesson, and Richard boisterously broke out:

> "The love of Monsieur Francatelli,
>   It was the ruin of—et cætera!"

Hippias blinked, exclaiming: "Really, my dear boy! I never saw you so excited."

"It's the Railway! It's the fun, Uncle!"

"Ah!" Hippias wagged a melancholy head, "you've got the Golden Bride! Keep her if you can. That's a pretty fable of your father's. I gave him the idea, though. Austin filches a great many of my ideas!"

"Here's the idea in verse, Uncle.

>   " 'O sunless walkers by the tide!
>   O have you seen the Golden Bridge?
>   They say that she is fair beyond
>   All women; faithful, and more fond!'

"You know, the young inquirer comes to a group of penitent sinners by the brink of a stream. They howl, and answer:

>   " 'Faithful she is, but she forsakes:
>   And fond, yet endless woe she makes:
>   And fair! but with this curse she's cross'd:
>   To know her not till she is lost!'

"Then the doleful party march off in single file solemnly, and the fabulist pursues:

>   " 'She hath a palace in the West:
>   Bright Hesper lights her to her rest:
>   And him the Morning-Star awakes
>   Whom to her charmèd arms she takes.
>   So lives he till he sees, alas!
>   The maids of baser metal pass:'

"And prodigal of the happiness she lends him, he asks to share it with one of them. There is the Silver Maid, and the Copper, and the Brassy Maid, and others of them. First, you know, he tries Argentine, and finds her only twenty to the pound, and has a worse experience with Copperina, till he descends to the scullery; and the lower he goes, the less obscure become the features of his Bride of Gold, and all her radiance shines forth, my Uncle!"

"Verse rather blunts the point.—Well, keep to her, now you've got her," says Hippias.

"We will, Uncle! Look how the farms fly past! Look at the cattle in the fields! And how the lines duck, and swim up!

> *" 'She claims the whole, and not the part—-*
> *The coin of an unusëd heart!*
> *To gain his Golden Bride again,*
> *He hunts with melancholy men,'*

—"and is waked no longer by the Morning-star!"

"Not if he doesn't sleep till an hour before it rises!" Hippias interjected. "You don't rhyme badly. But stick to Prose. Poetry's a Base-metal-maid. I'm not sure that any writing's good for the digestion. I'm almost afraid it has spoilt mine." Hippias did look doubtful.

"Fear nothing, Uncle!" laughed Richard. "You shall ride in the park with me every day to get an appetite. You, and I, and little Carola—a splendid little girl. I shall call her my Golden Bride. You know that little poem of Sandoe's?

> *" 'She rides in the park on a prancing bay,*
> *She and her squires together:*
> *Her dark locks gleam from a bonnet of grey,*
> *And toss with the tossing feather.*

> *" 'Too calmly proud for a glance of pride*
> *Is the beautiful face as it passes:*
> *The cockneys nod to each other aside,*
> *The coxcombs lift their glasses.*

> *" 'And throng to her, sigh to her, you that can breach*
> *The ice-wall that guards her securely:*
> *You have not such bliss, though she smile on you each,*
> *As the heart that can image her purely.'*

"Wasn't Sandoe once a friend of my father's? I suppose they quarrelled. He understands the heart. What does he make his 'Humble Lover' say?

> *" 'True, Madam, you may think to part*
> *Conditions by a glacier-ridge,*
> *But Beauty's for the largest heart,*
> *And all abysses Love can bridge!' "*

Hippias now laughed; grimly, as men laugh at the emptiness of words.

"Largest heart!" he sneered. "What's a 'glacier-ridge'? I've never seen one. I can't deny it rhymes with 'bridge.' But don't go parading your admiration of that person, Richard. Your father will speak to you on the subject when he thinks fit."

"I thought they had quarrelled," said Richard. "What a pity!" and he murmured to a pleased ear:

> *" 'Beauty's for the largest heart!' "*

The flow of their conversation was interrupted by the entrance of passengers at a station. Richard examined their faces with pleasure. All faces pleased him. Human nature sat tributary at the feet of him and his Golden Bride. As he could not well talk his thoughts before them, he looked out at the windows and enjoyed the changing landscape, projecting all sorts of delights for his old friend Ripton, and little Carola, and musing hazily on the wondrous things he was to do in the world; of the great service he was to be, of to his fellow-creatures. In the midst of his reveries he was landed in London. Tom Bakewell stood at the carriage-door. A glance told Richard that his squire had something curious on his mind, and he gave Tom the word to speak out. Tom edged his master out of hearing, and began sputtering a laugh.

"Dash'd if I can help it, Sir!" he said. "That young Tom! He've come to Town dressed that spicy! and he dunnow his way about no more than a stag. He's come to fetch somebody from another Rail, and he dunnow how to get there, and he ain't sure about which Rail 'tis. Look at 'un, Mr. Richard! There he goes."

Young Tom appeared to have all London on his beaver.

"Who has he come for?" Richard asked.

"Don't you know, Sir? You don't like me to mention the name," mumbled Tom, bursting to be perfectly intelligible.

"Is it for her, Tom?"

"Miss Lucy, Sir."

Richard turned away, and was seized by Hippias, who begged him to get out of the noise and pother, and caught hold of his slack arm to bear him into a conveyance; but Richard, by wheeling half to the right, or left, always got his face round to the point where young Tom was manœuvring to appear at his ease. Even when they were seated in the conveyance, Hippias could not persuade him to drive off. He made the excuse that he did not wish to start till there was a clear road. At last young Tom cast anchor by a policeman, and, doubtless at the official's suggestion, bashfully took seat in a cab, and was shot into the whirlpool of London. Richard then angrily asked his driver what he was waiting for.

"Are you ill, my boy?" said Hippias. "Where's your colour."

He laughed oddly, and made a random answer that he hoped the fellow would drive fast.

"I hate this slow motion after being in the Railway," he said.

Hippias assured him there was something the matter with him.

"Nothing, Uncle! nothing!" said Richard, looking fiercely candid.

They say, that when the skill and care of men rescue a drowned wretch from extinction, and warm the flickering spirit into steady flame, such pain it is, the blood forcing its way along the dry channels, and the heavily-ticking nerves, and the sullen heart—the struggle of Life and Death in him—grim Death relaxing his gripe: such pain it is, he cries out no thanks to them that pull him by inches from the depths of the dead River. And he who has thought a love extinct, and is surprised by the old fires, and the old tyranny, he rebels, and strives to fight clear of the cloud of forgotten sensations that settle on him; such pain it is, the old sweet music reviving through his frame, and the charm of his passion fixing him afresh. Still was fair Lucy the One woman to Richard. He had forbidden her name but from an instinct of self-defence. Must the maids of baser metal dominate him anew, it is in Lucy's shape. Thinking of her now so near him—his darling! all her graces, her sweetness, her truth—for, despite his bitter blame of her, he knew her true—swam in a thousand visions before his eyes: visions pathetic, and full of glory, that now wrung his heart, and now elated it. As well might a ship attempt to calm the sea, as this young man the violent emotion that began to rage in his breast. "I shall not see her!" he said to himself exultingly, and at the same instant thought, how black was every corner of the earth but that one spot where Lucy stood! how utterly cheerless the place he was going to! Then he determined to bear it; to live in darkness: there was a refuge in the idea of a voluntary martyrdom. "For if I chose I could see her—this day— within an hour!—I could see her, and touch her hand, and, oh, Heaven!—But I do not choose." And a great wave swelled through him, and was crushed down only to swell again more stormily.

Then Tom Bakewell's words recurred to him, that young Tom Blaize was uncertain where to go for her, and that she might be thrown on this Babylon alone. And flying from point to point, it struck him that they had known at Raynham of her return, and had sent him to Town to be out of the way,—they had been miserably plotting against him once more. "They shall see what right they have to

fear me. I'll shame them!" was the first turn taken by his
wrathful feelings, as he resolved to go, and see her safe,
and calmly return to his Uncle, whom he sincerely believed not to be one of the conspirators. Nevertheless, after
forming that resolve, he sat still, as if there were something
fatal in the wheels that bore him away from it—perhaps
because he knew, as some do when passion is lord, that his
intelligence juggled with him; though none the less keenly
did he feel his wrongs and suspicions. His Golden Bride
was waning fast. But when Hippias ejaculated to cheer
him: "We shall soon be there!" the spell broke. Richard
stopped the ·cab, saying he wanted to speak to Tom, and
would ride with him the rest of the journey. He knew
well enough which line of railway his Lucy must come by.
He had studied every town and station on the line. Before
his Uncle could express more than a mute remonstrance, he
jumped out and hailed Tom Bakewell, who came behind
with the boxes and baggage in a companion cab, his head
a yard beyond the window to make sure of his ark of safety,
the vehicle preceding.

"What an extraordinary, impetuous boy it is!" said Hippias. "We're in the very street!"

Within a minute, the stalwart Berry, despatched by the
Baronet to arrange everything for their comfort, had opened
the door, and made his bow.

"Mr. Richard, Sir?—evaporated?" was Berry's mod-
ulated inquiry.

"Behind—among the boxes, fool!" Hippias growled, as
he received Berry's muscular assistance to alight. "Lunch
ready—eh?"

"Luncheon was ordered precise at two o'clock, Sir—
been in attendance one quarter of an hour.—Heah!" Berry
sang out to the second cab, which, with its pyramid of lug-
gage, remained stationary some thirty paces distant. At
his voice the majestic pile deliberately turned its back on
them, and went off in a contrary direction.

CHAPTER XXX

RECORDS THE RAPID DEVELOPMENT OF THE HERO

On the stroke of the hour when Ripton Thompson was accustomed to consult his gold-watch for practical purposes, and sniff freedom and the forthcoming dinner, a burglarious foot entered the clerk's office where he sat, and a man of a scowling countenance, who looked a villain, and whom he was afraid he knew, slid a letter into his hands, nodding that it would be prudent for him to read, and be silent. Ripton obeyed in alarm. Apparently the contents of the letter relieved his conscience; for he reached down his hat, and told Mr. Beazley to inform his father that he had business of pressing importance in the West, and should meet him at the station. Mr. Beazley zealously waited upon the paternal Thompson without delay, and together making their observations from the window, they beheld a cab of many boxes, into which Ripton darted and was followed by one in groom's dress. It was Saturday, the day when Ripton gave up his Law-readings, magnanimously to bestow himself upon his family, and Mr. Thompson liked to have his son's arm as he walked down to the Station; but that third glass of port which always stood for his second, and the groom's suggestion of aristocratic acquaintances, prevented Mr. Thompson from interfering: so Ripton was permitted to depart.

In the cab Ripton made a study of the letter he held. It had the preciseness of an Imperial mandate.

"Dear Ripton,
"You are to get lodgings for a lady immediately. Not a word to a soul. Then come along with Tom.
                                        "R. D. F."

"Lodgings for a lady!" Ripton meditated aloud: "What

sort of lodgings? Where am I to get lodgings? Who's
the lady?—I say!" he addressed the mysterious messenger,
"so you're Tom Bakewell, are you, Tom?"

Tom grinned his identity.

"Do you remember the rick, Tom? Ha! ha! We got
out of that neatly, didn't we, Tom? We might all have
been transported, though. I could have convicted you,
Tom! safe! It's no use coming across a practised lawyer.—
Now tell me." Ripton, having flourished his powers, commenced his examination: "Who's this lady?"

"Better wait till ye see Mr. Richard, Sir." Tom resumed
his scowl to reply.

"Ah!" Ripton acquiesced. "Is she young, Tom!"

Tom said she was not old.

"Handsome, Tom?"

Some might think one thing, some another, Tom said.

"And where does she come from, now?" asked Ripton,
with the friendly cheerfulness of a baffled counsel.

"Comes from the coontry, Sir."

"A friend of the family, I suppose? a relation?"

Ripton left this insinuating query to be answered by a
look. Tom's face was a dead blank.

"Ah!" Ripton took a breath, and eyed the mask opposite
him. "Why, you're quite a scholar, Tom! Mr. Richard
is quite well? Father's quite well? All right at home?—
eh, Tom?"

"Come to Town this mornin' with his Uncle," said Tom.
"All quite well, thank'ee, Sir."

"Ha!" cried Ripton, more than ever puzzled, "now I see.
You all came to Town today, and these are your boxes
outside. So, so! But Mr. Richard writes for me to get
lodgings for a lady. There must be some mistake—he wrote
in a hurry. He wants lodgings for you all—eh?"

"'M sure I d'n know what he wants," said Tom.
"You'd better go by the letter, Sir."

Ripton re-consulted that document. "'Lodgings for a

lady, and then come along with Tom. Not a word to a soul.' I say! that looks like—But he never cared for *them*. You don't mean to say, Tom, he's been running away with anybody?"

Tom fell back upon his first reply: "Better wait till ye see Mr. Richard, Sir," and Ripton exclaimed: "Hanged if you ain't the tightest witness I ever saw! I shouldn't like to have you in a box. Some of you country fellows beat any number of cockneys. You do!"

Tom received the compliment stubbornly on his guard, and Ripton, as nothing was to be got out of him, set about considering how to perform his friend's injunctions; deciding firstly, that a lady fresh from the country ought to lodge near the parks, in which direction he told the cabman to drive. Thus, unaware of his high destiny, Ripton joined the hero, and accepted his character in the New Comedy.

It is, nevertheless, true that certain favoured people do have beneficent omens to prepare them for their parts, when the Hero is in full career, so that they really may be nerved to meet him; ay, and to check him in his course, had they that signal courage. For instance, Mrs. Elizabeth Berry, a ripe and wholesome landlady of advertised Lodgings, on the borders of Kensington, noted, as she sat rocking her contemplative person before the parlour fire this very March afternoon, a supernatural tendency in that fire to burn *all on one side*: which signifies that a Wedding approaches the house. Why—who shall say? Omens are as impassible as Heroes. It may be because in these affairs the fire is thought to be all on one side. Enough that the omen exists, and spoke its solemn warning to the devout woman. Mrs. Berry, in her circle, was known as a certificated lecturer against the snares of Matrimony. Still that was no reason why she should not like a Wedding. Expectant, therefore, she watched the one glowing cheek of Hymen, and with pleasing tremors beheld a cab of many boxes draw up by her bit of garden, and a gentleman emerge from it in the

act of consulting an Advertisement-paper. The gentleman
required lodgings for a lady. Lodgings for a lady Mrs.
Berry could produce, and a very roseate smile for a gentleman; so much so that Ripton forgot to ask about the terms;
which made the landlady in Mrs. Berry leap up to embrace him as the happy man. But her experienced woman's
eye checked her enthusiasm. He had not the air of a
bridegroom: he did not seem to have a weight on his chest,
or an itch to twiddle everything with his fingers. At any
rate, he was not the bridegroom for whom Omens fly
abroad. Promising to have all ready for the lady within an
hour, Mrs. Berry fortified him with her card, curtsied him
back to his cab, and floated him off on her smiles.

The remarkable vehicle which had woven this thread of
intrigue through London streets, now proceeded sedately to
finish its operations. Ripton was landed at an hotel in
Westminster. Ere he was halfway up the stairs, a door
opened, and his old comrade in adventure rushed down.
Richard allowed no time for salutations. "Have you done
it?" was all he asked. For answer Ripton handed him Mrs.
Berry's card. Richard took it, and left him standing there.
Five minutes elapsed, and then Ripton heard the gracious
rustle of feminine garments above. Richard came a little
in advance, leading and half-supporting a figure in a black-
silk mantle and small black-straw bonnet: young—that was
certain, though she held her veil so close he could hardly
catch the outlines of her face: girlishly slender, and sweet
and simple in appearance. The hush that came with her,
and her soft manner of moving, stirred the silly youth to
some of those ardours that awake the Knight of Dames in
our bosoms. He felt that he would have given considerable sums for her to lift her veil. He could see that she
was trembling—perhaps weeping. It was the master of
her fates she clung to. They passed him without speaking.
As she went by, her head passively bent, Ripton had a
glimpse of noble tresses and a lovely neck: great golden

curls hung loosely behind, pouring from under her bonnet. She looked a captive borne to the sacrifice. What Ripton, after a sight of those curls, would have given for her just to lift her veil an instant and strike him blind with beauty, was, fortunately for his exchequer, never demanded of him. And he had absolutely been composing speeches as he came along in the cab! gallant speeches for the lady, and sly congratulatory ones for his friend, to be delivered as occasion should serve, that both might know him a man of the world, and be at their ease. He forgot the smirking immoralities he had revelled in. This was clearly serious. Ripton did not require to be told that his friend was in love and meant that life-and-death business called marriage, parents and guardians consenting or not.

Presently Richard returned to him, and said hurriedly: 'I want you now to go to my uncle, at our hotel. Keep him quiet till I come. Say I had to see you—say anything. I shall be there by the dinner-hour. Rip! I must talk to you alone after dinner.'

Ripton feebly attempted to reply that he was due at home. He was very curious to hear the plot of the New Comedy: and besides, there was Richard's face questioning him sternly and confidently for signs of unhesitating obedience. He finished his grimaces by asking the name and direction of the hotel. Richard pressed his hand. It is much to obtain even that recognition of our devotion from the Hero.

Tom Bakewell also received his priming, and, to judge by his chuckles and grins, rather appeared to enjoy the work cut out for him. In a few minutes they had driven to their separate destinations: Ripton was left to the unusual exercise of his fancy. Such is the nature of youth and its thirst for Romance, that only to act as a subordinate is pleasant. When one unfurls the standard of Defiance to parents and guardians, he may be sure of raising a lawless troop of adolescent ruffians, born rebels, to any amount.

The beardless crew know that they have not a chance of pay: but what of that when the rosy prospect of thwarting their elders is in view? Though it is to see another eat the Forbidden Fruit, they will run all his risks with him. Gaily Ripton took rank as lieutenant in the enterprise, and the moment his heart had sworn the oaths, he was rewarded by an exquisite sense of the charms of existence. London streets wore a sly laugh to him. He walked with a dandi-fied heel. The generous youth ogled aristocratic carriages, and glanced intimately at the ladies, overflowingly happy. The crossing-sweepers blessed him. He hummed lively tunes, he turned over old jokes in his mouth unctuously, he hugged himself, he had a mind to dance down Piccadilly, and all because a friend of his was running away with a pretty girl, and he was in the secret!

It was only when he stood on the doorstep of Richard's hotel, that his jocund mood was a little dashed by re-membering that he had then to commence the duties of his office, and must fabricate a plausible story to account for what he knew nothing about—a part that the greatest of Sages would find it difficult to perform. The young, how-ever, whom Sages well may envy, seldom fail in lifting their inventive faculties to the level of their spirits, and two minutes of Hippias's angry complaints against the friend he serenely inquired for gave Ripton his cue.

"We're in the very street—within a stone's-throw of the house, and he jumps like a harlequin out of my cab into another,—he must be mad—that boy's got madness in him! —and carries off all the boxes—my dinner-pills, too! and keeps away the whole of the day, though he promised to go to the Doctor, and had a dozen engagements with me," said Hippias, venting an enraged snarl to sum up his grievances.

Ripton at once told him that the Doctor was not at home.

"Why, you don't mean to say he's been to the Doctor?" Hippias cried out.

"He has called on him twice, Sir," said Ripton, expressively. "On leaving me he was going a third time. I shouldn't wonder that's what detains him—he's so determined."

By fine degrees, beyond the reach of art, Ripton ventured to grow circumstantial, saying that Richard's case was urgent and required immediate medical advice; and that both he and his father were of opinion Richard should not lose an hour in obtaining it.

"He's dreadfully alarmed about himself," said Ripton, and tapped his chest, and threw up his lips and brows.

Hippias protested he had never heard a word from his nephew of any physical affliction.

"No," groaned Ripton, "he was afraid of making you anxious."

Algernon Feverel and Richard came in while he was hammering at the Alphabet to recollect the first letter of the Doctor's name. They had met in the hall below, and were laughing heartily as they entered the room. Ripton jumped up to get the initiative.

"Have you seen the Doctor?" he asked, significantly plucking at Richard's fingers.

Richard was all abroad at the question.

"Why, the Doctor you were going to for the third time when you left me," said Ripton, in a manner not to be mistaken. "What does he say?"

Richard sought in turn the countenances of all present, and settled upon Ripton's with a ludicrous stare.

Algernon clapped him on the back. "What the deuce do you want with Doctors, boy?"

The solid thump awakened him to see matters as they were. "Oh, ay! the Doctor!" he said, smiling frankly at his lieutenant. "Why, he tells me he'd back me to do Milo's trick in a week from the present day.—Uncle," he came forward to Hippias, "I hope you'll excuse me for running off as I did. I was in a hurry. I left something at the Railway. This stupid Rip thinks I went to the Doctor about myself. The fact was, I wanted to fetch the Doctor to see you here—so that you might have no trouble, you know. You can't bear the sight of his instruments and skeletons—I've heard you say so. You said, it set all your marrow in revolt—'fried your marrow,' I think were the words, and made you see twenty thousand different ways of sliding down to the chambers of the Grim King. Don't you remember?"

Hippias emphatically did not remember, and he did not believe the story. Irritation at the mad ravishment of his pill-box rendered him incredulous. As he had no means of confuting his nephew, all he could do safely to express his disbelief in him, was to utter petulant remarks on his powerlessness to appear at the dinner-table that day: upon which—Berry just then trumpeting dinner—Algernon seized one arm of the Dyspepsy, and Richard another, and the laughing couple bore him into the room where dinner was laid, Ripton, sniggering in the rear, the really happy man of the party.

They had fun at the dinner-table. Richard would have it; and his gaiety, his by-play, his princely superiority to truth and heroic promise of overriding all our Laws, his handsome face, the lord and possessor of Beauty that he looked, as it were a star shining on his forehead, gained the old complete mastery over Ripton, who had been, mentally at least, half patronizing him till then, because he knew more of London and life, and was aware that his friend now depended upon him almost entirely.

After a second circle of the claret, the hero caught his lieutenant's eye across the table, and said:

"We must go out and talk over that law-business, Rip, before you go. Do you think the old lady has any chance?"

"Not a bit!" said Ripton authoritatively.

"But it's worth fighting—eh, Rip?"

"Oh, certainly!" was Ripton's matured opinion.

Richard observed that Ripton's father seemed doubtful. Ripton cited his father's habitual caution. Richard made a playful remark on the necessity of sometimes acting in opposition to fathers. Ripton agreed to it—in certain cases.

"Yes, yes! in certain cases," said Richard.

"Pretty legal morality, gentlemen!" Algernon interjected; Hippias adding: "And lay, too!"

The pair of Uncles listened further to the fictitious dialogue, well kept up on both sides, and in the end desired a statement of the old lady's garrulous case; Hippias offering to decide what her chances were in Law, and Algernon to give a common-sense judgment.

"Rip will tell you," said Richard, deferentially signalling the lawyer. "I'm a bad hand at these matters. Tell them how it stands, Rip."

Ripton disguised his excessive uneasiness under endeavours to right his position on his chair, and, inwardly praying speed to the claret-jug to come and strengthen his wits, began with a careless aspect: "Oh, nothing! She—very curious old character! She—a—wears a wig. She—a— very curious old character indeed! She—a—quite the old style. There's no doing anything with her!" and Ripton took a long breath to relieve himself after his elaborate fiction.

"So it appears," Hippias commented, and Algernon asked: "Well? and about her wig? Somebody stole it?" while Richard, whose features were grim with suppressed laughter, bade the narrator continue.

Ripton lunged for the claret-jug. He had got an old lady like an oppressive bundle on his brain, and he was as helpless as she was. In the pangs of ineffectual authorship, his ideas shot at her wig, and then at her one characteristic of extreme obstinacy, and tore back again at her wig, but

she would not be animated. The obstinate old thing would
remain a bundle. Law-studies seemed light in comparison
with this tremendous task of changing an old lady from
a doll to a human creature. He flung off some claret,
perspired freely, and, with a mental tribute to the cleverness of those author-fellows, recommenced: "Oh, nothing!
She—a—wore a wig for a long time. She—Richard knows
her better than I do—an old lady—somewhere down in
Suffolk. I think we had better advise her not to proceed.
The expenses of litigation are enormous! She—I think
we had better advise her to stop short, and not make any
scandal."

"And not make any scandal!" Algernon took him up.
"Come, come! there's something more than a wig, then?"

Ripton was commanded to proceed, whether she did or
no. The luckless fictionist looked straight at his pitiless
leader, and blurted out dubiously: "She—there's a daughter."

"Born with effort!" ejaculated Hippias. "Must give
her pause after that! and I'll take the opportunity to
stretch my length on the sofa. Heigho! that's true what
Austin says: 'The general prayer should be for a full
stomach, and the individual for one that works well; for
on that basis only are we a match for temporal matters, and
able to contemplate eternal.' Sententious, but true. I
gave him the idea, though! Take care of your stomachs,
boys! and if ever you hear of a monument proposed to a
scientific cook, or gastronomic doctor, send in your sub-
scriptions. Or say to him while he lives, 'Go forth, and be
a Knight!' Ha! They have a good cook at this house. He
suits me better than ours at Raynham. I almost wish I
had brought my manuscript to Town, I feel so much better. Aha! I didn't expect to digest at all without my
regular incentive. I think I shall give it up.—What do you
say to the theatre tonight, boys?"

Richard shouted: "Bravo, Uncle!"

"Let Mr. Thompson finish first," said Algernon. "I want to hear the conclusion of the story. The old girl has a wig, and a daughter. I'll swear somebody runs away with one of the two! Fill your glass, Mr. Thompson, and forward!"

"So somebody does," Ripton received his impetus. "And they're found in Town together," he made a fresh jerk. "She—a—that is, the old lady—found them in company."

"She finds him with her wig on in company!" said Algernon. "Capital! Here's matter for the lawyers!"

"And you advise her not to proceed, under such circumstances of aggravation?" Hippias observed, humorously twinkling stomachic content.

"It's the daughter!" Ripton sighed, and surrendering to pressure, hurried on recklessly, "A runaway match—beautiful girl!—the only son of a Baronet—married by special license. A—the point is," he now brightened and spoke from his own element, "the point is whether the marriage can be annulled, as she's of the Catholic persuasion and he's a Protestant, and they're both married under age. That's the point."

Having come to the point he breathed extreme relief, and saw things more distinctly; not a little amazed at his leader's horrified face.

The two elders were making various absurd inquiries, when Richard sent his chair to the floor, crying: "What a muddle you're in, Rip! You're mixing half-a-dozen stories together. The old lady I told you about was old Dame Bakewell, and the dispute was concerning a neighbour of hers who encroached on her garden, and I said I'd pay the money to see her righted!"

"Ah, to be sure!" said Ripton humbly, "I was thinking of the other. Oh, of course! Yes—she a—her cabbages"—

"Here, come along," Richard beckoned to him savagely. "I'll be back in five minutes, Uncle," he nodded coolly to either.

The young men left the room, and put on their hats. In the hall-passage they met Berry, dressed to return to Raynham. Richard dropped a helper to the intelligence into his hand, and warned him not to gossip much of London. Berry bowed perfect discreetness.

"What on earth induced you to talk about Protestants and Catholics marrying, Rip!" said Richard, as soon as they were in the street.

"Why," Ripton answered, "I was so hard pushed for it, 'pon my honour, I didn't know what to say. I ain't an author, you know. I can't make a story. I was trying to invent a point, you know, and I couldn't think of any other, and I thought that was just the point likely to make a jolly good dispute. Capital dinners they give at those crack hotels.—Why did you throw it all upon me? I didn't begin on the old lady."

The Hero mused: "It's odd! It's impossible you could have known!—I'll tell you why, Rip! I wanted to try you. You fib well at long range, but you don't do at close quarters and single combat. You're good behind walls, but not worth a shot in the open. I just see what you're fit for. You're staunch—that I'm certain of. You always were. Lead the way to one of the Parks—down in that direction. You know?—where she is!"

Ripton led the way. His dinner had prepared this young Englishman to defy the whole Artillery of established morals. With the muffled roar of London around them, alone in a dark slope of green, the Hero, leaning on his henchman, and speaking in a harsh clear under-tone, delivered his explanations. Doubtless the true heroic insignia and point of view will be discerned, albeit in common private's uniform.

"They've been plotting against me for a year, Rip! When you see her, you'll know what it was to have such a creature taken away from you. It nearly killed me. Never mind what she is. She's the most perfect and noble creature God ever made! It's not only her beauty—I don't care so much about that!—but when you've once seen her, she seems to draw music from all the nerves of your body—but she's such an Angel. I worship her. And her mind's like her face. She's pure gold. There—you'll see her to-night.

"Well," he pursued, after inflating Ripton with this rapturous prospect, "they got her away, and I recovered. It was Mister Adrian's work.—What's my father's objection to her? Because of her birth? She's educated: her manners are beautiful—full of refinement—quick and soft! Can they show me one of their ladies like her?—she's the daughter of a naval lieutenant!—Because she's a Catholic? What has religion to do with"—he pronounced "Love!" a little modestly—as it were a blush in his voice.

"Well, when I recovered, I thought I did not care for her. It shows how we know ourselves! And I cared for nothing. I felt as if I had no blood. I tried to imitate my dear Austin. I wish to God he were here. I love Austin. He would understand her. He's coming back this year, and then—but it'll be too late then.—Well, my father's always scheming to make me perfect—he has never spoken to me a word about her, but I can see her in his eyes—he wanted to give me a change, he said, and asked me to come to Town with my Uncle Hippy, and I consented. It was another plot to get me out of the way! As I live I had no more idea of meeting her than of flying to Heaven!"

He lifted his face. "Look at those old elm-branches! How they seem to mix among the stars!—glittering fruits of Winter!"

Ripton tipped his comical nose upward and was in duty bound to say, Yes! though he observed no connection between them and the narrative.

"Well," the Hero went on, "I came to Town. There I heard she was coming, too—coming home. It must have been fate, Ripton! Heaven forgive me! I was angry

with her, and I thought I should like to see her once—
only once—and reproach her for being false—for she never
wrote to me. And, oh, the dear Angel! what she must have
suffered!—I gave my Uncle the slip, and got to the Railway
she was coming by. There was a fellow going to meet
her—a farmer's son—and, good God! they were going to
try and make her marry him! I remembered it all then.
A servant of the farm had told me. That fellow went to
the wrong station, I suppose, for we saw nothing of him.
There she was—not changed a bit!—looking lovelier than
ever! And when she saw me, I knew in a minute that she
must love me till death!—You don't know what it is yet,
Ripton!—Will you believe it?—Though I was as sure she
loved me and had been true as steel, as that I shall see her
tonight, I spoke bitterly to her. And she bore it meekly—
she looked like a saint. I told her there was but one hope
of life for me—she must prove she was true, and as I give
up all, so must she. I don't know what I said. The
thought of losing her made me mad. She tried to plead with
me to wait—it was for my sake, I know. I pretended, like
a miserable hypocrite, that she did not love me at all. I
think I said shameful things. Oh what noble creatures
women are! She hardly had strength to move. I took her
to that place where you found us.—Rip! she went down on
her knees to me. I never dreamed of anything in life so
lovely as she looked then. Her eyes were thrown up,
bright with a crowd of tears—her dark brows bent together,
like Pain and Beauty meeting in one: and her glorious
golden hair swept off her shoulders as she hung forward
to my hands.—Could I lose such a prize?—If anything
could have persuaded me, would not that?—I thought of
Dante's Madonna—Guido's Magdalen.—Is there sin in it?
I see none! And if there is, it's all mine! I swear she's
spotless of a thought of sin. I see her very soul! Cease
to love her? Who dares ask me? Cease to love her? Why
I live on her!—To see her little chin straining up from her

throat, as she knelt to me!—there was one curl that fell across her throat. . . ."

Ripton listened for more. Richard had gone off in a muse at the picture.

"Well?" said Ripton, "and how about that young farmer fellow?"

The Hero's head was again contemplating the starry branches. His lieutenant's question came to him after an interval.

"Young Tom? Why, it's young Tom Blaize—son of our old enemy, Rip! I like the old man now. Oh! I saw nothing of the fellow."

"Lord!" cried Ripton, "are we going to get into a mess with Blazes again? I don't like that!"

His commander quietly passed his likes or dislikes.

"But when he goes to the train, and finds she's not there?" Ripton suggested.

"I've provided for that. The fool went to the South-East, instead of the South-West. All warmth, all sweetness, comes with the South-West!—I've provided for that, friend Rip. My trusty Tom awaits him there, as if by accident. He tells him he has not seen her, and advises him to remain in Town, and go for her there tomorrow, and the day following. Tom has money for the work. Young Tom ought to see London, you know, Rip!—like you. We shall gain some good clear days. And when old Blaize hears of it—what then? I have her! she's mine!—Besides, he won't hear for a week. This Tom beats that Tom in cunning, I'll wager.—Ha! ha!" the Hero burst out at a recollection. "What do you think, Rip? My father has some sort of System with me, it appears, and when I came to Town the time before, he took me to some people—the Grandisons—and what do you think? one of the daughters is a little girl—a nice little thing enough—very funny —and he wants me to wait for her! He hasn't said so, but I know it. I know what he means. Nobody understands him but me. I know he loves me, and is one of the best of men—but just consider!—a *little girl* who just comes up to my elbow. Isn't it ridiculous? Did you ever hear such nonsense?"

Ripton emphasized his opinion that it certainly was foolish.

"No, no! The die's cast!" said Richard. "They've been plotting for a year up to this day, and this is what comes of it! If my father loves me, he will love her. And if he loves me, he'll forgive my acting against his wishes, and see it was the only thing to be done. Come! step out! what a Time we've been!" and away he went, compelling Ripton to the sort of strides a drummer-boy has to take beside a column of grenadiers.

Ripton began to wish himself in love, seeing that it endowed a man with wind so that he could breathe great sighs, while going at a tremendous pace, and experience no sensation of fatigue. The Hero was communing with the elements, his familiars, and allowed him to pant as he pleased. Some keen-eyed Kensington urchins, noticing the discrepancy between the pedestrian powers of the two, aimed their wit at Mr. Thompson junior's expense. The pace, and nothing but the pace, induced Ripton to proclaim that they had gone too far, when they discovered that they had overshot the mark by half a mile. In the street over which stood Love's star, the Hero thundered his presence at a door, and evoked a flying housemaid, who knew not Mrs. Berry. The Hero attached significance to the fact that his instincts should have betrayed him, for he could have sworn to that house. The door being shut he stood in dead silence.

"Haven't you got her card?" Ripton inquired, and heard that it was in the custody of the cabman. Neither of them could positively bring to mind the number of the house.

"You ought to have chalked it, like that fellow in the

Forty Thieves," Ripton hazarded a pleasantry which met with no response.

Betrayed by his instincts, the magic slaves of Love! The Hero heavily descended the steps.

Ripton murmured that they were done for. His commander turned on him, and said: "Take all the houses on the opposite side, one after another. I'll take these." With a wry face Ripton crossed the road, altogether subdued by his native superiority to adverse circumstances.

Then were families aroused. Then did mortals dimly guess that something portentous was abroad. Then were labourers all day in the vineyard, harshly wakened, from their evening's nap. Hope and Fear stalked the street, as again and again the loud companion summonses resounded. Finally Ripton sang out cheerfully. He had Mrs. Berry before him, profuse of mellow curtsies.

Richard ran to her and caught her hands: "She's well?— upstairs?"

"Oh, quite well! only a trifle tired with her journey, and fluttering-like," Mrs. Berry replied to Ripton alone. The lover had flown aloft.

The wise woman sagely ushered Ripton into her own private parlour, there to wait till he was wanted.

CHAPTER XXXI

CONTAINS AN INTERCESSION FOR THE HEROINE

'IN all cases where two have joined to commit an offence, punish one of the two lightly,' is the dictum of THE PILGRIM'S SCRIP.

It is possible for young heads to conceive proper plans of action, and occasionally, by sheer force of will, to check the wild horses that are ever fretting to gallop off with them. But when they have given the reins and the whip to another, what are they to do? They may go down on their knees, and beg and pray the furious charioteer to stop, or moderate his speed. Alas! each fresh thing they do redoubles his ardour. Lucy submitting, he chooses his pace. Lucy remonstrating, he is fired to madness. There is a power in their troubled beauty women learn the use of, and what wonder? They have seen it kindle Ilium to flames so often! But ere they grow matronly in the house of Menelaus, they weep, and implore, and do not in truth know how terribly two-edged is their gift of loveliness. They resign themselves to an incomprehensible frenzy; pleasant to them, because they attribute it to excessive love. And so the very sensible things which they can and do say, are vain.

I reckon it absurd to ask them to be quite in earnest. Are not those their own horses in yonder team? Certainly if they were quite in earnest they might soon have my gentleman as sober as a carter. A hundred different ways of disenchanting him exist, and Adrian will point you out one or two that shall be instantly efficacious. For Love, the charioteer, is easily tripped, while honest jog-trot Love keeps his legs to the end. Granted dear women are not quite in earnest, still the mere words they utter should be put to their good account. They do mean them, though their hearts are set the wrong way. 'Tis a despairing, pathetic, homage to the judgment of the majority, in whose faces they are flying. Punish Helen, very young, lightly. After a certain age you may select her for special chastisement. And innocent with Theseus, with Paris she is an advanced incendiary.

The fair young girl was sitting as her lover had left her; trying to recall her stunned senses. Her bonnet was unremoved; her hands clasped on her knees; dry tears in her eyes. Like a dutiful slave, she rose to him. And first he claimed her mouth. There was a speech, made up of all the pretty wisdom her wild situation and true love could gather, awaiting him there; but his kiss scattered it to fragments. She dropped to her seat weeping, and hiding shamed cheeks.

By his silence she divined his thoughts, and took his hand, and drew it to her lips.

"Keep your eyes so."

She could not.

"Do you fear me, Lucy?"

A throbbing pressure answered him.

"Do you love me, darling?"

She trembled from head to foot.

"Then why do you turn from me?"

She wept: "Oh, Richard! take me home! take me home!"

"Look at me, Lucy!"

Her head shrank timidly round.

"Keep your eyes on me, darling! Now speak!"

But she could not look, and speak too. The lover knew his mastery when he had her eyes.

"You wish me to take you home?"

She faltered: "Oh, Richard! it is not too late."

"You regret what you have done for me?"

"Dearest! it is ruin."

"You weep because you have consented to be mine?"

"Not for me! Oh, Richard!"

"For me you weep? Look at me! For me?"

"How will it end! Oh, Richard!"

"You weep for me?"

"Dearest! I would die for you!"

"Would you see me indifferent to everything in the world? Would you have me lost? Do you think I will live another day in England without you? I have staked all I have on you, Lucy. You have nearly killed me once. A second time, and earth will not be troubled by me. You ask me to wait, when they are plotting against us on all sides? Darling Lucy! look on me. Fix your fond eyes on me. You ask me to wait, when here you are given to me—when you have proved my faith—when we know we love as none have loved. Give me your eyes! Let them tell me I have your heart!"

Where was her wise little speech? How could she match such mighty eloquence? She sought to collect a few more of the scattered fragments.

"Dearest! your father may be brought to consent by and by, and then—Oh! if you take me home now—"

The lover stood up: "He who has been arranging that fine scheme to disgrace and martyrize you? True, as I live! that's the reason of their having you back. Your old servant heard him and your Uncle discussing it. He!—Lucy! he's a good man, but he must not step in between you and me. I say God has given you to me."

He was down by her side again, his arms enfolding her.

She had hoped to fight a better battle than in the morning, and she was weaker and softer.

Ah! why should she doubt that his great love was the first law to her? Why should she not believe that she would wreck him by resisting? And if she suffered, O sweet to think it was for his sake! Sweet to shut out Wisdom: accept total blindness, and be led by him!

The hag, Wisdom, annoyed them little further. She rustled her garments ominously, and vanished.

"Oh, my own Richard!" the fair girl just breathed.

He whispered: "Call me that name."

She blushed deeply.

"Call me that name," he repeated. "You said it once to-day."

"Dearest!"

"Not that."

"Oh, darling!"

"Not that."

"Husband!"

She was won. The rosy gate from which the word had issued was closed with a seal.

Ripton did not enjoy his introduction to the caged bird of beauty that night. He received a lesson in the art of pumping from the worthy landlady below, up to an hour when she yawned, and he blinked, and their common candle wore with dignity the brigand's hat of midnight, and cocked a drunken eye at them under it.

CHAPTER XXXII

RELATES HOW PREPARATIONS FOR ACTION WERE CONDUCTED UNDER THE APRIL OF LOVERS

BEAUTY, of course, is for the Hero. Nevertheless, it is not always he on whom Beauty works its most conquering influence. It is the dull, commonplace, man into whose slow brain she drops like a celestial light, and burns lastingly. The poet, for instance, is a connoisseur of Beauty: to the artist she is a model. These gentlemen by much contemplation of her charms wax critical. The days when they had hearts being gone, they are haply divided between the blonde, and the brunette; the aquiline nose, and the Proserpine; this shaped eye, and that. But go about among simple unprofessional fellows, boors, dunderheads, and here and there you shall find some barbarous intelligence which has had just strength enough to conceive, and has taken Beauty as its Goddess, and knows but one form to worship, in his poor stupid fashion, and would perish for her. Nay, more: the man would devote all his days to her, though he is dumb as a dog. And indeed, he is Beauty's Dog. Almost every Beauty has her Dog. The Hero possesses her; the poet proclaims her; the painter puts her upon canvass; and the faithful old Dog follows her: and the end of it is that the faithful old Dog is her single attendant. Sir Hero is revelling in the wars, or in Armida's bowers; Mr. Poet

has spied a wrinkle; the Brush is for the Rose in its Season.
She turns to her old Dog then. She hugs him; and he, who
has subsisted on a bone and a pat till there he squats decrepid, he turns his grateful old eyes up to her, and has not
a notion that she is hugging sad memories in him: Hero,
Poet, Painter, in one scrubby one! Then is she buried, and
the village hears languid howls, and there is a paragraph
in the newspapers concerning the extraordinary fidelity of an
Old Dog. So runs the round.

Excited by suggestive recollections of Nooredeen and the
Fair Persian, and the change in the obscure monotony of his
life by his having quarters in a crack hotel, and living
familiarly with West-End people—living on the fat of the
land (which forms a stout portion of an honest youth's
Romance), Ripton Thompson breakfasted next morning
with his chief at half-past eight. The meal had been fixed
overnight for seven, but Ripton slept a great deal more
than the nightingale, and (to chronicle his exact state) even
half-past eight rather afflicted his new aristocratic senses, and
reminded him too keenly of Law and bondage. He had
preferred to breakfast at Algernon's hour, who had left word
for eleven. Him, however, it was Richard's object to avoid,
so they fell to, and Ripton no longer envied Hippias in bed.
Breakfast done, they bequeathed the consoling information
for Algernon that they were off to hear a popular preacher,
and departed.

"How happy everybody looks!" said Richard, in the quiet
Sunday streets.

"Yes—jolly!" said Ripton.

Most young gentlemen speak from one part or other of
their interiors.

"When I'm—when this is over, I'll see that they are,
too—as many as I can make happy," said the Hero: adding
softly: "Her blind was down at a quarter to six. I think
she slept well!"

"You don't mean to say you've been there this morning?"

Ripton exclaimed. "Really?" and an idea of what Love was dawned upon his dull brain.

"Will she see me, Ricky?"

"Yes. She'll see you today. She was tired last night."

"Positively?"

Richard assured him that privilege would be his.

"Here," he said, coming under some trees in the park, "here's where I talked to you last night. What a time it seems! How I hate the night!"

"You'll soon—" Ripton darkly winked; but his Chief looked uninstructed, and he branched into the converse of daylight.

On the way, that Richard might have an exalted opinion of him, he hinted decorously at a somewhat intimate and mysterious acquaintance with the sex. Ripton Thompson had seen pretty girls, and pretty girls had seen Ripton Thompson. Ahem!—Headings of certain Random adventures he gave.

"Well!" said his Chief, "why don't you marry her?"

Then was Ripton shocked, and cried, "Oh, dear!" and had a taste of the feeling of superiority, destined that day to be crushed utterly.

He was again deposited in Mrs. Berry's charge for a term that caused him dismal fears that the Fair Persian still refused to show her face, but Richard called out to him, and up Ripton went, unaware of the transformation he was to undergo. Hero and Beauty stood together to receive him. From the bottom of the stairs he had his vivaciously agreeable smile ready for them, and by the time he entered the room his cheeks were painfully stiff, and his eyes strained beyond their exact meaning. Lucy, with one hand anchored to her lover, welcomed him kindly. He relieved her shyness by looking so extremely silly. They sat down, and tried to commence a conversation, but Ripton was as little master of his tongue as he was of his eyes. After an interval, the Fair Persian, having done duty by showing herself, was glad to quit the room. Her lord and possessor then turned inquiringly to Ripton.

"You don't wonder now, Rip?" he said.

"No, Richard!" Ripton waited to reply with sufficient solemnity, "indeed I don't!"

He spoke differently; he looked differently. He had the Old Dog's eyes in his head. They watched the door she had passed through; they listened for her, as dogs' eyes do. When she came in, bonneted for a walk, his agitation was dog-like. When she hung on her lover timidly, and went forth, he followed without an idea of envy, or anything save the secret raptures the sight of her gave him, which are the Old Dog's own. For beneficent Nature requites him. His sensations cannot be heroic, but they have a fulness, and a wagging delight, as good in their way. And this capacity for humble unaspiring worship has its peculiar guerdon. When Ripton comes to think of Miss Random now, what will he think of himself? Let no one despise the Old Dog. Through him doth Beauty vindicate her sex.

It did not please Ripton that others should have the bliss of beholding her, and as, to his perceptions, everybody did, and observed her offensively, and stared, and turned their heads back, and interchanged comments on her, and became in a minute madly in love with her, he had to smother low growls. They strolled about the pleasant Gardens of Kensington all the morning, under the young chestnut buds, and round the windless waters, talking, and soothing the wild excitement of their hearts. If Lucy spoke, Ripton pricked up his ears. She, too, made the remark that everybody seemed to look happy, and he heard it with thrills of joy. "So everybody is, where you are!" he would have wished to say, if he dared, but was restrained by fears that nis burning eloquence would commit him. Ripton knew the people he met twice. It would have been difficult to persuade him they were the creatures of accident.

From the Gardens, in contempt of Ripton's frowned protest, Richard boldly struck into the Park, where solitary carriages were beginning to perform the circuit. Here Ripton had some justification for his jealous pangs. The young girl's golden locks of hair; her sweet, now dreamily sad, face; her gentle graceful figure in the black straight dress she wore; a sort of half-conventual air she had—a mark of something not class, that was partly Beauty's, partly maiden innocence growing conscious, partly remorse at her weakness and dim fear of the Future it was sowing;—did attract the eye-glasses. Ripton had to learn that eyes are bearable, but eye-glasses an abomination. They fixed a spell upon his courage; for somehow the youth had always ranked them as emblems of our nobility, and hearing two exquisite eye-glasses, who had been to front and rear several times, drawl in gibberish generally imputed to lords, that his heroine was a charming little creature, just the size, but had no style,—he was abashed; he did not fly at them and tear them. He became dejected. Beauty's Dog is affected by the eye-glass in a manner not unlike the common animal's terror of the human eye.

Richard appeared to hear nothing, or it was homage that he heard. He repeated to Lucy Diaper Sandoe's verses:

> 'The cockneys nod to each other aside,
>   The coxcombs lift their glasses,'

and projected hiring a horse for her to ride every day in the park, and shine among the highest.

They had turned to the West, against the sky glittering through the bare trees across the water, and the bright-edged rack. The lover, his imagination just then occupied clothing earthly glories in celestial, felt where his senses were sharpest the hand of his darling falter, and instinctively looked ahead. His Uncle Algernon was leisurely jolting towards them on his one sound leg. The dismembered

Guardsman talked to a friend whose arm supported him, and speculated from time to time on the fair heralds of the crush driving by. The two white faces passed him unobserved. Unfortunately Ripton, coming behind, went plump upon the Captain's live toe—or so he pretended—crying: "Confound it, Mr. Thompson! you might have chosen the other."

The horrible apparition did confound Ripton, who stammered that it was extraordinary.

"Not at all," said Algernon. "Everybody makes up to that fellow. Instinct, I suppose!"

He had not to ask for his nephew. Richard turned to face the matter.

"Sorry I couldn't wait for you this morning, Uncle," he said, with the coolness of relationship. "I thought you never walked so far."

His voice was in perfect tone—the heroic mask admirable.

Algernon examined the downcast visage at his side, and contrived to allude to the popular preacher. He was instantly introduced to Ripton's sister, Miss Thompson.

The Captain bowed, smiling melancholy approval of his nephew's choice of a Minister. After a few stray remarks, and an affable salute to Miss Thompson, he hobbled away, and then the three sealed volcanoes breathed, and Lucy's arm ceased to be squeezed quite so much up to the heroic pitch.

This incident quickened their steps homeward to the sheltering wings of Mrs. Berry. All that passed between them on the subject comprised a stammered excuse from Ripton for his conduct, and a good-humoured rejoinder from Richard, that he had gained a sister by it: at which Ripton ventured to wish aloud Miss Desborough would only think so, and a faint smile twitched poor Lucy's lips to please him. She hardly had strength to reach her cage. She had none to eat of Mrs. Berry's nice little dinner. To be alone, that she might cry and ease her heart of its accusing weight of tears, was all she prayed for. Kind Mrs. Berry, slipping into her bedroom to take off her things, found the fair body in a fevered shudder, and finished by undressing her completely and putting her to bed.

"Just an hour's sleep, or so," the mellifluous woman explained the case to the two anxious gentlemen. "A quiet sleep and a cup of warm tea goes for more than twenty Doctors, it do—when there's the flutters," she pursued. "I know it by myself. And a good cry beforehand's better than the best of medicine."

She nursed them into a make-believe of eating, and retired to her softer charge and sweeter babe, reflecting, "Lord! Lord! the three of 'em don't make fifty! I'm as old as two and a half of 'em, to say the least." Mrs. Berry used her apron, and by virtue of their years took them all three into her heart.

Left alone, neither of the young men could swallow a morsel.

"Did you see the change come over her?" Richard whispered.

Ripton fiercely accused his prodigious stupidity.

The lover flung down his knife and fork: "What could I do? If I had said nothing, we should have been suspected. I was obliged to speak. And she hates a lie! See! it has struck her down. God forgive me!"

Ripton affected a serene mind: "It was a fright, Richard," he said. "That's what Mrs. Berry means by flutters. Those old women talk in that way. You heard what she said. And these old women know. I'll tell you what it is. It's this, Richard!—it's because you've got a fool for your friend."

"She regrets it," muttered the lover. "Good God! I think she fears me." He dropped his face in his hands.

Ripton went to the window, repeating energetically for his comfort: "It's because you've got a fool for your friend!"

Sombre grew the street they had last night aroused. The sun was buried alive in cloud. Ripton saw himself no more in the opposite window. He watched the deplorable objects passing on the pavement. His aristocratic visions had gone like his breakfast. Beauty had been struck down by his egregious folly, and there he stood—a Wretch!

Richard came to him! "Don't mumble on like that, Rip!" he said. "Nobody blames you."

"Ah! you're very kind, Richard," interposed the Wretch, moved at the face of misery he beheld.

"Listen to me, Rip! I shall take her home tonight. Yes! If she's happier away from me!—do you think me a brute, Ripton? Rather than have her shed a tear, I'd!—I'll take her home tonight!"

Ripton suggested that it was sudden; adding from his larger experience, people perhaps might talk.

The lover could not understand what they should talk about, but he said: "If I give him who came for her yesterday the clue? If no one sees or hears of me what can they say? Oh, Rip! I'll give her up. I'm wrecked for ever! what of that? Yes—let them take her! The world in arms should never have torn her from me, but when she cries— Yes! all's over. I'll find him at once."

He searched in out-of-the-way corners for the hat of resolve. Ripton looked on, wretcheder than ever.

"Suppose," the idea struck him, "Suppose, Richard, she doesn't want to go?"

The lover sternly continued his hunt. He found the propelling machine at last, and put it on, saying under its shadow: "I'm ready! Now!"

Here was sadness and gloom come upon them! Ripton likewise commenced the search for his doleful casque, and toppled it moodily on the back of his head in sign of glorious enterprise abandoned, and surrender to the enemy.

It was a moment when, perhaps, one who sided with parents and guardians and the old wise world, might have inclined them to pursue their righteous wretched course, and have given small Cupid a smack and sent him home to his naughty Mother. Alas! (it is THE PILGRIM'S SCRIP interjecting) women are the born accomplices of mischief! In bustles Mrs. Berry to clear away the refection, and finds the two knights helmed, and sees, though 'tis dusk, that they wear doubtful brows, and guesses bad things for her dear God Hymen in a twinkling.

"Dear! dear!" she exclaimed, "and neither of you eaten a scrap! And there's my dear young lady off into the prettiest sleep you ever see!"

"Ha!" cried the lover, illuminated.

"Soft as a baby!" Mrs. Berry averred. "I went to look at her this very moment, and there's not a bit of trouble in her breath. It come and it go like the sweetest regular instrument ever made. The Black Ox haven't trod on *her* foot yet! Most like it was the air of London. But only fancy, if you had called in a Doctor! Why, I shouldn't have let her take any of his quackery. Now, there!"

Ripton attentively observed his Chief, and saw him doff his hat with a curious caution, and peer into its recess, from which, during Mrs. Berry's speech, he drew forth a little glove—dropped there by some freak of chance.

"Keep me, keep me, now you have me!" sang the little glove, and amused the lover with a thousand concerts.

"When will she wake, do you think, Mrs. Berry?" he asked.

"Oh! we mustn't go for disturbing her," said the guileful good creature. "Bless ye! let her sleep it out. And if you young gentlemen was to take my advice, and go and take a walk for to get a appetite—everybody should eat! it's their sacred dooty, no so matter what their feelings be! and I say it who 'm no chicken!—I'll frickashee this—which is a chicken—against your return. I'm a Cook, I can assure ye!"

The lover seized her two hands. "You're the best old

soul in the world!" he cried.   Mrs. Berry appeared willing
to kiss him. "We won't disturb her. Let her sleep. Keep
her in bed, Mrs. Berry. Will you? And we'll call to inquire after her this evening, and come and see her tomorrow.
I'm sure you'll be kind to her. There! there!" Mrs. Berry
was preparing to whimper. "I trust her to you, you see.
Good-bye, you dear old soul."

He smuggled a handful of gold into her keeping, and
went to dine with his Uncles, happy and hungry.

Before they reached the hotel, they had agreed to draw
Mrs. Berry into their confidence, telling her (with embel-
lishments) all save their names, so that they might enjoy
the counsel and assistance of that trump of a woman, and
yet have nothing to fear from her. Lucy was to receive the
name of Letitia, Ripton's youngest and best-looking sister.
The heartless fellow proposed it in cruel mockery of an old
weakness of hers.

"Letitia!" mused Richard. "I like the name. Both begin
with L. There's something soft—womanlike—in the L's."

Material Ripton remarked that they looked like pounds
on paper. The lover roamed through his golden groves.
"Lucy Feverel! that sounds better! I wonder where Ralph
is. I should like to help him. He's in love with my cousin
Clare. He'll never do anything till he marries. No man
can. I'm going to do a hundred things when it's over.
We shall travel first. I want to see the Alps. One doesn't
know what the Earth is till one has seen the Alps. What a
delight it will be to her! I fancy I see her eyes gazing up
at them.

> "'And O your dear blue eyes, that heavenward glance
>   With kindred beauty! banished humbleness!
>   Past weeping for mortality's distress—
> Yet from your soul a tear hangs there in trance.
>   And fills, but does not fall:
>   Softly I hear it call

At Heaven's gate, till Sister Seraphs press
To look on you their old love from the skies:
Those are the eyes of Seraphs so bright on your blue eyes!'

Beautiful! Those lines, Rip, were written by a man who was once a friend of my father's. I intend to find him and make them friends again. You don't care for poetry. It's no use your trying to swallow it, Rip!"

"It sounds very nice," said Ripton, modestly shutting his mouth.

"The Alps! Italy! Rome! and then I shall go to the East," the Hero continued. "She's ready to go anywhere with me, the dear brave heart! Oh, the glorious golden East! I dream of the Desert. I dream I'm Chief of an Arab tribe, and we fly all white in the moonlight on our mares, and hurry to the rescue of my darling! And we push the spears, and we scatter them, and I come to the tent where she crouches, and catch her to my saddle, and away!— Rip! what a life!"

Ripton strove to imagine he could enjoy it. "And then we shall come home, and I shall lead Austin's life, with her to help me. First be virtuous, Rip! and then serve your country heart and soul. A wise man told me that. I think I shall do something."

Sunshine and cloud, cloud and sunshine passed over the lover. Now life was a narrow ring: now the distances extended. An hour ago and food was hateful. Now he manfully refreshed his nature, and joined in Algernon's encomiums on Miss Letitia Thompson.

Meantime Beauty slept, watched by the veteran volunteer of the Hero's band. Lucy awoke from dreams which seemed reality, to the reality which was a dream. She awoke calling for some friend, "Margaret!" and heard one say: "My name is Bessy Berry, my love! not Margaret." Then she asked piteously where she was, and where was

Margaret, her dear friend, and Mrs. Berry whispered: "Sure you've got a dearer!"

"Ah!" sighed Lucy, sinking on her pillow, overwhelmed by the strangeness of her state.

Mrs. Berry closed the frill of her nightgown and adjusted the bedclothes quietly.

Her name was breathed.

"Yes, my love?" she said.

"Is he here?"

"He's gone, my dear."

"Gone?—Oh, where?" The young girl started up in disorder.

"Gone, to be back, my love! Ah! that young gentleman!" Mrs. Berry chanted: "Not a morsel have he eat: not a drop have he drunk!"

"O Mrs. Berry! why did you not make him?" Lucy wept for the famine-struck hero who was just then feeding mightily.

Mrs. Berry explained that to make one eat who thought the darling of his heart like to die, was a sheer impossibility for the cleverest of women; and on this deep truth Lucy reflected, with her eyes wide at the candle. She wanted one to pour her feelings out to. She slid her hand from under the bedclothes, and took Mrs. Berry's, and kissed it. The good creature required no further avowal of her secret, but forthwith leaned her consummate bosom to the pillow, and petitioned Heaven to bless them both!—Then the little bride was alarmed, and wondered how Mrs. Berry could have guessed it.

"Why," said Mrs. Berry, "your love is out of your eyes, and out of everything ye do." And the little bride wondered more. She thought she had been so very cautious not to betray it. The common woman in them made cheer together after their own April fashion. Following which Mrs. Berry probed for the sweet particulars of this beautiful love-match: but the little bride's lips were locked. She only said her lover was above her in station.

"And you're a Catholic, my dear!"

"Yes, Mrs. Berry!"

"And him a Protestant."

"Yes, Mrs. Berry!"

"Dear, dear!—And why shouldn't ye be?" she ejaculated, seeing sadness return to the bridal babe. "So as you was born, so shall ye be! But you'll have to make arrangements about the children. The girls to worship with you: the boys with him. It's the same God, my dear! You mustn't blush at it, though you do look so pretty. If my young gentlemen could see you now!"

"Please, Mrs. Berry!" Lucy murmured.

"Why, he will, you know, my dear!"

"Oh, please, Mrs. Berry!"

"And you that can't bear the thoughts of it! Well, I do wish there was fathers and mothers on both sides, and dockments signed, and bridesmaids, and a breakfast! but love is love, and ever will be, in spite of them."

She made other and deeper dives into the little heart, but though she drew up pearls, they were not of the kind she searched for. The one fact that hung as a fruit upon her tree of Love, Lucy had given her: she would not, in fealty to her lover, reveal its growth and history, however sadly she yearned to pour out all to this dear old Mother Confessor.

Her conduct drove Mrs. Berry from the rosy to the Autumnal view of matrimony, generally heralded by the announcement that it is a Lottery.

"And when you see your ticket," said Mrs. Berry, "you shan't know whether it's a prize or a blank. And, Lord knows! some go on thinking it's a prize when it turns on 'em and tears 'em. I'm one of the blanks, my dear. I drew a blank in Berry. He was a black Berry to me, my dear! Smile away! he truly was, and I a prizin' him as proud as you can conceive! My dear!" Mrs. Berry pressed her hands flat on her apron, "we hadn't been a three months man and wife, when that man—it wasn't the Honeymoon, which some can't say—that man—Yes! he kicked me. His wedded wife he kicked! Ah!" she sighed to Lucy's large eyes, "I could have borne that. A blow don't touch the heart," the poor creature tapped her sensitive side. "I went on loving of him, for I'm a soft one. Tall as a Grenadier he is, and when out of service grows his moustache. I used to call him my body Guardsman—like a Queen! I flattered him like the fools we women are. For take my word for it, my dear, there's nothing here below so vain as a man! That I know. But I didn't deserve it. . . . I'm a superior Cook. . . . I did not deserve that noways." Mrs. Berry thumped her knee, and accentuated towards her climax: "I mended his linen. I saw to his adornments—he called his clothes, the bad man! I was a servant to him, my dear! and there—it was nine months—nine months from the day he swear to protect and cherish and that—nine calendar months, and my gentleman is off with another woman! Bone of his bone!—pish!" exclaimed Mrs. Berry, reckoning her wrongs over vividly. "Here's my Ring. A pretty ornament! What do it mean? I'm for tearin' it off my finger a dozen times in the day. It's a symbol? I call it a tomfoolery for the dead-alive to wear it, that's a widow and not a widow, and haven't got a name for what she is in any Dixonary. I've looked, my dear, and"—she spread out her arms—"Johnson haven't got a name for me!"

At this impressive woe Mrs. Berry's voice quavered into sobs. Lucy spoke gentle words to the poor outcast from Johnson. The sorrows of Autumn have no warning for April. The little bride, for all her tender pity, felt happier when she had heard her landlady's moving tale of the wickedness of man, which cast in bright relief the glory of that one Hero who was hers. Then from a short flight of inconceivable bliss, she fell, shot by one of her hundred Argus-eyed fears.

"Oh, Mrs. Berry! I'm so young! Think of me—only just seventeen!"

Mrs. Berry immediately dried her eyes to radiance. "Young, my dear! Nonsense! There's no so much harm in being young, here and there. I knew an Irish lady was married at fourteen. Her daughter married close on fourteen. She was a grandmother by thirty! When any strange man began, she used to ask him what pattern caps grandmothers wore. They'd stare! Bless you! the grandmother could have married over and over again. It was her daughter's fault, not hers, you know."

"She was three years younger," mused Lucy.

"She married beneath her, my dear. Ran off with her father's bailiff's son. 'Ah, Berry!' she'd say, 'if I hadn't been foolish, I should be my lady now—not Granny!' Her father never forgave her—left all his estates out of the family."

"Did her husband always love her?" Lucy preferred to know.

"In his way, my dear, he did," said Mrs. Berry, coming upon her matrimonial wisdom. "He couldn't help himself. If he left off, he began again. She was so clever, and did make him so comfortable. Cook! there wasn't such another cook out of a Alderman's ketchen; no, indeed! And she a born lady! That tells ye it's the dooty of all women! She had her saying—'When the parlour fire gets low, put coals on the ketchen fire!' and a good saying it is to treasure. Such is man! no use in havin' their hearts, if ye don't have their stomachs."

Perceiving that she grew abstruse, Mrs. Berry added briskly: "You know nothing about that yet, my dear. Only mind me and mark me: Don't neglect your Cookery. Kissing don't last: Cookery do!"

Here, with an Aphorism worthy a place in THE PILGRIM'S

SCRIP, she broke off to go posseting for her dear invalid. Lucy was quite well; very eager to be allowed to rise and be ready when the knock should come. Mrs. Berry, in her loving considerateness for the little bride, positively commanded her to lie down, and be quiet, and submit to be nursed and cherished. For Mrs. Berry well knew that ten minutes alone with the Hero could only be had while the little bride was in that unattainable position.

Thanks to her strategy, as she thought, her object was gained. The night did not pass before she learnt, from the Hero's own mouth, that Mr. Richards, the father of the Hero, and a stern lawyer, was adverse to his union with this young lady he loved, because of a ward of his, heiress to an immense property, whom he desired his son to espouse: and because his darling Letitia was a Catholic: Letitia, the sole daughter of a brave naval officer, deceased, and in the hands of a savage Uncle, who wanted to sacrifice this Beauty to a brute of a son. Mrs. Berry listened credulously to the emphatic narrative, and spoke to the effect that the wickedness of old people formed the excuse for the wildness of young ones. The ceremonious administration of oaths of secrecy and devotion over, she was enrolled in the Hero's band, which now numbered three, and entered upon the duties with feminine energy, for there are no conspirators like women. Ripton's lieutenancy became a sinecure, his rank merely titular. He had never been married—he knew nothing about licenses, except that they must be obtained and were not difficult—he had not an idea that so many days' warning must be given to the Clergyman of the Parish where one of the parties was resident. How should he? All his forethought was comprised in the Ring, and whenever the discussion of arrangements for the great event grew particularly hot and important, he would say, with a shrewd nod: "We mustn't forget the Ring, you know, Mrs. Berry!" and the new member was only prevented by natural complaisance from shouting: "Oh, drat ye! and your Ring,

too." Mrs. Berry had acted conspicuously in fifteen marriages, by banns, and by Licenses, and to have such an ob-
vious requisite dinned in her ears was exasperating. They
could not have contracted alliance with an auxiliar more
invaluable, an authority so profound, as they acknowledged
to themselves. The Hero marched like an automaton at her
bidding: Lieutenant Thompson was rejoiced to perform
services as errand-boy in the enterprise.

"It's in hopes you'll be happier than me, I do it," said
the devout and charitable Berry. "Marriages is made in
Heaven, they say; and if that's the case, I say they don't
take much account of us below!"

Her own woful experiences had been given to the Hero
in exchange for his story of cruel parents.

Richard vowed to her that he would henceforth hold it
a duty to hunt out the Wanderer from wedded bonds, and
bring him back, bound and suppliant.

"Oh, he'll come!" said Mrs. Berry, pursing prophetic
wrinkles: "He'll come of his own accord. Never anywheres will he meet such a cook as Bessy Berry! And he
know her value in his heart of hearts. And I do believe,
when he do come, I shall be opening these arms to him
again, and not slapping his impidence in the face—I'm that
soft! I always was—in matrimony, Mr. Richards!"

As when nations are secretly preparing for War, the
Docks and Arsenals hammer night and day, and busy con-
tractors measure Time by inches, and the air hums around
for leagues as it were myriads of bees, so the house and
neighbourhood of the matrimonial soft one resounded in the
heroic style, and knew little of the changes of light decreed
by Creation. Mrs. Berry was the general of the hour.
Down to Doctors' Commons she expedited the Hero, in-
structing him how boldly to face the Law, and fib: for that
the Law never could resist a fib and a bold face. Down the
Hero went, and proclaimed his presence. And lo! the Law
danced to him its sedatest lovely bear's-dance. Think ye

the Law less susceptible to him than flesh and blood? With
a beautiful confidence it put the few familiar questions to
him, and nodded to his replies; then stamped the bond, and
took the fee. It must be an old vagabond at heart that can
permit the irrevocable to go so cheap even to a Hero. For
only mark him when he is petitioned by heros and heroines
to undo what he does so easily! That small archway of
Doctors' Commons seems the eye of a needle, through
which the lean purse has a way, somehow, of slipping more
readily than the portly: but once through, all are camels
alike, the lean purse an especially big camel. Dispensing
tremendous Marriage as it does, the Law can have no conscience.

"I hadn't the slightest difficulty," says the exulting Hero.

"Of course not!" returns Mrs. Berry. "It's as easy, if
ye're in earnest, as buying a plum bun."

Likewise the Ambassador of the Hero went to claim the
promise of the Church to be attendance on a certain spot,
on a certain day, and there swear eternal fealty, and gird
him about with all its forces; which the Church, receiving a
wink from the Law, obsequiously engaged to do, for less
than the price of a plum-cake.

Meantime, while craftsmen and skilled women, directed
by Mrs. Berry, were toiling to deck the day at hand, Raynham and Belthorpe slept,—the former soundly; and one
day was as another to them. Regularly every morning a
letter arrived from Richard to his father, containing observations on the phenomena of London; remarks (mainly
cynical) on the speeches and acts of Parliament; and reasons
for not having yet been able to call on the Grandisons.
They were certainly rather monotonous, and spiritless. The
Baronet did not complain. The cold dutiful tone assured
him there was no internal trouble or distraction. "The letters of a healthful physique!" he said to Lady Blandish with
sure insight. Complacently he sat and smiled, little witting
that his son's Ordeal was imminent, and that his son's

Ordeal was to be his own. Hippias wrote that his Nephew was killing him by making appointments which he never kept, and altogether neglecting him in the most shameless way, so that his ganglionic centre was in a ten times worse state than when he left Raynham. He wrote very bitterly, but it was hard to feel compassion for his offended stomach.

On the other hand, young Tom Blaize was not forth-coming, and had despatched no tidings whatever. Farmer Blaize smoked his pipe evening after evening, vastly dis-turbed. London was a large place—young Tom might be lost in it, he thought: and young Tom had his weaknesses. A wolf at Belthorpe, he was likely to be a sheep in London, as yokels have proved. But what had become of Lucy? This consideration almost sent Farmer Blaize off to London direct, and he would have gone had not his pipe enlightened him. A young fellow might play truant and get into a scrape, but a young man and a young woman were sure to be heard of, *unless* they were acting in complicity:—Why, of course, young Tom had behaved like a man, the rascal! and married her outright there, while he had the chance. It was a long guess. Still it was the only reasonable way of accounting for his extraordinary silence, and therefore the farmer held to it that he had done the deed. He argued as modern men do who think the Hero, the upsetter of ordinary calculations, is gone from us. So, after despatching a letter to a friend in Town to be on the look-out for son Tom, he continued awhile to smoke his pipe, rather elated than not, and mused on the shrewd manner he should adopt when Master Honeymoon did appear.

Towards the middle of the second week of Richard's absence, Tom Bakewell came to Raynham for Cassandra, and privately handed a letter to the Eighteenth Century, containing a request for money, and a round sum. The Eighteenth Century was as good as her word, and gave Tom a letter in return, enclosing a cheque on her bankers, amply providing to keep the heroic engine in motion at a moderate pace. Tom went back, and Raynham and Lobourne slept and dreamed not of the morrow. The System, wedded to Time, slept, and knew not how he had been outraged—anticipated by seven pregnant seasons. For Time had heard the Hero swear to that legalizing instrument, and had also registered an oath. Ah me! venerable Hebrew Time! he is unforgiving. Half the confusion and fever of the world comes of this Vendetta he declares against the hapless Innocents who have once done him a wrong. They cannot escape him. They will never outlive it. The Father of jokes, he is himself no joke: which it seems the business of men to discover.

The days roll round. He is their servant now. Mrs. Berry has a new satin gown, a beautiful bonnet, a gold brooch, and sweet gloves, presented to her by the Hero, wherein to stand by his bride at the altar tomorrow; and, instead of being an old wary hen, she is as much a chicken as any of the party, such has been the magic of these articles. Fathers she sees accepting the facts produced for them by their children: a world content to be carved out as it pleases the Hero.

At last Time brings the bridal eve, and is blest as a benefactor. The final arrangements are made; the bridegroom does depart; and Mrs. Berry lights the little bride to her bed. Lucy stops on the landing where there is an old clock eccentrically correct that night. 'Tis the palpitating pause before the gates of her transfiguration. Mrs. Berry sees her put her rosy finger on the ONE about to strike, and touch all the hours successively till she comes to the TWELVE that shall sound 'Wife' in her ears on the morrow, moving her lips the while, and looking round archly solemn when she has done: and that sight so catches at Mrs. Berry's heart that, not guessing Time to be the poor child's enemy, she endangers her candle by folding Lucy warmly in her arms,

whimpering: "Bless you for a darling! you innocent lamb!
You shall be happy! You shall!"

Old Time gazes grimly ahead.

CHAPTER XXXIII

IN WHICH THE LAST ACT OF A COMEDY TAKES THE PLACE OF THE FIRST

ALTHOUGH it blew hard when Cæsar crossed the Rubicon,
the passage of that River is commonly calm; calm as
Acheron. So long as he gets his fare, the ferryman does not
need to be told whom he carries: he pulls with a will, and
Heroes may be over in half an hour. Some, by taking an
oar themselves, have done it in five minutes: some in two.
Only when they stand on the opposite banks, do they see
what a leap they have taken. The shores they have relinquished shrink to an infinite remoteness. There they have
dreamed: here they must act. There lie youth and irresolution: here manhood and purpose. They are veritably in
another land: a moral Acheron divides their life. Their
memories scarce seem their own! The PHILOSOPHICAL
GEOGRAPHY (about to be published) observes that each
man has, one time or other, a little Rubicon—a clear, or a
foul, water to cross. It is asked him: 'Wilt thou wed this
Fate, and give up all behind thee?' And 'I will,' firmly pronounced, speeds him over. The above-named Manuscript
authority informs us that by far the greater number of
carcases rolled by this heroic flood to its sister stream below,
are those of fellows who have repented their pledge, and
have tried to swim back to the banks they have blotted out.
For though every man of us may be a Hero for one fatal
minute, very few remain so after a day's march even: and
who wonders that Madam Fate is indignant, and wears the
features of the terrible Universal Fate to him? Fail before

her, either in heart, or in act, and lo, how the alluring loves in her visage wither and sicken to what it is modelled on! Be your Rubicon big or small, clear or foul, it is the same: you shall not return. On—or to Acheron!—I subscribe to that saying of THE PILGRIM'S SCRIP:

'The danger of a little knowledge of things is disputable: but beware the little knowledge of one's self!'

Richard Feverel was now crossing the River of his Ordeal. Already the mists were stealing over the land he had left: his life was cut in two, and he breathed but the air that met his nostrils. His father, his father's love, his boyhood and ambition, were shadowy. His poetic dreams had taken a living attainable shape. He had a distincter impression of the Autumnal Berry and her household, than of anything at Raynham. And yet the young man loved his father, loved his home: and I dare say Cæsar loved Rome: but whether he did or no, Cæsar when he killed the Republic was quite bald, and the Hero we are dealing with is scarce beginning to feel his despotic moustache. Did he know what he was made of? Doubtless, nothing at all. But honest passion has an instinct that can be safer than conscious wisdom. He was an arrow drawn to the head, flying from the bow. His audacious mendacities and subterfuges did not strike him as anyway criminal; for he was perfectly sure that the winning and securing of Lucy would in the end be boisterously approved of, and in that case were not the means justified? Not that he took trouble to argue thus, as older Heroes and self-convicting villains are in the habit of doing, to deduce a clear conscience. Conscience and Lucy went together.

It was a soft fair day. The Rubicon sparkled in the morning sun. One of those days when London embraces the prospect of Summer, and troops forth all its babies. The pavement, the squares, the parks, were early alive with the cries of young Britain. Violet and primrose girls, and organ boys with military monkeys, and systematic bands very determined in tone if not in tune, filled the atmosphere,

and crowned the blazing procession of omnibuses, freighted
with business men, Cityward, where a column of reddish
brown smoke,—blown aloft by the South-West, marked
the scene of conflict to which these persistent warriors re-
paired. Richard had seen much of early London that morning. His plans were laid. He had taken care to ensure
his personal liberty against accidents, by leaving his hotel
and his injured Uncle Hippias at sunrise. Today or tomorrow his father was to arrive. Farmer Blaize, Tom
Bakewell reported to him, was raging in Town. Another
day and she might be torn from him: but today this miracle
of creation would be his, and then from those glittering
banks yonder, let them summons him to surrender her who
dared! The position of things looked so propitious he naturally thought the powers that wait on Love conspiring in his
behalf. And she, too—since she must cross this River, she
had sworn to him to be brave, and do him honour, and wear
the true gladness of her heart in her face. So, without a
suspicion of folly in his acts, or fear of results, Richard
strolled into Kensington Gardens, breakfasting on the fore-
shadow of his great joy, now with a vision of his bride,
now of the new life opening to him. Mountain masses of
cloud, rounded in sunlight, swung up the blue. The flower-
ing chestnut pavilions overhead rustled and hummed. A
sound in his ears as of a banner unfolding in the joyful
distance lulled him.

He was to meet his bride at the Church at a quarter past
eleven. His watch said a quarter to ten. He strolled on beneath the long-stemmed trees towards the Well dedicated to
a Saint obscure. Some people were drinking at the Well.
A florid lady stood by a younger one, who had a little silver
mug half-way to her mouth, and evinced undisguised dislike
to the liquor of the salutary Saint.

"Drink, child!" said the maturer lady. "That is only
your second mug. I insist upon your drinking three full

ones every morning we're in Town. Your constitution positively requires iron!"

"But, Mama," the other expostulated, "it's so nasty. I shall be sick."

"Drink!" was the harsh injunction. "Nothing to the German waters, my dear. Here, let me taste." She took the mug and gave it a flying kiss. "I declare I think it almost nice—not at all objectionable. Pray taste it," she said to a gentleman standing below them to act as cup-bearer.

An unmistakable cis-Rubicon voice replied: "Certainly, if it's good fellowship; though I confess I don't think mutual sickness a very engaging ceremony."

"Can one never escape from one's relations?" Richard ejaculated inwardly.

Without a doubt those people were Mrs. Doria, Clare, and Adrian. He had them under his eyes.

Clare peeping up from her constitutional dose to make sure no man was near to see the possible consequences of it, was the first to perceive him. Her hand dropped.

"Now pray drink, and do not fuss!" said Mrs. Doria.

"Mama!" Clare gasped.

Richard came forward, and capitulated honourably, since retreat was out of the question. Mrs. Doria swam to meet him: "My own boy! My dear Richard!" profuse of exclamations. Clare shyly greeted him. Adrian kept in the background.

"Why, we were coming for you today, Richard," said Mrs. Doria, smiling effusion; and rattled on, "We want another cavalier. This is delightful! My dear nephew! You have grown from a boy to a man. And there's down on his lip! And what brings you down here at such an hour in the morning? Poetry, I suppose! Here, take my arm, child.—Clare, finish that mug and thank your Cousin for sparing you the third.—I always bring her, when we are by a chalybeate, to take the waters before breakfast. We have to get up at unearthly hours. Think, my dear boy! Mothers are sacrifices! And so you've been alone a fortnight with your agreeable Uncle! A charming time of it you must have had! Poor Hippy! what may be his last nostrum?"

"Nephew!" Adrian stretched his head round to the couple. "Doses of Nephew taken morning and night fourteen days! And he guarantees that it shall destroy an iron constitution in a month."

Richard mechanically shook Adrian's hand as he spoke.

"Quite well, Ricky?"

"Yes: well enough," Richard answered.

"Well?" resumed his vigorous Aunt, walking on with him, while Clare and Adrian followed. "I really never saw you looking so handsome. There's something about your face—look at me—you needn't blush. You've grown to an Apollo. That blue buttoned-up frock coat becomes you admirably—and those gloves—and that easy neck-tie. Your style is irreproachable—quite a style of your own! And nothing eccentric. You have the instinct of dress. Dress shows blood, my dear boy, as much as anything else. Boy!—you see, I can't forget old habits. You were a boy when I left, and now!—Do you see any change in him, Clare?" she turned half round to her daughter.

"Richard is looking very well, Mama," said Clare, glancing at him under her eyelids.

"I wish I could say the same of you, my dear—Take my arm, Richard. Are you afraid of your Aunt? I want to get used to you. Won't it be pleasant, our being all in Town together in the Season? How fresh the Opera will be to you! Austin, I hear, takes Stalls. You can come to the Foreys' box when you like. We are staying with the Foreys close by here. I think it's a little too far out, you know; but they like the neighbourhood. This is what I have always said: 'Give him more liberty!' Austin has seen it at last. How do you think Clare looking?"

The question had to be repeated. Richard surveyed his cousin hastily, and praised her looks.

"Pale!" Mrs. Doria sighed.

"Rather pale, Aunt."

"Grown very much—don't you think, Richard?"

"Very tall girl indeed, Aunt."

"If she had but a little more colour, my dear Richard! I'm sure I give her all the iron she can swallow, but that pallor still continues. I think she does not prosper away from her old companion. She was accustomed to look up to you, Richard—"

"Did you get Ralph's letter, Aunt?" Richard interrupted her.

"Absurd!" Mrs. Doria pressed his arm. "The nonsense of a boy! Why did you undertake to forward such stuff?"

"I'm certain he loves her," said Richard, in a serious way.

The maternal eyes narrowed on him. "Life, my dear Richard, is a game of cross-purposes," she observed, dropping her fluency, and was rather angered to hear him laugh. He excused himself by saying that she spoke so like his father.

"You breakfast with us," she freshened off again. "The Foreys wish to see you—the girls are dying to know you. Do you know, you have a reputation on account of that"— she crushed an intruding adjective—"System you were brought up on. You mustn't mind it. For my part I think you look a credit to it. Don't be bashful with young women, mind! As much as you please with the old ones. You know how to behave among men. There you have your Drawing-room Guide! I'm sure I shall be proud of you. Am I not?"

Mrs. Doria addressed his eyes coaxingly.

A benevolent idea struck Richard, that he might employ the minutes to spare, in pleading the case of poor Ralph; and, as he was drawn along, he pulled out his watch to note the precise number of minutes he could dedicate to this charitable office.

"Pardon me," said Mrs. Doria. "You want manners, my dear boy. I think it never happened to me before that a man consulted his watch in my presence."

Richard mildly replied that he had an engagement at a particular hour, up to which he was her servant.

"Fiddlededee!" the vivacious lady sang. "Now I've got you, I mean to keep you. Oh! I've heard all about you. This ridiculous indifference that your father makes so much of! Why, of course, you wanted to see the world! A strong healthy young man shut up all his life in a lonely house—no friends, no society, no amusements but those of rustics! Of course you were indifferent! Your intelligence and superior mind alone saved you from becoming a dissipated country boor.—Where are the others?"

Clare and Adrian came up at a quick pace.

"My damosel dropped something," Adrian explained.

Her mother asked what it was.

"Nothing, Mama," said Clara, demurely, and they proceeded as before.

Overborne by his Aunt's fluency of tongue, and occupied in acute calculation of the flying minutes, Richard let many pass before he edged in a word for Ralph. When he did, Mrs. Doria stopped him immediately.

"I must tell you, child, that I refuse to listen to such rank idiotcy."

"It's nothing of the kind, Aunt."

"The fancy of a boy."

"He's not a boy, Aunt. He's half a year older than I am!"

"You silly child! The moment you fall in love, you all think yourselves men."

"On my honour, Aunt! I believe he loves her thoroughly."

"Did he tell you so, child?"

"Men don't speak openly of those things," said Richard.

"Boys do," said Mrs. Doria.

"But listen to me in earnest, Aunt. I want you to be kind to Ralph. Don't drive him to— You may be sorry for it. Let him—do let him write to her, and see her. I believe women are as cruel as men in these things."

"I never encourage absurdity, Richard."

"What objection have you to Ralph, Aunt!"

"Oh, they're both good families. It's not that absurdity, Richard. It will be to his credit to remember that his first fancy wasn't a dairymaid."

Mrs. Doria pitched her accent tellingly. It did not touch her nephew.

"Don't you want Clare ever to marry?" he put the last point of reason to her.

Mrs. Doria laughed. "I hope so, child. We must find some comfortable old gentleman for her."

"What infamy!" mutters Richard.

"And I engage Ralph shall be ready to dance at her wedding, or eat a hearty breakfast—We don't dance at weddings now, and very proper. It's a horrid sad business, not to be treated with levity.—Is that his regiment?" she said, as they passed out of the hussar-sentinelled gardens. "Tush, tush, child! Master Ralph will recover, as—ahem! others have done. A little head-ache—you call it heart-ache—and up you rise again, looking better than ever. No doubt, to have a grain of sense forced into your brains, you poor dear children! must be painful. Girls suffer as much as boys, I assure you. More, for their heads are weaker, and their appetites less constant. Do I talk like your father now? Whatever makes the boy fidget at his watch so?"

Richard stopped short. Time spoke urgently.

"I must go," he said.

His face did not seem good for trifling. Mrs. Doria would trifle in spite.

"Listen, Clare! Richard is going. He says he has an engagement. What possible engagement can a young man have at eleven o'clock in the morning?---unless he's going

to be married?—Eh? Then of course!" Mrs. Doria
laughed at the ingenuity of her suggestion.

"Is the Church handy, Ricky?" said Adrian. "You can
still give us half an hour if it is. The celibate hours strike
at Twelve." And he also laughed in his fashion.

"Won't you stay with us, Richard?" Clare asked. She
blushed timidly, and her voice shook.

Something indefinite—a sharp-edged thrill in the tones
made the burning bridegroom speak gently to her.

"Indeed, I would, Clare—I should like to please you—
but I have a most imperative appointment—that is, I promised—I must go. I shall see you again. . . ."

Mrs. Doria took forcible possession of him. "Now do
come, and don't waste words. I insist upon your having
some breakfast first, and then, if you really must go, you
shall. Look! there's the house. At least you will accompany your Aunt to the door."

Richard conceded this. She little imagined what she required of him. Two of his golden minutes melted into
nothingness. They were growing to be jewels of price, one
by one more and more precious as they ran, and now so
costly-rare—rich as his blood! not to kindest relations, dearest friends, could he give another. The die is cast! Ferryman! push off!

"Good-bye!" he cried, nodding bluffly at the three as one,
and fled.

They watched his abrupt muscular stride through the
grounds of the house. He looked like Resolution on the
march. Mrs. Doria, as usual with her out of her brother's
hearing, began rating the System.

"See what comes of that nonsensical education! The
boy really does not know how to behave like a common
mortal. He has some paltry appointment, or is mad after
some ridiculous idea of his own, and everything must be
sacrificed to it! That's what Austin calls, Concentration of
the faculties. I think it's more likely to lead to downright

insanity than to Greatness of any kind. And so I shall tell
Austin. It's time he should be spoken to seriously about
him."

"He's an Engine, my dear Aunt," said Adrian. "He isn't
a boy, or a man, but an Engine. And he appears to have
been at high pressure since he came to Town—out all day
and half the night."

"He's mad!" Mrs. Doria interjected.

"Not at all. Extremely shrewd is Master Ricky, and
carries as open an eye ahead of him as the ships before Troy.
He's more than a match for any of us. He is for me, I confess."

"Then," said Mrs. Doria, "he does astonish me!"

Adrian begged her to retain her astonishment till the right
season, which would not be long arriving.

Their common wisdom counselled them not to tell the
Foreys of their hopeful relation's ungracious behaviour.
Clare had left them. When Mrs. Doria went to her room,
her daughter was there, gazing down at something in her
hand, which she guiltily closed.

In answer to an inquiry why she had not gone to take
off her things, Clare said she was not hungry. Mrs. Doria
lamented the obstinacy of a constitution that no quantity
of iron could affect, and eclipsed the looking-glass, saying:
"Take them off here, child, and learn to assist yourself."

She disentangled her bonnet from the array of her spread-
ing hair, talking of Richard, and his handsome appearance,
and extraordinary conduct. Clare kept opening and shutting her hand, in an attitude half pensive, half listless. She
did not stir to undress. A joyless dimple hung in one pale
cheek, and she drew long even breaths.

Mrs. Doria, assured by the glass that she was ready to
show, came to her daughter.

"Now really," she said, "you are too helpless, my dear.
You cannot do a thing without a dozen women at your

elbow. What will become of you? You will have to marry a millionaire.—What's the matter with you, child?"

Clare undid her tight-shut fingers, as if to some attraction of her eyes, and displayed a small gold hoop on the palm of a green glove.

"A Wedding-Ring!" exclaimed Mrs. Doria, inspecting the curiosity most daintily.

There on Clare's green glove lay a Wedding-Ring!

Rapid questions as to where, when, how, it was found, beset Clare, who replied: "In the Gardens, Mama. This morning. When I was walking behind Richard."

"Are you sure he did not give it you, Clare?"

"Oh no, Mama! he did not give it me."

"Of course not! only he does such absurd things! I thought, perhaps—these boys are so exceedingly ridiculous!" Mrs. Doria had an idea that it might have been concerted between the two young gentlemen, Richard and Ralph, that the former should present this token of hymeneal devotion from the latter to the young lady of his love; but a moment's reflection exonerated boys even from such preposterous behaviour.

"Now, I wonder," she speculated on Clare's cold face, "I do wonder whether it's lucky to find a Wedding-Ring? What very quick eyes you have, my darling!" Mrs. Doria kissed her. She thought it must be lucky, and the circumstance made her feel tender to her child. Her child did not move to the kiss.

"Let's see whether it fits," said Mrs. Doria almost infantine with surprise and pleasure.

Clare suffered her glove to be drawn off. The Ring slid down her long thin finger, and settled comfortably.

"It does!" Mrs. Doria whispered. To find a Wedding-Ring is open to any woman; but to find a Wedding-Ring that fits may well cause superstitious emotions. Moreover, that it should be found while walking in the neighbourhood of the identical youth whom a mother has destined for her daughter, gives significance to the gentle perturbation of ideas consequent on such a hint from Fortune.

"It really fits!" she pursued. "Now I never pay any attention to the nonsense of omens and that kind of thing" (had the Ring been a horseshoe Mrs. Doria would have picked it up and dragged it obediently home), "but this, I must say, is odd—to find a Ring that fits!—singular! It never happened to me. Sixpence is the most I ever discovered, and I have it now. Mind you keep it, Clare—this Ring. And," she laughed, "offer it to Richard when he comes; say, you think he must have dropped it."

The dimple in Clare's cheek quivered.

Mother and daughter had never spoken explicitly of Richard. Mrs. Doria, by exquisite management, had contrived to be sure that on one side there would be no obstacle to her project of general happiness, without, as she thought, compromising her daughter's feelings unnecessarily. It could do no harm to an obedient young girl to hear that there was no youth in the world like a certain youth. He the Prince of his generation, she might softly consent, when requested, to be his Princess; and, if never requested (for Mrs. Doria envisaged failure), she might easily transfer her softness to squires of lower degree. Clare had always been blindly obedient to her mother (Adrian called them, Mrs. Doria Battledoria and the fair Shuttlecockiana), and her mother accepted in this blind obedience the text of her entire character. It is difficult for those who think very earnestly for their children to know when their children are thinking on their own account. The exercise of their volition we construe as revolt. Our love does not like to be invalided and deposed from its command, and here I think yonder old thrush on the lawn who has just kicked the last of her lank offspring out of the nest to go shift for itself, much the kindest of the two, though sentimental people do shrug their shoulders at these unsentimental acts of the creatures who never wander from Nature. Now excess of obedience is, to one who manages most exquisitely, as bad as insurrection. Happily Mrs. Doria saw nothing in her daughter's manner save a want of iron. Her pallor, her lassitude, the tremulous nerves in her face, exhibited an imperious requirement of the mineral.

'The reason why men and women are mysterious to us, and prove disappointing,' we learn from THE PILGRIM'S SCRIP, 'is, that we will read them from our own book: just as we are perplexed by reading ourselves from theirs.'

Mrs. Doria read her daughter from her own book, and she was gay; she laughed with Adrian at the breakfast-table, and mock-seriously joined in his jocose assertion that Clare was positively and by all hymeneal auspices betrothed to the owner of that Ring, be he who he may, and must, whenever he should choose to come and claim her, give her hand to him (for everybody agreed the owner must be masculine, as no *woman* would drop a Wedding-Ring), and follow him whither he listed all the world over. Amiable giggling Forey girls called Clare, The Betrothed. Dark man, or Fair? was mooted. Adrian threw off the first strophe of Clare's fortune in burlesque rhymes, with an insinuating gypsy twang. Her Aunt Forey warned her to have her dresses in readiness. Her grandpapa Forey pretended to grumble at bridal presents being expected from grandpapas. This one smelt orange-flower, another spoke solemnly of an old shoe. The Finding of a Wedding-Ring was celebrated through all the palpitating accessories and rosy ceremonies involved by that famous instrument. In the midst of the general hilarity, Clare showed her deplorable want of iron by bursting into tears.

Did the poor mocked-at heart divine what might be then enacting? Perhaps, dimly, as we say: that is, without eyes.

At an altar stand two fair young creatures, ready with their Oaths. They are asked to fix all time to the moment, and they do so. If there is hesitation at the immense undertaking, it is but maidenly. She conceives as little mental doubt of the sanity of the act as he. Over them hangs a cool

young Curate in his raiment of office. Behind are two
apparently lucid people, distinguished from each other by
sex, and age: the foremost a bunch of simmering black satin,
under her shadow a cock-robin in the dress of a gentleman,
big joy swelling out his chest, and pert satisfaction cocking
his head. These be they who stand here in place of parents
to the young couple. All is well. The Service proceeds.

Firmly the bridegroom tells forth his words. This hour
of the complacent Giant at least is his, and that he means
to hold him bound through the Eternities, men may hear.
Clearly, and with brave modesty, speaks she: no less firmly,
though her body trembles: her voice just vibrating while the
tone travels on, like a smitten vase.

Time hears sentence pronounced on him: the frail hands
bind his huge limbs and lock the chains. He is used to it:
he lets them do as they will.

Then comes that period when they are to give their troth
to each other. The Man with his right hand takes the
Woman by her right hand: the Woman with her right hand
takes the Man by his right hand.—Devils dare not laugh at
whom Angels crowd to contemplate.

Their hands are joined: their blood flows as one stream.
Adam and Fair Eve front the generations. Are they not
lovely? Purer fountains of Life were never in two bosoms.

And then they loose their hands, and the cool Curate
doth bid the Man to put a Ring on the Woman's fourth
finger. And the Man thrusts his hand into one pocket, and
into another, forward and back many times: into all his
pockets. And his hand comes forth empty. And the Man
is ghastly to look at!

Yet, though Angels smile, shall not Devils laugh! The
Curate deliberates. The black-satin bunch ceases to simmer.
He in her shadow changes from a beaming cock-robin to an
inquisitive sparrow. Eyes multiply questions: lips have no
reply. Time ominously shakes his chain, and in the pause
a sound of mockery stings their ears.

Think ye a Hero one to be defeated in his first battle? Look at the clock! there are but seven minutes to the stroke of the celibate hours: the Veteran is surely lifting his two hands to deliver fire, and his shot will sunder them in twain so nearly united. All the Jewellers of London speeding down with sacks full of the Nuptial Circlet cannot save them!

The battle must be won on the field, and what does the Hero now? It is an inspiration! For who else would dream of such a reserve in the rear? None see what he does: only that the black-satin bunch is remonstratingly agitated, stormily shaken, and subdued: and as though the menacing Cloud had opened, and dropped the dear token from the skies at his demand, he produces the Symbol of their consent, and the Service proceeds: 'With this Ring I thee wed.'

They are prayed over, and blest. For good, or for ill, this deed is done. The names are registered: fees fly right and left: they thank and salute, the Curate, whose official coolness melts into a smile of monastic gallantry: the Beadle on the steps waves off a gaping world as they issue forth: bridegroom and bridesman recklessly scatter gold on him: carriage-doors are banged to: the coachmen drive off, and the scene closes, everybody happy.

CHAPTER XXXIV

CELEBRATES THE BREAKFAST

AND the next moment the Bride is weeping as if she would dissolve to one of Dian's Virgin Fountains from the clasp of the Sun-God. She has nobly preserved the mask imposed by Comedies, till the curtain has fallen, and now she weeps, streams with tears. Have patience, O impetuous young man! It is your profession to be a Hero. This poor heart is new to it, and her duties involve such wild acts,

such brigandage, such terrors and tasks, she is quite un-
nerved. She did you honour till now. Bear with her now.
She does not cry the cry of ordinary maidens in like cases.
While the struggle went on her tender face was brave; but
alas! Omens are against her: she holds an ever-present
dreadful one on that fatal fourth finger of hers, that has
coiled itself round her dream of delight, and takes her in
its clutch like a horrid Serpent. And yet she must love it.
She dares not part from it. She must love and hug it, and
feed on its strange honey, and all the bliss it gives her casts
all the deeper shadow on what is to come.

Say. Is it not enough to cause feminine apprehension for
a woman to be married in another woman's Ring?

You are amazons, ladies, at Saragossa, and a thousand
citadels—wherever there is strife, and Time is to be taken
by the throat. Then shall few men match your sublime
fury. But what if you see a Vulture, visible only to yourselves, hovering over the house you are gaily led by the Torch
to inhabit? Will you not crouch and be cowards?

As for the Hero, in the hour of Victory he pays no heed
to Omens. He does his best to win his darling to confidence by caresses. Is she not his? Is he not hers? And why,
when the battle is won, does she weep? Does she regret
what she has done?

Oh, never! never! her soft blue eyes assure him, steadfast Love seen swimming on clear depths of Faith in them,
through the shower.

He is silenced by her exceeding beauty, and sits perplexed, waiting for the shower to pass.

Alone with Mrs. Berry, in her bedroom, Lucy gave
tongue to her distress, and a second character in the Comedy
changed her face.

"Oh, Mrs. Berry! Mrs. Berry! what has happened!
what has happened!"

"My darlin' child!" The bridal Berry gazed at the
finger of doleful joy. "I'd forgot all about it! And that's

what've made me feel so queer ever since, then! I've been seemin' as if I wasn't myself somehow, without my Ring. Dear! dear! what a wilful young gentleman! We ain't a match for men in that state—Lord help us!"

Mrs. Berry sat on the edge of a chair: Lucy on the edge of the bed.

"What do you think of it, Mrs. Berry? Is it not terrible?"

"I can't say I should 'a liked it myself, my dear," Mrs. Berry candidly responded.

"Oh, why, why, why did it happen!" the young bride bent to a flood of fresh tears, murmuring that she felt already old—forsaken.

"Haven't you got a comfort in your Religion for all accidents?" Mrs. Berry inquired.

"None for this. I know it's wrong to cry when I am so happy. I hope he will forgive me."

Mrs. Berry vowed her bride was the sweetest, softest, beautifulest thing in life.

"I'll cry no more," said Lucy. "Leave me, Mrs. Berry, and come back when I ring."

She drew forth a little silver cross, and fell upon her knees to the bed. Mrs. Berry left the room tiptoe.

When she was called to return, Lucy was calm and tearless, and smiled kindly to her.

"It's over now," she said.

Mrs. Berry sedately looked for her Ring to follow.

"He does not wish me to go in to the breakfast you have prepared, Mrs. Berry. I begged to be excused. I cannot eat."

Mrs. Berry very much deplored it, as she had laid out a superior nuptial breakfast, but with her mind on her Ring she nodded assentingly.

"We shall not have much packing to do, Mrs. Berry."

"No, my dear. It's pretty well all done."

"We are going to the Isle of Wight, Mrs. Berry."

"And a very suitable spot ye've chose, my dear!"

"He loves the sea. He wishes to be near it."

"Don't ye cross tonight, if it's anyways rough, my dear. It isn't advisable," Mrs. Berry sank her voice to say, "Don't ye be soft and give way to him there, or you'll both be repenting it."

Lucy had only been staving off the unpleasantness she had to speak. She saw Mrs. Berry's eyes pursuing her Ring, and screwed up her courage at last.

"Mrs. Berry."

"Yes, my dear."

"Mrs. Berry, you shall have another Ring."

"Another, my dear?" Berry did not comprehend. "One's quite enough for the objeck," she remarked.

"I mean," Lucy touched her fourth finger, "I cannot part with this." She looked straight at Mrs. Berry.

That bewildered creature gazed at her, and at the Ring, till she had thoroughly exhausted the meaning of the words, and then exclaimed, horror-struck: "Deary me, now? you don't say that?"

The young wife repeated: "I never can part with it."

"But, my dear!" the wretched Berry wrung her hands. divided between compassion and a sense of injury. "My dear!" she kept expostulating like a mute.

"I know all that you would say, Mrs. Berry. I am very grieved to pain you. It is mine now, and must be mine. I cannot give it back."

There she sat, suddenly developed to the most inflexible little Heroine in the Three Kingdoms.

From her first perception of the meaning of the young bride's words, Mrs. Berry, a shrewd physiognomist, knew that her case was hopeless, unless she treated her as she herself had been treated, and seized the Ring by force of arms; and that she had not heart for.

"What!" she gasped faintly, "one's own lawful Wedding-Ring you wouldn't give back to a body?"

"Because it is mine, Mrs. Berry. It was yours, but it is mine now. You shall have whatever you ask for but that. Pray forgive me! It must be so."

Mrs. Berry rocked on her chair, and sounded her hands together. It amazed her that this soft little creature could be thus firm. She tried argument.

"Don't ye know, my dear, it's the fatalest thing you're inflictin' upon me, reelly! Don't ye know that bein' bereft of one's lawful Wedding-Ring's the fatalest thing in life, and there's no prosperity after it! For what stands in place o' that, when that's gone, my dear? And what *could* ye give me to compensate a body for the loss o' that? Don't ye know—Oh, deary me!" The little bride's face was so set that poor Berry wailed off in despair.

"I know it," said Lucy. "I know it all. I know what I do to you. Dear, dear Mrs. Berry! forgive me! If I parted with my Ring I know it would be fatal."

So this fair young freebooter took possession of her argument as well as her Ring.

Berry racked her distracted wits for a further appeal.

"But, my child," she counterargued, "you don't understand. It ain't as you think it. It ain't a hurt to you now. Not a bit, it ain't. It makes no difference now! Any Ring does while the wearer's a Maid. And your Mr. Richard'll find the very Ring he intended for ye. And, of course, that's the one you'll wear as his wife. It's all the same now, my dear. It's no shame to a Maid. Now do—now do—there's a darlin'!"

Wheedling availed as little as argument.

"Mrs. Berry," said Lucy, "you know what my—he spoke: 'With this Ring I thee wed.' It was with *this* Ring. Then how could it be with another?"

Berry was constrained despondently to acknowledge that was logic.

She hit upon an artful conjecture:

"Won't it be unlucky you're wearin' of that Ring which served me so? Think o' that!"

"It may! it may! it may!" cried Lucy.

"And arn't you rushin' into it, my dear?"

"Mrs. Berry," Lucy said again, "it was this Ring. It cannot—it never can be another. It was this. What it brings me I must bear. I shall wear it till I die!"

"Then what am I to do?" the ill-used woman groaned. "What shall I tell my husband when he come back to me, and see I've got a new Ring waitin' for him? Won't that be a welcome?"

Quoth Lucy: "How can he know it is not the same, in a plain gold Ring?"

"You never see so keen a eyed man in joolry as my Berry!" returned his solitary spouse. "Not know, my dear? Why, any one would know that've got eyes in his head. There's as much difference in Wedding-Rings as there's in Wedding People! Now, do pray be reasonable, my own sweet!"

"Pray do not ask me," pleads Lucy.

"Pray do think better of it," urges Berry.

"Pray, pray, Mrs. Berry!" pleads Lucy.

"—And not leave your old Berry all forlorn just when you're so happy!"

"Indeed I would not, you dear kind old creature!" Lucy faltered.

Mrs. Berry thought she had her.

"Just when you're going to be the happiest wife on earth —all you want yours!" she pursued the tender strain. "A handsome young gentleman! Love and Fortune smilin' on ye!" . . .

Lucy rose up.

"Mrs. Berry," she said, "I think we must not lose time in getting ready, or he will be impatient."

Poor Berry surveyed her in abject wonder from the edge of her chair. Dignity and resolve were in the ductile form she had hitherto folded under her wing. In an hour the

Heroine had risen to the measure of the Hero. Without being exactly aware what creature she was dealing with, Berry acknowledged to herself it was not one of the common run, and sighed, and submitted.

"It's like a Divorce, that it is!" she sobbed.

After putting the corners of her apron to her eyes, Berry bustled humbly about the packing. Then Lucy, whose heart was full to her, came and kissed her, and Berry bumped down and regularly cried. This over, she had recourse to fatalism.

"I suppose it was to be, my dear! It's my punishment for meddlin' with such matters. No, I'm not sorry. Bless ye both! Who'd 'a thought you was so wilful?—you that any one might have taken for one of the silly-softs! You're a pair, my dear! indeed you are! You was made to meet! But we musn't show him we've been crying.—Men don't like it when they're happy. Let's wash our faces and try to bear our lot."

So saying the black-satin bunch careened to a renewed deluge. She deserved some sympathy, for if it is sad to be married in another person's Ring, how much sadder to have one's own old accustomed lawful Ring violently torn off one's finger and eternally severed from one! But where you have Heroes and Heroines, these terrible complications ensue.

They had now both fought their battle of the Ring, and with equal honour and success.

In the Chamber of Banquet Richard was giving Ripton his last directions. Though it was a private wedding Mrs. Berry had prepared a sumptuous breakfast. Chickens offered their breasts: Pies hinted savoury secrets: things mystic, in a mash, with Gallic appellatives, jellies, creams, fruits, strewed the table: as a tower in the midst, the Cake colossal: the priestly vesture of its nuptial white relieved by hymeneal splendours.

Many hours, much labour and anxiety of mind, Mrs. Berry had expended upon this breakfast, and why? There is one who comes to all feasts that have their basis in Folly, whom criminals of trained instinct are careful to provide against: who will speak, and whose hateful voice must somehow be silenced while the feast is going on. This personage is THE PHILOSOPHER. Mrs. Berry knew him. She knew that he would come. She provided against him in the manner she thought most efficacious: that is, by cheating her eyes and intoxicating her conscience with the due and proper glories incident to Weddings where fathers dilate, mothers collapse, and marriage settlements are flourished on high by the family lawyer: and had there been no show of the kind to greet her on her return from the Church, she would, and she foresaw she would, have stared at squalor and emptiness, and repented her work. The Philosopher would have laid hold of her by the ear, and called her bad names. Entrenched behind a breakfast-table so legitimately adorned, Mrs. Berry defied him. In the presence of that Cake he dared not speak above a whisper. And there were wines to drown him in, should he still think of protesting; fiery wines, and cool: claret sent purposely by the bridegroom for the delectation of his friend.

For one good hour, therefore, the labour of many hours kept him dumb. Ripton was fortifying himself so as to forget him altogether, and the world as well, till the next morning. Ripton was excited, overdone with delight. He had already finished one bottle, and listened, pleasantly flushed, to his emphatic, and more abstemious, Chief. He had nothing to do but to listen, and to drink. The Hero would not allow him to shout Victory! or hear a word of toasts; and as, from the quantity of oil poured on it, his eloquence was becoming a natural force in his bosom, the poor fellow was afflicted with a sort of elephantiasis of suppressed emotion. At times he half rose from his chair and fell vacuously into it again; or he chuckled in the face of weighty, severely-worded, instructions; tapped his chest, stretched his arms, yawned, and in short behaved so singu

larly that Richard observed it, and said: "On my soul, I
don't think you know a word I'm saying."

"Every word, Ricky!" Ripton spirted through the opening. "I'm going down to your Governor, and tell him: 'Sir
Austin! Here's your only chance of being a happy father—'
no, no!—Oh! don't you fear me, Ricky! I shall talk the old
gentleman over. I feel tremendous! I feel, upon my honour, Ricky, I feel as if nobody *coul'* resis' me!" Ripton
stamped his might on the table. "I shall tell him the whole
affair point-blank. I can tell you that if it comes to argument 'tween us, I can lay on the man who'll have the best
of it. I shall tell him I was a witness. And I hope, Sir
Austin, in a year's time you'll have best witness of all, Sir!—
jolly 'ittle grandson!" Ripton's head went roguishly to right
and left, and he emptied his glass at a draught.

Richard arrested his resumption of speech, and he continued
slowly to fizz like an ill-corked effervescence, while his Chief
said:

"Look here. You had better not go down tonight. Go
down the first thing tomorrow—by the six o'clock train.
Give him my letter. Listen to me—give him my letter,
and don't speak a word till he speaks. His eyebrows will
go up and down; he won't say much. I know him. If he
asks you about her, don't be a fool, but say what you think
of her sensibly—"

No cork could hold in Ripton when she was alluded to.
He shouted: "She's an Angel!"

Richard checked him: "Speak sensibly, I say—quietly.
You can say how gentle and good she is—my fleur-de-luce!
And say, this was not her doing. If any one's to blame, it's
I. I made her marry me.—Then go to Lady Blandish, if
you don't find her at the house. You may say whatever you
please to her. Give her my letter, and tell her I want to hear
from her immediately. She has seen Lucy, and I know what
she thinks of her. You will then go to farmer Blaize. I told
you Lucy happens to be his niece—she has not lived long

there. She lived with her Aunt Desborough in France while she was a child, and can hardly be called a relation to the farmer—there's not a point of likeness between them. Poor darling! she never knew her mother. Go to Mr. Blaize, and tell him. You will treat him just as you would treat any other gentleman. If you are civil, he is sure to be. And if he abuses me, for my sake and hers you will still treat him with respect. You hear? And then write me a full account of all that has been said and done. You will have my address the day after tomorrow. By the way, Tom will be here this afternoon. Write out for him where to call on you the day after tomorrow, in case you have heard anything in the morning you think I ought to know at once, as Tom will join me that night. Don't mention to anybody about my losing the Ring, Ripton. I wouldn't have Adrian get hold of that for a thousand pounds. How on earth I came to lose it!—How well she bore it, Rip! How beautifully she behaved!"

Ripton again shouted: "She's an Angel!" He endeavoured to get a leap beyond the Angels, but being of tame imagination those commonplace hosts had to stand for what he felt. Throwing up the heels of his second bottle, he said:

"You may trust your friend, Richard. Your oldest friend, Ricky!—Eh? A cool head and a heart in the right place! A man who'd want to drink better wine than his—he'd bet' not drink any 't all. I think I was hem!—marking that we know what wine is. Talking of old Blaize, ain't it odd we should be drinking cleret 'gether, just married? I mean, when you come to think of it, Ricky? It strikes me 's odd. But as for your thinking there'll be much fuss, you know, there you're wrong. Let's have s' more cleret."

Richard hospitably opened another bottle for him, and sat knocking his finger-nails on his teeth, impatient for the bride, while Ripton freely flowed forth. In spite of the innocuousness of claret, his words were displaying an oily tendency to run into one another, and his eyes were growing vivaciously stupid.

"Strikes me, Richard, every fresh bottle's better than one before. Well, I was saying, you know, I shall make all right with your father. Oh! *he* won't stand out after a little talking. And mind you, Mr. Ricky, I *can* talk! I ought to have gone the Bar, you know. Fancy me in off'ces! Aha! Why, they haven't got so many good fellows at the Bar that they should keep me in off'ces.—cleret! cleret I keep saying:— claret, Sir! 'Minds me of Gravelkind. I'm always making 'stakes of that sort. Best of it is, it never 'fects you. You may drink as much as ever you like, and it never 'fects you. Gentleman's wine! When I'm in practice, you know, I—I never drink anything else! I—I never drink anything else! Though if you ask me point-blank which I p'fer, why, I'd rather go the Bar. I'm an only son, you know, and a mother and four sisters, and I must do as I'm tole. Ha! ha! that Letty! whar a face she'll make when she hears of it! sil' ittle thing!—ha! ha!—I do think this has been the jollies' day I ever knew! Behave, Sir? She did behave most beauriful! I hear her voice now—like that glass. Oh! I ain't going to get married. I can't see the girl to suit me. Tell you the truth, girls don't quite take to me—not in that way, you know. I don't know how to talk to them unless they begin, and look all right. It went as smooth, Ricky!—but lor! you're such a chap. You're sure to do if you say you will. Aha! when you pulled at old Mrs. Berry, I didn't know what was up. I do wish you'd let me drink her health?"

"Here's to Penelope!" said Richard, just wetting his mouth. The carriage was at the door: a couple of dire organs, each grinding the same tune, and a vulture-scented itinerant band (from which not the secretest veiled Wedding can ever escape) worked harmoniously without in the production of discord, and the noise acting on his nervous state made him begin to fume and send in messages for his bride by the maid.

Ripton drank Penelope, and afterwards had an idea that Penelope did not mean Lucy. He tried to tell Richard that the health proposed was that of his lovely wife, but Richard had no ear for him, and let him mumble on. By and by the lovely wife presented herself dressed for her journey, and smiling from stained eyes.

Mrs. Berry was requested to drink some wine, which Ripton poured out for her, enabling Mrs. Berry thereby to measure his condition. Ripton's expressive bibulous invitation was: "Aha! Mrs. Berry!"

Penelope bowed and bumped her duty to them all. Richard and Lucy talked apart. Ripton balanced his body against the back of his chair. A notion possessed his nodding head that it devolved upon him to make a formal speech, and that now was the time. If ever the Old Dog was to enunciate in human language his devoted appreciation of Beauty, the occasion was present. But how was he to fashion his phrases? Notwithstanding the state he was in, his sincere homage caused him to be critical of his capabilities: and then his brain whirled: innumerable phantom forms of sentences with a promise of glowing periods, offered their heads to him, and immediately cut themselves off from all consequence, so that he was afraid to commence. Speaking, moreover, he found to affect his balance. It became a problem whether he should talk, or retain his perpendicular. His latent sense of propriety counselled him not to risk it, and he stood mute, looking like a Mask of ancient Comedy, beneath which general embracing took place. The bride kissed Mrs. Berry, Mrs. Berry kissed the bridegroom, on the plea of her softness. Ripton's long tight smile elaborated as the mad idea, engendered by these proceedings, of claiming certain privileges due to him in his character of bridesman, flashed across him. Some one noticed that the Cake had not been cut, and his attention was drawn to the Cake, and he fell upon it, literally, rising sufficiently ashamed not to dare to look in the fair bride's face, much more to claim a privilege. Lucy, however, gave him her hand, with a musical: "Good-bye, Mr. Ripton," and her extreme graciousness made him just sensible enough to sit down before he murmured his fervent hopes for her happiness.

"I shall take good care of him," said Mrs. Berry, focussing her eyes to the comprehension of the company.

"Farewell, Penelope!" cries Richard. "I shall tell the Police everywhere to look out for him."

"Oh! no fear, my dears! he'll return. Good-bye! and Heaven bless ye both!"

Berry quavers, touched with compunction at the thoughts of approaching loneliness. Ripton, his mouth drawn like a bow to his ears, brought up the rear to the carriage, receiving a fair slap on the cheek from an old shoe precipitated by Mrs. Berry's enthusiastic female domestic.

White handkerchiefs were waved: the adieux had fallen to signs: they were off. Then did a thought of such urgency illumine Mrs. Berry, that she telegraphed, hands in air, awakening Ripton's lungs, for the coachman to stop, and ran back to the house. Richard chafed to be gone, but at his bride's intercession he consented to wait. Presently they beheld the old black-satin bunch stream through the street-door, down the bit of garden, and up the astonished street, halting, panting, capless at the carriage-door, a book in her hand,—a much-used, dog-leaved, steamy, greasy, book, which, at the same time calling out in breathless jerks, "There! never ye mind looks! I ain't got a new one. Read it, and don't ye forget it!" she discharged into Lucy's lap, and retreated to the railings, a signal for the Coachman to drive away for good.

How Richard laughed at the Berry's bridal gift! Lucy too, lost the Omen at her heart as she glanced at the title of the volume. It was Dr. Kitchener on Domestic Cookery! Mrs. Berry's beloved private copy, with the wisdom contained in which she trusted to allure back to home and its duties the wandering Ulysses of Footmen.

CHAPTER XXXV

THE PHILOSOPHER APPEARS IN PERSON

GENERAL withdrawing of heads from street-windows, emigration of organs and bands, and a relaxed atmosphere in the circle of Mrs. Berry's abode, proved that Dan Cupid had veritably flown to suck the life of fresh regions. With a pensive mind she grasped Ripton's arm to regulate his steps, and returned to the room where her Creditor awaited her. In the interval he had stormed her undefended fortress, the Cake, from which altitude he shook a dolorous head at the guilty woman. She smoothed her excited apron, sighing. Let no one imagine that she regretted her complicity. She was ready to cry torrents, but there must be absolute castigation before this criminal shall conceive the sense of regret; and probably then she will cling to her wickedness the more, —such is the Born Pagan's tenacity! Mrs. Berry sighed, and gave him back his shake of the head. 'O you wanton improvident creature!' said he. 'O you very wise old gentleman!' said she. He asked her the thing she had been doing. She enlightened him with the fatalist's reply. He sounded a Bogey's Alarum of contingent grave results. She retreated to the entrenched camp of the Fact she had helped to make. "It's done!" she exclaimed. How could she regret what she felt comfort to know was done? Convinced that events alone could stamp a mark on such stubborn flesh, he determined to wait for them, and crouched silent on the Cake, with one finger downward at Ripton's incision there, showing a crumbling chasm and gloomy rich recess.

The eloquent indication was understood. "Dear! dear!" cried Mrs. Berry, "what a heap o' Cake, and no one to send it to!"

Ripton had resumed his seat by the table and his embrace of the claret. Clear ideas of satisfaction had left him and resolved to a boiling geyser of indistinguishable transports. He bubbled, and waggled, and nodded amicably to nothing, and successfully, though not without effort, preserved his uppermost member from the seductions of the nymph, Gravitation, who was on the look-out for his whole length shortly.

"Ha! ha!" he shouted, about a minute after Mrs. Berry had spoken, and almost abandoned himself to the nymph on the spot. Mrs. Berry's words had just reached his wits.

"Why do you laugh, young man?" she inquired, familiar and motherly on account of his condition.

"Ha! hah!" Ripton laughed louder, and caught his chest on the edge of the table and his nose on a chicken. "That's goo'!" he said, recovering, and rocking under Mrs. Berry's eyes. "No frien' send to? I like that!"

Mrs. Berry searched him with a glance. Perhaps the inebriate youth might let her into a few sweet particulars of this interesting business, denied to her by the wary bridegroom and his obedient bride, she thought. She wanted to have the stern father and cruel Uncle described to her; their stature, complexion, and annual net incomes; also their places of residence.

"I did not say, no friend," she remarked. "I said, no one: meanin', I know not where for to send it to."

Ripton's response to this was: "You cut fair, Mizz Berry. There won't be much for'em, I sh . . . 'sure you. Take glass wine. Claret's my wine, Sh . . . herry's yours. Why 'n't you put Richard's crez' on that Cake?—Mr. Richards hah! ha—best fun the world!— Why 'n't you put a Griffin on that Cake, Mizz Berry? Wheatsheaves each si'. Plenty 't means and Plenty te-te-'tis! I'm very fond of Heraldry," he added with a reflective visage, and fell half asleep upon the attachment.

"His crest?" Mrs. Berry winningly waked him.

"Oldest Bar'netcy in England!" waved Ripton.

"Yes?" Mrs. Berry encouraged him on.

"Oldest Bar'netcy 'n England! If 'tisn't my name's not

Rip'm Thomps'—Es...quire. Gentleman, Ma'm, though he is arricled the Law. Take glass wine, M... Mizz Berry. Claret's my wine, Sh...herry's yours. This bom my third bod'l. What's three to a gentleman, though he isn't a Bar'net's son with fifty th—housand a-year."

"Fifty thousand! My goodness gracious me!" ejaculated Mrs. Berry in flattering accents.

"Na a penny less, M'm! And I'm his oldts friend. Very near transp...orted once, drinking claret 'gether. Nev' 'fects you! Do take glass wine. Ha! ha! you think he's Richard's. Nor a bir of it! No Bar'net Richards 's I know. We're 'bliged be secret, Mizz Berry." Ripton looked profoundly secret. "Anything if 't's your own dedriment. That's Law, Mizz Berry. And 't's not his own dedriment. It's his delaight—ha! hah!"

Here Gravitation gave Ripton a strong pull. He just saved himself, and went on, with a hideous mimicry of the God of Secrecy: "We're oblige' be very close. And she's the most lovely!—If I hear man say thing 'gainst her, I... I knock 'm down! I... I... I knock 'm down! She is such a poory creature!" he sang in falsetto.

"You needn't for to cry over her, young man," said Mrs. Berry, who was resolved to stop his claret the moment she had the secret, and indulged him for that sole object.

Ripton attempted the God of Secrecy again, but his lips would not protrude enough, and his eyebrows were disaffected. He laughed outright. "Wha' 's it matter now? They're married, Sir. Wha' 've you be 'shamed of?—eh? I can talk! Here, I say, Mizz Berry! come—bumper! La'ies and gen'l'men! I rise 'pose toas'd—hay!"

Filling Mrs. Berry's glass, and his own, to overflowing, and again splitting the solitary female who formed his audience into two sexes, Ripton commanded Silence, and pendulously swayed over Mrs. Berry's lap in total forgetfulness of what he had ventured on his legs to celebrate. Aware that they did duty for some purpose, he shut his eyes to meditate, but at this congenial action densest oblivion enwrapped his senses, and he was in danger of coming into Mrs. Berry's lap head foremost; a calamity she averted by rising likewise, and shaking him roughly, which brought him back to visionary consciousness, when he sank into his chair, and mildly asked: "Wha'm I 'bout? That you, Mizz Berry?"

A little asperity was in her voice as she replied. "You were going to propose a toast. And then, young man, you'd better lie down a bit, and cool yourself. Do it sitting," she gesticulated peremptorily, "I'll open the bottle and fill your glass for you. I declare you're drinking it out of tumblers. It's shocking! You're never going to have another full tumbler?"

Ripton chivalrously insisted on a bumper. She filled it for him, under mental protest, for conscience pricked her. Ripton drained his bumper in emphatic silence.

"Young man," said Mrs. Berry severely, "I wanted for to drink their right healths by their right names, and then go about my day's work, and I do hope you won't keep me."

As if by miracle, Ripton stood bolt upright at her words. "You do?" he said, and filling another bumper he with cheerfully vinous articulation and glibness of tongue proposed the healths of Richard and Lucy Feverel, of Raynham Abbey! and that mankind should not require an expeditious example of the way to accept the inspiriting toast, he drained his bumper at a gulp. It finished him. The farthing-rushlight of his reason leapt and expired. He staggered to the sofa, and there stretched. Ripton was far from being in practice.

Some minutes subsequent to Ripton's signalization of his devotion to the bridal pair, Mrs. Berry's maid entered the room to say that a gentleman was inquiring below after the young gentleman who had departed, and found her mistress with a tottering wineglass in her hand, exhibiting every symptom of unconsoled hysterics. Her mouth gaped, as if the fell Creditor had her by the swallow. She ejaculated with horrible exultation that she had been and done it, as her disastrous aspect seemed to testify, and her evident, but inexplicable, access of misery induced the sympathetic maid to tender those caressing words that were all Mrs. Berry wanted to go off into the self-caressing fit without delay; and she had already given the preluding demoniac ironic outburst, when the maid called Heaven to witness that the gentleman would hear her: upon which Mrs. Berry violently controlled her bosom, and ordered that he should be shown upstairs instantly to see her the wretch she was. She repeated the injunction.

"I'll be seen as I am!" screamed Mrs. Berry.

The maid did as she was told, and Mrs. Berry, wishing first to see herself as she was, mutely accosted the looking-glass, and tried to look a very little better. She dropped a shawl on Ripton and was settled, smoothing her agitation when her visitor was announced.

The gentleman was Adrian Harley. An interview with Tom Bakewell had put him on the track, and now a momentary survey of the table, and its white-vestured Cake, made him whistle.

Mrs. Berry plaintively begged him to do her the favour to be seated.

"A fine morning, Ma'am," said Adrian.

"It have been!" Mrs. Berry answered, glancing over her shoulder at the window, and gulping as if to get her heart down from her mouth.

"A very fine Spring," pursued Adrian, calmly anatomizing her countenance.

Mrs. Berry smothered an adjective to "weather" on a deep sigh. Her wretchedness was palpable. In proportion to it Adrian waxed cheerful and brisk. He divined enough of the business to see that there was some strange intelligence to be fished out of the culprit who sat compressing hysterics before him; and as he was never more in his element than when he had a sinner, and a repentant prostrate abject sinner, in hand, his affable countenance might well deceive poor Berry.

"I presume these are Mr. Thompson's lodgings?" he re-marked, with a look at the table.

Mrs. Berry's head and the whites of her eyes informed him that they were not Mr. Thompson's lodgings.

"No?" said Adrian, and threw a carelessly inquisitive eye about him. "Mr. Feverel is out, I suppose?"

A convulsive start at the name, and two corroborating hands dropped on her knees, formed Mrs. Berry's reply.

"Mr. Feverel's man," continued Adrian, "told me I should be certain to find him here. I thought he would be with his friend, Mr. Thompson. I'm too late, I perceive. Their entertainment is over. I fancy you have been having a party of them here, Ma'am?—bachelors' breakfast!"

In the presence of that Cake this observation seemed to mask an irony so shrewd that Mrs. Berry could barely con-tain herself. She felt she must speak. Making her face as deplorably propitiating as she could, she began:

"Sir, may I beg for to know your name?"

Mr. Harley accorded her request.

Groaning in the clutch of a pitiless truth, she continued:

"And you are Mr. Harley, that was—oh! and you've come for Mr. —?"

Mr. Richard Feverel was the gentleman Mr. Harley had come for.

"Oh! and it's no mistake, and he's of Raynham Abbey?" Mrs. Berry inquired.

Adrian, very much amused, assured her that he was born and bred there.

"His father's Sir Austin?" wailed the black-satin bunch from behind her handkerchief.

Adrian verified Richard's descent.

"Oh, then what have I been and done!" she cried, and stared blankly at her visitor. "I been and married my baby! I been and married the bread out of my own mouth! Oh, Mr. Harley! Mr. Harley! I knew you when you was a boy that big, and wore jackets; and all of you. And it's my

softness that's my ruin, for I never can resist a man's asking. Look at that Cake, Mr. Harley!"

Adrian followed her directions quite coolly. "Wedding-
Cake, Ma'am!" he said.

"Bride Cake it is, Mr. Harley!"

"Did you make it yourself, Ma'am?"

The quiet ease of the question overwhelmed Mrs. Berry,
and upset that train of symbolic representations by which
she was seeking to make him guess the catastrophe and spare
her the furnace of confession.

"I did not make it myself, Mr. Harley," she replied. "It's
a bought Cake, and I'm a lost woman. Little I dreamed
when I had him in my arms a baby that I should some day be
marrying him out of my own house! I little dreamed that!
Oh, why did he come to me! Don't you remember his old
nurse, when he was a baby in arms, that went away se
sudden, and no fault of hers, Mr. Harley! The very
mornin' after the night you got into Mr. Benson's cellar,
and got so tipsy on his Madeary—I remember it as clear
as yesterday!—and Mr. Benson was that angry he threated
to use the whip to you, and I helped put you to bed. I'm
that very woman."

Adrian smiled placidly at these reminiscences of his guileless youthful life.

"Well, Ma'am! well?" he said. He would bring her to
the furnace.

"Won't you see it all, kind Sir?" Mrs. Berry appealed to
him in pathetic dumb show.

Doubtless by this time Adrian did see it all, and was
mentally cursing at Folly, and reckoning the immediate consequences, but he looked uninstructed, his peculiar dimpled
smile was undisturbed, his comfortable full-bodied posture
was the same. "Well, Ma'am?" he spurred her on.

Mrs. Berry burst forth: "It were done this mornin', Mr.
Harley, in the Church, at half-past e-leven of the clock, o1

twenty to, by license;" adding from the bottom of her voice, "and I've never a ring to show for it!"

Adrian was now obliged to comprehend a case af Matrimony. "Oh!" he said, like one who is as hard as facts, and as little to be moved: "Somebody was married this morning; was it Mr. Thompson, or Mr. Feverel?"

Mrs. Berry shuffled up to Ripton, and removed the shawl from him, saying: "Do he look like a new married bridegroom, Mr. Harley?"

Adrian inspected the oblivious Ripton with philosophic gravity.

"This young gentleman was at Church this morning?" he asked.

"Oh! he were quite reasonable and proper, then," Mrs. Berry begged him to understand.

"Of course, Ma'am." Adrian lifted and let fall the stupid inanimate limbs of the gone wretch, puckering his mouth queerly. "You were all reasonable and proper, Ma'am. The principal male performer, then, is my cousin, Mr. Feverel? He was married by you this morning by license, at your parish Church, and came here, and ate a hearty breakfast, and left intoxicated."

Mrs. Berry flew out. "He never drink a drop, Sir. A more moderate young gentleman you never see. Oh! don't ye think now, Mr. Harley. He was as upright and master of his mind as you be."

"Ay!" the Wise Youth nodded thanks to her for the comparison, "I mean the other form of intoxication."

Mrs. Berry sighed. She could say nothing on that score.

Adrian desired her to sit down, and compose herself, and tell him circumstantially what had been done.

She obeyed, in utter perplexity at his perfectly composed demeanour.

Mrs. Berry, as her recital declared, was no other than that identical woman who once in old days had dared to behold the Baronet behind his mask, and had ever since lived in exile from the Raynham world on a little pension, regularly paid to her as an indemnity. She was that woman, and the thought of it made her almost accuse Providence for the betraying excess of softness it had endowed her with. How was she to recognize her baby grown a man? He came in a feigned name: not a word of the family was mentioned. He came like an ordinary mortal, though she felt something more than ordinary towards him, she knew she did. He came bringing a beautiful young lady, and on what grounds could she turn her back on them? Why, seeing that all was chaste and legal, why *should* she interfere to make them unhappy? so few the chances of happiness in this world! Mrs. Berry related the seizure of her Ring.

"One wrench," said the sobbing culprit, "one wrench, and my Ring went off like my Berry!"

She had no suspicions, and she had therefore never thought of looking at the signatures in the Vestry-book.

"And it's fort'nate I didn't!" she exclaimed, "for out I should 'a shrieked there and then, never mind where's the spot, to think I been and married my own baby unbeknown. Not till this Mr. Thompson proposed their healths tipsy by their right names, did I think—Feverel! Raynham Abbey! Oh! then I had been and married my baby! and so you found me, Mr. Harley, and I dare say I looked it."

"You looked as if you were suffering from a premature indigestion of Bride-Cake, Ma'am," said Adrian. "I dare say you were exceedingly sorry for what you had done."

"Indeed, Sir," dolorously moaned Berry, "I were, and am."

"And would do your best to rectify the mischief—eh, Ma'am?"

"Indeed, and indeed, Sir, I would!" she protested solemnly.

"—As, of course, you should—knowing the family. Where may these lunatics have gone to spend the Moon?"

Mrs. Berry swimmingly replied: "To the Isle o' ——

don't know, indeed, Sir!" she snapped the indication short, and jumped out of the pit she had fallen into. Repentant as she might be, those dears should not be pursued and cruelly baulked of their young bliss! Tomorrow, if you please, Mr. Harley: not today!

"A pleasant spot," Adrian observed, smiling at his easy prey.

By a measurement of dates he discovered that the bridegroom had brought his bride to the house on the day he had quitted Raynham, and this was enough to satisfy Adrian's mind that there had been concoction and chicanery. Chance, probably, had brought him to the old woman: Chance certainly had not brought him to the young one.

"Very well, Ma'am," he said, in answer to her petitions for his favourable offices with Sir Austin in behalf of her little pension, and the bridal pair, "I will tell him you were only a blind agent in the affair, being naturally soft, and that you trust he will bless the consummation. He will be in Town tomorrow morning; but one of you two must see him tonight. An emetic kindly administered will set our friend here on his legs. A bath, and a clean shirt, and he might go. I don't see why your name should appear at all. Brush him up, and send him to Bellingham by the seven o'clock train. He will find his way to Raynham; he knows the neighbourhood in the dark. Let him go and state the case. Remember, one of you must go."

With this fair prospect of leaving a choice of perdition between the couple of unfortunates, for them to fight and lose all their virtues over, Adrian said, "Good morning."

Mrs. Berry touchingly arrested him. "You won't refuse a piece of his Cake, Mr. Harley?"

"Oh, dear no, Ma'am." Adrian turned to the Cake with alacrity. "I shall claim a very large piece. Richard has a great many friends who will rejoice to eat his Wedding-Cake. Cut me a fair quarter, Mrs. Berry. Put it in paper, if you please. I shall be delighted to carry it to them, and apportion it equitably according to their several degrees of relationship."

Mrs. Berry cut the Cake. Somehow, as she sliced through it, the sweetness and hapless innocence of the bride was presented to her, and she launched into eulogies of Lucy, and clearly showed how little she regretted her conduct. She vowed that they seemed made for each other: that both were beautiful: both had spirit: both were innocent: and to part them, or make them unhappy, would be, Mrs. Berry wrought herself to cry aloud, Oh, such a pity!

Adrian listened to it as the expression of a matter-of-fact opinion. He took the huge quarter of Cake, nodded multitudinous promises, and left Mrs. Berry to bless his good heart.

"So dies the System!" was Adrian's comment in the street. "And now let prophets roar! He dies respectably in a marriage-bed, which is more than I should have foretold of the Monster. Meantime," he gave the Cake a dramatic tap, "I'll go sow nightmares."

CHAPTER XXXVI

PROCESSION OF THE CAKE

ADRIAN really bore the news he had heard with creditable disinterestedness, and admirable repression of anything beneath the dignity of a philosopher. When one has attained that felicitous point of wisdom from which one sees all mankind to be fools, the diminutive objects may make what new moves they please, one does not marvel at them: their sedateness is as comical as their frolic, and their frenzies more comical still. On this intellectual eminence the Wise Youth had built his Castle, and he had lived in it from an early period. Astonishment never shook the foundations, nor did envy of greater heights tempt him to relinquish the security of his stronghold, for he saw none. Jugglers he saw running up ladders that overtopped him, and air-balloons scaling the empyrean; but the former came precipitately down again, and the latter were at the mercy of the winds; while he remained tranquil on his solid unambitious ground, fitting his morality to the laws, his conscience to his morality, his comfort to his conscience. Not that voluntarily he cut himself off from his fellows: on the contrary, his sole amusement was their society. Alone he was rather dull, as a man who beholds but one thing must naturally be. Study of the animated varieties of that one thing, excited him sufficiently to think life a pleasant play; and the faculties he had forfeited to hold his elevated position, he could serenely enjoy by contemplation of them in others. Thus:—wonder at Master Richard's madness: though he himself did not experience it, he was eager to mark the effect on his beloved relations. As he carried along his vindictive hunch of cake, he shaped out their different attitudes of amaze, bewilderment, horror; passing by some personal chagrin in the prospect. For his patron had projected a journey this Summer, commencing with Paris, culminating on the Alps, and lapsing in Rome: a delightful journey to show Richard the highways of History and tear him from the risk of further ignoble fascinations, that his spirit might be altogether bathed in freshness and revived. This had been planned during Richard's absence to surprise him.

Now the dream of Travel was to Adrian what the Love of Woman is to the race of young men. It supplanted that foolishness. It was his Romance, as we say; that buoyant anticipation on which in youth we ride the airs, and which, as we wax older and too heavy for our atmosphere, hardens to the Hobby, which, if an obstinate animal, is a safer horse, and conducts man at a slower pace to the Sexton. Adrian had never travelled. He was aware that his Romance was earthly and had discomforts only to be evaded by the one potent talisman possessed by his patron. His Alp would hardly be grand to him without an obsequious landlord in the foreground: he must recline on Mammon's Imperial cushions in order to moralize becomingly on the Ancient World. The search for pleasure at the expense of discomfort, as frantic lovers woo their mistresses to partake the shelter of a hut and batten on a crust, Adrian deemed the bitterness of beggarliness. Let his sweet mistress be given him in the pomp and splendour due to his superior emotions, or not at all. Consequently the Wise Youth had long nursed an ineffectual passion, and it argued a great nature in him that, at the moment when his wishes were to be crowned, he should look with such slight touches of spleen at the gorgeous composite fabric of Parisian Cookery and Roman Antiquities crumbling into unsubstantial mockery. Assuredly very few even of the philosophers would have turned away uncomplainingly to meaner delights the moment after.

Hippias received the first portion of the Cake.

He was sitting by the window in his hotel reading. He had fought down his breakfast with more than usual success, and was looking forward to his dinner at the Foreys' with less than usual timidity.

"Ah! glad you've come, Adrian," he said, and expanded his chest. "I was afraid I should have to ride down. This is kind of you. We'll walk down together through the park. It's absolutely dangerous to walk alone in these streets. My opinion is that orange-peel lasts all through the year now, and will till the legislation puts a stop to it. We were free from that nuisance in the Summer—once; but now everybody's stupid inconsiderateness has multiplied tenfold the malignity of those boys who broke our necks in the Winter, and there's positively no relapse. I give you my word I slipped on a piece of orange-peel yesterday afternoon in Piccadilly, and I thought I was down—I thought I was down! I saved myself by miracle."

Adrian animadverted on everybody very sympathetically.

"You have an appetite, I hope?" he asked.

"I think I shall get one, after a bit of a walk," chirped Hippias. "Yes. I think I feel hungry now."

"Charmed to hear it," said Adrian, and began unpinning his parcel on his knees. "How should you define Folly?" he checked the process to inquire.

"Hm!" Hippias meditated, who always prided himself on being oracular when such questions were addressed to him. "I think I should define it to be, a Slide."

"Very good definition. In other words, a piece of orange-peel; once on it, your life and limbs are in danger, and you are saved by miracle. You must present that to the PILGRIM. And the Monument of Folly, what would that be?"

Hippias meditated anew. "All the human race on one another's shoulders." He chuckled at the sweeping sourness of the instance.

"Very good," Adrian applauded, "or in default of that, some symbol of the thing, say; such as this of which I have here brought you a chip."

Adrian displayed the Quarter of the Cake.

"This is the Monument made portable—eh?"

"Cake!" cried Hippias, retreating his chair with intense disgust. "Well! you're right of them that eat it. If I—if I don't mistake," he peered at it, "the noxious composition bedizened in that way is what they call Wedding-Cake. It's arrant poison! It's destruction to the stomach! Ugh! Who is it you want to kill? What are you carrying such stuff about for?"

Adrian rang the bell for a knife. "To present you with your due and proper portion."

"Me?" Hippias's face became venomous.

"Well," said Adrian, "you will have friends and relations, and can't be saved from them, not even by miracle. It is a habit which exhibits, perhaps, the unconscious inherent cynicism of the human mind, for people who consider that they have reached the acme of mundane felicity, to distribute this token of esteem to their friends, with the object prob-

ably" (he took the knife from a waiter and went to the
table to slice the Cake) "of enabling those friends (these
edifices require very delicate incision—each particular currant
and subtle condiment hangs to its neighbour—a Wedding-
Cake is evidently the most highly civilized of Cakes and
partakes of the evils as well as the advantages of Civilization!) I was saying, they send us these love-tokens, no doubt
(we shall have to weigh out the crumbs, if each is to have
his fair share) that we may the better estimate (got to the
bottom as last!) their state of Bliss, by passing some hours
in Purgatory. This, as far as I can apportion it without
weights and scales, is your share, my Uncle!"

He pushed the corner of the table bearing the Cake
towards Hippias.

"Get away!" Hippias vehemently motioned, and started
from his chair. "I'll have none of it, I tell you! It's
Death! It's fifty times worse than that beastly compound
Christmas pudding! What fool has been doing this, then?
Who dares send me Cake? Me! It's an insult."

"You are not compelled to eat any before dinner," said
Adrian, pointing the corner of the table after him, "but your
share you must take, and appear to consume. One who has
done so much to bring about the marriage cannot in conscience refuse his allotment of the fruits. Maidens, I hear,
first cook it under their pillows, and extract nuptial dreams
therefrom—said to be of a lighter class, taken that way.
It's a capital Cake, and, upon my honour, you have helped
to make it—you have indeed! So here it is."

The table again went at Hippias. He ran nimbly round
it, and flung on a sofa, exhausted, crying: "There! . . .
My appetite's gone for today!"

"Then shall I tell Richard that you won't touch a morsel
of his Cake?" said Adrian, leaning on his two hands over
the table and looking at his uncle.

"Richard?"

"Yes, your nephew: my cousin: Richard! Your companion since you've been in Town. He's married, you know. Married this morning at Kensington parish church, by license, at half-past eleven of the clock, or twenty to. Married, and gone to spend his Honeymoon in the Isle of Wight: a very delectable place for a month's residence. I have to announce to you that, thanks to your assistance, the Experiment is launched, Sir!—"

"Richard married!"

There was something to think and to say in objection to it, but the wits of poor Hippias were softened by the shock. His hand travelled half-way to his forehead, spread out to smooth the surface of that seat of reason, and then fell.

"Surely you knew all about it? you were so anxious to have him in Town under your charge. . . . "

"Married?" Hippias jumped up—he had it. "Why, he's under age! he's an infant."

"So he is. But the infant is not the less married. Fib like a man and pay your fee—what does it matter? Any one who is breeched can obtain a license in our noble country. And the interests of morality demand that it should not be difficult. Is it true—can you persuade anybody that you have known nothing about it?"

"Ha! infamous joke! I wish, Sir, you would play your pranks on somebody else," said Hippias, sternly, as he sank back on the sofa. "You've done me up for the day, I can assure you."

Adrian sat down to instil belief by gentle degrees and put an artistic finish to the work. He had the gratification of passing his Uncle through varied contortions, and at last Hippias perspired conviction, and exclaimed: "This accounts for his conduct to me. That boy must have a cunning nothing short of infernal! I feel . . . I feel it just here," he drew a hand along his midriff.

"I'm not equal to this world of fools," he added faintly, and shut his eyes. "No, I can't dine. Eat? ha! . . . no. Go without me!"

Shortly after, Hippias went to bed, saying to himself, as he undressed: "See what comes of our fine schemes! Poor Austin!" and as the pillow swelled over his ears: "I'm not sure that a day's fast won't do me good." The Dyspepsy had bought his philosophy at a heavy price: he had a right to use it.

Adrian resumed the Procession of the Cake.

He sighted his melancholy Uncle Algernon hunting an appetite in the Row, and looking as if the Hope before him were also one-legged. The Captain did not pass without querying the ungainly parcel.

"I hope I carry it ostentatiously enough?" said Adrian. "Enclosed is wherewithal to quiet the alarm of the land. Now may the maids and wives of merry England sleep secure! I had half a mind to fix it on a pole, and engage a band to parade it. This is our dear Richard's Wedding-Cake. Married at half-past eleven this morning, by license, at the Kensington parish church: his own Ring being lost he employed the Ring of his beautiful bride's lachrymose landlady, she standing adjacent by the altar. His farewell to you as a bachelor, and hers as a maid, you can claim on the spot if you think proper and digest according to your powers."

Algernon let off steam in a whistle. "Thompson, the solicitor's daughter!" he said. "I met them the other day, somewhere about here. He introduced me to her. A pretty little baggage."

"No." Adrian set him right. " 'Tis a Miss Desborough, a Roman Catholic dairymaid. Reminds one of pastoral England in the time of the Plantagenets! He's quite equal to introducing her as Thompson's daughter, and himself as Beelzebub's son. However, the wild animal is in Hymen's chains, and the Cake is cut. Will you have your morsel?"

"Oh, by all means!—not now." Algernon had an unwonted air of reflection.—"Father know it?"

"Not yet. He will tonight by nine o'clock."

"Then I must see him by seven. Don't say you met me."
He nodded, and pricked his horse.

"Wants money!" said Adrian, putting the combustible he carried once more in motion.

The women were the crowning joy of his contemplative mind. He had reserved them for his final discharge. Dear demonstrative creatures! Dyspepsia would not weaken their poignant outcries, or Self-interest check their fainting fits. On the generic woman one could calculate. Well might THE PILGRIM'S SCRIP say of her that, 'She is always at Nature's breast:' not intending it as a compliment. Each woman is Eve throughout the Ages: whereas the PILGRIM would have us believe that the Adam in men has become warier, if not wiser: and weak as he is, has learnt a lesson from Time. Probably the Pilgrim's meaning may be taken to be, that Man grows, and Woman does not.

At any rate, Adrian hoped for such natural choruses as you hear in the Nursery when a bauble is lost. He was awake to Mrs. Doria's maternal predestinations, and guessed that Clare stood ready with the best form of filial obedience. They were only a poor couple to gratify his Mephistophelian humour to be sure, but Mrs. Doria was equal to twenty, and they would proclaim the diverse ways with which Maidenhood and Womanhood took disappointment, while the surrounding Forey girls and other females of the family assembly were expected to develop the finer shades and tapering edges of an agitation to which no woman could be cold.

All went well. He managed cleverly to leave the Cake unchallenged in a conspicuous part of the Drawing-Room, and stept gaily down to dinner. Much of the conversation adverted to Richard. Mrs. Doria asked him if he had seen the youth, or heard of him.

"Seen him? no! Heard of him? yes!" said Adrian. "I have heard of him. I heard that he was sublimely happy, and had eaten such a breakfast that dinner was impossible; claret and cold chicken, cake and——"

"Cake at breakfast!" they all interjected.

"That seems to be his fancy just now."

"What an extraordinary taste!"

"You know, he is educated on a system."

One fast young male Forey allied the system and the cake in a miserable pun. Adrian, a hater of puns, looked at him, and held the table silent, as if he were going to speak; but he said nothing and the young gentleman vanished from the conversation in a blush, extinguished by his own spark.

Mrs. Doria peevishly exclaimed: "Oh! fishcake, I suppose! I wish he understood a little better the obligations of relationship."

"Whether he understands them, I can't say," observed Adrian, "but I assure you he is very energetic in extending them."

The Wise Youth talked innuendoes whenever he had an opportunity, that his dear relative might be rendered sufficiently inflammable by and by at the aspect of the Cake: but he was not thought more than commonly mysterious and deep.

"Was his appointment at the house of those Grandison people?" Mrs. Doria asked, with a hostile upper-lip.

Adrian warmed the blindfolded parties by replying: "Do they keep a Beadle at the door?"

Mrs. Doria's animosity to Mrs. Grandison made her treat this as a piece of satirical ingenuousness. "I dare say they do," she said.

"And a Curate on hand?"

"Oh, I should think a dozen!"

Old Mr. Forey advised his punning grandson Clarence to give that house a wide berth, where he might be disposed of and dished-up at a moment's notice, and the scent ran off at a jest.

The Foreys gave good dinners, and with the old gentleman the excellent old fashion remained in permanence of trooping off the ladies as soon as they had taken their sustenance and just exchanged a smile with the flowers and the dessert, when they rose to fade with a beautiful accord, and the gallant males breathed under easier waistcoats, and settled to the business of the table, sure then an hour was their own. Adrian took a chair by Brandon Forey, a barrister of standing.

"I want to ask you," he said, "whether an infant in Law can legally bind himself."

"If he's old enough to affix his signature to an instrument, I suppose he can," yawned Brandon.

"Is he responsible for his acts?"

"I've no doubt we could hang him."

"Then what he could do for himself, you could do for him?"

"Not quite so much: pretty near."

"For instance, he can marry?"

"That's not a criminal case, you know."

"And the marriage is valid?"

"You can dispute it."

"Yes, and the Greeks and the Trojans can fight. It holds then?"

"Both water and fire!"

The Patriarch of the table sang out to Adrian that he stopped the vigorous circulation of the claret.

"Dear me, Sir!" said Adrian, "I beg pardon. The circumstances must excuse me. The fact is, my cousin Richard got married to a dairymaid this morning, and I wanted to know whether it held."

It was amusing to watch the manly coolness with which the announcement was taken. Nothing was heard more energetic than, "Deuce he has!" and, "A dairymaid!"

"I thought it better to let the ladies dine in peace," Adrian continued. "I wanted to be able to console my Aunt . . ."

"Well, but—well, but," the old gentleman, much the most excited, puffed,—"eh, Brandon? He's a boy, this young ass! Do you mean to tell me a boy can go and marry when he pleases, and any trull he pleases, and the marriage is good? If I thought that I'd turn every woman off my premises. I would! from the housekeeper to the scullery-maid. I'd have no woman near him till—till . . ."

"Till the young greenhorn was grey, Sir?" suggested Brandon.

"Till he knew what women are made of, Sir!" the old gentleman finished his sentence vehemently. "What, d'ye think, will Feverel say to it, Mr. Adrian?"

"He has been trying the very System you have proposed, Sir,—one that does not reckon on the powerful action of Curiosity on the juvenile intelligence. I'm afraid it's the very worst way of solving the problem."

"Of course it is," said Clarence. "None but a fool. . . ."

"At your age," Adrian relieved his embarrassment, "it is natural, my dear Clarence, that you should consider the idea of an isolated or imprisoned manhood something monstrous, and we do not expect you to see what amount of wisdom it contains. You follow one extreme, and we the other. I don't say that a middle course exists. The History of mankind shows our painful efforts to find one, but they have invariably resolved themselves into asceticism, or laxity, acting and reacting. The moral question is, If a naughty little man, by reason of his naughtiness, releases himself from foolishness, does a foolish little man, by reason of his foolishness, save himself from naughtiness?"

A discussion peculiar to men of the world, succeeded the laugh at Mr. Clarence. Then coffee was handed round, and the footman informed Adrian, in a low voice, that Mrs. Doria Forey particularly wished to speak with him. Adrian preferred not to go in alone. "Very well," he said, and sipped his coffee. They talked on, sounding the depths of Law in Brandon Forey, and receiving nought but hollow echoes from that profound cavity. He would not affirm that the Marriage was invalid: he would not affirm that it could not be annulled. He thought not: still he thought it would be worth trying. A consummated, and a non-consummated, Union were two different things. . . .

"Dear me!" said Adrian, "does the Law recognize that? Why that's almost human!"

Another message was brought to Adrian that Mrs. Doria Forey *very* particularly wished to speak with him.

"What can be the matter?" he exclaimed, pleased to have his faith in Woman strengthened. The Cake had exploded, no doubt.

So it proved, when the gentlemen joined the fair society. All the younger ladies stood about the table, whereon the Cake stood displayed, gaps being left for those sitting to feast their vision, and intrude the comments and speculations continually arising from fresh shocks of wonder at the unaccountable Apparition. Entering with the half-guilty air of men who know they have come from a grosser atmosphere, the gallant males also ranged themselves round the common object of curiosity.

"Here! Adrian!" Mrs. Doria cried. "Where is Adrian? Pray come here. Tell me! Where did this Cake come from? Whose is it? What does it do here? You know all about it, for you brought it. Clare saw you bring it into the room. What does it mean? I insist upon a direct answer. Now do not make me impatient, Adrian."

Certainly Mrs. Doria was equal to twenty. By her concentrated rapidity and volcanic complexion it was evident that suspicion had kindled.

"I was really bound to bring it," Adrian protested.

"Answer me!"

The Wise Youth bowed: "Categorically. This Cake came from the house of a person, a female of the name of Berry. It belongs to you partly, partly to me, partly to Clare, and to the rest of our family, on the principle of equal division: for which purpose it is present. . . ."

"Yes! Speak!"

"It means, my dear Aunt, what that kind of Cake usually does mean."

"This, then, is the Breakfast! And the Ring! Adrian! where is Richard?"

Mrs. Doria still clung to unbelief in the monstrous horror. But when Adrian told her that Richard had left Town, her struggling hope sank. "The wretched boy has ruined himself!" she said, and sat down trembling.

Oh! that System! The delicate vituperations gentle ladies use instead of oaths, Mrs. Doria showered on that System. She hesitated not to say that her brother had got what he deserved. Opinionated, morbid, weak, justice had overtaken him. Now he would see! but at what a price! at what a sacrifice!

Mrs. Doria commanded Adrian to confirm her fears.

Sadly the Wise Youth capitulated Berry's words. "He was married this morning at half-past eleven of the clock, or twenty to, by license, at the Kensington Parish Church."

"Then that was his appointment!" Mrs. Doria murmured.

"That was the Cake for breakfast!" breathed a second of her sex.

"And it was his Ring!" exclaimed a third.

The men were silent, and made faces.

Clare stood cold and sedate. She and her mother avoided each other's eyes.

"Is it that abominable country person, Adrian?"

"The happy damsel is, I regret to say, the Papist dairy-maid," said Adrian, in sorrowful but deliberate accents.

Then arose a feminine hum, in the midst of which Mrs. Doria cried, "Brandon!" She was a woman of energy. Her thoughts resolved to action spontaneously.

"Brandon," she drew the barrister a little aside, "can they not be followed, and separated? I want your advice. Cannot we separate them? A boy! it is really shameful if he should be allowed to fall into the toils of a designing creature to ruin himself irrevocably. Can we not, Brandon?"

The worthy barrister felt inclined to laugh, but he answered her entreaties: "From what I hear of the young groom I should imagine the office perilous."

"I'm speaking of Law, Brandon. Can we not obtain an order from one of your Courts to pursue them and separate them instantly?"

"This evening?"

"Yes!"

Brandon was sorry to say she decidedly could not.

"You might call on one of your Judges, Brandon."

Brandon assured her that the Judges were a hard-worked race, and to a man slept heavily after dinner.

"Will you do so tomorrow, the first thing in the morning? Will you promise me to do so, Brandon?—Or a magistrate! A magistrate would send a policeman after them. My dear Brandon! I beg—I beg you to assist us in this dreadful extremity. It will be the death of my poor brother. I believe he would forgive anything but this. You have no idea what his notions are of blood."

Brandon tipped Adrian a significant nod to step in and aid.

"What is it, Aunt?" asked the Wise Youth. "You want them followed and torn asunder by wild policemen?"

"Tomorrow!" Brandon queerly interposed.

"Won't that be—just too late?" Adrian suggested.

Mrs. Doria sighed out her last spark of hope.

"You see," said Adrian. . . .

"Yes! yes!" Mrs. Doria did not require any of his elucidations. "Pray be quiet, Adrian, and let me speak. Brandon! it cannot be! it's quite impossible! Can you stand there and tell me that boy is legally married? I never will believe it! The Law cannot be so shamefully bad as to permit a boy—a mere child—to do such absurd things. Grandpapa!" she beckoned to the old gentleman. "Grandpapa! pray do make Brandon speak. These lawyers never will. He might stop it, if he would. If I were a man, do you think I would stand here?"

"Well, my dear," the old gentleman toddled to compose her, "I'm quite of your opinion. I believe he knows no more than you or I. My belief is they none oi them know anything till they join issue and go into Court. I want to see a few female lawyers."

"To encourage the bankrupt perruquier, Sir?" said Adrian. "They would have to keep a large supply of wigs on hand."

"And you can jest, Adrian!" his Aunt reproached him. "But I will not be beaten. I know—I am firmly convinced that no Law would ever allow a boy to disgrace his family and ruin himself like that, and nothing shall persuade me that it is so. Now tell me, Brandon, and pray do speak in answer to my questions, and please to forget you are dealing with a woman. *Can* my nephew be rescued from the consequences of his folly? *Is* what he has done legitimate? *Is* he bound for life by what he has done while a boy?"

"Well—a," Brandon breathed through his teeth. "A—hm! the matter's so very delicate, you see, Helen."

"You're to forget that," Adrian remarked.

"A—hm! well!" pursued Brandon. "Perhaps if you could arrest and divide them before nightfall, and make affidavit of certain facts. . . ."

"Yes?" the eager woman hastened his lagging mouth.

"Well . . . hm! a . . . in that case . . . a . . . Or if a lunatic, you could prove him to have been of unsound mind. . . ."

"Oh! there's no doubt of his madness on *my* mind, Brandon."

"Yes! well! in that case . . . Or if of different Religious persuasions. . . ."

"She *is* a Catholic!" Mrs. Doria joyfully interjected.

"Yes! well! in that case . . . objections might be taken to the form of the marriage. . . . Might be proved fictitious. . . . Or if he's under, say eighteen years. . . ."

"He *can't* be much more," cried Mrs. Doria. "I think," she appeared to reflect, and then faltered imploringly to Adrian, "What is Richard's age?"

The kind Wise Youth could not find it in his heart to strike away the phantom straw she caught at.

"Oh! about that, I should fancy," he muttered, and found it necessary at the same time to duck and turn his head for concealment. Mrs. Doria surpassed his expectations.

"Yes! well, then . . . " Brandon was resuming with a shrug which was meant to say he still pledged himself to nothing, when Clare's voice was heard from out the buzzing circle of her cousins: "Richard is nineteen years and six months old today, Mama."

"Nonsense, child."

"Yes, he is, Mama." Clare's voice was very steadfast.

"Non*sense,* I tell you. How *can* you know?"

"Richard is one year and nine months older than me, Mama."

Mrs. Doria fought the fact by years and finally by months. Clare was too strong for her.

"Singular child!" she mentally apostrophized the girl who scornfully rejected straws while drowning.

"But there's the Religion still!" she comforted herself, and sat down to cogitate.

The men smiled, and looked vacuous.

Music was proposed. There are times when soft Music hath not charms: when it is put to as base uses as Imperial Cæsar's dust and is simply taken to fill horrid pauses. Angelica Forey thumped the piano, and sang: *'I'm a laughing Gitana, ha—ha! ha—ha!'* Nobody believed her. Matilda Forey and her cousin Mary Branksburne wedded their voices and songfully incited all young people to *Haste to the bower that Love has built,* and defy the wise ones of the world; but the wise ones of the world were in a majority there, and very few places of assembly will be found where they are not, so the glowing appeal of the British Balladmonger passed into the bosom of the Emptiness he addressed. Clare was asked to entertain the company. The singular child calmly marched to the instrument, and turned over the exquisitely appropriate illustrations to the British Balladmonger's repertory.

"Sing this, dear," said Angelica. "This is pretty: *'I know I have not loved in vain!'* Eh? don't you like that? or this: *'He knew not that I watched his ways.'* What's this correction in the lines . . . ? *'I thought he knew not I wore—'* It's that Clarence! Really it's a shame how he treats our books. And here again: *'When I heard he was married.'* *Spliced!* he has written in. One of his dreadful slang words! I'll serve him out, though. Oh! he is too absurd. Look: *'I dare not breathe his name.'* He has written: *'For it is not pretty—Tomkins!'* Clarence has no idea of sentiment."

But Clarence candidly revealed the estimation in which the British Balladmonger is held by the applausive sons of Britain (not enamoured of the fair cantatrice), who murmur 'Beautiful!' 'Charming song!' and nightly receive Drawing-Room lessons of disgust at hearts, and bosoms, and bowers, that may partly account for their reticence and gaucherie when hearts, and bosoms and bowers, are things of earnest with them.

Clare rejected all pathetic anatomy, and sang a little Irish air. Her duty done, she marched from the piano. Mothers are rarely deceived by their daughters in these matters; but Clare deceived her mother; and Mrs. Doria only persisted in feeling an agony of pity for her child, that she might the more warrantably pity herself—a not uncommon form of the emotion: for there is no Juggler like that Heart the Balladmonger puts into our mouths so boldly. Remember that she saw years of self-denial, years of a ripening scheme, rendered fruitless in a minute, and by the System which had almost reduced her to the condition of constitutional hypocrite. She had enough of bitterness to brood over, and some excuse for self-pity.

Still, even when she was cooler, Mrs. Doria's energetic nature prevented her from giving up. Straws were straws, and the frailer they were the harder she clutched them.

She rose from her chair, and left the room, calling to Adrian to follow her.

"Adrian," she said, turning upon him in the passage, "you mentioned a house where this horrible Cake . . . where he was this morning. I desire you to take me to that woman immediately."

The Wise Youth had not bargained for personal servitude. He had hoped he should be in time for the last act of the Opera that night, after enjoying the Comedy of real life.

"My dear Aunt . . ." he was beginning to insinuate.

"Order a cab to be sent for, and get your hat," said Mrs. Doria.

There was nothing for it but to obey. He stamped his assent to the PILGRIM's dictum, that Women are practical creatures, and now reflected on his own account that relationship to a young fool may be a vexation and a nuisance. However, Mrs. Doria compensated him.

What Mrs. Doria intended to do, the practical creature did not plainly know; but her energy positively demanded to be used in some way or other, and her instinct directed her to the offender on whom she could use it in wrath. She wanted somebody to be angry with, somebody to abuse. She dared not abuse her brother to his face: him she would have to console. Adrian was a fellow-hypocrite to the System, and would, she was aware, bring her into painfully delicate, albeit highly philosophic, ground by a discussion of the case. So she drove to Bessy Berry's simply to inquire whither her nephew had flown.

When a soft woman, and that soft woman a sinner, is matched with a woman of energy, she does not show much fight and she meets no mercy. Bessy Berry's creditor came

to her in female form that night. She then beheld it in all
its terrors. Hitherto it had appeared to her as a male, a
disembodied spirit of her imagination possessing male attributes, and the peculiar male characteristic of being moved,
and ultimately silenced, by tears. As female, her Creditor
was terrible indeed. Still, had it not been a late hour,
Bessy Berry would have died rather than speak openly
that her babes had sped to make their nest in the Isle of
Wight. They had a long start, they were out of the reach
of pursuers, they were safe, and she told what she had to
tell. She told more than was wise of her to tell. She made
mention of her early service in the family, and of her little
pension. Alas! her little pension! Her Creditor had come
expecting no payment—come, as Creditors are wont in such
moods, just to take it out of her, to employ the familiar
term. At once Mrs. Doria pounced upon the pension.

"That, of course, you know is at an end," she said in
the calmest manner, and Berry did not plead for the little
bit of bread to her. She only asked a little consideration for
her feelings.

True admirers of Women had better stand aside from the
scene. Undoubtedly it was sad for Adrian to be compelled
to witness it. Mrs. Doria was not generous. The PILGRIM
may be wrong about the sex not growing: but its fashion of
conducting warfare we must allow to be barbarous, and according to what is deemed the pristine, or wild cat, method.
Ruin, nothing short of it, accompanied poor Berry to her
bed that night, and her character bled till morning on her
pillow.

The scene over, Adrian reconducted Mrs. Doria to her
home. Mice had been at the Cake during her absence, apparently. The ladies and gentlemen present put it on the greedy
mice, who were accused of having gorged and gone to bed.

"I'm sure they're quite welcome," said Mrs. Doria. "It's
a farce, this Marriage, and Adrian has quite come to my way
of thinking. I would not touch an atom of it. Why, they

were married in a married woman's Ring! Can *that* be legal
as you call it? Oh, I'm convinced! Don't tell me. Austin
will be in Town tomorrow, and if he is true to his principles,
he will instantly adopt measures to rescue his son from
infamy. I want no legal advice. I go upon common sense,
common decency. This Marriage is false."

Mrs. Doria's fine scheme had become so much a part of
her life, that she could not give it up. She took Clare to her
bed, and caressed and wept over her, as she would not have
done had she known the singular child, saying, "Poor Richard! my poor dear boy! we must save him, Clare! we must
save him!" Of the two the mother showed the greater
want of iron on this occasion. Clare lay in her arms rigid
and emotionless, with one of her hands tight-locked. All
she said was: "I knew it in the morning, Mama." She slept
clasping Richard's nuptial Ring.

By this time all specially concerned in the System knew
it. The Honeymoon was shining placidly above them. Is
not happiness like another Circulating Medium? When
we have a very great deal of it, some poor hearts are aching
for what is taken away from them. When we have gone
out and seized it on the highways, certain inscrutable laws
are sure to be at work to bring us to the Criminal bar, sooner
or later. Who knows the Honeymoon that did not steal
somebody's sweetness? Richard Turpin went forth, singing:
'Money or life' to the world: Richard Feverel has done the
same, substituting 'Happiness' for 'Money,' frequently syn-
onyms. The coin he wanted he would have, and was just
as much a highway robber as his fellow Dick, so that those
who failed to recognize him as a Hero before, may now regard him in that light. Meanwhile the world he has squeezed
looks exceeding patient and beautiful. His coin chinks
delicious music to him. Nature, and the order of things on
earth, have no warmer admirer than a jolly brigand, or a
young man made happy by the Jews.

CHAPTER XXXVII

NURSING THE DEVIL

AND now the author of the system was on trial under
the eyes of the lady who loved him. What so kind as they?
Yet are they very rigorous, those soft watchful woman's
eyes. If you fall below the measure they have made of you,
you will feel it in the fulness of time. She cannot but
show you that she took you for a giant, and has had to come
down a bit. You feel yourself strangely diminishing in
those sweet mirrors, till at last they drop on you complacently
level. But, oh beware, vain man, of ever waxing enamoured
of that wonderful elongation of a male creature you saw
reflected in her adoring upcast orbs! Beware of assisting to
delude her! A woman who is not quite a fool will forgive your being but a man, if you are surely that: she will
haply learn to acknowledge that no mortal tailor could have
fitted that figure she made of you respectably, and that practically (though she sighs to think it) her ideal of you was on
the pattern of an overgrown charity-boy in the regulation
jacket and breech. For this she first scorns the narrow
capacities of the tailor, and then smiles at herself. But
shouldst thou, when the hour says plainly, Be thyself, and
the woman is willing to take thee as thou art, shouldst thou
still aspire to be that thing of shanks and wrists, wilt thou not
seem contemptible as well as ridiculous? And when the fall
comes, will it not be flat on thy face, instead of to the common height of men? You may fall miles below her measure
of you, and be safe: nothing is damaged save an overgrown
charity-boy; but if you fall below the common height of
men, you must make up your mind to see her rustle her
gown, spy at the looking-glass, and transfer her allegiance.
The moral of which is, that if we pretend to be what we are
not, women, for whose amusement the farce is performed,

will find us out and punish us for it. And it is usually the end of a sentimental dalliance.

Had Sir Austin given vent to the pain and wrath it was natural he should feel, he might have gone to unphilosophic excesses, and however much he lowered his reputation as a sage, Lady Blandish would have excused him: she would not have loved him less for seeing him closer. But the poor gentleman tasked his soul and stretched his muscles to act up to her conception of him. He, a man of science in Life, who was bound to be surprised by nothing in Nature, it was not for him to do more than lift his eyebrows and draw in his lips at the news delivered by Ripton Thompson, that ill bird at Raynham.

All he said, after Ripton had handed the letters and carried his penitential headache to bed, was: "You see, Emmeline, it is useless to base any System on a human being."

A very philosophical remark for one who had been busily at work building for nearly twenty years. Too philosophical to seem genuine. It revealed where the blow struck sharpest. Richard was no longer the Richard of his creation: his pride and his joy: but simply a human being with the rest. The bright star had sunk among the mass.

And yet, what had the young man done? And in what had the System failed?

The lady could not but ask herself this, while she condoled with the offended father.

"My friend," she said, tenderly taking his hand before she retired, "I know how deeply you must be grieved. I know what your disappointment must be. I do not beg of you to forgive him now. You cannot doubt his love for this young person, and according to his light, has he not behaved honourably, and as you would have wished, rather than bring her to shame? You will think of that. It has been an accident—a misfortune—a terrible misfortune . . ."

"The God of this world is in the machine—not out of it,"

Sir Austin interrupted her, and pressed her hand to get the
Good night over.

At any other time her mind would have been arrested to
admire the phrase: now it seemed perverse, vain, false, and
she was tempted to turn the meaning that was in it against
himself, much as she pitied him.

"You know, Emmeline," he added, "I believe very little
in the fortune, or misfortune, to which men attribute their
successes and reverses. They are useful impersonations to
novelists; but my opinion is sufficiently high of flesh and
blood to believe that we make our own history without intervention. Accidents?—Terrible misfortunes?—What are
they?—Good night."

"Good night," she said, looking sad and troubled. "When
I said 'misfortune,' I meant of course, that he is to blame,
but—shall I leave you his letter to me?"

"I think I have enough to meditate upon," he replied,
coldly bowing.

"God bless you!" she whispered. "And—may I say it? do
not shut your heart."

He assured her that he hoped not to do so, and the moment
she was gone he set about shutting it as tight as he could.

If, instead of saying, Base no system on a human being,
he had said, Never experimentalize with one, he would
have been nearer the truth of his own case. He had experi-
mented on humanity in the person of the son he loved as his
life, and at once when the experiment appeared to have
failed, all humanity's failings fell on the shoulders of his son.
Richard's parting laugh in the train—it was explicable now:
it sounded in his ears like the mockery of this base nature
of ours at every endeavour to exalt and chasten it. The
young man had plotted this. From step to step Sir Austin
traced the plot. The curious mask he had worn since his ill-
ness; the selection of his incapable uncle Hippias for a companion in preference to Adrian; it was an evident, well-per-
fected, plot. That hideous laugh would not be silenced.

Base, like the rest, treacherous, a creature of passions using his abilities solely to gratify them—never surely had humanity such chances as in him! A Manichæan tendency, from which the sententious eulogist of Nature had been struggling for years (and which was partly at the bottom of the System), now began to cloud and usurp dominion of his mind. As he sat alone in the forlorn dead-hush of his library, he saw the Devil.

How are we to know when we are at the head and fountain of the fates of them we love?

There by the springs of Richard's future, his father sat: and the Devil said to him: "Only be quiet: do nothing: resolutely do nothing: your object now is to keep a brave face to the world, so that all may know you superior to this human nature that has deceived you. For it is the shameless Deception, not the Marriage, that has wounded you."

"Ay!" answered the Baronet, "the shameless Deception, not the Marriage! wicked and ruinous as it must be; a destroyer of my tenderest hopes! my dearest schemes! Not the Marriage:—the shameless Deception!" and he crumpled up his son's letter to him, and tossed it into the fire.

How are we to distinguish the dark chief of the Manichæans when he talks our own thoughts to us?

Further he whispered: "And your System:— if you would be brave to the world, have courage to cast the dream of it out of you: relinquish an impossible project; see it as it is— dead: too good for men!"

"Ay!" muttered the Baronet; "all who would save them perish on the Cross!"

And so he sat nursing the Devil.

By and by he took his lamp, and put on the old cloak and cap, and went to gaze at Ripton. That exhausted debauchee and youth without a destiny slept a dead sleep. A handkerchief was bound about his forehead, and his helpless sunken chin and snoring nose projected up the pillow, made him look absurdly piteous. The Baronet remembered how often he had compared his boy with this one: his own bright boy! And where was the difference between them?

"Mere outward gilding!" said his Familiar.

"Yes," he responded, "I dare say this one never positively plotted to deceive his father: he followed his appetites unchecked, and is internally the sounder of the two."

Ripton, with his sunken chin and snoring nose under the light of the lamp, stood for human nature, honest, however abject.

"Miss Random, I fear very much, is a necessary Establishment!" whispered the Monitor.

"Does the evil in us demand its natural food, or it corrupts the whole?" ejaculated Sir Austin. "And is no Angel of avail till that is drawn off? And is that our conflict—to see whether we can escape the contagion of its embrace, and come uncorrupted out of that?"

"The world is wise in its way," said the voice.

"Though it look on itself through Port?" he suggested, remembering his lawyer Thompson.

"Wise in not seeking to be too wise," said the voice.

"And getting intoxicated on its drug of comfort!"

"Human nature is weak."

"And Miss Random is an Establishment, and Wild Oats an Institution!"

"It always has been so."

"And always will be?"

"So I fear! in spite of your very noble efforts."

"And leads—whither? And ends—where?"

Richard's laugh, taken up by horrid reverberations, as it were through the lengths of the Lower Halls, replied.

This colloquy of two voices in a brain was concluded by Sir Austin asking again if there was no actual difference between the flower of his hopes and yonder drunken weed, and receiving for answer that there was a decided dissimilarity in the smell of the couple: becoming cognizant of which he retreated.

Sir Austin did not battle with the tempter. He took him into his bosom at once, as if he had been ripe for him, and received his suggestions, and bowed to his dictates. Because he suffered and decreed that he would suffer silently, and be the only sufferer, it seemed to him that he was great-minded in his calamity. He had stood against the world. The world had beaten him. What then? He must shut his heart and mask his face: that was all. To be far in advance of the mass, is as fruitless to mankind, he reflected, as straggling in the rear. For how do we know that they move behind us at all? or move in our track? What we win for them is lost; and where we are overthrown we lie!

It was thus that a fine mind and a fine heart at the bounds of a nature not great, chose to colour his retrogression and countenance his shortcoming: and it was thus that he set about ruining the work he had done. He might well say, as he once did, that there are hours when the clearest soul becomes a cunning fox. For a grief that was private and pe-culiar, he unhesitatingly cast the blame upon humanity; just as he had accused it in the period of what he termed his own ordeal. How had he borne that? By masking his face. And he prepared the ordeal for his son by doing the same. This was by no means his idea of a man's duty in tribulation, about which he could be strenuously eloquent. But it was his in-stinct so to act, and in times of trial great natures alone are not at the mercy of their instincts. Moreover it would cost him pain to mask his face: pain worse than that he endured when there still remained an object for him to open his heart to in proportion: and he always reposed upon the Spartan comfort of bearing pain and being passive. "Do nothing," said the Devil he nursed: which meant in his case, "Take me into you, and don't cast me out." Excellent and sane, I think, is the outburst of wrath to men, when it stops short of slaughter. For who that locks it up to eat it solitary, can say that it is consumed? Sir Austin had as weak a digestion for wrath, as poor Hippias for a green duckling. Instead of eating it, it ate him. The wild beast in him was not the less deadly because it did not roar, and the Devil in him not the less active because he resolved to do nothing.

He sat at the springs of Richard's future, in the forlorn dead-hush of his library there, hearing the cinders click in the extinguished fire, and that humming stillness in which one may fancy one hears the midnight Fates busily stirring their embryos. The lamp glowed mildly on the bust of Chatham.

Towards morning a gentle knock fell at his door. Lady Blandish glided in. With hasty step she came straight to him, and took both his hands.

"My friend," she said, speaking tearfully, and trembling, "I feared I should find you here. I could not sleep. How is it with you?"

"Well, Emmeline! well!" he replied, torturing his brows to fix the mask.

He wished it had been Adrian who had come to him. He had an extraordinary longing for Adrian's society. He knew that the Wise Youth would divine how to treat him, and he mentally confessed to just enough weakness to demand a certain kind of management. Besides, Adrian, he had not a doubt, would accept him entirely as he seemed, and not pester him in any way by trying to unlock his heart: whereas, a woman, he feared, would be waxing too womanly, and swelling from tears and supplications to a scene, of all things abhorred by him the most. So he rapped the floor with his foot, and gave the lady no very welcome face when he said it was well with him.

She sat down by his side, still holding one hand firmly, and softly detaining the other.

"Oh, my friend! may I believe you? May I speak to you?" She leaned close to him. "You know my heart. I have no better ambition than to be your friend. Surely I divide your grief, and may I not claim your confidence? Who has wept more over your great and dreadful sorrows?

I would not have come to you, but I do believe that sorrow
shared relieves the burden, and it is now that you may feel
a woman's aid, and something of what a woman could be
to you. . . ."

"Be assured," he gravely said, "I thank you, Emmeline,
for your intentions."

"No, no! not for my intentions! And do not thank me.
Think of him . . . think of your dear boy . . . Our
Richard, as we have called him—Oh! do not think it a
foolish superstition of mine, but I have had a thought this
night that has kept me in torment till I rose to speak to
you. . . . Tell me first you have forgiven him."

"A father bears no malice to his son, Emmeline."

"Your heart has forgiven him?"

"My heart has taken what he gave."

"And quite forgiven him?"

"You will hear no complaints of mine."

The lady paused despondingly, and looked at him in a
wistful manner, saying with a sigh, "Yes! I know how
noble you are, and different from others!"

He drew one of his hands from her relaxed hold.

"You ought to be in bed, Emmeline."

"I cannot sleep."

"Go, and talk to me another time."

"No, it must be now. You have helped me when I struggled to rise into a clearer world, and I think, humble as I am,
I can help you now. I have had a thought this night that
if you do not pray for him and bless him . . . it will end
miserably. My friend, have you done so?"

He was stung and offended, and could hardly help showing it in spite of his mask.

"Have you done so, Austin?"

"This is assuredly a new way of committing fathers to
the follies of their sons, Emmeline!"

"No, not that. But will you pray for your boy, and
bless him, before the day comes?"

He restrained himself to pronounce his words calmly:—
"And I must do this, or it will end in misery? How else
can it end? Can I save him from the seed he has sown?
Consider, Emmeline, what you say. He has repeated his
cousin's sin. You see the end of that. . . ."

"Oh, so different! This young person is *not,* is *not* of the
class poor Austin Wentworth allied himself to. Indeed it is
different. And he—be just and admit his nobleness. I
fancied you did. This young person has great beauty, she has
the elements of good-breeding, she—indeed I think, had she
been in another position, you would not have looked upon
her unfavourably."

"She may be too good for my son!" The Baronet spoke
with sublime bitterness.

"No woman is too good for Richard, and you know it."

"Pass her."

"Yes, I will speak only of him. He met her by a fatal
accident. We thought his love dead, and so did he till he
saw her again. He met her, he thought we were plotting
against him, he thought he should lose her for ever, and
in the madness of an hour he did this. . . ."

"My Emmeline pleads bravely for clandestine matches."

"Ah! do not trifle, my friend. Say: would you have had
him act as young men in his position generally do to young
women beneath them?"

Sir Austin did not like the question. It probed him
very severely.

"You mean," he said, "that fathers must fold their arms,
and either submit to infamous marriages, or have these
creatures ruined."

"I do *not* mean that," exclaimed the lady, striving for
what she did mean, and how to express it. "I mean that . . .
he loved her. Is it not a madness at his age? But what
I chiefly mean is—save him from the consequences. No, you
shall not withdraw your hand. Think of his pride, his sensitiveness, his great wild nature—wild when he is set wrong:

think, how intense it is, set upon love; think, my friend, do not forget his love for you."

Sir Austin smiled an admirable smile of pity.

"That I should save him, or any one, from consequences, is asking more than the order of things will allow to you, Emmeline, and is not in the disposition of this world. I cannot. Consequences are the natural offspring of acts. My child, you are talking sentiment, which is the distraction of our modern age in everything—a phantasmal vapour distorting the image of the life we live. You ask me to give him a golden age in spite of himself. All that could be done, by keeping him in the paths of Virtue and Truth, I did. He is become a man, as a man he must reap his own sowing."

The baffled lady sighed. He sat so rigid: he spoke so securely, as if wisdom were to him more than the love of his son. And yet he did love his son. Feeling sure that he loved his son while he spoke so loftily, she reverenced him still, baffled as she was, and sensible that she had been quibbled with.

"All I ask of you is to open your heart to him," she said. He was silent.

"Call him a man—he is, and must ever be the child of your education, my friend."

"You would console me, Emmeline, with the prospect that, if he ruins himself, he spares the world of young women. Yes, that is something! that is something!"

Closely she scanned the mask. It was impenetrable. He could meet her eyes, and respond to the pressure of her hand, and smile, and not show what he felt. Nor did he deem it hypocritical to seek to maintain his elevation in her soft soul, by simulating supreme philosophy over offended love. Nor did he know that he had an Angel with him then: a blind Angel, and a weak one, but one who struck upon his chance.

"Am I pardoned for coming to you?" she said after a pause.

"Surely I can read my Emmeline's intentions," he gently replied.

"Very poor ones. I feel my weakness. I cannot utter half I have been thinking. Oh, if I could!"

"You speak very well, Emmeline."

"At least, I am pardoned?"

"Surely so."

"And before I leave you, dear friend, shall I be forgiven? —may I beg it?—will you bless him?"

He was again silent.

"Pray for him, Austin! pray for him ere the night is over."

As she spoke she slid down to his feet and pressed his hand to her bosom.

The Baronet was startled. In very dread of the soft fit that wooed him, he pushed back his chair, and rose, and went to the window.

"It's day already!" he said with assumed vivacity, throwing open the shutters, and displaying the young light on the lawn.

Lady Blandish dried her eyes as she knelt, and then joined him, and glanced up silently at Richard's Moon standing in wane towards the West. She hoped it was because of her having been premature in pleading so earnestly, that she had failed to move him, and she accused herself more than the Baronet. But in acting as she had done, she had treated him as no common man, and she was compelled to perceive that his heart was at present hardly superior to the hearts of ordinary men, however composed his face might be, and apparently serene his wisdom. From that moment she grew critical of him, and began to study her Idol,—a process dangerous to Idols. He, now that she seemed to have relinquished the painful subject, drew to her, and, as one who wished to smooth a foregone roughness, murmured: "God's rarest blessing is, after all, a good woman! My Emmeline bears her sleepless night well. She does not shame the day." He gazed down on her with a fondling tenderness.

"I could bear many, many!" she replied meeting his eyes, "and you would see me look better and better, if . . . if only . . . " but she had no encouragement to end the sentence.

Perhaps he wanted some mute form of consolation: perhaps the handsome placid features of the dark-eyed dame touched him: at any rate their Platonism was advanced by his putting an arm about her. She felt the arm, and talked of the morning.

Thus proximate, they by-and-by both heard something very like a groan behind them, and looking round, beheld the Saurian eye. Lady Blandish smiled, but the Baronet's discomposure was not to be concealed. By a strange fatality every stage of their innocent loves was certain to have a human beholder.

"Oh, I'm sure I beg pardon," Benson mumbled, arresting his head in a melancholy pendulosity. He was ordered out of the room.

"And I think I shall follow him and try to get forty winks," said Lady Blandish. They parted with a quiet squeeze of hands.

The Baronet then called in Benson.

"Get me my breakfast as soon as you can," he said, regardless of the aspect of injured conscience Benson sombrely presented to him. "I am going to Town early. And Benson," he added, "you will also go to Town this afternoon, or tomorrow, if it suits you, and take your book with you to Mr. Thompson. You will not return here. A provision will be made for you. You can go."

The heavy butler essayed to speak, but the tremendous blow and the Baronet's gesture choked him. At the door he made another effort which shook the rolls of his loose skin pitiably. An impatient signal sent him out dumb,—and

Raynham was quit of the one believer in the Great Shaddock Dogma.

CHAPTER XXXVIII

CONQUEST OF AN EPICURE

It was the month of July. The Solent ran up green
waves before a full-blowing South-Wester. Gay little
yachts bounded out like foam, and flashed their sails, light
as sea-nymphs. A crown of deep Summer blue topped the
flying mountains of cloud.

By an open window that looked on the brine through
nodding roses, our young bridal pair were at breakfast, regaling worthily both of them. Had the Scientific Humanist
observed them, he could not have contested the fact that, as
a couple who had set up to be father and mother of Britons,
they were doing their duty. Files of egg-cups with disin-
tegrated shells, bore witness to it, and they were still at
work, hardly talking from rapidity of exercise. Both were
dressed for an expedition. She had her bonnet on, and he
his yachting-hat. His sleeves were turned over at the wrists,
and her gown showed its lining on her lap. At times a
chance word might spring a laugh, but eating was the business of the hour, as I would have you to know it always
will be where Cupid is in earnest. Tribute flowed in to
them from the subject land. Neglected lies Love's penny-
whistle on which they played so prettily, and charmed the
spheres to hear them. What do they care for the spheres,
who have one another? Come, eggs! come, bread and
butter! come, tea with sugar in it and milk! and welcome,
the jolly hours. That is a fair interpretation of the music
in them just now. Yonder instrument was good only for
the Overture. After all, what finer aspiration can lovers
have, than to be free man and woman in the heart of plenty?
And is it not a glorious level to have attained? Ah, wretched

Scientific Humanist! not to be by and mark the admirable sight of these young creatures feeding! It would have been a spell to exorcise the Manichee, methinks.

The mighty performance came to an end, and then, with a flourish of his table-napkin husband stood over wife, who met him on the confident budding of her mouth. The poetry of mortals is their daily prose. Is it not a glorious level to have attained? A short, quick-blooded kiss, radiant, fresh, and honest, as Aurora, and then Richard says, without lack of cheer, "No letter today, my Lucy!" whereat her sweet eyes dwell on him a little seriously, but he cries, "Never mind! he'll be coming down himself some morning. He has only to know her, and all's well! eh?" and so saying he puts a hand beneath her chin, and seems to frame her fair face in fancy, she smiling up to be looked at.

"But one thing I do want to ask my darling," says Lucy, and dropped into his bosom with hands of petition. "Take me on board his yacht with him to day—not leave me with those people! Will he? I'm a good sailor, he knows!"

"The best afloat!" laughs Richard, hugging her, "but, you know, you darling bit of a sailor, they don't allow more than a certain number on board for the race, and if they hear you've been with me, there'll be cries of foul play! Besides, there's Lady Judith to talk to you about Austin, and Lord Mountfalcon's compliments for you to listen to, and Mr. Morton to take care of you."

Lucy's eyes fixed sideways an instant.

"I hope I don't frown and blush as I did?" she said, screwing her pliable brows up to him winningly, and he bent his cheek against hers, and murmured something delicious.

"And we shall be separated for—how many hours? one, two, three hours!" she pouted to his flatteries.

"And then I shall come on board to receive my bride's congratulations."

"And then my husband will talk all the time to Lady Judith."

"And then I shall see my wife frowning and blushing at Lord Mountfalcon."

"Am I so foolish, Richard?" she forgot her trifling to ask in an earnest way, and had another Aurorean kiss, just brushing the dew on her lips, for answer.

After hiding a month in shyest shade, the pair of happy sinners had wandered forth one day to look on men and marvel at them, and had chanced to meet Mr. Morton of Poer Hall, Austin Wentworth's friend, and Ralph's uncle. Mr. Morton had once been intimate with the Baronet, but had given him up for many years as impracticable and hopeless, for which reason he was the more inclined to regard Richard's misdemeanour charitably, and to lay the faults of the son on the father: and thinking society to be the one thing requisite to the young man, he had introduced him to the people he knew in the island: among others to the Lady Judith Felle, a fair young dame, who introduced him to Lord Mountfalcon, a puissant nobleman; who introduced him to the yachtsmen beginning to congregate: so that in a few weeks he found himself in the centre of a brilliant company, and for the first time in his life tasted what it was to have free intercourse with his fellow-creatures of both sexes. The son of a System was, therefore, launched; not only through the surf, but in deep waters.

Now the Baronet had so far compromised between the recurrence of his softer feelings and the suggestions of his new Familiar, that he had determined to act towards Richard with justness. The world called it magnanimity, and even Lady Blandish had some thoughts of the same kind when she heard that he had decreed to Richard a handsome allowance, and had scouted Mrs. Doria's proposal for him to contest the legality of the marriage: but Sir Austin knew well he was simply just in not withholding money from a youth so situated. And here again the world deceived him by embellishing his conduct. For what is it to be just to whom we love? He knew it was not magnanimous, but the cry of the world somehow fortified him in the conceit that in dealing perfect justice to his son he was doing all that was possible, because so much more than common fathers would have done. He had shut his heart.

Consequently Richard did not want money. What he wanted more, and did not get, was a word from his father, and though he said nothing to sadden his young bride, she felt how much it preyed upon him to be at variance with the man whom, now that he had offended him and gone against him, he would have fallen on his knees to: the man who was as no other man to him. She heard him of nights when she lay by his side, and the darkness, and the tears, and the broken mutterings, of those nights clothed the figure of the strange stern man in her mind. Not that it affected the appetites of the pretty pair. We must not expect that of Cupid enthroned, and in condition; under the influence of sea-air, too. The files of egg-cups laugh at such an idea. Still the worm did gnaw them. Judge, then, of their delight when, on this pleasant morning, as they were issuing from the garden of their cottage to go down to the sea, they caught sight of Tom Bakewell rushing up the road with a portmanteau on his shoulders, and, some distance behind him, discerned Adrian.

"It's all right!" shouted Richard, and ran off to meet him, and never left his hand till he had hauled him up, firing questions at him all the way, to where Lucy stood.

"Lucy! this is Adrian, my cousin."—"Isn't he an Angel?" his eyes seemed to add; while Lucy's clearly answered, "That he is!"

The full-bodied Angel ceremoniously bowed to her, and acted with reserved unction the Benefactor he saw in their greetings. "I think we are not strangers," he was good enough to remark, and very quickly let them know he had not breakfasted; on hearing which they hurried him into the house, and Lucy put herself in motion to have him served.

"Dear old Rady," said Richard, tugging at his hand again,

"how glad I am you've come! I don't mind telling you we've been horridly wretched."

"Six, seven, eight, nine eggs," was Adrian's comment on a survey of the breakfast-table.

"Why wouldn't he write? Why didn't he answer one of my letters? But here you are, so I don't mind now. He wants to see us, does he? We'll go up tonight. I've a match on at eleven; my little yacht—I've called her the 'Blandish'—against Fred Currie's 'Begum.' I shall beat, but whether I do or not, we'll go up tonight? What's the news? What are they all doing?"

"My dear boy!" Adrian returned, sitting comfortably down, "let me put myself a little more on an equal footing with you before I undertake to reply. Half that number of eggs will be sufficient for an unmarried man, and then we'll talk. They're all very well, as well as I can recollect after the shaking my total vacuity has had this morning. I came over by the first boat, and the sea, the sea has made me love mother earth, and desire of her fruits."

Richard fretted restlessly opposite his cool relative.

"Adrian! what did he say when he heard of it? I want to know exactly what words he said."

"Well says the Sage, my son! 'Speech is the small change of Silence.' He said less than I do."

"That's how he took it!" cried Richard, and plunged in meditation.

Soon the table was cleared, and laid out afresh, and Lucy preceded the maid bearing eggs on the tray, and sat down, unbonneted, and like a thorough-bred housewife, to pour out the tea for him.

"Now we'll commence," said Adrian, tapping his egg with meditative cheerfulness; but his expression soon changed to one of pain, all the more alarming for his benevolent efforts to conceal it. Could it be possible the egg was bad? oh, horror! Lucy watched him, and waited in trepidation.

"This egg has boiled three minutes and three quarters," he observed, ceasing to contemplate it.

"Dear, dear!" said Lucy, "I boiled them myself exactly that time. Richard likes them so. And you like them hard, Mr. Harley?"

"On the contrary, I like them soft. Two minutes and a half, or three-quarters at the outside. An egg should never rashly verge upon hardness—never. Three minutes is the excess of temerity."

"If Richard had told me! If I had only known!" the lovely little hostess interjected ruefully, biting her lip.

"We mustn't expect him to pay attention to such matters," said Adrian, trying to smile.

"Hang it! there are more eggs in the house," cried Richard, and pulled savagely at the bell.

Lucy jumped up, saying, "Oh, yes! I will go and boil some exactly the time you like. Pray let me go, Mr. Harley."

Adrian restrained her departure with a motion of his hand. "No," he said, "I will be ruled by Richard's tastes, and heaven grant me his digestion!"

Lucy threw a sad look at Richard, who stretched on a sofa and left the burden of the entertainment entirely to her. The eggs were a melancholy beginning, but her ardour to please Adrian would not be damped, and she deeply admired his resignation. If she failed in pleasing this glorious herald of peace, no matter by what small misadventure, she apprehended calamity: so there sat this fair dove with brows at work above her serious smiling blue eyes, covertly studying every aspect of the plump-faced epicure, that she might learn how to propitiate him. "He shall not think me timid and stupid," thought this brave girl, and indeed Adrian was astonished to find that she could both chat and be useful, as well as look ornamental. When he had finished one egg, behold, two fresh ones came in, boiled according to his prescription. She had quietly given her orders to the maid, and he had them without fuss. Possibly his look of dismay at the offending eggs had not been altogether involuntary, and her woman's instinct, inexperienced as she was, may have told her that he had come prepared to be not very well satisfied with anything in Love's cottage. There was mental faculty in those pliable brows to see through, and combat, an unwitting Wise Youth.

How much she had achieved already she partly divined when Adrian said: "I think now I'm in case to answer your questions, my dear boy—thanks to Mrs. Richard," and he bowed to her his first direct acknowledgment of her position. Lucy thrilled with pleasure.

"Ah!" went Richard, and settled easily on his back.

"To begin, the Pilgrim has lost his Note-book, and has been persuaded to offer a reward which shall maintain the happy finder thereof in an asylum for life.—What's this? Caviare? No, thank you, nothing coming from the sea after this morning.—Benson—superlative Benson—has turned his shoulders upon Raynham. None know whither he has departed. It is believed that the sole surviving member of the sect of the Shaddock-Dogmatists is under a total eclipse of Woman."

"Benson gone?" Richard exclaimed. "What a tremendous time it seems since I left Raynham!"

"So it is, my dear boy. The Honeymoon is Mahomet's minute: or say, the Persian King's water-pail that you read of in the story: You dip your head in it, and when you draw it out, you discover that you have lived a life. To resume: your Uncle Algernon still roams in pursuit of the lost one—I should say, hops. Your Uncle Hippias has a new and most perplexing symptom; a determination of Bridecake to the nose. Ever since your generous present to him, though he declares he never consumed a morsel of it, he has been under the distressing illusion that his nose is enormous, and I assure you he exhibits quite a maidenly timidity in following it—through a doorway, for instance. He complains of its terrible weight. I have conceived that Benson invisible might be sitting on it. His hand, and the doctor's, are in hourly consultation with it, but I fear it will not grow smaller. The Pilgrim has begotten upon it a new Aphorism: that Size is a matter of opinion. It is the last in the Note-book, and if they do with Note-books as it is the fashion to treat novels—turn from the commencement to the conclusion —the happy finder will have rapidly qualified himself to appreciate the full meaning of the reward.

"Poor Uncle Hippy!" said Richard, "I wonder he doesn't believe in magic. There's nothing supernatural to rival the wonderful sensations he does believe in. Good God! fancy coming to that!"

"I'm sure I'm very sorry," Lucy protested, "but I can't help laughing."

Charming to the Wise Youth her pretty laughter sounded.

"The Pilgrim has your notion, Richard. Whom does he not forestall? 'Confirmed Dyspepsia is the apparatus of illusions,' and he accuses the Ages that put faith in sorcery, of universal Indigestion, which may have been the case, owing to their infamous Cookery. He says again, if you remember, that our own Age is travelling back to darkness and Ignorance through dyspepsia. He lays the seat of wisdom in the centre of our system, Mrs. Richard: for which reason you will understand how sensible I am of the vast obligation I am under to you at the present moment, for your especial care of mine."

Richard looked on at Lucy's little triumph, attributing Adrian's subjugation to her beauty and sweetness. She had latterly received a great many compliments on that score, which she did not care to hear, and Adrian's homage to a practical quality was far pleasanter to the young wife, who shrewdly guessed that her beauty would not help her much in the struggle she had now to maintain. Adrian continuing to lecture on the excelling virtues of wise Cookery, a thought struck her: Where, where had she tossed Mrs. Berry's book?

"So that's all about the home-people?" said Richard.

"All!" replied Adrian. "Or stay; you know Clara's going to be married? Not? Your Aunt Helen—"

"Oh, bother my Aunt Helen! What do you think she had the impertinence to write?—but never mind! Is it to Ralph?"

"Your Aunt Helen, I was going to say, my dear boy, is an extraordinary woman. It was from her originally that the Pilgrim first learned to call the female the practical animal. He studies us all, you know. THE PILGRIM'S SCRIP is the abstract portraiture of his surrounding relatives. Well, your Aunt Helen—"

"Mrs. Doria Battledoria!" laughed Richard.

"—being foiled in a little pet scheme of her own—call it a System if you like—of some ten or fifteen years' standing, with regard to Miss Clare—"

"The fair Shuttlecockiana!"

"—instead of fretting like a man, and questioning Providence, and turning herself and everybody else inside out, and seeing the world upside down, what does the practical animal do? She wanted to marry her to somebody she couldn't marry her to, so she resolved instantly to marry her to somebody she could marry her to: and as old gentlemen enter into these transactions with the practical animal the most readily, she fixed upon an old gentleman; an unmarried old gentleman, a rich old gentleman, and now a captive old gentleman. The ceremony takes place in about a week from the present time. No doubt you will receive your invitation in a day or two."

"And that cold, icy, wretched Clare has consented to marry an old man!" groaned Richard. "I'll put a stop to that when I go to Town."

"Don't," said Adrian.

Richard got up and strode about the room. Then he bethought him it was time to go on board and make preparations.

"I'm off," he said. "Adrian, you'll take her. She goes

in the Empress, Mountfalcon's vessel. He starts us. A little schooner-yacht—such a beauty! I'll have one like her some day. Good-bye, darling!" he whispered to Lucy, and his hand and eyes lingered on her, and hers on him, seeking to make up for the priceless kiss they were debarred from. But she quickly looked away from him as he held her:—Adrian was silent: his brows were up, and his mouth dubiously contracted. He spoke at last.

"Go on the water?"

"Yes. It's only to St. Helen's. Short and sharp."

"Do you grudge me the nourishment my poor system has just received, my son?"

"Oh, bother your system! Put on your hat, and come along. I'll put you on board in my boat."

"Richard! I have already paid the penalty of them who are condemned to come to an island. I will go with you to the edge of the sea, and I will meet you there when you return, and take up the Tale of the Tritons: but, though I forfeit the pleasure of Mrs. Richard's company, I refuse to quit the land."

"Yes, oh, Mr. Harley!" Lucy broke from her husband, "and I will stay with you, if you please. I don't want to go among those people, and we can see it all from the shore. Dearest! I don't want to go. You don't mind? Of course, I will go if you wish, but I would so much rather stay;" and she lengthened her plea in her attitude and look to melt the discontent she saw gathering.

Adrian protested that she had much better go; that he could amuse himself very well till their return, and so forth: but she had schemes in her pretty head, and held to it to be allowed to stay in spite of Lord Mountfalcon's disappointment cited by Richard, and at the great risk of vexing her darling, as she saw. Richard pished, and glanced contemptuously at Adrian. He gave way ungraciously.

"There, do as you like. Get your things ready to leave this evening. No, I'm not angry."—"Who could be?" he seemed as he looked up from her modest fondling to ask Adrian, and seized the indemnity of a kiss on her forehead, which, however, did not immediately disperse the shade of annoyance he felt.

"Good Heavens!" he exclaimed. "Such a day as this, and a fellow refuses to come on the water! Well, come along to the edge of the sea." Adrian's angelic quality had quite worn off to him. He never thought of devoting himself to make the most of the material there was: but somebody else did, and that fair somebody succeeded wonderfully in a few short hours. She induced Adrian to reflect that the Baronet had only to see her, and the family muddle would be smoothed at once. He came to it by degrees; still the gradations were rapid. Her manner he liked: she was certainly a nice picture: best of all, she was sensible. He forgot the farmer's niece in her, she was so very sensible. She appeared really to understand that it was a woman's duty to know how to cook.

But the difficulty was, by what means the Baronet could be brought to consent to see her. He had not yet consented to see his son, and Adrian, spurred by Lady Blandish, had ventured something in coming down. He was not inclined to venture more. The small debate in his mind ended by his throwing the burden on time. Time would bring the matter about. Christians as well as Pagans are in the habit of phrasing this excuse for folding their arms; 'forgetful,' says THE PILGRIM'S SCRIP, 'that the Devil's imps enter into no such armistice.'

As she loitered along the shore with her amusing companion, Lucy had many things to think of. There was her darling's match. The yachts were started by pistol-shot by Lord Mountfalcon on board the Empress, and her little heart beat after Richard's straining sails. Then there was the strangeness of walking with a relation of Richard's, one who had lived by his side so long. And the thought that perhaps this night she would have to appear before the dreaded father of her husband.

"Oh, Mr. Harley!" she said, "is it true—are we to go tonight? And me," she faltered, "will he see me?"

"Ah! that is what I wanted to talk to you about," said Adrian. "I made some reply to our dear boy which he has slightly misinterpreted. Our second person plural is liable to misconstruction by an ardent mind. I said 'see you,' and he supposed—now, Mrs. Richard, I am sure you will understand me. Just at present perhaps it would be advisable—when the father and son have settled their accounts, the daughter-in-law can't be a debtor. . . ."

Lucy threw up her blue eyes. A half-cowardly delight at the chance of a respite from the awful interview made her quickly apprehensive.

"Oh, Mr. Harley! you think he should go alone first?"

"Well, that is my notion. But the fact is, he is such an excellent husband and I fancy it will require more than a man's power of persuasion to get him to go."

"But I will persuade him, Mr. Harley."

"Perhaps, if you would . . ."

"There is nothing I would not do for his happiness," murmured Lucy.

The Wise Youth pressed her hand with lymphatic approbation. They walked on till the yachts had rounded the point.

"Is it tonight, Mr. Harley," she asked with some trouble in her voice now that her darling was out of sight.

"I don't imagine your eloquence even will get him to leave you tonight," Adrian replied gallantly. "Besides, I must speak for myself. To achieve the passage to an island is enough for one day. No necessity exists for any hurry, except in the brain of that impetuous boy. You must correct it, Mrs. Richard. Men are made to be managed, and women are born managers. Now, if you were to let him know that you don't want to go tonight, and let him guess, after a day or two, that you would very much rather . . . you might affect a peculiar repugnance. By taking it on your-self, you see, this wild young man will not require such frightful efforts of persuasion. Both his father and he are exceedingly delicate subjects, and his father unfortunately is not in a position to be managed directly. It's a strange office to propose to you, but it appears to devolve upon you to manage the father through the son. Prodigal having made his peace, you, who have done all the work from a distance, naturally come into the circle of the paternal smile, knowing it due to you. I see no other way. If Richard suspects that his father objects for the present to welcome his daughter-in-law, hostilities will be continued, the breach will be widened, bad will grow to worse, and I see no end to it."

Adrian looked in her face, as much as to say: Now are you capable of this piece of heroism? And it did seem hard to her that she should have to tell Richard she shrank from any trial. But the proposition chimed in with her fears and her wishes: she thought the Wise Youth very wise: the poor child was not insensible to his flattery, and the subtler flattery of making herself in some measure a sacrifice to the home she had disturbed. She agreed to simulate as Adrian had suggested.

Victory is the commonest heritage of the Hero, and when Richard came on shore proclaiming that the Blandish had beaten the Begum by seven minutes and three quarters, he was hastily kissed and congratulated by his bride with her fingers among the leaves of Dr. Kitchener, and anxiously questioned about wine.

"Dearest! Mr. Harley wants to stay with us a little, and he thinks we ought not to go immediately—that is, be-fore he has had some letters, and I feel . . . I would so much rather . . ."

"Ah! that's it, you coward!" said Richard. "Well, then, tomorrow. We had a splendid race. Did you see us?"

"Oh, yes! I saw you and was sure my darling would win." And again she threw on him the cold water of that solicitude about wine. "Mr. Harley must have the best, you know, and we never drink it, and I'm so silly I don't know good wine, and if you would send Tom where he can get *good* wine. I have seen to the dinner."

"So that's why you didn't come to meet me?"

"Pardon me, darling."

"Well, I do, but Mountfalcon doesn't and Lady Judith thinks you ought to have been there."

"Ah, but my heart was with you!"

Richard put his hand to feel for the little heart: her eyelids softened, and she ran away.

It is to say much of the dinner that Adrian found no fault with it, and was in perfect good humour at the conclusion of the service. He did not abuse the wine they were able to procure for him, which was also much. The coffee, too, had the honour of passing without comment. These were sound first steps towards the conquest of an epicure, and as yet Cupid did not grumble.

After coffee they strolled out to see the sun set from Lady Judith's grounds. The wind had dropped. The clouds had rolled from the zenith, and ranged in amphitheatre with distant flushed bodies over sea and land: Titanic crimson head and chest rising from the wave faced Hyperion falling. There hung Briareus with deep-indented trunk and ravined brows, stretching all his hands up to unattainable blue summits. North-west the range had a rich white glow, as if shining to the moon, and westward, streams of amber, melting into the upper rose, shot out from the dipping disk.

"What Sandoe calls the passion-flower of Heaven," said Richard under his breath to Adrian, who was serenely chanting Greek hexameters, and answered, in the swing of the cæsura: "He might as well have said cauliflower."

Lady Judith, with a black lace veil tied over her head,

met them in the walk. She was tall and dark; dark-haired, dark-eyed, sweet and persuasive in her accent and manner. "A second edition of the Blandish," thinks Adrian. She welcomed him as one who had claims on her affability. She kissed Lucy protectingly, and remarking on the wonders of the evening, appropriated her husband. Adrian and Lucy found themselves walking behind them.

The sun was under. All the spaces of the sky were alight, and Richard's fancy flamed.

"So you're not intoxicated with your immense triumph this morning?" said Lady Judith.

"Don't laugh at me. When it's over I feel ashamed of the trouble I've taken. Look at that glory!—I'm sure you despise me for it."

"Was I not there to applaud you? I only think such energies should be turned into some definitely useful channel. But you must not go into the Army."

"What else can I do?"

"You are fit for so much that is better."

"I never can be anything like Austin."

"But I think you can do more."

"Well, I thank you for thinking it, Lady Judith. Something I will do. A man must deserve to live, as you say."

"Sauces," Adrian was heard to articulate distinctly in the rear, "Sauces are the top of the tree of this science. A woman who has mastered Sauces sits on the apex of civilization."

Briareus reddened duskily seaward. The West was all a burning rose round the one star.

"How can men see such sights as those, and live idle?" Richard resumed. "I feel ashamed of asking my men to work for me.—Or I feel so now."

"Not when you're racing the Begum, I think. There's no necessity for you to turn democrat like Austin. Do you write now?"

"No. What is writing like mine? It doesn't deceive

me. I know it's only the excuse I'm making to myself for remaining idle. I haven't written a line since—lately."

"Because you are so happy."

"No, not because of that. Of course I'm very happy . . ." He did not finish.

Vague, shapeless ambition had replaced Love in yonder skies. No Scientific Humanist was by to study the natural development, and guide him. This lady would hardly be deemed a very proper guide to the undirected energies of the youth, yet they had established relations of that nature. She was five years older than he, and a woman, which may explain her serene presumption.

The cloud-giants had broken up: a brawny shoulder smouldered over the sea.

"We'll work together in Town, at all events," said Richard. "Why can't we go about together at night and find out people who want help?"

Lady Judith smiled, and only corrected his nonsense by saying, "I think we mustn't be too romantic. You will become a knight-errant, I suppose. You have the characteristics of one."

"Especially at breakfast," Adrian's unnecessarily emphatic gastronomical lessons to the young wife here came in.

"You must be our champion," continued Lady Judith: "the rescuer and succourer of distressed dames and damsels. We want one badly."

"You do," said Richard earnestly: "from what I hear: from what I know!" His thoughts flew off with him as knight-errant hailed shrilly at exceeding critical moments by distressed dames and damsels. Images of airy towers hung around. His fancy performed miraculous feats. The towers crumbled. The one star grew larger, seemed to throb with lustre. His fancy crumbled with the towers of air, his heart gave a leap, he turned to Lucy.

"My darling! what have you been doing?" And as if to

compensate her for his little knight-errant infidelity, he pressed very tenderly to her.

"We have been engaged in a charming conversation on Domestic Cookery," interposed Adrian.

"Cookery! such an evening as this?" His face was a handsome likeness of Hippias at the presentation of Bride-cake.

"Dearest! you know it's very useful," Lucy mirthfully pleaded.

"Indeed I quite agree with you, child," said Lady Judith, "and I think you have the laugh of us. I certainly will learn to cook, some day."

"Woman's mission, in so many words," ejaculated Adrian.

"And pray, what is man's?"

"To taste thereof, and pronounce thereupon."

"Let us give it up to them," said Lady Judith to Richard. "You and I never will make so delightful and beautifully balanced a world of it."

Richard appeared to have grown perfectly willing to give everything up to the fair face, his bridal Hesper.

Next day Lucy had to act the coward anew, and as she did so, her heart sank to see how painfully it affected him that she should hesitate to go with him to his father. He was patient, gentle; he sat down by her side to appeal to her reason, and used all the arguments he could think of to persuade her.

"If we go together and make him see us both; if he sees he has nothing to be ashamed of in you—rather everything to be proud of; if you are only near him, you will not have to speak a word, and I'm certain—as certain as that I live—that in a week we shall be settled happily at Raynham. I know my father so well, Lucy. Nobody knows him but me."

Lucy asked whether Mr. Harley did not.

"Adrian? Not a bit. Adrian only knows a part of people, Lucy; and not the best part."

Lucy was disposed to think more highly of the object of her conquest.

"Is it he that has been frightening you, Lucy?"

"No, no, Richard; oh, dear no!" she cried, and looked at him more tenderly because she was not quite truthful.

"He doesn't know my father at all," said Richard. But Lucy had another opinion of the Wise Youth, and secretly maintained it. She could not be won to imagine the Baronet a man of human mould, generous, forgiving, full of passionate love at heart, as Richard tried to picture him, and thought him, now that he beheld him again through Adrian's embassy. To her he was that awful figure, shrouded by the midnight. "Why are you so harsh?" she had heard Richard cry more than once. She was sure that Adrian must be right.

"Well, I tell you I won't go without you," said Richard, and Lucy begged for a little more time.

Cupid now began to grumble, and with cause. Adrian positively refused to go on the water unless that element were smooth as a plate. The South-west still joked boisterously at any comparison of the sort: the days were magnificent: Richard had yachting engagements: and Lucy always petitioned to stay to keep Adrian company, conceiving it her duty as hostess. Arguing with Adrian was an absurd idea. If Richard hinted at his retaining Lucy, the Wise Youth would remark: "It's a wholesome interlude to your extremely Cupidinous behaviour, my dear boy."

Richard asked his wife what they could possibly find to talk about.

"All manner of things," said Lucy; "not only cookery. He is so amusing, though he does make fun of THE PILGRIM'S SCRIP, and I think he ought not. And then, do you know, darling—you won't think me vain?—I think he is beginning to like me a little."

Richard laughed at the humble mind of his beauty.

"Doesn't everybody like you, admire you? Doesn't Lord Mountfalcon, and Mr. Morton, and Lady Judith?"

"But he is one of your family, Richard."

"And they all will, if she isn't a coward."

"Ah, no!" she sighs, and is chid.

The Conquest of an Epicure, or any young wife's conquest beyond her husband, however loyally devised for their mutual happiness, may be costly to her. Richard in his hours of excitement was thrown very much with Lady Judith. He consulted her regarding what he termed Lucy's cowardice. Lady Judith said:

"I think she's wrong, but you must learn to humour little women."

"Then would you advise me to go up alone?" he asked, with a cloudy forehead.

"What else can you do? Be reconciled yourself as quickly as you can. You can't drag her like a captive, you know?"

It is not pleasant for a young husband, fancying his bride the peerless flower of Creation, to learn that he must humour a little woman in her. It was revolting to Richard.

"What I fear," he said, "is that my father will make it smooth with me, and not acknowledge her: so that whenever I go to him, I shall have to leave her, and tit for tat—an abominable existence, like a ball on a billiard-table. I won't bear that ignominy. And this I know, I know! she might prevent it at once, if she would only be brave, and face it. You, you, Lady Judith, you wouldn't be a coward?"

"Where my old lord tells me to go, I go," the lady coldly replied. "There's not much merit in that. Pray don't cite me. Women are born cowards, you know."

"But I love the women who are not cowards."

"The little thing—your wife has not refused to go?"

"No—but tears! Who can stand tears?"

Lucy had come to drop them. Unaccustomed to have his will thwarted, and urgent where he saw the thing to do so clearly, the young husband had spoken strong words: and she, who knew that she would have given her life by inches for him; who knew that she was playing a part for his happiness, and hiding for his sake the nature that was worthy his esteem; the poor little martyr had been weak a moment.

She had Adrian's support. The Wise Youth was very comfortable. He liked the air of the island, and he liked being petted. "A nice little woman! a very nice little woman!" Tom Bakewell heard him murmur to himself according to a habit he had; and his air of rather succulent patronage as he walked or sat beside the innocent beauty, with his head thrown back and a smile that seemed always to be in secret communion with his marked abdominal prominence, showed that she was gaining part of what she played for. Wise Youths who buy their loves, are not unwilling, when opportunity offers, to try and obtain the commodity for nothing. Examinations of her hand, as for some occult purpose, and unctuous pattings of the same, were not infrequent. Adrian waxed now and then Anacreontic in his compliments. Lucy would say: "That's worse than Lord Mountfalcon."

"Better English than the noble lord deigns to employ— allow that?" quoth Adrian.

"He is very kind," said Lucy.

"To all, save to our noble vernacular," added Adrian. 'He seems to scent a rival to his dignity there."

It may be that Adrian scented a rival to his lymphatic emotions.

"We are at our ease here in excellent society," he wrote to Lady Blandish. "I am bound to confess that the Huron has a happy fortune, or a superlative instinct. Blindfold he has seized upon a suitable mate. She can look at a Lord, and cook for an Epicure. Besides Dr. Kitchener, she reads and comments on THE PILGRIM'S SCRIP. The 'Love' chapter, of course, takes her fancy. That picture of Woman, *'Drawn by Reverence and coloured by Love,'* she thinks beau-

tiful, and repeats it, tossing up pretty eyes. Also the lovers'
petition: *'Give me purity to be worthy the good in her, and
grant her patience to reach the good in me.'* 'Tis quite taking to hear her lisp it. Be sure that I am repeating the
petition! I make her read me her choice passages. She
has not a bad voice.

"The Lady Judith I spoke of is Austin's Miss Menteith
married to the incapable old Lord Felle, or Fellow, as the
wits here call him. Lord Mountfalcon is his cousin, and
her—what? She has been trying to find out, but they have
both got over their perplexity, and act respectively the bad
man reproved and the chaste counsellor; a position in which
our young couple found them, and haply diverted its perils.
They have quite taken them in hand. Lady Judith under-
takes to cure the fair Papist of a pretty, modest trick of
frowning and blushing when addressed, and his Lordship
directs the exuberant energies of the original man. 'Tis
thus we fulfil our destinies and are content. Sometimes
they change pupils; my Lord educates the little dame, and
my Lady the Hope of Raynham. Joy and blessings unto
all! as the German poet sings. Lady Judith accepted the
hand of her incapable lord that she might be of potent service
to her fellow-creatures. Austin, you know, had great hopes
of her.

"I have for the first time in my career a field of lords to
study. I think it is not without meaning that I am introduced to it by a yeoman's niece. The language of the two
social extremes is similar. I find it to consist in an instinctively lavish use of vowels and adjectives. My Lord and
farmer Blaize speak the same tongue, only my Lord's has
lost its backbone, and is limp, though fluent. Their pursuits are identical; but that one has money, or, as the Pilgrim terms it, *vantage,* and the other has not. Their ideas
seem to have a special relationship in the peculiarity of stopping where they have begun. Young Tom Blaize with
vantage would be Lord Mountfalcon. Even in the char-

acter of their parasites I see a resemblance, though I am bound to confess that the Hon. Peter Brayder, who is my Lord's parasite, is by no means noxious.

"This sounds dreadfully democratic. Pray don't be alarmed. The discovery of the affinity between the two extremes of the Royal British Oak has made me thrice conservative. I see now that the national love of a lord is less subservience than a form of self-love; putting a gold-lace hat on one's image, as it were, to bow to it. I see, too, the admirable wisdom of our system:—could there be a finer balance of power than in a community where men intellectually nil, have lawful vantage and a gold-lace hat on? How soothing it is to Intellect—that noble rebel, as the Pilgrim has it—to stand, and bow, and know itself superior! This exquisite compensation maintains the balance: whereas that period anticipated by the Pilgrim, when science shall have produced an intellectual aristocracy, is indeed horrible to contemplate. For what despotism is so black as one the mind cannot challenge? 'T will be an Iron Age. Wherefore, Madame, I cry, and shall continue to cry, 'Vive Lord Mountfalcon! long may he sip his Burgundy! long may the bacon-fed carry him on their shoulders!'

"Mr. Morton (who does me the honour to call me Young Mephisto, and Socrates missed) leaves tomorrow to get Master Ralph out of a scrape. Our Richard has just been elected member of a club for the promotion of nausea. Is he happy? you ask. As much so as one who has had the misfortune to obtain what he wanted can be. Speed is his passion. He races from point to point. In emulation of Leander and Don Juan, he swam, I hear, to the opposite shores the other day, or some world-shaking feat of the sort: himself the Hero whom he went to meet: or, as they who pun say, his Hero was a Bet. A pretty little domestic episode occurred this morning. He finds her abstracted in the fire of his caresses: she turns shy and seeks solitude: green jealousy takes hold of him: he lies in wait, and discovers her with his new rival—a veteran edition of the culinary Doctor! Blind to the Doctor's great national services, deaf to her wild music, he grasps the intruder, dismembers him, and performs upon him the treatment he has recommended for dressed cucumber. Tears and shrieks accompany the descent of the gastronome. Down she rushes to secure the cherished fragments: he follows: they find him, true to his character, alighted and straggling over a bed of blooming flowers. Yet ere a fairer flower can gather him, a heel black as Pluto's stamps him into earth, flowers and all:— happy burial! Pathetic tribute to his merit is watering his grave, when by saunters my Lord Mountfalcon. 'What's the mattah?' says his Lordship, soothing his moustache. They break apart, and 't is left to me to explain from the window. My Lord looks shocked, Richard is angry with her for having to be ashamed of himself, Beauty dries her eyes, and after a pause of general foolishness, the business of life is resumed. I may add that the Doctor has just been dug up, and we are busy, in the enemy's absence, renewing old Æson with enchanted threads."

A month had passed when Adrian wrote this letter. He was very comfortable; so of course he thought Time was doing his duty. Not a word did he say of Richard's return, and for some reason or other neither Richard nor Lucy spoke of it now.

Lady Blandish wrote back: "His father thinks he has refused to come to him. By your utter silence on the subject, I fear that it must be so. Make him come. Bring him by force. *Insist* on his coming. Is he mad? He must come *at once.*"

To this Adrian replied, after a contemplative comfortable lapse of a day or two, which might be laid to his efforts to adopt the lady's advice: "The point is that the half man declines to come without the whole man. The terrible question of sex is our obstruction."

Lady Blandish was in despair. She had no positive assurance that the Baronet would see his son: the Mask put them all in the dark: but she thought she saw irritation that the offender, at least when the opening to come and make his peace seemed to be before him, should let days and weeks go by. She saw through the mask sufficiently not to have any hope of his consenting to receive the couple at present: she was sure that his equanimity was fictitious: but she pierced no farther, or she might have started and asked herself: Is this the heart of a woman?

The lady at last wrote to Richard. She said: "Come instantly, and come alone." Then Richard, against his judgment, gave way. "My father is not the man I thought him!" he exclaimed sadly, and Lucy felt his eyes saying to her: "And you, too, are not the woman I thought you." Nothing could the poor little heart reply but strain to his bosom and pray in his arms sleeplessly all the night.

CHAPER XXXIX

CLARE'S MARRIAGE

THREE weeks after Richard arrived in Town, his cousin Clare was married, under the blessings of her energetic mother, and with the approbation of her kinsfolk, to the husband that had been expeditiously chosen for her. The gentleman, though something more than twice the age of his bride, had no idea of approaching senility for many long connubial years to come. Backed by his tailor and his hairdresser, he presented no such bad figure at the altar, and none would have thought that he was an ancient admirer of his bride's Mama, as certainly none knew he had lately proposed to Mrs. Doria before there was any question of her daughter. These things were secrets; and the elastic and happy appearance of Mr. John Todhunter did not betray them at the altar. Perhaps he would rather have married the mother. He was a man of property, well born, tolerably well educated, and had, when Mrs. Doria rejected him for the first time, the reputation of being a fool—which a wealthy man may have in his youth; but as he lived on, and did not squander his money—amassed it, on the contrary, and did not seek to go into Parliament, and did other negative wise things, the world's opinion, as usual, veered completely round, and John Todhunter was esteemed a shrewd sensible man—only not brilliant: that he was brilliant could not be said of him. In fact the man could hardly talk, and it was a fortunate provision that no impromptu deliveries were required of him in the Marriage-service.

Mrs. Doria had her own reasons for being in a hurry. She had discovered something of the strange impassive nature of her child; not from any confession of Clare's, but from signs a mother can read when her eyes are not resolutely shut. She saw with alarm and anguish Clare had fallen into the pit she had been digging for her so laboriously. In vain she entreated the Baronet to break the disgraceful, and, as she said, illegal alliance his son had contracted. Sir Austin would not even stop the little pension to poor Berry. "At least you will do that, Austin," she begged pathetically. "You will show your sense of that horrid woman's conduct?" He refused to offer up any victim to console her. Then Mrs. Doria told him her thoughts,—and when an outraged energetic lady is finally brought to exhibit these painfully hoarded treasures, she does not use half words as a medium. His System, and his conduct generally, were denounced to him, without analysis. She let him understand that the world laughed at him; and he heard this from her at a time when his mask was still soft and liable to be acted on by his nerves. "You are weak, Austin! weak, I tell you!" she said, and, like all angry and self-interested people, prophecy came easy to her. In her heart she accused him of her own fault, in imputing to him the wreck of her project. The Baronet allowed her to revel in the proclamation of a dire future, and quietly counselled her to keep apart from him, which his sister assured him she would do.

But to be passive in calamity is the province of no woman. Mark the race at any hour. 'What revolution and hubbub does not that little instrument, the needle, avert from us!' says THE PILGRIM'S SCRIP. Alas, that in calamity women cannot stitch! Now that she saw Clare wanted other than iron, it struck her she must have a husband, and be made secure as a woman and a wife. This seemed the thing to do: and, as she had forced the iron down Clare's throat, so she forced the husband, and Clare gulped at the latter as she had at the former. On the very day that Mrs. Doria had this new track shaped out before her, John Todhunter called at the Foreys'. "Old John!" sang out Mrs. Doria, "show him up to me. I want to see him particularly." He sat with her alone. He was a man multitudes of women would have married—whom will they not?—and who would have married any presentable woman: but women do want asking, and John never had the word. The rape of such men is left to the practical animal. So John sat alone with his old flame. He had become resigned to her perpetual lamentation and living Suttee for his defunct rival. But ha! what meant those soft glances now—addressed to him? His tailor and his hairdresser gave youth to John, but they had not the art to bestow upon him distinction, and an undistinguished man what woman looks at? John was an indistinguishable man. For that reason he was dry wood to a soft glance. He was quickly incandescent. He proposed, at the close of an hour's conflagration, thus: "Aren't you ever going to change your state, Helen?"

"Oh, no! never, indeed!" the fair widow replied.

"Then it's a shame," muttered John, thinking how many children and cries of 'Papa' this woman—to whom he fancied he had been constantly, utterly devoted—owed him.

Ere he could fall back upon his accustomed resignation, Mrs. Doria had assured the man that she knew of no one who would make so good a husband, no one she would like so well to have related to her.

"And you ought to be married, John: you know you ought."

"But if I can't have her?" returned John, staring stupidly at her enigmatical forefinger.

"Well, well! might you not have something better?"

Mr. Todhunter gallantly denied the possibility of that.

"Something younger is something better, John. No. I'm not young, and I intend to remain what I am. Put me by. You must marry a young woman, John. You are well preserved—younger than most of the young men of our day. You are eminently domestic, a good son, and will be a good husband and good father. Some one you must marry. —What do you think of Clare for a wife for you?"

At first John Todhunter thought it would be very much like his marrying a baby. However, he listened to it, and that was enough for Mrs. Doria. "I'll do the wooing for you, John," she said.

She did more. She went down to John's mother, and consulted with her on the propriety of the scheme of wedding her daughter to John in accordance with his position. Mrs. Todhunter's jealousy of any disturbing force in the influence she held over her son Mrs. Doria knew to be one of the causes of John's remaining constant to the impression she had aforetime produced on him. She spoke so kindly of John, and laid so much stress on the ingrained obedience and passive disposition of her daughter, that Mrs. Todhunter was led to admit she did think it almost time John should be seeking a mate, and that he—all things considered—would hardly find a fitter one. And this, John Todhunter—old John no more—heard to his amazement when, a day or two subsequently, he instanced the probable disapproval of his mother.

The match was arranged. Mrs. Doria did the wooing. It consisted in telling Clare that she had come to years when marriage was desirable, and that she had fallen into habits of moping which might have the worse effect on her future life, as it had on her present health and appearance, and which a husband would cure. Richard was told by Mrs. Doria that Clare had instantaneously consented to accept Mr. John Todhunter as lord of her days, and with more than obedience,—with alacrity. At all events, when Richard spoke to Clare, the strange passive creature did not admit restraint on her inclinations. Mrs. Doria allowed Richard to speak to her. She laughed at his futile endeavours to undo her work, and the boyish sentiments he uttered on the subject. "Let us see, child," she said, "let us see which turns out the best; a marriage of passion, or a marriage of common sense."

Heroic efforts were not wanting to arrest the union. Richard made repeated journeys to Hounslow, where Ralph was quartered, and if Ralph could have been persuaded to carry off a young lady who did not love him, from the bridegroom her mother averred she did love, Mrs. Doria might have been defeated. But Ralph in his cavalry quarters was cooler than Ralph in the Bursley meadows. "Women are oddities, Dick," he remarked, running a finger right and left along his upper lip. "Best leave 'em to their own freaks. She's a dear girl, though she don't talk: I like her for that. If she cared for me I'd go the race. She don't, and never did. It's no use asking a girl twice. *She* knows whether she cares a fig for a fellow. My belief, Mr. Dick, is that she's in love with you, if it's anybody."

The Hero quitted him with some contempt, saying to himself, "I believe he's nothing more than an embroidered jacket now." But as Ralph Morton was a young man, and he had determined that John Todhunter was an old man, he sought another private interview with Clare, and getting her alone, said: "Clare, I've come to you for the last time. Will you marry Ralph Morton?"

To which Clare replied: "I cannot marry two husbands, Richard."

"Will you refuse to marry this old man?"

"I must do as Mama wishes."

"Then you're going to marry an old man—a man you don't love, and can't love! Oh, good God! do you know what you're doing?" He flung about in a fury. "Do you know what it is? Clare!" he caught her two hands violently, "have you any idea of the horror you're going to commit?"

She shrank a little at his vehemence, but neither blushed nor stammered; answering: "I see nothing wrong in doing what Mama thinks right, Richard."

"Your mother! I tell you it's an infamy, Clare! It's a miserable sin! I tell you, if I had done such a thing I would not live an hour after it. And coldly to prepare for it! to be busy about your dresses! They told me when I came in that you were with the milliner. To be smiling over the horrible outrage! decorating yourself!" . . . He burst into tears.

"Dear Richard," said Clare, "you will make me very unhappy."

"That one of my blood should be so debased!" he cried, brushing angrily at his face. "Unhappy! I beg you to feel for yourself, Clare. But I suppose," and he said it scornfully, "girls don't feel this sort of shame."

She grew a trifle paler.

"Next to Mama, I would wish to please you, dear Richard."

"Have you no will of your own?" he exclaimed.

She looked at him softly; a look he interpreted for the meekness he detested in her.

"No, I believe you have none!" he added. "And what can I do? I can't step forward and stop this accursed marriage. If you would say a word I would save you: but you tie my hands. And they expect me to stand by, and see it done!"

"Will you not be there, Richard?" said Clare, following the question with her soft eyes. It was the same voice that had so thrilled him on his marriage-morn.

"Oh, my darling Clare!" he cried in the kindest way he had ever used to her, "if you knew how I feel this!" and now as he wept she wept, and came insensibly into his arms. "My darling Clare!" he repeated.

She said nothing, but seemed to shudder, weeping.

"You *will* do it, Clare? You will be sacrificed? So lovely as you are, too! Oh! to think of that mouth being given over to . . . O curses of Hell! to think . . . Clare! you cannot be quite blind. If I dared speak to you, and tell you all . . . Look up. Can you still consent?"

"I must not disobey Mama," Clare murmured, without looking up from the nest her cheek had made on his bosom.

"Then kiss me for the last time," said Richard. "I'll never kiss you after it, Clare."

He bent his head to meet her mouth, and she threw her arms wildly round him, and kissed him convulsively, and clung to his lips, shutting her eyes, her face suffused with a burning red.

Then he left her, unaware of the meaning of those passionate kisses.

Argument with Mrs. Doria was like firing paper-pellets against a stone-wall. To her indeed the young married Hero spoke almost indecorously, and that his delicacy withheld him from speaking to Clare. He could provoke nothing more responsive from the practical animal than, "Pooh-pooh!" "Tush, tush!" and "Fiddlesticks!"

"Really," Mrs. Doria said to her intimates, "that boy's education acts like a disease on him. He cannot regard anything sensibly. He is for ever in some mad excess of his fancy, and what he will come to at last Heaven only knows! I sincerely pray that Austin will be able to bear it."

Threats of prayer, however, that harp upon their sincerity, are not very well worth having. Mrs. Doria had embarked in a practical controversy, as it were, with her brother. Doubtless she did trust he would be able to bear his sorrows to come, but one who has uttered prophecy can barely help hoping to see it fulfilled: she had prophesied much grief to the Baronet.

Poor John Todhunter, who would rather have married the mother, and had none of your heroic notions about the sacred necessity for Love in Marriage, moved as one guiltless of offence, and that deserves his happiness. Mrs. Doria shielded him from the Hero. To see him smile at Clare's obedient figure, and try not to look paternal, was touching.

Meantime Clare's Marriage served one purpose. It completely occupied Richard's mind, and prevented him from chafing at the vexation of not finding his father ready to meet him when he came to Town. A letter had awaited Adrian at the hotel, which said: "Detain him till you hear further from me. Take him about with you into every form of society." No more than that. Adrian had to extemporize that the Baronet had gone down to Wales on pressing business, and would be back in a week or so. For ulterior inventions and devices wherewith to keep the young gentleman in Town, he applied to Mrs. Doria. "Leave him to me," said Mrs. Doria, "I'll manage him." And she did.

'Who can say,' asks THE PILGRIM'S SCRIP, 'when he is not walking a puppet to some woman?'

Mrs. Doria would hear no good of Lucy. "I believe," she observed, as Adrian ventured a shrugging protest in her behalf,—"it is my firm opinion that a scullery-maid would turn any of you men round her little finger—only give her time and opportunity." By dwelling on the arts of women, she reconciled it to her conscience to do her best to divide the young husband from his wife till it pleased his father they should live their unhallowed union again. Without compunction, or a sense of incongruity, she abused her brother and assisted the fulfilment of his behests.

So the puppets were marshalled by Mrs. Doria, happy, or sad, or indifferent. Quite against his set resolve and the tide of his feelings, Richard found himself standing behind Clare in the Church,—the very edifice that had witnessed his own marriage, and heard, "I Clare Doria take thee John Pemberton," clearly pronounced. He stood with black brows dissecting the arts of the tailor and hairdresser on unconscious John. The back, and much of the middle, of Mr. Todhunter's head was bald; the back shone like an egg-shell, but across the middle the artist had drawn two long dabs of hair from the sides, and plastered them cunningly, so that all save wilful eyes would have acknowledged the head to be well covered. The man's only pretension was to a respectable juvenility. He had a good chest, stout limbs, a face inclined to be jolly. Mrs. Doria had no cause to be put out of countenance at all by the exterior of her son-in-law: nor was she. Her splendid hair and gratified smile made a light in the Church. Playing puppets must be an immense pleasure to the practical animal. The Forey bridesmaids, five in number, and one Miss Doria, their cousin, stood as girls do stand at these sacrifices, whether happy, sad, or indifferent: a smile on their lips and tears in attendance. Old Mrs. Todhunter, an exceedingly small ancient woman, was also there. "I can't have my boy John married without seeing it done," she said, and throughout the ceremony she was muttering audible encomiums on her boy John's manly behaviour.

The Ring was affixed to Clare's finger: there was no Ring lost in this common-sense marriage. John had his disengaged hand at his waistcoat-pocket, and the instant the clergyman bade him employ it, he drew the Ring out, and dropped it on the finger of the cold passive hand in a business-like way, as one who had studied the matter. Mrs. Doria glanced aside at Richard. Richard observed

Clare spread out her fingers that the operation might be the more easily effected.

He did duty in the vestry a few minutes, and then said to his Aunt:

"Now I'll go."

"You'll come to the breakfast, child? The Foreys—"

He cut her short. "I've stood for the family, and I'll do no more. I won't pretend to eat and make merry over it."

"Richard!"

"Good-bye."

She had attained her object, and she wisely gave way.

"Well. Go and kiss Clare, and shake his hand. Pray, pray be civil."

She turned to Adrian, and said: "He is going. You must go with him, and find some means of keeping him, or he'll be running off to that woman. Now, no words —go!"

Richard bade Clare farewell. She put up her mouth to him humbly, but he kissed her on the forehead.

"Do not cease to love me," she said in a quavering whisper in his ear.

Mr. Todhunter stood beaming and endangering the art of the hairdresser with his pocket-handkerchief. Now he positively was married, he thought he would rather have the daughter than the mother, which is a reverse of the order of human thankfulness at a gift of the Gods.

"Richard, my boy!" he said heartily, "congratulate me."

"I should be happy to, if I could," sedately replied the Hero, to the consternation of those around. Nodding to the bridesmaids and bowing to the old lady, he passed out.

Adrian, who had been behind him, deputed to watch for a possible unpleasantness, just hinted to John: "You know, poor fellow, he has got into a mess with his marriage."

"Oh! ah! yes!" kindly said John, "poor fellow!"

All the puppets then rolled off to the breakfast.

Adrian hurried after Richard in an extremely disconsolate state of mind. Not to be at the breakfast and see the best of the fun, disgusted him. However, he remembered that he was a philosopher, and the strong disgust he felt was only expressed in concentrated cynicism on every earthly matter engendered by the conversation. They walked side by side into Kensington Gardens. The Hero was mouthing away to himself, talking by fits.

Presently he faced Adrian, crying: "And I might have stopped it! I see it now! I might have stopped it by going straight to him, and asking him if he dared marry a girl who did not love him. And I never thought of it. Good Heaven! I feel this miserable affair on my conscience."

"Ah!" went Adrian. "Hum! An unpleasant cargo for the conscience, that! I would rather carry anything on mine than a married couple. Do you purpose going to him now?"

The Hero soliloquized: "He's not a bad sort of man . . ."

"Well, he's not a Cavalier," said Adrian, "and that's why you wonder your Aunt selected him, no doubt? He's decidedly of the Roundhead type, with the Puritan extracted, or inoffensive, if latent."

"There's the double infamy!" cried Richard, "that a man you can't call bad, should do this damned thing!"

"Well, it's hard we can't find a villain."

"He would have listened to me, I'm sure."

"Go to him now, Richard, my son. Go to him now. It's not yet too late. Who knows? if he really has a noble elevated superior mind—though not a Cavalier in person, he may be one at heart—he might, to please you, and since you put such stress upon it, abstain . . . perhaps with some loss of dignity, but never mind. And the request might be singular, or seem so, but everything has happened before in this world, you know, my dear boy. And what an infinite consolation it is for the eccentric, that reflection!—Eh?"

The Hero was impervious to the Wise Youth. He stared at him as if he were but a speck in the universe he visioned.

It was provoking that Richard should be Adrian's best subject for cynical pastime, in the extraordinary heterodoxies he started, and his worst in the way he took it; and the Wise Youth, against his will, had to feel as conscious of the young man's imaginative mental armour, as he was of his muscular physical.

"The same sort of day!" mused Richard, looking up. "I suppose my father's right. We make our own fates, and Nature has nothing to do with it."

Adrian yawned.

"Some difference in the trees, though," Richard continued abstractedly.

"Growing bald at the top," said Adrian. "Do they suggest the bridegroom to you?"

"Will you believe that my Aunt Helen compared the conduct of that wretched slave Clare to Lucy's, who, she had the cruel insolence to say, entangled me into marriage?" the Hero broke out loudly and rapidly. "You know—I told you, Adrian—how I had to threaten and insist, and how she pleaded, and implored me to wait."

"Ah! Hum!" went Adrian.

"Don't you remember my telling you?" Richard was earnest to hear her exonerated.

"Pleaded and implored, my dear boy? Oh, no doubt she did. Where's the lass 'that doesn't."

"Call my wife by another name, if you please."

"The generic title can't be cancelled because of your having married one of the body, my son."

"She did all she could to persuade me to wait!" emphasized Richard.

Adrian shook his head with a deplorable smile.

"Come, come, my good Ricky; not all; not all!"

Richard bellowed: "What more could she have done?"

"She could have shaved her head, for instance."

This happy shaft did stick. With a furious exclamation Richard shot in front, Adrian following him; and asking him (merely to have the assumption verified), whether he did not think she might have shaved her head? and, presuming her to have done so, whether, in candour, he did not think he would have waited—at least till she looked less of a rank lunatic?

After a minute or so, the Wise Youth was but a fly buzzing about Richard's head. Three weeks of separation from Lucy, and an excitement deceased, caused him to have soft yearnings for the dear lovely home-face. He told Adrian it was his intention to go down that night. Adrian immediately became serious. He was at a loss what to invent to detain him, beyond the stale fiction that his father was coming tomorrow. He rendered homage to the genius of woman in these straits. "My Aunt," he thought, "would have the lie ready; and not only that, but she would take care it did its work."

At this juncture the voice of the cavalier in the Row hailed them, proving to be the Honourable Peter Brayder, Lord Mountfalcon's parasite. He greeted them very cordially; and Richard, remembering some fun they had in the island, asked him to dine with them; postponing his return till the next day. Lucy was his. It was even sweet to dally with the delight of seeing her.

The Honourable Peter was one who did honour to the body he belonged to. Though not so tall as a West of London footman, he was as shapely; and he had a power of making his voice insinuating, or arrogant, as it suited the exigencies of his profession. He had not a rap of money in the world; yet he rode a horse, lived high, expended largely. The world said that the Honourable Peter was salaried by his Lordship, and that, in common with that of Parasite, he exercised the ancient companion profession. This the world said, and still smiled at the Honourable

Peter; for he was an engaging fellow, and where he went not Lord Mountfalcon would not go.

They had a quiet little hotel dinner, ordered by Adrian, and made a square at the table, Ripton Thompson being the fourth. Richard sent down to his office to fetch him, and the two friends shook hands for the first time since the great deed had been executed. Deep was the Old Dog's delight to hear the praises of his Beauty sounded by such aristocratic lips as the Hon. Peter Brayder's. All through the dinner he was throwing out hints and small queries to get a fuller account of her; and when the claret had circulated, he spoke a word or two himself, and heard the Honourable Peter eulogize his taste, and wish him a bride as beautiful; at which Ripton blushed, and said, he had no hope of that, and the Honourable Peter assured him Marriage did not break the mould.

After the wine the Honourable Peter took his cigar on the balcony and found occasion to get some conversation with Adrian alone.

"Our young friend here—made it all right with the governor?" he asked carelessly.

"Oh, yes!" said Adrian. But it struck him that Brayder might be of assistance in showing Richard a little of the 'society in every form' required by his Chief's prescript. "That is," he continued, "we are not yet permitted an interview with the august author of our being, and I have rather a difficult post. 'T is mine both to keep him here, and also to find him the opportunity to measure himself with his fellow-man. In other words, his father wants him to see something of life before he enters upon housekeeping. Now I am proud to confess that I'm hardly equal to the task. The demi—or damned-monde—if it's that he wants him to observe—is one I have not got the walk to."

"Ha! ha!" laughed the Honourable Peter. "You do the keeping, I offer to parade the demi. I must say, though, it's a queer notion of the old gentleman."

"It's the continuation of a philosophic plan," said Adrian.

The Honourable Peter followed the curvings of the whiff of his cigar with his eyes, and ejaculated: "Infahnally philosophic!"

"Has Lord Mountfalcon left the island?" Adrian inquired.

"Mount? to tell the truth I don't know where he is. Chasing some light craft, I suppose. That's poor Mount's weakness. It's his ruin, poor fellow! He's so confoundedly in earnest at the game."

"He ought to know it by this time, if fame speaks true," remarked Adrian.

"He's a baby about women, and always will be," said Brayder. "He's been once or twice wanting to marry them. Now there's a woman—you've heard of Mrs. Mount? All the world knows her.—If that woman hadn't scandalized—" The young man joined them, and checked the communication. Brayder winked to Adrian, and pitifully indicated the presence of an innocent.

"A married man, you know," said Adrian.

"Yes, yes!—but we won't shock him," the Honourable Peter observed, patting Richard on the back. He appeared to study the young man while they talked.

Next morning Richard was surprised by a visit from his Aunt. Mrs. Doria took a seat by his side, and spoke as follows:

"My dear Nephew. Now you know I have always loved you, and thought of your welfare as if you had been my own child. More than that, I fear. Well, now, you are thinking of returning to—to that place—are you not? Yes. It is as I thought. Very well now, let me speak to you. You are in a much more dangerous position than you imagine. I don't deny your father's affection for you. It would be absurd to deny it. But you are of an age now to appreciate his character. Whatever you may do he will always give you money. That you are sure of. That

you know. Very well. But you are one to want
more than money: you want his love. Richard, I am
convinced you will never be happy, whatever base
pleasures you may be led into, if he should withhold
his love from you. Now, child, you know you have
grievously offended him. I wish not to animadvert on your
conduct.—You fancied yourself in love, and so on, and
you were rash. The less said of it the better now. But you
must now—it is your duty now to do something—to do
everything that lies in your power to show him you repent. No interruptions! Listen to me. You must consider
him. Austin is not like other men. Austin requires the most
delicate management. You must—whether you feel it or
no—present an appearance of contrition. I counsel it for
the good of all. He is just like a woman, and where
his feelings are offended he wants utter subservience. He
has you in Town, and he does not see you—now you
know that he and I are not in communication: we have
likewise our differences:—Well, he has you in Town, and
he holds aloof:—he is trying you, my dear Richard. No: he
is not at Raynham: I do not know where he is. He is
trying you, child, and you must be patient. You must con-
vince him that you do not care utterly for your own gratification. If this person—I wish to speak of her with respect, for your sake—well, if she loves you *at all*—if, I
says, she loves you *one atom,* she will repeat my solicitations
for you to stay and patiently wait here till he consents to
see you. I tell you candidly, it's your only chance of
ever getting him to receive *her*. That you should know.
And now, Richard, I may add that there is something else
you should know. You should know that it depends
entirely upon your conduct now, whether you are to see your
father's heart for ever divided towards you, and a new family at Raynham. You do not understand? I will explain.
Brothers and sisters are excellent things for young people, but
a new brood of them can hardly be acceptable to a young

man. In fact, they are, and must be, aliens. I only tell you what I have heard on good authority. Don't you understand now? Foolish boy! if you do not humour him, he will marry Lady Blandish. Oh! I am sure of it. I know it. And this you will drive him to. I do not warn you on the score of your prospects, but of your feelings. I should regard such a contingency, Richard, as a final division between you. Think of the scandal! but alas, that is the least of the evils."

It was Mrs. Doria's object to produce an impression, and avoid an argument. She therefore left him as soon as she had, as she supposed, made her mark on the young man. Richard was very silent during the speech, and, save for an exclamation or so, had listened attentively. He pondered on what his Aunt said. He loved Lady Blandish, and yet he did not wish to see her Lady Feverel. Mrs. Doria laid painful stress on the scandal, and though he did not give his mind to this, he thought of it. He thought of his mother. Where was she? But most his thoughts recurred to his father, and something akin to jealousy slowly awakened his heart to him. He had given him up, and had not latterly felt extremely filial; but he could not bear the idea of a division in the love of which he had ever been the idol and sole object. And such a man, too! so good! so generous! If it was jealousy that roused the young man's heart to his father, the better part of Love was also revived in it. He thought of old days: of his father's forbearance, his own wilfulness. He looked on himself, and what he had done, with the eyes of such a man. He determined to do all he could to regain his favour.

Mrs. Doria learnt from Adrian in the evening that her nephew intended waiting in Town another week.

"That will do," smiled Mrs. Doria. "He will be more patient at the end of a week."

"Oh! does Patience beget Patience?" said Adrian. "I was not aware it was a propagating virtue. I surrender him to

you. I shan't be able to hold him in after one week more.
I assure you, my dear Aunt, he's already . . ."

"Thank you, no explanation," Mrs. Doria begged.

When Richard saw her next, he was informed that she
had received a most satisfactory letter from Mrs. John
Todhunter: quite a glowing account of John's behaviour:
but on Richard's desiring to know the words Clare had
written, Mrs. Doria objected to be explicit, and shot into
worldly gossip.

"Clara seldom glows," said Richard.

"No, I mean for her," his Aunt remarked. "Don't look
like your father, child."

"I should like to have seen the letter," said Richard.

Mrs. Doria did not propose to show it.

CHAPTER XL

A DINNER PARTY AT RICHMOND

A LADY driving a pair of greys was noticed by Richard
in his rides and walks. She passed him rather obviously and
often. She was very handsome; a bold beauty, with shining
black hair, red lips, and eyes not afraid of men. The hair
was brushed from her temples, leaving one of those fine
reckless outlines which the action of driving, and the pace,
so admirably set off. She took his fancy. He liked the air
of petulant gallantry about her, and mused upon the picture,
rare to him, of a glorious dashing woman. He thought, too,
she looked at him. He was not at the time inclined to be
vain or he might have been sure she did. Once it struck
him she nodded slightly.

He asked Adrian one day in the park—who she was.

"I don't know her," said Adrian. "Probably a superior
priestess of Paphos."

"Now that's my idea of Bellona," Richard exclaimed.

"Not the Fury they paint, but a spirited, dauntless, eager-looking creature like that."

"Bellona?" returned the Wise Youth. "I don't think her hair was black. Red, wasn't it? I shouldn't compare her to Bellona; though, no doubt, she's as ready to spill blood. Look at her! She does seem to scent carnage. I see your idea. No; I should liken her to Diana emerged from the tutorship of Master Endymion, and at nice play among the Gods. Depend upon it—they tell us nothing of the matter —Olympus shrouds the story—but you may be certain that when she left the pretty shepherd she had greater vogue than Venus up aloft."

Brayder joined them.

"See Mrs. Mount go by?" he said.

"Oh, that's Mrs. Mount!" cried Adrian.

"Who's Mrs. Mount?" Richard inquired.

"A sister to Miss Random, my dear boy."

"Like to know her?" drawled the Honourable Peter.

Richard replied indifferently, "No," and Mrs. Mount passed out of sight and out of the conversation.

The young man wrote submissive letters to his father. "I have remained here waiting to see you now five weeks," he wrote. "I have written to you three letters, and you do not reply to them. Let me tell you again how sincerely I desire and pray that you will come, or permit me to come to you and throw myself at your feet, and beg my forgiveness, and hers. She as earnestly implores it. Indeed, I am very wretched, Sir. Believe me, there is nothing I would not do to regain your esteem and the love I fear I have unhappily forfeited. I will remain another week in the hope of hearing from you, or seeing you. I beg of you, Sir, not to drive me mad. Whatever you ask of me I will consent to."

"Nothing he would not do!" the Baronet commented as he read. "There is nothing he would not do! He will remain another week and give me that final chance! And it is I who drive him mad! Already he is beginning to cast his retribution on my shoulders."

Sir Austin had really gone down to Wales to be out of the way. A Shaddock-Dogmatist does not meet misfortune without hearing of it, and the author of THE PILGRIM'S SCRIP in trouble found London too hot for him. Miss Joy Blewins was not dead: she had a numerous progeny on the female Press of the land. It was but a choice of evils between the pathetic sympathy of Mrs. Grandison, and the Irish howl of the veteran M'Murphy. He quitted London to take refuge among the mountains; living there in solitary commune with a virgin Note-book.

Some indefinite scheme was in his head in this treatment of his son. Had he construed it, it would have looked ugly; and it settled to a vague principle that the young man should be tried and tested.

"Let him learn to deny himself something. Let him live with his equals for a term. If he loves me he will read my wishes." Thus he explained his principle to Lady Blandish.

The lady wrote: "You speak of a term. Till when? May I name one to him? It is the dreadful *uncertainty* that reduces him to despair. That, and nothing else. Pray be explicit."

In return, he distantly indicated Richard's majority.

How could Lady Blandish go and ask the young man to wait a year away from his wife? Her instinct began to open a wide eye on the idol she worshiped.

When people do not themselves know what they mean, they succeed in deceiving, and imposing upon, others. Not only was Lady Blandish mystified; Mrs. Doria, who pierced into the recesses of everybody's mind, and had always been in the habit of reading off her brother from infancy, and had never known herself to be once wrong about him, she confessed she was quite at a loss to comprehend Austin's principle. "For principle he has," said Mrs. Doria: "he never acts without one. But what it is I cannot at present perceive. If he would write, and command the boy to await his return, all would be clear. He allows us to go and fetch him, and then leaves us all in a quandary. It must be some woman's influence. That is the only way to account for it."

"Singular!" interjected Adrian, "what pride women have in their sex! Well, I have to tell you, my dear Aunt, that the day after tomorrow I hand my charge over to your keeping. I can't hold him in an hour longer. I've had to leash him with lies till my invention's exhausted. I petition to have them put down to the Chief's account, but when the stream runs dry I can do no more. The last was, that I had heard from him desiring me to have the South-west bedroom ready for him on Tuesday proximate. 'So!' says my son, 'I'll wait till then,' and from the gigantic effort he exhibited in coming to it, I doubt any human power's getting him to wait longer."

"We must, we must detain him," said Mrs. Doria. "If we do not, I am convinced Austin will do something rash that he will for ever repent. He will marry that woman, Adrian. Mark my words. Now with any other young man . . . But Richard's education! that ridiculous System! . . . Has he no distraction? nothing to amuse him?"

"Poor boy! I suppose he wants his own particular playfellow."

The Wise Youth had to bow to a reproof.

"I tell you, Adrian, he will marry that woman."

"My dear Aunt! Can a chaste man do ought more commendable?"

"Has the boy no object we can induce him to follow?— If he had but a profession!"

"What say you to the regeneration of the streets of London, and the profession of moral-scavenger, Aunt? I assure you I have served a month's apprenticeship with him. We sally forth on the tenth hour towards night. A female

passes. I hear him groan. 'Is *she* one of them, Adrian?'
I am compelled to admit she is not the Saint he deems it the
portion of every creature wearing petticoats to be. Another
groan: an evident internal, 'It cannot be—and yet!' . . .
that we hear on the stage. Rollings of eyes: impious questionings of the Creator of the universe: savage mutterings
against brutal males: and then we meet a second young person, and repeat the performance—of which I am rather
tired. It would be all very well, but he turns upon me, and
lectures me because I don't hire a house, and furnish it for
all the women one meets to live in in purity. Now that's
too much to ask of a quiet man. Master Thompson has
latterly relieved me, I'm happy to say."

Mrs. Doria thought her thoughts.

"Has Austin written to you since you were in Town?"

"Not an Aphorism!" returned Adrian.

"I must see Richard tomorrow morning," Mrs. Doria
ended the colloquy by saying.

The result of her interview with her nephew was, that
Richard made no allusion to a departure on the Tuesday;
and for many days afterwards he appeared to have an absorbing business on his hands: but what it was Adrian did not
then learn, and his admiration of Mrs. Doria's genius for
management rose to a very high pitch.

On a morning in October they had an early visitor in the
person of the Honourable Peter, whom they had not seen
for a week or more.

"Gentlemen," he said, flourishing his cane in his most
affable manner, "I've come to propose to you to join us in
a little dinner-party at Richmond. Nobody's in Town, you
know. London's as dead as a stock-fish. Nothing but the
scrapings to offer you. But the weather's fine: I flatter myself you'll find the company agreeable. What says my
friend Feverel?"

Richard begged to be excused.

"No, no: positively you must come," said the Honourable Peter. "I've had some trouble to get them together to relieve the dulness of your incarceration. Richmond's within the rules of your prison. You can be back by night. Moonlight on the water—lovely woman. We've engaged a Citybarge to pull us back. Eight oars—I'm not sure it isn't sixteen. Come—the word!"

Adrian was for going. Richard said he had an appointment with Ripton.

"You're in for another rick, you two," said Adrian. "Arrange that we go. You haven't seen the cockney's Paradise. Abjure Blazes, and taste of peace, my son."

After some persuasion, Richard yawned wearily,—and got up, and threw aside the care that was on him, saying, "Very well. Just as you like. We'll take old Rip with us."

Adrian consulted Brayder's eye at this. The Honourable Peter briskly declared he should be delighted to have Feverel's friend, and offered to take them all down in his drag.

"If you don't get a match on to swim there with the tide—eh, Feverel, my boy?"

Richard replied that he had given up that sort of thing, at which Brayder communicated a queer glance to Adrian, and applauded the youth.

Richmond was under a still October sun. The pleasant landscape, bathed in Autumn, stretched from the foot of the hill to a red horizon haze. The day was like none that Richard vividly remembered. It touched no link in the chain of his recollection. It was quiet, and belonged to the spirit of the Season.

Adrian had divined the character of the scrapings they were to meet. Brayder introduced them to one or two of the men, hastily, and in rather an undervoice, as a thing to get over. They made their bow to the first knot of ladies they encountered. Propriety was strictly observed, even to severity. The general talk was of the weather. Here and there a lady would seize a button-hole, or any little bit of the habiliments, of the man she was addressing; and if it came to her to chide him, she did it with more than a fore-finger. This, however, was only here and there, and a privilege of intimacy.

Where ladies are gathered together, the Queen of the assemblage may be known by her Court of males. The Queen of the present gathering leaned against a corner of the open window, surrounded by a stalwart Court, in whom a practised eye would have discerned guardsmen, and Ripton, with a sinking of the heart, apprehended lords. They were fine men, offering inanimate homage. The trim of their whiskerage, the cut of their coats, the high-bred indolence in their aspect, eclipsed Ripton's sense of self-esteem. But they kindly looked over him. Occasionally one committed a momentary outrage on him with an eye-glass, seeming to cry out in a voice of scathing scorn, "Who's this?" and Ripton got closer to his Hero to justify his humble pretensions to existence and an identity in the shadow of him. Richard gazed about. Heroes do not always know what to say or do; and the cold bath before dinner in strange company is one of the instances. He had recognized his superb Bellona in the lady by the garden window. For Brayder the men had nods and jokes, the ladies a pretty playfulness. He was very busy, passing between the groups, chatting, laughing, taking the feminine taps he received, and some-times returning them in sly whispers. Adrian sat down and crossed his legs, looking amused and benignant.

"Whose dinner is it?" Ripton heard a mignonne beauty ask of a cavalier.

"Mount's, I suppose," was the answer.

"Where is he? why don't he come?"

"An affaire, I fancy."

"There he is again! How shamefully he treats Mrs. Mount!"

"She don't seem to cry over it."

Mrs. Mount was flashing her teeth and eyes with laughter at one of her Court, who appeared to be Fool.

Dinner was announced. The ladies proclaimed extravagant appetites. Brayder posted his three friends. Ripton found himself under the lee of a dame with a bosom. On the other side of him was the mignonne. Adrian was at the lower end of the table. Ladies were in profusion, and he had his share. Brayder drew Richard from seat to seat. A happy man had established himself next to Mrs. Mount. Him Brayder hailed to take the head of the table. The happy man objected, Brayder continued urgent, the lady tenderly insisted, the happy man grimaced, dropped into the post of honour, strove to look placable. Richard usurped his chair, and was not badly welcomed by his neighbour.

Then the dinner commenced, and had all the attention of the company, till the flying of the first champagne-cork gave the signal, and a hum began to spread. Sparkling wine that looseneth the tongue, and displayeth the verity, hath also the quality of colouring it. The ladies laughed high; Richard only thought them gay and natural. They flung back in their chairs and laughed to tears; Ripton thought only of the pleasure he had in their society. The champagne-corks continued a regular file-firing.

"Where have you been lately? I haven't seen you in the park?" said Mrs. Mount to Richard.

"No," he replied, "I've not been there." The question seemed odd: she spoke so simply that it did not impress him. He emptied his glass, and had it filled again.

The Honourable Peter did most of the open talking, which related to horses, yachting, Opera, and sport generally: who was ruined; by what horse, or what woman. He told one or two of Richard's feats. Fair smiles rewarded the Hero.

"Do you bet?" said Mrs. Mount.

"Only on myself," returned Richard.

"Bravo!" cried his Bellona, and her eye sent a lingering delirious sparkle across her brimming glass at him.

"I'm sure you're a safe one to back," she added, and seemed to scan his points approvingly.

Richard's cheeks mounted bloom.

"Don't you adore champagne?" quoth the dame with a bosom to Ripton.

"Oh, yes!" answered Ripton, with more candour than accuracy, "I always drink it."

"Do you indeed?" said the enraptured bosom, ogling him. "You would be a friend, now! I hope you don't object to a lady joining you now and then. Champagne's my folly."

A laugh was circling among the ladies of whom Adrian was the centre; first low, and as he continued some narration, peals resounded, till those excluded from the fun demanded the cue, and ladies leaned behind gentlemen to take it up, and formed an electric chain of laughter. Each one, as her ear received it, caught up her handkerchief, and laughed, and looked shocked afterwards, or looked shocked, and then spouted laughter. The anecdote might have been communicated to the bewildered cavaliers, but coming to a lady of a demurer cast, she looked shocked without laughing, and reproved the female table, in whose breasts it was consigned to burial: but here and there a man's head was seen bent, and a lady's mouth moved, though her face was not turned towards him, and a man's broad laugh was presently heard, while the lady gazed unconsciously before her, and preserved her gravity if she could escape any other lady's eyes; failing in which handkerchiefs were simultaneously seized, and a second chime arose, till the tickling force subsided to a few chance bursts.

"What nonsense it is what my father writes about women!" thought Richard. "He says they can't laugh, and don't understand humour. It comes," he reflected, "of his shutting himself from the world." And the idea that he was seeing the world, and feeling wiser, flattered him. He talked fluently to his dangerous Bellona. He gave her some reminiscences of Adrian's whimsies.

"Oh!" said she, "that's your tutor, is it!" She eyed the young man as if she thought he must go far and fast.

Ripton felt a push. "Look at that:" said the bosom, fuming utter disgust. He was directed to see a manly arm around the waist of the mignonne. "Now that's what I don't like in company," the bosom inflated to observe with sufficient emphasis. "She always will allow it with everybody. Give her a nudge."

Ripton protested that he dared not; upon which she said, "Then I will;" and inclined her sumptuous bust across his lap, breathing wine in his face, and gave the nudge. The mignonne turned an inquiring eye on Ripton; a mischievous spark shot from it. She laughed, and said: "Aren't you satisfied with the old girl?"

"Impudence!" muttered the bosom, growing grander and redder.

"Do, do fill her glass, and keep her quiet,—she drinks port when there's no more champagne," said the mignonne.

The bosom revenged herself by whispering to Ripton scandal of the mignonne, and between them he was enabled to form a correcter estimate of the company, and quite recovered from his original awe; so much so as to feel a touch of jealousy at seeing his lively little neighbour still held in absolute possession.

Mrs. Mount did not come out much; but there was a deferential manner in the bearing of the men towards her, which those haughty creatures accord not save to clever women; and she contrived to hold the talk with three or four at the head of the table while she still had passages aside with Richard.

The Port and Claret went very well after the Champagne. The ladies here did not ignominiously surrender the field to the gentlemen; they maintained their position with honour. Silver was seen far out on Thames. The wine ebbed, and the laughter. Sentiment and cigars took up the wondrous tale.

"Oh, what a lovely night!" said the ladies, looking above.
"Charming," said the gentlemen, looking below.

The faint-smelling cool Autumn air was pleasant after
the feast. Fragrant weeds burned bright about the garden.

"We are split into couples," said Adrian to Richard, who
was standing alone, eyeing the landscape. " 'T is the influence of the moon! Apparently we are in Cyprus. How
has my son enjoyed himself? How likes he the society of
Aspasia? I feel like a wise Greek tonight."

Adrian was jolly, and rolled comfortably as he talked.
Ripton had been carried off by the sentimental bosom. He
came up to them and whispered: "By Jove, Ricky! do you
know what sort of women these are?"

Richard said he thought them a nice sort.

"Puritan!" exclaimed Adrian, slapping Ripton on the
back. "Why didn't you get tipsy, Sir? Don't you ever
intoxicate yourself but at lawful marriages? Reveal to us
what you have done with the portly dame?"

Ripton endured his bantering that he might hang about
Richard, and watch over him. He was jealous of his inno-
cent Beauty's husband being in proximity with such women.
Murmuring couples passed them to and fro.

"By Jove, Ricky!" Ripton favoured his friend with another hard whisper, "there's a woman smoking!"

"And why not, O Riptonus?" said Adrian. "Art unaware
that woman cosmopolitan is woman consummate? and dost
grumble to pay the small price for the splendid gem?"

"Well, I don't like women to smoke," said plain Ripton.

"Why mayn't they do what men do?" the Hero cried
impetuously. "I hate that contemptible narrow-mindedness.
It's that that makes the ruin and horrors I see. Why mayn't
they do what men do? I like the women who are brave
enough not to be hypocrites. By Heaven! if these women
are bad, I like them better than a set of hypocritical creatures
who are all show, and deceive you in the end."

"Bravo!" shouted Adrian. "There speaks the regener-ator."

Ripton, as usual, was crushed by his leader. He had no argument. He still thought women ought not to smoke; and he thought of one far away, lonely by the sea, who was perfect without being cosmopolitan.

THE PILGRIM'S SCRIP remarks that: 'Young men take joy in nothing so much as the thinking women Angels: and nothing sours men of experience more than knowing that all are not quite so.'

The Aphorist would have pardoned Ripton Thompson his first Random extravagance, had he perceived the simple warm-hearted worship of feminine goodness Richard's young bride had inspired in the breast of the youth. It might possibly have taught him to put deeper trust in Nature.

Ripton thought of her, and had a feeling of sadness. He wandered about the grounds by himself, went through an open postern, and threw himself down among some bushes on the slope of the hill. Lying there, and meditating, he became aware of voices conversing.

"What does he want?" said a woman's voice. "It's another of his villainies, I know. Upon my honour, Brayder, when I think of what I have to reproach him for, I think I must go mad, or kill him."

"Tragic!" said the Honourable Peter. "Haven't you revenged yourself, Bella, pretty often? Best deal openly. This is a commercial transaction. You ask for money, and you are to have it—on the conditions: double the sum, and debts paid."

"He applies to me!"

"You know, my dear Bella, it has long been all up between you. I think Mount has behaved very well, considering all he knows. He's not easily hoodwinked, you know. He resigns himself to his fate, and follows other game."

"Then the condition is that I am to seduce this young man?"

"My dear Bella! you strike your bird like a hawk. I didn't say seduce. Hold him in—play with him. Amuse him."

"I don't understand half-measures."

"Women seldom do."

"How I hate you, Brayder!"

"I thank your Ladyship."

The two walked further, and the result of the colloquy was shut from Ripton. He left the spot in a serious mood, apprehensive of something dark to the people he loved, though he had no idea of what the Honourable Peter's stipulation involved.

In the voyage back to Town, Richard was again selected to sit by Mrs. Mount. Brayder and Adrian started the jokes. The pair of parasites got on extremely well together. Soft fell the splash of the oars; softly the moonlight curled around them: softly the banks glided by. The ladies were in a state of high sentiment. They sang without request. All deemed the British balladmonger an appropriate interpreter of their emotions. After good wine, and plenty thereof, fair throats will make men of taste swallow the British balladmonger. Eyes, lips, hearts; darts and smarts and sighs; beauty, duty; bosom, blossom; false one, farewell! To this pathetic strain they melted. Mrs. Mount, though strongly requested, declined to sing. She preserved her state. Under the stately aspens of Brentfordait, and on they swept, the white moon in their wake. Richard's hand lay open by his side. Mrs. Mount's little white hand by misadventure fell into it. It was not pressed, or soothed for its fall, or made intimate with eloquent fingers. It lay there like a bit of snow on the cold ground. A yellow leaf wavering down from the aspens struck Richard's cheek, and he drew away the very hand to throw back his hair and smooth his face, and then folded his arms, unconscious of offence. He was thinking ambitiously of his life: his blood was untroubled: his brain calmly working.

'Which is the more perilous?' is a problem put by the PILGRIM: 'To meet the temptings of Eve, or to pique her?'

Mrs. Mount stared at the young man as at a curiosity, and turned to flirt with one of her Court. The Guardsmen were mostly sentimental. One or two rattled, and one was such a good-humoured fellow that Adrian could not make him ridiculous. The others seemed to give themselves up to a silent waxing in length of limb. However far they sat removed, everybody was entangled in their legs. Pursuing his studies, Adrian came to the conclusion that the same close intellectual and moral affinity which he had discovered to exist between our nobility and our yeomanry, is to be observed between the Guardsmen class, and that of the corps de ballet: they both live by the strength of their legs, where also their wits, if they do not altogether reside there, are principally developed: both are volage: wine, tobacco, and the moon, influence both alike; and admitting the one marked difference that does exist, it is, after all, pretty nearly the same thing to be coquetting and sinning on two legs as on the point of a toe.

A long Guardsman with a deep bass voice sang a doleful song about the twining tendrils of the heart ruthlessly torn, but required urgent persuasions and heavy trumpeting of his lungs to get to the end: before he had accomplished it, Adrian had contrived to raise a laugh in his neighbourhood, so that the company was divided, the camp was split: jollity returned to one-half, while sentiment held the other. Ripton, blotted behind the bosom, was only lucky in securing a higher degree of heat than was possible for the rest. "Are you cold?" she would ask, smiling charitably.

"I am," said the mignonne, as if to excuse her conduct, which was still evident to the decorous bosom, though more removed therefrom.

"You always appear to be," the bosom sniffed and snapped.

"Won't you warm two, Mrs. Mortimer?" said the naughty mignonne.

Disdain prevented any further notice of her. Those familiar with the ladies enjoyed their sparring, which was frequent. The mignonne was heard to whisper: "That poor fellow will certainly be baked."

Very prettily the ladies took and gave warmth, for the air on the water was chill and misty. Adrian had beside him the demure one who had stopped the circulation of his anecdote. She in nowise objected to the fair exchange, but said "Hush!" betweenwhiles.

Past Kew, and Hammersmith, on the cool smooth water; across Putney reach; through Battersea bridge; and the City grew around them, and the shadows of great mill-factories slept athwart the moonlight.

All the ladies said they had had a charming day when they alighted on land. Several cavaliers crushed for the honour of conducting Mrs. Mount home.

"My brougham's here; I shall go alone," said Mrs. Mount. "Some one arrange my shawl."

She turned her back to Richard, who had a view of a delicate neck as he manipulated with the bearing of a mailed-knight.

"Which way are you going?" she asked carelessly, and, to his reply, "Then I can give you a lift," and she took his arm with a matter-of-course air, and walked up the stairs with him.

Ripton saw what had happened. He was going to follow: the portly dame retained him, and desired him to get her a cab.

"O you happy fellow!" said the bright-eyed mignonne, passing by.

Ripton procured the cab, and stuffed it full without having to get into it himself.

"Try and let him come in, too?" said the persecuting mignonne, again passing.

"Take liberties with your men—you shan't with me,"
retorted the angry bosom, and drove off.

"So she's been and gone and run away and left him after
all his trouble!" cried the pert little thing, peering into
Ripton's eyes. "Now you'll never be so foolish as to pin
your faith to fat women again. There! he shall be made
happy another time." She gave his nose a comical tap, and
tripped away with her possessor.

Ripton rather forgot his friend for some minutes: random
thoughts laid hold of him. Cabs and carriages rattled past.
He was sure he had been among members of the nobility
that day, though when they went by him now they only
recognized him with an effort of the eyelids. He began to
think of the day with exultation, as an event. Recollections
of the mignonne were captivating. "Blue eyes—just what I
like! And such a little impudent nose, and red lips, pouting—the very thing I like! And her hair? darkish, I think
—say, brown. And so saucy, and light on her feet. And
kind she is, or she wouldn't have talked to me like that."
Thus, with a groaning soul, he pictured her. His reason
voluntarily consigned her to the aristocracy as a natural
appanage: but he did amorously wish that Fortune had made
a lord of him.

Then his mind reverted to Mrs. Mount, and the strange
conversation he had heard on the hill. He was not one to
suspect anybody positively. He was timid of fixing a suspicion. It hovered indefinitely, and clouded people, without
stirring him to any resolve. Still the attentions of the lady
towards Richard were queer. He endeavoured to imagine
they were in the nature of things, because Richard was so
handsome that any woman must take to him. "But he's married," said Ripton, "and he mustn't go near these people if
he's married." Not a high morality, perhaps: better than
none at all: better for the world were it practised more.
He thought of Richard along with that sparkling dame,
alone with her. The adorable beauty of his dear bride, her

pure heavenly face, swam before him. Thinking of her, he lost sight of the mignonne who had made him giddy.

He walked to Richard's hotel, and up and down the street there, hoping every minute to hear his step; sometimes fancying he might have returned and gone to bed. Two o'clock struck. Ripton could not go away. He was sure he should not sleep if he did. At last the cold sent him homeward, and leaving the street, on the moonlight side of Piccadilly he met his friend patrolling with his head up and that swing of the feet proper to men who are chanting verses.

"Old Rip!" cried Richard cheerily. "What on earth are you doing here at this hour of the morning?"

Ripton muttered of his pleasure at meeting him. "I wanted to shake your hand before I went home."

Richard smiled on him in an amused kindly way. "That all? You may shake my hand any day, like a true man as you are, old Rip! I've been speaking about you. Do you know, that—Mrs. Mount—never saw you all the time at Richmond, or in the boat!"

"Oh!" Ripton said, well-assured he was a dwarf: "You saw her safe home?"

"Yes. I've been there for the last couple of hours—talking. She talks capitally. She's wonderfully clever. She's very like a man, only much nicer. I like her."

"But Richard—excuse me—I'm sure I don't mean to offend you—but now you're married . . . perhaps you couldn't help seeing her home, but I think you really indeed oughtn't to have gone upstairs."

Ripton delivered this opinion with a modest impressiveness.

"What do you mean?" said Richard. "You don't suppose I care for any woman but my little darling down there." He laughed.

"No; of course not. That's absurd. What I mean is, that people perhaps will—you know, they do—they say all manner of things, and that makes unhappiness, and . . . I do wish you were going home tomorrow, Ricky. I mean, to your dear wife." Ripton blushed and looked away as he spoke.

The Hero gave one of his scornful glances. "So you're anxious about my reputation. I hate that way of looking at women. Because they have been once misled—look how much weaker they are!—because the world has given them an ill fame, you would treat them as contagious, and keep away from them for the sake of your character!"

"It would be different with me," quoth Ripton.

"How?" asked the Hero.

"Because I'm worse than you," was all the logical explanation Ripton was capable of.

"I do hope you will go home soon," he added.

"Yes," said Richard, "and I, so do I hope so. But I've work to do now. I dare not, I cannot, leave it. Lucy would be the last to ask me;—You saw her letter yesterday. Now listen to me, Rip. I want to make you just towards women."

Then he read Ripton a lecture on erring women, speaking of them as if he had known them and studied them for years. Clever, beautiful, but betrayed by Love, it was the first duty of all true men to cherish and redeem them. "We turn them into curses, Rip; these divine creatures." And the world suffered for it. That—that was the root of all the evil in the world!

"I don't feel anger or horror at these poor women, Rip! It's strange. I knew what they were when we came home in the boat. But I do—it tears my heart to see a young girl given over to an old man—a man she doesn't love. That's shame!—Don't speak of it."

Forgetting to contest the premiss, that all betrayed women are betrayed by Love, Ripton was silenced. He, like most young men, had pondered somewhat on this matter, and was inclined to be sentimental when he was not hungry. They walked in the moonlight by the railings of the park. Richard harangued at leisure, while Ripton's teeth chattered. Chiv-

alry might be dead, but there was still something to do, went
the strain. The lady of the day had not been thrown in
the Hero's path without an object, he said: and he was sadly
right there. He did not express the thing clearly: nevertheless Ripton understood him to mean that he intended to
rescue that lady from further transgressions, and show a
certain scorn for the world. That lady, and then other ladies
unknown, were to be rescued. Ripton was to help. He and
Ripton were to be the knights of this enterprise. When
appealed to, Ripton acquiesced, and shivered. Not only were
they to be knights, they would have to be Titans, for the
powers of the world, the spurious ruling Social Gods, would
have to be defied and overthrown. And Titan number one
flung up his handsome bold face as if to challenge base Jove
on the spot: and Titan number two strained the upper but-
ton of his coat to meet across his pocket-handkerchief on his
chest, and warmed his fingers under his coat-tails. The moon
had fallen from her high seat and was in the mists of the
West, when he was allowed to seek his blankets, and the
cold acting on his friend's eloquence made Ripton's flesh
very contrite. The poor fellow had thinner blood than the
Hero; but his heart was good. By the time he had got a
little warmth about him, his heart gratefully strove to encourage him in the conception of becoming a knight and a
Titan; and so striving Ripton fell asleep and dreamed of a
bosom.

CHAPTER XLI

MRS. BERRY ON MATRIMONY

BEHOLD the Hero embarked in the redemption of an err
ing beautiful woman.

"Alas!" writes the PILGRIM at this very time to Lady
Blandish, "I cannot get that legend of the Serpent from

me, the more I think. Has he not caught you, and ranked you foremost in his legions? For see: till you were fashioned, the fruits hung immobile on the boughs. They swayed before us, glistening and cold. The hand must be eager that plucked them. They did not come down to us, and smile, and speak our language, and read our thoughts, and know when to fly, when to follow! how surely to have us!

"Do but mark one of you standing openly in the track of the Serpent. What shall be done with her? I fear the world is wiser than its judges! Turn from her, says the world. By day the sons of the world do. It darkens, and they dance together downward. Then comes there one of the world's elect who deems old counsel devilish; indifference to the end of Evil worse than its pursuit. He comes to reclaim her. From deepest bane will he bring her back to highest blessing. Is not that a bait already? Poor fish! 'tis wondrous flattering. The Serpent has slimed her so to secure him! With slow weary steps he draws her into light: she clings to him; she is human; part of his work, and he loves it. As they mount upward, he looks on her more, while she, it may be, looks above. What has touched him? What has passed out of her, and into him? The Serpent laughs below. At the gateways of the Sun they fall together!"

This alliterative production was written without any sense of the peril that makes prophecy.

It suited Sir Austin to write thus. It was a channel to his acrimony moderated through his philosophy. The letter was a reply to a vehement entreaty from Lady Blandish for him to come up to Richard and forgive him thoroughly: Richard's name was not mentioned in it.

"He tries to be more than he is," thought the lady: and she began insensibly to conceive him less than he was.

The Baronet was conscious of a certain false gratification in his son's apparent obedience to his wishes, and complete submission: a gratification he chose to accept as his due, without dissecting or accounting for it. The intelligence re-iterating that Richard waited, and still waited; Richard's letters, and more his dumb abiding and practical penitence; vindicated humanity sufficiently to stop the course of viru-lent aphorisms. He could speak, we have seen, in sorrow for this frail nature of ours that he had once stood forth to champion. "But how long will this last?" he demanded with the air of Hippias. He did not reflect how long it had lasted. Indeed, his indigestion of wrath had made of him a moral Dyspepsy.

It was not mere obedience that held Richard from the arms of his young wife: nor was it this new Knightly enter-prise he had presumed to undertake. Hero as he was, a youth, open to the insane promptings of hot blood, he was not a fool. There had been talk between him and Mrs. Doria of his mother. Now that he had broken from his father, his heart spoke for her. She lived, he knew: he knew no more. Words painfully hovering along the borders of plain speech had been communicated to him, filling him with moody imaginings. If he thought of her, the red was on his face, though he could not have said why. But now, after canvassing the conduct of his father, and throwing him aside as a terrible riddle, he asked Mrs. Doria to tell him of his other parent. As softly as she could she told the story. To her the shame was past: she could weep for the poor lady. Richard dropped no tears. Disgrace of this kind is always present to a son, and, educated as he had been, these tidings were a vivid fire in his brain. He resolved to hunt her out, and take her from the man. Here was work set to his hand. All her dear husband did was right to Lucy. She encouraged him to stay for that purpose, thinking it also served another. There was Tom Bakewell to watch over Lucy: there was work for him to do. Whether it would please his father he did not stop to consider. As to the justice of the act let us say nothing.

On Ripton devolved the humbler task of grubbing for

Sandoe's place of residence; and as he was unacquainted
with the name by which the poet now went in private, his
endeavours were not immediately successful. The friends
met in the evening at Lady Blandish's town-house, or at the
Foreys', where Mrs. Doria procured the reverer of the
Royal Martyr, and staunch conservative, a favourable reception. Pity, deep pity for Richard's conduct Ripton saw
breathing out of Mrs. Doria. Algernon Feverel treated him
with a sort of rough commiseration, as a young fellow who
had spoilt his luck. Pity was in Lady Blandish's eyes, though
for a different cause. She doubted if she did well in seconding his father's unwise scheme—supposing him to have a
scheme. She saw the young husband encompassed by dangers
at a critical time. Not a word of Mrs. Mount had been
breathed to her, but the lady had some knowledge of life.
She touched on delicate verges to the Baronet in her letters, and he understood her well enough. "If he loves this
person to whom he has bound himself, what fear for him?
Or are you coming to think it something that bears the
name of love because we have to veil the rightful appellation?" So he responded remote among the mountains.
She tried very hard to speak plainly. She beat against a
wall of shrouded Manichæism. Finally he came to say
that he denied himself the pleasure of seeing his son specially,
that he for a time might be put to the test the lady seemed
to dread. This was almost too much for Lady Blandish.
Love's charity boy so loftily serene now that she saw him
half denuded—a thing of shanks and wrists—was a trial for
her true heart.

Going home at night Richard would laugh at the faces
made about his marriage. "We'll carry the day, Rip, my
Lucy and I! or I'll do it alone—what there is to do." He
slightly adverted to a natural want of courage in women
which Ripton took to indicate that his Beauty was deficient
in that quality. Up leapt the Old Dog: "I'm sure there
never was a braver creature upon earth, Richard! She's

as brave as she's lovely, I'll swear she is! Look how she behaved that day! How her voice sounded! She was trembling . . . Brave? She'd follow you into battle, Richard!"

And Richard rejoined: "Talk on, dear old Rip! She's my darling love, whatever she is! And she is gloriously lovely. No eyes are like hers. And when I make them bashful—by Heaven! I'll go down tomorrow morning the first thing."

Ripton only wondered the husband of such a treasure could remain apart from it. So thought Richard for a space.

"But if I go, Rip," he said despondently, "if I go for a day even I shall have undone all my work with my father. She says it herself—you saw it in her last letter."

"Yes," Ripton assented, and the words 'Please remember me to dear Mr. Thompson,' fluttered about the Old Dog's heart.

It came to pass that Mrs. Berry, having certain business that led her through Kensington Gardens, spied a figure that she had once dandled in long clothes, and helped make a man of, if ever woman did. He was walking under the trees beside a lady, talking to her, not indifferently. The gentleman was her bridegroom and her babe. "I know his back," said Mrs. Berry, as if she had branded a mark on it in infancy. But the lady was not her bride. Mrs. Berry diverged from the path, and got before them on the left flank; she stared, retreated, and came round upon the right. There was that in the lady's face which Mrs. Berry did not like. Her innermost question was, why he was not walking with his own wife? She stopped in front of them. They broke, and passed about her. She hemmed! at Richard's elbow. The lady presently made a laughing remark to him, whereat he turned to look, and Mrs. Berry bobbed. She had to bob a second time, and then he remembered the

worthy creature, and hailed her Penelope, shaking her hand
so that he put her in countenance again. Mrs. Berry was
extremely agitated. He dismissed her, promising to call
upon her in the evening. She heard the lady slip out something from a side of her lip, and they both laughed as she
toddled off to a sheltering tree to wipe a corner of each eye.
"I don't like the looks of that woman," she said and repeated it resolutely.

"Why doesn't he walk arm-in-arm with her?" was her
next inquiry. "Where's his wife?" succeeded it. After
many interrogations of the sort, she arrived at naming the
lady a bold-faced thing; adding subsequently, brazen. The
lady had apparently shown Mrs. Berry that she wished to
get rid of her, and had checked the outpouring of her emotions on the breast of her babe. "I know a lady when I
see one," said Mrs. Berry. "I haven't lived with 'em for
nothing; and if she's a lady bred and born, I wasn't married in the Church alive."

Then, if not a lady, what was she? Mrs. Berry desired
to know. "She's imitation lady, I'm sure she is!" Berry
vowed. "I say she don't look proper."

Establishing the lady to be a spurious article, however,
what was one to think of a married man in company with
such? "Oh, no! it ain't that!" Mrs. Berry returned immediately on the charitable tack. "Belike it's some one of
his acquaintance 've married her for her looks, and he've
just met her. . . . Why it'd be as bad as my Berry!" the
relinquished spouse of Berry ejaculated, in horror at the idea
of a second man being so monstrous in wickedness. "Just
coupled, too!" Mrs. Berry groaned on the suspicious side
of the debate. "And such a sweet young thing for his
wife! But no, I'll never believe it. Not if he tell me so
himself! And men don't do that," she whimpered.

Women are swift at coming to conclusions in these matters; soft women exceedingly swift: and soft women who
have been betrayed are rapid beyond measure. Mrs. Berry

had not cogitated long ere she pronounced distinctly and without a shadow of dubiosity: "My opinion is—married or not married, and wheresomever he pick her up—she's nothin' more nor less than a Beller Donner!" as which poisonous plant she forthwith registered the lady in the botanical notebook of her brain. It would have astonished Mrs. Mount to have heard her person so accurately hit off at a glance.

In the evening Richard made good his promise, accompanied by Ripton. Mrs. Berry opened the door to them. She could not wait to get him into the parlour. "You're my own blessed babe; and I'm as good as your mother,—though I didn't suck ye, bein' a maid!" she cried, falling into his arms, while Richard did his best to support the unexpected burden. Then, reproaching him tenderly for his guile—at mention of which Ripton chuckled, deeming it his own most honourable portion of the plot—Mrs. Berry led them into the parlour, and revealed to Richard who she was, and how she had tossed him, and hugged him, and kissed him all over, when he was only that big—showing him her stumpy fat arm. "I kissed ye from head to tail, I did," said Mrs. Berry, "and you needn't be ashamed of it. It's be hoped you'll never have nothin' worse come t'ye, my dear!"

Richard assured her he was not a bit ashamed, but warned her that she must not do it now, Mrs. Berry admitting it was out of the question now, and that he had a wife, moreover. The young men laughed, and Ripton laughing over-loudly drew on himself Mrs. Berry's attention: "But that Mr. Thompson there—however he can look me in the face after his inn'cence! helping blindfold an old 'oman!—though I ain't sorry for what I did—that I'm free for to say, and it's over, and blessed be all! Amen! So now where is she and how is she, Mr. Richard, my dear— it's only cuttin' of the 's' and you are as you was.—Why didn't ye bring her with ye to see old Berry?"

Richard hurriedly explained that Lucy was still in the Isle of Wight.

"Oh! and you've left her for a day or two?" said Mrs. Berry.

"Good God! I wish it had been a day or two," cried Richard.

"Ah! and how long have it been?" asked Mrs. Berry, her heart beginning to beat at his manner of speaking.

"Don't talk about it," said Richard.

"Oh! you never been dudgeonin' already? Oh! you haven't been peckin' at one another yet?" Mrs. Berry exclaimed.

Ripton interposed to tell her such fears were unfounded.

"Then how long ha' you been divided?"

In a guilty voice Ripton stammered "since September."

"September!" breathed Mrs. Berry, counting on her fingers, "September, October, Nov—two months and more! nigh three! A young married husband away from the wife of his bosom nigh three months! Oh my! Oh my! what do that mean?"

"My father sent for me—I'm waiting to see him," said Richard. A few more words helped Mrs. Berry to comprehend the condition of affairs. Then Mrs. Berry spread her lap, flattened out her hands, fixed her eyes, and spoke.

"My dear young gentleman! I'd like to call ye my darlin' babe! I'm going to speak as a mother to ye, whether ye likes it or no; and what old Berry says, ye won't mind, for she's had ye when there was no conventionals about ye, and she has the feelin's of a mother to ye, though humble her state. If there's one that know Matrimony it's me, my dear, though Berry did give me no more but nine months of it: and I've known the worst of Matrimony, which, if you wants to be woful wise, there it is for ye. For what have been my gain? That man gave me nothin' but his name; and Bessy Andrews was as good as Bessy Berry, though both is 'B's:' and says he, you was

'A,' and now you's 'B,' so you're my A. B. he says, write
yerself down that, he says, the bad man, with his jokes!—
Berry went to service." Mrs. Berry's softness came upon
her. "So I tell ye, Berry went to service. He left the wife
of his bosom forlorn and he went to service; because he
were al'ays an ambitious man, and wasn't, so to speak,
happy out of his uniform—which was his livery—not even in
my arms—and he let me know it. He got among them
kitchen sluts, which was my mournin' ready made, and
worse than a widow's cap to me, which is no shame to wear,
and some say becomin'. There's no man as ever lived know
better than my Berry how to show his legs to advantage,
and gals look at 'em. I don't wonder now that Berry was
prostrated. His temptations was strong, and his flesh was
weak. Then what I say is, that for a young married man—
be he whomsoever he may be—to be separated from the
wife of his bosom—a young sweet thing, and he a inn'cent
young gentleman!—so to sunder, in their state, and be kep'
from each other, I say it's as bad as bad can be! For what
is Matrimony, my dears? We're told it's a holy Ordnance.
And why are ye so comfortable in Matrimony? For that ye
are not a-sinnin'! And they that severs ye they tempts ye to
stray: and you learn too late the meanin' o' them blessin's of
the priest—as it was ordained. Separate—what comes?
Fust it's like the circylation of yer blood a-stoppin'—all goes
wrong. Then there's misunderstandings—ye've both lost
the key. Then, behold ye, there's birds o' prey hoverin' over
each on ye, and it's which 'll be snapped up fust. Then—
Oh, dear! Oh, dear! it be like the Devil come into the
world again." Mrs. Berry struck her hands, and moaned.
"A day I'll give ye: I'll go so far as a week: but there's the
outside. Three months' dwellin' apart! That's not Matrimony, it's divorcin'! what can it be to her but widerhood?
widerhood with no cap to show for it! And what can it be
to you, my dear? Think! you been a bachelor three months!
and a bachelor man," Mrs. Berry shook her head most dole-

fully, "he ain't a widow woman. I don't go to compare you
to Berry, my dear young gentleman. Some men's 'arts is
vagabonds born—they must go astray—it's their natur' to.
But all men are men, and I know the foundation of 'em,
by reason of my woe."

Mrs. Berry paused. Richard was respectfully attentive
to the sermon. The truth in the good creature's address
was not to be disputed, or despised, notwithstanding the
inclination to laugh provoked by her quaint way of putting
it. Ripton nodded encouragingly at every sentence, for he
saw her drift, and wished to second it.

Seeking for an illustration of her meaning, Mrs. Berry
solemnly continued: "We all know what checked prespiration is." But neither of the young gentlemen could resist
this. Out they burst in a roar of laughter.

"Laugh away," said Mrs. Berry. "I don't mind ye. I
say again, we all do know what checked prespiration is. It
fly to the lungs, it gives ye mortal inflammation, and it
carries ye off. Then I say checked Matrimony is as bad. It
fly to the 'art, and it carries off the virtue that's in ye, and
you might as well be dead! Them that is joined it's their
salvation not to separate! It don't so much matter before
it. That Mr. Thompson there—if he go astray, it ain't
from the blessed fold. He hurt himself alone—not double,
and belike treble, for who can say now what may be?
There's time for it. I'm for holding back young people so
that they knows their minds, howsomever they rattles about
their 'arts. I ain't a speeder of Matrimony, and good's
my reason! but where it's been done—where they're law-
fully joined, and their bodies made one, I do say this, that
to put division between 'em then, it's to make wanderin'
comets of 'em—creatures without a objeck, and no soul
can say what they's good for but to rush about!"

Mrs. Berry here took a heavy breath, as one who has said
her utmost for the time being.

"My dear old girl," Richard went up to her and applauding her on the shoulder, "you're a very wise old woman. But you mustn't speak to me as if I wanted to stop here. I'm compelled to. I do it for her good chiefly."

"It's yer father that's doin' it, my dear?"

"Well, I'm waiting his pleasure."

"A pretty pleasure! puttin' a snake in the nest of young turtle-doves! And why don't she come up to ye?"

"Well, that you must ask her. The fact is, she's a little timid girl—she wants me to see him first, and when I've made all right, then she'll come."

"A little timid girl!" cried Mrs. Berry. "Oh, lor, how she must ha' deceived ye to make ye think that! Look at that Ring," she held out her finger, "he's a stranger: he's not my lawful! You know what ye did to me, my dear. Could I get my own Wedding-Ring back from her? 'No!' says she, firm as a rock, 'he said, with this Ring I thee wed'—I think I see her now, with her pretty eyes and love-some locks—a darlin'.—And that Ring she'd keep to, come life, come death. And she must ha' been a rock for me to give in to her in that. For what's the conskence? Here am I," Mrs. Berry smoothed down the back of her hand mournfully, "here am I in a strange Ring, that's like a strange man holdin' of me, and me a wearin' of it just to seem decent, and feelin' all over no better than a b—— a big—that nasty name I can't abide!—I tell ye, my dear, she ain't soft, no!—except to the man of her 'art; and the best of women's too soft there—more's our sorrow!"

"Well, well!" went Richard, who thought he knew.

"I agree with you, Mrs. Berry," Ripton struck in, "Mrs. Richard would do anything in the world her husband asked her, I'm quite sure."

"Bless ye for yer good opinion, Mr. Thompson! Why, see her! she ain't frail on her feet; she looks ye straight in the eyes; she ain't one of yer hang-down Misses. Look how she behaved at the ceremony!"

"Ah!" sighed Ripton.

"And if you'd ha' seen her when she spoke to me about my Ring! Depend upon it, my dear Mr. Richard, if she blinded you about the nerve she've got, it was somethin' she thought she ought to do for your sake, and I wish I'd been by to counsel her, poor blessed babe!—And how much longer, now, can ye stay divided from that darlin'?"

Richard paced up and down uneasily.

"A father's will," urged Mrs. Berry, "that's a son's law: but he mustn't go again' the laws of his natur' to do it."

"Just be quiet at present—talk of other things, there's a good woman," said Richard.

Mrs. Berry meekly folded her arms.

"How strange, now, our meetin' like this! meetin' at all, too!" she remarked contemplatively. "It's them Advertisements! They brings people together from the ends of the earth, for good or for bad. I often say, there's more lucky accidents, or unlucky ones, since Advertisements was the rule, than ever there was before. They make a number of Romances, depend upon it! Do you walk much in the Gardens, my dear?"

"Now and then," said Richard.

"Very pleasant it is there with the fine folks and flowers and titled people," continued Mrs. Berry. "That was a handsome woman you was a-walkin' beside, this mornin'."

"Very," said Richard.

"She was a handsome woman! or I should say, is, for her day ain't past, and she know it. I thought at first— by her back—it might ha' been your Aunt, Mrs. Forey; for she do step out well and hold up her shoulders: straight as a dart she be! but when I come to see her face—Oh, dear me! says I, this ain't one of the family. They none of 'em got such bold faces—nor no *lady* as I know have. But she's a fine woman—that nobody can gainsay."

Mrs. Berry talked further of the fine woman. It was a liberty she took to speak in this disrespectful tone of her, and Mrs. Berry was quite aware that she was laying herself open to rebuke. She had her end in view. No rebuke was uttered, and during her talk she observed intercourse passing between the eyes of the young men.

"Look here, Penelope," Richard stopped her at last. "Will it make you comfortable if I tell you I'll obey the laws of my nature and go down at the end of the week?"

"I'll thank the Lord of Heaven if you do!" she exclaimed.

"Very well, then—be happy—I will. Now listen. I want you to keep your rooms for me—those she had. I expect, in a day or two, to bring a lady here—"

"A lady?" faltered Mrs. Berry.

"Yes. A lady."

"May I make so bold as to ask what lady?"

"You may not. Not now. Of course you will know."

Mrs. Berry's short neck made the best imitation it could of an offended swan's action. She was very angry. She said she did not like so many ladies, which natural objection Richard met by saying there was only one lady.

"And Mrs. Berry," he added, dropping his voice. "You will treat her as you did my dear girl, for she will require not only shelter but kindness. I would rather leave her with you than with any one. She has been very unfortunate."

His serious air and habitual tone of command fascinated the softness of Berry, and it was not until he had gone that she spoke out. "Unfort'nate! He's going to bring me an unfort'nate female? Oh! not from my babe can I bear that! Never will I have her here! I see it. It's that bold-faced woman he's got mixed-up in, and she've been and made the young man think he'll go for to reform her. It's one o' their arts—that is; and he's too inn'cent a young man to mean anythin' else. But I ain't a house of Magdalens— no! and sooner than have her here I'd have the roof fall over me, I would."

She sat down to eat her supper on the sublime resolve.

In Love Mrs. Berry's charity was all on the side of the

Law, and this is the case with many of her sisters. The PILGRIM sneers at them for it, and would have us credit that it is their admirable instinct which, at the expense of every virtue save one, preserves the artificial barrier simply to impose upon us. Men, I presume, are hardly fair judges, and should stand aside and mark.

Early next day Mrs. Berry bundled off to Richard's hotel to let him know her determination. She did not find him there. Returning homeward through the Park, she beheld him on horseback riding by the side of the identical lady. The sight of this public exposure shocked her more than the secret walk under the trees. "You don't look near yer reform yet," Mrs. Berry apostrophized her. "You don't look to me one that'd come the Fair Penitent till you've left off bein' fair—if then ye do, which some of ye don't. Laugh away and show yer airs! Spite o' yer hat and feather, and yer ridin'-habit, yer a beller donner." Setting her down again absolutely for such, whatever it might signify, Mrs. Berry had a virtuous glow.

In the evening she heard the noise of wheels stopping at the door. "Never!" she rose from her chair to exclaim. "He ain't rided her out in the mornin', and been and made a Magdalen of her afore dark?"

A lady veiled was brought into the house by Richard. Mrs. Berry feebly tried to bar his progress in the passage. He pushed past her, and conducted the lady into the parlour without speaking. Mrs. Berry did not follow. She heard him murmur a few sentences within. Then he came out. All her crest stood up, as she whispered vigorously: "Mr. Richard! if that woman stay here, I go forth. My house ain't a penitentiary for unfort'nate females, Sir—"

He frowned at her curiously; but as she was on the point of renewing her indignant protest, he clapped his hand across her mouth, and spoke words in her ear that had awful import to her. She trembled, breathing low: "My God, for-

give me! Lady Feverel is it? Your mother, Mr. Richard?"
And her virtue was humble before Lady Feverel.

CHAPTER XLII

AN ENCHANTRESS

ONE may suppose that a prematurely aged, oily little man
—a poet in bad circumstances—a decrepid butterfly chained
to a disappointed inkstand—will not put out strenuous energies to retain his ancient paramour when a robust young
man comes imperatively to demand his mother of him in her
person. The colloquy was short between Diaper Sandoe and
Richard. The question was referred to the poor spiritless
lady, who, seeing that her son made no question of it, cast
herself on his hands. Small loss to her was Diaper; but he
was the loss of habit, and that is something to a woman who
has lived. The blood of her son had been running so long
alien from her that the sense of her motherhood smote her
now with strangeness, and Richard's stern gentleness seemed
like dreadful justice come upon her. Her heart had almost
forgotten its maternal functions. She called him Sir, till he
bade her remember he was her son. Her voice sounded to
him like that of a broken-throated lamb, so painful and
weak it was, with the plaintive stop in the utterance. When
he kissed her, her skin was cold. Her thin hand fell out of
his when his grasp relaxed. "Can sin hunt one like this?"
he asked, bitterly reproaching himself for the shame she had
caused him to endure, and a deep compassion filled his breast.
Poetic justice had been dealt to Diaper the poet. He
thought of all he had sacrificed for this woman—the comfortable quarters, the friend, the happy flights. He could
not but accuse her of unfaithfulness in leaving him in his
old-age. Habit had legalized his union with her. He wrote
as pathetically of the break of habit as men feel at the death

of love; and when we are old and have no fair hope tossing golden looks before us, a wound to this second nature is quite as sad. I know not even if it be not actually sadder.

Day by day Richard visited his mother. Lady Blandish and Ripton alone were in the secret. Adrian let him do as he pleased. He thought proper to tell him that the public recognition he accorded to a particular lady was, in the present state of the world, scarcely prudent.

" 'Tis a proof to me of your moral rectitude, my son, but the world will not think so. No one character is sufficient to cover two—in a Protestant country especially. The divinity that doth hedge a Bishop would have no chance in contact with your Madame Danaë. Methinks I see the reverend man! though he takes excellent care to make it a contemptible hypothesis. That part of his pastoral duty he wisely leaves to weanling laymen. Drop the woman, my son. Or permit me to speak what you would have her hear."

Richard listened to him with disgust.

"Well, you've had my doctorial warning," said Adrian, and plunged back into his book.

When Lady Feverel had revived to take part in the consultations Mrs. Berry perpetually opened on the subject of Richard's matrimonial duty, another chain was cast about him. "Do not, oh, do not offend your father!" was her one repeated supplication. Sir Austin had grown to be a vindictive phantom in her mind. She never wept but when she said this.

So Mrs. Berry, to whom Richard had once made mention of Lady Blandish as the only friend he had among women, bundled off in her black-satin dress to obtain an interview with her, and an ally. After coming to an understanding on the matter of the visit, and reiterating many of her views concerning young married people, Mrs. Berry said: "My lady, if I may speak so bold, I'd say the sin that's bein' done is the sin o' the lookers on. And when everybody

appear frighted by that young gentleman's father, I'll say
—hopin' your pardon—they no cause be frighted at all.
For though it's nigh twenty year since I knew him, and
I knew him then just sixteen months—no more—I'll say his
'art's as soft as a woman's, which I've cause to know. And
that's it. That's where everybody's deceived by him, and
I was. It's because he keeps his face, and makes ye think
you're dealin' with a man of iron, and all the while there's
a woman underneath. And a man that's like a woman
he's the puzzle o' life! We can see through ourselves,
my Lady, and we can see through men, but one o' that
sort—he's like somethin' out o' natur'. Then I say—hopin'
be excused—what's to do is for to treat him *like* a woman,
and not for to let him 'ave his own way—which he don't
know himself, and is why nobody else do. Let that sweet
young couple come together, and be wholesome in spite of
him, I say; and then give him time to come round, just
like a woman; and round he'll come, and give 'em his
blessin', and we shall know we've made him comfortable.
He's angry because Matrimony have come between him and
his son, and he, woman-like, he's wantin' to treat what is
as if it isn't. But Matrimony's a holier than him. It
began long long before him, and it's be hoped will endoor
long's the time after, if the world's not coming to rack—
wishin' him no harm."

Now Mrs. Berry only put Lady Blandish's thoughts in
bad English. The lady took upon herself seriously to advise
Richard to send for his wife. He wrote, bidding her come.
Lucy, however, had wits, and inexperienced wits are as a
little knowledge. In pursuance of her sage plan to make
the family feel her worth, and to conquer the members of
it one by one, she had got up a correspondence with Adrian,
whom it tickled. Adrian constantly assured her all was
going well: Time would heal the wound if both the offenders
had the fortitude to be patient: he fancied he saw signs of
the Baronet's relenting: they must do nothing to arrest

those favourable symptoms. Indeed the Wise Youth was languidly seeking to produce them. He wrote, and felt, as Lucy's benefactor. So Lucy replied to her husband a cheerful rigmarole he could make nothing of, save that she was happy in hope, and still had fears. Then Mrs. Berry trained her fist to indite a lecture to her bride. Her bride answered it by saying she trusted to Time. "You poor marter," Mrs. Berry wrote back, "I know what your sufferins be. They is the only kind a wife should never hide from her husband. He thinks all sorts of things if she can abide being away. And you trusting to time, why it's like trusting not to catch a cold out of your natural clothes." There was no shaking Lucy's firmness.

Richard gave it up. He began to think that the life lying behind him was the life of a fool. What had he done in it? He had burnt a rick and got married! He associated the two facts of his existence. Where was the hero he was to have carved out of Tom Bakewell?—a wretch he had taught to lie and chicane: and for what? Great Heavens! how ignoble a flash from the light of his aspirations made his marriage appear! The young man sought amusement. He allowed his Aunt to drag him into society, and sick of that he made late evening calls on Mrs. Mount, oblivious of the purpose he had in visiting her at all. Her man-like conversation, which he took for honesty, was a refreshing change on fair lips.

"Call me Bella: I'll call you Dick," said she. And it came to be Bella and Dick between them. No mention of Bella occurred in Richard's letters to Lucy.

Mrs. Mount spoke quite openly of herself. "I pretend to be no better than I am," she said, "and I know I'm no worse than many a woman who holds her head high." To back this she told him stories of blooming dames of good repute, and poured a little social sewerage into his ears.

Also she understood him. "What you want, my dear Dick, is something to do. You went and got married like a—hum!—friends must be respectful. Go into the Army. Try the Turf. I can put you up to a trick or two—friends should make themselves useful."

She told him what she liked in him. "You're the only man I was ever alone with who don't talk to me of love and make me feel sick. I hate men who can't speak to a woman sensibly.—Just wait a minute." She left him and presently returned with, "Ah, Dick! old fellow! how are you?"—arrayed like a cavalier, one arm stuck in her side, her hat jauntily cocked, and a pretty oath on her lips to give reality to the costume. "What do you think of me? Wasn't it a shame to make a woman of me when I was born to be a man?"

"I don't know that," said Richard, for the contrast in her attire to those shooting eyes and lips, aired her sex bewitchingly.

"What! do you think I don't do it well?"

"Charming! but I can't forget . . ."

"Now that is too bad!" she pouted.

Then she proposed that they should go out into the midnight streets arm-in-arm, and out they went and had great fits of laughter at her impertinent manner of using her eye-glass, and outrageous affectation of the supreme dandy.

"They take up men, Dick, for going about in women's clothes, and vice versaw, I s'paus. You'll bail me, old fellaa, if I have to make my bow to the beak, won't ya? Say it's becas I'm an honest woman and dun't caa to haid the—a—unmentionables when I waa them—as the t'others do," sprinkled with the dandy's famous invocations.

He began to conceive Romance in that sort of fun.

"You're a woppa, my brave Dick! won't let any peelaw take me? by Jawve!"

And he with much assurance guaranteed to stand by her, while she bent her thin fingers trying the muscle of his arm, and reposed upon it more. There was delicacy in her dandyism. She was a graceful cavalier.

'Sir Julius,' as they named the dandy's attire, was frequently called for on his evening visits to Mrs. Mount. When he beheld Sir Julius he thought of the lady, and 'vice versaw,' as Sir Julius was fond of exclaiming.

Was ever Hero in this fashion wooed?

The woman now and then would peep through Sir Julius. Or she would sit, and talk, and altogether forget she was impersonating that worthy fop.

She never uttered an idea, or a reflection, but Richard thought her the cleverest woman he had ever met.

All kinds of problematic notions beset him. She was cold as ice, she hated talk about love, and she was branded by the world!

A rumour spread that reached Mrs. Doria's ears. She rushed to Adrian first. The Wise Youth believed there was nothing in it. She sailed full down upon Richard. "Is this true? that you have been seen going publicly about with an infamous woman, Richard? Tell me! pray relieve me!"

Richard knew of no person answering to his Aunt's description in whose company he could have been seen.

"Tell me, I say! Don't quibble. Do you know *any* woman of bad character?"

The acquaintance of a lady very much misjudged and ill used by the world, Richard admitted to.

Urgent grave advice Mrs. Doria tendered her nephew, both from the moral, and the worldly point of view, mentally ejaculating all the while: "That ridiculous System! That disgraceful Marriage!" Sir Austin in his mountain solitude was furnished with serious stuff to brood over.

The rumour came to Lady Blandish. She likewise lectured Richard, and with her he condescended to argue. But he found himself obliged to instance something he had quite neglected. "Instead of her doing me harm, it's I that will do her good."

Lady Blandish shook her head and held up her finger. "This person must be very clever to have given you that delusion, dear."

"She *is* clever. And the world treats her shamefully."

"She complains of her position to you?"

"Not a word. But I will stand by her. She has no friend but me."

"My poor boy! has she made you think that?"

"How unjust you all are!" cried Richard.

"How mad and wicked is the man who can let him be tempted so!" thought Lady Blandish.

He would pronounce no promise not to visit her, not to address her publicly. The world that condemned her and cast her out, was no better—worse for its miserable hypocrisy. He knew the world now, the young man said.

"My child! the world may be very bad. I am not going to defend it. But you have some one else to think of. Have you forgotten you have a wife, Richard?"

"Ay! you all speak of her now. There's my Aunt: 'Remember you have a wife!' Do you think I love any one but Lucy? poor little thing! Because I am married am I to give up the society of women?"

"Of women!"

"Isn't she a woman?"

"Too much so!" sighed the defender of her sex.

Adrian became more emphatic in his warnings. Richard laughed at him. The Wise Youth sneered at Mrs. Mount. The Hero then favoured him with a warning equal to in emphasis, and surpassing in sincerity, his own.

"We won't quarrel, my dear boy," said Adrian. "I'm a man of peace. Besides, we are not fairly proportioned for a combat. Ride your steed to Virtue's goal! All I say is, that I think he'll upset you, and it's better to go at a slow pace and in companionship with the children of the sun. You have a very nice little woman for a wife—well, good-bye!"

To have his wife and the world thrown at his face, was unendurable to the Hero: he associated them somewhat after the manner of the rick and the marriage. Charming Sir Julius, always gay, always honest, dispersed his black moods.

"Why, you're taller," Richard made the discovery.

"Of course I am. Don't you remember you said I was such a little thing when I came out of my woman's shell?"

"And how have you done it?"

"Grown, to please you."

"Now, if you can do that, you can do anything."

"And so I would do anything."

"You would?"

"Honour!"

"Then . . ." his project recurred to him. But the incongruity of speaking seriously to Sir Julius struck him dumb.

"Then what?" asked she.

"Then you're a gallant fellow."

"That all?"

"Isn't it enough?"

"Not quite. You were going to say something. I saw it in your eyes."

"You saw that I admired you."

"Yes, but a man mustn't admire a man."

"I suppose I had an idea you were a woman."

"What! when I had the heels of my boots raised half-an-inch," Sir Julius turned one heel, and volleyed out silver laughter.

"I don't come much above your shoulder even now," she said, and proceeded to measure her height beside him with arch up-glances.

"You must grow more."

" 'Fraid I can't, Dick! Bootmakers can't do it."

"I'll show you how," and he lifted Sir Julius lightly,

and bore the fair gentleman to the looking-glass, holding him there exactly on a level with his head. "Will that do?"

"Yes! Oh, but I can't stay here."

"Why can't you?"

"Why can't I?"

Their eyes met. He put her down instantly.

Sir Julius, charming as he was, lost his vogue. Seeing that, the wily woman resumed her shell. The memory of Sir Julius breathing about her still, doubled the feminine attraction.

"I ought to have been an actress," she said.

Richard told her he found all natural women had a similar wish.

"Yes! Ah! then! if I had been!" sighed Mrs. Mount, divining the pattern of the carpet.

He took her hand, and pressed it.

"You are not happy as you are?"

"No."

"May I speak to you?"

"Yes."

Her nearest eye, setting a dimple of her cheek in motion, slid to the corner towards her ear, as she sat with her head sideways to him listening. When he had gone, she said to herself: "Old hypocrites talk in that way; but I never heard of a young man doing it, and not making love at the same time."

Their next meeting displayed her quieter: subdued as one who had been set thinking. He lauded her fair looks. "Don't make me thrice ashamed," she petitioned.

But it was not only that mood with her. Dauntless defiance that splendidly befitted her gallant outline and gave a wildness to her bright bold eyes, when she would call out: "Happy? who dares say I'm not happy? D'you think if the world whips me I'll wince? D'you think I care for what they say or do? Let them kill me! they shall never get one cry out of me!" and flashing on the

young man as if he were the congregated enemy, add:
"There! now you know me!"—that was a mood that well
became her, and helped the work. She ought to have
been an actress.

"This must not go on," said Lady Blandish and Mrs.
Doria in unison. A common object brought them together.
They confined their talk to it, and did not disagree. Mrs.
Doria engaged to go down to the Baronet. Both ladies knew
it was a dangerous, likely to turn out a disastrous, expedition.
They agreed to it because it was something to do, and doing
anything is better than doing nothing. "Do it," said the
Wise Youth, when they made him a third, "do it, if you
want him to be a hermit for life. You will bring back nothing but his dead body, ladies—a Hellenic, rather than a
Roman, triumph. He will listen to you—he will accompany
you to the station—he will hand you into the carriage—and
when you point to his seat he will bow profoundly, and
retire into his congenial mists."

Adrian spoke their thoughts. They fretted; they relapsed.

"Speak to him, you, Adrian," said Mrs. Doria. "Speak
to the boy solemnly.. It would be almost better he should
go back to that little thing he has married."

"Almost?" Lady Blandish opened her eyes. "I have
been advising it for the last month and more."

"A choice of evils," said Mrs. Doria's sour-sweet face and
shake of the head.

Each lady saw a point of dissension, and mutually agreed,
with heroic effort, to avoid it by shutting their mouths.
What was more, they preserved the peace in spite of the
Wise Youth's clever artifices.

"Well, I'll talk to him again," he said. "I'll try to get
the Engine on the conventional line."

"Command him!" exclaimed the practical animal.

"Command an Engine, Ma'am?"

"Gentle means are, I think, the only means with Richard,"
said Lady Blandish.

"Appeal to his reason," the practical animal iterated.

"The reason of an Engine, Ma'am?"

Throwing banter aside, as much as he could, Adrian spoke to Richard. "You want to reform this woman. Her manner is open—fair and free—the traditional characteristic. We won't stop to canvass how that particular honesty of deportment that wins your approbation has been gained. In her college it is not uncommon. Girls, you know, are not like boys. At a certain age they can't be quite natural. It's a bad sign if they don't blush, and fib, and affect this and that. It wears off when they're women. But a woman who speaks like a man, and has all those excellent virtues you admire—where has she learnt the trick? She tells you. You don't surely approve of the school? Well, what is there in it then? Reform her, of course. The task is worthy of your energies. But, if you are appointed to do it, don't do it publicly, and don't attempt it just now. May I ask you whether your wife participates in this undertaking?"

Richard walked away from the interrogation. The Wise Youth, who hated long unrelieved speeches and had healed his conscience, said no more.

Dear tender Lucy! Poor darling! Richard's eyes moistened. Her letters seemed sadder latterly. Yet she never called to him to come, or he would have gone. His heart leapt up to her. He announced to Adrian that he should wait no longer for his father. Adrian placidly nodded.

The Enchantress observed that her knight had a clouded brow and an absent voice.

"Richard—I can't call you Dick now, I really don't know why—" she said, "I want to beg a favour of you."

"Name it. I can still call you Bella, I suppose?"

"If you care to. What I want to say is this: when you meet me out—to cut it short—please not to recognize me."

"And why?"

"Do you ask to be told *that?*"

"Certainly I do."

"Then look: I won't compromise you."

"I see no harm, Bella."

"No," she caressed his hand, "and there is none. I know that. But," modest eyelids were drooped, "other people do," struggling eyes were raised.

"What do we care for other people?"

"Nothing. I don't. Not that!" snapping her finger. "I care for you, though." A prolonged look followed the declaration.

"You're foolish, Bella."

"Not quite so giddy—that's all."

He did not combat it with his usual impetuosity. Adrian's abrupt inquiry had sunk in his mind, as the Wise Youth intended it should. He had instinctively refrained from speaking to Lucy of this lady. But what a noble creature this lady was!

So they met in the Park; Mrs. Mount whipped past him; and secrecy added a new sense to their intimacy.

Adrian was gratified at the result produced by his eloquence.

Though this lady never expressed an idea, Richard was not mistaken in her cleverness. She could make evenings pass gaily, and one was not the fellow to the other. She could make you forget she was a woman, and then bring the fact startlingly home to you. She could read men with one quiver of her half-closed eyelashes. She could catch the coming mood in a man, and fit herself to it. What does a woman want with ideas, who can do thus much? Keenness of perception, conformity, delicacy of handling, these be all the qualities necessary to parasites.

Love would have scared the youth: she banished it from her tongue. It may also have been true that it sickened her. She played on his higher nature. She understood spontaneously what would be most strange and taking to him in a woman. Various as the Serpent of old Nile, she acted fallen Beauty, humorous indifference, reckless daring, arrogance in ruin. And acting thus, what think you?—She did it so well because she was growing half in earnest.

"Richard! I am not what I was since I knew you. You will not give me up quite?"

"Never, Bella."

"I am not so bad as I'm painted?"

"You are only unfortunate."

"Now that I know you I think so, and yet I am happier."

She told him her history when this soft horizon of repentance seemed to throw Heaven's twilight across it. A woman's history, you know: certain chapters expunged. It was dark enough to Richard.

"Did you love the man?" he asked. "You say you love no one now."

"Did I love him? He was a nobleman and I a tradesman's daughter. No. I did not love him. I have lived to learn it. And now I should hate him, if I did not despise him."

"Can you be deceived in love?" said Richard, more to himself than to her.

"Yes. When we're young we can be very easily deceived. If there is such a thing as love, we discover it after we have tossed about and roughed it. Then we find the man, or the woman, that suits us:—and then it's too late! we can't have him."

"Singular!" murmured Richard, "she says just what my father said."

He spoke aloud: "I could forgive you if you had loved him."

"Don't be harsh, grave judge! How is a girl to distinguish?"

"You had some affection for him? He was the first?"

She chose to admit that. "Yes. And the first who talks of love to a girl must be a fool if he doesn't blind her."

"That makes what is called first love, nonsense."

"Isn't it?"

He repelled the insinuation. "Because I know it is not, Bella."

Nevertheless she had opened a wider view of the world to him, and a colder. He thought poorly of girls. A woman— a sensible, brave, beautiful woman seemed, on comparison, infinitely nobler than those weak creatures.

She was best in her character of lovely rebel accusing foul injustice. "What am I to do? You tell me to be different. How can I? What am I to do? Will virtuous people let me earn my bread? I could not get a housemaid's place! They wouldn't have me—I see their noses smelling! Yes: I can go to a hospital and sing behind a screen! Do you expect me to bury myself alive? Why, man, I have blood: I can't become a stone. You say I am honest, and I will be. Then let me tell you that I have been used to luxuries, and I can't do without them. I might have married men—lots would have had me. But who marries one like me but a fool? and I could not marry a fool. The man I marry I must respect. He could not respect me—I should know him to be a fool, and I should be worse off than I am now. As I am now they may look as pious as they like—I laugh at them!"

And so forth: direr things. Imputations upon wives: horrible exultation at the universal peccancy of husbands. This lovely outcast almost made him think she had the right on her side, so keenly her Parthian arrows pierced the holy centres of society, and exposed its rottenness.

Mrs. Mount's house was discreetly conducted: nothing ever occurred to shock him there. The young man would ask himself where the difference was between her and the women of society? How base, too, was the army of banded hypocrites! He was ready to declare war against them on her behalf. His casus belli, accurately worded, would have read curiously. Because the world refused to lure the lady to virtue with the offer of a housemaid's place, our knight threw down his challenge. But the lady had scornfully rebutted this prospect of a return to chastity. Then the form of the challenge must be: Because the world declined to support the lady in luxury for nothing! But what did that mean? In other words: she was to receive the Devil's wages without rendering him her services. Such an arrangement appears hardly fair on the world, or on the Devil. Heroes will have to conquer both before they will get them to subscribe to it.

Heroes, however, are not in the habit of wording their declarations of war at all. Lance in rest they challenge, and they charge. Like women they trust to instinct, and graft on it the muscle of men. Wide fly the leisurely-remonstrating hosts: institutions are scattered, they know not wherefore, heads are broken that have not the balm of a reason why. 'Tis instinct strikes! Surely there is something divine in instinct.

Still, war declared, where were these hosts? The Hero could not charge down on the ladies and gentlemen in a ball-room, and spoil the quadrille. He had sufficient reticence to avoid sounding his challenge in the Law-Courts; nor could he well go into the Houses of Parliament with a trumpet, though to come to a tussle with the nation's direct representatives did seem the likelier method. It was likewise out of the question that he should enter every house, and shop, and battle with its master in the cause of Mrs. Mount. Where, then, was his enemy? Everybody was his enemy, and everybody was nowhere! Shall he convoke multitudes on Wimbledon Common? Blue Policemen, and a distant dread of ridicule, bar all his projects. Alas for the Hero in our day!

Nothing teaches a strong arm its impotence so much as knocking at empty air.

"What can I do for this poor woman?" cried Richard, after fighting his phantom enemy till he was worn out.

"Oh, Rip! old Rip!" he addressed his friend, "I'm distracted. I wish I was dead! What good am I for? Miserable! selfish! What have I done but make every soul I know wretched about me? I follow my own inclinations —I make people help me by lying as hard as they can—and I'm a liar. And when I've got it I'm ashamed of myself. And now when I do see something unselfish for me to do, I come upon grins—I don't know where to turn—how to act—and I laugh at myself like a devil!"

It was only friend Ripton's ear that was required, so his words went for little: but he did say he thought there was small matter to be ashamed of in winning and wearing the Beauty of Earth. Richard added his customary comment of "Poor little thing!"

He fought his duello with empty air till he was exhausted. A last letter written to his father procured him no reply. "Then," said he, "I have tried my utmost. I have tried to be dutiful—my father won't listen to me. One thing I can do—I can go down to my dear girl, and make her happy, and save her at least from some of the consequences of my rashness."

"There's nothing better for me!" the Hero groaned. His great ambition must be covered by a house-top: he and the cat must warm themselves on the domestic hearth! The Hero was not aware that his heart moved him to this. His heart was not now in open communion with his mind.

Mrs. Mount heard that her friend was going—would go. She knew he was going to his wife. Far from discouraging him, she said nobly: "Go—I believe I have kept you. Let us have an evening together, and then go: for good, if you like. If not, then to meet again another time. Forget me. I shan't forget you. You're the best fellow I ever knew, Richard. You are, on my honour! I swear I would not step in between you and your wife to cause either of you a moment's unhappiness. When I can be another woman I will, and I shall think of you then."

Lady Blandish heard from Adrian that Richard was positively going to his wife. The Wise Youth modestly veiled his own merit in bringing it about by saying: "I couldn't see that poor little woman left alone down there any longer."

"Well! Yes!" said Mrs. Doria, to whom the modest speech was repeated, "I suppose, poor boy, it's the best he can do now."

Richard bade them adieu, and went to spend his last evening with Mrs. Mount.

The Enchantress received him in state.

"Do you know this dress? No? It's the dress I wore when I first met you—not when I first saw you. I think I remarked you, Sir, before you deigned to cast an eye upon humble me. When we first met we drank Champagne together, and I intend to celebrate our parting in the same liquor. Will you liquor with me, old boy?"

She was gay. She revived Sir Julius occasionally. He, dispirited, left the talking all to her.

Mrs. Mount kept a footman. At a late hour the man of calves dressed the table for supper. It was a point of honour for Richard to sit down to it and try to eat. Drinking, thanks to the kindly mother Nature, who loves to see her children made fools of, is always an easier matter. The footman was diligent: the Champagne-corks feebly recalled the file-firing at Richmond.

"We'll drink to what we might have been, Dick," said the Enchantress.

Oh, the glorious wreck she looked!

His heart choked as he gulped the buzzing wine.

"What! down, my boy? They shall never see me hoist signals of distress. We must all die, and the secret of the thing is to die game, by Jove! Did you ever hear of Laura Fenn? a superb girl! handsomer than your humble servant—if you'll believe it—a 'Miss' in the bargain, and as a consequence, I suppose, a much greater rake. She was in the hunting-field. Her horse threw her, and she fell

plump on a stake. It went into her left breast. All the
fellows crowded round her, and one young man, who was
in love with her—he sits in the House of Peers now—we
used to call him 'Duck' because he was such a dear—he
dropped from his horse to his knees: 'Laura! Laura! my
darling! speak a word to me!—the last!' She turned over
all white and bloody: 'I—I shan't be in at the death!' and
gave up the ghost! Wasn't that dying game? Here's to
the example of Laura Fenn! Why, what's the matter?
See! it makes a man turn pale to hear how a woman can
die. Fill the glasses, John. Why, you're as bad!"

"It's give me a turn, my Lady," pleaded John, and the
man's hand was unsteady as he poured out the wine.

"You ought not to listen. Go, and drink some brandy."

John footman went from the room.

"My brave Dick! Richard! what a face you've got!"

He showed a deep frown on a colourless face.

"Can't you bear to hear of blood? You know, it was
only one naughty woman out of the world. The clergyman
of the parish didn't refuse to give her decent burial. We
are Christians! Hurrah!"

She cheered, and laughed. A lurid splendour glanced
about her like lights from the pit.

"Pledge me, Dick! Drink, and recover yourself. Who
minds? We must all die—the good and the bad. Ashes
to ashes—dust to dust—and wine for living lips! That's
poetry—almost. Sentiment: 'May we never say die till
we've drunk our fill!' Not bad—eh? A little vulgar, perhaps, by Jove! Do you think me horrid?"

"Where's the wine?" Richard shouted. He drank a
couple of glasses in succession, and stared about. Was he
in Hell, with a lost soul raving to him?

"Nobly spoken! and nobly acted upon, my brave Dick!
Now we'll be companions. 'She wished that Heaven had
made her such a man.' Ah, Dick! Dick! too late! too late!"

Softly fell her voice. Her eyes threw slanting beams.

"Do you see this?"

She pointed to a symbolic golden anchor studded with gems and coiled with a rope of hair in her bosom. It was a gift of his.

"Do you know when I stole the lock? Foolish Dick! you gave me an anchor without a rope. Come and see."

She rose from the table, and threw herself on the sofa.

"Don't you recognize your own hair? I should know a thread of mine among a million."

Something of the strength of Samson went out of him as he inspected his hair on the bosom of Delilah.

"And you knew nothing of it! You hardly know it now you see it! What couldn't a woman steal from you? But you're not vain, and that's a protection. You're a miracle, Dick: a man that's not vain! Sit here." She curled up her feet to give him place on the sofa. "Now let us talk like friends that part to meet no more. You found a ship with fever on board, and you weren't afraid to come alongside and keep her company. The fever isn't catching, you see. Let us mingle our tears together. Ha! ha! a man said that once to me. The hypocrite wanted to catch the fever, but he was too old. How old are you, Dick?"

Richard pushed a few months forward.

"Twenty-one? You just look it, you blooming boy. Now tell me my age, Adonis!—Twenty—*what?*"

Richard had given the lady twenty-five years.

She laughed violently. "You don't pay compliments, Dick. Best to be honest! Guess again. You don't like to? Not twenty-five, or twenty-four, or twenty-three, or— see how he begins to stare!—twenty-two. Just twenty-one, my dear. I think my birthday's somewhere in next month. Why, look at me, close—closer. Have I a wrinkle?"

"And when, in Heaven's name! . . ." he stopped short.

"I understand you. When did I commence for to live? At the ripe age of sixteen I saw a nobleman in despair because of my beauty. He vowed he'd die. I didn't want him to do that. So to save the poor man for his family, I ran away with him, and I dare say they didn't appreciate the sacrifice, and he soon forgot to, if he ever did. It's the way of the world!"

"Where's the wine?" cried Richard. He seized some dead champagne, emptied the bottle into a tumbler, and drank it off.

John footman entered to clear the table, and they were left without further interruption.

"Bella! Bella!" Richard uttered in a deep sad voice, as he walked the room.

She leaned on her arm, her hair crushed against a reddened cheek, her eyes half-shut and dreamy.

"Bella!" he dropped beside her. "You are unhappy."

She blinked and yawned, as one who is awaked suddenly. "I think you spoke," said she.

"You are unhappy, Bella. You can't conceal it. Your laugh sounds like madness. You must be unhappy. So young, too! Only twenty-one!"

"What does it matter? Who cares for me?"

The mighty pity falling from his eyes took in her whole shape. She did not mistake it for tenderness, as another would have done.

"Who cares for you, Bella? I do. What makes my misery now, but to see you there, and know of no way of helping you? Father of mercy! it seems too much to have to stand by powerless while such a ruin is going on!"

Her hand was shaken in his by the passion of torment with which his frame quaked.

Involuntarily a tear started between her eyelids. She glanced up at him quickly, then looked down, drew her hand from his, and smoothed it, eyeing it.

"Bella! you have a father alive?"

"A linen draper, dear. He wears a white neckcloth."

This article of apparel instantaneously changed the tone of the conversation, for he, rising abruptly, nearly squashed the lady's lap-dog, whose squeaks and howls were piteous, and demanded the most fervent caresses of its mistress. It was: "Oh, my poor pet Mumpsy, and he didn't like a nasty great big ugly heavy foot on his poor soft silky—mum—mum—back, he didn't, and he soodn't, that he—mum—mum—soodn't; and he cried out, and knew the place to come to, and was oh so sorry for what had happened to him—mum—mum—mum—and now he was going to be made happy, his mistress make him happy—mum—mum—mum—moo-o-o-o."

"Yes!" said Richard savagely, from the other end of the room, "you care for the happiness of your dog."

"A course se does," Mumpsy was simperingly assured in the thick of his silky flanks.

Richard looked for his hat. Mumpsy was deposited on the sofa in a twinkling.

"Now," said the lady, "you must come and beg Mumpsy's pardon whether you meant to do it or no, because little doggies can't tell that—how should they? And there's poor Mumpsy thinking you're a great terrible rival that tries to squash him all flat to nothing on purpose, pretending you didn't see; and he's trembling, poor dear wee pet! And I may love my dog, Sir, if I like; and I do; and I won't have him ill-treated, for he's never been jealous of you, and he is a darling, ten times truer than men, and I love him fifty times better. So come to him with me."

First a smile changed Richard's face; then, laughing, a melancholy laugh, he surrendered to her humour, and went through the form of begging Mumpsy's pardon.

"The dear dog! I do believe he saw we were getting dull," said she.

"And immolated himself intentionally? Noble animal!"

"Well, we'll act as if we thought so. Let us be gay, Richard, and not part like ancient fogies. Where's your fun? You can rattle; why don't you? You haven't seen me in one of my characters—not Sir Julius: wait a couple of minutes." She ran out.

A white visage reappeared behind a spring of flame. Her black hair was scattered over her shoulders and fell half across her brows. She moved slowly, and came up to him, fastening weird eyes on him, pointing a finger at the region of witches. Sepulchral cadences accompanied the representation. He did not listen, for he was thinking what a deadly charming and exquisitely horrid witch she was. Something in the way her underlids worked seemed to remind him of a forgotten picture; but a veil hung on the picture. There could be no analogy, for this was beautiful and devilish, and that, if he remembered rightly, had the beauty of seraphs.

His reflections and her performance were stayed by a shriek. The spirits of wine had run over the plate she held to the floor. She had the coolness to put the plate down on the table, while he stamped out the flame on the carpet. Again she shrieked: she thought she was on fire. He fell on his knees and clasped her skirts all round, drawing his arms down them several times.

Still kneeling, he looked up, and asked: "Do you feel safe now?"

She bent her face glaring down till the ends of her hair touched his cheek.

Said she, "Do you?"

Was she a witch verily? There was sorcery in her breath; sorcery in her hair: the ends of it stung him like little snakes.

"How do I do it, Dick?" She flung back laughing.

"Like you do everything, Bella," he said, and took a breath.

"There! I won't be a witch; I won't be a witch; they may burn me to a cinder, but I won't be a witch!"

She sang, throwing her hair about, and stamping her feet.

"I suppose I look a figure. I must go and tidy myself."

"No, don't change. I like to see you so." He gazed at her with a mixture of wonder and admiration. "I can't think you the same person—not even when you laugh."

"Richard," her tone was serious, "you were going to speak to me of my parents."

"How wild and awful you looked, Bella!"

"My father, Richard, was a very respectable man."

"Bella, you'll haunt me like a ghost."

"My mother died in my infancy, Richard."

"Don't put up your hair, Bella."

"I was an only only child!"

Her head shook sorrowfully at the glistening fire-irons. He followed the abstracted intentness of her look, and came upon her words.

"Ah, yes! speak of your father, Bella. Speak of him."

"Shall I haunt you, and come to your bedside, and cry: ' 'Tis time!'?"

"Dear Bella! if you will tell me where he lives, I will go to him. He shall receive you. He shall not refuse—he shall forgive you."

"If I haunt you, you can't forget me, Richard."

"Let me go to your father, Bella—let me go to him tomorrow. I'll give you my time. It's all I can give. Oh, Bella! let me save you."

"So you like me best dishevelled, do you, you naughty boy! Ha! ha!" and away she burst from him, and up flew her hair, as she danced across the room, and fell at full length on the sofa.

He felt giddy; bewitched.

"We'll talk of everyday things, Dick," she called to him from the sofa. "It's our last evening. Our last? Heigho! It makes me sentimental. How's that Mr. Ripson, Pipson, Nipson?—it's not complimentary, but I can't remember names of that sort. Why do you have friends of that sort? He's not a gentleman. Better, is he? Well, he's rather *too* insignificant for me. Why do you sit off there? Come to me instantly. There—I'll sit up, and be proper, and you'll have plenty of room. Talk, Dick!"

He was reflecting on the fact that her eyes were brown. They had a haughty sparkle when she pleased, and when she pleased a soft languor circled them. Excitement had dyed her cheeks deep red. He was a youth, and she an Enchantress. He a Hero: she a female Will o' the Wisp.

The eyes were languid now, set in rosy colour.

"You will not leave me yet, Richard? not yet?"

He had no thought of departing.

"It's our last night—I suppose it's our last hour together in this world—and I don't want to meet you in the next, for poor Dick will have to come to such a very very disagreeable place to make the visit."

He grasped her hand at this.

"Yes, he will! too true! can't be helped: They say I'm handsome."

"You're lovely, Bella."

She drank in his homage.

"Well, we'll admit it. His Highness below likes lovely women, I hear say. A gentleman of taste! You don't know all my accomplishments yet, Richard."

"I shan't be astonished at anything new, Bella."

"Then hear, and wonder." Her voice trolled out some lively roulades. "Don't you think he'll make me his prima donna below? It's nonsense to tell me there's no singing there. And the atmosphere will be favourable to the voice. No *damp,* you know. You saw the piano—why didn't you ask me to sing before? I can sing Italian. I had a master —who made love to me. I forgave him because of the music-stool—men can't help it on a music-stool, poor dears!"

She went to the piano, struck the notes, and sang:

'*My heart, my heart—I think 't will break.*'

"Because I'm such a rake. I don't know any other

reason. No; I hate sentimental songs. Won't sing that.
Ta-tiddy-tiddy-iddy—a . . . e! How ridiculous those
women were, coming home from Richmond!

> "'Once the sweet Romance of story
> Clad thy moving form with grace:
> Once the world and all its glory
> Was but framework to thy face.
> Ah, too fair!—what I remember,
> Might my soul recall—but no!
> To the winds this wretched ember
> Of a fire that falls so low!'

"Hum! don't much like that. Tum-te-tum-tum—accanto
al fuoco—heigho! I don't want to show off, Dick—or to
break down—so I won't try that.

> "'Oh! but for thee, Oh! but for thee,
> I might have been a happy wife,
> And nursed a baby on my knee,
> And never blushed to give it life.'

"I used to sing that when I was a girl, sweet Richard,
and didn't know at all, at all, what it meant. Mustn't
sing that sort of song in company. We're Oh! so proper—
even we!

> "'If I had a husband, what think you I'd do?
> I'd make it my business to keep him a lover:
> For when a young gentleman ceases to woo,
> Some other amusement he'll quickly discover.'

"For such are young gentlemen made of—made of: such
are young gentlemen made of!"
After this trifling she sang a Spanish ballad sweetly. He
was in the mood when the imagination intensely vivifies
everything. Mere suggestions of music sufficed. The lady

in the ballad had been wronged. Lo! it was the lady before him; and soft horns blew; he smelt the languid night-flowers; he saw the stars crowd large and close above the arid plain; this lady leaning at her window desolate, pouring out her abandoned heart.

Heroes know little what they owe to Champagne.

The lady wandered to Venice. Thither he followed her at a leap. In Venice she was not happy. He was prepared for the misery of any woman anywhere. But, oh! to be with her! To glide with phantom-motion through throbbing streets; past houses muffled in shadow and gloomy legends; under storied bridges; past palaces charged with full life in dead quietness; past grand old towers, colossal squares, gleaming quays, and out, and on with her, on into the silver infinity shaking over seas!

Was it the Champagne? the music? or the poetry? Something of the two former, perhaps: but most the Enchantress playing upon him. How many instruments cannot clever women play upon at the same moment! And this Enchantress was not too clever, or he might have felt her touch. She was no longer absolutely bent on winning him, or he might have seen a manœuvre. She liked him—liked none better. She wished him well. Her pique was satisfied. Still he was handsome, and he was going. What she liked him for, she rather—very slightly—wished to do away with, or see if it could be done away with: just as one wishes to catch a pretty butterfly, without hurting its patterned wings. No harm intended to the innocent insect, only one wants to inspect it thoroughly, and enjoy the marvel of it, in one's tender possession, and have the felicity of thinking one could crush it, if one would.

He knew her what she was, this lady. In Seville, or in Venice, the spot was on her. Sailing the pathways of the moon it was not celestial light that illumined her beauty. Her sin was there: but in dreaming to save, he was soft to her sin—drowned it in deep mournfulness.

Silence, and the rustle of her dress, awoke him from his musing. She swam wave-like to the sofa. She was at his feet.

"I have been light and careless tonight, Richard. Of course I meant it. I *must* be happy with my best friend going to leave me."

Those witch underlids were working brightly.

"You will not forget me? and I shall try . . . try . . ."

Her lips twitched. She thought him such a very handsome fellow.

"If I change—if I can change . . . Oh! if you could know what a net I'm in, Richard!"

Now at those words, as he looked down on her haggard loveliness, not divine sorrow but a devouring jealousy sprang like fire in his breast, and set him rocking with horrid pain. He bent closer to her pale beseeching face. Her eyes still drew him down.

"Bella! No! no! promise me! swear it!"

"Lost, Richard! lost for ever! give me up!"

He cried: "I never will!" and strained her in his arms, and kissed her passionately on the lips.

She was not acting now as she sidled and slunk her half-averted head with a kind of maiden shame under his arm, sighing heavily, weeping, clinging to him. It was wicked truth.

Not a word of Love between them!

Was ever Hero in this fashion won?

CHAPTER XLIII

THE LITTLE BIRD AND THE FALCON: A BERRY TO THE RESCUE!

AT a season when the pleasant south-western Island has few attractions to other than invalids and hermits enamoured of wind and rain, the potent nobleman, Lord Mountfalcon, still lingered there to the disgust of his friends and special parasite. "Mount's in for it again," they said among themselves. "Hang the women!" was a natural sequence. For, don't you see, what a shame it was of the women to be always kindling such a very inflammable subject! All understood that Cupid had twanged his bow, and transfixed a peer of Britain for the fiftieth time: but none would perceive, though he vouched for it with his most eloquent oaths, that this was a totally different case from the antecedent ones. So it had been sworn to them too frequently before. He was as a man with mighty tidings, and no language: intensely communicative, but inarticulate. Good round oaths had formerly compassed and expounded his noble emotions. They were now quite beyond the comprehension of blasphemy, even when emphasized, and by this the poor lord divinely felt the case was different. There is something impressive in a great human hulk writhing under the unutterable torments of a mastery he cannot contend with, or account for, or explain by means of intelligible words. At first he took refuge in the depths of his contempt for women. Cupid gave him line. When he had come to vent his worst of them, the fair face stamped on his brain beamed the more triumphantly: so the harpooned whale rose to the surface, and after a few convulsions, surrendered his huge length. My lord was in love with Richard's young wife. He gave proofs of it by burying himself beside her. To her, could she have seen it, he gave further proofs of a real devotion, in affecting, and in her presence feeling, nothing beyond a lively interest in her well-being. This wonder, that when near her he should be cool and composed, and when away from her wrapped in a tempest of desires, was matter for what powers of cogitation the heavy nobleman possessed.

The Honourable Peter, tired of his journeys to and fro, urged him to press the business. Lord Mountfalcon was wiser, or more scrupulous than his parasite. Almost every

evening he saw Lucy. The inexperienced little wife apprehended no harm in his visits. Moreover, Richard had com-
mended her to the care of Lord Mountfalcon, and Lady
Judith. Lady Judith had left the island for London: Lord
Mountfalcon remained. There could be no harm. If she
had ever thought so, she no longer did. Secretly, perhaps,
she was flattered. Lord Mountfalcon was as well educated
as it is the fortune of the run of titled elder sons to be:
he could talk and instruct: he was a lord: and he let her
understand that he was wicked, very wicked, and that she
improved him. The Heroine, in common with the Hero,
has her ambition to be of use in the world—to do some
good: and the task of reclaiming a bad man is extremely
seductive to good women. Dear to their tender bosoms as
old china is a bad man they are mending! Lord Mountfalcon had none of the arts of a libertine: his gold, his
title, and his person, had hitherto preserved him from having
long to sigh in vain, or sigh at all, possibly: the Honourable
Peter did his villainies for him. No alarm was given to
Lucy's pure instinct, as might have been the case had my
lord been over-adept. It was nice in her martyrdom to have
a true friend to support her, and really be able to do something for that friend. Too simple-minded to think much of
his lordship's position, she was yet a woman. "He, a great
nobleman, does not scorn to acknowledge me, and think
something of me," may have been one of the half-thoughts
passing through her now and then, as she reflected in self-
defence on the proud family she had married into.

January was watering and freezing old earth by turns,
when the Honourable Peter travelled down to the sun of
his purse with great news. He had no sooner broached his
lordship's immediate weakness, than Mountfalcon began to
plunge like a heavy dragoon in difficulties. He swore by
this and that he had come across an angel for his sins, and
would do her no hurt. The next moment he swore she
must be his, though she cursed like a cat. His lordship's

illustrations were not choice. "I haven't advanced an inch," he groaned. "Brayder! upon my soul, that little woman could do anything with me. By heaven! I'd marry her to-morrow. Here I am, seeing her every day in the week out or in, and what do you think she gets me to talk about?—History! Isn't it enough to make a fellow mad? and there am I lecturing like a prig, and by Heaven! while I'm at it I feel a pleasure in it; and when I leave the house I should feel an immense gratification in shooting somebody. What do they say in Town?"

"Not much," said Brayder significantly.

"When's that fellow—her husband—coming down?"

"I rather hope we've settled him for life, Mount."

Nobleman and parasite exchanged looks.

"How d'ye mean?"

Brayder hummed an air, and broke it to say: "He's in for Don Juan at a gallop, that's all."

"The deuce! Has Bella got him?" Mountfalcon asked with eagerness.

Brayder handed my lord a letter. It was dated from the Sussex coast, signed 'Richard,' and was worded thus:

"My beautiful Devil!

"Since we're both devils together, and have found each other out, come to me at once, or I shall be going somewhere in a hurry. Come, my bright Hell-star! I ran away from you, and now I ask you to come to me! You have taught me how devils love, and I can't do without you. Come an hour after you receive this."

Mountfalcon turned over the letter to see if there was anything more. "Complimentary love-epistle!" he remarked, and rising from his chair and striding about, muttered, "The dog! how infamously he treats his wife!"

"Very bad," said Brayder.

"How did you get hold of this?"

"Strolled into Bella's dressing-room, waiting for her—

turned over her pincushion haphazard. You know her trick."

"By Jove! I think that girl does it on purpose. Thank Heaven! I haven't written her any letters for an age. Is she going to him?"

"Not she! But it's odd, Mount!—did you ever know her refuse money before? She tore up the cheque in style, and presented me the fragments with two or three of the delicacies of language she learnt at your Academy. I rather like to hear a woman swear. It embellishes them!"

Mountfalcon took counsel of his parasite as to the end the letter could be made to serve. Both conscientiously agreed that Richard's behaviour to his wife was infamous, and that he at least deserved no mercy. "But," said his lordship, "it won't do to show the letter. At first she'll be swearing it's false, and then she'll stick to him closer. I know the sluts."

"The rule of contrary," said Brayder, carelessly. "She must see the trahison with her eyes. They believe their eyes. There's your chance, Mount. You step in: you give her revenge and consolation—two birds at one shot. That's what they like."

"You're an ass, Brayder," the nobleman exclaimed. "You're an infernal blackguard. You talk of this little woman as if she and other women were all of a piece. I don't see anything I gain by this confounded letter. Her husband's a brute—that's clear."

"Will you leave it to me, Mount?"

"Be damned before I do!" muttered my lord.

"Thank you. Now see how this will end. You're too soft, Mount. You'll be made a fool of."

"I tell you, Brayder, there's nothing to be done. If I carry her off—I've been on the point of doing it every day—what'll come of that? She'll look—I can't stand her eyes—I shall be a fool—worse off with her than I am now."

Mountfalcon yawned despondently. "And what do you

think?" he pursued. "Isn't it enough to make a fellow gnash his teeth? She's . . ." he mentioned something in an underbreath, and turned red as he said it.

"Hm!" Brayder put up his mouth and rapped the handle of his cane on his chin. "That's disagreeable, Mount. You don't exactly want to act in that character. You haven't got a diploma. Bother!"

"Do you think I love her a bit less?" broke out my lord in a frenzy. "By Heaven! I'd read to her by her bedside, and talk that infernal History to her, if it pleased her, all day and all night."

"You're evidently graduating for a midwife, Mount."

The nobleman appeared silently to accept the imputation.

"What do they say in Town?" he asked again.

Brayder said the sole question was, whether it was maid, wife, or widow.

"I'll go to her this evening," Mountfalcon resumed, after —to judge by the cast of his face—reflecting deeply. "I'll go to her this evening. She shall know what infernal torment she makes me suffer."

"Do you mean to say she don't know it?"

"Hasn't an idea—thinks me a friend. And so, by Heaven! I'll be to her."

"A—hm!" went on the Honourable Peter. "This way to the sign of the Green Man, ladies!"

"Do you want to be pitched out of the window, Brayder?"

"Once was enough, Mount. The Savage Man is strong. I may have forgotten the trick of alighting on my feet. There—there! I'll be sworn she's excessively innocent, and thinks you a disinterested friend."

"I'll go to her this evening," Mountfalcon repeated. "She shall know what damned misery it is to see her in such a position. I can't hold out any longer. Deceit's horrible to such a girl as that. I'd rather have her cursing me than—"

"Caressing?" the Honourable Peter ventured to suggest.

"—speaking and looking as she does," continued my lord, not heeding him. "Dear little girl!—she's only a child. You haven't an idea how sensible that little woman is."

"Have you?" inquired the cunning one.

"My belief is, Brayder, that there are angels among women," said Mountfalcon, evading his parasite's eye as he spoke.

To the world Lord Mountfalcon was the thoroughly wicked man; his parasite simply ingenuously dissipated. Full many a man of God had thought it the easier task to reclaim the Honourable Peter.

Lucy received her noble friend by firelight that evening, and sat much in the shade. She offered to have the candles brought in. He begged her to allow the room to remain as it was. "I have something to say to you," he observed with a certain solemnity.

"Yes—to me?" said Lucy quickly.

Lord Mountfalcon knew he had a great deal to say, but how to say it, and what it exactly was, he did not know.

"You conceal it admirably," he began, "but you must be very lonely here—I fear, unhappy."

"I should have been lonely, but for your kindness, my lord," said Lucy. "I am not unhappy." Her face was in shade and could not belie her.

"Is there any help that one who would really be your friend might give you, Mrs. Feverel?"

"None indeed that I know of," Lucy replied. "Who can help us to pay for our sins?"

"At least you may permit me to endeavour to pay my debts, since you have helped me to wash out some of *my* sins."

"Ah, my lord!" said Lucy, not displeased. It is sweet for a woman to believe she had drawn the serpent's teeth.

"I tell you the truth," Lord Mountfalcon went on. "What object could I have in deceiving you? I know you quite above flattery—so different from other women!"

"Oh, pray do not say that," interposed Lucy.

"According to my experience, then."

"But you say you have met such—such very bad women."

"I have. And now that I meet a good one, it is my misfortune."

"Your misfortune, Lord Mountfalcon?"

"Yes, and I might say more."

His Lordship held impressively mute.

"How strange men are!" thought Lucy. "He has some unhappy secret."

Tom Bakewell, who had a habit of coming into the room on various pretences during the nobleman's visits, put a stop to the revelation, if his lordship intended to make any.

When they were alone again, Lucy said, smiling: "Do you know, I am always ashamed to ask you to begin to read."

Mountfalcon stared. "To read?—oh! ha! yes!" he remembered his evening duties. "Very happy, I'm sure. Let me see. Where were we?"

"The life of the Emperor Julian. But indeed I feel quite ashamed to ask you to read, my lord. It's new to me; like a new world—hearing about Emperors, and armies, and things that really have been on the earth we walk upon. It fills my mind. But it must have ceased to interest you, and I was thinking that I would not tease you any more."

"Your pleasure is mine, Mrs. Feverel. 'Pon my honour, I'd read till I was hoarse, to hear your remarks."

"Are you laughing at me?"

"Do I look so?"

Lord Mountfalcon had fine full eyes, and by merely dropping the lids he could appear to endow them with mental expression.

"No, you are not," said Lucy. "I must thank you for your forbearance."

The nobleman went on his honour loudly.

Now it was an object of Lucy's to have him reading; for
his sake, for her sake, and for somebody else's sake; which
somebody else was probably considered first in the matter.
When he was reading to her, he seemed to be legitimizing
his presence there; and though she had no doubts or suspicions whatever, she was easier in her heart while she
had him employed in that office. So she rose to fetch the
book, laid it open on the table at his lordship's elbow, and
quietly waited to ring for candles when he should be willing
to commence.

That evening Lord Mountfalcon could not get himself
up to the farce, and he felt a pity for the strangely innocent
unprotected child with anguish hanging over her, that withheld the words he wanted to speak, or insinuate. He sat
silent and did nothing.

"What I do not like him for," said Lucy meditatively,
"is his changing his Religion. He would have been such a
hero, but for that. I could have loved him."

"Who is it you could have loved, Mrs. Feverel?" Lord
Mountfalcon asked.

"The Emperor Julian."

"Oh! the Emperor Julian! Well, he was an apostate:
but then, you know, he meant what he was about. He didn't
even do it for a woman."

"For a woman!" cried Lucy. "What man would for a
woman?"

"I would."

"You, Lord Mountfalcon?"

"Yes. I'd turn Catholic tomorrow."

"You make me very unhappy if you say that, my lord."

"Then I'll unsay it."

Lucy slightly shuddered. She put her hand upon the bell
to ring for lights.

"Do you reject a convert, Mrs. Feverel?" said the nobleman.

"Oh yes! yes! I do. One who does not give his conscience I would not have."

"If he gives his heart and body, can he give more?"

Lucy's hand pressed the bell. She did not like the doubtful light with one who was so unscrupulous. Lord Mountfalcon had never spoken in this way before. He spoke better, too. She missed the aristocratic twang in his voice, and the hesitation for words, and fluid lordliness with which he rolled over difficulties in speech.

Simultaneously with the sounding of the bell the door opened, and presented Tom Bakewell. There was a double knock at the same instant at the street-door. Lucy delayed to give orders.

"Can it be a letter, Tom?—so late!" she said, changing colour. "Pray run and see."

"That an't a powst," Tom remarked, as he obeyed his mistress.

"Are you very anxious for a letter, Mrs. Feverel?" Lord Mountfalcon inquired.

"Oh, no!—yes, I am, very!" said Lucy. Her quick ear caught the tones of a voice she remembered. "That dear old thing has come to see me," she cried, starting up.

Tom ushered a bunch of black satin into the room.

"Mrs. Berry!" said Lucy, running up to her and kissing her.

"Me, my darlin'!" Mrs. Berry, breathless and rosy with her journey, returned the salute. "Me truly it is, in fault of a better, for I ain't one to stand by and give the devil his license—roamin'! and the salt sure enough have spilte my bridegown at the beginnin', which ain't the best sign. Bless ye!—Oh, here he is." She beheld a male figure in a chair by the half light, and swung round to address him. "You bad man!" she held aloft one of her fat fingers, "I've come on ye like a bolt, I have, and goin' to make ye do yer dooty, naughty boy! But you're my darlin' babe," she melted, as was her custom, "and I'll never meet ye and not give to ye the kiss of a mother."

Before Lord Mountfalcon could find time to expostulate, the soft woman had him by the neck, and was down among his luxurious whiskers.

"Ha!" She gave a smothered shriek, and fell back. "What hair's that?"

Tom Bakewell just then illumined the transaction.

"Oh, my gracious!" Mrs. Berry breathed with horror, "I been and kiss a strange man!"

Lucy, half-laughing, but in dreadful concern, begged the noble lord to excuse the woful mistake.

"Extremely flattered, highly favoured, I'm sure," said his lordship, re-arranging his disconcerted moustache, "May I beg the pleasure of an introduction?"

"My husband's dear old nurse—Mrs. Berry," said Lucy, taking her hand to lend her countenance. "Lord Mountfalcon, Mrs. Berry."

Mrs. Berry sought grace while she performed a series of apologetic bobs, and wiped the perspiration from her forehead. "'M sure, my lord! 'm sure, my lord! had I 'a known—yer lordship know I never should 'a presume. Oh, dear! oh, dear! my lord! it was accidentals, quite, my lord! mistakin' of yer lordship for another. I never, never kiss a man but my babe and my Berry, never! no, indeed! not bein' the woman to—"

"Pray don't exclude me now," said the affable nobleman.

Lucy put her into a chair: Lord Mountfalcon asked for an account of her passage over to the island; receiving distressingly full particulars, by which it was revealed that the softness of her heart was only equalled by the weakness of her stomach. The recital calmed Mrs. Berry down.

"Well, and where's my—where's Mr. Richard? 'yer husband, my dear?" Mrs. Berry turned from her tale to question.

"Did you expect to see him here?" said Lucy in a broken voice.

"And where else, my love, since he haven't been seen in London a whole fort-night?"

Lucy did not speak.

"We will dismiss the Emperor Julian till tomorrow, I think," said Lord Mountfalcon rising, and bowing.

Lucy gave him her hand with mute thanks. He touched it distantly, embraced Mrs. Berry in a farewell bow, and was shown out of the house by Tom Bakewell.

The moment he was satisfactorily gone, Mrs. Berry threw up her arms. "Did ye ever know sich a horrid thing to go and happen to a virtuous woman!" she exclaimed. "I could cry at it, I could! To be goin' and kissin' a strange hairy man! Oh, dear me! what's comin' next, I wonder? Whiskers! thinks I—for I know the touch o' whiskers—'t ain't like other hair—what! have he growed a crop that sudden, I says to myself; and it kind o' flashed on me I been and made a awful mistake! and the lights come in, and I see that great hairy man—beggin' his pardon—nobleman, and if I could 'a dropped through the floor out o' sight o' men, drat 'em! they're al'ays in the way, that they are!"—

"Mrs. Berry," Lucy checked her, "did you expect to find him here?"

"Askin' that solemn!" retorted Berry. "What him? your husband? O' course I did! and you got him—somewheres hid."

"I have not heard from my husband for fifteen days," said Lucy, and her tears rolled heavily off her cheeks.

"Not heer from him!—fifteen days!" Berry echoed.

"Oh, Mrs. Berry! dear kind Mrs. Berry! have you no news? nothing to tell me? I've borne it so long. They're cruel to me, Mrs. Berry. Oh! do you know if I have offended him—my husband? While he wrote I did not complain. I could live on his letters for years. But not to hear from him! To think I have ruined him, and that he repents! Do they want to take him from me? Do they want me dead? Oh, Mrs. Berry! I've had no one to speak out my heart to all this time, and I cannot, cannot help crying, Mrs. Berry!"

Mrs. Berry was inclined to be miserable at what she heard from Lucy's lips, and she was herself full of dire apprehension; but it was never this excellent creature's system to be miserable in company. The sight of a sorrow that was not positive, and could not refer to proof, set her resolutely the other way.

"Fiddle-faddle," she said. "I'd like to see him repent! He won't find anywheres a beauty like his own dear little wife, and he know it. Now, look you here, my dear—you blessed weepin' pet—the man that could see ye with that hair of yours there in ruins, and he backed by the law, and not rush into yer arms and hold ye squeezed for life, he an't got much man in him, I say; and no one can say that of my babe! I was sayin', look here, to comfort ye—Oh, why, to be sure he've got some surprise for ye. And so 've I, my lamb! Hark now! His father 've come to town, like a good reasonable man at last, to u-nite ye both, and bring yer bodies together, as yer 'arts is, for everlastin'. Now ain't that news?"

"Oh!" cried Lucy, "that takes my last hope away. I thought he had gone to his father." She burst into fresh tears.

Mrs. Berry paused, disturbed.

"Belike he's travellin' after him," she suggested.

"Fifteen days, Mrs. Berry!"

"Ah, fifteen weeks, my dear, after sich a man as that. He's a reg'lar mete-or, is Sir Austin Feverel, Raynham Abbey. Well, so hark you here. I says to myself, that knows him—for I did think my babe *was* in his nat'ral nest— I says, the Bar'net 'll never write for you both to come up and beg forgiveness, so down I'll go and fetch y' up. For there was your mistake, my dear, ever to leave your husband to go away from ye one hour in a young marriage. It's dangerous, it's mad, it's wrong, and it's ony to be righted by your obeyin' of me, as I commands it: for I has my fits, though I *am* a soft 'un. Obey me, and ye'll be happy to-morrow—or the next to it."

Lucy was willing to see comfort. She was weary of her self-inflicted martyrdom, and glad to give herself up to somebody else's guidance utterly.

"But why does he not write to me, Mrs. Berry?"

" 'Cause, 'cause—who can tell the why of men, my dear? But that he love ye faithful, I'll swear. Haven't he groan in my arms that he couldn't come to ye?—weak wretch? Hasn't he swore how he loved ye to me, poor young man? But this is your fault, my sweet. Yes, it be. You should 'a followed my 'dvice at the fust—'stead o' going into your 'eroics about this and t'other." Here Mrs. Berry poured forth fresh sentences on matrimony, pointed especially at young couples. "I should 'a been a fool if I hadn't suffered myself," she confessed, "so I'll thank my Berry if I makes you wise in season."

Lucy smoothed her ruddy plump cheeks, and gazed up affectionately into the soft woman's kind brown eyes. Endearing phrases passed from mouth to mouth. And as she gazed, Lucy blushed, as one who has something very secret to tell, very sweet, very strange, but cannot quite bring herself to speak it.

"Well! there's three men in my life I kissed," said Mrs. Berry, too much absorbed in her extraordinary adventure to notice the young wife's struggling bosom, "three men, and one a nobleman! He've got more whisker than my Berry. I wonder what the man thought. Ten to one he'll think, now, I was glad o' my chance—they're that vain, whether they's lords or commons. How was I to know? I nat'ral thinks none but her husband 'd sit in that chair. Ha! and in the dark? and alone with ye?" Mrs. Berry hardened her eyes, "and yer husband away? What do this mean? Tell to me, child, what it mean his bein' here alone without ere a candle?"

"Lord Mountfalcon is the only friend I have here," said Lucy. "He is very kind. He comes almost every evening."

"Lord Muntfalcon—that's his name!" Mrs. Berry exclaimed. "I been that flurried by the man, I didn't mind it at first. He come every evenin', and yer husband out o' sight! My goodness me! it's gettin' wus and wus. And what do he come for, now, Ma'am? Now tell me candid what ye do together here in the dark of an evenin'."

Mrs. Berry glanced severe.

"Oh, Mrs. Berry! please not to speak in that way—I don't like it," said Lucy, pouting.

"What do he come for, I ask?"

"Because he is so kind, Mrs. Berry. He sees me very lonely, and wishes to amuse me. And he tells me of things I know nothing about and—"

"And wants to be a-teachin' some of his things, mayhap," Mrs. Berry interrupted with a ruffled breast.

"You are a very ungenerous, suspicious, naughty old woman," said Lucy, chiding her.

"And you're a silly, unsuspectin' little bird," Mrs. Berry retorted, as she returned her taps on the cheek. "You haven't told me what ye do together, and what's his excuse for comin'."

"Well, then, Mrs. Berry, almost every evening that he comes we read history, and he explains the battles, and talks to me about the great men. And *he* says I'm not silly, Mrs. Berry."

"That's one bit o' lime on yer wings, my bird. History, indeed! History to a young married lovely woman alone in the dark! a pretty history! Why, I know that man's name, my dear. He's note-horious rake, that Lord Muntfalcon. No woman's safe with him."

"Ah, but he hasn't deceived me, Mrs. Berry. He has not pretended he was good."

"More's his art," quoth the experienced dame. "So you read history together in the dark, my dear!"

"I was unwell tonight, Mrs. Berry. I wanted him not to see my face. Look! there's the book open ready for him when the candles come in. And now you dear kind darling old thing, let me kiss you for coming to me. I do love you. Talk of other things."

"So we will," said Mrs. Berry, softening to Lucy's caresses. "So let us. A nobleman, indeed! alone with a young wife in the dark, and she sich a beauty! I say this shall be put a stop to now and 'enceforth, on the spot, it shall! He won't meneuvle Bessy Berry with his arts. There! I drop him. I'm dying for a cup o' tea, my dear."

Lucy got up to ring the bell, and as Mrs. Berry, incapable of quite dropping him, was continuing to say: "Let him go and boast I kiss him; he an't nothin' to be 'shamed of in a chaste woman's kiss—unawares—which men don't get too often in their lives, I can assure 'em:"—her eye surveyed Lucy's figure.

Lo, when Lucy returned to her, Mrs. Berry surrounded her with her arms, and drew her into feminine depths. "Oh, you blessed!" she cried in most meaning tone, "you good, lovin', proper, little wife, you!"

"What is it, Mrs. Berry?" lisps Lucy, opening innocent blue eyes.

"As if I couldn't see, you pet! It was my flurry blinded me, or I'd 'a marked ye the fust shock. Thinkin' to deceive me!"

Mrs. Berry's eyes spoke generations. Lucy's wavered; she coloured all over, and hid her face on the bounteous breast that mounted to her.

"You're a sweet one," murmured the soft woman, patting her back, and rocking her. "You're a rose, you are! and a bud on yer stalk. Haven't told a word to yer husband, my dear?" she asked quickly.

Lucy shook her head, looking sly and shy.

"That's right. We'll give him a surprise: let it come all at once on him, and thinks he—losin' breath—'I'm a father!' Nor a hint even you haven't give him?"

Lucy kissed her, to indicate it was quite a secret.

"Oh! you *are* a sweet one," said Bessy Berry, and rocked her more closely and lovingly.

Then these twain had a whispered conversation, from which let all of male persuasion retire a space nothing under one mile.

Returning, after a due interval, we see Mrs. Berry counting dates on her fingers' ends. Concluding the sum, she cries prophetically: "Now this right everything—a baby in the balance! Now I say this angel-infant come from on high. It's God's messenger, my love! and it's not wrong to say so. He thinks you worthy, or you wouldn't 'a had one—not for all the tryin' in the world, you wouldn't, and some tries hard enough, poor creatures! Now let us rejice and make merry! I'm for cryin' and laughin', one and the same. This is the blessed seal of Matrimony, which Berry never stamp on me. It's be hoped it's a boy. Make that man a gran'father, and his gran'child a son, and you got him safe. Oh! this is what I call 'appiness, and I'll have my tea a little stronger in conskence. I declare I could get tipsy to know this joyful news."

So Mrs. Berry carolled. She had her tea a little stronger. She ate and she drank: she rejoiced and made merry. The bliss of the chaste was hers.

Says Lucy demurely: "Now you know why I read history, and that sort of books."

"Do I?" replies Berry. "Belike I do. Since what you done's so good, my darlin', I'm agreeable to anything. A fig for all the lords! They can't come anigh a baby. You may read Voyages and Travels, my dear, and Ro-mances, and Tales of Love and War. You cut the riddle in yer own dear way, and that's all I cares for."

"No, but you don't understand," persists Lucy. "I only

read sensible books, and talk of serious things, because I'm sure . . . because I have heard say . . . dear Mrs. Berry! don't you understand now?"

Mrs. Berry smacked her knees. "Ony to think of her bein' that thoughtful! and she a Catholic, too! Never tell me that people of one Religion ain't as good as another, after that. Why, you want to make him a Historian, to be sure! And that rake of a lord who've been comin' here playin' at wolf, you been and made him—unbeknown to himself—sort o' tuter to the unborn blessed! Ha! ha! say that little women ain't got art ekal to the cunningest of 'em. Oh! I understand. Why, to be sure, didn't I know a lady, a widow of a clergyman: he was a postermost child, and afore his birth that woman read nothin' but Blair's 'Grave' over and again, from the end toe the beginnin';—that's a serious book! —very hard readin'!—and at four year of age that child that come of it reelly was the piousest infant!—he was like a little curate. His eyes was up; he talked se solemn." Mrs. Berry imitated the little curate's appearance and manner of speaking. "So she got her wish, for one!"

But at this lady Lucy laughed.

They chattered on happily till bed-time. Lucy arranged for Mrs. Berry to sleep with her. "If it's not dreadful to ye, my sweet, sleepin' beside a woman," said Mrs. Berry. "I know it were to me shortly after my Berry, and I felt it. It don't somehow seem nat'ral after Matrimony—a woman in yer bed! I was 'bliged t' ave somebody, for the cold sheets do give ye the creeps when you've been used to that that's different."

Upstairs they went together, Lucy not sharing these objections. Then Lucy opened certain drawers, and exhibited pretty caps, and laced linen, all adapted for a very small body, all the work of her own hands; and Mrs. Berry praised them and her. "You been guessin' a boy—womanlike," she said. Then they cooed, and kissed, and undressed by the fire, and knelt at the bedside, with their arms about each other, praying; both praying for the unborn child; and Mrs. Berry pressed Lucy's waist the moment she was about to breathe the petition to Heaven to shield and bless that coming life: and thereat Lucy closed to her, and felt a strong love for her. Then Lucy got into bed first, leaving Berry to put out the light, and before she did so, Berry leaned over her, and eyed her roguishly, saying, "I never see ye like this, but I'm half in love with ye myself, you blushin' beauty! Sweet's your eyes, and yer hair do take one so—lyin' back. I'd never forgive my father if he kep me away from ye four-and-twenty hours just. Husband o' that!" Berry pointed at the young wife's loveliness. "Ye look so ripe with kisses, and there they are a-langishin'! . . . You never look so but in yer bed, ye beauty!—just as it ought to be." Lucy had to pretend to rise to put out the light before Berry would give up her amorous chaste soliloquy. Then they lay in bed, and Mrs. Berry fondled her, and arranged for their departure tomorrow, and reviewed Richard's emotions when he came to hear he was going to be made a father by her, and hinted at Lucy's delicious shivers when Richard was again in his rightful place, which she, Bessy Berry, now usurped; and all sorts of amorous sweet things; enough to make one fancy the adage subverted, that stolen fruits are sweetest; she drew such glowing pictures of bliss within the Law, and the limits of the conscience, till at last, worn out, Lucy murmured, "Peepy, dear Berry," and the soft woman gradually ceased her chirp.

Bessy Berry did not sleep. She lay thinking of the sweet brave heart beside her, and listening to Lucy's breath as it came and went; squeezing the fair sleeper's hand now and then, to ease her love as her reflections warmed. A storm of wind came howling over the Hampshire hills, and sprang white foam on the water, and shook the bare trees. It passed, leaving a thin cloth of snow on the wintry land. The moon shone brilliantly. Berry heard the house-dog bark. His bark was savage and persistent. She was roused by the noise. By and by she fancied she heard a movement in the house; then it seemed to her that the house-door opened. She cocked her ears, and could almost make out voices in the midnight stillness. She slipped from the bed, locked and bolted the door of the room, assured herself of Lucy's unconsciousness, and went on tiptoe to the window. The trees all stood white to the north; the ground glittered; the cold was keen. Berry wrapped her fat arms across her bosom, and peeped as close over into the garden as the situation of the window permitted. Berry was a soft, not a timid, woman; and it happened this night that her thoughts were above the fears of the dark. She was sure of the voices; curiosity without a shade of alarm held her on the watch; and gathering bundles of her day-apparel round her neck and shoulders, she silenced the chattering of her teeth as well as she could, and remained stationary. The low hum of the voices came to a break; something was said in a louder tone; the house-door quietly shut; a man walked out of the garden into the road. He paused opposite her window, and Berry let the blind go back to its place, and peeped from behind an edge of it. He was in the shadow of the house, so that it was impossible to discern much of his figure. After some minutes he walked rapidly away, and Berry returned to the bed an icicle, from which Lucy's limbs sensitively shrank.

Next morning Mrs. Berry asked Tom Bakewell if he had been disturbed in the night. Tom, the mysterious, said he had slept like a top. Mrs. Berry went into the garden. The snow was partially melted; all save one spot, just under the portal, and there she saw the print of a man's foot. By some strange guidance it occurred to her to go and find one of Richard's boots. She did so, and unperceived she measured the sole of the boot in that solitary footmark. There could be no doubt that it fitted. She tried it from heel to toe a dozen times.

CHAPTER XLIV

CLARE'S DIARY

SIR Austin Feverel had come to Town with the serenity of a philosopher who says, 'Tis now time; and the satisfaction of a man who has not arrived thereat without a struggle. He had almost forgiven his son. His deep love for him had well-nigh shaken loose from wounded pride and more tenacious vanity. Stirrings of a remote sympathy for the creature who had robbed him of his son and hewed at his System, were in his heart of hearts. This he knew; and in his own mind he took credit for his softness. But the world must not suppose him soft; the world must think he was still acting on his System. Otherwise what would his long absence signify?—Something highly unphilosophic. So, though Love was strong, and was moving him to a straightforward course, the last tug of vanity drew him still aslant.

The Aphorist read himself so well, that to juggle with himself was a necessity. As he wished the world to see him, he beheld himself: one who entirely put aside mere personal feelings: one in whom parental duty, based on the science of Life, was paramount: a Scientific Humanist, in short.

He was, therefore, rather surprised at a coldness in Lady Blandish's manner when he did appear. "At last!" said the lady, in a sad way that sounded reproachfully. Now the Scientific Humanist had, of course, nothing to reproach himself with.

But where was Richard?

Adrian positively averred he was not with his wife.

"If he had gone," said the Baronet, "he would have anticipated me by a few hours."

This, when repeated to Lady Blandish, should have propitiated her, and shown his great forgiveness. She, however, sighed, and looked at him wistfully.

Their converse was not happy and deeply intimate. Philosophy did not seem to catch her mind; and fine phrases encountered a rueful assent, more flattering to their grandeur than to their influence.

Days went by. Richard did not present himself. Sir Austin's pitch of self-command was to await the youth without signs of impatience.

Seeing this, the lady told him her fears for Richard, and mentioned the rumour of him that was about.

"If," said the Baronet, "this person, his wife, is what you paint her, I do not share your fears for him. I think too well of him. If she is one to inspire the sacredness of that union, I think too well of him. It is impossible."

The lady saw one thing to be done.

"Call her to you," she said. "Have her with you at Raynham. Recognize her. It is the disunion and doubt that so confuses him and drives him wild. I confess to you I hoped he had gone to her. It seems not. If she is with you his way will be clear. Will you do that?"

Science is notoriously of slow movement. Lady Blandish's proposition was far too hasty for Sir Austin. Women, rapid by nature, have no idea of Science.

"We shall see her there in time, Emmeline. At present let it be between me and my son."

He spoke loftily. In truth it offended him to be asked to do anything, when he had just brought himself to do so much.

A month elapsed, and Richard appeared on the scene.

The meeting between him and his father was not what his father expected, and had crooned over in the Welsh mountains, among the echoes of his Aphorisms. Richard shook his hand respectfully, and inquired after his health with the common social solicitude. He then said: "During your absence, Sir, I have taken the liberty, without consulting you, to do something in which you are more deeply concerned than myself. I have taken upon myself to find out

my mother and place her under my care. I trust you will
not think I have done wrong. I acted as I thought best."

Sir Austin replied: "You are of an age, Richard, to judge
for yourself in such a case. I would have you simply beware
of deceiving yourself in imagining that you considered any
one but yourself in acting as you did."

"I have not deceived myself, Sir," said Richard, and the
interview was over. Both hated an exposure of the feelings,
and in that both were satisfied: but the Baronet, as one who
loves, hoped and looked for tones indicative of trouble and
delight in the deep heart; and Richard gave him none of
those. The young man did not even face him as he spoke:
if their eyes met by chance, Richard's were defiantly cold.
His whole bearing was changed.

"This rash Marriage has altered him," said the very just
man of Science in life: and that meant: 'It has debased him.'

He pursued his reflections: "I see in him the desperate
maturity of a suddenly-ripened nature: and but for my faith
that good work is never lost, what should I think of the toil
of my years? Lost, perhaps, to me! lost to him! It may
show itself in his children."

The Philosopher, we may conceive, has contentment in
benefiting embryos: but it was a somewhat bitter prospect
to Sir Austin. Bitterly he felt the injury to himself.

One little incident spoke well of Richard. A poor woman
called at the hotel while he was missing. The Baronet saw
her, and she told him a tale that threw Christian light on
one part of Richard's nature. But this might gratify the
father in Sir Austin; it did not touch the man of Science.
A Feverel, his son, would not do less, he thought. He sat
down deliberately to study his son.

No definite observations enlightened him. Richard ate
and drank; joked and laughed. He was generally before
Adrian in calling for a fresh bottle. He talked easily of
current topics: his gaiety did not sound forced. In all he
did, nevertheless, there was not the air of a youth who sees

a future before him. Sir Austin put that down. It might
be carelessness, and wanton blood, for no one could say he
had much on his mind. The man of Science was not reckoning that Richard also might have learned to act and wear a
mask. Dead subjects—that is to say, people not on their
guard—he could penetrate and dissect. It is by a rare
chance, as scientific men well know, that one has an opportunity of examining the structure of the living.

However, that rare chance was granted to Sir Austin.
They were engaged to dine with Mrs. Doria at the Foreys,
and walked down to her in the afternoon, father and son
arm-in-arm, Adrian beside them. Previously the offended
father had condescended to inform his son that it would
shortly be time for him to return to his wife, indicating that
arrangements would ultimately be ordered to receive her at
Raynham. Richard had replied nothing; which might mean
excess of gratitude, or hypocrisy in concealing his pleasure,
or any one of the thousand shifts by which gratified human
nature expresses itself when all is made to run smooth with
it. Now Mrs. Berry had her surprise ready charged for the
young husband. She had Lucy in her own house waiting for
him. Every day she expected him to call and be overcome
by the rapturous surprise, and every day, knowing his habit
of frequenting the park, she marched Lucy thither, under the
plea that Master Richard, whom she had already christened,
should have an airing.

The round of the red winter sun was behind the bare
Kensington chestnuts, when these two parties met. Happily
for Lucy and the hope she bore in her bosom, she was per-
versely admiring a fair horsewoman galloping by at the
moment. Mrs. Berry plucked at her gown once or twice to
prepare her eyes for the shock, but Lucy's head was still half
averted, and thinks Mrs. Berry, " 'Twon't hurt her if she
go into his arms head foremost." They were close; Mrs.
Berry performed the bob preliminary. Richard held her
silent with a terrible face; he grasped her arm, and put

her behind him. Other people intervened. Lucy saw nothing to account for Berry's excessive flutter. Berry threw it on the air and some breakfast bacon, which, she said, she knew in the morning while she ate it, was bad for the bile, and which probably was the cause of her bursting into tears, much to Lucy's astonishment.

"What you ate makes you cry, Mrs. Berry?"

"It's all—" Mrs. Berry pressed at her heart and leaned sideways, "it's all stomach, my dear. Don't ye mind," and becoming aware of her unfashionable behaviour, she trailed off to the shelter of the elms.

"You have a singular manner with old ladies," said Sir Austin to his son, after Berry had been swept aside. "Scarcely courteous. She behaved like a mad woman, certainly.—Are you ill, my son?"

Richard was death-pale, his strong form smitten through with weakness. The Baronet sought Adrian's eye. Adrian had seen Lucy as they passed, and he had a glimpse of Richard's countenance while disposing of Berry. Had Lucy recognized them, he would have gone to her unhesitatingly. As she did not, he thought it well, under the circumstances, to leave matters as they were. He answered the Baronet's look with a shrug.

"Are you ill, Richard?" Sir Austin again asked his son.

"Come on, Sir! come on!" cried Richard.

His father's further meditations, as they stepped briskly to the Foreys, gave poor Berry a character which one who lectures on Matrimony, and has kissed but three men in her life, shrieks to hear the very title of.

"Richard will go to his wife tomorrow," Sir Austin said to Adrian some time before they went in to dinner.

Adrian asked him if he had chanced to see a young fair-haired lady by the side of the old one Richard had treated so peculiarly; and to the Baronet's acknowledgment that he remembered to have observed such a person, Adrian said: "That was his wife, Sir."

Sir Austin could now dissect the living subject. As if a bullet had torn open the young man's skull, and some blast of battle laid his palpitating organization bare, he watched every motion of his brain and his heart; and with the grief and terror of one whose mental habit was ever to pierce to extremes. Not altogether conscious that he had hitherto played with life, he felt that he was suddenly plunged into the stormful reality of it. He projected to speak plainly to his son on all points that night.

"Richard is very gay," Mrs. Doria whispered her brother.

"All will be right with him tomorrow," he replied; for the game had been in his hands so long, so long had he been the God of the machine, that having once resolved to speak plainly and to act, he was to a certain extent secure, bad as the thing to mend might be.

"I notice he has a rather wild laugh—I don't exactly like his eyes," said Mrs. Doria.

"You will see a change in him tomorrow," the man of Science remarked.

It was reserved for Mrs. Doria herself to experience that change. In the middle of the dinner a telegraphic message from her son-in-law, worthy John Todhunter, reached the house, stating that Clare was alarmingly ill, bidding her come instantly. She cast about for some one to accompany her, and fixed on Richard. Before he would give his consent for Richard to go, Sir Austin desired to speak with him apart, and in that interview he said to his son: "My dear Richard! it was my intention that we should come to an understanding together this night. But the time is short— poor Helen cannot spare many minutes. Let me then say that you deceived me, and that I forgive you. We fix our seal on the Past. You will bring your wife to me when you return." And very cheerfully the Baronet looked down on the generous future he thus founded.

"Will you have her at Raynham at once, Sir?" said Richard.

"Yes, my son, when you bring her."

"Are you mocking me, Sir?"

"Pray, what do you mean?"

"I ask you to receive her at once."

"Well! the delay cannot be long. I do not apprehend that you will be kept from your happiness many days."

"I think it will be some time, Sir!" said Richard, sighing deeply.

"And what mental freak is this that can induce you to postpone it and play with your first duty?"

"What is my first duty, Sir?"

"Since you are married, to be with your wife."

"I have heard that from an old woman called Berry!" said Richard to himself, not intending irony.

"Will you receive her at once, Sir?" he asked resolutely.

The Baronet was clouded by his son's reception of his graciousness. His grateful prospect had formerly been Richard's marriage—the culmination of his System. Richard had destroyed his participation in that. He now looked for a pretty scene in recompense:—Richard leading up his wife to him, and both being welcomed by him paternally, and so held one ostentatious minute in his embrace.

He said: "Before you return, I demur to receiving her."

"Very well, Sir," replied his son, and stood as if he had spoken all.

"Really you tempt me to fancy you already regret your rash proceeding!" the Baronet exclaimed; and the next moment it pained him he had uttered the words, Richard's eyes were so sorrowfully fierce. It pained him, but he divined in that look a history, and he could not refrain from glancing acutely and asking: "Do you?"

"Regret it, Sir?" The question aroused one of those struggles in the young man's breast which a passionate storm of tears may still, and which sink like leaden death into the soul when tears come not. Richard's eyes had the light of the desert.

"Do you?" his father repeated. "You tempt me—I al-most fear you do." At the thought—for he expressed his mind—the pity that he had for Richard was not pure gold.

"Ask me what I think of her, Sir! Ask me what she is! Ask me what it is to have taken one of God's precious Angels and chained her to misery! Ask me what it is to have plunged a sword into her heart, and to stand over her and see such a creature bleeding! Do I regret that? Why, yes, I do! Would you?"

His eyes flew hard at his father under the ridge of his eyebrows.

Sir Austin winced and reddened. Did he understand? There is ever in the mind's eye a certain wilfulness. We see and understand; we see and won't understand.

"Tell me why you passed by her as you did this after-noon," he said gravely: and in the same voice Richard answered: "I passed her because I could not do otherwise."

"Your wife, Richard?"

"Yes! my wife!"

"If she had seen you, Richard?"

"God spared her that!"

Mrs. Doria, bustling in practical haste, and bearing Richard's hat and greatcoat in her energetic hands, came between them at this juncture. Dimples of commiseration were in her cheeks while she kissed her brother's perplexed forehead. She forgot her trouble about Clare, deploring his fatuity.

Sir Austin was forced to let his son depart. As of old, he took counsel with Adrian, and the Wise Youth was soothing. "Somebody has kissed him, Sir, and the chaste boy can't get over it." This absurd suggestion did more to appease the Baronet than if Adrian had given a veritable reasonable key to Richard's conduct. It set him thinking that it might be a prudish strain in the young man's mind, due to the System in difficulties.

"I may have been wrong in one thing," he said, with an

air of the utmost doubt of it. "I, perhaps, was wrong in allowing him so much liberty during his Probation."

Adrian pointed out to him that he had distinctly commanded it.

"Yes, yes; that is on me."

His was an order of mind that would accept the most burdensome charges, and by some species of moral usury make a profit out of them.

Clare was little talked of. Adrian attributed the employment of the telegraph to John Todhunter's uxorious distress at a toothache, or possibly the first symptoms of an heir to his house.

"That child's mind has disease in it. She is not sound," said the Baronet.

On the door-step of the hotel, when they returned, stood Mrs. Berry. Her wish to speak a few words with the Baronet reverentially communicated, she was ushered upstairs into his room.

Mrs. Berry compressed her person in the chair she was beckoned to occupy.

"Well, Ma'am, you have something to say," observed the Baronet, for she seemed loath to commence.

"Wishin' I hadn't!" Mrs. Berry took him up, and mindful of the good rule to begin at the beginning, pursued: "I dare say, Sir Austin, you don't remember me, and I little thought when last we parted our meeting'd be like this. Twenty year don't go over one without showin' it, no more than twenty ox. It's a might o' time—twenty year! Leastways not quite twenty, it an't."

"Round figures are best," Adrian remarked.

"In them round figures a be-loved son have growed up, and got himself married!" said Mrs. Berry, diving straight into the case.

Sir Austin then learnt that he had before him the culprit who had assisted his son in that venture. It was a stretch of his patience to hear himself addressed on a family matter, but he was naturally courteous.

"He kem to my house, Sir Austin, a stranger! If twenty year alters us as have knowed each other on the earth, how must they alter they that we parted with just come from Heaven! And a heavenly babe he were! se sweet, se strong! *so* fat!"

Adrian laughed aloud.

Mrs. Berry bumped a curtsey to him in her chair, continuing: "I wished afore I spoke to say how thankful am I bound to be for my pension not cut short, as have offended so, but that I know Sir Austin Feverel, Raynham Abbey, ain't one o' them that likes to hear their good deeds pumlished. And a pension to me now, it's something more than it were. For a pension and pretty rosy cheeks in a maid, which I was—that's a bait many a man'll bite, that won't so a forsaken wife!"

"If you will speak to the point, Ma'am, I will listen to you," the Baronet interrupted her.

"It's the beginnin' that's the worst, and that's over, thank the Lord! So I'll speak, Sir Austin, and say my say:— Lord speed me! Believin' our idees o' Matrimony to be sim'lar, then, I'll say, once married—married for life! Yes! I don't even like widows. For I can't stop at the grave. Not at the tomb I can't stop. My husband's my husband, and if I'm a body at the Resurrection, I say, speakin' humbly, my Berry is the husband o' my body; and to think of two claimin' of me then—it makes me hot all over. Such is my notion of that state 'tween man and woman. No givin' in marriage, o' course I know, and if so I'm single."

The Baronet suppressed a smile. "Really my good woman, you wander very much."

"Beggin' pardon, Sir Austin; but I has my point before me all the same, and I'm comin' to it. Ac-knowledgin' our error, it's done, and bein' done, it's writ aloft. Oh! if you ony knew what a sweet young creature she be! Indeed 'tain't all of humble birth that's unworthy, Sir Austin. And she got her ideas, too. She read History! She talk that sensible as would surprise ye. But for all that she's a prey to the artful o' men—unpertected. And it's a young marriage—but there's no fear for her, as far as she go. The fear's t'other way. There's that in a man—at the commencement—which make of him Lord knows what! if you any way interferes: whereas a woman bides quiet. It's consolation catch her, which is what we mean by seducin'. Whereas a man—he's a savage!"

Sir Austin turned his face to Adrian, who was listening with huge delight.

"Well, Ma'am, I see you have something in your mind, if you would only come to it quickly."

"Then here's my point, Sir Austin. I say you bred him so as there ain't another young gentleman like him in England, and proud he make me. And as for her, I'll risk sayin'—it's done, and no harm—you might search England through, and nowheres will ye find a maid that's his match like his own wife. Then there they be. Are they together as should be? Oh Lord no! Months they been divided. Then she all lonely and exposed, I went, and fetched her out of seducers' ways—which they may say what they like, but the inn'cent is most open to when they're healthy and confidin'—I fetch her, and—the liberty—boxed her safe in my own house. So much for that sweet! That you may do with women. But it's him—Mr. Richard—I *am* bold, I know, but there—I'm in for it, and the Lord'll help me! It's him, Sir Austin, in this great Metropilis, warm from a young marriage. It's him, and—I say nothin' of her, and how sweet she bears it, and it's eating her at a time when Natur' should have no other trouble but the one that's goin' on— it's him, and I ask—so bold—shall there—and a Christian gentleman his father—shall there be a tug 'tween him as a son and him as a husband—soon to be somethin' else? I speak bold out—I'd have sons obey ther fathers, but the

priest's words spoke over him, which they're now in my
ears, I say I ain't a doubt on earth—I'm sure there ain't one
in Heaven—which dooty's the holier of the two."

Sir Austin heard her to an end. Their views on the junction of the sexes were undoubtedly akin. To be lectured on
his prime subject, however, was slightly disagreeable, and to
be obliged mentally to assent to this old lady's doctrine was
rather humiliating, when it could not be averred that he had
latterly followed it out. He sat cross-legged and silent, a
finger to his temple.

"One gets so addle-pated thinkin' many thinks," said Mrs.
Berry, simply. "That's why we see wonder clever people
al'ays goin' wrong—to my mind. I think it's al'ays the
plan in a dielemmer to pray God and walk forward."

The keen-witted soft woman was tracking the Baronet's
thoughts, and she had absolutely run him down and taken an
explanation out of his mouth, by which Mrs. Berry was to
have been informed that he had acted from a principle of his
own, and devolved a wisdom she could not be expected to
comprehend.

Of course he became advised immediately that it would
be waste of time to direct such an explanation to her inferior capacity.

He gave her his hand, saying, "My son has gone out of
Town to see his cousin who is ill. He will return in two
or three days, and then they will both come to me at Raynham."

Mrs. Berry took the tips of his fingers, and went half-way
to the floor perpendicularly. "He pass her like a stranger
in the park this evenin'," she faltered.

"Ah?" said the Baronet. "Yes, well! they will be at
Raynham before the week is over."

Mrs. Berry was not quite satisfied. "Not of his own
accord he pass that sweet young wife of his like a stranger
this day, Sir Austin?"

"I must beg you not to intrude further, Ma'am."

Mrs. Berry bobbed her bunch of a body out of the room. "All's well as ends well," she said to herself. "It's bad inquirin' too close among men. We must take 'em somethin' like Providence—*as* they come. Thank Heaven! I kep' back the baby."

In Mrs. Berry's eyes the baby was the victorious reserve. Adrian asked his chief what he thought of that specimen of woman.

"I think I have not met a better in my life," said the Baronet, mingling praise and sarcasm.

Clare lies in her bed as placid as in the days when she breathed; her white hands stretched their length along the coverlid, at peace from head to feet. She needs iron no more. Richard is face to face with Death for the first time. He sees the sculpture of clay—the spark gone.

Clare gave her mother the welcome of the dead. This child would have spoken nothing but kind commonplaces had she been alive. She was dead, and none knew her malady. On her fourth finger were two wedding-rings.

When hours of weeping had silenced the mother's anguish, she, for some comfort she saw in it, pointed out that strange thing to Richard, speaking low in the chamber of the dead; and then he learnt that it was his own lost ring Clare wore in the two worlds. He learnt from her husband Clare's last request had been that neither of the Rings should be removed. She had written it: she would not speak it.

"I beg of my husband, and all kind people who may have the care of me between this and the grave, to bury me with my right hand untouched."

The tracing of the words showed the bodily torment she was suffering, as she wrote them on a scrap of paper found beside her pillow.

In wonder as the dim idea grew from the waving of Clare's dead hand, Richard paced the house, and hung about the awful room; dreading to enter it, reluctant to quit it.

The secret Clare had buried while she lived, arose with her death. He saw it play like flame across her marble features. The memory of her voice was like a knife at his nerves. His coldness to her started up accusingly: her meekness was bitter blame.

On the evening of the fourth day, her mother came to him in his bedroom, with a face so white he asked himself if aught worse could happen to a mother than the loss of her child. Choking she said to him, "Read this," and thrust a leather-bound pocket-book trembling in his hand. She would not breathe to him what it was. She entreated him not to open it before her.

"Tell me," she said, "tell me what you think. John must not hear of it. I have nobody to consult but you—oh, Richard!"

"My Diary" was written in the round hand of Clare's childhood on the first page. The first name his eye encountered was his own.

"Richard's fourteenth birthday. I have worked him a purse and put it under his pillow, because he is going to have plenty of money. He does not notice me now because he has a friend now, and he is ugly, but Richard is not, and never will be."

The occurrences of that day were subsequently recorded, and a childish prayer to God for him set down. Step by step he saw her growing mind in his history. As she advanced in years she began to look back, and made much of little trivial remembrances, all bearing upon him.

"We went into the fields and gathered cowslips together, and pelted each other, and I told him he used to call them 'coals-sleeps' when he was a baby, and he was angry at my telling him, for he does not like to be told he was ever a baby."

He remembered the incident, and remembered his stupid scorn of her meek affection. Little Clare! how she lived

before him in her white dress and pink ribbons, and soft
dark eyes! Upstairs she was lying dead. He read on:

"Mama says there is no one in the world like Richard,
and I am sure there is not, not in the whole world. He
says he is going to be a great General and going to the wars.
If he does I shall dress myself as a boy and go after him,
and he will not know me till I am wounded. Oh I pray he
will never never be wounded. I wonder what I should
feel if Richard was ever to die."

Upstairs Clare was lying dead.

"Lady Blandish said there is a likeness between Richard
and me. Richard said I hope I do not hang down my head
as she does. He is angry with me because I do not look
people in the face and speak out, but I know I am not looking after earth-worms."

Yes. He had told her that. A shiver seized him at the
recollection.

Then it came to a period when the words: "Richard kissed
me," stood by themselves, and marked a day in her life.

Afterwards it was solemnly discovered that Richard wrote
poetry. He read one of his old forgotten compositions penned
when he had that ambition.

> *"Thy truth to me is truer*
>   *Than horse, or dog, or blade:*
> *Thy vows to me are fewer*
>   *Than ever maiden made.*
> *Thou steppest from thy splendour*
>   *To make my life a song:*
> *My bosom shall be tender*
>   *As thine has risen strong."*

All the verses were transcribed. "It is he who is the
humble knight," Clare explained at the close, "and his lady
is a Queen. Any Queen would throw her crown away for
him."

It came to that period when Clare left Raynham with her mother.

"Richard was not sorry to lose me. He only loves boys and men. Something tells me I shall never see Raynham again. He was dressed in blue. He said Good-bye, Clare, and kissed me on the cheek. Richard never kisses me on the mouth. He did not know I went to his bed and kissed him while he was asleep. He sleeps with one arm under his head, and the other out on the bed. I moved away a bit of his hair that was over his eyes. I wanted to cut it. I have one piece. I do not let anybody see I am unhappy, not even Mama. She says I want iron. I am sure I do not. I like to write my name. Clare Doria Forey. Richard's is Richard Doria Feverel."

His breast rose convulsively. Clare Doria Forey! He knew the music of that name. He had heard it somewhere. It sounded faint and mellow now behind the hills of Death.

He could not read for tears. It was midnight. The hour seemed to belong to her. The awful stillness and the darkness was Clare's. Clare's voice clear and cold from the grave possessed it.

Painfully, with blinded eyes, he looked over the breathless pages. She spoke of his Marriage, and her finding the Ring.

"I knew it was his. I knew he was going to be married that morning. I saw him stand by the altar when they laughed at breakfast. His wife must be so beautiful! Richard's wife! Perhaps he will love me better now he is married. Mama says they must be separated. That is shameful. If I can help him I will. I pray so that he may be happy. I hope God hears poor sinners' prayers. I am very sinful. Nobody knows it as I do. They say I am good, but I know. When I look on the ground I am not looking after earth-worms, as he said. Oh, do forgive me, God!"

Then she spoke of her own marriage, and that it was her duty to obey her mother. A blank in the Diary ensued.

"I have seen Richard. Richard despises me," was the next entry.

But now as he read his eyes were fixed, and the delicate feminine handwriting like a black thread drew on his soul to one terrible conclusion.

"I cannot live. Richard despises me. I cannot bear the touch of my fingers or the sight of my face. Oh! I understand him now. He should not have kissed me so that last time. I wished to die while his mouth was on mine."

Further:

"I have no escape. Richard said he would die rather than endure it. I know he would. Why should I be afraid to do what he would do? I think if my husband whipped me I could bear it better. He is so kind, and tries to make me cheerful. He will soon be very unhappy. I pray to God half the night. I seem to be losing sight of Him the more I pray."

Richard laid the book open on the table. Phantom surges seemed to be mounting and travelling for his brain. Had Clare taken his wild words in earnest? Did she lie there dead—he shrouded the thought.

He wrapped the thoughts in shrouds, but he was again reading.

"A quarter to one o'clock. I shall not be alive this time tomorrow. I shall never see Richard now. I dreamed last night we were in the fields together, and he walked with his arm round my waist. We were children, but I thought we were married, and I showed him I wore his Ring, and he said—if you always wear it, Clare, you are as good as my wife. Then I made a vow to wear it for ever and ever. . . . It is not Mama's fault. She does not think as Richard and I do of these things. He is not a coward, nor am I. He hates cowards.

"I have written to his father to make him happy. Perhaps when I am dead he will hear what I say.

"I heard just now Richard call distinctly—Clari, come

out to me. Surely he has not gone. I am going I know not where. I cannot think. I am very cold."

The words were written larger, and staggered towards the close, as if her hand had lost mastery over the pen.

"I can only remember Richard now a boy. A little boy and a big boy. I am not sure now of his voice. I can only remember certain words. 'Clari,' and 'Don Ricardo,' and his laugh. He used to be full of fun. Once we laughed all day together tumbling in the hay. Then he had a friend, and began to write poetry, and be proud. If I had married a young man he would have forgiven me, but I should not have been happier. I must have died. God never looks on me.

"It is past two o'clock. The sheep are bleating outside. It must be very cold in the ground. Good-bye, Richard."

With his name it began and ended. Even to herself Clare was not over-communicative. The book was slender, yet her nineteen years of existence left half the number of pages white.

Those last words drew him irresistibly to gaze on her. There she lay, the same impassive Clare. For a moment he wondered she had not moved—to him she had become so different. She who had just filled his ears with strange tidings—it was not possible to think her dead! She seemed to have been speaking to him all through his life. His image was on that still heart.

He dismissed the night-watchers from the room, and remained with her alone, till the sense of Death oppressed him, and then the shock sent him to the window to look for sky and stars. Behind a low broad pine, hung with frosty mist, he heard a bell-wether of the flock in the silent fold. Death in life it sounded.

The mother found him praying at the foot of Clare's bed. She knelt by his side, and they prayed, and their joint sobs shook their bodies, but neither of them shed many tears.

They held a dark unspoken secret in common. They prayed God to forgive her.

Clare was buried in the family-vault of the Todhunters. Her mother breathed no wish to have her lying at Lobourne.

After the funeral, what they alone upon earth knew brought them together.

"Richard," she said, "the worst is over for me. I have no one to love but you, dear. We have all been fighting against God, and this . . . Richard! you will come with me, and be united to your wife, and spare my brother what I suffer."

He answered the broken spirit: "I have killed one. She sees me as I am. I cannot go with you to my wife, because I am not worthy to touch her hand, and were I to go, I should do *this* to silence my self-contempt. Go you to her, and when she asks of me, say I have a death upon my head that——No! say that I am abroad, seeking for that which shall cleanse me. If I find it I shall come to claim her. If not, God help us all!"

She had no force to contest his solemn words, or stay him, and he went forth.

CHAPTER XLV

AUSTIN RETURNS

A MAN with a beard saluted the Wise Youth Adrian in the full blaze of Piccadilly with a clap on the shoulder. Adrian glanced leisurely behind.

"Do you want to try my nerves, my dear fellow? I'm not a man of fashion, happily, or you would have struck the seat of them:—vital! How are you?"

That was his welcome to Austin Wentworth after his long absence.

Austin took his arm, and asked for news with the hunger of one who had been in the wilderness five years.

"The Whigs have given up the ghost, my dear Austin. The free Briton is to receive Liberty's pearl, the Ballot. The Aristocracy has had a cycle's notice to quit. The Monarchy and old Madeira are going out; Demos and Cape wines are coming it. They call it Reform. So, you see, your absence has worked wonders. Depart for another five years, and you will return to ruined stomachs, cracked sconces, general upset, and an Equality made perfect by universal prostration."

Austin indulged him in a laugh. "I want to hear about ourselves. How is old Ricky?"

"You know of his—what do they call it when greenhorns are licensed to jump into the milk-pails of dairymaids?—a very charming little woman she makes, by the way—presentable! quite old Anacreon's rose in milk. Well! everybody thought the System must die of it. Not a bit. It continued to flourish in spite. It's in a consumption now, though—emaciated, lean, raw, spectral! I've this morning escaped from Raynham to avoid the sight of it. I have brought our genial Uncle Hippias to Town—a delightful companion! I said to him: 'We've had a fine Spring.' 'Ugh!' he answers, 'there's a time when you come to think the Spring old.' You should have heard how he trained out the 'old.' I felt something like decay in my sap just to hear him. In the prize-fight of life, my dear Austin, our Uncle Hippias has been unfairly hit below the belt. Let's guard ourselves there, and go and order dinner."

"But where's Ricky now, and what is he doing?" said Austin.

"Ask what he has done. The miraculous boy has gone and got a baby!"

"A child? Richard has one?" Austin's clear eyes shone with pleasure.

"I suppose it's not common among your tropical savages. He has one: one as big as two. 'Tis that has been the death-blow to the System. It bore the Marriage—the baby was too much for it. Could it swallow the baby, 't would live.

She, the wonderful woman, has produced a large boy. I assure you it's quite amusing to see the System opening its mouth every hour of the day, trying to gulp him down, aware that it would be a consummate cure, or a happy release."

By degrees Austin learnt the Baronet's proceedings, and smiled sadly.

"How has Ricky turned out?" he asked. "What sort of a character has he?"

"The poor boy is ruined by his excessive anxiety about it. Character? he has the character of a bullet with a treble charge of powder behind it. Enthusiasm is the powder. That boy could get up an enthusiasm for the maiden days of Ops! He was going to reform the world, after your fashion, Austin,—you have something to answer for. Unfortunately he began with the feminine side of it. Cupid proud of Phœbus newly slain, or Pluto wishing to people his kingdom, if you like, put it into the soft head of one of the guileless grateful creatures to kiss him for his good work. Oh, horror! he never expected that. Conceive the System in the flesh, and you have our Richard. The consequence is that this male Peri refuses to enter his Paradise, though the gates are open for him, the trumpets blow, and the fair unspotted one awaits him fruitful within. We heard of him last that he was trying the German waters—preparatory to his undertaking the release of Italy from the subjugation of the Teuton. Let's hope they'll wash him. He is in the company of Lady Judith Felle—your old friend, the ardent female Radical who married the decrepid lord to carry out her principles. They always marry English lords, or foreign princes. I admire their tactics."

"Judith is bad for him in such a state. I like her, but she was always too sentimental," said Austin.

"Sentiment made her marry the old lord, I suppose? I like her *for* her sentiment, Austin. Sentimental people are sure to live long and die fat. 'T is feeling that's the slayer,

coz. Sentiment! 'tis the cajolery of existence: the soft bloom
which whoso weareth, he or she is enviable. Would that J
had more!"

"You're not much changed, Adrian."

"I'm not a Radical, Austin."

Further inquiries, responded to in Adrian's figurative
speech, instructed Austin that the Baronet was waiting for
his son, in a posture of statuesque offended paternity, before
he would receive his daughter-in-law and grandson. That
was what Adrian meant by the efforts of the System to
swallow the baby.

"We're in a tangle," said the Wise Youth. "Time will
extricate us, I presume, or what is the venerable Seignor
good for?"

Austin mused some minutes, and asked for Lucy's place
of residence.

"We'll go to her by and by," said Adrian.

"I shall go and see her now," said Austin.

"Well, we'll go and order the dinner first, coz."

"Give me her address."

"Really, Austin, you carry matters with too long a beard,"
Adrian objected. "Don't you care what you eat?" he roared
hoarsely, looking humorously hurt. "I dare say not. A slice
out of him that's handy—sauce du ciel! Go, batten on the
baby, cannibal. Dinner at seven."

Adrian gave him his own address, and Lucy's, and strolled
off to do the better thing.

Overnight Mrs. Berry had observed a long stranger in her
tea-cup. Posting him on her fingers and starting him with
a smack, he had vaulted lightly and thereby indicated that
he was positively coming the next day. She forgot him in
the bustle of her duties and the absorption of her faculties
in thoughts of the incomparable stranger Lucy had presented to the world, till a knock at the street-door reminded
her. "There he is!" she cried, as she ran to open to him.
"There's my stranger come!" Never was a woman's faith

in omens so justified. The stranger desired to see Mrs. Richard Feverel. He said his name was Mr. Austin Wentworth. Mrs. Berry clasped her hands, exclaiming, "Come at last!" and ran bolt out of the house to look up and down the street. Presently she returned with many excuses for her rudeness, saying: "I 'xpected to see her comin' home, Mr. Wentworth. Every day twice a day she go out to give her blessed Angel an airing. No leavin' the child with nuss-maids for her! She *is* a mother! and good milk, too, thank the Lord! though her 'art's se low—nat'ral!"

Indoors Mrs. Berry stated who she was, related the history of the young couple, and her participation in it, and admired the beard. "Though I'd swear you don't wear it for orn'-ment, now!" she said, having in the first impulse designed a stroke at man's vanity.

Ultimately Mrs. Berry spoke of the family-complication, and with dejected head and joined hands threw out dark hints about Richard.

While Austin was giving his cheerfuller views of the case, Lucy came in, preceding the baby.

"I am Austin Wentworth," he said, taking her hand. They read each other's faces, these two, and smiled kinship.

"Your name is Lucy?"

She affirmed it softly.

"And mine is Austin, as you know."

Mrs. Berry allowed time for Lucy's charms to subdue him, and presented Richard's representative, who, seeing a new face, suffered himself to be contemplated before he commenced crying aloud, and knocking at the doors of Nature for something that was due to him.

"Ain't he a lusty darlin'?" says Mrs. Berry. "Ain't he like his own father? There can't be no doubt about zoo, zoo pitty pet. Look at his fists. Ain't he got passion? Ain't he a splendid roarer? Oh!" and she went off rapturously into baby-language.

A fine boy, certainly. Mrs. Berry exhibited his legs for

further proof, desiring Austin's confirmation as to their being dumplings.

Lucy murmured a word of excuse, and bore the splendid roarer out of the room.

"She might 'a done it here," said Mrs. Berry. "There's no prettier sight, I say. If her dear husband could but see that! He's off in his 'eroics—he want to be doin' all sorts o' things: I say he'll never do anything grander than that baby. You should 'a seen her uncle over that baby—he came here, for I said, you *shall* see your own fam'ly, my dear, and so she thinks. He come, and he laughed over that baby in the ji of his 'art, poo' man! he cried, he did. You should see that Mr. Thompson, Mr. Wentworth—a friend o' Mr. Richard's, and a very modest-minded young gentleman—he worships her, in his inn'cence. It's a sight to see him with that baby. My belief is he's unhappy 'cause he can't anyways be nussmaid to him. Lor! and there everything so beautiful, and just that one screw loose. Oh, Mr. Wentworth! what *do* you think of her, Sir?"

Austin's reply was as satisfactory as a man's poor speech could make it. He heard that Lady Feverel was in the house, and Mrs. Berry prepared the way for him to pay his respects to her. Then Mrs. Berry ran to Lucy, and the house buzzed with new life. The simple creatures felt in Austin's presence something good among them. "He don't speak much," said Mrs. Berry, "but I see by his eye he mean a deal. He ain't one o' yer long-word gentry, who's all gay deceivers, every one of 'em."

Lucy pressed the hearty suckling into her breast. "I wonder what he thinks of me, Mrs. Berry? I could not speak to him. I loved him before I saw him. I knew what his face was like."

"He looks proper even with a beard, and that's a trial for a virtuos man," said Mrs. Berry. "One sees straight *through* the hair with him. Think! he'll think what any *man* 'd think—you a-suckin' spite o' all yer sorrow, my sweet,—and my Berry talkin' of his Roman Matrons!—here's a English wife 'll match 'em all! that's what he thinks. And now that leetle dark under yer eye 'll clear, my darlin', now he've come."

Mrs. Berry looked to no more than that; Lucy to no more than the peace she had in being near Richard's best friend. When she sat down to tea it was with a sense that the little room that held her was her home perhaps for many a day.

A chop procured and cooked by Mrs. Berry formed Austin's dinner. During the meal he entertained them with anecdotes of his travels. Poor Lucy had no temptation to try to conquer Austin. That heroic weakness of hers was gone.

Mrs. Berry had said: "Three cups—I goes no further," and Lucy had rejected the proffer of more tea, when Austin, who was in the thick of a Brazilian forest, asked her if she was a good traveller.

"I mean, can you start at a minute's notice?"

Lucy hesitated, and then said, "Yes," decisively, to which Mrs. Berry added, that she was not a "luggage-woman."

"There used to be a train at seven o'clock," Austin remarked, consulting his watch.

The two women were silent.

"Could you get ready to come with me to Raynham in ten minutes?"

Austin looked as if he had asked a commonplace question. Lucy's lips parted to speak. She could not answer.

Loud rattled the teaboard to Mrs. Berry's dropping hands.

"Ji and deliverance!" she exclaimed with a foundering voice.

"Will you come?" Austin kindly asked again.

Lucy tried to stop her beating heart, as she answered, "Yes." Mrs. Berry cunningly pretended to interpret the irresolution in her tones with a mighty whisper: "She's thinking what's to be done with baby."

"He must learn to travel, too," said Austin.

"Oh!" cried Mrs. Berry, "and I'll be his nuss, and bear him, a sweet! Oh! and think of it! me nussmaid once more at Raynham Abbey! but it's a nusswoman now, you must say. Let us be goin' on the spot."

She started up and away in hot haste, fearing delay would cool the heaven-sent resolve. Austin smiled, eyeing his watch and Lucy alternately. She was wishing to ask a multitude of questions. His face reassured her, and saying: "I will be dressed instantly," she also left the room. Talking, bustling, preparing, wrapping up my lord, and looking to their neatnesses, they were nevertheless ready within the time prescribed by Austin, and Mrs. Berry stood humming over the baby. "He'll sleep it through," she said. "He's had enough for an alderman, and goes to sleep sound after his dinner, he do, a duck!" Before they departed, Lucy ran up to Lady Feverel. She returned for the small one.

"One moment, Mr. Wentworth?"

"Just two," said Austin.

Master Richard was taken up, and when Lucy came back her eyes were full of tears.

"She thinks she is never to see him again, Mr. Wentworth."

"She shall," Austin said simply.

Off they went, and with Austin near her, Lucy forgot to dwell at all upon the great act of courage she was performing.

"I do hope baby will not wake," was her chief solicitude.

"He!" cries nusswoman Berry from the rear, "his little tum-tum's *as* tight *as* he can hold, a pet! a lamb! a bird! a beauty! and ye may take yer oath he never wakes till that's slack. He've got character of his own, a blessed!"

There are some tremendous citadels that only want to be taken by storm. The Baronet sat alone in his library, sick of resistance, and rejoicing in the pride of no surrender; a terror to his friends and to himself. Hearing Austin's name sonorously pronounced by the man of calves, he looked up from his book, and held out his hand. "Glad to see you, Austin." His appearance betokened complete security. The next minute he found himself escaladed.

It was a cry from Mrs. Berry that told him others were in the room besides Austin. Lucy stood a little behind the lamp; Mrs. Berry close to the door. The door was half open, and passing through it might be seen the petrified figure of a fine man. The Baronet glancing over the lamp rose at Mrs. Berry's signification of a woman's personality. Austin stepped back and led Lucy to him by the hand. "I have brought Richard's wife, Sir," he said with a pleased, perfectly uncalculating, countenance, that was disarming. Very pale and trembling Lucy bowed. She felt her two hands taken, and heard a kind voice. Could it be possible it belonged to the dreadful father of her husband? She lifted her eyes nervously: her hands were still detained. The Baronet contemplated Richard's choice. Had he ever had a rivalry with those pure eyes? He saw the pain of her position shooting across her brows, and uttering gentle inquiries as to her health placed her in a seat. Mrs. Berry had already fallen into a chair. "What aspect do you like for your bedroom?—East?" said the Baronet.

Lucy was asking herself wonderingly: "Am I to stay?"

"Perhaps you had better take to Richard's room at once," he pursued. "You have the Lobourne valley there and a good morning air, and will feel more at home."

Lucy's colour mounted. Mrs. Berry gave a short cough, as who should say, "The day is ours!" Undoubtedly— strange as it was to think it—the fortress was carried.

"Lucy is rather tired," said Austin, and to hear her Christian name thus bravely spoken brought grateful dew to her eyes.

The Baronet was about to touch the bell. "But have you come alone?" he asked.

At this Mrs. Berry came forward. Not immediately: it seemed to require effort for her to move, and when she was within the region of the lamp, her agitation could not escape notice. The blissful bundle shook in her arms.

"By the way, what is he to me?" Austin inquired generally, as he went and unveiled the younger Hope of Raynham. "My relationship is not so defined as yours, Sir."

An observer might have supposed that the Baronet peeped at his grandson with the courteous indifference of one who merely wished to compliment the mother of anybody's child.

"I really think he's like Richard," Austin laughed. Lucy looked: "I am sure he is."

"As like as one to one," Mrs. Berry murmured feebly; but Grandpapa not speaking she thought it incumbent on her to pluck up. "And he's as healthy as his father was, Sir Austin—spite o' the might 'a beens. Reg'lar as the clock! We never want a clock since he come. We knows the hour o' the day, and *of* the night."

"You nurse him yourself, of course?" the Baronet spoke to Lucy, and was satisfied on that point.

Mrs. Berry was going to display the prodigious legs. Lucy, fearing the consequent effect on the prodigious lungs, begged her not to wake him. " 'T'd take a deal to do that," said Mrs. Berry, and harped on Master Richard's health and the small wonder it was that he enjoyed it, considering the superior quality of his diet, and the lavish attentions of his mother, and then suddenly fell silent on a deep sigh.

"He looks healthy," said the Baronet, "but I am not a judge of babies."

Thus, having capitulated, Raynham chose to acknowledge its new commandant, who was now borne away, under the directions of the housekeeper, to occupy the room Richard had slept in as an infant.

Austin cast no thought on his success. The Baronet said: "She is extremely well-looking." He replied: "A person you take to at once." There it ended.

But a much more animated colloquy was taking place aloft, where Lucy and Mrs. Berry sat alone. Lucy expected her to talk about the reception they had met with, and the house, and the peculiarities of the rooms, and the solid happiness that seemed in store. Mrs. Berry all the while would persist in consulting the looking-glass. Her first distinct answer was, "My dear! tell me candid, how do I look?"

"Very nice indeed, Mrs. Berry; but could you have believed he would be so kind, so considerate?"

"I'm sure I looked a frump," returned Mrs. Berry. "Oh, dear! two birds at a shot. What *do* you think, now?"

"I never saw so wonderful a likeness," says Lucy.

"Likeness! look at me." Mrs. Berry was trembling and hot in the palms.

"You're very feverish, dear Berry. What can it be?"

"Ain't it like the love-flutters of a young gal, my dear?"

"Go to bed, Berry, dear," says Lucy, pouting in her soft caressing way. "I will undress you, and see to you, dear heart! You've had so much excitement."

"Ha! ha!" Berry laughed hysterically, "she thinks it's about this business of hers. Why, it's child's-play, my darlin'. But I didn't look for tragedy tonight. Sleep in this house I can't, my love!"

Lucy was astonished. "Not sleep here, Mrs. Berry?— Oh! why, you silly old thing? I know."

"Do ye!" said Mrs. Berry with a sceptical nose.

"You're afraid of ghosts."

"Belike I am when they're six foot two in their shoes, and bellows when you stick a pin into their calves. I seen my Berry!"

"Your husband?"

"Large as life!"

Lucy meditated on optical delusions, but Mrs. Berry described him as the Colossus who had marched them into the library, and vowed that he had recognized her, and quaked. "Time ain't aged him," said Mrs. Berry, "whereas me! he 've got his excuse now. I *know* I look a frump."

Lucy kissed her: "You look the nicest, dearest old thing."

"You may say an old thing, my dear."

"And your husband is really here?"

"Berry's below!"

Profoundly uttered as this was, it chased every vestige of incredulity.

"What will you do, Mrs. Berry?"

"Go, my dear. Leave him to be happy in his own way. It's over atween us, I see that. When I entered the house I felt there was something comin' over me, and lo, and behold ye! no sooner was we in the hall-passage—if it hadn't been for that blessed infant I sh'd 'a dropped. I must 'a known his step, for my heart began thumpin', and I knew I hadn't got my hair straight—that Mr. Wentworth was in such a hurry—nor my best gown. I knew he'd scorn me. He hates frumps."

"Scorn you!" cried Lucy angrily. "He who has behaved so wickedly!"

Mrs. Berry attempted to rise. "I may as well go at once," she whimpered. "If I see him I shall ony be disgracin' of myself. I feel it all on my side already. Did ye mark him, my dear? He's in his uniform. His uni*corn* I used to call it, vexin' him. I know I was vexin' to him at times, I was. Those big men are se touchy about their dignity—nat'ral. Hark at me! I'm goin' all soft in a minute. Let me leave the house, my dear. I dare say it was good half my fault. Young women don't understand men sufficient—not altogether—and I was a young woman then—and then what they goes and does they ain't quite answerable for: they feels, I dare say, pushed from behind. Yes. I'll go. I'm a frump. I'll go. 'Tain't in natur' for me to sleep in the same house."

Lucy laid her hands on Mrs. Berry's shoulders, and forcibly fixed her in her seat. "Leave baby, naughty woman?

I tell you he shall come to you, and fall on his knees to you, and beg your forgiveness."

"Berry on his knees!"

"Yes. And he shall beg and pray you to forgive him."

"If you get more from Martin Berry than breath-away words, great 'll be my wonder!" said Mrs. Berry.

"We will see," said Lucy, thoroughly determined to do something for the good creature that had befriended her.

Mrs. Berry examined her gown. "Won't it seem we're runnin' after him?" she murmured faintly.

"He is your husband, Mrs. Berry. He may be wanting to come to you now."

"Oh! where is all I was goin' to say to that man when we met!" Mrs. Berry ejaculated. Lucy had left the room.

On the landing outside the door Lucy met a lady dressed in black, who stopped her and asked if she was Richard's wife, and kissed her, passing from her immediately. Lucy despatched a message for Austin, and related the Berry history. Austin sent for the great man, and said: "Do you know your wife is here?" Before Berry had time to draw himself up to enunciate his longest, he was requested to step upstairs, and as his young mistress at once led the way, Berry could not refuse to put his legs in motion and carry the stately edifice aloft.

Of the interview Mrs. Berry gave Lucy a slight sketch that night. "He began in the old way, my dear, and says I, a true 'art and plain words, Martin Berry. So there he cuts himself and his Johnson short, and down he goes— down *on* his knees. I never could 'a believed it. I kep my dignity as a woman till I see that sight, but that done for me. I was a ripe apple in his arms 'fore I knew where I was. There's something about a fine man on his knees that's too much for us women. And it reely was the penitent on his two knees, not the lover on his one. If he mean it! But ah! what do you think he begs of me, my dear?—not to make it known in the house just yet! I can't, I can't say that look well."

Lucy attributed it to his sense of shame at his conduct, and Mrs. Berry did her best to look on it in that light.

"Did the Bar'net kiss ye when you wished him good night?" she asked. Lucy said he had not. "Then bide awake as long as ye can," was Mrs. Berry's rejoinder. "And now let us pray blessings on that simple-speaking gentleman who does se much 'cause he says se little."

Like many other natural people, Mrs. Berry was only silly where her own soft heart was concerned. As she secretly anticipated, the Baronet came into her room when all was quiet. She saw him go and bend over Richard the Second, and remain earnestly watching him. He then went to the half-opened door of the room where Lucy slept, leaned his ear a moment, knocked gently, and entered. Mrs. Berry heard low words interchanging within. She could not catch a syllable, yet she would have sworn to the context. "He've called her his daughter, promised her happiness, and given a father's kiss to her." When Sir Austin passed out she was in a deep sleep.

CHAPTER XLVI

NATURE SPEAKS

BRIAREUS reddening angrily over the sea—where is that vaporous Titan? And Hesper set in his rosy garland—why looks he so implacably sweet? It is that one has left that bright home to go forth and do cloudy work, and he has got a stain with which he dare not return. Far in the west fair Lucy beckons him to come. Ah, Heaven! if he might! How strong and fierce the temptation is! how subtle the sleepless desire! it drugs his reason, his honour. For he loves her; she is still the first and only woman to him.

Otherwise would this black spot be Hell to him? otherwise would his limbs be chained while her arms spread open to him? And if he loves her, why then what is one fall in the pit, or a thousand? Is not Love the password to that beckoning bliss? So may we say; but here is one whose body has been made a temple to him, and it is desecrated.

A temple, and desecrated! For what is it fit but for a dance of devils?

He can blame nothing but his own baseness. But to feel base and accept the bliss that beckons—he has not fallen so low as that.

Ah, happy English home! sweet wife! what mad miserable Wisp of the Fancy led him away from you, high in his conceit? Poor wretch! that thought to be he of the hundred hands, and war against the absolute Gods. Jove whispered a light commission to the Laughing Dame; she met him; and how did he shake Olympus?—with laughter.

Sure it were better to be Orestes, the Furies howling in his ears, than one called to by a heavenly soul from whom he is for ever outcast. He has not the oblivion of madness. Clothed in the lights of his first passion, robed in the splendour of old skies, she meets him everywhere; morning, evening, and night, she shines above him; waylays him suddenly in forest depths; drops palpably on his heart. At moments he forgets; he rushes to embrace her; calls her his beloved, and lo, her innocent kiss brings agony of shame to his face.

Daily the struggle endured. His father wrote to him begging him by the love he had for him to return. From that hour Richard burnt unread all the letters he received. He knew too well how easily he could persuade himself: words from without might tempt him and quite extinguish the spark of honourable feeling that tortured him, and that he clung to in desperate self-vindication.

To arrest young gentlemen on the downward slope is both a dangerous and a thankless office. It is, nevertheless, one fair women greatly prize, and certain of them professionally follow. Lady Judith, as far as her sex would permit, was also of the Titans in their battle against the absolute Gods; for which purpose, mark you, she had married a lord incapable in all save his acres. Her achievements she kept to her own mind: she did not look happy over them. She met Richard accidentally in Paris; she saw his state; she let him learn that she alone on earth understood him. The consequence was that he was forthwith enrolled in her train. It soothed him to be near a woman. Did she venture her guess as to the cause of his conduct, she blotted it out with a facility women have, and cast on it a melancholy hue he was taught to participate in. She spoke of sorrows, personal sorrows, much as he might speak of his—vaguely, and with self-blame. And she understood him. How the dark unfathomed wealth within us gleams to a woman's eye! We are at compound interest immediately: so much richer than we knew!—almost as rich as we dreamed! But then the instant we are away from her we find ourselves bankrupt, beggared. How is that? We do not ask. We hurry to her and bask hungrily in her orbs. The eye must be feminine to be thus creative: I cannot say why. Lady Judith understood Richard, and he feeling infinitely vile, somehow held to her more feverishly, as one who dreaded the worst in missing her. The spirit must rest; he was weak with what he suffered.

Austin found them among the hills of Nassau in Rhineland: Titans, male and female, who had not displaced Jove, and were now adrift prone on floods of sentiment. The blue-frocked peasant swinging behind his oxen of a morning, the gaily-kerchiefed fruit-woman, the jackass-driver, even the doctor of those regions, have done more for their fellows. Horrible reflection! Lady Judith is serene above it, but it frets at Richard when he is out of her shadow. Often wretchedly he watches the young men of his own age trooping to their work. Not cloud-work theirs! Work solid, unambitious, fruitful!

Lady Judith had nobler in prospect for the Hero. He gaped for anything blindfolded, and she gave him the map of Europe in tatters. He swallowed it comfortably. It was an intoxicating cordial. Himself on horseback over-riding wrecks of Empires! Well might common sense cower with the meaner animals at the picture. Tacitly they agreed to recast the civilized globe. The quality of vapour is to melt and shape itself anew; but it is never the quality of vapour to reassume the same shapes. Briareus of the hundred unoccupied hands may turn to a monstrous donkey with his hind legs aloft, or twenty thousand jabbering apes. The phantasmic groupings of the young brain are very like those we see in the skies, and equally the sport of the wind. Lady Judith blew. There was plenty of vapour in him, and it always resolved into some shape or other. You that mark those clouds of eventide, and know youth, will see the similitude: it will not be strange, it will barely seem foolish to you, that a young man of Richard's age, Richard's education and position, should be in this wild state. Had he not been nursed to believe he was born for great things? Did she not say she was sure of it? And to feel base, and yet born for better, is enough to make one grasp at anything cloudy. Suppose the Hero with a game leg. How intense is his faith in quacks! with what a passion of longing is he not seized to break somebody's head! They spoke of Italy in low voices: "The time will come," said she. "And I shall be ready," said he. What rank was he to take in the liberating army? Captain, colonel, general in chief, or simple private? Here, as became him, he was much more positive and specific than she was. Simple private, he said. Yet he saw himself caracoling on horseback. Private in the cavalry, then, of course. Private in the cavalry over-riding wrecks of Empires. She looked forth under her brows with mournful indistinctness at that object in the distance. They read Petrarch to get up the necessary fires. Italia mia! Vain indeed was this speaking to those thick and mortal wounds in her fair body, but their sighs went with the Tiber, the Arno, and the Po, and their hands joined. Who has not wept for Italy? I see the aspirations of a world arise for her, thick and frequent as the puffs of smoke from cigars of Pannonian sentries!

So when Austin came Richard said he could not leave Lady Judith, Lady Judith said she could not part with him. For his sake, mind! This Richard verified. Perhaps he had reason to be grateful. The highroad of Folly may have led him from one that terminates worse. He is foolish, God knows; but for my part I will not laugh at the Hero, because he has not got his occasion. Meet him when he is, as it were, anointed by his occasion, and he is no laughing matter.

Richard felt his safety in this which, to please the world, we must term Folly. Exhalation of vapours was a wholesome process to him, and somebody who gave them shape and hue a beneficent Iris. He told Austin plainly he could not leave her, and did not anticipate the day when he could.

"Why can't you go to your wife, Richard?"

"For a reason you would be the first to approve, Austin."

He welcomed Austin with every show of manly tenderness, and sadness at heart. Austin he had always associated with his Lucy in that Hesperian palace of the West. Austin waited patiently. Lady Judith's old lord played on all the baths in Nassau without evoking the tune of health. Whithersoever he listed she changed her abode. So admirable a wife was to be pardoned for espousing an old man. She was an enthusiast even in her connubial duties. She had the brows of an enthusiast. With occasion she might have been a Charlotte Corday. So let her also be shielded from the ban of ridicule. Nonsense of enthusiasts is very different from nonsense of ninnies. She was truly a high-minded person, of that order who always do what they see to be right, and always have confidence in their optics. She was not unworthy of a young man's admiration, if she was unfit to be his guide. She resumed her ancient intimacy with Austin easily, while she preserved her new footing with Richard. She and Austin were not unlike, only Austin never dreamed, and had not married an old lord.

The three were walking on the bridge at Limburg on the Lahn, where the shadow of a stone bishop is thrown by the moonlight on the water brawling over slabs of slate. A woman passed them bearing in her arms a baby, whose mighty size drew their attention.

"What a wopper!" Richard laughed.

"Well, that is a fine fellow," said Austin, "but I don't think he's much bigger than your boy."

"He'll do for a nineteenth-century Arminius," Richard was saying. Then he looked at Austin.

"What was that you said?" Lady Judith asked of Austin.

"What have I said that deserves to be repeated?" Austin counterqueried quite innocently.

"Richard has a son?"

"You didn't know it?"

"His modesty goes very far," said Lady Judith, sweeping a curtsey to Richard's paternity.

Richard's heart throbbed with violence. He looked again in Austin's face. Austin took it so much as a matter of course that he said nothing more on the subject.

"Well!" murmured Lady Judith.

The moment the two men were alone, Richard said in a quick voice: "Austin! were you in earnest?"

"I hope so," Austin replied. "When?"

"In what you said on the bridge."

"On the bridge?"

"You said I had a—" he could hardly get the words out— "a son."

"You didn't know it, Richard?"

"No."

"Why, they all wrote to you. Lucy wrote to you: your father, your aunt. I believe Adrian wrote, too."

"I tore up their letters," said Richard.

"He's a noble fellow, I can tell you. You've nothing to be ashamed of, my dear boy. He'll soon be coming to ask about you. I made sure you knew."

"No, I never knew." Richard walked away, and then said: "What is he like?"

"Well, he really is like you, but he has his mother's eyes."

"And she's—quite well!"

"Yes. I think the child has kept her so."

"And they're both at Raynham?"

"Both."

Hence, fantastic vapours! What are ye to this? Where are the dreams of the Hero when he learns that he has a child? Nature is taking him to her bosom. She will speak presently. Every domesticated boor in these hills can boast the same, yet marvels the Hero at none of his visioned prodigies as he does when he comes to hear of this most common performance. A father? Richard fixed his eyes as if he were trying to make out the lineaments of his child.

Telling Austin he would be back in a few minutes, he sallied into the air, and walked on and on. "A father!" he kept repeating to himself: "a child!" And though he knew it not, he was striking the key-notes of Nature. But he did know of a singular harmony that suddenly burst over his whole being.

The moon was surpassingly bright: the summer air heavy and still. He left the highroad and pierced into the forest. His walk was rapid: the leaves on the trees brushed his cheeks; the dead leaves heaped in the dells noised to his feet. Something of a religious joy—a strange sacred pleasure—was in him. By degrees it wore: he remembered himself: and now he was possessed by a proportionate anguish. A father! he dared never see his child. And he had no longer his phantasies to fall upon. He was utterly bare to his sin. In his troubled mind it seemed to him that Clare looked down on him—Clare who saw him as he was—and that to her eyes it would be infamy for him to go and print his kiss upon his child. Then came stern efforts to command his misery and make the nerves of his face iron.

By the log of an ancient tree half-buried in dead leaves of past summers, beside a brook, he halted as one who has reached his journey's end. There he discovered he had a companion in Lady Judith's little dog. He gave the friendly animal a pat of recognition, and both were silent in the forest-silence.

It was impossible for Richard to return; his heart was surcharged. He must advance, and on he footed, the little dog following.

An oppressive slumber hung about the forest-branches. In the dells and on the heights was the same dead heat. Here where the brook tinkled it was no cool-lipped sound, but metallic, and without the spirit of water. Yonder in a space of moonlight on lush grass, the beams were as white fire to sight and feeling. No haze spread around. The valleys were clear, defined to the shadows of their verges; the distances sharply distinct; and with the colours of day but slightly softened. Richard beheld a roe moving across a slope of sward far out of rifle-mark. The breathless silence was significant, yet the moon shone in a broad blue Heaven. Tongue out of mouth trotted the little dog after him; couched panting when he stopped an instant; rose weariedly when he started afresh. Now and then a large white night-moth flitted through the dusk of the forest.

On a barren corner of the wooded highland looking in-land stood grey topless ruins set in nettles and rank grass-blades. Richard mechanically sat down on the crumbling flints to rest, and listened to the panting of the dog. Sprinkled at his feet were emerald lights: hundreds of glow-worms studded the dark dry ground.

He sat and eyed them, thinking not at all. His energies were expended in action. He sat as a part of the ruins, and the moon turned his shadow westward from the South. Overhead, as she declined, long ripples of silver cloud were imperceptibly stealing towards her. They were the van of a tempest. He did not observe them, or the leaves beginning to chatter. When he again pursued his course with his face set to the Rhine, a huge mountain appeared to rise sheer over him, and he had it in his mind to scale it. He got no nearer to the base of it for all his vigorous outstepping. The ground began to dip; he lost sight of the sky. Then heavy thunderdrops struck his cheek, the leaves were singing, the earth breathed, it was black before him and behind. All at once the thunder spoke. The mountain he had marked was bursting over him.

Up started the whole forest in violet fire. He saw the country at the foot of the hills to the bounding Rhine gleam, quiver, extinguished. Then there were pauses; and the lightning seemed as the eye of Heaven, and the thunder as the tongue of Heaven, each alternately addressing him; filling him with awful rapture. Alone there—sole human creature among the grandeurs and mysteries of storm—he felt the representative of his kind, and his spirit rose, and marched, and exulted, let it be glory, let it be ruin! Lower down the lightened abysses of air rolled the wrathful crash: then white thrusts of light were darted from the sky, and great curving ferns, seen steadfast in pallor a second, were supernaturally agitated and vanished. Then a shrill song roused in the leaves and the herbage. Prolonged and louder it sounded, as deeper and heavier the deluge pressed. A mighty force of water satisfied the desire of the earth. Even in this, drenched as he was by the first outpouring, Richard had a savage pleasure. Keeping in motion he was scarcely conscious of the wet, and the grateful breath of the weeds was refreshing. Suddenly he stopped short, lifting a curious nostril. He fancied he smelt meadow-sweet. He had never seen the flower in Rhineland—never thought of it; and it would hardly be met with in a forest. He was sure he smelt it fresh in dews. His little companion wagged a miserable wet tail some way in advance. He went on slowly, thinking indistinctly. After two or three steps he stooped and stretched out his hand to feel for the flower, having, he knew not why, a strong wish to verify its growth there. Groping about, his hand encountered something warm that started at his touch, and he, with the instinct we have, seized it, and lifted it to look at it. The creature was very small, evidently quite young. Richard's eyes, now accustomed to the darkness, were able to discern it for what it was, a tiny leveret, and he supposed that the dog had probably frightened its dam just before he found it. He put the little thing on one hand in his breast, and stepped out rapidly as before.

The rain was now steady; from every tree a fountain poured. So cool and easy had his mind become that he was speculating on what kind of shelter the birds could find, and how the butterflies and moths saved their coloured wings from washing. Folded close they might hang under a leaf, he thought. Lovingly he looked into the dripping darkness of the coverts on each side, as one of their children. Then he was musing on a strange sensation he experienced. It ran up one arm with an indescribable thrill, but communicated nothing to his heart. It was purely physical, ceased for a time, and recommenced, till he had it all through his blood, wonderfully thrilling. He grew aware that the little thing he carried in his breast was licking his hand there. The small rough tongue going over and over the palm of his hand produced this strange sensation he felt. Now that he knew the cause, the marvel ended; but now that he knew the cause, his heart was touched and made more of it. The gentle scraping continued without intermission as on he walked. What did it say to him? Human tongue could not have said so much just then.

A pale grey light on the skirts of the flying tempest displayed the dawn. Richard was walking hurriedly. The green drenched weeds lay all about in his path, bent thick, and the forest drooped glimmeringly. Impelled as a man who feels a revelation mounting obscurely to his brain, Richard was passing one of those little forest-chapels, hung with votive wreaths, where the peasant halts to kneel and pray. Cold, still, in the twilight it stood, rain-drops pattering round it. He looked within, and saw the Virgin holding her child. He moved by. But not many steps had he gone ere his strength went out of him, and he shuddered. What was it? He asked not. He was in other hands. Vivid as lightning the Spirit of Life illumined him. He felt in his heart the cry of his child, his darling's touch. With shut eyes he saw them both. They drew him from the depths; they led him a blind and tottering man. And as they led him he had a sense of purification so sweet he shuddered again and again.

When he looked out from his trance on the breathing world, the small birds hopped and chirped; warm fresh sunlight was over all the hills. He was on the edge of the forest, entering a plain clothed with ripe corn under a spacious morning sky.

CHAPTER XLVII

AGAIN THE MAGIAN CONFLICT

THEY heard at Raynham that Richard was coming. Lucy had the news first in a letter from Ripton Thompson, who met him at Bonn. Ripton did not say that he had employed his vacation holiday on purpose to use his efforts to induce his dear friend to return to his wife; and finding Richard already on his way, of course Ripton said nothing to him, but affected to be travelling for his pleasure like any cockney. Richard also wrote her. In case she should have gone to the sea he directed her to send word to his hotel that he might not lose an hour. His letter was sedate in tone, very sweet to her. Assisted by the faithful female Berry she was conquering an Aphorist.

'Woman's Reason is in the milk of her breasts,' was one of his rough notes, due to an observation of Lucy's maternal cares. Let us remember, therefore, we men who have drunk of it largely there, that she has it, though it is never more for us!

Mrs. Berry zealously apprised him how early Master Richard's education had commenced, and the great future Historian he must consequently be. This trait in Lucy was of itself sufficient to win Sir Austin.

"Here my plan with Richard was false," he reflected: "in presuming that anything save blind fortuity would bring him such a mate as he should have." He came to add: "And has got!"

He could admit now that Instinct had so far beaten Science; for as Richard was coming, as all were to be happy, his wisdom embraced them all paternally as the author of their happiness. Between him and Lucy a tender intimacy grew.

"I told you she could talk, Sir," said Adrian.

"She thinks!" said the Baronet.

The delicate question how she was to treat her Uncle he settled generously. Farmer Blaize should come up to Raynham when he would: Lucy must visit him at least three times a week. He had Farmer Blaize and Mrs. Berry to study, and really excellent Aphorisms sprang from the plain human bases this natural couple presented.

"It will do us no harm," he thought, "some of the honest blood of the soil in our veins." And he was content in musing on the parentage of the little cradled boy. A common sight for those who had the entry to the library was the Baronet cherishing the hand of his daughter-in-law.

So Richard was crossing the sea, and hearts at Raynham were beating quicker measures as the minutes progressed. That night he would be with them. Sir Austin gave Lucy a longer, warmer, salute when she came down to break-fast in the morning. Mrs. Berry waxed thrice amorous. "It's yer second bridals, ye sweet livin' widow!" she said. "Thanks be the Lord! it's the same man, too! and a baby over the bedpost," she appended seriously.

"Strange," Berry declared it to be, "strange I feel none o' this to my Berry now. All my feelin's o' love seem t' ave gone into you two sweet chicks."

In fact the faithless male Berry complained of being treated badly, and affected a superb jealousy of the baby; but the good dame told him that if he suffered at all he suffered his due. Berry's position was decidedly uncomfortable. It could not be concealed from the lower household that he had a wife in the establishment, and for the complications this gave rise to his wife would not legitimately console him. He devised to petition the Baronet. Lucy did intercede for him, but Mrs. Berry was obdurate. She averred she would not give up the child till he was weaned. "Then perhaps," she said prospectively. "You see I ain't se soft as you thought for."

"You're a very unkind vindictive old woman," said Lucy.

"Belike I am," Mrs. Berry was proud to agree. We like a new character, now and then. Berry had delayed too long.

She explained herself: "Let me see my Berry with his toes up, and I'm his tender nuss. It's a nusswoman he've found—not a wife. 'Tain't revengin' him, my darlin'! She never is to a baby—not a woman isn't—what she grow to a man. I had to see my Berry again to learn that, it sim. We goes off—somehow—to a man. Hard on 'em, it may be. Nat'ral, it is. The Scriptures tells of concubines. And there was Abram, we read. But it's all a puzzle, man *and* woman! and we purplexes each other on toe the end. Nor 'tain't that Berry's alter. That man's much as he was, in body both and in spirit. It's me am changed, and Berry—like—discovers it to me I am. It's a mis'rable truth, it be, my feelin's as a wedded wife sim gone now I got him. 'Kiss me,' says he. I gives him my cheek. 'So cold, Bessy Berry,' he says reproachful. I don't say nothin', for how'd he understand if I tell him I gone back to a spinster? So it is! and was I to see my Berry kissin' another woman now, I'd only feel p'rhaps—just that," Mrs. Berry simulated a short spasm. "And it makes me feel different about Eternal Life now," she continued. "I was always a-marriagin' in it before:—couldn't think of it without partners:—all for sex! But now them words 'No givin' in Marriage' comes home to me. A man and a woman they does their work below, and it's ended long afore they lays their bodies in the grave—leastways the woman. It's be hoped you won't feel that, my darlin', yet awhile—you se rosy simmerin' there!"

"Be quiet, Mrs. Berry," says Lucy, wishing to be pensive.

"Boilin', then. Bless her! she knows she is!" And Mrs. Berry, in contemplation of the reunion of the younger couple, went into amorous strophes immediately.

Were it not notorious that the straightlaced prudish dare not listen to the natural chaste, certain things Mrs. Berry thought it advisable to impart to the young wife with regard to Berry's infidelity, and the charity women should have towards sinful men, might here be reproduced. Enough that she thought proper to broach the matter, and cite her own Christian sentiments.

Oily calm is on the sea. At Raynham they look up at the sky and speculate that Richard is approaching fairly speeded. He comes to throw himself on his darling's mercy. Lucy irradiated over forest and sea, tempest and peace— to her the Hero comes humbly. Great is that day when we see our folly! Ripton and he were the friends of old. Richard encouraged him to talk of the two he could be eloquent on, and Ripton, whose secret vanity was in his powers of speech, never tired of enumerating Lucy's virtues, and the peculiar attributes of the baby.

"She did not say a word against me, Rip?"

"Against you, Richard! The moment she knew she was to be a mother, she thought of nothing but her duty to the child. She's one who can't think of herself."

"You've seen her at Raynham, Rip?"

"Yes, once. They asked me down. And your father's so fond of her—I'm sure he thinks no woman like her, and he's right. She is so lovely, and so good."

Richard was too full of blame of himself to blame his father: too British to expose his emotions. Ripton divined how deep and changed they were by his manner. He had cast aside the Hero, and however Ripton had obeyed him and looked up to him in the heroic time, he loved him tenfold now. He told his friend how much Lucy's mere womanly sweetness and excellence had done for him, and Richard contrasted his own profitless extravagance with the patient beauty of his dear home-Angel. He was not one to take her on the easy terms that offered. There was that to do which made his cheek burn as he thought of it, but he was going to do it, even though it lost her to him. Just to see her and kneel to her was joy sufficient to sustain him, and warm his blood in the prospect. They marked the white cliffs growing over the water. Nearer the sun made them lustrous. Houses and people seemed to welcome the wild youth to common-sense, simplicity, and home.

They were in Town by midday. Richard had a momentary idea of not driving to his hotel for letters. After a short debate he determined to go there. The porter said he had two letters for Mr. Richard Feverel—one had been waiting some time. He went to the box and fetched them. The first Richard opened was from Lucy, and as he read it, Ripton observed the colour deepen on his face, while a quivering smile played about his mouth. He then opened the other indifferently. It began without any form of address. Richard's forehead darkened at the signature. This

letter was in a sloping feminine hand, and flourished with
light strokes all over, like a field of the bearded barley.
Thus it ran:

"I know you are in a rage with me because I would
not consent to ruin you, you foolish fellow. What do you
call it? Going to that unpleasant place together. Thank
you, my milliner is not ready yet, and I want to make a
good appearance when I do go. I suppose I shall have to
some day. Your health, Sir Richard. Now let me speak to
you seriously. *Go home to your wife at once.* But I know
the sort of fellow you are, and I must be plain with you.
Did I ever say I loved you? You may hate me as much
as you please, but I will save you from being a fool.

"Now listen to me. You know my relations with Mount.
That beast Brayder offered to pay all my debts and set me
afloat, if I would keep you in Town. I declare on my
honour I had no idea why, and I did not agree to it. But
you were such a handsome fellow—I noticed you in the park
before I heard a word of you. But then you fought shy—
you were just as tempting as a girl. You *stung* me. Do you
know what that is? I would make you care for me, and
we know how it ended, without any intention of mine, I
swear. I'd have cut off my hand rather than do you any
harm, upon my honour. Circumstances! Then I saw it was
all up between us. Brayder came and began to chaff about
you. I dealt the animal a stroke on the face with my riding-whip—I shut him up pretty quick. Do you think I
would let a man speak about you?—I was going to swear.
You see I remember Dick's lessons. O my God! I do feel
unhappy.—Brayder offered me money. Go and think I took
it, if you like. What do I care what anybody thinks!
Something that blackguard said made me suspicious. I
went down to the Isle of Wight where Mount was, and your
wife was just gone with an old lady who came and took
her away. I should so have liked to see her. You said,

you remember, she would take me as a sister, and treat me—
I laughed at it then. My God! how I could cry now, if
water did any good to a *devil,* as you politely call poor me.
I called at your house and saw your man-servant, who said
Mount had just been there. In a minute it struck me. I
was sure Mount was after a woman, but it never struck
me that woman was your wife. Then I saw why they
wanted me to keep you away. I went to Brayder. You
know how I hate him. I made love to the man to get
it out of him. Richard! my word of honour they have
planned to carry her off, if Mount finds he cannot seduce
her. Talk of devils! He's one; but he is not so bad as
Brayder. I cannot forgive a mean dog his villainy.

"Now after this, I am quite sure you are too much of a
man to stop away from her another moment. I have no
more to say. I suppose we shall not see each other again,
so good-bye, Dick! I fancy I hear you cursing me. Why
can't you feel like other men on the subject? But if you
were like the rest of them I should not have cared for you
a farthing. I have not worn lilac since I saw you last.
I'll be buried in your colour, Dick. That will not offend
you—will it?

"You are not going to believe I took the money? If I
thought you thought that—it makes me *feel* like a devil
only to fancy you think it.

"The first time you meet Brayder, *cane him publicly.*

"Adieu! Say it's because you don't like his face. I suppose devils must not say *Adieu.* Here's plain old good-bye,
then, between you and me. Good-bye, dear Dick! You
won't think that of me?

"May I eat dry bread to the day of my death if I took
or ever will touch a scrap of their money!

"BELLA."

Richard folded up the letter silently.

"Jump into the cab," he said to Ripton.

"Anything the matter, Richard?"

"No."

The driver received directions. Richard sat without speaking. His friend knew that face. He asked whether there was bad news in the letter. For answer he had the lie circumstantial. He ventured to remark that they were going the wrong way.

"It's the right way," cried Richard, and his jaws were hard and square, and his eyes looked heavy and full.

Ripton said no more, but thought.

The cabman pulled up at a club. A gentleman, in whom Ripton recognized the Honourable Peter Brayder, was just then swinging a leg over his horse, with one foot in the stirrup. Hearing his name called, the Honourable Peter turned about, and stretched an affable hand.

"Is Mountfalcon in Town?" said Richard, taking the horse's reins instead of the gentlemanly hand. His voice and aspect were quite friendly.

"Mount?" Brayder replied, curiously watching the action, "yes. He's off this evening."

"He *is* in Town?" Richard released the horse. "I want to see him. Where is he?"

The young man looked pleasant: that which might have aroused Brayder's suspicions was an old affair in his parasitical register by this time. "Want to see him? What about?" he said carelessly, and gave the address.

"By the way," he sung out, "we thought of putting your name down, Feverel." He indicated the lofty structure. "What do you say?"

Richard nodded back to him, crying, "Hurry." Brayder returned the nod, and those who promenaded the district soon beheld his body in elegant motion to the stepping of his well-earned horse.

"What do you want to see Lord Mountfalcon for, Richard?" said Ripton.

"I just want to see him," Richard replied.

Ripton was left in the cab at the door of my lord's residence. He had to wait there a space of about ten minutes, when Richard returned with a clearer visage, though somewhat heated. He stood outside the cab, and Ripton was conscious of being examined by those strong grey eyes. As clear as speech he understood them to say to him, "You won't do," but which of the many things on earth he would not do for he was at a loss to think.

"Go down to Raynham, Ripton. Say I shall be there tonight certainly. Don't bother me with questions. Drive off at once. Or wait. Get another cab. I'll take this."

Ripton was ejected, and found himself standing alone in the street. As he was on the point of rushing after the galloping cab-horse to get a word of elucidation, he heard some one speak behind him.

"You are Feverel's friend?"

Ripton had an eye for lords. An ambrosial footman, standing at the open door of Lord Mountfalcon's house, and a gentleman on the door-step, told him that he was addressd by that nobleman. He was requested to step into the house. When they were alone, Lord Mountfalcon, slightly ruffled, said: "Feverel has insulted me grossly. I must meet him, of course. It's a piece of infernal folly!—I suppose he's not quite mad?"

Ripton's only definite answer was a gasping iteration of "My lord."

My lord resumed: "I am perfectly guiltless of offending him, as far as I know. In fact I had a friendship for him. Is he liable to fits of this sort of thing?"

Not yet at conversation-point, Ripton stammered: "Fits, my lord?"

"Ah!" went the other, eyeing Ripton in lordly cognizant style. "You know nothing of this business perhaps?"

Ripton said he did not.

"Have you any influence with him?"

"Not much, my lord. Only now and then—a little."

"You are not in the Army?"

The question was quite unnecessary. Ripton confessed to the Law, and my lord did not look surprised.

"I will not detain you," he said, distantly bowing.

Ripton gave him a commoner's obeisance; but getting to the door, the sense of the matter enlightened him.

"It's a duel, my lord?"

"No help for it, if his friends don't shut him up in Bedlam between this and tomorrow morning."

Of all horrible things a duel was the worst in Ripton's imagination. He stood holding the handle of the door, revolving this last chapter of calamity suddenly opened where happiness had promised.

"A duel! but he won't, my lord,—he mustn't fight, my lord."

"He must come on the ground," said my lord positively.

Ripton ejaculated unintelligible stuff. Finally Lord Mountfalcon said: "I went out of my way, Sir, in speaking to you. I saw you from the window. Your friend is mad. Deuced methodical, I admit, but mad. I have particular reasons to wish not to injure the young man, and if an apology is to be got out of him when we're on the ground, I'll take it, and we'll stop the damned scandal, if possible. You understand? I'm the insulted party, and I shall only require of him to use formal words of excuse to come to an amicable settlement. Let him just say he regrets it. Now, Sir," the nobleman spoke with considerable earnestness, "should anything happen—I have the honour to be known to Mrs. Feverel—and I beg you will tell her. I very particularly desire you to let her know that I was not to blame."

Mountfalcon rang the bell, and bowed him out. With this on his mind Ripton hurried down to those who were waiting in joyful trust at Raynham.

CHAPTER XLVIII

THE LAST SCENE

THE watch consulted by Hippias alternately with his pulse, in occult calculation hideous to mark, said half-past eleven towards midnight. Adrian wearing a composedly amused expression on his dimpled plump face,—held slightly sideways, aloof from paper and pen,—sat writing at the library table. Round the Baronet's chair, in a semicircle, were Lucy, Lady Blandish, Mrs. Doria, and Ripton, that very ill bird at Raynham. They were silent as are those who question the flying minutes. Ripton had said that Richard was sure to come; but the feminine eyes reading him ever and anon, had gathered matter for disquietude, which increased as time sped. Sir Austin persisted in his habitual air of speculative repose.

Remote as he appeared from vulgar anxiety, he was the first to speak and betray his state.

"Pray put up that watch. Impatience serves nothing," he said, half-turning hastily to his brother behind him.

Hippias relinquished his pulse and mildly groaned: "It's no nightmare, this!"

His remark was unheard, and the bearing of it remained obscure. Adrian's pen made a louder flourish on his manuscript; whether in commiseration or infernal glee, none might say.

"What are you writing?" the Baronet inquired testily of Adrian, after a pause; twitched, it may be, by a sort of jealousy of the Wise Youth's coolness.

"Do I disturb you, Sir?" rejoined Adrian. "I am engaged on a portion of a Proposal for uniting the Empires and Kingdoms of Europe under one Paternal Head, on the model of the ever to be admired and lamented Holy Roman. This treats of the management of Youths and Maids, and of certain magisterial functions connected therewith. 'It is decreed that these officers be all and every men of Science,' etc." And Adrian cheerily drove his pen afresh.

Mrs. Doria took Lucy's hand, mutely addressing encouragement to her, and Lucy brought as much of a smile as she could command to reply with.

"I fear we must give him up tonight," observed Lady Blandish.

"If he said he would come, he will come," Sir Austin interjected. Between him and the lady there was something of a contest secretly going on. He was conscious that nothing save perfect success would now hold this self-emancipating mind. She had seen him through.

"He declared to me he would be certain to come," said Ripton; but he could look at none of them as he said it, for he was growing aware that Richard might have deceived him, and was feeling like a black conspirator against their happiness. He determined to tell the Baronet what he knew, if Richard did not come by twelve.

"What is the time?" he asked Hippias in a modest voice.

"Time for me to be in bed," growled Hippias, as if everybody present had been treating him badly.

Mrs. Berry came in to apprise Lucy that she was wanted above. She quietly rose. Sir Austin kissed her on the forehead, saying: "You had better not come down again, my child." She kept her eyes on him. "Oblige me by retiring for the night," he added. Lucy shook their hands, and went out accompanied by Mrs. Doria.

"This agitation will be bad for the child," he said, speaking to himself aloud.

Lady Blandish remarked: "I think she might just as well have returned. She will not sleep."

"She will control herself for the child's sake."

"You ask too much of her."

"Of her not," he emphasized.

It was twelve o'clock when Hippias shut his watch, and

said with vehemence: "I'm convinced my circulation gradually and steadily decreases."

"Going back to the pre-Harvey period," murmured Adrian as he wrote.

Sir Austin and Lady Blandish knew well that any comment would introduce them to the interior of his machinery, the external view of which was sufficiently harrowing; so they maintained a discreet reserve. Taking it for acquiescence in his deplorable condition, Hippias resumed despairingly. "It's a fact. I've brought you to see that. No one can be more moderate than I am, and yet I get worse. My system is organically sound—I believe: I do every possible thing, and yet I get worse. Nature never forgives! I'll go to bed."

The Dyspepsy departed unconsoled.

Sir Austin took up his brother's thought: "I suppose nothing short of a miracle helps us when we have offended her."

"Nothing short of a quack satisfies us," said Adrian, applying wax to an envelope of official dimensions.

Ripton sat accusing his soul of cowardice while they talked; haunted by Lucy's last look at him. He got up his courage presently and went round to Adrian who, after a few whispered words, deliberately rose and accompanied him out of the room, shrugging. When they had gone, Lady Blandish said to the Baronet:

"He is not coming."

"Tomorrow, then, if not tonight," he replied. "But I say he will come tonight."

"You do really wish to see him united to his wife?"

The question made the Baronet raise his brows with some displeasure.

"Can you ask me?"

"I mean," said the ungenerous woman, "your System will require no further sacrifices from either of them?"

When he did answer, it was to say: "I think her altogether a superior person. I confess I should scarcely have hoped to find one like her."

"Admit that your Science does not accomplish everything."

"No: it was presumptuous—beyond a certain point," said the Baronet, meaning deep things.

Lady Blandish eyed him. "Ah me!" she sighed, "if we would always be true to our own wisdom!"

"You are very singular tonight, Emmeline." Sir Austin stopped his walk in front of her.

In truth, was she not unjust? Here was an offending son freely forgiven. Here was a young woman of humble birth freely accepted into his family and permitted to stand upon her qualities. Who would have done more—or as much? This lady, for instance, had the case been hers, would have fought it. All the people of position that he was acquainted with would have fought it, and that without feeling it so peculiarly. But while the Baronet thought this, he did not think of the exceptional education his son had received. He took the common ground of fathers, forgetting his System when it was absolutely on trial. False to his son it could not be said that he had been: false to his System he was. Others saw it plainly, but he had to learn his lesson by-and-by.

Lady Blandish gave him her face; then stretched her hand to the table, saying, "Well! well!" She fingered a half-opened parcel lying there, and drew forth a little book she recognized. "Ha! what is this?" she said.

"Benson returned it this morning," he informed her. "The stupid fellow took it away with him—by mischance, I am bound to believe."

It was nothing other than the old Note-book. Lady Blandish turned over the leaves, and came upon the later jottings.

She read: 'A maker of Proverbs—what is he but a narrow mind the mouthpiece of narrower?'

"I do not agree with that," she observed. He was in no humour for argument.

"Was your humility feigned when you wrote it?"

He merely said: "Consider the sort of minds influenced by set sayings. A proverb is the halfway-house to an Ideal, I conceive; and the majority rest there content: can the keeper of such a house be flattered by his company?"

She felt her feminine intelligence swaying under him again. There must be greatness in a man who could thus speak of his own special and admirable aptitude.

Further she read, 'Which is the coward among us?—He who sneers at the failings of Humanity.'

"Oh! that is true! How much I admire that!" cried the dark-eyed dame as she beamed intellectual raptures.

Another Aphorism seemed closely to apply to him: 'There is no more grievous sight, as there is no greater perversion, than a wise man at the mercy of his feelings.'

"He must have written it," she thought, "when he had himself for an example—strange man that he is!"

Lady Blandish was still inclined to submission, though decidedly insubordinate. She had once been fairly conquered: but if what she reverenced as a great mind could conquer her, it must be a great man that should hold her captive. The Autumn Primrose blooms for the loftiest manhood; is a vindictive flower in lesser hands. Nevertheless Sir Austin had only to be successful, and this lady's allegiance was his for ever. The trial was at hand.

She said again: "He is not coming tonight," and the Baronet, on whose visage a contemplative pleased look had been rising for a minute past, quietly added: "He is come."

Richard's voice was heard in the hall.

There was commotion all over the house at the return of the young heir. Berry, seizing every possible occasion to approach his Bessy now that her involuntary coldness had enhanced her value—"Such is men!" as the soft woman reflected—Berry ascended to her and delivered the news in pompous tones and wheedling gestures. "The best word you've spoke for many a day," says she, and leaves him unfeed, in an attitude, to hurry and pour bliss into Lucy's ears.

"Lord be praised!" she entered the adjoining room exclaiming, "we're goin' to be happy at last. They men have come to their senses. I could cry to your Virgin and kiss yer Cross, you sweet!"

"Hush!" Lucy admonished her, and crooned over the child on her knees. The tiny open hands, full of sleep, clutched; the large blue eyes started awake; and his mother, all trembling and palpitating, knowing, but thirsting to hear it, covered him with her tresses, and tried to still her frame, and rocked, and sang low, interdicting even a whisper from bursting Mrs. Berry.

Richard had come. He was under his father's roof, in the old home that had so soon grown foreign to him. He stood close to his wife and child. He might embrace them both: and now the fulness of his anguish and the madness of the thing he had done smote the young man: now first he tasted hard earthy misery.

Had not God spoken to him in the tempest? Had not the finger of Heaven directed him homeward? And he had come: here he stood: congratulations were thick in his ears: the cup of happiness was held to him, and he was invited to drink of it. Which was the dream? his work for the morrow, or this? But for a leaden load he felt like a bullet in his breast, he might have thought the morrow with Death sitting on it was the dream. Yes: he was awake. Now first the cloud of phantasms cleared away: he beheld his real life, and the colours of true human joy: and on the morrow perhaps he was to close his eyes on them. That leaden bullet dispersed all unrealities.

They stood about him in the hall, his father, Lady Blandish, Mrs. Doria, Adrian, Ripton; people who had known him long. They shook his hand: they gave him greetings he had never before understood the worth of or the meaning. Now that he did they mocked him. There was Mrs. Berry in the background bobbing, there was Martin Berry bowing, there was Tom Bakewell grinning. Somehow he loved the sight of these better.

"Ah, my old Penelope!" he said, breaking through the circle of his relations to go to her, "so you've found him at last? Tom! how are you? Berry! I hope you're going to behave like a man."

Berry inclined with dignified confusion, and drew up to man's height—to indicate his honourable intentions, let us hope. Tom Bakewell performed a motion as if to smear his face with an arm, but decided on making his grin vocal.

"Bless ye, my Mr. Richard," whimpered Mrs. Berry, and whispered rosily, "all's agreeable now. She's waiting up in bed for ye, like a new-born."

The person who betrayed most agitation was Mrs. Doria. She held close to him, and eagerly studied his face and every movement as one accustomed to masks. "You are pale, Richard?" He pleaded exhaustion. "What detained you, dear?" "Business," he said. She drew him imperiously apart from the others. "Richard! is it over?" He asked what she meant. "The dreadful duel, Richard." He looked darkly. "Is it over? is it done, Richard?" Getting no immediate answer, she continued—and such was her agitation that the words were shaken by pieces from her mouth: "Don't pretend not to understand me, Richard! Is it over? Are you going to die the death of my child—Clare's death? Is not one in a family enough? Think of your dear young wife—we love her so!—your child!—your father! Will you kill us all?"

Mrs. Doria had chanced to overhear a trifle of Ripton's communication to Adrian, and had built thereon with the dark forces of a stricken soul.

Wondering how this woman could have divined it, Richard calmly said: "It's arranged—the matter you allude to."

"Indeed! truly, dear?"

"Yes."

"Tell me—" but he broke away from her, saying: "You shall hear the particulars tomorrow," and she, not alive to double meaning just then, allowed him to leave her.

He had eaten nothing for twelve hours, and called for food, but he would only take dry bread and claret, which was served on a tray in the library. He said, without any show of feeling, that he must eat before he saw the younger Hope of Raynham: so there he sat, breaking bread, and eating great mouthfuls, and washing them down with wine, talking of what they would. His father's studious mind felt itself years behind him, he was so completely altered. He had the precision of speech, the bearing of a man of thirty. Indeed he had all that the necessity for commanding and cloaking infinite misery gives. But let things be as they might, he was *there*. For one night in his life Sir Austin's perspective of the future was bounded by the night.

"Will you go to your wife now?" he had asked, and Richard had replied with a strange indifference. The Baronet thought it better that their meeting should be private, and sent word for Lucy to wait upstairs. The others perceived that father and son should now be left alone. Adrian went up to him, and said: "I can no longer witness this painful sight, so Good night, Sir Famish! You may cheat yourself into the belief that you've made a meal, but depend upon it your progeny—and it threatens to be numerous—will cry aloud and rue the day. Nature never forgives! A lost dinner can never be replaced! Good night, my dear boy. And here—oblige me by taking this," he handed Richard the enormous envelope containing what he had written that evening. "Credentials!" he exclaimed humorously, slapping Richard on the shoulder. Ripton heard also the words "propagator—species," but had no idea of their import. The Wise Youth looked: "You see we've made matters all right for you here," and quitted the room on that unusual gleam of earnestness.

Richard shook his hand, and Ripton's. Then Lady Blandish said her Good-night, praising Lucy, and promising to pray for their mutual happiness. The two men who knew what was hanging over him, spoke together outside. Ripton was for getting a positive assurance that the duel would not be fought, but Adrian said: "Time enough tomorrow. He's safe enough while he's here. I'll stop it tomorrow:" ending with banter of Ripton and allusions to his adventures with Miss Random, which must, Adrian said, have led him into many affairs of the sort. Certainly Richard was there, and while he was there he must be safe. So thought Ripton, and went to his bed. Mrs. Doria deliberated likewise, and likewise thought him safe while he was there. For once in her life she thought it better not to trust her instinct, for fear of useless disturbance where peace should be. So she said not a syllable of it to her brother. She only looked more deeply into Richard's eyes, as she kissed him, praising Lucy, "I have found a second daughter in her, dear. Oh! may you both be happy!"

They all praised Lucy now. His father commenced the moment they were alone. "Poor Helen! Your wife has been a great comfort to her, Richard. I think Helen must have sunk without her. So lovely a young person, possessing mental faculty, and a conscience for her duties, I have never before met."

He wished to gratify his son by these eulogies of Lucy, and some hours back he would have succeeded. Now it had the contrary effect.

"You compliment me on my choice, Sir?"

Richard spoke sedately, but the irony was perceptible, and he could speak no other way, his bitterness was so intense.

"I think you very fortunate," said his father.

Sensitive to tone and manner as he was, his ebullition of paternal feeling was frozen. Richard did not approach him.

He leaned against the chimney-piece, glancing at the floor, and lifting his eyes only when he spoke. Fortunate! very fortunate! As he revolved his later history, and remembered how clearly he had seen that his father must love Lucy if he but knew her, and remembered his efforts to persuade her to come with him, a sting of miserable rage blackened his brain. But could he blame that gentle soul? Whom could he blame? Himself? Not utterly. His father? Yes, and no. The blame was here, the blame was there: it was everywhere and nowhere, and the young man cast it on the Fates, and looked angrily at Heaven, and grew reckless.

"Richard," said his father, coming close to him, "it is late tonight. I do not wish Lucy to remain in expectation longer, or I should have explained myself to you thoroughly, and I think—or at least hope—you would have justified me. I had cause to believe that you had not only violated my confidence, but grossly deceived me. It was not so I now know. I was mistaken. Much of our misunderstanding has resulted from that mistake. But you were married—a boy: you knew nothing of the world, little of yourself. To save you in after-life—for there is a period when mature men and women who have married young are more impelled to temptation than in youth,—though not so exposed to it,—to save you, I say, I decreed that you should experience self-denial and learn something of your fellows of both sexes, before settling into a state that must have been otherwise precarious, however excellent the woman who is your mate. My System with you would have been otherwise imperfect, and you would have felt the effects of it. It is over now. You are a man. The dangers to which your nature was open are, I trust, at an end. I wish you to be happy, and I give you both my blessing, and pray God to conduct and strengthen you both."

Sir Austin's mind was unconscious of not having spoken

devoutly. True or not, his words were idle to his son: his talk of dangers over, and happiness, mockery.

Richard coldly took his father's extended hand.

"We will go to her," said the Baronet. "I will leave you at her door."

Not moving: looking fixedly at his father with a hard face on which the colour rushed, Richard said: "A husband who has been unfaithful to his wife may go to her there, Sir?"

It was horrible, it was cruel: it was uncalled for—Richard knew that. He wanted no advice on such a matter, having fully resolved what to do. Yesterday he would have listened to his father, and blamed himself alone, and done what was to be done humbly before God and her: now in the recklessness of his misery he had as little pity for any other soul as for his own.

Sir Austin's brows were deep drawn down.

"What did you say, Richard?"

Clearly his intelligence had taken it, but this—the worst he could hear—this that he had dreaded once, and doubted, and smoothed over, and cast aside—could it be?

Richard said: "I told you all but the very words when we last parted. What else do you think would have kept me from her?"

Angered at his callous aspect, his father cried: "What brings you to her now?"

"That will be between us two," was the reply.

Sir Austin fell into his chair. Meditation was impossible. He spoke from a wrathful heart: "You will not dare to take her without—"

"No, Sir," Richard interrupted him, "I shall not. Have no fear."

"Then you did not love your wife?"

"Did I not?" A smile passed faintly over Richard's face.

"Did you care so much for this—this other person?"

"So much? If you ask me whether I had affection for her, I can say I had none."

O base human nature! Then how? then why? A thousand questions rose in the Baronet's mind. Bessy Berry could have answered them every one.

"Poor child! poor child!" he apostrophized Lucy, pacing the room. Thinking of her, knowing her deep love for his son—her true forgiving heart—it seemed she should be spared this misery.

He proposed to Richard to spare her. Vast is the distinction between women and men in this one sin, he said, and supported it with physical and moral citations. His argument carried him so far that to hear him one would have imagined he thought the sin in men small indeed. His words were idle.

"She must know it," said Richard sternly. "I will go to her now, Sir, if you please."

Sir Austin detained him, expostulated, contradicted himself, confounded his principles, made nonsense of all his theories. He could not induce his son to waver in his resolve. Ultimately, their Good-night being interchanged, he understood that the happiness of Raynham depended on Lucy's mercy. He had no fears of her sweet heart, but it was a strange thing to have come to.

On which should the accusation fall—on Science, or on Human nature?

He remained in the library pondering over the question, at times breathing contempt for his son, and again seized with unwonted suspicion of his own wisdom: troubled, much to be pitied, even if he deserved that blow from his son which had plunged him into wretchedness.

Richard went straight to Tom Bakewell, roused the heavy sleeper, and told him to have his mare saddled and waiting at the park gates East within an hour. Tom's nearest approach to a Hero was to be a faithful slave to his master, and in doing this he acted to his conception of that high and glorious character. He got up and heroically dashed his head into cold water. "She shall be ready, Sir," he nodded.

"Tom! if you don't see me back here at Raynham, your money will go on being paid to you."

"Rather see you than the money, Mr. Richard," said Tom.

"And you will always watch and see no harm comes to her, Tom."

"Mrs. Richard, Sir?" Tom stared. "God bless me, Mr. Richard—"

"No questions. You'll do what I say."

"Ay, Sir; that will. Did 'n Oisle o' Woight."

The very name of the Island shocked Richard's blood, and he had to walk up and down before he could knock at Lucy's door. That infamous conspiracy to which he owed his degradation and misery scarce left him the feelings of a man when he thought of it.

The soft beloved voice responded to his knock. He opened the door, and stood before her. Lucy was halfway towards him. In the moment that passed ere she was in his arms, he had time to observe the change in her. He had left her a girl: he beheld a woman—a blooming woman: for pale at first, no sooner did she see him than the colour was rich and deep on her face and neck and bosom half shown through the loose dressing-robe, and the sense of her exceeding beauty made his heart thump and his eyes swim.

"My darling!" each cried, and they clung together, and her mouth was fastened on his.

They spoke no more. His soul was drowned in her kiss. Supporting her, whose strength was gone, he, almost as weak as she, hung over her, and clasped her closer, closer, till they were as one body, and in the oblivion her lips put upon him he was free to the bliss of her embrace. Heaven granted him that.

He placed her in a chair and knelt at her feet with both arms around her. Her bosom heaved; her eyes never quitted him: their light as the light on a rolling wave. This young creature, commonly so frank and straightforward, was broken with bashfulness in her husband's arms—womanly bashfulness on the torrent of womanly love; tenfold more seductive than the bashfulness of girlhood. Terrible tenfold the loss of her seemed now, as distantly—far on the horizon the memory—the fatal truth returned to him.

Lose her? lose this? He looked up as if to ask God to confirm it.

The same sweet blue eyes; the eyes that he had often seen in the dying glories of evening; on him they dwelt, shifting, and fluttering, and glittering, but constant: the light of them as the light on a rolling wave.

And true to him! true, good, glorious, as the Angels of Heaven! And his she was! a woman—his wife! The temptation to take her, and be dumb, was all-powerful: the wish to die against her bosom so strong as to be the prayer of his vital forces. Again he strained her to him, but this time it was as a robber grasps priceless treasure—with fierce exultation, and defiance. One instant of this. Lucy, whose pure tenderness had now surmounted the first wild passion of their meeting, bent back her head from her surrendered body, and said almost voiceless, her underlids wistfully quivering: "Come and see him—baby;" and then in great hope of the happiness she was going to give her husband, and share with him, and in tremor and doubt of what his feelings would be, she blushed, and her brows worked: she tried to throw off the strangeness of a year's separation, misunderstanding, and uncertainty.

"Darling! come and see him. He is here." She spoke more clearly, though no louder.

Richard had released her, and she took his hand, and he suffered himself to be led to the other side of the bed. His heart began rapidly throbbing at the sight of a little rosy-curtained cot covered with lace like milky summer cloud.

It seemed to him he would lose his manhood if he looked on that child's face.

"Stop," he cried suddenly.

Lucy turned first to him, and then to her infant, fearing it should have been disturbed.

"Lucy, come back."

"What is it, darling?" said she, in alarm at his voice and the gripe he had unwittingly given her hand.

O God! what an Ordeal was this! that tomorrow he must face Death, perhaps die and be torn from his darling—his wife and his child; and that ere he went forth, ere he could dare to see his child and lean his head reproachfully on his young wife's breast—for the last time, it might be—he must stab her to the heart, shatter the image she held of him.

"Lucy!" She saw him wrenched with agony, and her own face took the whiteness of his—she bending forward to him, all her faculties strung to hearing.

He held her two hands that she might look on him and not spare the horrible wound he was going to lay open to her eyes.

"Lucy. Do you know why I came to you tonight?"

She moved her lips repeating his words.

"Lucy. Have you guessed why I did not come before?"

Her head shook widened eyes.

"Lucy. I did not come because I was not worthy of my wife! Do you understand?"

Again the widened eyes were shaken negatively.

"You do not?"

"Darling," she faltered plaintively, and hung crouching under him, "what have I done to make you angry with me?"

"Oh, beloved!" cried he, the tears bursting out of his eyes. "Oh, beloved!" was all he could say, kissing her hands passionately.

She waited reassured, but in terror.

"Lucy. I stayed away from you—I could not come to you, because . . . I dared not come to you, my wife, my beloved! I could not come because I was a coward: because

—hear me—this was the reason: I have broken my Marriage oath."

Again her lips moved repeating his words. She caught at a dim fleshless meaning in them. "But you love me? Richard! My husband! you love me?"

"Yes. I have never loved, I never shall love, woman but you."

"Darling! Kiss me."

"Have you understood what I have told you?"

"Kiss me," she said.

He did not join lips. "I have come to you tonight to ask your forgiveness."

Her answer was still: "Kiss me."

"Can you forgive a man so base?"

"But you love me, Richard?"

"Yes: that I can say before God. I love you, and I have betrayed you, and am unworthy of you—not worthy to touch your hand, to kneel at your feet, to breathe the same air with you."

Her eyes shone brilliantly. "You love me! you love me, darling!" And as one who has sailed through dark fears into daylight, she said: "My husband! my darling! you will never leave me? We never shall be parted again?"

He drew his breath painfully. To smooth her face growing rigid with fresh fears at his silence, he met her mouth. That kiss in which she spoke what her soul had to say, calmed her, and she smiled happily from it, and in her manner reminded him of his first vision of her on the summer morning in the field of the meadow-sweet. He held her to him, and thought then of a holier picture: of mother and child: of the sweet wonders of life she had made real to him.

Had he not absolved his conscience? At least the pangs to come made him think so. He now followed her leading hand. Lucy whispered: "You mustn't disturb him—mustn't touch him, dear!" and with dainty fingers drew off the covering to the little shoulder. One arm of the child was out along the pillow; the small hand open. His baby-mouth was pouted full; the dark lashes of his eyes seemed to lie on his plump cheeks. Richard stooped lower down to him, hungering for some movement as a sign that he lived. Lucy whispered: "He sleeps like you, Richard—one arm under his head." Great wonder, and the stir of a grasping tenderness was in Richard. He breathed quick and soft, bending lower, till Lucy's curls, as she nestled and bent with him, rolled on the crimson quilt of the cot. A smile went up the plump cheeks: forthwith the bud of a mouth was in rapid motion. The young mother whispered, blushing: "He's dreaming of me," and the simple words did more than Richard's eyes to make him see what was. Then Lucy began to hum and buzz sweet baby-language, and some of the tiny fingers stirred, and he made as if to change his cosy position, but reconsidered, and deferred it, with a peaceful little sigh. Lucy whispered: "He is such a big fellow. Oh! when you see him awake he is so like you, Richard." He did not hear her immediately: it seemed a bit of heaven dropped there in his likeness: the more human the fact of the child grew the more heavenly it seemed. His son! his child! should he ever see him awake? At the thought he took the words that had been spoken, and started from the dream he had been in.

"Will he wake soon, Lucy?"

"Oh, no! not yet, dear: not for hours. I would have kept him awake for you, but he was *so* sleepy."

Richard stood back from the cot. He thought that if he saw the eyes of his boy, and had him once on his heart, he never should have force to leave him. Then he looked down on him, again struggled to tear himself away. Two natures warred in his bosom, or it may have been the Magian Conflict still going on. He had come to see his child once, and to make peace with his wife before it should be too late. Might he not stop with them? Might he not relinquish that devilish pledge? Was not divine happiness here offered to him?—If foolish Ripton had not delayed to tell him of his interview with Mountfalcon all might have been well. But Pride said it was impossible. And then Injury spoke. For why was he thus base and spotted to the darling of his love? A mad pleasure in the prospect of wreaking vengeance on the villain who had laid the trap for him, once more blackened his brain. If he would stay he could not. So he resolved, throwing the burden on Fate. The struggle was over, but oh, the pain! Lucy beheld the tears streaming hot from his face on the child's cot. She marvelled at such excess of emotion. But when his chest heaved, and the extremity of mortal anguish appeared to have seized him, her heart sank, and she tried to get him in her arms. He turned away from her and went to the window. A half-moon was over the lake.

"Look," he said, "do you remember our rowing there one night, and we saw the shadow of the cypress? I wish I could have come early tonight that we might have had another row, and I have heard you sing there!"

"Darling!" said she, "will it make you happier if I go with you now? I will."

"No, Lucy. Lucy, you are brave!"

"Oh, no! that I'm not. I thought so once. I know I am not now."

"Yes! to have lived—the child on your heart—and never to have uttered a complaint!—you are brave. Oh, my Lucy! my wife! you that have made me man! I called you a coward. I remember it. *I* was the coward—*I* the wretched vain fool! Darling! I am going to leave you now. You are brave, and you will bear it. Listen: in two days, or three, I may be back—back for good, if you will accept me. Promise me to go to bed quietly. Kiss the child for me, and tell him his father has seen him. He will learn to speak soon. Will he soon speak, Lucy?"

Dreadful suspicion kept her speechless; she could only clutch one arm of his with both her hands.

"Going?" she presently gasped.

"For two or three days. No more—I hope."

"Tonight?"

"Yes. Now."

"Going now? my husband!" Her faculties abandoned her.

"You will be brave, my Lucy!"

"Richard! my darling husband! Going? What is it takes you from me?" But questioning no further, she fell on her knees, and cried piteously to him to stay—not to leave them. Then she dragged him to the little sleeper, and urged him to pray by his side, and he did, but rose abruptly from his prayer when he had muttered a few broken words—she praying on with tight-strung nerves in the faith that what she said to the interceding Mother above would be stronger than human hands on him. Nor could he go while she knelt there.

And he wavered. He had not reckoned on her terrible suffering.

She came to him quiet. "I knew you would remain." And taking his hand, innocently fondling it: "Am I so changed from her he loved? You will not leave me, dear?" But dread returned, and the words quavered as she spoke them.

He was almost vanquished by the loveliness of her womanhood. She drew his hand to her heart, and strained it there under one breast. "Come: lie on my heart," she murmured with a smile of holy sweetness.

He wavered more, and drooped to her, but summoning the powers of Hell, kissed her suddenly, cried the words of parting, and hurried to the door. It was over in an instant. She cried out his name, clinging to him wildly, and was adjured to be brave, for he would be dishonoured if he did not go. Then she was shaken off.

Mrs. Berry was aroused by an unusual prolonged wailing

of the child, which showed that no one was comforting it, and failing to get any answer to her applications for admittance, she made bold to enter. There she saw Lucy, the child in her lap, sitting on the floor senseless:—she had taken it from its sleep and tried to follow her husband with it as her strongest appeal to him, and had fainted.

"O my! O my!" Mrs. Berry moaned, "and I just now thinkin' they was so happy that was a gender!"

Warming and caressing the poor infant, she managed by degrees to revive Lucy, and heard what had brought her to that situation.

"Go to his father," said Mrs. Berry. "Ta-te-tiddle-te-heighty-O! Go, my love, and every horse in Raynham shall be out after'm. This is what men brings us to! Heighty-oighty-iddlety-Ah! Or you take blessed baby, and I'll go."

The Baronet himself knocked at the door. "What is this?" he cried. "I heard a noise and a step descend."

"It's Mr. Richard have gone, Sir Austin! have gone from his wife and babe! Rum-te-um-te-iddledy—Oh, my goodness! what sorrow's come on us!" and Mrs. Berry wept, and sang to baby, and baby cried vehemently, and Lucy, sobbing, took him and danced him and sang to him with drawn lips and tears dropping over him. And if the Scientific Humanist to the day of his death forgets the sight of those two poor true women jigging on their wretched hearts to calm the child, he must have very little of the human in him.

There was no more sleep for Raynham that night.

CHAPTER XLIX

LADY BLANDISH TO AUSTIN WENTWORTH

"His Ordeal is over. I have just come from his room and seen him bear the worst that could be. Return at once—he has asked for you. I can hardly write intelligibly, but I will tell you what we know.

"Two days after the dreadful night when he left us, his father heard from Ralph Morton. Richard had fought a duel in France with Lord Mountfalcon, and was lying wounded at a hamlet on the coast. His father started immediately with his poor wife, and I followed in company with his aunt and his child. The wound was not dangerous. He was shot in the side somewhere, but the ball injured no vital part. We thought all would be well. Oh! how sick I am of theories, and Systems, and the pretensions of men! There was his son lying all but dead, and the man was still unconvinced of the folly he has been guilty of. I could hardly bear the sight of his composure. I shall hate the name of Science till the day I die. Give me nothing but commonplace unpretending people!

"They were at a wretched French cabaret, smelling vilely, where we still remain, and the people try as much as they can do to compensate for our discomforts by their kindness. The French poor people are very considerate where they see suffering. I will say that for them. The Doctors had not allowed his poor Lucy to go near him. She sat outside his door, and none of us dared disturb her. That was a sight for Science. His father, and myself, and Mrs. Berry, were the only ones permitted to wait on him, and whenever we came out, there she sat, not speaking a word—for she had been told it would endanger his life—but she looked such awful eagerness. She had the sort of eye I fancy mad persons have. I was sure her reason was going. We did everything we could think of to comfort her. A bed was made up for her and her meals were brought to her there. Of course there was no getting her to eat. What do you suppose *his* alarm was fixed on? He absolutely said to me—but I have not patience to repeat his words. He thought her to blame for not *commanding* herself for the sake of her *maternal duties*. He had absolutely an idea of insisting that she should make an effort to suckle the child. I shall love that Mrs. Berry to the end of my days. I really

believe she has *twice* the sense of any of us—Science and all.
She asked him plainly if he wished to poison the child, and
then he gave way, but with a bad grace.

"Poor man! perhaps I am hard on him. I remember that
you said Richard had done wrong. Yes; well, that may be.
But his father eclipsed his wrong in a greater wrong—a
crime, or quite as bad; for if he deceived himself in the
belief that he was acting righteously in separating husband
and wife, and exposing his son as he did, I can only say
that there are some who are worse than people who deliberately commit *crimes*. No doubt Science will benefit by it.
They kill little animals for the sake of Science.

"We have with us Doctor Bairam, and a French physi-
sian from Dieppe, a very skilful man. It was he who told
us where the real danger lay. We thought all would be
well. A week had passed, and no fever supervened. We
told Richard that his wife was coming to him, and he could
bear to hear it. I went to her and began to circumlocute,
thinking she listened—she had the same eager look. When
I told her she might go in with me to see her dear husband,
her features did not change. M. Desprès, who held her
pulse at the time, told me, in a whisper, it was cerebral
fever—brain-fever coming on. We have talked of her since.
I noticed that though she did not seem to understand me,
her bosom heaved, and she appeared to be trying to repress
it, and choke something. I am sure now, from what I know
of her character, that she—even in the approaches of de-
lirium—was preventing herself from crying out. Her last
hold of reason was a thought for Richard. It was against
a creature like this that we plotted! I have the comfort of
knowing that I did my share in helping to destroy her.
Had she seen her husband a day or two before—but no!
there was a new System to interdict that! Or had she not
so violently controlled her nature as she did, I believe she
might have been saved.

"He said once of a man, that his conscience was a cox

comb. Will you believe that when he saw his son's wife—
poor victim! lying delirious, he could not even then see his
error. You said he wished to take Providence out of God's
hands. His mad self-deceit would not leave him. I am
positive that, while he was standing over her, he was blam-
ing her for not having considered the child. Indeed he made
a remark to me that it was unfortunate—'disastrous,' I think
he said—that the child should have to be fed by hand. I
dare say it is. All I pray is that this young child may be
saved from him. I cannot bear to see him look on it. He
does not spare himself *bodily* fatigue—but what is that? that
is the vulgarest form of love. I know what you will say.
You will say I have lost all charity, and I have. But I
should not feel so, Austin, if I could be *quite sure* that he is
an altered man even now the blow has struck him. He is
reserved and simple in speech, and his grief is evident, but I
have doubts. He heard her while she was senseless call him
cruel and harsh, and cry that she had suffered, and I saw
then his mouth contract as if he had been touched. Perhaps,
when he thinks, his mind will be clearer, but what he has
done cannot be undone. I do not imagine he will abuse
women any more. The Doctor called her a 'forte et belle
jeune femme:' and *he* said she was as noble a soul as ever
God moulded clay upon. A noble soul 'forte et belle!'
She lies upstairs. If he can look on her and not see his
sin, I almost fear God will never enlighten him.

"She died five days after she had been removed. The
shock had utterly deranged her. I was with her. She died
very quietly, breathing her last breath without pain, asking
for no one. A death I should like to die.

"Her cries at one time were dreadfully loud. She
screamed that she was 'drowning in fire,' and her husband
would not come to her to save her. We deadened the sound
as much as we could, but it was impossible to prevent Richard
from hearing. He knew her voice, and it produced an
effect like fever on him. Whenever she called he answered.

You could not hear them without weeping. Mrs. Berry sat with her, and I sat with him, and his father moved from one to the other.

"But the trial for us came when she was gone. How to communicate it to Richard—or whether to do so at all! His father consulted with us. We were quite decided that it would be madness to breathe it while he was in that state. I can admit now—as things have turned out—we were wrong. His father left us—I believe he spent the time in prayer—and then leaning on me, he went to Richard, and said in so many words, that his Lucy was no more. I thought it must kill him. He listened, and smiled. I never saw a smile so sweet and so sad. He said he had seen her die, as if he had passed through his suffering a long time ago. He shut his eyes. I could see by the motion of his eyeballs up that he was straining his sight to some inner Heaven—I cannot go on.

"I think Richard is safe. Had we postponed the tidings till he came to his clear senses, it must have killed him. His father was right for once then. But if he has saved his son's body, he has given the death-blow to his heart. Richard will never be what he promised.

"A letter found on his clothes tells us the origin of the quarrel. I have had an interview with Lord M. this morning. I cannot say I think him exactly to blame: Richard forced him to fight. At least I do not select him the foremost for blame. He was deeply and sincerely affected by the calamity he has caused. Alas! he was only an instrument. Your poor aunt is utterly prostrate and talks strange things of her daughter's death. She is only happy in *drudging*. Dr. Bairam says we must under any circumstances keep her employed. While she is doing something, she can chat freely, but the moment her hands are not occupied she gives me an idea that she is going into a fit.

"We expect the dear child's uncle today. Mr. Thompson

is here. I have taken him upstairs to look at her. That poor young man has a true heart.

"Come at once. You will not be in time to see her. She will lie at Raynham. If you could you would see an Angel. *He* sits by her side for hours. I can give you no description of her beauty.

"You will not delay, I know, dear Austin, and I want you, for your presence will make me more charitable than I find it possible to be. Have you noticed the expression in the eyes of blind men? That is just how Richard looks, as he lies there silent in his bed—striving to image her on his brain."

THE END

Modern Library of the World's Best Books

COMPLETE LIST OF TITLES IN

THE MODERN LIBRARY

For convenience in ordering
please use number at right of title

ADAMS, HENRY	The Education of Henry Adams 76
AIKEN, CONRAD	A Comprehensive Anthology of American Verse 101
AIKEN, CONRAD	Modern American Poetry 127
ANDERSON, SHERWOOD	Winesburg, Ohio 104
BALZAC	Droll Stories 193
BEEBE, WILLIAM	Jungle Peace 30
BEERBOHM, MAX	Zuleika Dobson 116
BENNETT, ARNOLD	The Old Wives' Tale 184
BIERCE, AMBROSE	In the Midst of Life 133
BLAKE, WILLIAM	Poems 91
BOCCACCIO	The Decameron 71
BRONTE, CHARLOTTE	Jane Eyre 64
BRONTE, EMILY	Wuthering Heights 106
BUCK, PEARL	The Good Earth 2
BURTON, RICHARD	The Arabian Nights 201
BUTLER, SAMUEL	Erewhon and Erewhon Revisited 136
BUTLER, SAMUEL	The Way of All Flesh 13
CABELL, JAMES BRANCH	Jurgen 15
CALDWELL, ERSKINE	God's Little Acre 51
CANFIELD, DOROTHY	The Deepening Stream 200
CARROLL, LEWIS	Alice in Wonderland, etc. 79
CASANOVA, JACQUES	Memoirs of Casanova 165
CELLINI, BENVENUTO	Autobiography of Cellini 3
CERVANTES	Don Quixote 174
CHAUCER	The Canterbury Tales 161
CHAUCER	Troilus and Cressida 126
CONFUCIUS	The Wisdom of Confucius 7
CONRAD, JOSEPH	Heart of Darkness (In Great Modern Short Stories 168)
CONRAD, JOSEPH	Lord Jim 186
CONRAD, JOSEPH	Victory 34
CORNEILLE and RACINE	Six Plays of Corneille and Racine 194
CORVO, FREDERICK BARON	A History of the Borgias 192
CUMMINGS, E. E.	The Enormous Room 214
DANTE	The Divine Comedy 208
DAUDET, ALPHONSE	Sapho 85
DEFOE, DANIEL	Moll Flanders 122
DEWEY, JOHN	Human Nature and Conduct 173
DICKENS, CHARLES	A Tale of Two Cities 189
DICKENS, CHARLES	David Copperfield 110

DICKENS, CHARLES	Pickwick Papers 204
DINESEN, ISAK	Seven Gothic Tales 54
DOS PASSOS, JOHN	The 42nd Parallel 88
DOS PASSOS, JOHN	Three Soldiers 205
DOSTOYEVSKY, FYODOR	Crime and Punishment 199
DOSTOYEVSKY, FYODOR	The Brothers Karamazov 151
DOSTOYEVSKY, FYODOR	The Possessed 55
DOUGLAS, NORMAN	South Wind 5
DOWSON, ERNEST	Poems and Prose 74
DREISER, THEODORE	Sister Carrie 8
DUMAS, ALEXANDRE	Camille 69
DUMAS, ALEXANDRE	The Three Musketeers 143
DU MAURIER, GEORGE	Peter Ibbetson 207
EDMAN, IRWIN	The Philosophy of Plato 181
EDMONDS, WALTER D.	Rome Haul 191
ELLIS, HAVELOCK	The Dance of Life 160
FAULKNER, WILLIAM	Sanctuary 61
FERBER, EDNA	Show Boat 35
FEUCHTWANGER, LION	Power 206
FIELDING, HENRY	Joseph Andrews 117
FIELDING, HENRY	Tom Jones 185
FINEMAN, IRVING	Hear, Ye Sons 130
FLAUBERT, GUSTAVE	Madame Bovary 28
FORSTER, E. M.	A Passage to India 218
FRANCE, ANATOLE	Crime of Sylvestre Bonnard 22
FRANCE, ANATOLE	Penguin Island 210
FRANKLIN, BENJAMIN	Autobiography, etc. 39
GALSWORTHY, JOHN	The Apple Tree (In Great Modern Short Stories 168)
GAUTIER, THEOPHILE	Mlle. De Maupin, One of Cleopatra's Nights 53
GEORGE, HENRY	Progress and Poverty 36
GIDE, ANDRE	The Counterfeiters 187
GISSING, GEORGE	New Grub Street 125
GISSING, GEORGE	Private Papers of Henry Ryecroft 46
GLASGOW, ELLEN	Barren Ground 25
GOETHE	Faust 177
GOETHE	The Sorrows of Werther (In Collected German Stories 108)
GOGOL, NIKOLAI	Dead Souls 40
GRAVES, ROBERT	I, Claudius 20
HAMMETT, DASHIELL	The Maltese Falcon 45
HAMSUN, KNUT	Growth of the Soil 12
HARDY, THOMAS	Jude the Obscure 135
HARDY, THOMAS	The Mayor of Casterbridge 17
HARDY, THOMAS	The Return of the Native 121
HARDY, THOMAS	Tess of the D'Urbervilles 72
HART, LIDDELL	The War in Outline 16
HAWTHORNE, NATHANIEL	The Scarlet Letter 93
HEMINGWAY, ERNEST	A Farewell to Arms 19

HEMINGWAY, ERNEST	The Sun Also Rises 170
HEMON, LOUIS	Maria Chapdelaine 10
HEYWARD, DUBOSE	Porgy 148
HOMER	The Iliad 166
HOMER	The Odyssey 167
HORACE	The Complete Works of 141
HUDSON, W. H.	Green Mansions 89
HUDSON, W. H.	The Purple Land 24
HUGHES, RICHARD	A High Wind in Jamaica 112
HUNEKER, JAMES G.	Painted Veils 43
HUXLEY, ALDOUS	Antic Hay 209
HUXLEY, ALDOUS	Point Counter Point 180
IBSEN, HENRIK	A Doll's House, Ghosts, etc. 6
JAMES, HENRY	The Portrait of a Lady 107
JAMES, HENRY	The Turn of the Screw 169
JAMES, WILLIAM	The Philosophy of William James 114
JAMES, WILLIAM	The Varieties of Religious Experience 70
JEFFERS, ROBINSON	Roan Stallion; Tamar and Other Poems 118
JOYCE, JAMES	Dubliners 124
JOYCE, JAMES	A Portrait of the Artist as a Young Man 145
KUPRIN, ALEXANDRE	Yama 203
LAWRENCE, D. H.	The Rainbow 128
LAWRENCE, D. H.	Sons and Lovers 109
LAWRENCE, D. H.	Women in Love 68
LEWIS, SINCLAIR	Arrowsmith 42
LEWISOHN, LUDWIG	The Island Within 123
LONGFELLOW, HENRY W.	Poems 56
LOUYS, PIERRE	Aphrodite 77
LUDWIG, EMIL	Napoleon 95
LUNDBERG, FERDINAND	Imperial Hearst 81
MACHIAVELLI	The Prince and The Discourses of Machiavelli 65
MALRAUX, ANDRE	Man's Fate 33
MANN, THOMAS	Buddenbrooks 57
MANN, THOMAS	Death in Venice (In Collected German Stories 108)
MANSFIELD, KATHERINE	The Garden Party 129
MARQUAND, JOHN P.	The Late George Apley 182
MARX, KARL	Capital and Other Writings 202
MAUGHAM, W. SOMERSET	Of Human Bondage 176
MAUGHAM, W. SOMERSET	The Moon and Sixpence 27
MAUPASSANT, GUY DE	Best Short Stories 98
McFEE, WILLIAM	Casuals of the Sea 195
MELVILLE, HERMAN	Moby Dick 119
MEREDITH, GEORGE	Diana of the Crossways 14
MEREDITH, GEORGE	The Ordeal of Richard Feverel 134
MEREJKOWSKI, DMITRI	The Death of the Gods 153
MEREJKOWSKI, DMITRI	Peter and Alexis 175
MEREJKOWSKI, DMITRI	The Romance of Leonardo da Vinci 138

MISCELLANEOUS	An Anthology of American Negro Literature 163
	An Anthology of Light Verse 48
	Best Ghost Stories 73
	Best Amer. Humorous Short Stories 87
	Best Russian Short Stories, including Bunin's The Gentleman from San Francisco 18
	Eight Famous Elizabethan Plays 94
	Four Famous Greek Plays 158
	Fourteen Great Detective Stories 144
	Great German Short Novels and Stories 108
	Great Modern Short Stories 168
	The Making of Man: An Outline of Anthropology 149
	The Making of Society: An Outline of Sociology 183
	Outline of Abnormal Psychology 152
	Outline of Psychoanalysis 66
	The Sex Problem in Modern Society 198
MOLIERE	Plays 78
MORLEY, CHRISTOPHER	Parnassus on Wheels 190
NEWTON, A. EDWARD	The Amenities of Book-Collecting 164
NIETZSCHE, FRIEDRICH	Thus Spake Zarathustra 9
NORRIS, FRANK	The Pit 92
ODETS, CLIFFORD	Six Plays of 67
O'NEILL, EUGENE	The Emperor Jones, Anna Christie and The Hairy Ape 146
O'NEILL, EUGENE	Seven Plays of the Sea 111
PATER, WALTER	The Renaissance 86
PATER, WALTER	Marius the Epicurean 90
PEARSON, EDMUND	Studies in Murder 113
PEPYS, SAMUEL	Samuel Pepys' Diary 103
PETRONIUS ARBITER	The Satyricon 156
PLATO	The Philosophy of Plato 181
POE, EDGAR ALLAN	Best Tales 82
POLO, MARCO	The Travels of Marco Polo 196
PREVOST, ANTOINE	Manon Lescaut 85
PROUST, MARCEL	The Guermantes Way 213
PROUST, MARCEL	Swann's Way 59
PROUST, MARCEL	Within a Budding Grove 172
PROUST, MARCEL	Cities of the Plain 220
RABELAIS	Gargantua and Pantagruel 4
READE, CHARLES	The Cloister and the Hearth 62
REED, JOHN	Ten Days that Shook the World 215
RENAN, ERNEST	The Life of Jesus 140
ROSTAND, EDMOND	Cyrano de Bergerac 154
RUSSELL, BERTRAND	Selected Papers of Bertrand Russell 137
SCHOPENHAUER	The Philosophy of Schopenhauer 52
SCHREINER, OLIVE	The Story of an African Farm 132

SHEEAN, VINCENT	Personal History 32
SMOLLETT, TOBIAS	Humphry Clinker 159
SPINOZA	The Philosophy of Spinoza 60
STEIN, GERTRUDE	Three Lives 211
STEINBECK, JOHN	In Dubious Battle 115
STEINBECK, JOHN	Tortilla Flat 216
STEINBECK, JOHN	Of Mice and Men 29
STENDHAL	The Charterhouse of Parma 150
STENDHAL	The Red and the Black 157
STERNE, LAURENCE	Tristram Shandy 147
STOKER, BRAM	Dracula 31
STONE, IRVING	Lust for Life 11
STRACHEY, LYTTON	Eminent Victorians 212
SUDERMANN, HERMANN	The Song of Songs 162
SUETONIUS	Lives of the Twelve Caesars 188
SWIFT, JONATHAN	Gulliver's Travels, A Tale of a Tub, The Battle of the Books 100
SWINBURNE, CHARLES	Poems 23
SYMONDS, JOHN A.	The Life of Michelangelo 49
TCHEKOV, ANTON	Short Stories 50
TCHEKOV, ANTON	Sea Gull, Cherry Orchard, Three Sisters, etc. 171
THACKERAY, WILLIAM	Henry Esmond 80
THACKERAY, WILLIAM	Vanity Fair 131
THOMPSON, FRANCIS	Complete Poems 38
THOREAU, HENRY DAVID	Walden and Other Writings 155
THUCYDIDES	The Complete Writings of 58
TOLSTOY, LEO	Anna Karenina 37
TOMLINSON, H. M.	The Sea and the Jungle 99
TROLLOPE, ANTHONY	Barchester Towers and The Warden 41
TURGENEV, IVAN	Fathers and Sons 21
VAN LOON, HENDRIK W.	Ancient Man 105
VEBLEN, THORSTEIN	The Theory of the Leisure Class 63
VIRGIL'S WORKS	Including The Aeneid, Eclogues, and Georgics 75
VOLTAIRE	Candide 47
WALLACE, LEW	Ben Hur 139
WALPOLE, HUGH	Fortitude 178
WALTON, IZAAK	The Compleat Angler 26
WAUGH, EVELYN	Vile Bodies 120
WEBB, MARY	Precious Bane 219
WELLS, H. G.	Tono Bungay 197
WHITMAN, WALT	Leaves of Grass 97
WILDE, OSCAR	Dorian Gray, De Profundis 1
WILDE, OSCAR	The Plays of Oscar Wilde 83
WILDE, OSCAR	Poems and Fairy Tales 84
WOOLF, VIRGINIA	Mrs. Dalloway 96
WOOLF, VIRGINIA	To the Lighthouse 217
YEATS, W. B.	Irish Fairy and Folk Tales 44
YOUNG, G. F.	The Medici 179
ZOLA, EMILE	Nana 142
ZWEIG, STEFAN	Amok (In Collected German Stories 108)

MODERN LIBRARY GIANTS

*A series of full-sized library editions of books that formerly
were available only in cumbersome and expensive sets.*

THE TEXTS OF THE GIANTS ARE GUARANTEED TO BE COMPLETE AND UNABRIDGED

Many are illustrated and some of them are over 1200 pages long.

G1. TOLSTOY, LEO. War and Peace.

G2. BOSWELL, JAMES. Life of Samuel Johnson.

G3. HUGO, VICTOR. Les Miserables.

G4. THE COMPLETE POEMS OF KEATS AND SHELLEY.

G5. PLUTARCH'S LIVES (The Dryden Translation).

G6.⎱ GIBBON, EDWARD. The Decline and Fall of the Roman
G7.⎰ Empire (Complete in two volumes).

G8. THE COMPLETE NOVELS OF JANE AUSTEN.

G9. YOUNG, G. F.. The Medici (Illustrated).

G10. TWELVE FAMOUS RESTORATION PLAYS (1660-1820)
  (Congreve, Wycherley, Gay, Goldsmith, Sheridan, etc.)

G11. THE ESSAYS OF MONTAIGNE (The Florio Translation).

G12. THE MOST POPULAR NOVELS OF SIR WALTER
  SCOTT (Quentin Durward, Ivanhoe, and Kenilworth).

G13. CARLYLE, THOMAS. The French Revolution (Illustrated).

G14. BULFINCH'S MYTHOLOGY (Illustrated).

G15. CERVANTES. Don Quixote (Illustrated).

G16. WOLFE, THOMAS. Look Homeward, Angel.

G17. THE POEMS AND PLAYS OF ROBERT BROWNING.

G18. ELEVEN PLAYS OF HENRIK IBSEN.

G19. THE COMPLETE WORKS OF HOMER.

G20.⎱ SYMONDS, JOHN ADDINGTON. Renaissance in Italy.
G21.⎰ (Complete in two volumes).

G22. STRACHEY, JOHN. The Coming Struggle for Power.

G23. TOLSTOY, LEO. Anna Karenina.

G24. LAMB, CHARLES. The Complete Works and Letters of
  Charles Lamb.

G25. THE COMPLETE PLAYS OF GILBERT AND SULLIVAN

G26. MARX, KARL. Capital.

G27. DARWIN, CHARLES. The Origin of Species and The Descent
  of Man.

G28. THE COMPLETE WORKS OF LEWIS CARROLL.

G29. PRESCOTT, WILLIAM H. The Conquest of Mexico and The Conquest of Peru.

G30. MYERS, GUSTAVUS. History of the Great American Fortunes.

G31. WERFEL, FRANZ. The Forty Days of Musa Dagh.

G32. SMITH, ADAM. The Wealth of Nations.

G33. COLLINS, WILKIE. The Moonstone and The Woman in White.

G34. NIETZSCHE, FRIEDRICH. The Philosophy of Nietzsche.

G35. BURY, J. B. A History of Greece.

G36. DOSTOYEVSKY, FYODOR. The Brothers Karamazov.

G37. THE COMPLETE NOVELS AND SELECTED TALES OF NATHANIEL HAWTHORNE.

G38. ROLLAND, ROMAIN. Jean-Christophe.

G39. THE BASIC WRITINGS OF SIGMUND FREUD.

G40. THE COMPLETE TALES AND POEMS OF EDGAR ALLAN POE.

G41. FARRELL, JAMES T. Studs Lonigan.

G42. THE POEMS AND PLAYS OF TENNYSON.

G43. DEWEY, JOHN. Intelligence in the Modern World: John Dewey's Philosophy.

G44. DOS PASSOS, JOHN. U. S. A.

G45. LEWISOHN, LUDWIG. The Story of American Literature.

G46. A NEW ANTHOLOGY OF MODERN POETRY.

G47. THE ENGLISH PHILOSOPHERS FROM BACON TO MILL.

G48. THE METROPOLITAN OPERA GUIDE.

G49. TWAIN, MARK. Tom Sawyer and Huckleberry Finn.

G50. WHITMAN, WALT. Leaves of Grass.

G51. THE BEST-KNOWN NOVELS OF GEORGE ELIOT.